"THE PAGES PRACTICALLY TURN THEMSELVES . . . Gabaldon is a born storyteller. . . . She writes a prose that is brisk, lucid, good-humored and often felicitous. Gabaldon is obviously just over the threshold of a long and prolific career."
—*Arizona Republic*

Praise for
DRAGONFLY IN AMBER
and Diana Gabaldon

"I LOVED EVERY PAGE . . . DIANA GABALDON WEAVES A POWERFUL TALE LAYERED IN HISTORY AND MYTH." —Nora Roberts

"MARVELOUS . . . IT IS A LARGE CANVAS THAT GABALDON PAINTS, FILLED WITH STRONG PASSIONS AND DERRING-DO." —*San Francisco Chronicle*

"COMPULSIVELY READABLE . . . INTRIGUING . . . Gabaldon offers a fresh and offbeat historical view."
—*Publishers Weekly*

"ENGAGING TIME-TRAVEL . . . AN APPEALING MODERN HEROINE AND A MAGNETIC ROMANTIC HERO . . . a most entertaining mix of history and fantasy whose author, like its heroine, exhibits a winning combination of vivid imagination and good common sense."
—*Kirkus Reviews*

"BRILLIANT, ASTONISHING . . . A RIVETING HISTORICAL NOVEL THAT RIVALS THE BEST."
—*Rave Reviews*

By Diana Gabaldon

DIANA GABALDON

DRAGONFLY IN AMBER

A Novel

BANTAM BOOKS | NEW YORK

2016 Bantam Books Trade Paperback Tie-in Edition

Published in the United States by Bantam Books, an imprint of Random House, a division of Penguin Random House LLC, New York.

BANTAM BOOKS and the HOUSE colophon are registered trademarks of Penguin Random House LLC.

Originally published in hardcover in the United States by Delacorte Press, an imprint of Random House, a division of Penguin Random House LLC, in 1992.

ISBN 978-0-399-17768-2
eBook ISBN 978-0-440-33518-4

Printed in the United States of America on acid-free paper

randomhousebooks.com

2 4 6 8 9 7 5 3 1

Prologue

I woke three times in the dark predawn. First in sorrow, then in joy, and at the last, in solitude. The tears of a bone-deep loss woke me slowly, bathing my face like the comforting touch of a damp cloth in soothing hands. I turned my face to the wet pillow and sailed a salty river into the caverns of grief remembered, into the subterranean depths of sleep.

I came awake then in fierce joy, body arched bowlike in the throes of physical joining, the touch of him fresh on my skin, dying along the paths of my nerves as the ripples of consummation spread from my center. I repelled consciousness, turning again, seeking the sharp, warm smell of a man's satisfied desire, in the reassuring arms of my lover, sleep.

The third time I woke alone, beyond the touch of love or grief. The sight of the stones was fresh in my mind. A small circle, standing stones on the crest of a steep green hill. The name of the hill is Craigh na Dun; the fairies' hill. Some say the hill is enchanted, others say it is cursed. Both are right. But no one knows the function or the purpose of the stones.

Except me.

For my husband, Doug Watkins—
In thanks for the Raw Material

PART ONE

*Through a
Looking Glass,
Darkly*

Inverness, 1968

Mustering the Roll

Roger Wakefield stood in the center of the room, feeling surrounded. He thought the feeling largely justified, insofar as he *was* surrounded: by tables covered with bric-a-brac and mementos, by heavy Victorian-style furniture, replete with antimacassars, plush and afghans, by tiny braided rugs that lay on the polished wood, craftily awaiting an opportunity to skid beneath an unsuspecting foot. Surrounded by twelve rooms of furniture and clothing and papers. And the books—my God, the books!

The study where he stood was lined on three sides by bookshelves, every one crammed past bursting point. Paperback mystery novels lay in bright, tatty piles in front of calf-bound tomes, jammed cheek by jowl with book-club selections, ancient volumes pilfered from extinct libraries, and thousands upon thousands of pamphlets, leaflets, and hand-sewn manuscripts.

A similar situation prevailed in the rest of the house. Books and papers cluttered every horizontal surface, and every closet groaned and squeaked at the seams. His late adoptive father had lived a long, full life, a good ten years past his biblically allotted threescore and ten. And in eighty-odd years, the Reverend Mr. Reginald Wakefield had never thrown anything away.

Roger repressed the urge to run out of the front door, leap into his Morris Minor, and head back to Oxford, abandoning the manse and its contents to the mercy of weather and vandals. Be calm, he told himself, inhaling deeply. You can deal with this. The books are the easy part; nothing more than a matter of sorting through them and then calling someone to come and haul them away. Granted, they'll need a lorry the size of a railcar, but it can be done. Clothes—no problem. Oxfam gets the lot.

He didn't know what Oxfam was going to do with a lot of vested black serge suits, circa 1948, but perhaps the deserving poor weren't all that picky. He began to breathe a little easier. He had taken a month's leave from the History department at Oxford in order to clear up the Reverend's affairs. Perhaps that would be enough, after all. In his more depressed moments, it had seemed as though the task might take years.

He moved toward one of the tables and picked up a small china dish. It was filled with small metal rectangles; lead "gaberlunzies," badges issued to eighteenth-century beggars by parishes as a sort of license. A collection of stoneware bottles stood by the lamp, a ramshorn snuff mull, banded in silver, next to them. Give them to a museum? he thought dubiously. The house was filled with Jacobite artifacts; the Reverend had been an amateur historian, the eighteenth century his favorite hunting ground.

His fingers reached involuntarily to caress the surface of the snuff mull, tracing the black lines of the inscriptions—the names and dates of the Deacons and Treasurers of the Incorporation of Tailors of the Canongate, from Edinburgh, 1726. Perhaps he should keep a few of the Reverend's choicer acquisitions . . . but then he drew back, shaking his head decidedly. "Nothing doing, cock," he said aloud, "this way lies madness." Or at least the incipient life of a pack rat. Get started saving things, and he'd end up keeping the lot, living in this monstrosity of a house, surrounded by generations of rubbish. "Talking to yourself, too," he muttered.

The thought of generations of rubbish reminded him of the garage, and he sagged a bit at the knees. The Reverend, who was in fact Roger's great-uncle, had adopted him at the age of five when his parents had been killed in World War II; his mother in the Blitz, his father out over the dark waters of the Channel. With his usual preservative instincts, the Reverend had kept all of Roger's parents' effects, sealed in crates and cartons in the back of the garage. Roger knew for a fact that no one had opened one of those crates in the past twenty years.

Roger uttered an Old Testament groan at the thought of pawing through his parents' memorabilia. "Oh, God," he said aloud. "Anything but that!"

The remark had not been intended precisely as prayer, but the doorbell pealed as though in answer, making Roger bite his tongue in startlement.

The door of the manse had a tendency to stick in damp weather, which meant that it was stuck most of the time. Roger freed it with a rending screech, to find a woman on the doorstep.

"Can I help you?"

She was middle height and very pretty. He had an overall impression of fine bones and white linen, topped with a wealth of curly brown hair in a sort of half-tamed chignon. And in the middle of it all, the most extraordinary pair of light eyes, just the color of well-aged sherry.

The eyes swept up from his size-eleven plimsolls to the face a foot above her. The sidelong smile grew wider. "I hate to start right off with a cliché," she said, "but my, how you have grown, young Roger!"

Roger felt himself flushing. The woman laughed and extended a hand. "You *are* Roger, aren't you? My name's Claire Randall; I was an old friend of the Reverend's. But I haven't seen you since you were five years old."

"Er, you said you *were* a friend of my father's? Then, you know already. . . ."

The smile vanished, replaced by a look of regret.

"Yes, I was awfully sorry to hear about it. Heart, was it?"

"Um, yes. Very sudden. I've only just come up from Oxford to start dealing with . . . everything." He waved vaguely, encompassing the Reverend's death, the house behind him, and all its contents.

"From what I recall of your father's library, that little chore ought to last you 'til next Christmas," Claire observed.

"In that case, maybe we shouldn't be disturbing you," said a soft American voice.

"Oh, I forgot," said Claire, half-turning to the girl who had stood out of sight in the corner of the porch. "Roger Wakefield—my daughter, Brianna."

Brianna Randall stepped forward, a shy smile on her face. Roger stared for a moment, then remembered his manners. He stepped back and swung the door open wide, momentarily wondering just when he had last changed his shirt.

"Not at all, not at all!" he said heartily. "I was just wanting a break. Won't you come in?"

He waved the two women down the hall toward the Reverend's study, noting that as well as being moderately attractive, the daughter was one of the tallest girls he'd ever seen close-to. She had to be easily six feet, he thought, seeing her head even with the top of the hall stand as she passed. He unconsciously straightened himself as he followed, drawing up to his full six feet three. At the last moment, he ducked, to avoid banging his head on the study lintel as he followed the women into the room.

➤

"I'd meant to come before," said Claire, settling herself deeper in the huge wing chair. The fourth wall of the Reverend's study was equipped with floor-to-ceiling windows, and the sunlight winked off the pearl clip in her light-brown hair. The curls were beginning to escape from their confinement, and she tucked one absently behind an ear as she talked.

"I'd arranged to come last year, in fact, and then there was an emergency at the hospital in Boston—I'm a doctor," she explained, mouth curling a little at the look of surprise Roger hadn't quite managed to conceal. "But I'm sorry that we didn't; I would have liked so much to see your father again."

Roger rather wondered why they had come now, knowing the Reverend was dead, but it seemed impolite to ask. Instead, he asked, "Enjoying a bit of sightseeing, are you?"

"Yes, we drove up from London," Claire answered. She smiled at her daughter. "I wanted Bree to see the country; you wouldn't think it to hear her talk, but she's as English as I am, though she's never lived here."

"Really?" Roger glanced at Brianna. She didn't really look English, he thought; aside from the height, she had thick red hair, worn loose over her shoulders, and strong, sharp-angled bones in her face, with the nose long and straight—maybe a touch too long.

"I was born in America," Brianna explained, "but both Mother and Daddy are—were—English."

"Were?"

"My husband died two years ago," Claire explained. "You knew him, I think—Frank Randall."

"*Frank* Randall! Of course!" Roger smacked himself on the forehead, and felt his cheeks grow hot at Brianna's giggle. "You're going to think me a complete fool, but I've only just realized who you are."

The name explained a lot; Frank Randall had been an eminent historian, and a good friend of the Reverend's; they had exchanged bits of Jacobite arcana for years, though it was at least ten years since Frank Randall had last visited the manse.

"So—you'll be visiting the historical sites near Inverness?" Roger hazarded. "Have you been to Culloden yet?"

"Not yet," Brianna answered. "We thought we'd go later this week." Her answering smile was polite, but nothing more.

"We're booked for a trip down Loch Ness this afternoon," Claire explained. "And perhaps we'll drive down to Fort William tomorrow, or just poke about in Inverness; the place has grown a lot since I was last here."

"When was that?" Roger wondered whether he ought to volunteer his services as tour guide. He really shouldn't take the time, but the Randalls had been good friends of the Reverend's. Besides, a car trip to Fort William in company with two attractive women seemed a much more appealing prospect than cleaning out the garage, which was next on his list.

"Oh, more than twenty years ago. It's been a long time." There was an odd note in Claire's voice that made Roger glance at her, but she met his eyes with a smile.

"Well," he ventured, "if there's anything I can do for you, while you're in the Highlands . . ."

Claire was still smiling, but something in her face changed. He could almost think she had been waiting for an opening. She glanced at Brianna, then back to Roger.

"Since you mention it," she said, her smile broadening.

"Oh, Mother!" Brianna said, sitting up in her chair. "You don't want to bother Mr. Wakefield! Look at all he's got to do!" She waved a hand at the crowded study, with its overflowing cartons and endless stacks of books.

"Oh, no bother at all!" Roger protested. "Er . . . what is it?"

Claire shot her daughter a quelling look. "I wasn't planning to knock him on the head and drag him off," she said tartly. "But he might well know someone who could help. It's a small historical project," she explained to Roger. "I need someone who's fairly well versed in the eighteenth-century Jacobites—Bonnie Prince Charlie and all that lot."

Roger leaned forward, interested. "Jacobites?" he said. "That period's not one of my specialties, but I do know a bit—hard not to, living so close to Culloden. That's where the final battle was, you know," he explained to Brianna. "Where the Bonnie Prince's lot ran up against the Duke of Cumberland and got slaughtered for their pains."

"Right," said Claire. "And that, in fact, has to do with what I want to find out." She reached into her handbag and drew out a folded paper.

Roger opened it and scanned the contents quickly. It was a list of names—maybe thirty, all men. At the top of the sheet was a heading: "JACOBITE RISING, 1745—CULLODEN"

"Oh, the '45?" Roger said. "These men fought at Culloden, did they?"

"They did," Claire replied. "What I want to find out is—how many of the men on this list survived that battle?"

Roger rubbed his chin as he perused the list. "That's a simple question," he said, "but the answer might be hard to find. So many of the Highland clansmen who followed Prince Charles were killed on Culloden Field that they weren't buried individually. They were put into mass graves, with no more than a single stone bearing the clan name as a marker."

"I know," Claire said. "Brianna hasn't been there, but I have—a long time ago." He thought he saw a fleeting shadow in her eyes, though it was quickly hidden as she reached into her handbag. No wonder if there was, he thought. Culloden Field was an affecting place; it brought tears to his own eyes, to look out over that expanse of moorland and remember the gallantry and courage of the Scottish Highlanders who lay slaughtered beneath the grass.

She unfolded several more typed sheets and handed them to him. A long white finger ran down the margin of one sheet. Beautiful hands, Roger noted; delicately molded, carefully kept, with a single ring on each hand. The silver one on her right hand was especially striking; a wide Jacobean band in the Highland interlace pattern, embellished with thistle blossoms.

"These are the names of the wives, so far as I know them. I thought that might help, since if the husbands were killed at Culloden, you'd likely find these women remarrying or emigrating afterward. Those records would surely be in the parish register? They're all from the same parish; the church was in Broch Mordha—it's a good bit south of here."

"That's a very helpful idea," Roger said, mildly surprised. "It's the sort of thing an historian would think of."

"I'm hardly an historian," Claire Randall said dryly. "On the other hand, when you live with one, you do pick up the occasional odd thought."

"Of course." A thought struck Roger, and he rose from his chair. "I'm being a terrible host; please, let me get you a drink, and then you can tell me a bit more about this. Perhaps I could help you with it myself."

Despite the disorder, he knew where the decanters were kept, and quickly had his guests supplied with whisky. He'd put quite a lot of soda in Brianna's, but noticed that she sipped at it as though her glass contained ant spray, rather than the best Glenfiddich single malt. Claire, who took her whisky neat by request, seemed to enjoy it much more.

"Well." Roger resumed his seat and picked up the paper again. "It's an interesting problem, in terms of historical research. You said these men came from the same parish? I suppose they came from a single clan or sept—I see a number of them were named Fraser."

Claire nodded, hands folded in her lap. "They came from the same estate; a small Highland farm called Broch Tuarach—it was known locally as Lallybroch. They were part of clan Fraser, though they never gave a formal allegiance to Lord Lovat as chief. These men joined the Rising early; they fought in the Battle of Prestonpans—while Lovat's men didn't come until just before Culloden."

"Really? That's interesting." Under normal eighteenth-century conditions, such small tenant-farmers would have died where they lived, and be filed tidily away in the village churchyard, neatly docketed in the parish register. However, Bonnie Prince Charlie's attempt to regain the throne of Scotland in 1745 had disrupted the normal course of things in no uncertain terms.

In the famine after the disaster of Culloden, many Highlanders had emigrated to the New World; others had drifted from the glens and moors toward the cities, in search of food and employment. A few stayed on, stubbornly clinging to their land and traditions.

"It would make a fascinating article," Roger said, thinking aloud. "Follow the fate of a number of individuals, see what happened to them all. Less interesting if they all *were* killed at Culloden, but chances were that a few made it out." He would be inclined to take on the project as a welcome break even were it not Claire Randall who asked.

"Yes, I think I can help you with this," he said, and was gratified at the warm smile she bestowed on him.

"Would you really? That's wonderful!" she said.

"My pleasure," Roger said. He folded the paper and laid it on the table. "I'll start in on it directly. But tell me, how did you enjoy your drive up from London?"

The conversation became general as the Randalls regaled him with tales of their transatlantic journey, and the drive from London. Roger's attention drifted slightly, as he began to plan the research for this project. He felt mildly guilty about taking it on; he really shouldn't take the time. On the other hand, it was an interesting question. And it was possible that he could combine the project with some of the necessary clearing-up of the Reverend's material; he knew for a fact that there were forty-eight cartons in the garage, all labeled JACOBITES, MISCELLANEOUS. The thought of it was enough to make him feel faint.

With a wrench, he tore his mind away from the garage, to find that the conversation had made an abrupt change of subject.

"Druids?" Roger felt dazed. He peered suspiciously into his glass, checking to see that he really had added soda.

"You hadn't heard about them?" Claire looked slightly disappointed. "Your father—the Reverend—he knew about them, though only unofficially. Perhaps he didn't think it worth telling you; he thought it something of a joke."

Roger scratched his head, ruffling the thick black hair. "No, I really don't recall. But you're right, he may not have thought it anything serious."

"Well, I don't know that it is." She crossed her legs at the knee. A streak of sunlight gleamed down the shin of her stockings, emphasizing the delicacy of the long bone beneath.

"When I was here last with Frank—God, that was twenty-three years ago! —the Reverend told him that there was a local group of—well, modern Druids, I suppose you'd call them. I've no idea how authentic they might be; most likely not very." Brianna was leaning forward now, interested, the glass of whisky forgotten between her hands.

"The Reverend couldn't take official notice of them—paganism and all that, you know—but his housekeeper, Mrs. Graham, was involved with the group, so he got wind of their doings from time to time, and he tipped Frank that there would be a ceremony of some kind on the dawn of Beltane—May Day, that is."

Roger nodded, trying to adjust to the idea of elderly Mrs. Graham, that extremely proper person, engaging in pagan rites and dancing round stone circles in the dawn. All he could remember of Druid ceremonies himself was that some of them involved burning sacrificial victims in wicker cages, which seemed still more unlikely behavior for a Scottish Presbyterian lady of advanced years.

"There's a circle of standing stones on top of a hill, fairly nearby. So we went up there before dawn to, well, to spy on them," she continued, shrugging apologetically. "You know what scholars are like; no conscience at all when it comes to their own field, let alone a sense of social delicacy." Roger winced slightly at this, but nodded in wry agreement.

"And there they were," she said. "Mrs. Graham included, all wearing bedsheets, chanting things and dancing in the midst of the stone circle. Frank was fascinated," she added, with a smile. "And it *was* impressive, even to me."

She paused for a moment, eyeing Roger rather speculatively.

"I'd heard that Mrs. Graham had passed away a few years ago. But I wonder . . . do you know if she had any family? I believe membership in such groups is often hereditary; maybe there's a daughter or granddaughter who could tell me a bit."

"Well," Roger said slowly. "There is a granddaughter—Fiona's her name, Fiona Graham. In fact, she came to help out here at the manse after her grandmother died; the Reverend was really too elderly to be left all on his own."

If anything could displace his vision of Mrs. Graham dancing in a bed-sheet, it was the thought of nineteen-year-old Fiona as a guardian of ancient mystic knowledge, but Roger rallied gamely and went on.

"She isn't here just now, I'm afraid. I could ask her for you, though."

Claire waved a slender hand in dismissal. "Don't trouble yourself. Another time will do. We've taken up too much of your time already."

To Roger's dismay, she set down her empty glass on the small table between the chairs and Brianna added her own full one with what looked like alacrity. He noticed that Brianna Randall bit her nails. This small evidence of imperfection gave him the nerve to take the next step. She intrigued him, and he didn't want her to go, with no assurance that he would see her again.

"Speaking of stone circles," he said quickly. "I believe I know the one you mentioned. It's quite scenic, and not too far from town." He smiled directly at Brianna Randall, registering automatically the fact that she had three small freckles high on one cheekbone. "I thought perhaps I'd start on this project with a trip down to Broch Tuarach. It's in the same direction as the stone circle, so maybe . . . aaagh!"

With a sudden jerk of her bulky handbag, Claire Randall had bumped both whisky glasses off the table, showering Roger's lap and thighs with single malt whisky and quite a lot of soda.

"I'm terribly sorry," she apologized, obviously flustered. She bent and began picking up pieces of shattered crystal, despite Roger's half-coherent attempts to stop her.

Brianna, coming to assist with a handful of linen napkins seized from the sideboard, was saying "Really, Mother, how they ever let you do surgery, I don't know. You're just not safe with anything smaller than a bread-box. Look, you've got his shoes soaked with whisky!" She knelt on the floor, and began busily mopping up spilled Scotch and fragments of crystal. "And his pants, too."

Whipping a fresh napkin from the stack over her arm, she industriously polished Roger's toes, her red mane floating deliriously around his knees. Her head was rising, as she peered at his thighs, dabbing energetically at damp spots on the corduroy. Roger closed his eyes and thought frantically of terrible car crashes on the motorway and tax forms for the Inland Revenue and the Blob from Outer Space—anything that might stop him disgracing himself utterly as Brianna Randall's warm breath misted softly through the wet fabric of his trousers.

"Er, maybe you'd like to do the rest yourself?" The voice came from somewhere around the level of his nose, and he opened his eyes to find a pair of deep blue eyes facing him above a wide grin. He rather weakly took the napkin she was offering him, breathing as though he had just been chased by a train.

Lowering his head to scrub at his trousers, he caught sight of Claire Randall watching him with an expression of mingled sympathy and amusement.

There was nothing else visible in her expression; nothing of that flash he thought he'd seen in her eyes just before the catastrophe. Flustered as he was, it was probably his imagination, he thought. For why on earth should she have done it on purpose?

―――――――――

"Since when are you interested in Druids, Mama?" Brianna seemed disposed to find something hilarious in the idea; I had noticed her biting the insides of her cheeks while I was chatting with Roger Wakefield, and the grin she had been hiding then was now plastered across her face. "You going to get your own bedsheet and join up?"

"Bound to be more entertaining than hospital staff meetings every Thursday," I said. "Bit drafty, though." She hooted with laughter, startling two chickadees off the walk in front of us.

"No," I said, switching to seriousness. "It isn't the Druid ladies I'm after, so much. There's someone I used to know in Scotland that I wanted to find, if I can. I haven't an address for her—I haven't been in touch with her for more than twenty years—but she had an interest in odd things like that: witchcraft, old beliefs, folklore. All that sort of thing. She once lived near here; I thought if she was still here, she might be involved with a group like that."

"What's her name?"

I shook my head, grabbing at the loosened clip as it slid from my curls. It slipped through my fingers and bounced into the deep grass along the walk.

"Damn!" I said, stooping for it. My fingers were unsteady as I groped through the dense stalks, and I had trouble picking up the clip, slippery with moisture from the wet grass. The thought of Geillis Duncan tended to un-nerve me, even now.

"I don't know," I said, brushing the curls back off my flushed face. "I mean—it's been such a long time, I'm sure she'd have a different name by now. She was widowed; she might have married again, or be using her maiden name."

"Oh." Brianna lost interest in the topic, and walked along in silence for a little. Suddenly she said, "What did you think of Roger Wakefield, Mama?"

I glanced at her; her cheeks were pink, but it might be from the spring wind.

"He seems a very nice young man," I said carefully. "He's certainly intelligent; he's one of the youngest professors at Oxford." The intelligence I had known about; I wondered whether he had any imagination. So often scholarly types didn't. But imagination would be helpful.

"He's got the grooviest eyes," Brianna said, dreamily ignoring the question of his brain. "Aren't they the greenest you've ever seen?"

"Yes, they're very striking," I agreed. "They've always been like that; I remember noticing them when I first met him as a child."

Brianna looked down at me, frowning.

"Yes, Mother, really! Did you have to say 'My, how you've grown?' when he answered the door? How embarrassing!"

I laughed.

"Well, when you've last seen someone hovering round your navel, and suddenly you find yourself looking up his nose," I defended myself, "you can't help remarking the difference."

"Mother!" But she fizzed with laughter.

"He has a very nice bottom, too," I remarked, just to keep her going. "I noticed when he bent over to get the whisky."

"Mo-THERRR! They'll hear you!"

We were nearly at the bus stop. There were two or three women and an elderly gentleman in tweeds standing by the sign; they turned to stare at us as we came up.

"Is this the place for the Loch-side Tours bus?" I asked, scanning the bewildering array of notices and advertisements posted on the signboard.

"Och, aye," one of the ladies said kindly. "The bus will be comin' along in ten minutes or so." She scanned Brianna, so clearly American in blue jeans and white windbreaker. The final patriotic note was added by the flushed face, red with suppressed laughter. "You'll be going to see Loch Ness? Your first time, is it?"

I smiled at her. "I sailed down the loch with my husband twenty-odd years ago, but this is my daughter's first trip to Scotland."

"Oh, is it?" This attracted the attention of the other ladies and they crowded around, suddenly friendly, offering advice and asking questions until the big yellow bus came chugging round the corner.

Brianna paused before climbing the steps, admiring the picturesque drawing of green serpentine loops, undulating through a blue-paint lake, edged with black pines.

"This will be fun," she said, laughing. "Think we'll see the monster?"

"You never know," I said.

———

Roger spent the rest of the day in a state of abstraction, wandering absently from one task to another. The books to be packed for donation to the Society for the Preservation of Antiquities lay spilling out of their carton, the Reverend's ancient flatbed lorry sat in the drive with its bonnet up, halfway through a motor check, and a cup of tea sat half-drunk and milk-scummed at his elbow as he gazed blankly out at the falling rain of early evening.

What he should do, he knew, was get at the job of dismantling the heart of the Reverend's study. Not the books; massive as that job was, it was only a matter of deciding which to keep himself, and which should be dispatched to the SPA or the Reverend's old college library. No, sooner or later he would have to tackle the enormous desk, which had papers filling each huge drawer to the brim and protruding from its dozens of pigeonholes. And he'd have to take down and dispose of all of the miscellany decorating the cork wall that filled one side of the room; a task to daunt the stoutest heart.

Aside from a general disinclination to start the tedious job, Roger was hampered by something else. He didn't *want* to be doing these things, necessary as they were; he wanted to be working on Claire Randall's project, tracking down the clansmen of Culloden.

It was an interesting enough project in its way, though probably a minor research job. But that wasn't it. No, he thought, if he were being honest with himself, he wanted to tackle Claire Randall's project because he wanted to go round to Mrs. Thomas's guesthouse and lay his results at the feet of Brianna Randall, as knights were supposed to have done with the heads of dragons. Even if he didn't get results on that scale, he urgently wanted some excuse to see her and talk with her again.

It was a Bronzino painting she reminded him of, he decided. She and her mother both gave that odd impression of having been outlined somehow, drawn with such vivid strokes and delicate detail that they stood out from their background as though they'd been engraved on it. But Brianna had that brilliant coloring, and that air of absolute physical presence that made Bronzino's sitters seem to follow you with their eyes, to be about to speak from their frames. He'd never seen a Bronzino painting making faces at a glass of whisky, but if there had been one, he was sure it would have looked precisely like Brianna Randall.

"Well, bloody hell," he said aloud. "It won't take a lot of time just to look over the records at Culloden House tomorrow, will it? You," he said, addressing the desk and its multiple burdens, "can wait for a day. So can you," he said to the wall, and defiantly plucked a mystery novel from the shelf. He glanced around belligerently, as though daring any of the furnishings to object, but there was no sound but the whirring of the electric fire. He switched it off and, book under his arm, left the study, flicking off the light.

A minute later, he came back, crossing the room in the dark, and retrieved the list of names from the table.

"Well, bloody hell anyway!" he said, and tucked it into the pocket of his shirt. "Don't want to forget the damn thing in the morning." He patted the pocket, feeling the soft crackle of the paper just over his heart, and went up to bed.

We had come back from Loch Ness blown with wind and chilled with rain, to the warm comfort of a hot supper and an open fire in the parlor. Brianna had begun to yawn over the scrambled eggs, and soon excused herself to go and take a hot bath. I stayed downstairs for a bit, chatting with Mrs. Thomas, the landlady, and it was nearly ten o'clock before I made my way up to my own bath and nightgown.

Brianna was an early riser and an early sleeper; her soft breathing greeted me as I pushed open the bedroom door. An early sleeper, she was also a sound one; I moved carefully around the room, hanging up my clothes and tidying things away, but there was little danger of waking her. The house grew quiet as I went about my work, so that the rustle of my own movements seemed loud in my ears.

I had brought several of Frank's books with me, intending to donate them to the Inverness Library. They were laid neatly in the bottom of my suitcase, forming a foundation for the more squashable items above. I took them out one by one, laying them on the bed. Five hardbound volumes, glossy in bright dust covers. Nice, substantial things; five or six hundred pages each, not counting index and illustrations.

My late husband's Collected Works, in the Fully Annotated editions. Inches of admiring reviews covered the jacket flaps, comments from every recognized expert in the historical field. Not bad for a Life's Work, I thought. An accomplishment to be proud of. Compact, weighty, authoritative.

I stacked the books neatly on the table next to my bag, so as not to forget them in the morning. The titles on the spines were different, of course, but I stacked them so that the uniform "Frank W. Randall"'s at the ends lined up, one above the other. They glowed jewel-bright in the small pool of light from the bedside lamp.

The bed-and-breakfast was quiet; it was early in the year for guests, and those there were had long since gone to sleep. In the other twin bed, Brianna made a small whuffling noise and rolled over in her sleep, leaving long strands of red hair draped across her dreaming face. One long, bare foot protruded from the bedclothes, and I pulled the blanket gently over it.

The impulse to touch a sleeping child never fades, no matter that the child is a good deal larger than her mother, and a woman—if a young one—in her own right. I smoothed the hair back from her face and stroked the crown of her head. She smiled in her sleep, a brief reflex of contentment, gone as soon as it appeared. My own smile lingered as I watched her, and whispered to her sleep-deaf ears, as I had so many times before, "God, you are so like him."

I swallowed the faint thickening in my throat—it was nearly habit, by now—and took my dressing gown from the chairback. It was bloody cold at night in the Scottish Highlands in April, but I wasn't yet ready to seek the warm sanctuary of my own twin bed.

I had asked the landlady to leave the fire burning in the sitting room, assuring her that I would bank it before retiring. I closed the door softly, still seeing the sprawl of long limbs, the splash and tumble of red silk across the quilted blue spread.

"Not bad for a Life's Work, either," I whispered to the dark hallway. "Maybe not so compact, but damned authoritative."

The small parlor was dark and cozy, the fire burnt down to a steady glow of flame along the backbone of the main log. I pulled a small armchair up before the fire and propped my feet on the fender. I could hear all the small usual sounds of modern life around me; the faint whirr of the refrigerator in the basement below, the hum and whoosh of the central heating that made the fire a comfort rather than a necessity; the passing rush of an occasional car outside.

But under everything was the deep silence of a Highland night. I sat very still, reaching for it. It had been twenty years since I last felt it, but the soothing power of the dark was still there, cradled between the mountains.

I reached into the pocket of my dressing gown and pulled out the folded paper—a copy of the list I had given Roger Wakefield. It was too dark to read by firelight, but I didn't need to see the names. I unfolded the paper on my silk-clad knee and sat blindly staring at the lines of illegible type. I ran my finger slowly across each line, murmuring each man's name to myself like a prayer. They belonged to the cold spring night, more than I did. But I kept looking into the flames, letting the dark outside come to fill the empty places inside me.

And speaking their names as though to summon them, I began the first steps back, crossing the empty dark to where they waited.

———————————

2

The Plot Thickens

Roger left Culloden House next morning with twelve pages of notes and a growing feeling of bafflement. What had at first seemed a fairly straightforward job of historical research was turning up some odd twists, and no mistake.

He had found only three of the names from Claire Randall's list among the rolls of the dead of Culloden. This in itself was nothing remarkable. Charles Stuart's army had rarely had a coherent roll of enlistment, as some clan chieftains had joined the Bonnie Prince apparently on whim, and many had left for even less reason, before the names of their men could be inscribed on any official document. The Highland army's record-keeping, haphazard at best, had disintegrated almost completely toward the end; there was little point in keeping a payroll, after all, if you had nothing with which to pay the men on it.

He carefully folded his lanky frame and inserted himself into his ancient Morris, automatically ducking to avoid bumping his head. Taking the folder from under his arm, he opened it and frowned at the pages he had copied. What was odd about it was that nearly all of the men on Claire's list *had* been shown on another army list.

Within the ranks of a given clan regiment, men might have deserted as the dimensions of the coming disaster became clearer; that would have been nothing unusual. No, what made the whole thing so incomprehensible was that the names on Claire's list had shown up—entire and complete—as part of the Master of Lovat's regiment, sent late in the campaign to fulfill a promise of support made to the Stuarts by Simon Fraser, Lord Lovat.

Yet Claire had definitely said—and a glance at her original sheets confirmed it—that these men had all come from a small estate called Broch Tuarach, well to the south and west of the Fraser lands—on the border of the MacKenzie clan lands, in fact. More than that, she had said these men had been with the Highland army since the Battle of Prestonpans, which had occurred near the beginning of the campaign.

Roger shook his head. This made no kind of sense. Granted, Claire might have mistaken the timing—she had said herself that she was no historian. But not the location, surely? And how could men from the estate of Broch Tuarach, who had given no oath of allegiance to the chief of clan Fraser, have been at the disposal of Simon Fraser? True, Lord Lovat had been known as "the Old Fox," and for good reason, but Roger doubted that even that redoubtable old Earl had had sufficient wiliness to pull off something like this.

Frowning to himself, Roger started the car and pulled out of the parking lot. The archives at Culloden House were depressingly incomplete; mostly a lot of picturesque letters from Lord George Murray, beefing about supply problems, and things that looked good in the museum displays for the tourists. He needed a lot more than that.

"Hold on, cock," he reminded himself, squinting in the rearview mirror at the turn. "You're meant to be finding out what happened to the ones that *didn't* cark it at Culloden. What does it matter how they got there, so long as they left the battle in one piece?"

But he couldn't leave it alone. It was such an odd circumstance. Names got muddled with enormous frequency, especially in the Highlands, where half the population at any given moment seemed to be named "Alexander." Consequently, men had customarily been known by their place-names, as well as their clan or surnames. Sometimes *instead* of the surnames. "Lochiel," one of the most prominent Jacobite chieftains, was in fact Donald Cameron, *of* Lochiel, which distinguished him nicely from the hundreds of other Camerons named Donald.

And all the Highland men who hadn't been named Donald or Alec had been named John. Of the three names that he'd found on the death rolls that matched Claire's list, one was Donald Murray, one was Alexander MacKenzie Fraser, and one was John Graham Fraser. All without place-names attached; just the plain name, and the regiment to which they'd belonged. The Master of Lovat's regiment, the Fraser regiment.

But without the place-name, he couldn't be sure that they *were* the same men as the names on Claire's list. There were at least six John Frasers on the death roll, and even that was incomplete; the English had given little attention to completeness or accuracy—most of the records had been compiled after the fact, by clan chieftains counting noses and determining who hadn't come home. Frequently the chieftains themselves hadn't come home, which complicated matters.

He rubbed his hand hard through his hair with frustration, as though scalp massage might stimulate his brain. And if the three names *weren't* the same men, the mystery only deepened. A good half of Charles Stuart's army had been slaughtered at Culloden. And Lovat's men had been in the thick of it, right in the center of the battle. It was inconceivable that a group of thirty men had survived in that position without one fatality. The Master of Lovat's men had come late to the Rising; while desertion had been rife in other regiments, who had served long enough to have some idea what they were in for, the Frasers had been remarkably loyal—and suffered in consequence.

A loud horn-blast from behind startled him out of his concentration, and he pulled to the side to let a large, annoyed lorry rumble past. Thinking and driving were not compatible activities, he decided. End up smashed against a stone wall, if he kept this up.

He sat still for a moment, pondering. His natural impulse was to go to Mrs. Thomas's bed-and-breakfast, and tell Claire what he had found to date. The fact that this might involve basking for a few moments in the presence of Brianna Randall enhanced the appeal of this idea.

On the other hand, all his historian's instincts cried out for more data. And he wasn't at all sure that Claire was the person to provide it. He couldn't imagine why she should commission him to do this project, and at the same time, interfere with its completion by giving him inaccurate information. It wasn't sensible, and Claire Randall struck him as an eminently sensible person.

Still, there was that business with the whisky. His cheeks grew hot in memory. He was positive she'd done it on purpose—and as she didn't really seem the sort for practical jokes, he was compelled to assume she'd done it to stop him inviting Brianna to Broch Tuarach. Did she want to keep him away from the place, or only to stop him taking Brianna there? The more he thought about the incident, the more convinced he became that Claire Randall was keeping something from her daughter, but what it was, he couldn't imagine. Still less could he think what connection it had with him, or the project he had undertaken.

He'd give it up, were it not for two things. Brianna, and simple curiosity. He wanted to know what was going on, and he bloody well intended to find out.

He rapped his fist softly against the wheel, thinking, ignoring the rush of passing traffic. At last, decision made, he started the engine again and pulled into the road. At the next roundabout, he went three-quarters round the circle and headed for the town center of Inverness, and the railroad station.

The Flying Scotsman could have him in Edinburgh in three hours. The curator in charge of the Stuart Papers had been a close friend of the Reverend. And he had one clue to start with, puzzling as it was. The roll that had listed the names in the Master of Lovat's regiment had shown those thirty men as being under the command of a Captain James Fraser—of Broch Tuarach. This man was the only apparent link between Broch Tuarach and the Frasers of Lovat. He wondered why James Fraser had not appeared on Claire's list.

The sun was out; a rare event for mid-April, and Roger made the most of it by cranking down the tiny window on the driver's side, to let the bright wind blow past his ear.

He had had to stay overnight in Edinburgh, and coming back late the next day, had been so tired from the long train ride that he had done little more than eat the hot supper Fiona insisted on fixing him before he fell into bed. But today he had risen full of renewed energy and determination, and motored down to the small village of Broch Mordha, near the site of the estate called Broch Tuarach. If her mother didn't want Brianna Randall going to Broch Tuarach, there was nothing stopping *him* from having a look at the place.

He had actually found Broch Tuarach itself, or at least he assumed so; there was an enormous pile of fallen stone, surrounding the collapsed remnant of one of the ancient circular brochs, or towers, used in the distant past both for living and for defense. He had sufficient Gaelic to know that the name meant "north-facing tower," and had wondered briefly just how a circular tower could have come by such a name.

There was a manor house and its outbuildings nearby, also in ruins, though a good deal more of it was left. An estate agent's sign, weathered almost to illegibility, stood tacked to a stake in the dooryard. Roger stood on the slope above the house, looking around. At a glance, he could see nothing that would explain Claire's wanting to keep her daughter from coming here.

He parked the Morris in the dooryard, and climbed out. It was a beautiful site, but very remote; it had taken him nearly forty-five minutes of careful maneuvering to get his Morris down the rutted country lane from the main highway without fracturing his oil pan.

He didn't go into the house; it was plainly abandoned, and possibly dangerous—there would be nothing there. The name FRASER was carved into the lintel, though, and the same name adorned most of the small tombstones in what must have been the family graveyard—those that were legible. Not a great help, that, he reflected. None of these stones bore the names of men on his list. He'd have to go on along the road; according to the AA map, the village of Broch Mhorda was three miles farther on.

As he'd feared, the small village church had fallen into disuse and been knocked down years ago. Persistent knockings on doors elicited blank stares, dour looks, and finally a doubtful speculation from an aged farmer that the old parish records might have gone to the museum in Fort William, or maybe up to Inverness; there was a minister up that way who collected such rubbish.

Tired and dusty, but not yet discouraged, Roger trudged back to his car, sheltering in the lane by the village pub. This was the sort of setback that so often attended historical field research, and he was used to it. A quick pint—well, two, maybe, it was an unusually warm day—and then on to Fort William.

Serve him right, he reflected wryly, if the records he was looking for turned out to be in the Reverend's archives all along. That's what he got for neglecting his work to go on wild-goose chases to impress a girl. His trip to Edinburgh had done little more than serve to eliminate the three names he'd found at Culloden House; all three men proved to have come from different regiments, not the Broch Tuarach group.

The Stuart Papers took up three entire rooms, as well as untold packing cases in the basement of the museum, so he could hardly claim to have made an exhaustive study. Still, he had found a duplicate of the payroll he'd seen at

Culloden House, listing the joining of the men as part of a regiment under the overall command of the Master of Lovat—the Old Fox's son, that would have been, Young Simon. Cagy old bastard split his vote, Roger thought; sent the heir to fight for the Stuarts, and stayed home himself, claiming to have been a loyal subject of King Geordie all along. Much good it did him.

That document had listed Simon Fraser the Younger as commander, and made no mention of James Fraser. A James Fraser was mentioned in a number of army dispatches, memoranda, and other documents, though. If it was the same man, he'd been fairly active in the campaign. Still, with only the name "James Fraser," it was impossible to tell if it was the Broch Tuarach one; James was as common a Highland name as Duncan or Robert. In only one spot was a James Fraser listed with additional middle names that might help in identification, but that document made no mention of his men.

He shrugged, irritably waving off a sudden cloud of voracious midges. To go through those records in coherent fashion would take several years. Unable to shake the attentions of the midges, he ducked into the dark, brewery atmosphere of the pub, leaving them to mill outside in a frenzied cloud of inquiry.

Sipping the cool, bitter ale, he mentally reviewed the steps taken so far, and the options open to him. He had time to go to Fort William today, though it would mean getting back to Inverness late. And if the Fort William museum turned up nothing, then a good rummage through the Reverend's archives was the logical, if ironic, next step.

And after that? He drained the last drops of bitter, and signaled the landlord for another glass. Well, if it came down to it, a tramp round every kirkyard and burying ground in the general vicinity of Broch Tuarach was likely the best he could do in the short term. He doubted that the Randalls would stay in Inverness for the next two or three years, patiently awaiting results.

He felt in his pocket for the notebook that is the historian's constant companion. Before he left Broch Mhorda, he should at least have a look at what was left of the old kirkyard. You never knew what might turn up, and it would at least save him coming back.

The next afternoon, the Randalls came to take tea at Roger's invitation, and to hear his progress report.

"I've found several of the names on your list," he told Claire, leading the way into the study. "It's very odd; I haven't yet found any who died for sure at Culloden. I thought I had three, but they turned out to be different men with the same names." He glanced at Dr. Randall; she was standing quite still, one hand clasping the back of a wing chair, as though she'd forgotten where she was.

"Er, won't you sit down?" Roger invited, and with a small, startled jerk, she nodded and sat abruptly on the edge of the seat. Roger eyed her curiously, but went on, pulling out his folder of research notes and handing it to her.

"As I say, it's odd. I haven't tracked down all the names; I think I'll need to go nose about among the parish registers and graveyards near Broch Tuarach. I found most of these records among my father's papers. But you'd think I'd have turned up one or two battle-deaths at least, given that they were all at Culloden. Especially if, as you say, they were with one of the Fraser regiments; those were nearly all in the center of the battle, where the fighting was thickest."

"I know." There was something in her voice that made him look at her, puzzled, but her face was invisible as she bent over the desk. Most of the records were copies, made in Roger's own hand, as the exotic technology of photocopying had not yet penetrated to the government archive that guarded the Stuart Papers, but there were a few original sheets, unearthed from the late Reverend Wakefield's hoard of eighteenth-century documents. She turned over the records with a gentle finger, careful not to touch the fragile paper more than necessary.

"You're right; that *is* odd." Now he recognized the emotion in her voice —it was excitement, but mingled with satisfaction and relief. She had been in some way expecting this—or hoping for it.

"Tell me . . ." She hesitated. "The names you've found. What happened to them, if they didn't die at Culloden?"

He was faintly surprised that it should seem to matter so much to her, but obligingly pulled out the folder that held his research notes and opened it. "Two of them were on a ship's roll; they emigrated to America soon after Culloden. Four died of natural causes about a year later—not surprising, there was a terrible famine after Culloden, and a lot of people died in the Highlands. And this one I found in a parish register—but not the parish he came from. I'm fairly sure it's one of your men, though."

It was only as the tension went out of her shoulders that he noticed it had been there.

"Do you want me to look for the rest, still?" he asked, hoping that the answer would be "yes." He was watching Brianna over her mother's shoulder. She was standing by the cork wall, half-turned as though uninterested in her mother's project, but he could see a small vertical crease between her brows.

Perhaps she sensed the same thing he did, the odd air of suppressed excitement that surrounded Claire like an electric field. He had been aware of it from the moment she walked into the room, and his revelations had only increased it. He imagined that if he touched her, a great spark of static electricity would leap between them.

A knock on the study door interrupted his thoughts. The door opened and Fiona Graham came in, pushing a tea cart, fully equipped with teapot, cups, doilies, three kinds of sandwiches, cream-cakes, sponge cake, jam tarts, and scones with clotted cream.

"Yum!" said Brianna at the sight. "Is that all for us, or are you expecting ten other people?"

Claire Randall looked over the tea preparations, smiling. The electric field was still there, but damped down by major effort. Roger could see one of her hands, clenched so hard in the folds of her skirt that the edge of her ring cut into the flesh.

"That tea is so high, we won't need to eat for weeks," she said. "It looks wonderful!"

Fiona beamed. She was short, plump and pretty as a small brown hen. Roger sighed internally. While he was pleased to be able to offer his guests hospitality, he was well aware that the lavish nature of the refreshments was intended for his appreciation, not theirs. Fiona, aged nineteen, had one burning ambition in life. To be a wife. Preferably of a professional man. She had taken one look at Roger when he arrived a week earlier to tidy up the Reverend's affairs, and decided that an assistant professor of history was the best prospect Inverness offered.

Since then, he had been stuffed like a Christmas goose, had his shoes polished, his slippers and toothbrush laid out, his bed turned down, his coat brushed, the evening paper bought for him and laid alongside his plate, his neck rubbed when he had been working over his desk for long hours, and constant inquiries made concerning his bodily comfort, state of mind, and general health. He had never before been exposed to such a barrage of domesticity.

In short, Fiona was driving him mad. His current state of unshaven dishabille was more a reaction to her relentless pursuit than it was a descent into that natural squalor enjoyed by men temporarily freed from the demands of job and society.

The thought of being united in bonds of holy wedlock with Fiona Graham was one that froze him to the marrow. She would drive him insane within a year, with her constant pestering. Aside from that, though, there was Brianna Randall, now gazing contemplatively at the tea cart, as though wondering where to start.

He had been keeping his attention firmly fixed on Claire Randall and her project this afternoon, avoiding looking at her daughter. Claire Randall was lovely, with the sort of fine bones and translucent skin that would make her look much the same at sixty as she had at twenty. But looking at Brianna Randall made him feel slightly breathless.

She carried herself like a queen, not slumping as tall girls so often do. Noting her mother's straight back and graceful posture, he could see where that particular attribute had come from. But not the remarkable height, the cascade of waist-length red hair, sparked with gold and copper, streaked with amber and cinnamon, curling casually around face and shoulders like a mantle. The eyes, so dark a blue as almost to be black in some lights. Nor that wide, generous mouth, with a full lower lip that invited nibbling kisses and biting passion. Those things must have come from her father.

Roger was on the whole rather glad that her father was not present, since he would certainly have taken paternal umbrage at the sorts of thoughts Roger was thinking; thoughts he was desperately afraid showed on his face.

"Tea, eh?" he said heartily. "Splendid. Wonderful. Looks delicious, Fiona. Er, thanks, Fiona. I, um, don't think we need anything else."

Ignoring the broad hint to depart, Fiona nodded graciously at the compliments from the guests, laid out the doilies and cups with deft economy of motion, poured the tea, passed round the first plate of cake, and seemed prepared to stay indefinitely, presiding as lady of the house.

"Have some cream on your scones, Rog—I mean, Mr. Wakefield," she suggested, ladling it on without waiting for his reply. "You're much too thin; you want feeding up." She glanced conspiratorially at Brianna Randall, saying, "You know what men are; never eat properly without a woman to look after them."

"How lucky that he's got you to take care of him," Brianna answered politely.

Roger took a deep breath, and flexed his fingers several times, until the urge to strangle Fiona had passed.

"Fiona," he said. "Would you, um, could you possibly do me a small favor?"

She lit up like a small jack-o'-lantern, mouth stretched in an eager grin at the thought of doing something for him. "Of course, Rog—Mr. Wakefield! Anything at all!"

Roger felt vaguely ashamed of himself, but after all, he argued, it was for her good as much as his. If she didn't leave, he was shortly going to cease being responsible and commit some act they would both regret.

"Oh, thanks, Fiona. It's nothing much; only that I'd ordered some . . . some"—he thought frantically, trying to remember the name of one of the village merchants—"some tobacco, from Mr. Buchan in the High Street. I wonder if you'd be willing to go and fetch it for me; I could just do with a good pipe after such a wonderful tea."

Fiona was already untying her apron—the frilly, lace-trimmed one, Roger noted grimly. He closed his eyes briefly in relief as the study door shut behind her, dismissing for the moment the fact that he didn't smoke. With a sigh of relief, he turned to conversation with his guests.

"You were asking whether I wanted you to look for the rest of the names on my list," Claire said, almost at once. Roger had the odd impression that she shared his relief at Fiona's departure. "Yes, I do—if it wouldn't be too much trouble?"

"No, no! Not at all," Roger said, with only slight mendacity. "Glad to do it."

Roger's hand hovered uncertainly amid the largesse of the tea cart, then snaked down to grasp the crystal decanter of twelve-year-old Muir Breame whisky. After the skirmish with Fiona, he felt he owed it to himself.

"Will you have a bit of this?" he asked his guests politely. Catching the look of distaste on Brianna's face, he quickly added, "Or maybe some tea?"

"Tea," Brianna said with relief.

"You don't know what you're missing," Claire told her daughter, inhaling the whisky fumes with rapture.

"Oh yes I do," Brianna replied. "That's why I'm missing it." She shrugged and quirked an eyebrow at Roger.

"You have to be twenty-one before you can drink legally in Massachusetts," Claire explained to Roger. "Bree has another eight months to go, so she really isn't used to whisky."

"You act as though not liking whisky was a crime," Brianna protested, smiling at Roger above her teacup.

He raised his own brows in response. "My dear woman," he said severely. "This is *Scotland*. Of course not liking whisky is a crime!"

"Oh, aye?" said Brianna sweetly, in a perfect imitation of his own slight Scots burr. "Well, we'll hope it's no a capital offense like murrderrr, shall we?"

Taken by surprise, he swallowed a laugh with his whisky and choked. Coughing and pounding himself on the chest, he glanced at Claire to share the joke. A forced smile hung on her lips, but her face had gone quite pale. Then she blinked, the smile came back more naturally, and the moment passed.

Roger was surprised at how easily conversation flowed among them—both about trivialities, and about Claire's project. Brianna clearly had been interested in her father's work, and knew a great deal more about the Jacobites than did her mother.

"It's amazing they ever made it as far as Culloden," she said. "Did you know the Highlanders won the battle of Prestonpans with barely two thousand men? Against an English army of eight thousand? Incredible!"

"Well, and the Battle of Falkirk was nearly that way as well," Roger chimed in. "Outnumbered, outarmed, marching on foot . . . they should never have been able to do what they did . . . but they did!"

"Um-hm," said Claire, taking a deep gulp of her whisky. "They did."

"I was thinking," Roger said to Brianna, with an assumed air of casualness. "Perhaps you'd like to come with me to some of the places—the battle sites and other places? They're interesting, and I'm sure you'd be a tremendous help with the research."

Brianna laughed and smoothed back her hair, which had a tendency to drop into her tea. "I don't know about the help, but I'd love to come."

"Terrific!" Surprised and elated with her agreement, he fumbled for the decanter and nearly dropped it. Claire fielded it neatly, and filled his glass with precision.

"The least I can do, after spilling it the last time," she said, smiling in answer to his thanks.

Seeing her now, poised and relaxed, Roger was inclined to doubt his earlier suspicions. Maybe it had been an accident after all? That lovely cool face told him nothing.

A half-hour later, the tea table lay in shambles, the decanter stood empty, and the three of them sat in a shared stupor of content. Brianna shifted once or twice, glanced at Roger, and finally asked if she might use his "rest room."

"Oh, the W.C.? Of course." He heaved himself to his feet, ponderous with Dundee cake and almond sponge. If he didn't get away from Fiona soon, he'd weigh three hundred pounds before he got back to Oxford.

"It's one of the old-fashioned kind," he explained, pointing down the hall in the direction of the bathroom. "With a tank on the ceiling and a pull-chain."

"I saw some of those in the British Museum," Brianna said, nodding. "Only they weren't in with the exhibits, they were in the ladies' room." She hesitated, then asked, "You haven't got the same sort of toilet paper they have in the British Museum, do you? Because if you do, I've got some Kleenex in my purse."

Roger closed one eye and looked at her with the other. "Either that's a very odd non sequitur," he said, "or I've drunk a good deal more than I thought." In fact, he and Claire had accounted very satisfactorily for the Muir Breame, though Brianna had confined herself to tea.

Claire laughed, overhearing the exchange, and got up to hand Brianna several folded facial tissues from her own bag. "It won't be waxed paper stamped with 'Property of H. M. Government,' like the Museum's, but it likely won't be much better," she told her daughter. "British toilet paper is commonly rather a stiff article."

"Thanks." Brianna took the tissues and turned to the door, but then turned back. "Why on earth would people deliberately make toilet paper that feels like tinfoil?" she demanded.

"Hearts of oak are our men," Roger intoned, "stainless steel are their bums. It builds the national character."

"In the case of Scots, I expect it's hereditary nerve-deadening," Claire added. "The sort of men who could ride horse-back wearing a kilt have bottoms like saddle leather."

Brianna fizzed with laughter. "I'd hate to see what they used for toilet paper *then*," she said.

"Actually, it wasn't bad," Claire said, surprisingly. "Mullein leaves are really very nice; quite as good as two-ply bathroom tissue. And in the winter or indoors, it was usually a bit of damp rag; not very sanitary, but comfortable enough."

Roger and Brianna both gawked at her for a moment.

"Er . . . read it in a book," she said, and blushed amazingly.

As Brianna, still giggling, made her way off in search of the facilities, Claire remained standing by the door.

"It was awfully nice of you to entertain us so grandly," she said, smiling at Roger. The momentary discomposure had vanished, replaced by her usual poise. "And remarkably kind of you to have found out about those names for me."

"My pleasure entirely," Roger assured her. "It's made a nice change from cobwebs and mothballs. I'll let you know as soon as I've found out anything else about your Jacobites."

"Thank you." Claire hesitated, glanced over her shoulder, and lowered her voice. "Actually, since Bree's gone for the moment . . . there's something I wanted to ask you, in private."

Roger cleared his throat and straightened the tie he had donned in honor of the occasion.

"Ask away," he said, feeling cheerfully expansive with the success of the tea party. "I'm completely at your service."

"You were asking Bree if she'd go with you to do field research. I wanted to ask you . . . there's a place I'd rather you didn't take her, if you don't mind."

Alarm bells went off at once in Roger's head. Was he going to find out what the secret was about Broch Tuarach?

"The circle of standing stones—they call it Craigh na Dun." Claire's face was earnest as she leaned slightly closer. "There's an important reason, or I wouldn't ask. I want to take Brianna to the circle myself, but I'm afraid I can't tell you why, just now. I will, in time, but not quite yet. Will you promise me?"

Thoughts were chasing themselves through Roger's mind. So it hadn't been Broch Tuarach she wanted to keep the girl away from, after all! One mystery was explained, only to deepen another.

"If you like," he said at last. "Of course."

"Thank you." She touched his arm once, lightly, and turned to go. Seeing her silhouetted against the light, he was suddenly reminded of something. Perhaps it wasn't the moment to ask, but it couldn't do any harm.

"Oh, Dr. Randall—Claire?"

Claire turned back to face him. With the distractions of Brianna removed, he could see that Claire Randall was a very beautiful woman in her own right. Her face was flushed from the whisky, and her eyes were the most unusual light golden-brown color, he thought—like amber in crystal.

"In all the records that I found dealing with these men," Roger said, choosing his words carefully, "there was a mention of a Captain James Fraser, who seems to have been their leader. But he wasn't on your list. I only wondered; did you know about him?"

She stood stock-still for a moment, reminding him of the way she had behaved upon her arrival that afternoon. But after a moment, she shook herself slightly, and answered with apparent equanimity.

"Yes, I knew about him." She spoke calmly, but all the color had left her face, and Roger could see a small pulse beating rapidly at the base of her throat.

"I didn't put him on the list because I already knew what happened to him. Jamie Fraser died at Culloden."

"Are you sure?"

As though anxious to leave, Claire scooped up her handbag, and glanced down the hall toward the bathroom, where the rattling of the ancient knob indicated Brianna's attempts to get out.

"Yes," she said, not looking back. "I'm quite sure. Oh, Mr. Wakefield . . . Roger, I mean." She swung back now, fixing those oddly colored eyes on him. In this light, they looked almost yellow, he thought; the eyes of a big cat, a leopard's eyes.

"Please," she said, "don't mention Jamie Fraser to my daughter."

It was late, and he should have been abed long since, but Roger found himself unable to sleep. Whether from the aggravations of Fiona, the puzzling contradictions of Claire Randall, or from exaltation over the prospect of doing field research with Brianna Randall, he was wide-awake, and likely to remain so. Rather than toss, turn, or count sheep, he resolved to put his wakefulness to good use. A rummage through the Reverend's papers would probably put him to sleep in no time.

Fiona's light down the hall was still on, but he tiptoed down the stair, not to disturb her. Then, snapping on the study light, he stood for a moment, contemplating the magnitude of the task before him.

The wall exemplified the Reverend Wakefield's mind. Completely covering one side of the study, it was an expanse of corkboard measuring nearly twenty feet by twelve. Virtually none of the original cork was visible under the layers upon layers of papers, notes, photographs, mimeographed sheets, bills, receipts, bird feathers, torn-off corners of envelopes containing interesting postage stamps, address labels, key rings, postcards, rubber bands, and other impedimenta, all tacked up or attached by bits of string.

The trivia lay twelve layers deep in spots, yet the Reverend had always been able to set his hand unerringly on the bit he wanted. Roger thought that the wall must have been organized according to some underlying principle so subtle that not even American NASA scientists could discern it.

Roger viewed the wall dubiously. There was no logical point at which to start. He reached tentatively for a mimeographed list of General Assembly meeting dates sent out by the bishop's office, but was distracted by the sight underneath of a crayoned dragon, complete with artistic puffs of smoke from the flaring nostrils, and green flames shooting from the gaping mouth.

ROGER was written in large, straggling capitals at the bottom of the sheet. He vaguely remembered explaining that the dragon breathed green fire because it ate nothing but spinach. He let the General Assembly list fall back into place, and turned away from the wall. He could tackle that lot later.

The desk, an enormous oak rolltop with at least forty stuffed-to-bursting pigeonholes, seemed like pie by comparison. With a sigh, Roger pulled up the battered office chair and sat down to make sense of all the documents the Reverend thought worth keeping.

One stack of bills yet to be paid. Another of official-looking documents: automobile titles, surveyor's reports, building-inspection certificates. Another for historical notes and records. Another for family keepsakes. Another—by far the largest—for rubbish.

Deep in his task, he didn't hear the door open behind him, or the approaching footsteps. Suddenly a large teapot appeared on the desk next to him.

"Eh?" He straightened up, blinking.

"Thought you might do with some tea, Mr. Wake—I mean, Roger." Fiona set down a small tray containing a cup and saucer and a plate of biscuits.

"Oh, thanks." He was in fact hungry, and gave Fiona a friendly smile that sent the blood rushing into her round, fair cheeks. Seemingly encouraged by this, she didn't go away, but perched on the corner of the desk, watching him raptly as he went about his job between bites of chocolate biscuit.

Feeling obscurely that he ought to acknowledge her presence in some way, Roger held up a half-eaten biscuit and mumbled, "Good."

"Are they? I made them, ye know." Fiona's flush grew deeper. An attractive little girl, Fiona. Small, rounded, with dark curly hair and wide brown eyes. He found himself wondering suddenly whether Brianna Randall could cook, and shook his head to clear the image.

Apparently taking this as a gesture of disbelief, Fiona leaned closer. "No, really," she insisted. "A recipe of my gran's, it is. She always said they were a favorite of the Reverend's." The wide brown eyes grew a trifle misty. "She left me all her cookbooks and things. Me being the only granddaughter, ye see."

"I was sorry about your grandmother," Roger said sincerely. "Quick, was it?"

Fiona nodded mournfully. "Oh, aye. Right as rain all day, then she said after supper as she felt a bit tired, and went up to her bed." The girl lifted her shoulders and let them fall. "She went to sleep, and never woke up."

"A good way to go," Roger said. "I'm glad of it." Mrs. Graham had been a fixture in the manse since before Roger himself had come, a frightened, newly orphaned five-year-old. Middle-aged even then, and widowed with grown children, still she had provided an abundant supply of firm, no-nonsense maternal affection during school holidays when Roger came home to the manse. She and the Reverend made an odd pair, and yet between them they had made the old house definitely a home.

Moved by his memories, Roger reached out and squeezed Fiona's hand. She squeezed back, brown eyes suddenly melting. The small rosebud mouth parted slightly, and she leaned toward Roger, her breath warm on his ear.

"Uh, thank you," Roger blurted. He pulled his hand out of her grasp as though scorched. "Thanks very much. For the . . . the . . . er, tea and things. Good. It was good. Very good. Thanks." He turned and reached hastily for another stack of papers to cover his confusion, snatching a rolled bundle of newspaper clippings from a pigeonhole chosen at random.

He unrolled the yellowed clippings and spread them on the desk, holding them down between his palms. Frowning in apparent deep concentration, he bent his head lower over the smudged text. After a moment Fiona rose with a deep sigh, and her footsteps receded toward the door. Roger didn't look up.

Letting out a deep sigh of his own, he closed his eyes briefly and offered a quick prayer of thanks for the narrow escape. Yes, Fiona was attractive. Yes, she was undoubtedly a fine cook. She was also nosy, interfering, irritating, and firmly bent on marriage. Lay one hand on that rosy flesh again, and they'd be calling the banns by next month. But if there was any bann-calling to be done, the name linked with Roger Wakefield in the parish register was going to be Brianna Randall's, if Roger had anything to say about it.

Wondering just how much he *would* have to say about it, Roger opened his eyes and then blinked. For there in front of him was the name he had been envisioning on a wedding license—Randall.

Not, of course, Brianna Randall. Claire Randall. The headline read RE-TURNED FROM THE DEAD. Beneath was a picture of Claire Randall, twenty years younger, but looking little different than she did now, bar the expression on her face. She had been photographed sitting bolt upright in a hospital bed, hair tousled and flying like banners, delicate mouth set like a steel trap, and those extraordinary eyes glaring straight into the camera.

With a sense of shock, Roger thumbed rapidly through the bundle of clippings, then returned to read them more carefully. Though the papers had made as much sensation as possible of the story, the facts were sparse.

Claire Randall, wife of the noted historian Dr. Franklin W. Randall, had disappeared during a Scottish holiday in Inverness, late in the spring of 1946. A car she had been driving had been found, but the woman herself was gone without trace. All searches having proved futile, the police and bereaved husband had at length concluded that Claire Randall must have been murdered, perhaps by a roving tramp, and her body concealed somewhere in the rocky crags of the area.

And in 1948, nearly three years later, Claire Randall had returned. She had been found, disheveled and dressed in rags, wandering near the spot at which she had disappeared. While appearing to be in good physical health, though slightly malnourished, Mrs. Randall was disoriented and incoherent.

Raising his eyebrows slightly at the thought of Claire Randall ever being incoherent, Roger thumbed through the rest of the clippings. They contained little more than the information that Mrs. Randall was being treated for exposure and shock at a local hospital. There were photographs of the presumably overjoyed husband, Frank Randall. He looked stunned rather than overjoyed, Roger thought critically, not that one could blame him.

He examined the pictures curiously. Frank Randall had been a slender, handsome, aristocratic-looking man. Dark, with a rakish grace that showed in the angle of his body as he stood poised in the door of the hospital, surprised by the photographer on his way to visit his newly restored wife.

He traced the line of the long, narrow jaw, and the curve of the head, and realized that he was searching for traces of Brianna in her father. Intrigued by the thought, he rose and fetched one of Frank Randall's books from the shelves. Turning to the back jacket, he found a better picture. The jacket photograph showed Frank Randall in color, in full-face view. No, the hair was definitely dark brown, not red. That blazing glory must have come from a grandparent, along with the deep blue eyes, slanted as a cat's. Beautiful they were, but nothing like her mother's. And not like her father's either. Try as he might, he could see nothing of the flaming goddess in the face of the famous historian.

With a sigh, he closed the book and gathered up the clippings. He really must stop this mooning about and get on with the job, or he'd be sitting here for the next twelvemonth.

He was about to put the clippings into the keepsake pile, when one, headlined KIDNAPPED BY THE FAIRIES?, caught his eye. Or rather, not the clipping, but the date that appeared just above the headline. May 6, 1948.

He set the clipping down gently, as though it were a bomb that might go off in his hand. He closed his eyes and tried to summon up that first conversation with the Randalls. "You have to be twenty-one to drink in Massachusetts," Claire had said. "Brianna still has eight months to go." Twenty, then. Brianna Randall was twenty.

Unable to count backward fast enough, he rose and scrabbled through the perpetual calendar that the vicar had kept, in a clear space to itself on his cluttered wall. He found the date and stood with his finger pressed to the paper, blood draining from his face.

Claire Randall had returned from her mysterious disappearance disheveled, malnourished, incoherent—and pregnant.

In the fullness of time, Roger slept at last, but in consequence of his wakefulness, woke late and heavy-eyed, with an incipient headache, which neither a cold shower nor Fiona's chirpiness over breakfast did much to dispel.

The feeling was so oppressive that he abandoned his work and left the house for a walk. Striding through a light rain, he found the fresh air improved his headache, but unfortunately cleared his mind enough to start thinking again about the implications of last night's discovery.

Brianna didn't know. That was clear enough, from the way she spoke about her late father—or about the man she *thought* was her father, Frank Randall. And presumably Claire didn't mean her to know, or she would have told the girl herself. Unless this Scottish trip were meant to be a prelude to such a confession? The real father must have been a Scot; after all, Claire had disappeared—and reappeared—in Scotland. Was he still here?

That was a staggering thought. Had Claire brought her daughter to Scotland in order to introduce her to her real father? Roger shook his head doubtfully. Bloody risky, a thing like that. Bound to be confusing to Brianna, and painful as hell to Claire herself. Scare the shoes and socks off the father, too. And the girl plainly was devoted to Frank Randall. What was she going to feel like, realizing that the man she'd loved and idolized all her life in fact had no blood ties to her at all?

Roger felt bad for all concerned, including himself. He hadn't asked to have any part of this, and wished himself in the same state of blissful ignorance as yesterday. He liked Claire Randall, liked her very much, and he found the thought of her committing adultery distasteful. At the same time, he jeered at himself for his old-fashioned sentimentality. Who knew what her life with Frank Randall had been like? Perhaps she'd had good reason for going off with another man. But then why had she come back?

Sweating and moody, Roger wandered back to the house. He shed his jacket in the hallway and went up to have a bath. Sometimes bathing helped to soothe him, and he felt much in need of soothing.

He ran a hand along the row of hangers in his closet, groping for the fuzzy shoulder of his worn white toweling robe. Then, pausing for a moment, he reached instead far to the back of the closet, sweeping the hangers along the rod until he could grasp the one he wanted.

He viewed the shabby old dressing gown with affection. The yellow silk of the background had faded to ochre, but the multicolored peacocks were bold as ever, spreading their tails with lordly insouciance, regarding the viewer with eyes like black beads. He brought the soft fabric to his nose and inhaled deeply, closing his eyes. The faint whiff of Borkum Riff and spilled whisky brought back the Reverend Wakefield as not even his father's wall of trivia could do.

Many were the times he had smelled just that comforting aroma, with its upper note of Old Spice cologne, his face pressed against the smooth slickness of this silk, the Reverend's chubby arms wrapped protectively around him, promising him refuge. He had given the old man's other clothes to Oxfam, but somehow he couldn't bear to part with this.

On impulse, he slipped the robe over his bare shoulders, mildly surprised at the light warmth of it, like the caress of fingers across his skin. He shifted his shoulders pleasurably under the silk, then wrapped it closely about his body, tying the belt in a careless knot.

Keeping a wary eye out in case of raids by Fiona, he made his way along the upper hall to the bathroom. The hot-water geyser stood against the head of the bath like the guardian of a sacred spring, squat and eternal. Another of his youthful memories was the weekly terror of trying to light the geyser with a flint striker in order to heat the water for his bath, the gas escaping past his head with a menacing hiss as his hands, sweaty with the fear of explosion and imminent death, slipped ineffectively on the metal of the striker.

Long since rendered automatic by an operation on its mysterious innards, the geyser now gurgled quietly to itself, the gas ring at its base rumbling and whooshing with unseen flame beneath the metal shield. Roger twisted the cracked "Hot" tap as far as it would go, added a half-turn of the "Cold," then stood to study himself in the mirror while waiting for his bath to fill.

Nothing much wrong with him, he reflected, sucking in his stomach and pulling himself upright before the full-length reflection on the back of the door. Firm. Trim. Long-legged, but not spindle-shanked. Possibly a bit scrawny through the shoulders? He frowned critically, twisting his lean body back and forth.

He ran a hand through his thick black hair, until it stood on end like a shaving brush, trying to envision himself with a beard and long hair, like some of his students. Would he look dashing, or merely moth-eaten? Possibly an earring, while he was about it. He might look piratical then, like Edward Teach or Henry Morgan. He drew his brows together and bared his teeth.

"Grrrrr," he said to his reflection.

"Mr. Wakefield?" said the reflection.

Roger leaped back, startled, and stubbed his toe painfully against the protruding claw-foot of the ancient bath.

"Ow!"

"Are you all right, Mr. Wakefield?" the mirror said. The porcelain doorknob rattled.

"Of course I am!" he snapped testily, glaring at the door. "Go away, Fiona, I'm bathing!"

There was a giggle from the other side of the door.

"Ooh, twice in one day. *Aren't* we the dandy, though? Do you want some of the bay-rum soap? It's in the cupboard there, if you do."

"No, I don't," he snarled. The water level had risen midway in the tub, and he cut off the taps. The sudden silence was soothing, and he drew a deep breath of steam into his lungs. Wincing slightly at the heat, he stepped into the water and lowered himself gingerly, feeling a light sweat break out on his face as the heat rushed up his body.

"Mr. Wakefield?" The voice was back, chirping on the other side of the door like a hectoring robin.

"Go *away*, Fiona," he gritted, easing himself back in the tub. The steaming water rose around him, comforting as a lover's arms. "I have everything I want."

"No, you haven't," said the voice.

"Yes, I have." His eye swept the impressive lineup of bottles, jars, and implements arrayed on the shelf above the tub. "Shampoo, three kinds. Hair conditioner. Shaving cream. Razor. Body soap. Facial soap. After-shave. Cologne. Deodorant stick. I don't lack a thing, Fiona."

"What about towels?" said the voice, sweetly.

After a wild glance about the completely towel-less confines of the bathroom, Roger closed his eyes, clenched his teeth and counted slowly to ten. This proving insufficient, he made it twenty. Then, feeling himself able to answer without foaming at the mouth, he said calmly.

"All right, Fiona. Set them outside the door, please. And then, please . . . please, Fiona. . . . *go*."

A rustle outside was succeeded by the sound of reluctantly receding footsteps, and Roger, with a sigh of relief, gave himself up to the joys of privacy. Peace. Quiet. No Fiona.

Now, able to think more objectively about his upsetting discovery, he found himself more than curious about Brianna's mysterious real father. Judging from the daughter, the man must have had a rare degree of physical attractiveness; would that alone have been sufficient to lure a woman like Claire Randall?

He had wondered already whether Brianna's father might have been a Scot. Did he live—or *had* he lived—in Inverness? He supposed such proximity might account for Claire's nervousness, and the air she had of keeping secrets. But did it account for the puzzling requests she had made of him? She didn't want him to take Brianna to Craigh na Dun, nor to mention the captain of the Broch Tuarach men to her daughter. Why on earth not?

A sudden thought made him sit upright in the tub, water sloshing heedlessly against the cast-iron sides. What if it were not the eighteenth-century Jacobite soldier she was concerned about, but *only his name*? What if the man who had fathered her daughter in 1947 was also named James Fraser? It was a common enough name in the Highlands.

Yes, he thought, that might very well explain it. As for Claire's desire to show her daughter the stone circle herself, perhaps that was also connected with the mystery of her father; maybe that's where she'd met the man, or perhaps that's where Brianna had been conceived. Roger was well aware that the stone circle was commonly used as a trysting spot; he'd taken girls there himself in high school, relying on the circle's air of pagan mystery to loosen their reserve. It always worked.

He had a sudden startling vision of Claire Randall's fine white limbs, locked in wild abandon with the naked, straining body of a red-haired man, the two bodies slick with rain and stained with crushed grass, twisting in ecstasy among the standing stones. The vision was so shocking in its specificity that it left him trembling, sweat running down his chest to vanish into the steaming water of the bath.

Christ! How was he going to meet Claire Randall's eyes, next time they met? What was he going to say to Brianna, for that matter? "Read any good books lately?" "Seen any good flicks?" "D'you know you're illegitimate?"

He shook his head, trying to clear it. The truth was that he didn't know what to do next. It was a messy situation. He wanted no part in it, and yet he did. He liked Claire Randall; he liked Brianna Randall, too—much more than liked her, truth be told. He wanted to protect her, and save her whatever pain he could. And yet there seemed no way to do that. All he could do was keep his mouth shut until Claire Randall did whatever it was she planned to do. And then be there to pick up the pieces.

3

Mothers and Daughters

I wondered just how many tiny tea shops there were in Inverness. The High Street is lined on both sides with small cafes and tourist shops, as far as the eye can see. Once Queen Victoria had made the Highlands safe for travelers by giving her Royal approval of the place, tourists had flocked north in ever-increasing numbers. The Scots, unaccustomed to receiving anything from the South but armed invasions and political interference, had risen to the challenge magnificently.

You couldn't walk more than a few feet on the main street of any Highland town without encountering a shop selling shortbread, Edinburgh rock, handkerchiefs embroidered with thistles, toy bagpipes, clan badges of cast aluminum, letter-openers shaped like claymores, coin purses shaped like sporrans (some with an anatomically correct "Scotchman" attached underneath), and an eye-jangling assortment of spurious clan tartans, adorning every conceivable object made of fabric, from caps, neckties, and serviettes down to a particularly horrid yellow "Buchanan" sett used to make men's nylon Y-front underpants.

Looking over an assortment of tea towels stenciled with a wildly inaccurate depiction of the Loch Ness monster singing "Auld Lang Syne," I thought Victoria had a lot to answer for.

Brianna was wandering slowly down the narrow aisle of the shop, head tilted back as she stared in amazement at the assortment of merchandise hanging from the rafters.

"Do you think those are *real*?" she said, pointing upward at a set of mounted stag's antlers, poking their tines inquisitively through an absolute forest of bagpipe drones.

"The antlers? Oh, yes. I don't imagine plastics technology's got quite *that* good, yet," I replied. "Besides, look at the price. Anything over one hundred pounds is very likely real."

Brianna's eyes widened, and she lowered her head.

"Jeez. I think I'll get Jane a skirt-length of tartan instead."

"Good-quality wool tartan won't cost a lot less," I said dryly, "but it will be a lot easier to get home on the plane. Let's go across to the Kiltmaker store, then; they'll have the best quality."

It had begun to rain—of course—and we tucked our paper-wrapped parcels underneath the raincoats I had prudently insisted we wear. Brianna snorted with sudden amusement.

"You get so used to calling these things 'macs,' you forget what they're really called. I'm not surprised it was a Scot that invented them," she added, looking up at the water sheeting down from the edge of the canopy overhead. "Does it rain *all* the time here?"

"Pretty much," I said, peering up and down through the downpour for oncoming traffic. "Though I've always supposed Mr. Macintosh was rather a lily-livered sort; most Scots I've known were relatively impervious to rain." I bit my lip suddenly, but Brianna hadn't noticed the slip, minor as it was; she was eyeing the ankle-deep freshet running down the gutter.

"Tell you what, Mama, maybe we'd better go up to the crossing. We aren't going to make it jaywalking here."

Nodding assent, I followed her up the street, heart pounding with adrenaline under the clammy cover of my mac. *When are you going to get it over with?* my mind demanded. *You can't keep watching your words and swallowing half the things you start to say. Why not just tell her?*

Not yet, I thought to myself. I'm not a coward—or if I am, it doesn't matter. But it isn't quite time yet. I wanted her to see Scotland first. Not this lot—as we passed a shop offering a display of tartan baby booties—but the countryside. And Culloden. Most of all, I want to be able to tell her the end of the story. And for that, I need Roger Wakefield.

As though my thought had summoned it into being, the bright orange top of a battered Morris caught my eye in the parking lot to the left, glowing like a traffic beacon in the foggy wet.

Brianna had seen it too—there couldn't be many cars in Inverness of that specific color and disreputability—and pointed at it, saying, "Look, Mama, isn't that Roger Wakefield's car?"

"Yes, I think so," I said. There was a cafe on the right, from which the scent of fresh scones, stale toast, and coffee drifted to mingle with the fresh, rainy air. I grabbed Brianna's arm and pulled her into the cafe.

"I think I'm hungry after all," I explained. "Let's have some cocoa and biscuits."

Still child enough to be tempted by chocolate, and young enough to be willing to eat at any time, Bree offered no argument, but sat down at once and picked up the tea-stained sheet of green paper that served as the daily menu.

I didn't particularly want cocoa, but I did want a moment or two to think. There was a large sign on the concrete wall of the parking lot across the street, reading PARKING FOR SCOTRAIL ONLY, followed by various lowercase threats as to what would happen to the vehicles of people who parked there without being train riders. Unless Roger knew something about the forces of law and order in Inverness that I didn't know, chances were that he had taken a train. Granted that he could have gone anywhere, either Edinburgh or London seemed most likely. He was taking this research project seriously, dear lad.

We had come up on the train from Edinburgh ourselves. I tried to remember what the schedule was like, with no particular success.

"I wonder if Roger will be back on the evening train?" Bree said, echoing my thoughts with an uncanniness that made me choke on my cocoa. The fact that she wondered about Roger's reappearance made *me* wonder just how much notice she had taken of young Mr. Wakefield.

A fair amount, apparently.

"I was thinking," she said casually, "maybe we should get something for Roger Wakefield while we're out—like a thank-you for that project he's doing for you?"

"Good idea," I said, amused. "What do you think he'd like?"

She frowned into her cocoa as though looking for inspiration. "I don't know. Something nice; it looks like that project could be a lot of work." She glanced up at me suddenly, brows raised.

"Why did you ask him?" she said. "If you wanted to trace people from the eighteenth century, there're companies that do that. Genealogies and like that, I mean. Daddy always used Scot-Search, if he had to figure out a genealogy and didn't have time to do it himself."

"Yes, I know," I said, and took a deep breath. We were on shaky ground here. "This project—it was something special to . . . to your father. He would have wanted Roger Wakefield to do it."

"Oh." She was silent for a while, watching the rain spatter and pearl on the cafe window.

"Do you miss Daddy?" she asked suddenly, nose buried in her cup, lashes lowered to avoid looking at me.

"Yes," I said. I ran a forefinger up the edge of my own untouched cup, wiping off a drip of spilled cocoa. "We didn't always get on, you know that, but . . . yes. We respected each other; that counts for a lot. And we liked each other, in spite of everything. Yes, I do miss him."

She nodded, wordless, and put her hand over mine with a little squeeze. I curled my fingers around hers, long and warm, and we sat linked for a little while, sipping cocoa in silence.

"You know," I said at last, pushing back my chair with a squeak of metal on linoleum, "I'd forgotten something. I need to post a letter to the hospital. I'd meant to do it on the way into town, but I forgot. If I hurry, I think I can just catch the outgoing post. Why don't you go to the Kiltmaker's—it's just down the street, on the other side—and I'll join you there after I've been to the post office?"

Bree looked surprised, but nodded readily enough.

"Oh. Okay. Isn't the post office a long way, though? You'll get soaked."

"That's all right. I'll take a cab." I left a pound note on the table to pay for the meal, and shrugged back into my raincoat.

In most cities, the usual response of taxicabs to rain is to disappear, as though they were soluble. In Inverness, though, such behavior would render the species rapidly extinct. I'd walked less than a block before finding two squatty black cabs lurking outside a hotel, and I slid into the warm, tobacco-scented interior with a cozy feeling of familiarity. Besides the greater leg room and comfort, British cabs smelled different than American ones; one of those tiny things I had never realized I'd missed during the last twenty years.

"Number sixty-four? Tha's the auld manse, aye?" In spite of the efficiency of the cab's heater, the driver was muffled to the ears in a scarf and thick jacket, with a flat cap guarding the top of his head from errant drafts. Modern Scots had gone a bit soft, I reflected; a long way from the days when sturdy High-landers had slept in the heather in nothing but shirt and plaid. On the other hand, I wasn't all that eager to go sleep in the heather in a wet plaid, either. I nodded to the driver, and we set off in a splash.

I felt a bit subversive, sneaking round to interview Roger's housekeeper while he was out, and fooling Bree into the bargain. On the other hand, it would be difficult to explain to either of them just what I was doing. I hadn't yet determined exactly how or when I would tell them what I had to say, but I knew it wasn't time yet.

My fingers probed the inner pocket of my mac, reassured by the scrunch of the envelope from Scot-Search. While I hadn't paid a great deal of attention to Frank's work, I did know about the firm, which maintained a staff of half a dozen professional researchers specializing in Scottish genealogy; not the sort of place that gave you a family tree showing your relationship to Robert the Bruce and had done with it.

They'd done their usual thorough, discreet job on Roger Wakefield. I knew who his parents and grandparents had been, back some seven or eight generations. What I didn't know was what he might be made of. Time would tell me that.

I paid off the cab and splashed up the flooded path to the steps of the old minister's house. It was dry on the porch, and I had a chance to shake off the worst of the wet before the door was opened to my ring.

Fiona beamed in welcome; she had the sort of round, cheerful face whose natural expression was a smile. She was attired in jeans and a frilly apron, and the scent of lemon polish and fresh baking wafted from its folds like incense.

"Why, Mrs. Randall!" she exclaimed. "Can I be helpin' ye at all, then?"

"I think perhaps you might, Fiona," I said. "I wanted to talk to you about your grandmother."

"Are you sure you're all right, Mama? I could call Roger and ask him to go tomorrow, if you'd like me to stay with you." Brianna hovered in the doorway of the guesthouse bedroom, an anxious frown creasing her brow. She was dressed for walking, in boots, jeans, and sweater, but she'd added the brilliant orange and blue silk scarf Frank had brought her from Paris, just before his death two years before.

"Just the color of your eyes, little beauty," he'd said, smiling as he draped the scarf around her shoulders, "—orange." It was a joke between them now, the "little beauty," as Bree had topped Frank's modest five feet ten since she was fifteen. It was what he'd called her since babyhood, though, and the tenderness of the old name lingered as he reached up to touch the tip of her nose.

The scarf—the blue part—was in fact the color of her eyes; of Scottish lochs and summer skies, and the misty blue of distant mountains. I knew she treasured it, and revised my assessment of her interest in Roger Wakefield upward by several notches.

"No, I'll be fine," I assured her. I gestured toward the bedside table, adorned with a small teapot, carefully keeping warm under a knitted cozy, and a silver-plated toast rack, just as carefully keeping the toast nice and cold. "Mrs. Thomas brought me tea and toast; perhaps I'll be able to nibble a little later on." I hoped she couldn't hear the rumbling of my empty stomach under the bedclothes, registering appalled disbelief at this prospect.

"Well, all right." She turned reluctantly to the door. "We'll come right back after Culloden, though."

"Don't hurry on my account," I called after her.

I waited until I heard the sound of the door closing below, and was sure she was on her way. Only then did I reach into the drawer of the bedtable for the large Hershey bar with almonds that I had hidden there the night before.

Cordial relations with my stomach reestablished, I lay back against the pillow, idly watching the gray haze thicken in the sky outside. The tip of a budding lime branch flicked intermittently against the window; the wind was rising. It was warm enough in the bedroom, with the central-heating vent roaring away at the foot of the bed, but I shivered nonetheless. It would be cold on Culloden Field.

Not, perhaps, as cold as it had been in the April of 1746, when Bonnie Prince Charlie led his men onto that field, to stand in the face of freezing sleet and the roar of English cannon fire. Accounts of the day reported that it was bitterly cold, and the Highland wounded had lain heaped with the dead, soaked in blood and rain, awaiting the mercies of their English victors. The Duke of Cumberland, in command of the English army, had given no quarter to the fallen.

The dead were heaped up like cordwood and burned to prevent the spread of disease, and history said that many of the wounded had gone to a similar fate, without the grace of a final bullet. All of them lay now beyond the reach of war or weather, under the greensward of Culloden Field.

I had seen the place once, nearly thirty years before, when Frank had taken me there on our honeymoon. Now Frank was dead, too, and I had brought my daughter back to Scotland. I wanted Brianna to see Culloden, but no power on earth would make me set foot again on that deadly moor.

I supposed I had better stay in bed, to maintain credence in the sudden indisposition that had prevented me accompanying Brianna and Roger on their expedition; Mrs. Thomas might blab if I got up and put in an order for lunch. I peeked into the drawer; three more candy bars and a mystery novel. With luck, those would get me through the day.

The novel was good enough, but the rush of the rising wind outside was hypnotic, and the embrace of the warm bed welcoming. I dropped peacefully into sleep, to dream of kilted Highland men, and the sound of soft-spoken Scots, burring round a fire like the sound of bees in the heather.

4

Culloden

"What a mean little piggy face!" Brianna stooped to peer fascinated at the red-coated mannequin that stood menacingly to one side of the foyer in the Culloden Visitors Centre. He stood a few inches over five feet, powdered wig thrust belligerently forward over a low brow and pendulous, pink-tinged cheeks.

"Well, he was a fat little fellow," Roger agreed, amused. "Hell of a general, though, at least as compared to his elegant cousin over there." He waved a hand at the taller figure of Charles Edward Stuart on the other side of the foyer, gazing nobly off into the distance under his blue velvet bonnet with its white cockade, loftily ignoring the Duke of Cumberland.

"They called him 'Butcher Billy.' " Roger gestured at the Duke, stolid in white knee breeches and gold-braided coat. "For excellent reason. Aside from what they did here"—he waved toward the expanse of the spring-green moor outside, dulled by the lowering sky—"Cumberland's men were responsible for the worst reign of English terror ever seen in the Highlands. They chased the survivors of the battle back into the hills, burning and looting as they went. Women and children were turned out to starve, and the men shot down where they stood—with no effort to find out whether they'd ever fought for Charlie. One of the Duke's contemporaries said of him, 'He created a desert and called it peace'—and I'm afraid the Duke of Cumberland is still rather noticeably unpopular hereabouts."

This was true; the curator of the visitors' museum, a friend of Roger's, had told him that while the figure of the Bonnie Prince was treated with reverent respect, the buttons off the Duke's jacket were subject to constant disappearance, while the figure itself had been the butt of more than one rude joke.

"He said one morning he came in early and turned on the light, to find a genuine Highland dirk sticking in His Grace's belly," Roger said, nodding at the podgy little figure. "Said it gave him a right turn."

"I'd think so," Brianna murmured, looking at the Duke with raised brows. "People still take it that seriously?"

"Oh, aye. Scots have long memories, and they're not the most forgiving of people."

"Really?" She looked at him curiously. "Are you Scottish, Roger? Wakefield doesn't sound like a Scottish name, but there's something about the way you talk about the Duke of Cumberland . . ." There was the hint of a smile around her mouth, and he wasn't sure whether he was being teased, but he answered her seriously enough.

"Oh, aye." He smiled as he said it. "I'm Scots. Wakefield's not my own name, see; the Reverend gave it me when he adopted me. He was my mother's uncle—when my parents were killed in the War, he took me to live with him. But my own name is MacKenzie. As for the Duke of Cumberland"—he nodded at the plate-glass window, through which the monuments of Culloden Field were plainly visible. "There's a clan stone out there, with the name of MacKenzie carved on it, and a good many of my relatives under it."

He reached out and flicked a gold epaulet, leaving it swinging. "I don't feel quite so personal about it as some, but I haven't forgotten, either." He held out a hand to her. "Shall we go outside?"

It was cold outside, with a gusty wind that lashed two pennons, flying atop the poles set at either side of the moor. One yellow, one red, they marked the positions where the two commanders had stood behind their troops, awaiting the outcome of the battle.

"Well back out of the way, I see," Brianna observed dryly. "No chance of getting in the way of a stray bullet."

Roger noticed her shivering, and drew her hand further through his arm, bringing her close. He thought he might burst from the sudden swell of happiness touching her gave him, but tried to disguise it with a retreat into historical monologue. "Well, that was how generals led, back then—from the rear. Especially Charlie; he ran off so fast at the end of the battle that he left behind his sterling silver picnic set."

"A *picnic* set? He brought a picnic to the battle?"

"Oh, aye." Roger found that he quite liked being Scottish for Brianna. He usually took pains to keep his accent modulated under the all-purpose Oxbridge speech that served him at the university, but now he was letting it have free rein for the sake of the smile that crossed her face when she heard it.

"D'ye know why they called him 'Prince Charlie'?" Roger asked. "English people always think it was a nickname, showing how much his men loved him."

"It wasn't?"

Roger shook his head. "No, indeed. His men called him Prince *Tcharlach*" —he spelled it carefully—"which is the Gaelic for Charles. *Tcharlach mac Seamus,* 'Charles, son of James.' Very formal and respectful indeed. It's only that *Tcharlach* in Gaelic sounds the hell of a lot like 'Charlie' in English."

Brianna grinned. "So he never was 'Bonnie Prince Charlie'?"

"Not then." Roger shrugged. "Now he is, of course. One of those little historical mistakes that get passed on for fact. There are a lot of them."

"And you a historian!" Brianna said, teasing.

Roger smiled wryly. "That's how I know."

They wandered slowly down the graveled paths that led through the battlefield, Roger pointing out the positions of the different regiments that had fought there, explaining the order of battle, recounting small anecdotes of the commanders.

As they walked, the wind died down, and the silence of the field began to assert itself. Gradually their conversation died away as well, until they were talking only now and then, in low voices, almost whispers. The sky was gray with cloud from horizon to horizon, and everything beneath its bowl seemed muted, with only the whisper of the moor plants speaking in the voices of the men who fed them.

"This is the place they call the Well of Death." Roger stooped by the small spring. Barely a foot square, it was a tiny pool of dark water, welling under a ridge of stone. "One of the Highland chieftains died here; his followers washed the blood from his face with the water from this spring. And over there are the graves of the clans."

The clan stones were large boulders of gray granite, rounded by weather and blotched with lichens. They sat on patches of smooth grass, widely scattered near the edge of the moor. Each one bore a single name, the carving so faded by weather as to be nearly illegible in some cases. MacGillivray. MacDonald. Fraser. Grant. Chisholm. MacKenzie.

"Look," Brianna said, almost in a whisper. She pointed at one of the stones. A small heap of greenish-gray twigs lay there; a few early spring flowers mingled, wilted, with the twigs.

"Heather," Roger said. "It's more common in the summer, when the heather is blooming—then you'll see heaps like that in front of every clan stone. Purple, and here and there a branch of the white heather—the white is for luck, and for kingship; it was Charlie's emblem, that and the white rose."

"Who leaves them?" Brianna squatted on her heels next to the path, touching the twigs with a gentle finger.

"Visitors." Roger squatted next to her. He traced the faded letters on the stone—FRASER. "People descended from the families of the men who were killed here. Or just those who like to remember them."

She looked sidelong at him, hair drifting around her face. "Have you ever done it?"

He looked down, smiling at his hands as they hung between his knees.

"Yes. I suppose it's very sentimental, but I do."

Brianna turned to the thicket of moor plants that edged the path on the other side.

"Show me which is heather," she said.

On the way home, the melancholy of Culloden lifted, but the feeling of shared sentiment lingered, and they talked and laughed together like old friends.

"It's too bad Mother couldn't come with us," Brianna remarked as they turned into the road where the Randalls' bed-and-breakfast was.

Much as he liked Claire Randall, Roger didn't agree at all that it was too bad she hadn't come. Three, he thought, would have been a crowd, and no mistake. But he grunted noncommittally, and a moment later asked, "How *is* your mother? I hope she's not terribly ill."

"Oh, no, it's just an upset stomach—at least that's what she says." Brianna frowned to herself for a moment, then turned to Roger, laying a hand lightly on his leg. He felt the muscles quiver from knee to groin, and had a hard time keeping his mind on what she was saying. She was still talking about her mother.

". . . think she's all right?" she finished. She shook her head, and copper glinted from the waves of her hair, even in the dull light of the car. "I don't know; she seems awfully preoccupied. Not ill, exactly—more as though she's kind of worried about something."

Roger felt a sudden heaviness in the pit of his stomach.

"Mphm," he said. "Maybe just being away from her work. I'm sure it will be all right." Brianna smiled gratefully at him as they pulled up in front of Mrs. Thomas's small stone house.

"It was great, Roger," she said, touching him lightly on the shoulder. "But there wasn't much here to help with Mama's project. Can't I help you with some of the grubby stuff?"

Roger's spirits lightened considerably, and he smiled up at her. "I think that might be arranged. Want to come tomorrow and have a go at the garage with me? If it's filth you want, you can't get much grubbier than that."

"Great." She smiled, leaning on the car to look back in at him. "Maybe Mother will want to come along and help."

He could feel his face stiffen, but kept gallantly smiling.

"Right," he said. "Great. I hope so."

In the event, it was Brianna alone who came to the manse the next day.

"Mama's at the public library," she explained. "Looking up old phone directories. She's trying to find someone she used to know."

Roger's heart skipped a beat at that. He had checked the Reverend's phonebook the night before. There were three local listings under the name "James Fraser," and two more with different first names, but the middle initial "J."

"Well, I hope she finds him," he said, still trying for casualness. "You're really sure you want to help? It's boring, filthy work." Roger looked at Brianna dubiously, but she nodded, not at all discomposed at the prospect.

"I know. I used to help my father sometimes, dredging through old records and finding footnotes. Besides, it's Mama's project; the least I can do is help you with it."

"All right." Roger glanced down at his white shirt. "Let me change, and we'll go have a look."

The garage door creaked, groaned, then surrendered to the inevitable and surged suddenly upward, amid the twanging of springs and clouds of dust.

Brianna waved her hands back and forth in front of her face, coughing. "Gack!" she said. "How long since anyone's been in this place?"

"Eons, I expect." Roger replied absently. He shone his torch around the inside of the garage, briefly lighting stacks of cardboard cartons and wooden crates, old steamer trunks smeared with peeling labels, and amorphous tarpaulin-draped shapes. Here and there, the upturned legs of furniture poked through the gloom like the skeletons of small dinosaurs, protruding from their native rock formations.

There was a sort of fissure in the junk; Roger edged into this and promptly disappeared into a tunnel bounded by dust and shadows, his progress marked by the pale spot of his torch as it shone intermittently on the ceiling. At last, with a cry of triumph, he seized the dangling tail of a string hanging from above, and the garage was suddenly illuminated in the glare of an oversized bulb.

"This way," Roger said, reappearing abruptly and taking Brianna by the hand. "There's sort of a clear space in back."

An ancient table stood against the back wall. Perhaps originally the centerpiece of the Reverend Wakefield's dining room, it had evidently gone through several successive incarnations as kitchen block, toolbench, sawhorse, and painting table, before coming to rest in this dusty sanctuary. A heavily cobwebbed window overlooked it, through which a dim light shone on the nicked, paint-splattered surface.

"We can work here," Roger said, yanking a stool out of the mess and dusting it perfunctorily with a large handkerchief. "Have a seat, and I'll see if I can pry the window open; otherwise, we'll suffocate."

Brianna nodded, but instead of sitting down, began to poke curiously through the nearer piles of junk, as Roger heaved at the warped window frame. He could hear her behind him, reading the labels on some of the boxes. "Here's 1930–33," she said, "And here's 1942–46. What are these?"

"Journals," said Roger, grunting as he braced his elbows on the grimy sill. "My father—the Reverend, I mean—he always kept a journal. Wrote it up every night after supper."

"Looks like he found plenty to write about." Brianna hoisted down several of the boxes, and stacked them to the side, in order to inspect the next layer. "Here's a bunch of boxes with names on them—'Kerse,' 'Livingston,' 'Balnain.' Parishioners?"

"No. Villages." Roger paused in his labors for a moment, panting. He wiped his brow, leaving a streak of dirt down the sleeve of his shirt. Luckily both of them were dressed in old clothes, suitable for rootling in filth. "Those will be notes on the history of various Highland villages. Some of those boxes ended up as books, in fact; you'll see them in some of the local tourist shops through the Highlands."

He turned to a pegboard from which hung a selection of dilapidated tools, and selected a large screwdriver to aid his assault on the window.

"Look for the ones that say 'Parish Registers,' he advised. "Or for village names in the area of Broch Tuarach."

"I don't know any of the villages in the area," Brianna pointed out.

"Oh, aye, I was forgetting." Roger inserted the point of the screwdriver between the edges of the window frame, grimly chiseling through layers of ancient paint. "Look for the names Broch Mordha . . . um, Mariannan, and . . . oh, St. Kilda. There's others, but those are ones I know had fair-sized churches that have been closed or knocked down."

"Okay." Pushing aside a hanging flap of tarpaulin, Brianna suddenly leaped backward with a sharp cry.

"What? What is it?" Roger whirled from the window, screwdriver at the ready.

"I don't know. Something skittered away when I touched that tarp." Brianna pointed, and Roger lowered his weapon, relieved.

"Oh, that all? Mouse, most like. Maybe a rat."

"A *rat!* You have *rats* in here?" Brianna's agitation was noticeable.

"Well, I hope not, because if so, they'll have been chewing up the records we're looking for," Roger replied. He handed her the torch. "Here, shine this in any dark places; at least you won't be taken by surprise."

"Thanks a lot." Brianna accepted the torch, but still eyed the stacks of cartons with some reluctance.

"Well, go on then," Roger said. "Or did you want me to do you a rat satire on the spot?"

Brianna's face split in a wide grin. "A rat satire? What's that?"

Roger delayed his answer, long enough for another try at the window. He pushed until he could feel his biceps straining against the fabric of his shirt, but at last, with a rending screech, the window gave way, and a reviving draft of cool air whooshed in through the six-inch gap he'd created.

"God, that's better." He fanned himself exaggeratedly, grinning at Brianna. "Now, shall we get on with it?"

She handed him the torch, and stepped back. "How about *you* find the boxes, and *I'll* sort through them? And what's a rat satire?"

"Coward," he said, bending to rummage beneath the tarpaulin. "A rat satire is an old Scottish custom; if you had rats or mice in your house or your barn, you could make them go away by composing a poem—or you could sing it—telling the rats how poor the eating was where they were, and how good it was elsewhere. You told them where to go, and how to get there, and presumably, if the satire was good enough—they'd go."

He pulled out a carton labeled JACOBITES, MISCELLANEOUS, and carried it to the table, singing,

"Ye rats, ye are too many,
If ye would dine in plenty,
Ye mun go, ye mun go."

Lowering the box with a thump, he bowed in response to Brianna's giggling and turned back to the stacks, continuing in stentorian voice.

"Go to Campbell's garden,
Where nae cat stands warden,
And the kale, it grows green.

Go and fill your bellies,
Dinna stay and gnaw my wellies—
Go, ye rats, go!"

Brianna snorted appreciatively. "Did you just make that up?"

"Of course." Roger deposited another box on the table with a flourish. "A good rat satire must always be original." He cast a glance at the serried ranks of cartons. "After that performance, there shouldn't be a rat within miles of this place."

"Good." Brianna pulled a jackknife from her pocket and slit the tape that sealed the topmost carton. "You should come do one at the bed-and-breakfast place; Mama says she's sure there's mice in the bathroom. Something chewed on her soap case."

"God knows what it would take to dislodge a mouse capable of eating bars of soap; far beyond my feeble powers, I expect." He rolled a tattered round hassock out from behind a teetering stack of obsolete encyclopedias, and plumped down next to Brianna. "Here, you take the parish registers, they're a bit easier to read."

They worked through the morning in amiable companionship, turning up occasional interesting passages, the odd silverfish, and recurrent clouds of dust, but little of value to the project at hand.

"We'd better stop for lunch soon," Roger said at last. He felt a strong reluctance to go back into the house, where he would once more be at Fiona's mercy, but Brianna's stomach had begun to growl almost as loudly as his own.

"Okay. We can do some more after we eat, if you're not worn out." Brianna stood and stretched herself, her curled fists almost reaching the rafters of the old garage. She wiped her hands on the legs of her jeans, and ducked between the stacks of boxes.

"Hey!" She stopped short, near the door. Roger, following her, was brought up sharp, his nose almost touching the back of her head.

"What is it?" he asked. "Not another rat?" He noted with approval that the sun lit her thick single braid with glints of copper and gold. With a small golden nimbus of dust surrounding her, and the light of noon silhouetting her long-nosed profile, he thought she looked quite medieval; Our Lady of the Archives.

"No. Look at this, Roger!" She pointed at a cardboard carton near the middle of a stack. On the side, in the Reverend's strong black hand, was a label with the single word "Randall."

Roger felt a stab of mingled excitement and apprehension. Brianna's excitement was unalloyed.

"Maybe that's got the stuff we're looking for!" she exclaimed. "Mama said it was something my father was interested in; maybe he'd already asked the Reverend about it."

"Could be." Roger forced down the sudden feeling of dread that had struck him at sight of the name. He knelt to extract the box from its resting place. "Let's take it in the house; we can look in it after lunch."

The box, once opened in the Reverend's study, held an odd assortment of things. There were old photostats of pages from several parish registers, two or three army muster lists, a number of letters and scattered papers, a small, thin notebook, bound in gray cardboard covers, a packet of elderly photographs, curling at the edges, and a stiff folder, with the name "Randall" printed on the cover.

Brianna picked up the folder and opened it. "Why, it's Daddy's family tree!" she exclaimed. "Look." She passed the folder to Roger. Inside were two sheets of thick parchment, with lines of descent neatly ruled across and down. The beginning date was 1633; the final entry, at the foot of the second page, showed

Frank Wolverton Randall m. Claire Elizabeth Beauchamp, 1937

"Done before you were born," Roger murmured.

Brianna peered over his shoulder as his finger passed slowly down the lines of the genealogical table. "I've seen it before; Daddy had a copy in his study. He used to show it to me all the time. His had me at the bottom, though; this must be an early copy."

"Maybe the Reverend did some of the research for him." Roger handed Brianna back the folder, and picked up one of the papers from the stack on the desk.

"Now here's an heirloom for you," he said. He traced the coat of arms embossed at the head of the sheet. "A letter of commission in the army, signed by His Royal Majesty, King George II."

"George the *Second*? Jeez, that's even before the American Revolution."

"Considerably before. It's dated 1735. In the name of Jonathan Wolverton Randall. Know that name?"

"Yeah." Brianna nodded, stray wisps of hair falling in her face. She wiped them back carelessly and took the letter. "Daddy used to talk about him every now and then; one of the few ancestors he knew much about. He was a captain in the army that fought Bonnie Prince Charlie at Culloden." She looked up at Roger, blinking. "I think maybe he was killed in that battle, in fact. He wouldn't have been buried there, would he?"

Roger shook his head. "I shouldn't think so. It was the English who cleared up after the battle. They shipped most of their own dead back home for burial—the officers, anyway."

He was prevented from further observation by the sudden appearance in the doorway of Fiona, bearing a feather duster like a battle standard.

"Mr. Wakefield," she called. "There's the man come to take awa' the Reverend's truck, but he canna get it started. He says will ye be givin' him a hand, like?"

Roger started guiltily. He had taken the battery to a garage for testing, and it was still sitting in the backseat of his own Morris. No wonder the Reverend's truck wasn't starting.

"I'll have to go sort this out," he told Brianna. "I'm afraid it might take a while."

"That's okay." She smiled at him, blue eyes narrowing to triangles. "I should go too. Mama will be back by now; we thought we might go out to the Clava Cairns, if there was time. Thanks for the lunch."

"My pleasure—and Fiona's." Roger felt a stab of regret at being unable to offer to go with her, but duty called. He glanced at the papers spread out on the desk, then scooped them up and deposited them back in the box.

"Here," he said. "This is all your family records. You take it. Maybe your mother would be interested."

"Really? Well, thanks, Roger. Are you sure?"

"Absolutely," he said, carefully laying the folder with the genealogical chart on top. "Oh, wait. Maybe not all of it." The corner of the gray notebook stuck out from under the letter of commission; he pulled it free, and tidied the disturbed papers back into the box. "This looks like one of the Reverend's journals. Can't think what it's doing in there, but I suppose I'd better put it with the others; the historical society says they want the whole lot."

"Oh, sure." Brianna had risen to go, clutching the box to her chest, but hesitated, looking at him. "Do you—would you like me to come back?"

Roger smiled at her. There were cobwebs in her hair, and a long streak of dirt down the bridge of her nose.

"Nothing I'd like better," he said. "See you tomorrow, eh?"

The thought of the Reverend's journal stayed with Roger, all during the tedious business of getting the ancient truck started, and the subsequent visit of the furniture appraiser who came to sort the valuable antiques from the rubbish, and set a value on the Reverend's furnishings for auction.

This disposition of the Reverend's effects gave Roger a sense of restless melancholy. It was, after all, a dismantling of his own youth, as much as the clearing away of useless bric-a-brac. By the time he sat down in the study after dinner, he could not have said whether it was curiosity about the Randalls that compelled him to pick up the journal, or simply the urge somehow to regain a tenuous connection with the man who had been his father for so many years.

The journals were kept meticulously, the even lines of ink recording all major events of the parish and the community of which the Reverend Mr. Wakefield had been a part for so many years. The feel of the plain gray notebook and the sight of its pages conjured up for Roger an immediate vision of the Reverend, bald head gleaming in the glow of his desk lamp as he industriously inscribed the day's happenings.

"It's a discipline," he had explained once to Roger. "There's a great benefit to doing regularly something that orders the mind, you know. Catholic monks have services at set times every day, priests have their breviaries. I'm afraid I haven't the knack of such immediate devotion, but writing out the happenings of the day helps to clear my mind; then I can say my evening prayers with a calm heart."

A calm heart. Roger wished he could manage that himself, but calmness hadn't visited him since he'd found those clippings in the Reverend's desk.

He opened the book at random, and slowly turned the pages, looking for a mention of the name "Randall." The dates on the notebook's cover were January–June, 1948. While what he had told Brianna about the historical society was true, that had not been his chief motive in keeping the book. In May of 1948, Claire Randall had returned from her mysterious disappearance. The Reverend had known the Randalls well; such an event was sure to have found mention in his journal.

Sure enough, the entry for May 7:

"Visit w. Frank Randall this evening; this business about his wife. So distressing! Saw her yesterday—so frail, but those eyes staring—made me uneasy to sit w. her, poor woman, though she talked sensibly.

Enough to unhinge anyone, what she's been through—whatever it was. Terrible gossip about it all—so careless of Dr. Bartholomew to let on that she's pregnant. So hard for Frank—and for her, of course! My heart goes out to them both.

Mrs. Graham ill this week—she could have chosen a better time; jumble sale next week, and the porch full of old clothes . . ."

Roger flipped rapidly through the pages, looking for the next mention of the Randalls, and found it, later the same week.

"May 10—Frank Randall to dinner. Doing my best to associate publicly both w. him and his wife; I sit with her for an hour most days, in hopes of quelling some of the gossip. It's almost pitying now; word's gone round that she's demented. Knowing Claire Randall, I'm not sure that she would not be more offended at being thought insane than at being considered immoral— must be one or the other though?

Tried repeatedly to talk to her about her experiences, but she says nothing of that. Talks all right about anything else, but always a sense that she's thinking of something else.

Must make a note to preach this Sunday on the evils of gossip—though I'm afraid calling attention to the case with a sermon will only make it worse."

"May 12—. . . Can't get free of the notion that Claire Randall is not deranged. Have heard the gossip, of course, but see nothing in her behaviour that seems unstable in the slightest.

Do think she carries some terrible secret; one she's determined to keep. Spoke—cautiously—to Frank of this; he's reticent, but I'm convinced she has said something to him. Have tried to make it clear I wish to help, in any way I can."

"May 14—A visit from Frank Randall. Very puzzling. He has asked my help, but I can't see why he asked what he has. Seems very important to him, though; he keeps himself under close rein, but wound tight as a watch. I fear the release—if it comes.

Claire well enough to travel—he means to take her back to London this week. Assured him I would communicate any results to him by letter at his University address; no hint to his wife.

Have several items of interest on Jonathan Randall, though I can't imagine the significance of Frank's ancestor to this sorry business. Of James Fraser, as I told Frank—no inkling; a complete mystery."

A complete mystery. In more ways than one, Roger thought. What had Frank Randall asked the Reverend to do? To find out what he could about Jonathan Randall and about James Fraser, apparently. So Claire had told her husband about James Fraser—told him something, at least, if not everything.

But what conceivable connection could there be between an English army captain who had died at Culloden in 1746, and the man whose name seemed inextricably bound up with the mystery of Claire's disappearance in 1945—and the further mystery of Brianna's parentage?

The rest of the journal was filled with the usual miscellany of parish happenings; the chronic drunkenness of Derick Gowan, culminating in that parishioner's removal from the River Ness as a water-logged corpse in late May; the hasty wedding of Maggie Brown and William Dundee, a month before the christening of their daughter, June; Mrs. Graham's appendectomy, and the Reverend's attempts to cope with the resultant influx of covered dishes from the generous ladies of the parish—Herbert, the Reverend's current dog, seemed to have been the beneficiary of most of them.

Reading through the pages, Roger found himself smiling, hearing the Reverend's lively interest in his flock come to life once more in the old minister's words. Browsing and skimming, he nearly missed it—the last entry concerning Frank Randall's request.

> *"June 18—Had a brief note from Frank Randall, advising me that his wife's health is somewhat precarious; the pregnancy is dangerous and he asks my prayers.*
>
> *Replied with assurances of prayers and good wishes for both him and his wife. Enclosed also the information I had so far found for him; can't say what use it will be to him, but that must be his own judgement. Told him of the surprising discovery of Jonathan Randall's grave at St. Kilda; asked if he wishes me to photograph the stone."*

And that was all. There was no further mention of the Randalls, or of James Fraser. Roger laid the book down and massaged his temples; reading the slanting lines of handwriting had given him a mild headache.

Aside from confirming his suspicions that a man named James Fraser was mixed up in all this, the matter remained as impenetrable as ever. What in the name of God did Jonathan Randall have to do with it, and why on earth was the man buried at St. Kilda? The letter of commission had given Jonathan Randall's place of birth as an estate in Sussex; how did he end up in a remote Scottish kirkyard? True, it wasn't all that far from Culloden—but why hadn't he been shipped back to Sussex?

"Will ye be needin' anything else tonight, Mr. Wakefield?" Fiona's voice roused him from his fruitless meditations. He sat up, blinking, to see her holding a broom and a polishing cloth.

"What? Er, no. No, thanks, Fiona. But what are you doing with all that clobber? Not still cleaning at this time of night?"

"Well, it's the church ladies," Fiona explained. "You remember, ye told them they could hold their regular monthly meeting here tomorrow? I thought I'd best tidy up a bit."

The church ladies? Roger quailed at the thought of forty housewives, oozing sympathy, descending on the manse in an avalanche of tweeds, twin-sets, and cultured pearls.

"Will ye be takin' tea with the ladies?" Fiona was asking. "The Reverend always did."

The thought of entertaining Brianna Randall and the church ladies simul-taneously was more than Roger could contemplate with equanimity.

"Er, no," he said abruptly. "I've . . . I've an engagement tomorrow." His hand fell on the telephone, half-buried in the debris of the Reverend's desk. "If you'll excuse me, Fiona, I've got to make a call."

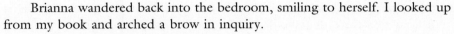

Brianna wandered back into the bedroom, smiling to herself. I looked up from my book and arched a brow in inquiry.

"Phone call from Roger?" I said.

"How'd you know?" She looked startled for a moment, then grinned, shucking off her robe. "Oh, because he's the only guy I know in Inverness?"

"I didn't think any of your boyfriends would be calling long-distance from Boston," I said. I peered at the clock on the table. "Not at this hour, anyway; they'll all be at football practice."

Brianna ignored this, and shoved her feet under the covers. "Roger's in-vited us to go up to a place called St. Kilda tomorrow. He says it's an interest-ing old church."

"I've heard of it," I said, yawning. "All right, why not? I'll take my plant press; maybe I can find some crown vetch—I promised some to Dr. Abernathy for his research. But if we're going to spend the day tramping round reading old gravestones, I'm turning in now. Digging up the past is strenuous work."

There was a brief flicker in Brianna's face, and I thought she was about to say something. But she merely nodded, and reached to turn out the light, the secretive smile still lurking in the corners of her mouth.

I lay looking up into the darkness, hearing her small tossings and turnings fade into the regular cadences of her sleeping breath. St. Kilda, eh? I had never been there, but I knew of the place; it was an old church, as Brianna had said, long deserted and out of the way for tourists—only the occasional researcher ever went there. Perhaps this was the opportunity I had been waiting for, then?

I would have Roger and Brianna together there, and alone, with little fear of interruption. And perhaps it was a suitable place to tell them—there among the long-dead parishioners of St. Kilda. Roger had not yet verified the where-abouts of the rest of the Lallybroch men, but it seemed fairly sure that they had at least left Culloden Field alive, and that was really all I needed to know, now. I could tell Bree the end of it, then.

My mouth grew dry at the thought of the coming interview. Where was I to find the words for this? I tried to visualize how it might go; what I might say,

and how they might react, but imagination failed me. More than ever, I regret-
ted my promise to Frank that had kept me from writing to the Reverend
Wakefield. If I had, Roger at least might already know. Or perhaps not; the
Reverend might not have believed me.

I turned restlessly, seeking inspiration, but weariness crept over me. And at
last I gave up and turned onto my back, closing my eyes on the dark above me.
As though my thinking of him had summoned the Reverend's spirit, a biblical
quotation drifted into my fading consciousness: *Sufficient unto the day,* the
Reverend's voice seemed to murmur to me, *sufficient unto the day is the evil
thereof.* And then I slept.

I woke up in the shadowed dark, hands clenched in the bedclothes, heart
beating with a force that shook me like the skin of a kettledrum. "Jesus!" I
said.

The silk of my nightgown was hot and clinging; looking down, I could
dimly see my nipples thrusting through it, hard as marbles. The quivering
spasms were still rippling through wrists and thighs, like the aftershocks of an
earthquake. I hoped I hadn't cried out. Probably not; I could hear Brianna's
breathing, untroubled and regular across the room.

I fell back on the pillow, shaking with weakness, the sudden flush washing
my temples with damp.

"Jesus H. Roosevelt Christ," I muttered, breathing deeply as my heart
slowly returned to normal.

One of the effects of a disturbed sleep cycle is that one stops dreaming
coherently. Through the long years of early motherhood, and then of intern-
ship, residency, and nights on-call, I had got used to falling at once into oblivion when I lay down, with such dreams as occurred nothing more than fragments and flashes, restless flickers in the dark as synapses fired at random,
recharging themselves for the work of the day that would come too soon.

In more recent years, with the resumption of something resembling a
normal schedule, I had begun to dream again. The usual kinds of dreams,
whether nightmare or good dream—long sequences of images, wanderings in
the wood of the mind. And I was familiar with this kind of dream, too; it was
common to what might politely be called periods of deprivation.

Usually, though, such dreams came floating, soft as the touch of satin
sheets, and if they woke me, I fell at once back into sleep, glowing dimly with a
memory that would not last 'til morning.

This was different. Not that I remembered much about it, but I had a
vague impression of hands that gripped me, rough and urgent, not wooing but
compelling. And a voice, nearly shouting, that echoed in the chambers of my
inner ear, along with the sound of my fading heartbeat.

I put my hand on my chest over the leaping pulse, feeling the soft fullness of my breast beneath the silk. Brianna's breath caught in a soft snore, then resumed its even cadence. I remembered listening for that sound when she was small; the slow, stertorous rhythm of reassurance, sounding through the darkened nursery, even as a heartbeat.

My own heartbeat was slowing under my hand, under the deep rose silk, the color of a baby's sleep-flushed cheek. When you hold a child to your breast to nurse, the curve of the little head echoes exactly the curve of the breast it suckles, as though this new person truly mirrors the flesh from which it sprang.

Babies are soft. Anyone looking at them can see the tender, fragile skin and know it for the rose-leaf softness that invites a finger's touch. But when you live with them and love them, you feel the softness going inward, the round-cheeked flesh wobbly as custard, the boneless splay of the tiny hands. Their joints are melted rubber, and even when you kiss them hard, in the passion of loving their existence, your lips sink down and seem never to find bone. Holding them against you, they melt and mold, as though they might at any moment flow back into your body.

But from the very start, there is that small streak of steel within each child. That thing that says "I am," and forms the core of personality.

In the second year, the bone hardens and the child stands upright, skull wide and solid, a helmet protecting the softness within. And "I am" grows, too. Looking at them, you can almost see it, sturdy as heartwood, glowing through the translucent flesh.

The bones of the face emerge at six, and the soul within is fixed at seven. The process of encapsulation goes on, to reach its peak in the glossy shell of adolescence, when all softness then is hidden under the nacreous layers of the multiple new personalities that teenagers try on to guard themselves.

In the next years, the hardening spreads from the center, as one finds and fixes the facets of the soul, until "I am" is set, delicate and detailed as an insect in amber.

I had thought I was well beyond that stage, had lost all trace of softness and was well set on my way to a middle age of stainless steel. But now I thought that Frank's death had cracked me in some way. And the cracks were widening, so that I could no longer patch them with denial. I had brought my daughter back to Scotland, she with those bones strong as the ribs of Highland mountains, in the hope that her shell was strong enough to hold her together, while the center of her "I am" might still be reachable.

But my own core held no longer in the isolation of "I am," and I had no protection to shield me from the softness from within. I no longer knew what I was or what she would be; only what I must do.

For I had come back, and I dreamed once more, in the cool air of the Highlands. And the voice of my dream still echoed through ears and heart, repeated with the sound of Brianna's sleeping breath.

"You are mine," it had said. "Mine! And I will not let you go."

Beloved Wife

The kirkyard of St. Kilda lay quiet in the sun. Not entirely flat, it occupied a plateau carved from the side of the hill by some geological freak. The land sloped and curved, so that the gravestones lay hidden in small hollows or jutted suddenly from the crest of a rise. The shifting of the earth had moved many, tilting them drunkenly or toppling them altogether, to lie flattened and broken in the long grass.

"It's a bit untidy," Roger said, apologetically. They paused in the kirkyard gate, looking over the small collection of ancient stones, overgrown and shadowed by the row of giant yews, planted long ago as a windbreak against the storms that rolled in from the northern sea. Clouds massed there now, far out over the distant firth, but the sun shone on the hilltop, and the air was still and warm.

"My father used to get together a gang of men from the church once or twice a year, and bring them up to keep the place in order, but I'm afraid it's rather gone to seed lately." He swung the lych-gate experimentally, noting the cracked hinge and the latch-fitting, dangling by one nail.

"It's a lovely, quiet place." Brianna edged carefully past the splintery gate. "Really old, isn't it?"

"Aye, it is. Dad thought the kirk itself was built on the site of an early church or an even older temple of some kind; that's why it's up here in such an inconvenient spot. One of his friends from Oxford was always threatening to come up and excavate the place to see what was under it, but of course he couldn't get clearance from the Church authorities, even though the place has been deconsecrated for years."

"It's kind of a climb." The flush of exertion was beginning to fade from Brianna's face as she fanned her cheeks with a guidebook. "Beautiful, though." She eyed the facade of the kirk with appreciation. Built into a natural opening in the crag, the stones and timbers of the kirk had been fitted by hand, the chinks caulked with peat and mud, so that it seemed to have grown there, a natural part of the cliff face. Ancient carvings decorated door sill and window frame, some showing the symbols of Christianity, some obviously much older.

"Is Jonathan Randall's stone over there?" She waved toward the kirkyard, visible beyond the gate. "Mother will be so surprised!"

"Aye, I expect so. Haven't seen it myself." He hoped the surprise would be a pleasant one; when he had mentioned the stone cautiously to Brianna over the phone the night before, she had been enthusiastic.

"I know about Jonathan Randall," she was telling Roger. "Daddy always admired him; said he was one of the few interesting people in the family tree. I guess he was a good soldier; Daddy had lots of commendations and things he'd gotten."

"Really?" Roger looked back, in search of Claire. "Does your mother need help with that plant press?"

Brianna shook her head. "Nah. She just found a plant by the path she couldn't resist. She'll be up in a minute."

It was a silent place. Even the birds were quiet as midday approached, and the dark evergreens that edged the plateau were still, with no breeze to stir their branches. Without the raw scars of recent graves or the flags of plastic flowers as testimony to still-fresh grief, the kirkyard breathed only the peace of the long-dead. Removed from strife and trouble, only the fact of their life remained to give the comfort of a human presence on the lonely heights of an empty land.

The progress of the three visitors was slow; they wandered their way casually through the old kirkyard, Roger and Brianna pausing to read aloud quaint inscriptions from the weathered stones, Claire, on her own, stooping now and then to clip a vine or uproot a small flowering plant.

Roger bent over one stone, and grinning, beckoned Brianna to read the inscription.

" 'Approach and read, not with your hats on,' " she read. " 'For here lies Bailie William Watson / Who was famous for his thinking / And moderation in his drinking.' " Brianna rose from examining the stone, her face flushed with laughter. "No dates—I wonder when William Watson lived."

"Eighteenth century, most likely," Roger said. "The seventeenth-century stones are mostly too weathered to read, and no one's been buried here in two hundred years; the church was deconsecrated in 1800."

A moment later, Brianna let out a muffled whoop. "Here it is!" She stood up and waved to Claire, who was standing on the far side of the kirkyard, peering inquisitively at a length of greenery she held in one hand. "Mama! Come look at this!"

Claire waved back, and made her way to where they stood beside the flat, square stone, stepping carefully across the crowded graves.

"What is it?" she asked. "Find an interesting grave?"

"I think so. Recognize this name?" Roger stepped back, so she could have a clear view.

"Jesus H. Roosevelt Christ!" Mildly startled, Roger glanced at Claire, and was alarmed to see how pale she was. She stared down at the weathered stone, and the muscles of her throat moved in a convulsive swallow. The plant she had pulled was crushed in her hand, unregarded.

"Dr. Randall—Claire—are you all right?"

The amber eyes were blank, and she appeared not to hear him for a moment. Then she blinked, and looked up. She was still pale, but seemed better now; back in control.

"I'm fine," she said, voice flat. She stooped, and ran her fingers over the letters of the stone as though reading them in Braille.

"Jonathan Wolverton Randall," she said softly, "1705–1746. I told you, didn't I? You bastard, I *told* you!" Her voice, so flat an instant before, was suddenly vibrant, filled with a restrained fury.

"Mama! Are you all right?" Brianna, obviously upset, pulled at her mother's arm.

Roger thought it was as though a shade had dropped behind Claire's eyes; the feeling that had shone there was suddenly hidden, as she snapped back to a realization of the two people staring at her, aghast. She smiled, a brief, mechanical grimace, and nodded.

"Yes. Yes, of course. I'm fine." Her hand opened, and the stalk of limp greenery dropped to the ground.

"I thought you'd be surprised." Brianna was looking worriedly at her mother. "Isn't this Daddy's ancestor? The soldier who died at Culloden?"

Claire glanced down at the gravestone near her feet.

"Yes, it is," she said. "And he *is* dead, isn't he?"

Roger and Brianna exchanged looks. Feeling responsible, Roger touched Claire on the shoulder.

"It's rather a hot day," he said, trying for a note of casual matter-of-factness. "Perhaps we should go into the church for a little shade. There are some very interesting carvings on the font; well worth seeing."

Claire smiled at him. A real smile this time, a little tired, but eminently sane.

"You go," she said, including Brianna with a tilt of her head. "I need a little air. I'll stay out here for a bit."

"I'll stay with you." Brianna was hovering, clearly unwilling to leave her mother on her own, but Claire had recovered both her equanimity and her air of command.

"Nonsense," she said briskly. "I'm perfectly all right. I'll go sit in the shade of the trees over there. You go along. I'd rather be by myself for a bit," she added firmly, seeing Roger opening his mouth to protest.

With no further ado, she turned and walked off, toward the line of dark yew trees that edged the kirkyard to the west. Brianna hesitated, looking after her, but Roger took the girl by the elbow, and drew her toward the church.

"Best leave her alone," he murmured. "After all, your mother's a doctor, isn't she? She'll know if it's all right."

"Yeah . . . I suppose so." With a final troubled glance after Claire's retreating figure, Brianna allowed him to lead her away.

The kirk was no more than an empty wood-floored room, with the abandoned font left in place only because it could not be removed. The shallow basin had been scooped out of the stone ledge that ran along one side of the room. Above the basin, the carved visage of St. Kilda gazed emptily toward the ceiling, eyes piously upturned.

"It was probably one of the pagan gods to start with," Roger said, tracing the line of the carving with a finger. "You can see where they added the veil and wimple to the original figure—not to mention the eyes."

"Like poached eggs," Brianna agreed, rolling her own up in imitation. "What's this carving over here? It looks a lot like the patterns on those Pictish stones outside Clava."

They strolled casually around the walls of the kirk, breathing the dusty air, examining the ancient carvings in the stone walls, and reading the small wooden plaques affixed by long-vanished parishioners in memory of ancestors gone still longer. They spoke quietly, both keeping an ear out for any sounds from the kirkyard, but all was quiet, and slowly they began to relax again.

Roger followed Brianna toward the front of the room, watching the curling tendrils that escaped from her braid to coil damply on her neck.

All that remained now at the front of the kirk was a plain wooden ledge above the hole where the altarstone had been removed. Still, Roger felt something of a quiver up his spine as he stood beside Brianna, facing the vanished altar.

The sheer intensity of his feelings seemed to echo in the empty place. He hoped she couldn't hear them. They had known each other barely a week, after all, and had had scarcely any private conversation. She would be taken aback, surely, or frightened, if she knew what he felt. Or worse yet, she would laugh.

Yet, when he stole a glance at her, her face was calm and serious. It was also looking back at him, with an expression in the dark blue of her eyes that turned him toward her and made him reach for her without conscious thought.

The kiss was brief and gentle, scarcely more than the formality that concludes a wedding, yet as striking in its impact as though they had this minute plighted a troth.

Roger's hands fell away, but the warmth of her lingered, in hands and lips and body, so that he felt as though he held her still. They stood a moment, bodies grazing, breathing each other's air, and then she stepped back. He could still feel the touch of her on the palms of his hands. He curled his fingers into fists, seeking to hold the feeling.

The still air of the church shivered suddenly into bits, the echoes of a scream scattering the dust motes. Without conscious thought, Roger was outside, running, stumbling and scrambling over the tumbled stones, heading for the dark line of the yews. He pushed his way between the overgrown branches, not bothering to hold back the scaly twigs for Brianna, hot on his heels.

Pale in the shadows, he saw Claire Randall's face. Completely drained of color, she looked like a wraith against the dark branches of the yew. She stood for a moment, swaying, then sank to her knees in the grass, as though her legs would no longer support her.

"Mother!" Brianna dropped to her knees beside the crouching figure, chafing one of the limp hands. "Mama, what is it? Are you faint? You should put your head between your knees. Here, why don't you lie down?"

Claire resisted the helpful proddings of her offspring, and the drooping head came upright on its slender neck once more.

"I don't want to lie down," she gasped. "I want. . . . oh, God. Oh, dear holy God." Kneeling among the unmowed grass she stretched out a trembling hand to the surface of the stone. It was carved of granite, a simple slab.

"Dr. Randall! Er, Claire?" Roger dropped to one knee on her other side, putting a hand under her other arm to support her. He was truly alarmed at her appearance. A fine sweat had broken out on her temples and she looked as though she might keel over at any moment. "Claire," he said again, urgently, trying to rouse her from the staring trance she had fallen into. "What is it? Is it a name you know?" Even as he spoke, his own words were ringing in his ears. *No one's been buried here since the eighteenth century,* he'd told Brianna. *No one's been buried here in two hundred years.*

Claire's fingers brushed his own away, and touched the stone, caressing, as though touching flesh, gently tracing the letters, the grooves worn shallow, but still clear.

" 'JAMES ALEXANDER MALCOLM MACKENZIE FRASER,' " she read aloud. "Yes, I know him." Her hand dropped lower, brushing back the grass that grew thickly about the stone, obscuring the line of smaller letters at its base.

" 'Beloved husband of Claire,' " she read.

"Yes, I knew him," she said again, so softly Roger could scarcely hear her. "I'm Claire. He was my husband." She looked up then, into the face of her daughter, white and shocked above her. "And your father," she said.

Roger and Brianna stared down at her, and the kirkyard was silent, save for the rustle of the yews above.

"No!" I said, quite crossly. "For the fifth time—no! I don't want a drink of water. I have not got a touch of the sun. I am not faint. I am not ill. And I haven't lost my mind, either, though I imagine that's what you're thinking."

Roger and Brianna exchanged glances that made it clear that that was precisely what they were thinking. They had, between them, got me out of the kirkyard and into the car. I had refused to be taken to hospital, so we had gone back to the manse. Roger had administered medicinal whisky for shock, but his eyes darted toward the telephone now as though wondering whether to dial for additional help—like a straitjacket, I supposed.

"Mama." Brianna spoke soothingly, reaching out to try to smooth the hair back from my face. "You're upset."

"Of course I'm upset!" I snapped. I took a long, quivering breath and clamped my lips tight together, until I could trust myself to speak calmly.

"I am certainly upset," I began, "but I'm not mad." I stopped, struggling for control. This wasn't the way I'd intended to do it. I didn't know quite what I *had* intended, but not this, blurting out the truth without preparation or time to organize my own thoughts. Seeing that bloody grave had disrupted any plan I might have formed.

"Damn you, Jamie Fraser!" I said, furious. "What are you doing there anyway; it's *miles* from Culloden!"

Brianna's eyes were halfway out on stalks, and Roger's hand was hovering near the telephone. I stopped abruptly and tried to get a grip on myself.

Be calm, Beauchamp, I instructed myself. Breathe deeply. Once . . . twice . . . once more. Better. Now. It's very simple; all you have to do is tell them the truth. That's what you came to Scotland for, isn't it?

I opened my mouth, but no sound came out. I closed my mouth, and my eyes as well, hoping that my nerve would return, if I couldn't see the two ashen faces in front of me. Just . . . let . . . me . . . tell . . . the . . . truth, I prayed, with no idea who I was talking to. Jamie, I thought.

I'd told the truth once before. It hadn't gone well.

I pressed my eyelids shut more tightly. Once more I could smell the carbolic surroundings of a hospital, and feel the unfamiliar starched pillowcase beneath my cheek. From the corridor outside came Frank's voice, choked with baffled rage.

"What do you mean, don't press her? Don't *press* her? My wife's been gone for nearly three years, and come back filthy, abused, and *pregnant,* for God's sake, and I'm not to ask *questions*?"

And the doctor's voice, murmuring soothingly. I caught the words "delusion," and "traumatic state," and "leave it for later, old man—just for a bit" as Frank's voice, still arguing and interrupting, was gently but firmly eased down the hall. That so-familiar voice, which raised anew the storm of grief and rage and terror inside me.

I had curled my body into a defensive ball, pillow clutched to my chest, and bitten it, as hard as I could, until I felt the cotton casing give way and the silky grit of feathers grinding between my teeth.

I was grinding them now, to the detriment of a new filling. I stopped, and opened my eyes.

"Look," I said, as reasonably as I could. "I'm sorry, I know how it sounds. But it's true, and nothing I can do about it."

This speech did nothing to reassure Brianna, who edged closer to Roger.

Roger himself had lost that green-about-the-gills look, though, and was exhibiting signs of cautious interest. Could it be possible that he really did have enough imagination to be able to grasp the truth?

I took hope from his expression, and unclenched my fists.

"It's the bloody stones," I said. "You know, the standing stone circle, on the fairies' hill, to the west?"

"Craigh na Dun," Roger murmured. "That one?"

"Right." I exhaled consciously. "You may know the legends about fairy hills—do you? About people who get trapped in rocky hills and wake up two hundred years later?"

Brianna was looking more alarmed by the moment.

"Mother, I really think you ought to go up and lie down," she said. She half-rose from her seat. "I could go get Fiona . . ."

Roger put a hand on her arm to stop her.

"No, wait," he said. He looked at me, with the sort of suppressed curiosity a scientist shows when putting a new slide under the microscope. "Go ahead," he said to me.

"Thanks," I said dryly. "Don't worry, I'm not going to start driveling about fairies; I just thought you'd like to know there's some basis to the legends. I haven't any idea what it actually is up there, or how it works, but the fact is . . ." I took a deep breath, "Well, the fact is, that I walked through a bloody cleft stone in that circle in 1945, and I ended up on the hillside below in 1743."

I'd said exactly that to Frank. He'd glared at me for a moment, picked up a vase of flowers from my bedside table, and smashed it on the floor.

Roger looked like a scientist whose new microbe has come through a winner. I wondered why, but was too engrossed in the struggle to find words that sounded halfway sane.

"The first person I ran into was an English dragoon in full fig," I said. "Which rather gave me a hint that something was wrong."

A sudden smile lighted Roger's face, though Brianna went on looking horrified. "I should think it might," he said.

"The difficulty was that I couldn't get back, you see." I thought I'd better address my remarks to Roger, who at least seemed disposed to listen, whether he believed me or not.

"The thing is, ladies then didn't go about the place unescorted, and if they did, they didn't do it wearing print dresses and oxford loafers," I explained. "Everyone I met, starting with that dragoon captain, knew there was something wrong about me—but they didn't know what. How could they? I couldn't explain then any better than I can now—and lunatic asylums back then were much less pleasant places than they are now. No basket weaving," I added, with an effort at a joke. It wasn't noticeably successful; Brianna grimaced and looked more worried than ever.

"That dragoon," I said, and a brief shudder went over me at the memory of Jonathan Wolverton Randall, Captain of His Majesty's Eighth Dragoons. "I thought I was hallucinating at first, because the man looked so very like Frank; at first glance, I thought it was he." I glanced at the table where a copy of one of Frank's books lay, with its back-cover photograph of a dark and handsome lean-faced man.

"That's quite a coincidence," Roger said. His eyes were alert, fixed on mine.

"Well, it was and it wasn't," I told him, wrenching my eyes with an effort from the stack of books. "You know he was Frank's ancestor. All the men in that family have a strong family resemblance—physically, at least," I added, thinking of the rather striking nonphysical differences.

"What—what was he like?" Brianna seemed to be coming out of her stupor, at least slightly.

"He was a bloody filthy pervert," I said. Two pairs of eyes snapped open wide and turned to each other with an identical look of consternation.

"You needn't look like that," I said. "They had perversion in the eighteenth century; it isn't anything new, you know. Only it was worse then, maybe, since no one really cared, so long as things were kept quiet and decent on the surface. And Black Jack Randall was a soldier; he captained a garrison in the Highlands, charged with keeping the clans under control—he had considerable scope for his activities, all officially sanctioned." I took a restorative gulp from the whisky glass I still held.

"He liked to hurt people," I said. "He liked it a lot."

"Did he . . . hurt you?" Roger put the question with some delicacy, after a rather noticeable pause. Bree seemed to be drawing into herself, the skin tightening across her cheekbones.

"Not directly. Or not much, at least." I shook my head. I could feel a cold spot in the pit of my stomach, which the whisky was doing little to thaw. Jack Randall had hit me there, once. I felt it in memory, like the ache of a long-healed wound.

"He had fairly eclectic tastes. But it was Jamie that he. . . . wanted." Under no circumstances would I have used the word "loved." My throat felt thick, and I swallowed the last drops of whisky. Roger held up the decanter, one brow raised questioningly, and I nodded and held out my glass.

"Jamie. That's Jamie Fraser? And he was . . ."

"He was my husband," I said.

Brianna shook her head like a horse driving off flies.

"But you *had* a husband," she said. "You couldn't . . . even if . . . I mean . . . you *couldn't.*"

"I had to," I said flatly. "I didn't do it on purpose, after all."

"Mother, you can't get married accidentally!" Brianna was losing her kindly-nurse-with-mental-patient attitude. I thought this was probably a good thing, even if the alternative was anger.

"Well, it wasn't precisely an accident," I said. "It was the best alternative to being handed over to Jack Randall, though. Jamie married me to protect me —and bloody generous of him, too," I finished, glaring at Bree over my glass. "He didn't have to do it, but he did."

I fought back the memory of our wedding night. He was a virgin; his hands had trembled when he touched me. I had been afraid too—with better reason. And then in the dawn he had held me, naked back against bare chest, his thighs warm and strong behind my own, murmuring into the clouds of my hair, "Dinna be afraid. There's the two of us now."

"See," I turned to Roger again, "I couldn't get back. I was running away from Captain Randall when the Scots found me. A party of cattle-raiders. Jamie was with them, they were his mother's people, the MacKenzies of Leoch. They didn't know what to make of me, but they took me with them as a captive. And I couldn't get away again."

I remembered my abortive efforts to escape from Castle Leoch. And then the day when I had told Jamie the truth, and he—not believing, any more than Frank had, but at least willing to act as though he did—had taken me back to the hill and the stones.

"He thought I was a witch, perhaps," I said, eyes closed, smiling just a bit at the thought. "Now they think you're mad; then they thought you were a witch. Cultural mores," I explained, opening my eyes. "Psychology is just what they call it these days instead of magic. Not the hell of a lot of difference." Roger nodded, seeming a little stunned.

"They tried me for witchcraft," I said. "In the village of Cranesmuir, just below the castle. Jamie saved me, though, and then I told him. And he took me to the hill, and told me to go back. Back to Frank." I paused and drew a deep breath, remembering that October afternoon, where control of my destiny, taken from me for so long, had been suddenly thrust back into my hands, and the choice not given, but demanded of me.

"Go back!" he had said. "There's nothing here for ye! Nothing save danger."

"Is there really nothing here for me?" I had asked. Too honorable to speak, he had answered nonetheless, and I had made my choice.

"It was too late," I said, staring down at my hands, lying open on my knees. The day was darkening to rain, but my two wedding rings still gleamed in the fading light, gold and silver. I hadn't taken Frank's gold band from my left hand when I married Jamie, but had worn Jamie's silver ring on the fourth finger of my right hand, for every day of the twenty-odd years since he put it there.

"I loved Frank," I said quietly, not looking at Bree. "I loved him a lot.

But by that time, Jamie was my heart and the breath of my body. I couldn't leave him. I *couldn't*," I said, raising my head suddenly to Bree in appeal. She stared back at me, stone-faced.

I looked down at my hands again, and went on.

"He took me to his own home—Lallybroch, it was called. A beautiful place." I shut my eyes again, to get away from the look on Brianna's face, and deliberately summoned the image of the estate of Broch Tuarach—Lallybroch, to the people who lived there. A beautiful Highland farm, with woods and streams; even a bit of fertile ground—rare for the Highlands. A lovely, peaceful place, sealed within high hills above a mountain pass that kept it remote from the recurrent strife that troubled the Highlands. But even Lallybroch had proved only a temporary sanctuary.

"Jamie was an outlaw," I said, seeing behind my closed eyelids the scars of flogging that the English had left on his back. A network of thin white lines that webbed the broad shoulders like a branded grid. "There was a price on his head. One of his own tenants betrayed him to the English. They captured him, and took him to Wentworth Prison—to hang him."

Roger gave a long, low whistle.

"Hell of a place," he remarked. "Have you seen it? The walls must be ten feet thick!"

I opened my eyes. "They are," I said wryly. "I've been inside them. But even the thickest walls have doors." I felt a small flicker of the blaze of desperate courage that had taken me inside Wentworth Prison, in pursuit of my heart. If I could do that for you, I told Jamie silently, I can do this as well. But help me, you bloody big Scot—help me!

"I got him out," I said, taking a deep breath. "What was left of him. Jack Randall commanded the garrison at Wentworth." Now I didn't want to remember the images that my words brought back, but they wouldn't stop. Jamie, naked and bloody, on the floor of Eldridge Manor, where we had found sanctuary.

"I wilna let them take me back again, Sassenach," he'd said to me, teeth clenched against the pain as I'd set the crushed bones of his hand and cleansed his wounds. "Sassenach." He had called me that from the first; the Gaelic word for an outlander, a stranger. An Englishman. First in jest, and then in affection.

And I hadn't let them find him; with the help of his kinsman, a little Fraser clansman called Murtagh, I'd gotten him across the Channel to France, and to refuge in the Abbey of Ste. Anne de Beaupré, where one of his Fraser uncles was abbot. But once there in safety, I had found that saving his life was not the end of the task set me.

What Jack Randall had done to him had sunk into his soul as surely as the flails of the lash had sunk in his back, and had left scars every bit as permanent. I was not sure, even now, what I had done, when I had summoned his demons and fought them single-handed, in the dark of his mind; there is very little difference between medicine and magic, when it comes to some kinds of healing.

I could still feel the cold, hard stone that bruised me, and the strength of the fury that I had drawn from him, the hands that closed round my neck and the burning creature who had hunted me through the dark.

"But I did heal him," I said softly. "He came back to me."

Brianna was shaking her head slowly back and forth, bewildered, but with a stubborn set to her head that I knew very well indeed. "Grahams are stupid, Campbells are deceitful, MacKenzies are charming but sly, and Frasers are stubborn," Jamie had told me once, giving me his view of the general characteristics of the clans. He hadn't been far wrong, either; Frasers *were* extremely stubborn, not least him. Nor Bree.

"I don't believe it," she said flatly. She sat up straighter, eyeing me closely. "I think maybe you've been thinking too much about those men at Culloden," she said. "After all, you've been under a strain lately, and maybe Daddy's death . . ."

"Frank wasn't your father," I said bluntly.

"He was!" She flashed back with it immediately, so fast that it startled both of us.

Frank had, in time, bowed to the doctors' insistence that any attempt to "force me to accept reality," as one of them put it, might be harmful to my pregnancy. There had been a lot of murmuring in corridors—and shouting, now and then—but he had given up asking me for the truth. And I, in frail health and sick at heart, had given up telling it to him.

I wasn't going to give up, this time.

"I promised Frank," I said. "Twenty years ago, when you were born. I tried to leave him, and he wouldn't let me go. He loved you." I felt my voice soften as I looked at Brianna. "He couldn't believe the truth, but he knew—of course—that he wasn't your father. He asked me not to tell you—to let him be your only father—as long as he lived. After that, he said, it was up to me." I swallowed, licking dry lips.

"I owed him that," I said. "Because he loved you. But now Frank's dead —and you have a right to know who you are."

"If you doubt it," I said, "go to the National Portrait Gallery. They've a picture there of Ellen MacKenzie; Jamie's mother. She's wearing these." I touched the pearl necklace at my throat. A string of baroque freshwater pearls from Scottish rivers, strung with roundels of pierced gold. "Jamie gave them to me on our wedding day."

I looked at Brianna, sitting tall and stiff, the bones of her face stark in protest. "Take along a hand mirror," I said. "Take a good look at the portrait and then in the mirror. It's not an exact likeness, but you're very like your grandmother."

Roger stared at Brianna as though he'd never seen her before. He glanced back and forth between us, then, as though making up his mind, suddenly squared his shoulders and rose from the sofa where he had been sitting beside her.

"I've something I think you should see," he said firmly. He crossed quickly to the Reverend's old rolltop desk and pulled a rubber-banded bundle of yellowed newspaper clippings from one of the pigeonholes.

"When you've read them, look at the dates," he told Brianna, handing them to her. Then, still standing, he turned to me and looked me over, with the long, dispassionate gaze that I recognized as a that of a scholar, schooled in objectivity. He didn't yet believe, but he had the imagination to doubt.

"Seventeen forty-three," he said, as though to himself. He shook his head, marveling. "And I thought it was a man you'd met here, in 1945. God, I would *never* have thought—well, Christ, who would?"

I was surprised. "You knew? About Brianna's father?"

He nodded at the clippings in Brianna's hands. She hadn't yet looked at them, but was staring at Roger, half-bewildered, half-angry. I could see the storm gathering in her eyes, and so, I thought, could Roger. He looked hastily away from her, turning back to me in question.

"Then those men whose names you gave me, the ones who fought at Culloden—you *knew* them?"

I relaxed, ever so slightly. "Yes, I knew them." There was a grumble of thunder to the east, and the rain broke in a spatter against the long windows that lined the study from floor to ceiling on one side. Brianna's head was bent over the clippings, the wings of her hair hiding everything but the tip of her nose, which was bright red. Jamie always went red when he was furious or upset. I was all too familiar with the sight of a Fraser on the verge of explosion.

"And you were in France," Roger murmured as though to himself, still studying me closely. The shock in his face was fading into surmise, and a kind of excitement. "I don't suppose you knew . . ."

"Yes, I did," I told him. "That's why we went to Paris. I'd told Jamie about Culloden—the '45, and what would happen. We went to Paris to try to stop Charles Stuart."

PART TWO

The Pretenders

———

Le Havre, France
February 1744

Making Waves

"Bread," I muttered feebly, keeping my eyes tightly closed. There was no response from the large, warm object next to me, other than the faint sigh of his breathing.

"Bread!" I said, a little louder. There was a sudden startled heave of the bedclothes, and I grasped the edge of the mattress and tightened all my muscles, hoping to stabilize the pitch and yaw of my internal organs.

Fumbling noises came from the far side of the bed, followed by the sliding of a drawer, a muffled exclamation in Gaelic, the soft thud of a bare foot stamping planks, and then the sinking of the mattress under the weight of a heavy body.

"Here, Sassenach," said an anxious voice, and I felt the touch of a dry bread crust against my lower lip. Groping blindly without opening my eyes, I grasped it and began to chew gingerly, forcing each choking bite down a parched throat. I knew better than to ask for water.

The dessicated wads of bread crumbs gradually made their way down my throat and took up residence in my stomach, where they lay like small heaps of ballast. The nauseating roll of my inner waves slowly calmed, and at last my innards lay at anchor. I opened my eyes, to see the anxious face of Jamie Fraser hovering a few inches above me.

"Ak!" I said, startled.

"All right, then?" he asked. When I nodded and feebly began to sit up, he put an arm around my back to help me. Sitting down beside me on the rough inn bed, he pulled me gently against him and stroked my sleep-tousled hair.

"Poor love," he said. "Would a bit of wine help? There's a flask of hock in my saddlebag."

"No. No, thank you." I shuddered briefly at the thought of drinking hock —I seemed to smell the dark, fruity fumes, just at the mention of it—and pushed myself upright.

"I'll be fine in a moment," I said, with forced cheerfulness. "Don't worry, it's quite normal for pregnant women to feel sick in the morning."

With a dubious look at me, Jamie rose and went to retrieve his clothes from the stool near the window. France in February is cold as hell frozen over, and the bubbled-glass panes of the window were coated thick with frost.

He was naked, and a ripple of gooseflesh brushed his shoulders and raised the red-gold hairs on his arms and legs. Accustomed to cold, though, he nei-ther shivered nor hurried as he pulled on stockings and shirt. Pausing in his dressing, he came back to the bed and hugged me briefly.

"Go back to bed," he suggested. "I'll send up the chambermaid to light the fire. Perhaps ye can rest a bit, now you've eaten. You won't be sick now?" I wasn't entirely sure, but nodded reassuringly.

"I don't think so." I cast an eye back at the bed; the quilts, like most coverings supplied by public inns, were none too clean. Still, the silver in Ja-mie's purse had procured us the best room in the inn, and the narrow bed was stuffed with goose feathers rather than with chaff or wool.

"Um, perhaps I *will* just lie down a moment," I murmured, pulling my feet off the freezing floor and thrusting them under the quilts, in search of the last remnants of warmth. My stomach seemed to have settled sufficiently to risk a sip of water, and I poured a cupful from the cracked bedroom ewer.

"What were you stamping on?" I asked, sipping carefully. "There aren't spiders up here, are there?"

Fastening his kilt about his waist, Jamie shook his head.

"Och, no," he said. Hands busy, he tilted his head toward the table. "Just a rat. After the bread, I expect."

Glancing down, I saw the limp gray form on the floor, a small pearl of blood glistening on the snout. I made it out of bed just in time.

"It's all right," I said faintly, a bit later. "There isn't anything left to throw up."

"Rinse your mouth, Sassenach, but don't swallow, for God's sake." Jamie held the cup for me, wiped my mouth with a cloth as though I were a small and messy child, then lifted me and laid me carefully back in the bed. He frowned worriedly down at me.

"Perhaps I'd better stay here," he said. "I could send word."

"No, no, I'm all right," I said. And I was. Fight as I would to keep from vomiting in the mornings, I could hold nothing down for long. Yet once the bout was over, I felt entirely restored. Aside from a sour taste in my mouth, and a slight soreness in the abdominal muscles, I felt quite my normal self. I threw back the covers and stood up, to demonstrate.

"See? I'll be fine. And you have to go; it wouldn't do to keep your cousin waiting, after all."

I was beginning to feel cheerful again, despite the chilly air rushing under the door and beneath the folds of my nightgown. Jamie was still hesitating, reluctant to leave me, and I went to him and hugged him tightly, both in reassurance and because he was delightfully warm.

"Brrr," I said. "How on earth can you be warm as toast, dressed in nothing but a kilt?"

"I've a shirt on as well," he protested, smiling down at me.

We clung together for a bit, enjoying each other's warmth in the quiet cold of the early French morning. In the corridor, the clash and shuffle of the chambermaid with her scuttle of kindling grew nearer.

Jamie shifted a bit, pressing against me. Because of the difficulties of traveling in the winter, we had been nearly a week on the road from Ste. Anne to Le Havre. And between the late arrivals at dismal inns, wet, filthy, and shivering with fatigue and cold, and the increasingly unsettled wakenings as my morning sickness got worse, we had scarcely touched each other since our last night at the Abbey.

"Come to bed with me?" I invited, softly.

He hesitated. The strength of his desire was obvious through the fabric of his kilt, and his hands were warm on the cool flesh of my own, but he didn't move to take me in his arms.

"Well . . ." he said doubtfully.

"You want to, don't you?" I said, sliding a chilly hand under his kilt to make sure.

"Oh! er . . . aye. Aye, I do." The evidence at hand bore out this statement. He groaned faintly as I cupped my hand between his legs. "Oh, Lord. Don't do that, Sassenach; I canna keep my hands from ye."

He did hug me then, wrapping long arms about me and pulling my face into the snowy tucks of his shirt, smelling faintly of the laundry starch Brother Alfonse used at the Abbey.

"Why should you?" I said, muffled in his linen. "You've a bit of time to spare, surely? It's only a short ride to the docks."

"It isna that," he said, smoothing my riotous hair.

"Oh, I'm too fat?" In fact, my stomach was still nearly flat, and I was thinner than usual because of the sickness. "Or is it . . . ?"

"No," he said, smiling. "Ye talk too much." He bent and kissed me, then scooped me up and sat down on the bed, holding me on his lap. I lay down and pulled him determinedly down on top of me.

"Claire, no!" he protested as I started unbuckling his kilt.

I stared at him. "Whyever not?"

"Well," he said awkwardly, blushing a bit. "The child . . . I mean, I dinna want to hurt it."

I laughed.

"Jamie, you can't hurt it. It's no bigger than the tip of my finger yet." I held up a finger in illustration, then used it to trace the full, curving line of his lower lip. He seized my hand and bent to kiss me abruptly, as though to erase the tickle of my touch.

"You're sure?" he asked. "I mean . . . I keep thinking he wouldna like being jounced about . . ."

"He'll never notice," I assured him, hands once more busy with the buckle of his kilt.

"Well . . . if you're sure of it."

There was a peremptory rap at the door, and with impeccable Gallic timing, the chambermaid pushed her way in backward, carelessly gouging the door with a billet of wood as she turned. From the scarred surfaces of door and jamb, it appeared that this was her usual method of operations.

"*Bonjour,* Monsieur, Madame," she muttered, with a curt nod toward the bed as she shuffled toward the hearth. All right for *some* people, said her attitude, louder than words. Used by this time to the matter-of-factness with which servants treated the sight of inn patrons in any form of dishabille, I merely murmured "*Bonjour,* Mademoiselle," in return and let it go at that. I also let go of Jamie's kilt, and slid under the covers, pulling the quilt up to hide my scarlet cheeks.

Possessed of somewhat greater sang-froid, Jamie placed one of the bolsters strategically across his lap, parked his elbows on it, rested his chin on upturned palms, and made pleasant conversation with the maid, praising the cuisine of the house.

"And from where do you procure the wine, Mademoiselle?" he asked politely.

"From here, from there." She shrugged, stuffing kindling rapidly under the sticks with a practiced hand. "Wherever it's cheapest." The woman's plump face creased slightly as she gave Jamie a sidelong look from the hearth.

"I gathered as much," he said, grinning at her, and she gave a brief snort of amusement.

"I'll wager I can match the price you're getting, and double the quality," he offered. "Tell your mistress."

One eyebrow rose skeptically. "And what's your own price, Monsieur?"

He made an altogether Gallic gesture of self-abnegation. "Nothing, Mademoiselle. I go to call upon a kinsman who sells wine. Perhaps I can bring him some new business to ensure my welcome, no?"

She nodded, seeing the wisdom of this, and grunted as she rose from her knees.

"Well enough, Monsieur. I'll speak to the *patronne.*"

The door thumped to behind the maid, aided by a skillful swing of her hip in passing. Putting the bolster aside, Jamie stood up and began to rebuckle his kilt.

"Where do you think you're going?" I protested.

He glanced down at me, and a reluctant smile curved the wide mouth.

"Oh. Well . . . you're sure you're up to it, Sassenach?"

"I am if you are," I said, unable to resist.

He eyed me austerely.

"Just for that, I should go at once," he said. "Still, I've heard that ye ought to humor expectant mothers." He let the kilt fall to the floor and sat down beside me in his shirt, the bed creaking beneath his weight.

His breath rose in a faint cloud as he turned back the quilt and spread the front of the nightdress to expose my breasts. Bending his head, he kissed each one, touching the nipple delicately with his tongue, so it rose as though by magic, a swelling dark pink against the white skin of my breast.

"God, they're so lovely," he murmured, repeating the process on the other side. He cupped both breasts, admiring them.

"They're heavier," he said, "just a bit. And the nipples are darker, too." One forefinger traced the springing curve of a single fine hair that rose near the dark areola, silver in the frosted light of the morning.

Lifting the quilt, he rolled next to me and I turned into his arms, clasping the solid curves of his back, letting my hands cup the firm rounds of his buttocks. His bare flesh was chilled by the morning air, but the goose bumps smoothed away under the warmth of my touch.

I tried to bring him to me at once, but he resisted me gently, forcing me down onto the pillow as he nibbled the edges of neck and ear. One hand slid up my thigh, the thin material of the nightgown gliding in waves before it.

His head dipped lower, and his hands gently spread my thighs apart. I shivered momentarily as the cold air hit the bare skin of my legs, then relaxed completely into the warm demand of his mouth.

His hair was loose, not yet laced back for the day, and the soft red tickle of it brushed my thighs. The solid weight of his body rested comfortably between my legs, broad hands cupped on the roundness of my hips.

"Mmmm?" came a interrogative sound from below.

I arched my hips slightly in response, and a brief chuckle grazed my skin with warmth.

The hands slid beneath my hips and raised me, and I relaxed into deliquescence as the tiny shudder grew and spread, rising in seconds to a fulfillment that left me limp and gasping, Jamie's head resting on my thigh. He waited a moment for me to recover, caressing the slope of my leg, before returning to his self-appointed task.

I smoothed the tumbled hair back, caressing those ears, so incongruously small and neat for such a large, blunt man. The upper curve glowed with a faint, translucent pink, and I ran my thumb along the edge of the curve.

"They're pointed at the tips," I said. "Just a bit. Like a faun's."

"Oh, aye?" he said, interrupting his labors for a moment. "Like a small deer, ye mean, or the things ye see in classical paintings wi' goat's legs, chasing naked women?"

I lifted my head and peered down across the roil of bedclothes, nightgown, and naked flesh, to the deep blue cat-eyes, gleaming above damp curls of brown hair.

"If the shoe fits," I said, "wear it." And let my head fall back on the pillow as the resultant muffled laugh vibrated against my all too sensitive flesh.

"Oh," I said, straining upward. "Oh, my. Jamie, come here."

"Not yet," he said, doing something with the tip of his tongue that made me squirm uncontrollably.

"Now," I said.

He didn't bother to reply, and I had no more breath to speak with.

"Oh," I said, a bit later. "That's . . ."

"Mmmm?"

"Good," I murmured. "Come here."

"No, I'll do," he said, face invisible behind the tangle of roan and cinnamon. "Would ye like it if I . . ."

"Jamie," I said. "I want you. Come *here*."

Sighing in resignation, he rose to his knees and let me pull him upward, settling at last with his weight balanced on his elbows, but comfortingly solid on top of me, belly to belly and lips to lips. He opened his mouth to protest further, but I promptly kissed him, and he slid between my thighs before he could stop himself. He moaned slightly in involuntary pleasure as he entered me, muscles tensing as he gripped my shoulders.

He was gentle and slow, pausing now and then to kiss me deeply, moving again only at my silent urging. I ran my hands softly down the slope of his back, careful not to press on the healing ridges of the fresh scars. The long muscles of his thigh trembled briefly against my own, but he held back, unwilling to move as quickly as he needed to.

I moved my hips against him, to bring him deeper.

He closed his eyes, and his brow furrowed slightly in concentration. His mouth was open, and his breath came hard.

"I can't . . ." he said. "Oh, God, I canna help it." His buttocks clenched suddenly, taut beneath my hands.

I sighed with deep satisfaction, and pulled him hard against me.

"You're all right?" he asked, a few moments later.

"I won't break, you know," I said, smiling into his eyes.

He laughed huskily. "Maybe not, Sassenach, but *I* may." He gathered me close against him, his cheek pressed against my hair. I flipped the quilt up and tucked it around his shoulders, sealing us in a pocket of warmth. The heat of the fire had not yet reached the bed, but the ice on the window was thawing, the crusted edge of the rime melted into glowing diamonds.

We lay quiet for a time, listening to the occasional crack of the burning applewood in the hearth and the faint sounds of the inn as the guests stirred to life. There were callings to and fro from the balconies across the courtyard, the swish and clop of hooves on the slushy stones outside, and the odd squeal now and then from below, from the piglets the landlady was raising in the kitchen behind the stove.

"Très français, n'est-ce pas?" I said, smiling at the sounds of an altercation drifting up through the floorboards, an amiable settling of accounts between the innkeeper's wife and the local vintner.

"Diseased son of a pox-ridden whore," the female voice remarked. "The brandy from last week tasted like horse-piss."

I didn't need to see the reply to imagine the one-shouldered shrug that went with it.

"How would you know, Madame? After the sixth glass, it all tastes the same, is it not so?"

The bed shook slightly as Jamie laughed with me. He lifted his head from the pillow and sniffed appreciatively at the scent of frying ham that filtered through the drafty chinks of the floorboards.

"Aye, it's France," he agreed. "Food, and drink—and love." He patted my bare hip before tugging the wrinkled gown down over it.

"Jamie," I said softly, "are you happy about it? About the baby?" Outlawed in Scotland, barred from his own home, and with only vague prospects in France, he could pardonably have been less than enthused about acquiring an additional obligation.

He was silent for a moment, only hugging me harder, then sighed briefly before answering.

"Aye, Sassenach." His hand strayed downward, gently rubbing my belly. "I'm happy. And proud as a stallion. But I am most awfully afraid, too."

"About the birth? I'll be all right." I could hardly blame him for apprehension; his own mother had died in childbirth, and birth and its complications were the leading cause of death for women in these times. Still, I knew a thing or two myself, and I had no intention whatever of exposing myself to what passed for medical care here.

"Aye, that—and everything," he said softly. "I want to protect ye, Sassenach—spread myself over ye like a cloak and shield you and the child wi' my body." His voice was soft and husky, with a slight catch in it. "I would do anything for ye . . . and yet . . . there's nothing I *can* do. It doesna matter how strong I am, or how willing; I canna go with you where ye must go . . . nor even help ye at all. And to think of the things that might happen, and me helpless to stop them . . . aye, I'm afraid, Sassenach.

"And yet"—he turned me toward him, hand closing gently over one breast—"yet when I think of you wi' my child at your breast . . . then I feel as though I've gone hollow as a soap bubble, and perhaps I shall burst with joy."

He pressed me tight against his chest, and I hugged him with all my might.

"Oh, Claire, ye do break my heart wi' loving you."

I slept for some time, and woke slowly, hearing the clang of a church bell ringing in the nearby square. Fresh from the Abbey of Ste. Anne, where all the day's activities took place to the rhythm of bells, I automatically glanced at the window, to gauge the intensity of the light and guess the time of day. Bright, clear light, and a window free of ice. The bells rang for the Angelus then, and it was noon.

I stretched, enjoying the blissful knowledge that I needn't get up at once. Early pregnancy made me tired, and the strain of travel had added to my fatigue, making the long rest doubly welcome.

It had rained and snowed unceasingly on the journey as the winter storms battered the French coast. Still, it could have been worse. We had originally intended to go to Rome, not Le Havre. That would have been three or four weeks' travel, in this weather.

Faced with the prospect of earning a living abroad, Jamie had obtained a recommendation as a translator to James Francis Edward Stuart, exiled King of Scotland—or merely the Chevalier St. George, Pretender to the Throne, depending on your loyalties—and we had determined to join the Pretender's court near Rome.

It had been a near thing, at that; we had been on the point of leaving for Italy, when Jamie's uncle Alexander, Abbot of Ste. Anne's, had summoned us to his study.

"I have heard from His Majesty," he announced without preamble.

"Which one?" Jamie asked. The slight family resemblance between the two men was exaggerated by their posture—both sat bolt upright in their chairs, shoulders squared. On the abbot's part, the posture was due to natural asceticism; on Jamie's, to reluctance to let the newly healed scars on his back contact the wood of the chair.

"His Majesty King James," his uncle replied, frowning slightly at me. I was careful to keep my face blank; my presence in Abbot Alexander's study was a mark of trust, and I didn't want to do anything to jeopardize it. He had known me a bare six weeks, since the day after Christmas, when I had appeared at his gate with Jamie, who was near death from torture and imprisonment. Subsequent acquaintance had presumably given the abbot some confidence in me. On the other hand, I was still English. And the English King's name was George, not James.

"Aye? Is he not in need of a translator, then?" Jamie was still thin, but he had been working outdoors with the Brothers who minded the stables and fields of the Abbey, and his face was regaining tinges of its normal healthy color.

"He is in need of a loyal servant—and a friend." Abbot Alexander tapped his fingers on a folded letter that lay on his desk, the crested seal broken. He pursed his lips, glancing from me to his nephew and back.

"What I tell you now must not be repeated," he said sternly. "It will be common knowledge soon, but for now—" I had tried to look trustworthy and close-mouthed; Jamie merely nodded, with a touch of impatience.

"His Highness, Prince Charles Edward, has left Rome, and will arrive in

France within the week," the Abbot said, leaning slightly forward as though to emphasize the importance of what he was saying.

And it was important. James Stuart had mounted an abortive attempt to regain his throne in 1715—an ill-considered military operation that had failed almost immediately for lack of support. Since then—according to Alexander— the exiled James of Scotland had worked tirelessly, writing ceaselessly to his fellow monarchs, and particularly to his cousin, Louis of France, reiterating the legitimacy of his claim to the throne of Scotland and England, and the position of his son, Prince Charles, as heir to that throne.

"His royal cousin Louis has been distressingly deaf to these entirely proper claims," the Abbot had said, frowning at the letter as though it were Louis. "If he's now come to a realization of his responsibilities in the matter, it's cause for great rejoicing among those who hold dear the sacred right of kingship."

Among the Jacobites, that was, James's supporters. Of whom Abbot Alexander of the Abbey of Ste. Anne—born Alexander Fraser of Scotland—was one. Jamie had told me that Alexander was one of the exiled King's most frequent correspondents, in touch with all that touched the Stuart cause.

"He's well placed for it," Jamie had explained to me, discussing the endeavor on which we were about to embark. "The papal messenger system crosses Italy, France, and Spain faster than almost any other. And the papal messengers canna be interfered with by government customs officers, so the letters they carry are less likely to be intercepted."

James of Scotland, exiled in Rome, was supported in large part by the Pope, in whose interest it very much was to have a Catholic monarchy restored to England and Scotland. Therefore, the largest part of James's private mail was carried by papal messenger—and passed through the hands of loyal supporters within the Church hierarchy, like Abbot Alexander of Ste. Anne de Beaupré, who could be depended on to communicate with the King's supporters in Scotland, with less risk than sending letters openly from Rome to Edinburgh and the Highlands.

I watched Alexander with interest, as he expounded the importance of Prince Charles's visit to France. A stocky man of about my own height, he was dark, and considerably shorter than his nephew, but shared with him the faintly slanted eyes, the sharp intelligence, and the talent for discerning hidden motive that seemed to characterize the Frasers I had met.

"So," he finished, stroking his full, dark-brown beard, "I cannot say whether His Highness is in France at Louis's invitation, or has come uninvited, on behalf of his father."

"It makes a wee bit of difference," Jamie remarked, raising one eyebrow skeptically.

His uncle nodded, and a wry smile showed briefly in the thicket of his beard.

"True, lad," he said, letting a faint hint of his native Scots emerge from his usual formal English. "Very true. And that's where you and your wife may be of service, if ye will."

The proposal was simple; His Majesty King James would provide travel expenses and a small stipend, if the nephew of his most loyal and most esteemed friend Alexander would agree to travel to Paris, there to assist his son, His Highness Prince Charles Edward, in whatever ways the latter might require.

I was stunned. We had meant originally to go to Rome because that seemed the best place to embark on our quest: the prevention of the second Jacobite Rising—the '45. From my own knowledge of history, I knew that the Rising, financed from France and carried out by Charles Edward Stuart, would go much farther than had his father's attempt in 1715—but not nearly far enough. If matters progressed as I thought they would, then the troops under Bonnie Prince Charlie would meet with disastrous defeat at Culloden in 1746, and the people of the Highlands would suffer the repercussions of defeat for two centuries thereafter.

Now, in 1744, apparently Charles himself was just beginning his search for support in France. Where better to try to stop a rebellion, than at the side of its leader?

I glanced at Jamie, who was looking over his uncle's shoulder at a small shrine set into the wall. His eyes rested on the gilded figure of Ste. Anne herself and the small sheaf of hothouse flowers laid at her feet, while his thoughts worked behind an expressionless face. At last he blinked once, and smiled at his uncle.

"Whatever assistance His Highness might require? Aye," he said quietly, "I think I can do that. We'll go."

And we had. Instead of proceeding directly to Paris, though, we had come down the coast from Ste. Anne to Le Havre, to meet first with Jamie's cousin, Jared Fraser.

A prosperous Scottish émigré, Jared was an importer of wines and spirits, with a small warehouse and large town house in Paris, and a very large warehouse indeed here in Le Havre, where he had asked Jamie to meet him, when Jamie had written to say we were en route to Paris.

Sufficiently rested by now, I was beginning to feel hungry. There was food on the table; Jamie must have told the chambermaid to bring it while I slept.

I had no dressing gown, but my heavy velvet traveling cloak was handy; I sat up and pulled the warm weight of it over my shoulders before rising to relieve myself, add another stick of wood to the fire, and sit down to my late breakfast.

I chewed hard rolls and baked ham contentedly, washing them down with the jug of milk provided. I hoped Jamie was being adequately fed as well; he insisted that Jared was a good friend, but I had my doubts about the hospitality of some of Jamie's relatives, having met a few of them by now. True, Abbot

Alexander had welcomed us—insofar as a man in the abbot's position could be said to welcome having an outlaw nephew with a suspect wife descend upon him unexpectedly. But our sojourn with Jamie's mother's people, the MacKenzies of Leoch, had come within inches of killing me the autumn before, when I had been arrested and tried as a witch.

"Granted," I'd said, "this Jared's a Fraser, and they seem a trifle safer than your MacKenzie relatives. But have you actually met him before?"

"I lived with him for a time when I was eighteen," he told me, dribbling candle-wax onto his reply and pressing his father's wedding ring on the resultant greenish-gray puddle. A small cabochon ruby, its mount was engraved with the Fraser clan motto, *je suis prest:* "I am ready."

"He had me to stay with him when I came to Paris to finish my schooling, and learn a bit of the world. He was verra kind to me; a good friend of my father's. And there's no one knows more about Parisian society than the man who sells it drink," he added, cracking the ring loose from the hardened wax. "I want to talk to Jared before I walk into Louis's court by the side of Charles Stuart; I should like to feel that I have some chance of getting out again," he finished wryly.

"Why? Do you think there'll be trouble?" I asked. "Whatever assistance His Highness might require" seemed to offer quite a bit of latitude.

He smiled at my worried look.

"No, I dinna expect any difficulty. But what is it the Bible says, Sassenach? 'Put not your trust in princes'?" He rose and kissed me quickly on the brow, tucking the ring back in his sporran. "Who am I to ignore the word of God, eh?"

I spent the afternoon in reading one of the herbals that my friend Brother Ambrose had pressed upon me as a parting gift, then in necessary repairs with needle and thread. Neither of us owned many clothes, and while there were advantages in traveling light, it meant that holey socks and undone hems demanded immediate attention. My needlecase was nearly as precious to me as the small chest in which I carried herbs and medicines.

The needle dipped in and out of the fabric, winking in the light from the window. I wondered how Jamie's visit with Jared was going. I wondered still more what Prince Charles would be like. He would be the first historically famous person I had met, and while I knew better than to believe all the legends that had (not had, *would,* I reminded myself) sprung up around him, the reality of the man was a mystery. The Rising of the '45 would depend almost entirely on the personality of this one young man—its failure or success. Whether it took place at all might depend upon the efforts of another young man—Jamie Fraser. And me.

I was still absorbed in my mending and my thoughts, when heavy footsteps in the corridor aroused me to the realization that it was late in the day; the drip of water from the eaves had slowed as the temperature dropped, and the flames of the sinking sun glowed in the ice spears hanging from the roof. The door opened, and Jamie came in.

He smiled vaguely in my direction, then stopped dead by the table, face absorbed as though he were trying to remember something. He took his cloak off, folded it, and hung it neatly over the foot of the bed, straightened, marched over to the other stool, sat down on it with great precision, and closed his eyes.

I sat still, my mending forgotten in my lap, watching this performance with considerable interest. After a moment, he opened his eyes and smiled at me, but didn't say anything. He leaned forward, studying my face with great attention, as though he hadn't seen me in weeks. At last, an expression of profound revelation passed over his face, and he relaxed, shoulders slumping as he rested his elbows on his knees.

"Whisky," he said, with immense satisfaction.

"I see," I said cautiously. "A lot of it?"

He shook his head slowly from side to side, as though it were very heavy. I could almost hear the contents sloshing.

"Not me," he said, very distinctly. "You."

"Me?" I said indignantly.

"Your eyes," he said. He smiled beatifically. His own eyes were soft and dreamy, cloudy as a trout pool in the rain.

"My eyes? What have my eyes got to do with . . ."

"They're the color of verra fine whisky, wi' the sun shining through them from behind. I thought this morning they looked like sherry, but I was wrong. Not sherry. Not brandy. It's whisky. That's what it is." He looked so gratified as he said this that I couldn't help laughing.

"Jamie, you're terribly drunk. What have you been doing?"

His expression altered to a slight frown.

"I'm not drunk."

"Oh, no?" I laid the mending aside and came over to lay a hand on his forehead. It was cool and damp, though his face was flushed. He at once put his arms about my waist and pulled me close, nuzzling affectionately at my bosom. The smell of mingled spirits rose from him like a fog, so thick as almost to be visible.

"Come here to me, Sassenach," he murmured. "My whisky-eyed lass, my love. Let me take ye to bed."

I thought it a debatable point as to who was likely to be taking whom to bed, but didn't argue. It didn't matter why he thought he was going to bed, after all, provided he got there. I bent and got a shoulder under his armpit to help him up, but he leaned away, rising slowly and majestically under his own power.

"I dinna need help," he said, reaching for the cord at the neck of his shirt. "I told ye, I'm not drunk."

"You're right," I said. " 'Drunk' isn't anywhere near sufficient to describe your current state. Jamie, you're completely pissed."

His eyes traveled down the front of his kilt, across the floor, and up the front of my gown.

"No, I'm not," he said, with great dignity. "I did that outside." He took a step toward me, glowing with ardor. "Come here to me, Sassenach; I'm ready."

I thought "ready" was a bit of an overstatement in one regard; he'd gotten his buttons half undone, and his shirt hung askew on his shoulders, but that was as far as he was likely to make it unaided.

In other respects, though . . . the broad expanse of his chest was exposed, showing the small hollow in the center where I was accustomed to rest my chin, and the small curly hairs sprang up joyous around his nipples. He saw me looking at him, and reached for one of my hands, clasping it to his breast. He was startlingly warm, and I moved instinctively toward him. The other arm swept round me and he bent to kiss me. He made such a thorough job of it that I felt mildly intoxicated, merely from sharing his breath.

"All right," I said, laughing. "If you're ready, so am I. Let me undress you first, though—I've had enough mending today."

He stood still as I stripped him, scarcely moving. He didn't move, either, as I attended to my own clothes and turned down the bed.

I climbed in and turned to look at him, ruddy and magnificent in the sunset glow. He was finely made as a Greek statue, long-nosed and high-cheeked as a profile on a Roman coin. The wide, soft mouth was set in a dreamy smile, and the slanted eyes looked far away. He was perfectly immobile.

I viewed him with some concern.

"Jamie," I said, "how, exactly, do you decide whether you're drunk?"

Aroused by my voice, he swayed alarmingly to one side, but caught himself on the edge of the mantelpiece. His eyes drifted around the room, then fixed on my face. For an instant, they blazed clear and pellucid with intelligence.

"Och, easy, Sassenach. If ye can stand up, you're not drunk." He let go of the mantelpiece, took a step toward me, and crumpled slowly onto the hearth, eyes blank, and a wide, sweet smile on his dreaming face.

"Oh," I said.

The yodeling of roosters outside and the clashing of pots below woke me just after dawn the next morning. The figure next to me jerked, waking abruptly, then froze as the sudden movement jarred his head.

I raised up on one elbow to examine the remains. Not too bad, I thought critically. His eyes were screwed tightly shut against stray beams of sunlight, and his hair stuck out in all directions like a hedgehog's spines, but his skin was pale and clear, and the hands clutching the coverlet were steady.

I pried up one eyelid, peered within, and said playfully, "Anybody home?"

The twin to the eye I was looking at opened slowly, to add its baleful glare to the first. I dropped my hand and smiled charmingly at him.

"Good morning."

"That, Sassenach, is entirely a matter of opinion," he said, and closed both eyes again.

"Have you got any idea how much you weigh?" I asked conversationally.

"No."

The abruptness of the reply suggested that he not only didn't know, he didn't care, but I persisted in my efforts.

"Something around fifteen stone, I make it. About as much as a good-sized boar. Unfortunately, I didn't have any beaters to hang you upside down from a spear and carry you home to the smoking shed."

One eye opened again, and looked consideringly at me, then at the hearth-stone on the far side of the room. One corner of his mouth lifted in a reluctant smile.

"How did you get me in bed?"

"I didn't. I couldn't budge you, so I just laid a quilt over you and left you on the hearth. You came to life and crawled in under your own power, some-where in the middle of the night."

He seemed surprised, and opened the other eye again.

"I did?"

I nodded and tried to smooth down the hair that spiked out over his left ear.

"Oh, yes. Very single-minded, you were."

"Single-minded?" He frowned, thinking, and stretched, thrusting his arms up over his head. Then he looked startled.

"No. I couldn't have."

"Yes, you could. Twice."

He squinted down his chest, as though looking for confirmation of this improbable statement, then looked back at me.

"Really? Well, that's hardly fair; I dinna remember a thing about it." He hesitated for a moment, looking shy. "Was it all right, then? I didna do any-thing foolish?"

I flopped down next to him and snuggled my head into the curve of his shoulder.

"No, I wouldn't call it foolish. You weren't very conversational, though."

"Thank the Lord for small blessings," he said, and a small chuckle rum-bled through his chest.

"Mm. You'd forgotten how to say anything except 'I love you,' but you said that a lot."

The chuckle came back, louder this time. "Oh, aye? Well, could have been worse, I suppose."

He drew in his breath, then paused. He turned his head and sniffed suspiciously at the soft tuft of cinnamon under his raised arm.

"Christ!" he said. He tried to push me away. "Ye dinna want to put your head near my oxter, Sassenach. I smell like a boar that's been dead a week."

"And pickled in brandy after," I agreed, snuggling closer. "How on earth did you get so—ahem—stinking drunk, anyway?"

"Jared's hospitality." He settled himself in the pillows with a deep sigh, arm round my shoulder.

"He took me down to show me his warehouse at the docks. And the storeroom there where he keeps the rare vintages and the Portuguese brandy and the Jamaican rum." He grimaced slightly, recalling. "The wine wasna so bad, for that you just taste, and spit it on the floor when you've done wi' a mouthful. But neither of us could see wasting the brandy that way. Besides, Jared said ye need to let it trickle down the back of your throat, to appreciate it fully."

"How much of it did you appreciate?" I asked curiously.

"I lost count in the middle of the second bottle." Just then, a church bell started to ring nearby; the summons to early Mass. Jamie sat bolt upright, staring at the windowpane, bright with sun.

"Christ, Sassenach! What time is it?"

"About six, I suppose," I said, puzzled. "Why?"

He relaxed slightly, though he stayed sitting up.

"Oh, that's all right, then. I was afraid it was the Angelus bell. I'd lost all track of time."

"I'd say so. Does it matter?"

In a burst of energy, he threw back the quilts and stood up. He staggered a moment, but kept his balance, though both hands went to his head, to make sure it was still attached.

"Aye," he said, gasping a bit. "We've an appointment this morning down at the docks, at Jared's warehouse. The two of us."

"Really?" I clambered out of bed myself, and groped for the chamber pot under the bed. "If he's planning to finish the job, I shouldn't think he'd want witnesses."

Jamie's head popped through the neck of his shirt, eyebrows raised.

"Finish the job?"

"Well, most of your other relatives seem to want to kill you or me; why not Jared? He's made a good start at poisoning you, seems to me."

"Verra funny, Sassenach," he said dryly. "Have ye something decent to wear?"

I had been wearing a serviceable gray serge gown on our travels, acquired through the good offices of the almoner at the Abbey of Ste. Anne, but I did also have the gown in which I had escaped from Scotland, a gift from Lady Annabelle MacRannoch. A pretty leaf-green velvet, it made me look rather pale, but was stylish enough.

"I think so, if there aren't too many saltwater stains on it."

I knelt by the small traveling chest, unfolding the green velvet. Kneeling next to me, Jamie flipped back the lid of my medicine box, studying the layers of bottles and boxes and bits of gauze-wrapped herbs.

"Have ye got anything in here for a verra vicious headache, Sassenach?"

I peered over his shoulder, then reached in and touched one bottle.

"Horehound might help, though it's not the best. And willow-bark tea with sow fennel works fairly well, but it takes some time to brew. Tell you what —why don't I make you up a recipe for hobnailed liver? Wonderful hangover cure."

He bent a suspicious blue eye on me.

"That sounds nasty."

"It is," I said cheerfully. "But you'll feel lots better after you throw up."

"Mphm." He stood up and nudged the chamber pot toward me with one toe.

"Vomiting in the morning is *your* job, Sassenach," he said. "Get it over with and get dressed. I'll stand the headache."

Jared Munro Fraser was a small, spare, black-eyed man, who bore more than a passing resemblance to his distant cousin Murtagh, the Fraser clansman who had accompanied us to Le Havre. When I first saw Jared, standing majestically in the gaping doors of his warehouse, so that streams of longshoremen carrying casks were forced to go around him, the resemblance was strong enough that I blinked and rubbed my eyes. Murtagh, so far as I knew, was still at the inn, attending a lame horse.

Jared had the same lank, dark hair and piercing eyes; the same sinewy, monkey-like frame. But there all resemblance stopped, and as we drew closer, Jamie gallantly clearing a path for me through the mob with elbows and shoulders, I could see the differences as well. Jared's face was oblong, rather than hatchet-shaped, with a cheerful snub nose that effectively ruined the dignified air conferred at a distance by his excellent tailoring and upright carriage.

A successful merchant rather than a cattle-raider, he also knew how to smile—unlike Murtagh, whose natural expression was one of unrelieved dourness—and a broad grin of welcome broke out on his face as we were jostled and shoved up the ramp into his presence.

"My dear!" he exclaimed, clutching me by the arm and yanking me deftly out of the way of two burly stevedores rolling a gigantic cask through the huge door. "So pleased to see you at last!" The cask bumped noisily on the boards of the ramp, and I could hear the rolling slosh of its contents as it passed me.

"You can treat rum like that," Jared observed, watching the ungainly progress of the enormous barrel through the obstructions of the warehouse, "but not port. I always fetch that up myself, along with the bottled wines. In fact, I was just setting off to see to a new shipment of Belle Rouge port. Would you perhaps be interested in accompanying me?"

I glanced at Jamie, who nodded, and we set off at once in Jared's wake, sidestepping the rumbling traffic of casks and hogsheads, carts and barrows, and men and boys of all descriptions carrying bolts of fabric, boxes of grain and foodstuffs, rolls of hammered copper, sacks of flour, and anything else that could be transported by ship.

Le Havre was an important center of shipping traffic, and the docks were the heart of the city. A long, solid wharf ran nearly a quarter-mile round the edge of the harbor, with smaller docks protruding from it, along which were anchored three-masted barks and brigantines, dories and small galleys; a full range of the ships that provisioned France.

Jamie kept a firm hold on my elbow, the better to yank me out of the way of oncoming handcarts, rolling casks, and careless merchants and seamen, who were inclined not to look where they were going but rather to depend on sheer momentum to see them through the scrum of the docks.

As we made our way down the quay, Jared shouted genteelly into my ear on the other side, pointing out objects of interest as we passed, and explaining the history and ownership of the various ships in a staccato, disjointed manner. The *Arianna,* which we were on our way to see, was in fact one of Jared's own ships. Ships, I gathered, might belong to a single owner, more often to a company of merchants who owned them collectively, or, occasionally, to a captain who contracted his vessel, crew, and services for a voyage. Seeing the number of company-owned vessels, compared to the relatively few owned by individuals, I began to form a very respectful idea of Jared's worth.

The *Arianna* was in the middle of the anchored row, near a large warehouse with the name FRASER painted on it in sloping, whitewashed letters. Seeing the name gave me an odd little thrill, a sudden feeling of alliance and belonging, with the realization that I shared that name, and with it, an acknowledged kinship with those who bore it.

The *Arianna* was a three-masted ship, perhaps sixty feet long, with a wide bow. There were two cannon on the side of the ship that faced the dock; in case of robbery on the high seas, I supposed. Men were swarming all over the deck with what I assumed was some purpose, though it looked like nothing so much as an ant's nest under attack.

All sails were reefed and tied, but the rising tide shifted the vessel slightly, swinging the bowsprit toward us. It was decorated with a rather grim-visaged figurehead; with her formidable bare bosom and tangled curls all spangled with salt, the lady looked as though she didn't enjoy sea air all that much.

"Sweet little beauty, is she not?" Jared asked, waving a hand expansively. I assumed he meant the ship, not the figurehead.

"Verra nice," said Jamie politely. I caught his uneasy glance at the boat's waterline, where the small waves lapped dark gray against the hull. I could see that he was hoping we would not be obliged to go on board. A gallant warrior, brilliant, bold, and courageous in battle, Jamie Fraser was also a landlubber.

Definitely not one of the hardy, seafaring Scots who hunted whales from Tarwathie or voyaged the world in search of wealth, he suffered from a seasickness so acute that our journey across the Channel in December had nearly killed him, weakened as he then was by the effects of torture and imprisonment. And while yesterday's drinking orgy with Jared wasn't in the same league, it wasn't likely to have made him any more seaworthy.

I could see dark memories crossing his face as he listened to his cousin extolling the sturdiness and speed of the *Arianna,* and drew near enough to whisper to him.

"Surely not while it's at anchor?"

"I don't know, Sassenach," he replied, with a look at the ship in which loathing and resignation were nicely mingled. "But I suppose we'll find out." Jared was already halfway up the gangplank, greeting the captain with loud cries of welcome. "If I turn green, can ye pretend to faint or something? It will make a poor impression if I vomit on Jared's shoes."

I patted his arm reassuringly. "Don't worry. I have faith in you."

"It isna *me,*" he said, with a last, lingering glance at terra firma, "it's my stomach."

The ship stayed comfortingly level under our shoes, however, and both Jamie and his stomach acquitted themselves nobly—assisted, perhaps, by the brandy poured out for us by the captain.

"A nice make," Jamie said, passing the glass briefly under his nose and closing his eyes in approval of the rich, aromatic fumes. "Portuguese, isn't it?"

Jared laughed delightedly and nudged the captain.

"You see, Portis? I told you he had a natural palate! He's only tasted it once before!"

I bit the inside of my cheek and avoided Jamie's eye. The captain, a large, scruffy-looking specimen, looked bored, but grimaced politely in Jamie's direction, exhibiting three gold teeth. A man who liked to keep his wealth portable.

"Ung," he said. "This the lad's going to keep your bilges dry, is it?"

Jared looked suddenly embarrassed, a slight flush rising under the leathery skin of his face. I noticed with fascination that one ear was pierced for an earring, and wondered just what sort of background had led to his present success.

"Aye, well," he said, betraying for the first time a hint of Scots accent, "that's to be seen yet. But I think—" He glanced through the port at the activity taking place on the dock, then back at the captain's glass, drained in three gulps while the rest of us were sipping. "Um, I say, Portis, would you allow me to use your cabin for a moment? I should like to confer with my nephew and his wife—and I see that the aft hold seems to be having a bit of trouble with the cargo nets, from the sound of it." This craftily added observation was enough to send Captain Portis out of the cabin like a charging boar, hoarse voice uplifted in a Spanish-French patois that I luckily didn't understand.

Jared stepped delicately to the door and closed it firmly after the captain's bulky form, cutting down the noise level substantially. He returned to the tiny captain's table and ceremoniously refilled all our glasses before speaking. Then he looked from Jamie to me and smiled once more, in charming deprecation.

"It's a bit more precipitous than I'd meant to make such a request," he said. "But I see the good captain has rather given away my hand. The truth of the matter is"—he raised his glass so the watery reflections from the port shivered through the brandy, striking patches of wavering light from the brass fittings of the cabin—"I need a man." He tipped the cup in Jamie's direction, then brought it to his lips and drank.

"A good man," he amplified, lowering the glass. "You see, my dear," bowing to me, "I have the opportunity of making an exceptional investment in a new winery in the Moselle region. But the evaluation of it is not one I should feel comfortable in entrusting to a subordinate; I should need to see the facilities myself, and advise in their development. The undertaking would require several months."

He gazed thoughtfully into his glass, gently swirling the fragrant brown liquid so its perfume filled the tiny cabin. I had drunk no more than a few sips from my own glass, but began to feel slightly giddy, more from a rising excitement than from drink.

"It's too good a chance to be missed," Jared said. "And there's the chance of making several good contracts with the wineries along the Rhône; the products there are excellent, but relatively rare in Paris. God, they'd sell among the nobility like snow in summer!" His shrewd black eyes gleamed momentarily with visions of avarice, then sparkled with humor as he looked at me.

"But—" he said.

"But," I finished for him, "you can't leave your business here without a guiding hand."

"Intelligence as well as beauty and charm. I congratulate you, Cousin." He tilted a well-groomed head toward Jamie, one eyebrow cocked in humorous approval.

"I confess that I was at something of a loss to see how I was to proceed," he said, setting the glass down on the small table with the air of a man putting aside social frivolity for the sake of serious business. "But when you wrote from Ste. Anne, saying you intended to visit Paris . . ." He hesitated a moment, then smiled at Jamie, with an odd little flutter of the hands.

"Knowing that you, my lad"—he nodded to Jamie—"have a head for figures, I was strongly inclined to consider your arrival an answer to prayer. Still, I thought that perhaps we should meet and become reacquainted before I took the step of making you a definite proposal."

You mean you thought you'd better see how presentable *I* was, I thought cynically, but smiled at him nonetheless. I caught Jamie's eye, and one of his brows twitched upward. This was our week for proposals, evidently. For a dispossessed outlaw and a suspected English spy, our services seemed to be rather in demand.

Jared's proposal was more than generous; in return for Jamie's running the French end of the business during the next six months, Jared would not only pay him a salary but would leave his Paris town house, complete with staff, at our disposal.

"Not at all, not at all," he said, when Jamie tried to protest this provision. He pressed a finger on the end of his nose, grinning charmingly at me. "A pretty woman to host dinner parties is a great asset in the wine business, Cousin. You have no idea how much wine you can sell, if you let the customers taste it first." He shook his head decidedly. "No, it will be a great service to me, if your wife would allow herself to be troubled by entertaining."

The thought of hosting supper parties for Parisian society was in fact a trifle daunting. Jamie looked at me, eyebrows raised in question, but I swallowed hard and smiled, nodding. It was a good offer; if he felt competent to take over the running of an importing business, the least I could do was order dinner and brush up my sprightly conversational French.

"Not at all," I murmured, but Jared had taken my agreement for granted, and was going on, intent black eyes fixed on Jamie.

"And then, I thought perhaps you'd be needing an establishment of sorts —for the benefit of the other interests which bring you to Paris."

Jamie smiled noncommittally, at which Jared uttered a short laugh and picked up his brandy glass. We had each been provided a glass of water as well, for cleansing the palate between sips, and he pulled one of these close with the other hand.

"Well, a toast!" he exclaimed. "To our association, Cousin—and to His Majesty!" He lifted the brandy glass in salute, then passed it ostentatiously over the glass of water and brought it to his lips.

I watched this odd behavior in surprise, but it apparently meant something to Jamie, for he smiled at Jared, picked up his own glass and passed it over the water.

"To His Majesty," he repeated. Then, seeing me staring at him in bewilderment, he smiled and explained, "To His Majesty—over the water, Sassenach."

"Oh?" I said, then, realization dawning, "oh!" The king over the water— King James. Which did a bit to explain this sudden urge on the part of everyone to see Jamie and myself established in Paris, which would otherwise have seemed an improbable coincidence.

If Jared were also a Jacobite, then his correspondence with Abbot Alexander was very likely more than coincidental; chances were that Jamie's letter announcing our arrival had come together with one from Alexander, explaining the commission from King James. And if our presence in Paris fitted in with Jared's own plans—then so much the better. With a sudden appreciation for the complexities of the Jacobite network, I raised my own glass, and drank to His Majesty across the water—and our new partnership with Jared.

Jared and Jamie then settled down to a discussion of the business, and were soon head to head, bent over inky sheets of paper, evidently manifests and bills of lading. The tiny cabin reeked of tobacco, brandy fumes, and unwashed sailor, and I began to feel a trifle queasy again. Seeing that I wouldn't be needed for a while, I stood up quietly and found my way out on deck.

I was careful to avoid the altercation still going on around the rear cargo hatch, and picked my way through coils of rope, objects which I assumed to be belaying pins, and tumbled piles of sail fabric, to a quiet spot in the bow. From here, I had an unobstructed view over the harbor.

I sat on a chest against the taffrail, enjoying the salty breeze and the tarry, fishy smells of ships and harbor. It was still cold, but with my cloak pulled tight around me, I was warm enough. The ship rocked slowly, rising on the incoming tide; I could see the beards of algae on nearby dock pilings lifting and swirling, obscuring the shiny black patches of mussels between them.

The thought of mussels reminded me of the steamed mussels with butter I had had for dinner the night before, and I was suddenly starving. The absurd contrasts of pregnancy seemed to keep me always conscious of my digestion; if I wasn't vomiting, I was ravenously hungry. The thought of food led me to the thought of menus, which led back to a contemplation of the entertaining Jared had mentioned. Dinner parties, hm? It seemed an odd way to begin the job of saving Scotland, but then, I couldn't really think of anything better.

At least if I had Charles Stuart across a dinner table from me, I could keep an eye on him, I thought, smiling to myself at the joke. If he showed signs of hopping a ship for Scotland, maybe I could slip something into his soup.

Perhaps that wasn't so funny, after all. The thought reminded me of Geillis Duncan, and my smile faded. Wife of the procurator fiscal in Cranesmuir, she had murdered her husband by dropping powdered cyanide into his food at a banquet. Accused as a witch soon afterward, she had been arrested while I was with her, and I had been taken to trial myself; a trial from which Jamie had rescued me. The memories of several days spent in the cold dark of the thieves' hole at Cranesmuir were all too fresh, and the wind seemed suddenly very cold.

I shivered, but not altogether from chill. I could not think of Geillis Duncan without that cold finger down my spine. Not so much because of what she had done, but because of who she had been. A Jacobite, too; one whose support of the Stuart cause had been more than slightly tinged with madness. Worse than that, she was what I was—a traveler through the standing stones.

I didn't know whether she had come to the past as I had, by accident, or whether her journey had been deliberate. Neither did I know precisely *where* she had come from. But my last vision of her, screaming defiance at the judges who would condemn her to burn, was of a tall, fair woman, arms stretched high, showing on one arm the telltale round of a vaccination scar. I felt automatically for the small patch of roughened skin on my own upper arm, beneath the comforting folds of my cloak, and shuddered when I found it.

I was distracted from these unhappy memories by a growing commotion on the next quay. A large knot of men had gathered by a ship's gangway, and there was considerable shouting and pushing going on. Not a fight; I peered over at the altercation, shading my eyes with my hand, but could see no blows exchanged. Instead, an effort seemed to be under way to clear a pathway through the milling crowd to the doors of a large warehouse on the upper end of the quay. The crowd was stubbornly resisting all such efforts, surging back like the tide after each push.

Jamie suddenly appeared behind me, closely followed by Jared, who squinted at the mob scene below. Absorbed by the shouting, I hadn't heard them come up.

"What is it?" I stood and leaned back into Jamie, bracing myself against the increasing sway of the ship underfoot. I was aware at close quarters of his scent; he had bathed at the inn and he smelled clean and warm, with a faint hint of sun and dust. A sharpening of the sense of smell was another effect of pregnancy, apparently; I could smell him even among the myriad stenches and scents of the seaport, much as you can hear a low-pitched voice close by in a noisy crowd.

"I don't know. Some trouble with the other ship, looks like." He reached down and put a hand on my elbow, to steady me. Jared turned and barked an order in gutteral French to one of the sailors nearby. The man promptly hopped over the rail and slid down one of the ropes to the quay, tarred pigtail dangling toward the water. We watched from the deck as he joined the crowd, prodded another seaman in the ribs, and received an answer, complete with expressive gesticulations.

Jared was frowning, as the pigtailed man scrambled back up the crowded gangplank. The sailor said something to him in that same thick-sounding French, too fast for me to follow it. After a few more words' conversation, Jared swung abruptly around and came to stand next to me, lean hands gripping the rail.

"He says there's sickness aboard the *Patagonia*."

"What sort of sickness?" I hadn't thought of bringing my medicine box with me, so there was little I could do in any case, but I was curious. Jared looked worried and unhappy.

"They're afraid it might be smallpox, but they don't know. The port's inspector and the harbor master have been called."

"Would you like me to have a look?" I offered. "I might at least be able to tell you whether it's a contagious disease or not."

Jared's sketchy eyebrows disappeared under the lank black fringe of his hair. Jamie looked mildly embarrassed.

"My wife's well known as a healer, Cousin," he explained, but then turned and shook his head at me.

"No, Sassenach. It wouldna be safe."

I could see the *Patagonia*'s gangway easily; now the gathered crowd moved suddenly back, jostling and stepping on each other's toes. Two seamen stepped down from the deck, a length of canvas slung between them as a stretcher. The white sail-fabric sagged heavily under the weight of the man they carried, and a bare, sun-darkened arm lolled from the makeshift hammock.

The seamen wore strips of cloth tied round their noses and mouths, and kept their faces turned away from the stretcher, jerking their heads as they growled at each other, maneuvering their burden over the splintered planks. The pair passed under the fascinated noses of the crowd and disappeared into a nearby warehouse.

Making a quick decision, I turned and headed for the rear gangplank of the *Arianna*.

"Don't worry," I called to Jamie over one shoulder, "if it is smallpox, I can't get that." One of the seamen, hearing me, paused and gaped, but I just smiled at him and brushed past.

The crowd was still now, no longer surging to and fro, and it was not so difficult to make my way between the muttering clusters of seamen, many of whom frowned or looked startled as I ducked past them. The warehouse was disused; no bales or casks filled the echoing shadows of the huge room, but the scents of sawn lumber, smoked meat, and fish lingered, easily distinguishable from the host of other smells.

The sick man had been hastily dumped near the door, on a pile of discarded straw packing. His attendants pushed past me as I entered, eager to get away.

I approached him cautiously, stopping a few feet away. He was flushed with fever, his skin a queer dark red, scabbed thick with white pustules. He moaned and tossed his head restlessly from side to side, cracked mouth working as though in search of water.

"Get me some water," I said to one of the sailors standing nearby. The man, a short, muscular fellow with his beard tarred into ornamental spikes, merely stared as though he had found himself suddenly addressed by a fish.

Turning my back on him impatiently, I sank to my knees by the sick man and opened his filthy shirt. He stank abominably; probably none too clean to start with, he had been left to lie in his own filth, his fellows afraid to touch him. His arms were relatively clear, but the pustules clustered thickly down his chest and stomach, and his skin was burning to the touch.

Jamie had come in while I made my examination, accompanied by Jared. With them was a small, pear-shaped man in a gold-swagged official's coat and two other men, one a nobleman or a rich bourgeois by his dress; the other a tall, lean individual, clearly a seafarer from his complexion. Probably the captain of the plague ship, if that's what it was.

And that's what it appeared to be. I had seen smallpox many times before, in the uncivilized parts of the world to which my uncle Lamb, an eminent archaeologist, had taken me during my early years. This fellow wasn't pissing blood, as sometimes happened when the disease attacked the kidneys, but otherwise he had every classic symptom.

"I'm afraid it is smallpox," I said.

The *Patagonia*'s captain gave a sudden howl of anguish, and stepped toward me, face contorted, raising his hand as though to strike me.

"No!" he shouted. "Fool of a woman! *Salope! Femme sans cervelle!* Do you want to ruin me?"

The last word was cut off in a gurgle as Jamie's hand closed on his throat. The other hand twisted hard in the man's shirtfront, lifting him onto his toes.

"I should prefer you to address my wife with respect, Monsieur," Jamie said, rather mildly. The captain, face turning purple, managed a short, jerky nod, and Jamie dropped him. He took a step back, wheezing, and sidled behind his companion as though for refuge, rubbing his throat.

The tubby little official was bending cautiously over the sick man, holding a large silver pomander on a chain close to his nose as he did so. Outside, the level of noise dropped suddenly as the crowd pulled back from the warehouse doors to admit another canvas stretcher.

The man before us sat up suddenly, startling the little official so that he nearly fell over. The man stared wildly around the warehouse, then his eyes rolled back in his head, and he fell back onto the straw as though he'd been poleaxed. He hadn't, but the end result was much the same.

"He's dead," I said, unnecessarily.

The official, recovering his dignity along with his pomander, stepped in once more, looked closely at the body, straightened up and announced, "Smallpox. The lady is correct. I'm sorry, Monsieur le Comte, but you know the law as well as anyone."

The man he addressed sighed impatiently. He glanced at me, frowning, then jerked his head at the official.

"I'm sure this can be arranged, Monsieur Pamplemousse. Please, a moment's private conversation . . ." He motioned toward the deserted foreman's hut that stood some distance away, a small derelict structure inside the larger building. A nobleman by dress as well as by title, Monsieur le Comte was a slender, elegant sort, with heavy brows and thin lips. His entire attitude proclaimed that he was used to getting his way.

But the little official was backing away, hands held out before him as though in self-defense.

"*Non*, Monsieur le Comte," he said, "*Je le regrette, mais c'est impossible.* . . . It cannot be done. Too many people know about it already. The news will be all over the docks by now." He glanced helplessly at Jamie and Jared, then waved vaguely at the warehouse door, where the featureless heads of spectators showed in silhouette, the late afternoon sun rimming them with gold halos.

"No," he said again, his pudgy features hardening with resolve. "You will excuse me, Monsieur—and Madame," he added belatedly, as though noticing me for the first time. "I must go and institute proceedings for the destruction of the ship."

The captain uttered another choked howl at this, and clutched at his sleeve, but he pulled away, and hurried out of the building.

The atmosphere following his departure was a trifle strained, what with Monsieur le Comte and his captain both glaring at me, Jamie glowering menacingly at them, and the dead man staring sightlessly up at the ceiling forty feet above.

The Comte took a step toward me, eyes glittering. "Have you any notion what you have done?" he snarled. "Be warned, Madame; you will pay for this day's work!"

Jamie moved suddenly in the Comte's direction, but Jared was even faster, tugging at Jamie's sleeve, pushing me gently in the direction of the door, and murmuring something unintelligible to the stricken captain, who merely shook his head dumbly in response.

"Poor bugger," Jared said outside, shaking his head. "Phew!" It was chilly on the quay, with a cold gray wind that rocked the ships at anchor, but Jared mopped his face and neck with a large, incongruous red sailcloth handkerchief pulled from the pocket of his coat. "Come on, laddie, let's find a tavern. I'm needing a drink."

Safely ensconced in the upper room of one of the quayside taverns, with a pitcher of wine on the table, Jared collapsed into a chair, fanning himself, and exhaled noisily.

"God, what luck!" He poured a large dollop of wine into his cup, tossed it off, and poured another. Seeing me staring at him, he grinned and pushed the pitcher in my direction.

"Well, there's wine, lassie," he explained, "and then there's stuff you drink to wash the dust away. Toss it back quick, before you have time to taste it, and it does the job handily." Taking his own advice, he drained the cup and reached for the pitcher again. I began to see exactly what had happened to Jamie the day before.

"Good luck or bad?" I asked Jared curiously. I would have assumed the answer to be "bad," but the little merchant's air of jovial exhilaration seemed much too pronounced to be due to the red wine, which strongly resembled battery acid. I set down my own cup, hoping the enamel on my molars was intact.

"Bad for St. Germain, good for me," he said succinctly. He rose from his chair and peered out the window.

"Good," he said, sitting down again with a satisfied air. "They'll have the wine off and into the warehouse by sunset. Safe and sound."

Jamie leaned back in his chair, surveying his cousin with one eyebrow raised, a smile on his lips.

"Do we take it that Monsieur le Comte St. Germain's ship also carried spirits, Cousin?"

An ear-to-ear grin in reply displayed two gold teeth in the lower jaw, which made Jared look still more piratical.

"The best aged port from Pinhão," he said happily. "Cost him a fortune. Half the vintage from the Noval vineyards, and no more available for a year."

"And I suppose the other half of the Noval port is what's being unloaded into your warehouse?" I began to understand his delight.

"Right, my lassie, right as rain!" Jared chortled, almost hugging himself at the thought. "D'ye know what that will sell for in Paris?" he demanded, rocking forward and banging his cup down on the table. "A limited supply, and me with the monopoly? God, my profit's made for the year!"

I rose and looked out the window myself. The *Arianna* rode at anchor, already noticeably higher in the water, as the huge cargo nets swung down from the boom mounted on the rear deck, to be carefully unloaded, bottle by bottle, into handcarts for the trip to the warehouse.

"Not to impair the general rejoicing," I said, a little diffidently, "but did you say that your port came from the same place as St. Germain's shipment?"

"Aye, I did." Jared came to stand next to me, squinting down at the procession of loaders below. "Noval makes the best port in the whole of Spain and Portugal; I'd have liked to take the whole bottling, but hadn't the capital. What of it?"

"Only that if the ships are coming from the same port, there's a chance that some of your seamen might have smallpox too," I said.

The thought blanched the wine flush from Jared's lean cheeks, and he reached for a restorative gulp.

"God, what a thought!" he said, gasping as he set the cup down. "But I think it's all right," he said, reassuring himself. "The port's half unloaded already. But I'd best speak to the captain, anyway," he added, frowning. "I'll have him pay the men off as soon as the loading's finished—and if anyone looks ill, they can have their wages and leave at once." He turned decisively and shot out of the room, pausing at the door just long enough to call over his shoulder, "Order some supper!" before disappearing down the stair with a clatter like a small herd of elephants.

I turned to Jamie, who was staring bemusedly into his undrunk cup of wine.

"He shouldn't do that!" I exclaimed. "If he has got smallpox on board, he could spread it all over the city by sending men off with it."

Jamie nodded slowly.

"Then I suppose we'll hope he hasna got it," he observed mildly.

I turned uncertainly toward the door. "But . . . shouldn't we do something? I could at least go have a look at his men. And tell them what to do with the bodies of the men from the other ship . . ."

"Sassenach." The deep voice was still mild, but held an unmistakable note of warning.

"What?" I turned back to find him leaning forward, regarding me levelly over the rim of his cup. He looked at me thoughtfully for a minute before speaking.

"D'ye think what we've set ourselves to do is important, Sassenach?"

My hand dropped from the door handle.

"Stopping the Stuarts from starting a rising in Scotland? Yes, of course I do. Why do you ask?"

He nodded, patient as an instructor with a slow pupil.

"Aye, well. If ye do, then you'll come here, sit yourself down, and drink wine wi' me until Jared comes back. And if ye don't . . ." He paused and blew out a long breath that stirred the ruddy wave of hair above his forehead.

"If ye don't, then you'll go down to a quay full of seamen and merchants who think women near ships are the height of ill luck, who are already spreading gossip that you've put a curse on St. Germain's ship, and you'll tell them what they must do. With luck, they'll be too afraid of ye to rape you before they cut your throat and toss you in the harbor, and me after you. If St. Germain himself doesna strangle you first. Did ye no see the look on his face?"

I came back to the table and sat down, a little abruptly. My knees were a trifle wobbly.

"I saw it," I said. "But could he . . . he wouldn't . . ."

Jamie raised his brows and pushed a cup of wine across the table to me.

"He could, and he would if he thought it could be managed inconspicuously. For the Lord's sake, Sassenach, you've cost the man close on a year's income! And he doesna look the sort to take such a loss philosophically. Had ye not told the harbor master it was smallpox, out loud in front of witnesses, a few discreet bribes would have taken care of the matter. As it is, why do ye think Jared brought us up here so fast? For the quality of the drink?"

My lips felt stiff, as though I'd actually drunk a good bit of the vitriol from the pitcher.

"You mean . . . we're in danger?"

He sat back, nodding.

"Now you've got it," he said kindly. "I dinna suppose Jared wanted to alarm you. I expect he's gone to arrange a guard of some kind for us, as well as to see to his crew. He'll likely be safe enough—everyone knows him, and his crew and loaders are right outside."

I rubbed my hands over the gooseflesh that rippled up my forearms. There was a cheerful fire in the hearth, and the room was warm and smoky, but I felt cold.

"How do you know so much about what the Comte St. Germain might do?" I didn't doubt Jamie at all—I remembered all too well the malevolent black glare the Comte had shot at me in the warehouse—but I did wonder how he knew the man.

Jamie took a small sip of the wine, made a face and put it down.

"For the one thing, he's some reputation for ruthlessness—and other things. I heard a bit about him when I lived in Paris before, though I had the luck never to run afoul of the man then. For another, Jared spent some time yesterday warning me about him; he's Jared's chief business rival in Paris."

I rested my elbows on the battered table, and parked my chin on my folded hands.

"I've made rather a mess of things, haven't I?" I said ruefully. "Got you off on a fine footing in business."

He smiled, then got up and came behind me, bending to put his arms around me. I was still rather unnerved from his sudden revelations, but felt much better to feel the strength and the bulk of him behind me. He kissed me lightly on top of the head.

"Dinna worry, Sassenach," he said. "I can take care of myself. And I can take care of you, too—and you'll let me." There was a smile in his voice, but a question as well, and I nodded, letting my head fall back against his chest.

"I'll let you," I said. "The citizens of Le Havre will just have to take their chances with the pox."

It was nearly an hour before Jared came back, ears reddened with cold, but throat unslit, and apparently none the worse for wear. I was happy to see him.

"It's all right," he announced, beaming. "Nothing but scurvy and the usual fluxes and chills aboard. No pox." He looked around the room, rubbing his hands together. "Where's supper?"

His cheeks were wind-reddened and he looked cheerful and capable. Apparently dealing with business rivals who settled contentions by assassination was all in a day's work to this merchant. And why not? I thought cynically. He was a bloody Scot, after all.

As if to confirm this view, Jared ordered the meal, acquired an excellent wine to go with it by the simple expedient of sending to his own warehouse for it, and sat down to a genial postprandial discussion with Jamie on ways and means of dealing with French merchants.

"Bandits," he said. "Every man jack o' them would stab ye in the back as soon as look at ye. Filthy thieves. Don't trust them an inch. Half on deposit, half on delivery, and never let a nobleman pay on credit."

Despite Jared's assurances that he had left two men below on watch, I was still a bit nervous, and after supper, I placed myself near the window, where I could see the comings and goings along the pier. Not that my watching out was likely to do a lot of good, I thought; every second man on the dock looked like an assassin to me.

The clouds were closing in over the harbor; it was going to snow again tonight. The reefed sails fluttered wildly in the rising wind, rattling against the spars with a noise that nearly overwhelmed the shouts of the loaders. The harbor glowed with a moment of dull green light as the setting sun was driven into the water by the pressing clouds.

As it grew darker, the bustle to and fro died down, the loaders with their handcarts disappearing up the streets into the town, and the sailors disappearing into the lighted doors of establishments like the one in which I sat. Still, the place was far from deserted; in particular, there was a small crowd still gathered near the ill-fated *Patagonia*. Men in some sort of uniform formed a cordon at the foot of the gangplank; no doubt to prevent anyone going aboard or bringing the cargo off. Jared had explained that the healthy members of the crew would be allowed to come ashore, but not permitted to bring anything off the ship save the clothes that they wore.

"Better than they'd do under the Dutch," he said, scratching the rough black stubble that was beginning to emerge along his jaw. "If a ship's coming in from a port known to have plague of some kind, the damned Hollanders make the sailors swim ashore naked."

"What do they do for clothes once they get ashore?" I asked curiously.

"I don't know," said Jared absently, "but since they'll find a brothel within moments of stepping on land, I don't suppose they'd need any—begging your pardon, m'dear," he added hastily, suddenly remembering that he was talking to a lady.

Covering his momentary confusion with heartiness, he rose and came to peer out of the window beside me.

"Ah," he said. "They're getting ready to fire the ship. Given what she's carrying, they'd best tow it a good way out into the harbor first."

Towropes had been attached to the doomed *Patagonia*, and a number of small boats manned by oarsmen were standing ready, waiting for a signal. This was given by the harbor master, whose gold braid was barely visible as a gleam in the dying light of the day. He shouted, waving both hands slowly back and forth above his head like a semaphore.

His shout was echoed by the captains of the rowboats and galleys, and the towropes slowly lifted from the water as they tautened, water sluicing down the heavy hemp spirals with a splash audible in the sudden silence that struck the docks. The shouts from the towboats were the only sound as the dark hulk of the condemned ship creaked, quivered, and turned into the wind, shrouds groaning as she set out on her last brief voyage.

They left her in the middle of the harbor, a safe distance away from the other ships. Her decks had been soaked with oil, and as the towropes were cast off and the galleys pulled away, the small round figure of the harbor master rose from the seat of the dinghy that had rowed him out. He bent down, head close to one of the seated figures, then rose with the bright sudden flame of a torch in one hand.

The rower behind him leaned away as he drew back his arm and threw the torch. A heavy club wrapped with oil-soaked rags, it turned end over end, the fire shrinking to a blue glow, and landed out of sight behind the railing. The harbor master didn't wait to see the effects of his action; he sat down at once, gesturing madly to the rower, who heaved on the oars, and the small boat shot away across the dark water.

For long moments, nothing happened, but the crowd on the dock stood still, murmuring quietly. I could see the pale reflection of Jamie's face, floating above my own in the dark glass of the window. The glass was cold, and misted over quickly with our breath; I rubbed it clear with the edge of my cloak.

"There," Jamie said softly. The flame ran suddenly behind the railing, a small blue glowing line. Then a flicker, and the forward shrouds sprang out, orange-red lines against the sky. A silent leap, and the tongues of fire danced along the oil-drenched rails, and one furled sail sparked and burst into flame.

In less than a minute, the shrouds of the mizzen had caught, and the mainsail unfurled, its moorings burnt through, a falling sheet of flame. The fire spread too rapidly then to watch its progress; everything seemed alight at once.

"Now," Jared said suddenly. "Come downstairs. The hold will catch in a minute, and that will be the best time to make away. No one will notice us."

He was right; as we crept cautiously out of the tavern door, two men materialized beside Jared—his own seamen, armed with pistols and marlin-spikes—but no one else noticed our appearance. Everyone was turned toward the harbor, where the superstructure of the *Patagonia* was visible now as a black skeleton inside a body of rippling flame. There was a series of pops, so close together they sounded like machine-gun fire, and then an almighty explosion that rose from the center of the ship in a fountain of sparks and burning timbers.

"Let's go." Jamie's hand was firm on my arm, and I made no protest. Following Jared, guarded by the sailors, we stole away from the quay, surreptitious as though we had started the fire.

7

Royal Audience

Jared's house in Paris stood in the Rue Tremoulins. It was a wealthy district, with stone-faced houses of three, four, and five stories crowded cheek by jowl together. Here and there a very large house stood alone in its own park, but for the most part, a reasonably athletic burglar could have leaped from rooftop to rooftop with no difficulty.

"Mmphm" was Murtagh's solitary observation, upon beholding Jared's house. "I'll find my own lodging."

"And it makes ye nervous to have a decent roof above your head, man, ye can sleep in the stables," Jamie suggested. He grinned down at his small, dour godfather. "We'll ha' the footman bring ye out your parritch on a silver tray."

Inside, the house was furnished with comfortable elegance, though as I was later to realize, it was Spartan by comparison with most of the houses of the nobility and the wealthy bourgeois. I supposed that this was at least in part because the house had no lady; Jared had never married, though he showed no signs of feeling the lack of a wife.

"Well, he has a mistress, of course," Jamie had explained when I speculated about his cousin's private life.

"Oh, of course," I murmured.

"But she's married. Jared told me once that a man of business should never form entanglements with unmarried ladies—he said they demand too much in terms of expense and time. And if ye marry them, they'll run through your money and you'll end up a pauper."

"Fine opinion he's got of wives," I said. "What does he think of your marrying, in spite of all this helpful advice?"

Jamie laughed. "Well, I havena got any money to start with, so I can hardly be worse off. He thinks you're verra decorative; he says I must buy ye a new gown, though."

I spread the skirt of the apple-green velvet, more than a little the worse for wear.

"I suppose so," I agreed. "Or I'll go round wrapped in a bedsheet after a while; this is already tight in the waist."

"Elsewhere, too," he said, grinning as he looked me over. "Got your appetite back, have ye, Sassenach?"

"Oaf," I said coldly. "You know perfectly well that Annabelle MacRannoch is the general size and shape of a shovel handle, whereas I am not."

"You are not," he agreed, eyeing me with appreciation. "Thank God." He patted me familiarly on the bottom.

"I'm to join Jared at the warehouse this morning to go over the ledgers, then we're going to call on some of his clients, to introduce me. Will ye be all right by yourself?"

"Yes, of course," I said. "I'll explore the house a bit, and get acquainted with the servants." I had met the servants en masse when we had arrived late in the previous afternoon, but since we had dined simply in our room, I had seen no one since but the footman who brought the food, and the maid who had come in early in the morning to put back the curtains, lay and light the fire, and carry away the chamber pot. I quailed a bit at the thought of suddenly being in charge of a "staff," but reassured myself by thinking that it couldn't be much different from directing orderlies and junior nurses, and I'd done that before, as a senior nurse at a French field station in 1943.

After Jamie's departure, I took my time in making what toilette could be made with a comb and water, which were the only grooming implements available. If Jared was serious about my holding dinner parties, I could see that a new gown was going to be merely the start of it.

I did have, in the side pocket of my medicine chest, the frayed willow twigs with which I cleaned my teeth, and I got one of these and set to work, thinking over the amazing fortune which had brought us here.

Essentially barred from Scotland, we would have had to find a place to make our future, either in Europe or by emigrating to America. And given what I now knew about Jamie's attitude toward ships, I wasn't at all surprised that he should have looked to France from the start.

The Frasers had strong ties with France; many of them, like Abbot Alexander and Jared Fraser, had made lives here, seldom if ever returning to their native Scotland. And there were many Jacobites as well, Jamie had told me, those who had followed their king into exile, and now lived as best they could in France or Italy while awaiting his restoration.

"There's always talk of it," he had said. "In the houses, mostly, not the taverns. And that's why nothing's come of it. When it gets to the taverns, you'll know it's serious."

"Tell me," I said, watching him brush the dust from his coat, "are all Scots born knowing about politics, or is it just you?"

He laughed, but quickly sobered as he opened the huge armoire and hung up the coat. It looked worn and rather pathetic, hanging by itself in the enormous, cedar-scented space.

"Well, I'll tell ye, Sassenach, I'd as soon not know. But born as I was, between the MacKenzies and the Frasers, I'd little choice in the matter. And ye don't spend a year in French society and two years in an army without learning how to listen to what's being said, and what's being meant, and how to tell the difference between the two. Given these times, though, it isna just me; there's neither laird nor cottar in the Highlands who can stand aside from what's to come."

"What's to come." What *was* to come? I wondered. What *would* come, if we were not successful in our efforts here, was an armed rebellion, an attempt at restoration of the Stuart monarchy, led by the son of the exiled king, Prince Charles Edward (Casimir Maria Sylvester) Stuart.

"Bonnie Prince Charlie," I said softly to myself, looking over my reflection in the large pier glass. He was here, now, in the same city, perhaps not too far away. What would he be like? I could think of him only in terms of his usual historical portrait, which showed a handsome, slightly effeminate youth of sixteen or so, with soft pink lips and powdered hair, in the fashion of the times. Or the imagined paintings, showing a more robust version of the same thing, brandishing a broadsword as he stepped out of a boat onto the shore of Scotland.

A Scotland he would ruin and lay waste in the effort to reclaim it for his father and himself. Doomed to failure, he would attract enough support to cleave the country, and lead his followers through civil war to a bloody end on the field of Culloden. Then he would flee back to safety in France, but the retribution of his enemies would be exacted upon those he left behind.

It was to prevent such a disaster that we had come. It seemed incredible, thinking about it in the peace and luxury of Jared's house. How did one stop a rebellion? Well, if risings were fomented in taverns, perhaps they could be stopped over dinner tables. I shrugged at myself in the mirror, blew an errant curl out of one eye, and went down to cozen the cook.

The staff, at first inclined to view me with frightened suspicion, soon realized that I had no intention of interfering with their work, and relaxed into a mood of wary obligingness. I had thought at first, in my blur of fatigue, that there were at least a dozen servants lined up in the hallway for my inspection. In fact, there were sixteen of them, counting the groom, the stable-lad and the knife-boy, whom I hadn't noticed in the general scrum. I was still more impressed at Jared's success in business, until I realized just how little the servants were paid: a new pair of shoes and two livres per year for the footmen, a trifle less for the housemaids and kitchenmaids, a little more for such exalted personages as Madame Vionnet, the cook, and the butler, Magnus.

While I explored the mechanics of the household and stored up what information I could glean at home from the gossip of the parlormaids, Jamie was out with Jared every day, calling upon customers, meeting people, preparing himself to "assist His Highness" by making those social connections that might prove of value to an exiled prince. It was among the dinner guests that we might find allies—or enemies.

"St. Germain?" I said, suddenly catching a familiar name in the midst of Marguerite's chatter as she polished the parquet floor. "The Comte St. Germain?"

"*Oui,* Madame." She was a small, fat girl, with an oddly flattened face and popeyes that made her look like a turbot, but she was friendly and eager to please. Now she pursed her mouth up into a tiny circle, portending the imparting of some really scandalous tidbit. I looked as encouraging as possible.

"The Comte, Madame, has a very bad reputation," she said portentously.

Since this was true—according to Marguerite—of virtually everyone who came to dinner, I arched my brows and waited for further details.

"He has sold his soul to the Devil, you know," she confided, lowering her voice and glancing around as though that gentleman might be lurking behind the chimney breast. "He celebrates the Black Mass, at which the blood and flesh of innocent children are shared amongst the wicked!"

A fine specimen you picked to make an enemy of, I thought to myself.

"Oh, everyone knows, Madame," Marguerite assured me. "But it does not matter; the women are mad for him, anyway; wherever he goes, they throw themselves at his head. But then, he is rich." Plainly this last qualification was at least sufficient to balance, if not to outweigh, the blood-drinking and flesh-eating.

"How interesting," I said. "But I thought that Monsieur le Comte was a competitor of Monsieur Jared; doesn't he also import wines? Why does Monsieur Jared invite him here, then?"

Marguerite looked up from her floor-polishing and laughed.

"Why, Madame! It is so that Monsieur Jared can serve the best Beaune at dinner, tell Monsieur le Comte that he has just acquired ten cases, and at the conclusion of the meal, generously offer him a bottle to take home!"

"I see," I said, grinning. "And is Monsieur Jared similarly invited to dine with Monsieur le Comte?"

She nodded, white kerchief bobbing over her oil-bottle and rag. "Oh, yes, Madame. But not as often!"

The Comte St. Germain was fortunately not invited for this evening. We dined simply en famille, so that Jared could rehearse Jamie in the few details left to be arranged before his departure. Of these, the most important was the King's *lever* at Versailles.

Being invited to attend the King's *lever* was a considerable mark of favor, Jared explained over dinner.

"Not to you, lad," he said kindly, waving a fork at Jamie. "To me. The King wants to make sure I'm coming back from Germany—or Duverney, the Minister of Finance, does, at least. The latest wave of taxes hit the merchants hard, and a good many of the foreigners left—with the ill effects on the Royal

Treasury you can imagine." He grimaced at the thought of taxes, scowling at the baby eel on his fork.

"I mean to be gone by Monday-week. I'm waiting only for word that the *Wilhelmina*'s come in safe to Calais; then I'm off." Jared took another bite of eel and nodded at Jamie, talking around the mouthful of food. "I'm leaving the business in good hands, lad; I've no worry on that score. We might talk a bit before I go about other matters, though. I've arranged with the Earl Marischal that we'll go with him to Montmartre two days hence, for you to pay your respects to His Highness, Prince Charles Edward."

I felt a sudden thump of excitement in the pit of my stomach, and exchanged a quick glance with Jamie. He nodded at Jared, as though this were nothing startling, but his eyes sparkled with anticipation as he looked at me. So this was the start of it.

"His Highness lives a very retired life in Paris," Jared was saying as he chased the last eels, slick with butter, around the edge of the plate. "It wouldn't be appropriate for him to appear in society, until and unless the King receives him officially. So His Highness seldom leaves his house, and sees few people, save those supporters of his father who come to pay their respects."

"That isn't what I've heard," I interjected.

"What?" Two pairs of startled eyes turned in my direction, and Jared laid down his fork, abandoning the final eel to its fate.

Jamie arched an eyebrow at me. "What have ye heard, Sassenach, and from whom?"

"From the servants," I said, concentrating on my own eels. Seeing Jared's frown, it occurred to me for the first time that it might not be considered quite the thing for the lady of the house to be gossiping with parlormaids. Well, the hell with it, I thought rebelliously. There wasn't much else for me to do.

"The parlormaid says that His Highness Prince Charles has been paying calls on the Princesse Louise de La Tour de Rohan," I said, plucking a single eel off the fork and chewing slowly. They were delicious, but felt rather disconcerting if swallowed whole, as though the creature were still alive. I swallowed carefully. So far, so good.

"In the absence of the lady's husband," I added delicately.

Jamie looked amused, Jared horrified.

"The Princesse de Rohan?" Jared said. "Marie-Louise-Henriette-Jeanne de La Tour d'Auvergne? Her husband's family are very close to the King." He rubbed his fingers across his lips, leaving a buttery shine around his mouth. "That could be very dangerous," he muttered, as though to himself. "I wonder if the wee fool . . . but no. Surely he's more sense than that. It must be only inexperience; he's not been so much in society, and things are different in Rome. Still . . .." He left off muttering and turned to Jamie with decision.

"That will be your first task, lad, in the service of His Majesty. You're much of an age with His Highness, but you have the experience and the judgment of your time in Paris—and my training, I flatter myself." He smiled briefly at Jamie. "You can befriend his Highness; smooth his path as much as may be with those men that will be of use to him; you've met most of them by now. And explain to His Highness—as tactfully as ye can—that gallantry in the wrong direction may do considerable damage to the aims of his father."

Jamie nodded absently, plainly thinking of something else.

"How does our parlormaid come to know about His Highness's vists, Sassenach?" he asked. "She doesna leave the house more than once a week, to go to Mass, does she?"

I shook my head, and swallowed the next mouthful in order to reply.

"So far as I've worked it out, our kitchenmaid heard it from the knife-boy, who heard it from the stable-lad, who got it from the groom next door. I don't know how many people there are in between, but the Rohan house is three doors down the street. I'd imagine the Princesse knows all about us, too," I added cheerfully. "At least she does, if she talks to her kitchenmaid."

"Ladies do *not* gossip with their kitchenmaids," Jared said coldly. He narrowed his eyes at Jamie in a silent adjuration to keep his wife in better order.

I could see the corner of Jamie's mouth twitching, but he merely sipped his Montrachet and changed the subject to a discussion of Jared's latest venture; a shipment of rum, on its way from Jamaica.

When Jared rang the bell for the dishes to be cleared and the brandy brought out, I excused myself. One of Jared's idiosyncrasies was the enjoyment of long black cheroots with his brandy, and I had the distinct feeling that, carefully chewed or not, the eels I had eaten wouldn't benefit from being smoked.

I lay on my bed and tried, with limited success, not to think about eels. I closed my eyes and tried to think of Jamaica—pleasant white beaches under tropical sun. But thoughts of Jamaica led to thoughts of the *Wilhelmina* and thought of ships made me think of the sea, which led directly back to images of giant eels, coiling and writhing through the heaving green waves. I greeted the distraction of Jamie's appearance with relief, sitting up as he came in.

"Phew!" He leaned against the closed door, fanning himself with the loose end of his jabot. "I feel like a smoked sausage. I'm fond of Jared, but I shall be verra pleased when he's taken his damned cheroots to Germany."

"Well, don't come near me, if you smell like a cheroot," I said. "The eels don't like smoke."

"I dinna blame them a bit." He took off his coat and unbuttoned his shirt. "I think it's a plan, ye ken," he confided, tossing his head toward the door as he took his shirt off. "Like the bees."

"Bees?"

"How ye move a hive of bees," he explained, opening the window and hanging his shirt outside from the crank of the casement. "You get a pipe full of the strongest tobacco ye can find, stick it into the hive and blow smoke up into the combs. The bees all fall down stunned, and you can take them where ye like. I think that's what Jared does to his customers; he smokes them into insensibility, and they've signed orders for three times more wine than they meant to before they recover their senses."

I giggled and he grinned, putting a finger to his lips as the sound of Jared's light footsteps came down the corridor, passing our door on his way to his own room.

Danger of discovery past, he came and stretched out beside me, wearing only his kilt and stockings.

"Not too bad?" he asked. "I can sleep in the dressing room, if it is. Or put my head out of the window for airing."

I sniffed his hair, where the scent of tobacco lingered among the ruddy waves. The candlelight shot the red with strands of gold, and I ruffled my fingers through it, enjoying the thick softness of it, and the hard, solid feel of the bone beneath.

"No, it's not too bad. You're not worried about Jared leaving so soon, then?"

He kissed my forehead and lay down, head on the bolster. He smiled up at me, shaking his head.

"No. I've met all the chief customers and the captains, I know all the warehousemen and the officials, I've the price lists and the inventories committed to memory. What's left to learn about the business I must just learn by trying; Jared canna teach me more."

"And Prince Charles?"

He half-closed his eyes and gave a small grunt of resignation. "Aye, well. For that, I must trust to the mercy of God, not Jared. And I daresay it will be easier if Jared isn't here to see what I'm doing."

I lay down beside him, and he turned toward me, sliding an arm around my waist so that we lay close together.

"What *shall* we do?" I asked. "Have you any idea, Jamie?"

His breath was warm on my face, scented with brandy, and I tilted my head up to kiss him. His soft, wide mouth opened on mine, and he lingered in the kiss for a moment before answering.

"Oh, I've ideas," he said, drawing back with a sigh. "God knows what they'll amount to, but I've ideas."

"Tell me."

"Mmphm." He settled himself more comfortably, turning on his back and cradling me in one arm, head on his shoulder.

"Well," he began, "as I see it, it's a matter of money, Sassenach."

"Money? I should have thought it was a matter of politics. Don't the French want James restored because it will cause the English trouble? From the little I recall, Louis wanted—*will* want"—I corrected myself—"Charles Stuart to distract King George from what Louis is up to in Brussels."

"I daresay he does," he said, "but restoring kings takes money. And Louis hasna got so much himself that he can be using it on the one hand to fight wars in Brussels, and on the other to finance invasions of England. You heard what Jared said about the Royal Treasury and the taxes?"

"Yes, but . . ."

"No, it isna Louis that will make it happen," he said, instructing me. "Though he's something to say about it, of course. No, there are other sources of money that James and Charles will be trying as well, and those are the French banking families, the Vatican, and the Spanish Court."

"James covering the Vatican and the Spanish, and Charles the French bankers, you think?" I asked, interested.

He nodded, staring up at the carved panels of the ceiling. The walnut panels were a soft, light brown in the flickering candle-glow, darker rosettes and ribbons twining from each corner.

"Aye, I do. Uncle Alex showed me correspondence from His Majesty King James, and I should say the Spanish are his best opportunity, judging from that. The Pope's compelled to support him, ye ken, as a Catholic monarch; Pope Clement supported James for a good many years, and now Clement's dead, Benedict continues it, but not at such a high level. But both Philip of Spain and Louis are James's cousins; it's the obligation of Bourbon blood he calls on there." He smiled wryly at me, sidelong. "And from the things I've seen, I can tell ye that Royal blood runs damn thin when it comes to money, Sassenach."

Lifting one foot at a time, he stripped off his stockings one handed and tossed them onto the bedroom stool.

"James got some money from Spain thirty years ago," he observed. "A small fleet of ships, and some men as well. That was the Rising in 1715. But he had ill luck, and James's forces were defeated at Sheriffsmuir—before James himself even arrived. So I'd say the Spanish are maybe none too eager to finance a second try at the Stuart restoration—not without a verra good idea that it might succeed."

"So Charles has come to France to work on Louis and the bankers," I mused. "And according to what I know of history, he'll succeed. Which leaves us where?"

Jamie's arm left my shoulders as he stretched, the shift of his weight tilting the mattress under me.

"It leaves me selling wine to bankers, Sassenach," he said, yawning. "And you talking to parlormaids. And if we blow enough smoke, perhaps we'll stun the bees."

Just before Jared's departure, he took Jamie to the small house in Montmartre where His Highness, Prince Charles Edward Louis Philip Casimir, etc. Stuart was residing, biding his time while waiting to see what Louis would or would not do for an impecunious cousin with aspirations to a throne.

I had seen them off, both dressed in their best, and spent the time while they were gone picturing the encounter in my mind, wondering how it had gone.

"How did it go?" I asked Jamie, the moment I got him alone upon his return. "What was he like?"

He scratched his head, thinking.

"Well," he said at last, "he had a toothache."

"What?"

"He said so. And it looked verra painful; he kept his face screwed up to one side with his jaw puffed a bit. I canna say whether he's stiff in his manner usually, or if it was only that it hurt him to talk, but he didna say much."

After the formal introductions, in fact, the older men, Jared, the Earl Marischal, and a rather seedy-looking specimen referred to casually as "Balhaldy," had gravitated together and begun talking Scottish politics, leaving Jamie and His Highness more or less to themselves.

"We had a cup of brandywine each," Jamie obediently reported, under my goading. "And I asked him how he found Paris, and he said he was finding it rather tiresomely confining, as he couldna get any hunting. And so then we talked of hunting. He prefers hunting wi' dogs to hunting with beaters, and I said I did, too. Then he told me how many pheasants he'd shot on one hunting trip in Italy. He talked about Italy until he said the cold air coming in through the window was hurting his tooth—it's no a verra well-built house; just a small villa. Then he drank some more brandywine for his tooth, and I told him about stag-hunting in the Highlands, and he said he'd like to try that sometime, and was I a good shot with a bow? And I said I was, and he said he hoped he would have the opportunity to invite me to hunt with him in Scotland. And then Jared said he needed to stop at the warehouse on the way back, so His Highness gave me his hand and I kissed it and we left."

"Hmm," I said. While reason asserted that naturally the famous—or about-to-be-famous, or possibly-famous, at any rate—were bound to be much like everyone else in their daily behavior, I had to admit that I found this report of the Bonnie Prince a bit of a letdown. Still, Jamie had been invited back. The important thing, as he pointed out, was to become acquainted with His Highness, in order to keep an eye on his plans as any developed. I wondered whether the King of France would be a trifle more impressive in person.

We were not long in finding out. A week later, Jamie rose in the cold, black dark and dressed himself for the long ride to Versailles, to attend the King's *lever*. Louis awoke punctually at six o'clock every morning. At this hour, the favored few chosen to attend the King's toilette should be assembled in the antechamber, ready to join the procession of nobles and attendants who were necessary to assist the monarch in greeting the new day.

Wakened in the small hours by Magnus the butler, Jamie stumbled sleepily out of bed and made ready, yawning and muttering. At this hour, my insides were tranquil, and I luxuriated in that delightful feeling that comes when we observe someone having to do something unpleasant that we are not required to do ourselves.

"Watch carefully," I said, my voice husky with sleep. "So you can tell me everything."

With a sleepy grunt of assent, he leaned over to kiss me, then shuffled off, candle in hand, to see to the saddling of his horse. The last I heard before sinking back under the surface of sleep was Jamie's voice downstairs, suddenly clear and alert in the crisp night air, exchanging farewells with the groom in the street outside.

Given the distance to Versailles, and the chance—of which Jared had warned—of being invited to lunch, I wasn't surprised when he didn't return before noon, but I couldn't help being curious, and waited in increasing impatience until his arrival—finally—near teatime.

"And how was the King's *lever*?" I asked, coming to help Jamie remove his coat. Wearing the tight pigskin gloves de rigueur at Court, he couldn't manage the crested silver buttons on the slippery velvet.

"Oh, that feels better," he said, flexing his broad shoulders in relief as the buttons sprang free. The coat was much too tight in the shoulders; peeling him out of it was like shelling an egg.

"Interesting, Sassenach," he said, in answer to my question, "at least for the first hour or so."

As the procession of nobles came into the Royal Bedchamber, each bearing his ceremonial implement—towel, razor, alecup, royal seal, etc.—the gentlemen of the bedchamber drew back the heavy curtains that kept out the dawn, unveiled the draperies of the great bed of state, and exposed the face of *le roi Louis* to the interested eye of the rising sun.

Assisted to a sitting position on the edge of his bed, the King had sat yawning and scratching his stubbled chin while his attendants pulled a silk robe, heavy with embroidery of silver and gold, over the royal shoulders, and knelt to strip off the heavy felt stockings in which the King slept, to be replaced with hose of lighter silk, and soft slippers lined with rabbit fur.

One by one, the nobles of the court came to kneel at the feet of their sovereign, to greet him respectfully and ask how His Majesty had passed the night?

"Not verra well, I should say," Jamie broke off to observe here. "He looked like he'd slept little more than an hour or two, and bad dreams with it."

Despite bloodshot eyes and drooping jowls, His Majesty had nodded graciously to his courtiers, then risen slowly to his feet and bowed to those favored guests hovering in the back of the chamber. A dispirited wave of the hand summoned a gentleman of the bedchamber, who led His Majesty to the waiting chair, where he sat with closed eyes, enjoying the ministrations of his attendants, while the visitors were led forward one at a time by the Duc d'Orléans, to kneel before the King and offer a few words of greeting. Formal petitions would be offered a little later, when there was a chance of Louis being awake enough to hear them.

"I wasna there for petitioning, but only as a mark of favor," Jamie explained, "so I just knelt and said, 'Good morning, Your Majesty,' while the Duc told the King who I was."

"Did the King say anything to you?" I asked.

Jamie grinned, hands linked behind his head as he stretched. "Oh, aye. He opened one eye and looked at me as though he didna believe it."

One eye still open, Louis had surveyed his visitor with a sort of dim interest, then remarked, "Big, aren't you?"

"I said, 'Yes, Your Majesty,'" Jamie said. "Then he said, 'Can you dance?' and I said I could. Then he shut his eye again, and the Duc motioned me back."

Introductions complete, the gentlemen of the bedchamber, ceremoniously assisted by the chief nobles, had then proceeded to make the King's toilette. As they did so, the various petitioners came forward at the beckoning of the Duc d'Orléans, to murmur into the King's ear as he twisted his head to accommodate the razor, or bent his neck to have his wig adjusted.

"Oh? And were you honored by being allowed to blow His Majesty's nose for him?" I asked.

Jamie grinned, stretching his linked hands until the knuckles cracked.

"No, thank God. I skulked about against the wardrobe, trying to look like part of the furniture, wi' the bitty wee comtes and ducs all glancing at me out of the sides of their eyes as though Scottishness were catching."

"Well, at least you were tall enough to see everything?"

"Oh, aye. That I did, even when he eased himself on his *chaise percée.*"

"He really did that? In front of everyone?" I was fascinated. I'd read about it, of course, but found it difficult to believe.

"Oh, aye, and everyone behaving just as they did when he washed his face and blew his nose. The Duc de Neve had the unspeakable honor," he added ironically, "of wiping His Majesty's arse for him. I didna notice what they did wi' the towel; took it out and had it gilded, no doubt.

"A verra wearisome business it was, too," he added, bending over and setting his hands on the floor to stretch the muscles of his legs. "Took forever; the man's tight as an owl."

"Tight as an owl?" I asked, amused at the simile. "Constipated, do you mean?"

"Aye, costive. And no wonder, the things they eat at Court," he added censoriously, stretching backward. "Terrible diet, all cream and butter. He should eat parritch every morning for breakfast—that'd take care of it. Verra good for the bowels, ye ken."

If Scotsmen were stubborn about anything—and, in fact, they tended to be stubborn about quite a number of things, truth be known—it was the virtues of oatmeal parritch for breakfast. Through eons of living in a land so poor there was little to eat but oats, they had as usual converted necessity into a virtue, and insisted that they liked the stuff.

Jamie had by now thrown himself on the floor and was doing the Royal Air Force exercises I had recommended to strengthen the muscles of his back.

Returning to his earlier remark, I said, "Why did you say 'tight as an owl'? I've heard that before, to mean drunk, but not costive. Are owls constipated, then?"

Completing his course, he flipped over and lay on the rug, panting.

"Oh, aye." He blew out a long sigh, and caught his breath. He sat up and pushed the hair out of his eyes. "Or not really, but that's the story ye hear. Folk will tell ye that owls havena got an arsehole, so they canna pass the things they eat—like mice, aye? So the bones and the hairs and such are all made up into a ball, and the owl vomits them out, not bein' able to get rid of them out the other end."

"Really?"

"Oh, aye, that's true enough, they do. That's how ye find an owl-tree; look underneath for the pellets on the ground. Make a terrible mess, owls do," he added, pulling his collar away from his neck to let air in.

"But they have got arseholes," he informed me. "I knocked one out of a tree once wi' a slingshot and looked."

"A lad with an inquiring mind, eh?" I said, laughing.

"To be sure, Sassenach." He grinned. "And they do pass things that way, too. I spent a whole day sitting under an owl-tree with Ian, once, just to make sure."

"Christ, you *must* have been curious," I remarked.

"Well, I wanted to know. Ian didna want to sit still so long, and I had to pound on him a bit to make him stop fidgeting." Jamie laughed, remembering. "So he sat still wi' me until it happened, and then he snatched up a handful of owl pellets, jammed them down the neck of my shirt, and was off like a shot. God, he could run like the wind." A tinge of sadness crossed his face, his memory of the fleet-footed friend of his youth clashing with more recent memories of his brother-in-law, hobbling stiffly, if good-naturedly, on the wooden leg a round of grapeshot taken in a foreign battle had left him with.

"That sounds an awful way to live," I remarked, wanting to distract him. "Not watching owls, I don't mean—the King. No privacy, ever, not even in the loo."

"I wouldna care for it myself," Jamie agreed. "But then he's the King."

"Mmm. And I suppose all the power and luxury and so forth makes up for a lot."

He shrugged. "Well, if it does or no, it's the bargain God's made for him, and he's little choice but to make the best of it." He picked up his plaid and drew the tail of it through his belt and up to his shoulder.

"Here, let me." I took the silver ring-brooch from him and fastened the flaming fabric at the crest of his shoulder. He arranged the drape, smoothing the vivid wool between his fingers.

"I've a bargain like that myself, Sassenach," he said quietly, looking down at me. He smiled briefly. "Though thank God it doesna mean inviting Ian to wipe my arse for me. But I was born laird. I'm the steward of that land and the people on it, and I must make the best of my own bargain wi' them."

He reached out and touched my hair lightly.

"That's why I was glad when ye said we'd come, to try and see what we might do. For there's a part of me would like no better than to take you and the bairn and go far away, to spend the rest of my life working the fields and the beasts, to come in in the evenings and lie beside ye, quiet through the night."

The deep blue eyes were hooded in thought, as his hand returned to the folds of his plaid, stroking the bright checks of the Fraser tartan, with the faint white stripe that distinguished Lallybroch from the other septs and families.

"But if I did," he went on, as though speaking more to himself than to me, "there's a part of my soul would feel forsworn, and I think—I think I would always hear the voices of the people that are mine, calling out behind me."

I laid a hand on his shoulder, and he looked up, a faint lopsided smile on the wide mouth.

"I think you would, too," I said. "Jamie . . . whatever happens, whatever we're able to do . . ." I stopped, looking for words. As so often before, the sheer enormity of the task we had taken on staggered me and left me speechless. Who were we, to alter the course of history, to change the course of events not for ourselves, but for princes and peasants, for the entire country of Scotland?

Jamie laid his hand over mine and squeezed it reassuringly.

"No one can ask more of us than our best, Sassenach. Nay, if there's blood shed, it wilna lie on our hands at least, and pray God it may not come to that."

I thought of the lonely gray clanstones on Culloden Moor, and the Highland men who might lie under them, if we were unsuccessful.

"Pray God," I echoed.

8

Unlaid Ghosts and Crocodiles

Between Royal audiences and the daily demands of Jared's business, Jamie seemed to be finding life full. He disappeared with Murtagh soon after breakfast each morning, to check new deliveries to the warehouse, make inventories, visit the docks on the Seine, and conduct tours of what sounded from his description to be extremely unsavory taverns.

"Well, at least you've got Murtagh with you," I remarked, taking comfort from the fact, "and the two of you can't get in too much trouble in broad daylight." The wiry little clansman was unimpressive to look at, his attire varying from that of the ne'er-do-wells on the docks only by the fact that the lower half was tartan plaid, but I had ridden through half of Scotland with Murtagh to rescue Jamie from Wentworth Prison, and there was no one in the world whom I would sooner have trusted with his welfare.

After luncheon, Jamie would make his rounds of calls—social and business, and an increasing number of both—and then retire into his study for an hour or two with the ledgers and account books before dinner. He was busy.

I was not. A few days of polite skirmishing with Madame Vionnet, the head-cook, had left it clear who was in charge of the household, and it wasn't me. Madame came to my sitting room each morning, to consult me on the menu for the day, and to present me with the list of expenditures deemed necessary for the provisioning of the kitchen—fruit, vegetables, butter, and milk from a farm just outside the city, delivered fresh each morning, fish caught from the Seine and sold from a barrow in the street, along with fresh mussels that poked their sealed black curves from heaps of wilting waterweed. I looked over the lists for form's sake, approved everything, praised the dinner of the night before, and that was that. Aside from the occasional call to open the linen cupboard, the wine cellar, the root cellar, or the pantry with a key from my bunch, my time was then my own, until the hour came to dress for dinner.

The social life of Jared's establishment continued much as it had when he was in residence. I was still cautious about entertaining on a large scale, but we held small dinners every night, to which came nobles, chevaliers, and ladies, poor Jacobites in exile, wealthy merchants and their wives.

However, I found that eating and drinking and preparing to eat and drink

was not really sufficient occupation. I fidgeted to the point that Jamie at last
suggested I come and copy ledger entries for him.

"Better do that than be gnawin' yourself," he said, looking critically at my
bitten nails. "Beside, ye write a fairer hand than the warehouse clerks."

So it was that I was in the study, crouched industriously over the enormous ledger books, when Mr. Silas Hawkins came late one afternoon, with an
order for two tuns of Flemish brandy. Mr. Hawkins was stout and prosperous;
an émigré like Jared, he was an Englishman who specialized in the export of
French brandies to his homeland.

I supposed that a merchant who looked like a teetotaler would find it
rather difficult to sell people wines and spirits in quantity. Mr. Hawkins was
fortunate in this regard, in that he had the permanently flushed cheeks and jolly
smile of a reveler, though Jamie had told me that the man never tasted his own
wares, and in fact seldom drank anything beyond rough ale, though his appetite
for food was a legend in the taverns he visited. An expression of alert calculation lurked at the back of his bright brown eyes, behind the smooth bonhomie
that oiled his transactions.

"My best suppliers, I do declare," he declared, signing a large order with a
flourish. "Always dependable, always of the first quality. I shall miss your cousin
sorely in his absence," he said, bowing to Jamie, "but he's done well in his
choice of a substitute. Trust a Scotsman to keep the business in the family."

The small, bright eyes lingered on Jamie's kilt, the Fraser red of it bright
against the dark wood paneling of the drawing room.

"Just over from Scotland recently?" Mr. Hawkins asked casually, feeling
inside his coat.

"Nay, I've been in France for a time." Jamie smiled, turning the question
away. He took the quill pen from Mr. Hawkins, but finding it too blunted for
his taste, tossed it aside, pulling a fresh one from the bouquet of goose feathers
that sprouted from a small glass jug on the sideboard.

"Ah. I see from your dress that you are a Highland Scot; I had thought
perhaps you would be able to advise me as to the current sentiments prevailing
in that part of the country. One hears such rumors, you know." Mr. Hawkins
subsided into a chair at the wave of Jamie's hand, his round, rosy face apparently intent on the fat leather purse he had drawn from his pocket.

"As for rumors—well, that's the normal state of affairs in Scotland, no?"
Jamie said, studiously sharpening the fresh quill. "But sentiments? Nay, if ye
mean politics, I'm afraid I've little attention for such things myself." The small
penknife made a sharp snicking sound as the horny slivers shaved off the thick
stem of the quill.

Mr. Hawkins brought out several silver pieces from his purse, stacking
them neatly in a tidy column between the two men.

" 'Strewth?" he said, almost absently. "If so, you're the first Highlander
I've met who hadn't."

Jamie finished his sharpening and held the point of the quill up, squinting to judge its angle.

"Mm?" he said vaguely. "Aye, well, I've other matters that concern me; the running of a business such as this is time-consuming, as you'll know yourself, I imagine."

"So it is." Mr. Hawkins counted over the coins in his column once more and removed one, replacing it with two smaller ones. "I've heard that Charles Stuart has recently arrived in Paris," he said. His round tippler's face showed no more than mild interest, but the eyes were alert in their pockets of fat.

"Oh, aye," Jamie muttered, his tone of voice leaving it open whether this was acknowledgment of fact, or merely an expression of polite indifference. He had the order before him, and was signing each page with excessive care, crafting the letters rather than scribbling them, as was his usual habit. A left-handed man forced as a boy to write right-handed, he always found letters difficult, but he seldom made such a fuss of it.

"You do not share your cousin's sympathies in that direction, then?" Hawkins sat back a little, watching the crown of Jamie's bent head, which was naturally rather noncommittal.

"Is that any concern of yours, sir?" Jamie raised his head, and fixed Mr. Hawkins with a mild blue stare. The plump merchant returned the look for a moment, then waved a podgy hand in airy dismissal.

"Not at all," he said smoothly. "Still, I am familiar with your cousin's Jacobite leanings—he makes no secret of them. I wondered only whether all Scots were of one mind on this matter of the Stuart pretensions to the throne."

"If you've had much to do wi' Highland Scots," Jamie said dryly, handing across a copy of the order, "then ye'll know that it's rare to find two of them in agreement on anything much beyond the color of the sky—and even that is open to question from time to time."

Mr. Hawkins laughed, his comfortable paunch shaking under his waistcoat, and tucked the folded paper away in his coat. Seeing that Jamie was not eager to have this line of inquiry pursued, I stepped in at this point with a hospitable offer of Madeira and biscuits.

Mr. Hawkins looked tempted for a moment, but then shook his head regretfully, pushing back his chair to rise.

"No, no, I thank you, milady, but no. The *Arabella* docks this Thursday, and I must be at Calais to meet her. And the devil of a lot there is to do before I set foot in the carriage to leave." He grimaced at a large sheaf of orders and receipts he had pulled from his pocket, added Jamie's receipt to the heap, and stuffed them back into a large leather traveling wallet.

"Still," he said, brightening, "I can do a bit of business on the way; I shall call in at the inns and public houses between here and Calais."

"If ye call in at *all* the taverns 'twixt here and the coast, you'll no reach

Calais 'til next month," observed Jamie. He fished his own purse from his sporran and scooped the small column of silver into it.

"Too true, milord," Mr. Hawkins said, frowning ruefully. "I suppose I must give one or two the miss, and catch them up on my way back."

"Surely you could send someone to Calais in your place, if your time is so valuable?" I suggested.

He rolled his eyes expressively, pursing his jolly little mouth into something as close to mournfulness as could be managed within the limitations of its shape.

"Would that I could, milady. But the shipment the *Arabella* carries is, alas, nothing I can consign to the good offices of a functionary. My niece Mary is aboard," he confided, "bound even as we speak for the French coast. She is but fifteen, and has never been away from her home before. I am afraid I could scarce leave her to find her way to Paris alone."

"I shouldn't think so," I agreed politely. The name seemed familiar, but I couldn't think why. Mary Hawkins. Undistinguished enough; I couldn't connect it with anything in particular. I was still musing over it when Jamie rose to see Mr. Hawkins to the door.

"I trust your niece's journey will be pleasant," he said politely. "Does she come for schooling, then? Or to visit relatives?"

"For marriage," said her uncle with satisfaction. "My brother has been fortunate in securing a most advantageous match for her, with a member of the French nobility." He seemed to expand with pride at this, the plain gold buttons straining the fabric of his waistcoat. "My elder brother is a baronet, you know."

"She's fifteen?" I said, uneasily. I knew that early marriages were not uncommon, but fifteen? Still, I had been married at nineteen—and again at twenty-seven. I knew the hell of a lot more at twenty-seven.

"Er, has your niece been acquainted with her fiancé for very long?" I asked cautiously.

"Never met him. In fact"—Mr. Hawkins leaned close, laying a finger next to his lips and lowering his voice—"she doesn't yet know about the marriage. The negotiations are not quite complete, you see."

I was appalled at this, and opened my mouth to say something, but Jamie clutched my elbow tightly in warning.

"Well, if the gentleman is of the nobility, perhaps we shall see your niece at Court, then," he suggested, shoving me firmly toward the door like the blade of a bulldozer. Mr. Hawkins, moving perforce to avoid my stepping on him, backed away, still talking.

"Indeed you may, milord Broch Tuarach. Indeed, I should deem it a great honor for yourself and your lady to meet my niece. I am sure she would derive great comfort from the society of a countrywoman," he added with a smarmy smile at me. "Not that I would presume upon what is merely a business acquaintance, to be sure."

The hell you wouldn't presume, I thought indignantly. You'd do anything you could to squeeze your family into the French nobility, including marrying your niece to . . . to . . .

"Er, who *is* your niece's fiancé?" I asked bluntly.

Mr. Hawkins's face grew cunning, and he leaned close enough to whisper hoarsely into my ear.

"I really should not say until the contracts have been signed, but seeing as it is your ladyship. . . . I can tell you that it is a member of the House of Gascogne. And a very high-ranking member indeed!"

"Indeed," I said.

Mr. Hawkins went off rubbing his hands together in a perfect frenzy of anticipation, and I turned at once to Jamie.

"Gascogne! He must mean . . . but he can't, can he? That revolting old beast with the snuff stains on his chin who came to dinner last week?"

"The Vicomte Marigny?" Jamie said, smiling at my description. "I suppose so; he's a widower, and the only single male of that house, so far as I know. I dinna think it's snuff, though; it's only the way his beard grows. A bit moth-eaten," he admitted, "but it's bound to be a hellish shave, wi' all those warts."

"He can't marry a fifteen-year-old girl to . . . to . . . *that*! And without even asking her!"

"Oh, I expect he can," Jamie said, with infuriating calmness. "In any case, Sassenach, it isna your affair." He took me firmly by both arms and gave me a little shake.

"D'ye hear me? I know it's strange to ye, but that's how matters are. After all"—the long mouth curled up at one corner—"you were made to wed against your will. Reconciled yourself to it yet, have ye?"

"Sometimes I wonder!" I yanked, trying to pull my arms free, but he merely gathered me in, laughing, and kissed me. After a moment, I gave up fighting. I relaxed into his embrace, admitting surrender, if only temporarily. I *would* meet with Mary Hawkins, I thought, and we'd see just what she thought about this proposed marriage. If she didn't want to see her name on a marriage contract, linked with the Vicomte Marigny, then . . . Suddenly I stiffened, pushing away from Jamie's embrace.

"What is it?" he looked alarmed. "Are ye ill, lass? You've gone all white!"

And little wonder if I had. For I had suddenly remembered where I had seen the name of Mary Hawkins. Jamie was wrong. This *was* my affair. For I had seen the name, written in a copperplate hand at the top of a genealogy chart, the ink old and faded by time to a sepia brown. Mary Hawkins was not meant to be the wife of the decrepit Vicomte Marigny. She was to marry Jonathan Randall, in the year of our Lord 1745.

"Well, she can't, can she?" Jamie said. "Jack Randall is dead." He finished pouring the glass of brandy, and held it out to me. His hand was steady on the crystal stem, but the line of his mouth was set and his voice clipped the word "dead," giving it a vicious finality.

"Put your feet up, Sassenach," he said. "You're still pale." At his motion, I obediently pulled up my feet and stretched out on the sofa. Jamie sat down near my head, and absently rested a hand on my shoulder. His fingers felt warm and strong, gently massaging the small hollow of the joint.

"Marcus MacRannoch told me he'd seen Randall trampled to death by cattle in the dungeons of Wentworth Prison," he said again, as though seeking to reassure himself by repetition. "A 'rag doll, rolled in blood.' That's what Sir Marcus said. He was verra sure about it."

"Yes." I sipped my brandy, feeling the warmth come back into my cheeks. "He told me that, too. No, you're right, Captain Randall is dead. It just gave me a turn, suddenly remembering about Mary Hawkins. Because of Frank." I glanced down at my left hand, resting on my stomach. There was a small fire burning on the hearth, and the light of it caught the smooth gold band of my first wedding ring. Jamie's ring, of Scottish silver, circled the fourth finger of my other hand.

"Ah." Jamie's touch on my shoulder stilled. His head was bent, but he glanced up to meet my gaze. We had not spoken of Frank since I had rescued Jamie from Wentworth, nor had Jonathan Randall's death been mentioned between us. At the time it had seemed of little importance, except insofar as it meant that no more danger menaced us from that direction. And since then, I had been reluctant to bring back any memory of Wentworth to Jamie.

"You know he is dead, do ye not, *mo duinne*?" Jamie spoke softly, his fingers resting on my wrist, and I knew he spoke of Frank, not Jonathan.

"Maybe not," I said, my eyes still fixed on the ring. I raised my hand, so the metal gleamed in the fading afternoon light. "If he's dead, Jamie—if he won't exist, because Jonathan is dead—then why do I still have the ring he gave me?"

He stared at the ring, and I saw a small muscle twitch near his mouth. His face was pale, too, I saw. I didn't know whether it would do him harm to think of Jonathan Randall now, but there seemed little choice.

"You're sure that Randall had no children before he died?" he asked. "That would be an answer."

"It would," I said, "but no, I'm sure not. Frank"—my voice trembled a bit on the name, and Jamie's grip on my wrist tightened—"Frank made quite a bit of the tragic circumstances of Jonathan Randall's death. He said that he—Jack Randall—had died at Culloden Field, in the last battle of the Rising, and his son—that would be Frank's five-times great-grandfather—was born a few months after his father's death. His widow married again, a few years later. Even if there were an illegitimate child, it wouldn't be in Frank's line of descent."

Jamie's forehead was creased, and a thin vertical line ran between his brows. "Could it be a mistake, then—that the child was not Randall's at all? Frank may come only of Mary Hawkins's line—for we know she still lives."

I shook my head helplessly.

"I don't see how. If you'd known Frank—but no, I suppose I've never told you. When I first met Jonathan Randall, I thought for the first moment that he *was* Frank—they weren't the same, of course, but the resemblance was . . . startling. No, Jack Randall was Frank's ancestor, all right."

"I see." Jamie's fingers had grown damp; he took them away and wiped them absently on his kilt.

"Then . . . perhaps the ring means nothing, *mo duinne*," he suggested gently.

"Perhaps not." I touched the metal, warm as my own flesh, then dropped my hand helplessly. "Oh, Jamie, I don't know! I don't know anything!"

He rubbed his knuckles tiredly on the crease between his eyes. "Neither do I, Sassenach." He dropped his hand and tried to smile at me.

"There's the one thing," he said. "You said that Frank told you Jonathan Randall would die at Culloden?"

"Yes. In fact, I told Jack Randall that myself, to scare him—at Wentworth, when he put me out in the snow, before . . . before going back to you." His eyes and mouth clamped shut in sudden spasm, and I swung my feet down, alarmed.

"Jamie! Are you all right?" I tried to put a hand on his head, but he pulled away from my touch, rising and going to the window.

"No. Yes. It's all right, Sassenach. I've been writing letters all the morning, and my head's fit to burst. Dinna worry yourself." He waved me away, pressing his forehead against the cold pane of the window, eyes tight closed. He went on speaking, as though to distract himself from the pain.

"Then, if you—and Frank—knew that Jack Randall would die at Culloden, but we know that he shall not . . . then it can be done, Claire."

"What can be done?" I hovered anxiously, wanting to help, but not knowing what to do. Clearly he didn't want to be touched.

"What you know will happen can be changed." He raised his head from the window and smiled tiredly at me. His face was still white, but the traces of that momentary spasm were gone. "Jack Randall died before he ought, and Mary Hawkins will wed another man. Even if that means that your Frank wilna be born—or perhaps will be born some other way," he added, to be comforting, "then it also means that we have a chance of succeeding in what we've set ourselves to do. Perhaps Jack Randall didna die at Culloden Field, because the battle there will never happen."

I could see him make the effort to stir himself, to come to me and put his arms around me. I held him about the waist, lightly, not moving. He bent his head, resting his forehead on my hair.

"I know it must grieve ye, *mo duinne*. But may it not ease ye, to know that good may come of it?"

"Yes," I whispered at last, into the folds of his shirt. I disengaged myself gently from his arms and laid my hand along his cheek. The line between his eyes was deeper, and his eyes slightly unfocused, but he smiled at me.

"Jamie," I said, "go and lie down. I'll send a note to the d'Arbanvilles, to say we can't come tonight."

"Och, no," he protested. "I'll be fine. I know this kind of headache, Sassenach; it's only from the writing, and an hour's sleep will cure it. I'll go up now." He turned toward the door, then hesitated and turned back, half-smiling.

"And if I should call out in my sleep, Sassenach, just lay your hand upon me, and say to me, 'Jack Randall's dead.' And it will aye be well wi' me."

Both food and company at the d'Arbanvilles were good. We came home late, and I fell into a sound sleep the instant my head hit the pillow. I slept dreamlessly, but waked suddenly in the middle of the night, knowing something was wrong.

The night was cold, and the down quilt had slithered off onto the floor, as was its sneaky habit, leaving only the thin woolen blanket over me. I rolled over, half-asleep, reaching for Jamie's warmth. He was gone.

I sat up in bed, looking for him, and saw him almost at once, sitting on the window seat, head in his hands.

"Jamie! What is it? Have you got headache again?" I groped for the candle, meaning to find my medicine box, but something in the way he sat made me abandon the search and go to him at once.

He was breathing hard, as though he had been running, and cold as it was, his body was drenched with sweat. I touched his shoulder and found it hard and cold as a metal statue.

He jerked back at my touch and sprang to his feet, eyes wide and black in the night-filled room.

"I didn't mean to startle you," I said. "Are you all right?"

I wondered briefly if he were sleepwalking, for his expression didn't change; he looked straight through me, and whatever he saw, he didn't like it.

"Jamie!" I said sharply. "Jamie, wake up!"

He blinked then, and saw me, though his expression stayed fixed in the desperate lines of a hunted beast.

"I'm all right," he said. "I'm awake." He spoke as though wanting to convince himself of the fact.

"What is it? Did you have a nightmare?"

"A dream. Aye. It was a dream."

I stepped forward and put a hand on his arm.

"Tell me. It will go away if you tell me about it."

He grasped me hard by the forearms, as much to keep me from touching him as for support. The moon was full, and I could see that every muscle of his body was tensed, hard and motionless as stone, but pulsing with furious energy, ready to explode into action.

"No," he said, still sounding dazed.

"Yes," I said. "Jamie, talk to me. Tell me. Tell me what you see."

"I canna . . . see anything. Nothing. I can't see."

I pulled, turning him from the shadows of the room to face the bright moonlight from the window. The light seemed to help, for his breathing slowed, and in halting, painful bits, the words came out.

It was the stones of Wentworth Prison that he dreamed of. And as he spoke, the shape of Jonathan Randall walked the room. And lay naked in my bed, atop the woolen blanket.

There had been the sound of hoarse breathing close behind him, and the feel of sweat-drenched skin, sliding against his own. He gritted his teeth in an agony of frustration. The man behind him sensed the small movement and laughed.

"Oh, we've some time yet before they hang you, my boy," he whispered. "Plenty of time to enjoy it." Randall moved suddenly, hard and abrupt, and he made a small involuntary sound.

Randall's hand stroked back the hair from his brow and smoothed it around his ear. The hot breath was close to his ear and he turned his head to escape, but it followed him, breathing words.

"Have you ever seen a man hanged, Fraser?" The words went on, not waiting for him to reply, and a long, slim hand came around his waist, gently stroking the slope of his belly, teasing its way lower with each word.

"Yes, of course you have; you were in France, you'll have seen deserters hanged now and then. A hanged man looses his bowels, doesn't he? As the rope tightens fast round his neck." The hand was gripping him, lightly, firmly, rubbing and stroking. He clenched his good hand tight around the edge of the bed and turned his face hard into the scratchy blanket, but the words pursued him.

"That will happen to you, Fraser. Just a few more hours, and you'll feel the noose." The voice laughed, pleased with itself. "You'll go to your death with your arse burning from my pleasure, and when you lose your bowels, it will be my spunk running down your legs and dripping on the ground below the gallows."

He made no sound. He could smell himself, crusted with filth from his imprisonment, acrid with the sweat of fear and anger. And the man behind him, the rank stench of the animal breaking through the delicate scent of the lavender toilet water.

"The blanket," he said. His eyes were closed, face strained in the moonlight. "It was rough under my face, and all I could see were the stones of the wall before me. There was nothing there to fix my mind to . . . nothing I could see. So I kept my eyes closed and thought of the blanket under my cheek. It was all I could feel besides the pain . . . and him. I . . . held to it."

"Jamie. Let me hold you." I spoke quietly, trying to calm the frenzy I could feel running through his blood. His grip on my arms was tight enough to numb them. But he wouldn't let me move closer; he held me away as surely as he clung to me.

Suddenly he freed me, jerking away and turning toward the moon-filled window. He stood tense and quivering as a bowstring just fired, but his voice was calm.

"No. I willna use ye that way, lassie. Ye shallna be part of it."

I took a step toward him, but he stopped me with a quick motion. He turned his face back to the window, calm now, and blank as the glass he looked through.

"Get ye to bed, lassie. Leave me to myself a bit; I'll be well enough presently. There's naught to worry ye now."

He stretched his arms out, grasping the window frame, blotting out the light with his body. His shoulders swelled with effort, and I could tell that he was pushing against the wood with all his might.

"It was only a dream. Jack Randall is dead."

I had at length fallen asleep, with Jamie still poised at the window, staring out into the face of the moon. When I woke at dawn, though, he was asleep, curled in the window seat, wrapped in his plaid, with my cloak dragged over his legs for warmth.

He woke to my stirring, and seemed his normal, irritatingly cheerful morning self. But I was not likely to forget the happenings of the night, and went to my medicine box after breakfast.

To my annoyance, I lacked several of the herbs I needed for the sleeping tonic I had in mind. But then I remembered the man Marguerite had told me about. Raymond the herb-seller, in the Rue de Varennes. A wizard, she had said. A place worth seeing. Well, then. Jamie would be at the warehouse all the morning. I had a coach and a footman at my disposal; I would go and see it.

A clean wooden counter ran the length of the shop on both sides, with shelves twice the height of a man extending from floor to ceiling behind it. Some of the shelves were enclosed with folding glass doors, protecting the rarer and more expensive substances, I supposed. Fat gilded cupids sprawled abandonedly above the cupboards, tooting horns, waving their draperies, and generally looking as though they had been imbibing some of the more alcoholic wares of the shop.

"Monsieur Raymond?" I inquired politely of the young woman behind the counter.

"*Maître* Raymond," she corrected. She wiped a red nose inelegantly on her sleeve and gestured toward the end of the shop, where sinister clouds of a brownish smoke floated out over the transom of a half-door.

Wizard or not, Raymond had the right setting for it. Smoke drifted up from a black slate hearth to coil beneath the low black beams of the roof. Above the fire, a stone table pierced with holes held glass alembics, copper "pelicans"—metal cans with long noses from which sinister substances dripped into cups—and what appeared to be a small but serviceable still. I sniffed cautiously. Among the other strong odors in the shop, a heady alcoholic note was clearly distinguishable from the direction of the fire. A neat lineup of clean bottles along the sideboard reinforced my original suspicions. Whatever his trade in charms and potions, Master Raymond plainly did a roaring business in high-quality cherry brandy.

The distiller himself was crouched over the fire, poking errant bits of charcoal back into the grate. Hearing me come in, he straightened up and turned to greet me with a pleasant smile.

"How do you do?" I said politely to the top of his head. So strong was the impression that I had stepped into an enchanter's den that I would not have been surprised to hear a croak in reply.

For Master Raymond resembled nothing so much as a large, genial frog. A touch over four feet tall, barrel-chested and bandy-legged, he had the thick, clammy skin of a swamp dweller, and slightly bulbous, friendly black eyes. Aside from the minor fact that he wasn't green, all he lacked was warts.

"Madonna!" he said, beaming expansively. "What may I have the pleasure of doing for you?" He lacked teeth altogether, enhancing the froggy impression still more, and I stared at him in fascination.

"Madonna?" he said, peering up at me questioningly.

Snapped abruptly to a realization of how rudely I had been staring, I blushed and said without thinking, "I was just wondering whether you'd ever been kissed by a beautiful young girl."

I went still redder as he shouted with laughter. With a broad grin, he said "Many times, madonna. But alas, it does not help. As you see. *Ribbit.*"

We dissolved in helpless laughter, attracting the notice of the shopgirl, who peered over the half-door in alarm. Master Raymond waved her away, then hobbled to the window, coughing and clutching his sides, to open the leaded panes and allow some of the smoke to escape.

"Oh, that's better!" he said, inhaling deeply as the cold spring air rushed in. He turned to me, smoothing back the long silver hair that brushed his shoulders. "Now, madonna. Since we are friends, perhaps you will wait a moment while I attend to something?"

Still blushing, I agreed at once, and he turned to his firing shelf, still hiccupping with laughter as he refilled the canister of the still. Taking the opportunity to restore my poise, I strolled about the workroom, looking at the amazing array of clutter.

A fairly good-sized crocodile, presumably stuffed, hung from the ceiling. I gazed up at the yellow belly-scutes, hard and shiny as pressed wax.

"Real, is it?" I asked, taking a seat at the scarred oak table.

Master Raymond glanced upward, smiling.

"My *crocodile?* Oh, to be sure, madonna. Gives the customers confidence." He jerked his head toward the shelf that ran along the wall just above eye height. It was lined with white fired-porcelain jars, each ornamented with gilded curlicues, painted flowers and beasts, and a label, written in elaborate black script. Three of the jars closest to me were labeled in Latin, which I translated with some difficulty—crocodile's blood, and the liver and bile of the same beast, presumably the one swinging sinisterly overhead in the draft from the main shop.

I picked up one of the jars, removed the stopper and sniffed delicately.

"Mustard," I said, wrinkling my nose, "and thyme. In walnut oil, I think, but what did you use to make it nasty?" I tilted the jar, critically examining the sludgy black liquid within.

"Ah, so your nose is not purely decorative, madonna!" A wide grin split the toadlike face, revealing hard blue gums.

"The black stuff is the rotted pulp of a gourd," he confided, leaning closer and lowering his voice. "As for the smell . . . well, that actually *is* blood."

"Not from a crocodile," I said, glancing upward.

"Such cynicism in one so young," Raymond mourned. "The ladies and gentlemen of the Court are fortunately more trusting in nature, not that trust is the emotion that springs immediately to mind when one thinks of an aristocrat. No, in fact it is pig's blood, madonna. Pigs being so much more available than crocodiles."

"Mm, yes," I agreed. "That one must have cost you a pretty penny."

"Fortunately, I inherited it, along with much of my present stock, from the previous owner." I thought I saw a faint flicker of unease in the depths of the soft black eyes, but I had become oversensitive to nuances of expression of late, from watching the faces at parties for tiny clues that might be useful to Jamie in his manipulations.

The stocky little proprietor leaned still closer, laying a hand confidentially on mine.

"A professional, are you?" he said. "I must say, you don't look it."

My first impulse was to jerk my hand away, but his touch was oddly comfortable; quite impersonal, but unexpectedly warm and soothing. I glanced at the frost riming the edge of the leaded-glass panes, and thought that that was it; his ungloved hands were warm, a highly unusual condition for anyone's hands at this time of year.

"That depends entirely upon what you mean by the term 'professional,' " I said primly. "I'm a healer."

"Ah, a healer?" He tilted back in his chair, looking me over with interest. "Yes, I thought so. Anything else, though? No fortune-telling, no love philtres?"

I felt a twinge of conscience, recalling my days on the road with Murtagh, when we had sought Jamie through the Highlands of Scotland, telling fortunes and singing for our suppers like a couple of Gypsies.

"Nothing like that," I said, blushing only slightly.

"Not a professional liar, at any rate," he said, eyeing me in amusement. "Rather a pity. Still, how may I have the pleasure of serving you, madonna?"

I explained my needs, and he nodded sagely as he listened, the thick gray hair swinging forward over his shoulders. He wore no wig within the sanctum of his shop, nor did he powder his hair. It was brushed back from a high, wide forehead, and fell straight as a stick to his shoulders, where it ended abruptly, as though cut with a blunt pair of scissors.

He was easy to talk to, and very knowledgeable indeed about the uses of herbs and botanicals. He took down small jars of this and that, shaking bits out and crushing the leaves in his palm for me to smell or taste.

Our conversation was interrupted by the sound of raised voices in the shop. A nattily-dressed footman was leaning across the counter, saying something to the shopgirl. Or rather, trying to say something. His feeble attempts were being thrown back in his teeth by a gale of withering Provençale from the other side of the counter. It was too idiomatic for me to follow entirely, but I caught the general drift of her remarks. Something involving cabbages and sausages, none of it complimentary.

I was musing on the odd tendency of the French to bring food into virtually any kind of discussion, when the shop door banged suddenly open. Reinforcements swept in behind the footman, in the guise of a rouged and flounced Personage of some sort.

"Ah," murmured Raymond, peering interestedly beneath my arm at the drama unfolding in his shop. "La Vicomtesse de Rambeau."

"You know her?" The shopgirl evidently did, for she abandoned her attack on the footman and shrank back against the cabinet of purges.

"Yes, madonna," said Raymond, nodding. "She's rather expensive."

I saw what he meant, as the lady in question picked up the evident source of altercation, a small jar containing a pickled plant of some kind, took aim, and flung it with considerable force and accuracy into the glass front of the cabinet.

The crash silenced the commotion at once. The Vicomtesse pointed one long, bony finger at the girl.

"You," she said, in a voice like metal shavings, "fetch me the black potion. At once."

The girl opened her mouth as though to protest, then, seeing the Vicomtesse reaching for another missile, shut it and fled for the back room.

Anticipating her entrance, Raymond reached resignedly above his head and thrust a bottle into her hand as she came through the door.

"Give it to her," he said, shrugging. "Before she breaks something else."

As the shopgirl timidly returned to deliver the bottle, he turned to me, pulling a wry face.

"Poison for a rival," he said. "Or at least she thinks so."

"Oh?" I said. "And what is it really? Bitter cascara?"

He looked at me in pleased surprise.

"You're very good at this," he said. "A natural talent, or were you taught? Well, no matter." He waved a broad palm, dismissing the matter. "Yes, that's right, cascara. The rival will fall sick tomorrow, suffer visibly in order to satisfy the Vicomtesse's desire for revenge and convince her that her purchase was a good one, and then she will recover, with no permanent harm done, and the Vicomtesse will attribute the recovery to the intervention of the priest or a counterspell done by a sorcerer employed by the victim."

"Mm," I said. "And the damage to your shop?" The late-afternoon sun glinted on the shards of glass on the counter, and on the single silver écu that the Vicomtesse had flung down in payment.

Raymond tilted a palm from side to side, in the immemorial custom of a man indicating equivocation.

"It evens out," he said calmly. "When she comes in next month for an abortifacient, I shall charge her enough not only to repair the damage but to build three new cases. And she'll pay without argument." He smiled briefly, but without the humor he had previously shown. "It's all in the timing, you know."

I was conscious of the black eyes flickering knowledgeably over my figure. I didn't show at all yet, but I was quite sure he knew.

"And does the medicine you'll give the Vicomtesse next month work?" I asked.

"It's all in the timing," he replied again, tilting his head quizzically to one side. "Early enough, and all is well. But it is dangerous to wait too long."

The note of warning in his voice was clear, and I smiled at him.

"Not for me," I said. "For reference only."

He relaxed again.

"Ah. I didn't think so."

A rumble from the street below proclaimed the passing of the Vicomtesse's blue-and-silver carriage. The footman waved and shouted from behind as pedestrians were forced to scramble for the shelter of doors and alleyways to avoid being crushed.

"*A la lanterne,*" I murmured under my breath. It was rare that my unusual perspective on current affairs afforded me much satisfaction, but this was certainly one occasion when it did.

"Ask not for whom the tumbril calls," I remarked, turning to Raymond. "It calls for thee."

He looked mildly bewildered.

"Oh? Well, in any case, you were saying that black betony is what you use for purging? I would use the white, myself."

"Really? Why is that?"

And with no further reference to the recent Vicomtesse, we sat down to complete our business.

9

The Splendors of Versailles

I closed the door of the drawing room quietly behind me and stood still a moment, gathering courage. I essayed a restorative deep breath, but the tightness of the whalebone corseting made it come out as a strangled gasp.

Jamie, immersed in a handful of shipping orders, glanced up at the sound and froze, eyes wide. His mouth opened, but he made no sound.

"How do you like it?" Handling the train a bit gingerly, I stepped down into the room, swaying gently as the seamstress had instructed, to show off the filmy gussets of silk plissé let into the overskirt.

Jamie shut his mouth and blinked several times.

"It's . . . ah . . . red, isn't it?" he observed.

"Rather." *Sang-du-Christ*, to be exact. Christ's blood, the most fashionable color of the season, or so I had been given to understand.

"Not every woman could wear it, Madame," the seamstress had declared, speech unhampered by a mouthful of pins. "But you, with that skin! Mother of God, you'll have men crawling under your skirt all night!"

"If one tries, I'll stamp on his fingers," I said. That, after all, was not at all the intended effect. But I did mean to be visible. Jamie had urged me to have something made that would make me stand out in the crowd. Early-morning fog notwithstanding, the King had evidently remembered him from his appearance at the *lever*, and we had been invited to a ball at Versailles.

"I'll need to get the ears of the men with the money," Jamie had said, making plans with me earlier. "And as I've neither great position nor power myself, it will have to be managed by making them seek my company." He heaved a sigh, looking at me, decidedly unglamorous in my woolen bedgown.

"And I'm afraid in Paris that means we'll have to go out a bit in society; appear at Court, if it can be managed. They'll know I'm a Scot; it will be natural for folk to ask me about Prince Charles, and whether Scotland is eagerly awaiting the return of the Stuarts. Then I can assure them discreetly that most Scots would pay a good price *not* to have the Stuarts back again—though it goes against the grain a bit to say so."

"Yes, you'd better be discreet," I agreed. "Or the Bonnie Prince may set the dogs on you next time you go to visit." In accordance with his plan to keep abreast of Charles's activities, Jamie had been paying weekly duty calls on the small house at Montmartre.

Jamie smiled briefly. "Aye. Well, so far as His Highness, and the Jacobite supporters are concerned, I'm a loyal upholder of the Stuart cause. And so long as Charles Stuart is not received at Court and I am, the chances of his finding out what I'm saying there are not great. The Jacobites in Paris keep to themselves, as a rule. For the one thing, they haven't the money to appear in fashionable circles. But we have, thanks to Jared."

Jared had concurred—for entirely different reasons—in Jamie's proposal that we widen the scope of Jared's usual business entertaining, so that the French nobility and the heads of the wealthy banking families might beat a path to our door, there to be seduced and cozened with Rhenish wine, good talk, fine entertainment, and large quantities of the good Scotch whisky that Murtagh had spent the last two weeks shepherding across the Channel and overland to our cellars.

"It's entertainment of one kind or another that draws them, ye ken," Jamie had said, sketching out plans on the back of a broadsheet poem describing the scurrilous affair between the Comte de Sévigny and the wife of the Minister of Agriculture. "All the nobility care about is appearances. So to start with, we must offer them something interesting to look at."

Judging from the stunned look on his face now, I had made a good beginning. I sashayed a bit, making the huge overskirt swing like a bell.

"Not bad, is it?" I asked. "Very visible, at any rate."

He found his voice at last.

"Visible?" he croaked. "*Visible?* God, I can see every inch of ye, down to the third rib!"

I peered downward.

"No, you can't. That isn't me under the lace, it's a lining of white charmeuse."

"Aye well, it *looks* like you!" He came closer, bending to inspect the bodice of the dress. He peered into my cleavage.

"Christ, I can see down to your navel! Surely ye dinna mean to go out in public like that!"

I bristled a bit at this. I had been feeling a trifle nervous myself over the general revealingness of the dress, the fashionable sketches the seamstress had shown me notwithstanding. But Jamie's reaction was making me feel defensive, and thus rebellious.

"*You* told me to be visible," I reminded him. "And this is absolutely nothing, compared to the latest Court fashions. Believe me, I shall be modesty personified, in comparison with Madame de Pérignon and the Duchesse de Rouen." I put my hands on my hips and surveyed him coldly. "Or do you want me to appear at Court in my green velvet?"

Jamie averted his eyes from my décolletage and tightened his lips.

"Mphm," he said, looking as Scotch as possible.

Trying to be conciliatory, I came closer and laid a hand on his arm.

"Come now," I said. "You've been at Court before; surely you know what ladies dress like. You know this isn't terribly extreme by those standards."

He glanced down at me and smiled, a trifle shamefaced.

"Aye," he said. "Aye, that's true. It's only . . . well, you're my wife, Sassenach. I dinna want other men to look at you the way I've looked at those ladies."

I laughed and put my hands behind his neck, pulling him down to kiss me. He held me around the waist, his thumbs unconsciously stroking the softness of the red silk where it sheathed my torso. His touch traveled upward, sliding across the slipperiness of the fabric to the nape of my neck. His other hand grasped the soft roundness of my breast, swelling up above the tethering grip of the corsets, voluptuously free under a single layer of sheer silk. He let go at last and straightened up, shaking his head doubtfully.

"I suppose ye'll have to wear it, Sassenach, but for Christ's sake be careful."

"Careful? Of what?"

His mouth twisted in a rueful smile.

"Lord, woman, have ye no notion what ye look like in that gown? It makes me want to commit rape on the spot. And these damned frog-eaters havena got my restraint." He frowned slightly. "You couldna . . . cover it up at bit at the top?" He waved a large hand vaguely in the direction of his own lace jabot, secured with a ruby stickpin. "A . . . ruffle or something? A handkerchief?"

"Men," I told him, "have no notion of fashion. But not to worry. The seamstress says that's what the fan is for." I flipped the matching lace-trimmed fan open with a gesture that had taken fifteen minutes' practice to perfect, and fluttered it enticingly over my bosom.

Jamie blinked meditatively at this performance, then turned to take my cloak from the wardrobe.

"Do me the one favor, Sassenach," he said, draping the heavy velvet over my shoulders. "Take a larger fan."

In terms of attracting notice, the dress was an unqualified success. In terms of the effects on Jamie's blood pressure, it was somewhat more equivocal.

He hovered protectively at my elbow, glaring ferociously at any male who glanced in my direction, until Annalise de Marillac, spotting us from across the room, came floating in our direction, her delicate features wreathed in a welcoming smile. I felt the smile freezing on my own face. Annalise de Marillac was an "acquaintance"—he said—of Jamie's, from his former residence in Paris. She was also beautiful, charming, and exquisitely tiny.

"Mon petit sauvage!" she greeted Jamie. "I have someone you must meet. Several someones, in fact." She tilted a head like a china doll in the direction of

a group of men, gathered around a chess table in the corner, arguing heatedly about something. I recognized the Duc d'Orléans, and Gérard Gobelin, a prominent banker. An influential group, then.

"Come and play chess for them," Annalise urged, placing a mothlike hand on Jamie's arm. "It will be a good place for His Majesty to meet you, later."

The King was expected to appear after the supper he was attending, sometime in the next hour or two. In the meantime, the guests wandered to and fro, conversing, admiring the paintings on the walls, flirting behind fans, consuming confits, tartlets, and wine, and disappearing at more or less discreet intervals into the odd little curtained alcoves. These were cleverly fitted into the paneling of the rooms, so that you scarcely noticed them, unless you got close enough to hear the sounds inside.

Jamie hesitated, and Annalise pulled a bit harder.

"Come along," she urged. "Have no fear for your lady"—she cast an appreciative glance at my gown—"she won't be alone long."

"That's what I'm afraid of," Jamie muttered under his breath. "All right, then, in a moment." He disengaged himself momentarily from Annalise's grasp and bent to whisper in my ear.

"If I find ye in one of those alcoves, Sassenach, the man you're with is dead. And as for you . . ." His hands twitched unconsciously in the direction of his swordbelt.

"Oh no you don't," I said. "You swore on your dirk you'd never beat me again. What price the Holy Iron, eh?"

A reluctant grin tugged at his mouth.

"No, I wilna beat ye, much as I'd like to."

"Good. What do you mean to do, then?" I asked, teasing.

"I'll think of something," he replied, with a certain grimness. "I dinna ken what, but ye wilna like it."

And with a final glare round and a proprietary squeeze of my shoulder, he allowed Annalise to lead him away, like a small but enthusiastic tug towing a reluctant barge.

Annalise was right. No longer deterred by Jamie's glowering presence, the gentlemen of the Court descended upon me like a flock of parrots on a ripe passion fruit.

My hand was kissed repeatedly and held lingeringly, dozens of flowery compliments were paid me, and cups of spiced wine were brought me in endless procession. After half an hour of this, my feet began to hurt. So did my face, from smiling. And my hand, from fan-wielding.

I had to admit some gratitude to Jamie for his intransigence in the matter of the fan. Bowing to his sensibilities, I had brought the largest I possessed, a foot-long whopper painted with what purported to be Scottish stags leaping through the heather. Jamie had been critical of the artistry, but approving of the size. Graciously fanning away the attentions of an ardent young man in purple, I then spread the thing inconspicuously beneath my chin to deflect crumbs while I nibbled at a piece of toast with salmon on it.

And not only toast crumbs. While Jamie, from his vantage point a foot above me, had claimed to be able to see my navel, my umbilicus was by and large safe from scrutiny by the French courtiers, most of whom were shorter than I was. On the other hand . . .

I had often enjoyed snuggling into Jamie's chest, my nose fitting comfortably into the small hollow in the center. A few of the shorter and bolder souls among my admirers seemed bent on enjoying a similar experience, and I was kept busy, flapping my fan hard enough to blow their curls back from their faces, or if that didn't suffice to discourage them, snapping the fan shut and rapping them smartly on the head with it.

It came as a considerable relief to hear the footman at the door suddenly draw himself up and intone, *"Sa Majesté, Le Roi Louis!"*

While the King might rise at dawn, apparently he blossomed at night. Not much taller than my own five feet six, Louis entered with the carriage of a much taller man, glancing left and right, nodding in gracious acknowledgment of his bowing subjects.

Now this, I thought, looking him over, was a good deal more in line with my ideas of what a king *ought* to look like. Not particularly handsome, he acted as though he were; an impression enhanced not only by the richness of his clothes, but by the attitude of those around him. He wore the latest backswept wig, and his coat was cut velvet, embroidered all over with hundreds of frivolous silk butterflies. It was cut away at the middle to display a waistcoat of voluptuous cream-colored silk with diamond buttons, matching the wide, butterfly-shaped buckles on his shoes.

The dark, hooded eyes swept restlessly over the crowd, and the haughty Bourbon nose lifted as though smelling out any item of interest.

Dressed in kilt and plaid, but with a coat and waistcoat of stiffened yellow silk, and with his flaming hair loose to his shoulders, a single small braid down one side in ancient Scots fashion, Jamie definitely qualified. At least I thought it was Jamie who had attracted the King's attention, as *Le Roi Louis* purposefully changed direction and swerved toward us, parting the crowd before him like the waves of the Red Sea. Madame Nesle de La Tourelle, whom I recognized from a previous party, followed close behind him like a dinghy in his wake.

I had forgotten the red dress; His Majesty halted directly in front of me and bowed extravagantly, hand over his waist.

"Chère Madame!" he said. "We are enchanted!"

I heard a deep intake of breath from Jamie, and then he stepped forward and bowed to the King.

"May I present my wife, Your Majesty—my lady Broch Tuarach." He rose and stepped back. Attracted by a quick flutter of Jamie's fingers, I stared at him for a moment of incomprehension, before suddenly realizing that he was signaling me to curtsy.

I dipped automatically, struggling to keep my eyes on the floor and wondering where I would look when I bobbed up again. Madame Nesle de la Tourelle was standing just behind Louis, watching the introduction with a slightly bored look on her face. Gossip said that "Nesle" was Louis's current favorite. She was, in current vogue, wearing a gown cut *below* both breasts, with a bit of supercedent gauze which was clearly meant for the sake of fashion, as it couldn't possibly function for either warmth or concealment.

It was neither the gown nor the prospect it revealed that had rattled me, though. The breasts of "Nesle," while reasonably adequate in size, pleasant in proportion, and tipped with large brownish areolae, were further adorned with a pair of nipple jewels that caused their settings to recede into insignificance. A pair of diamond-encrusted swans with ruby eyes stretched their necks toward each other, swinging precariously in their gold-hooped perches. The workmanship was superb and the materials stunning, but it was the fact that each gold hoop passed *through* her nipple that made me feel rather faint. The nipples themselves were rather seriously inverted, but this fact was disguised by the large pearl that covered each one, dangling on a thin gold chain that looped from side to side of the main hoop.

I rose, red-faced and coughing, and managed to excuse myself, hacking politely into a handkerchief as I backed away. I felt a presence in my rear and stopped just in time to avoid backing into Jamie, who was watching the King's mistress with no pretense whatever of tactful obliviousness.

"She told Marie d'Arbanville that Master Raymond did the piercing for her," I remarked under my breath. His fascinated gaze didn't waver.

"Shall I make an appointment?" I asked. "I imagine he'd do it for me if I gave him the recipe for caraway tonic."

Jamie glanced down at me at last. Taking my elbow, he steered me toward a refreshment alcove.

"If you so much as *speak* to Master Raymond again," he said, out of the corner of his mouth, "I'll pierce them for ye myself—wi' my teeth."

The King had by now wandered off toward the Salon of Apollo, the space left by his passage quickly filled by others coming from the supper room. Seeing Jamie distracted into conversation with a Monsieur Genet, head of a wealthy shipping family, I looked surreptitiously about for a place in which to remove my shoes for a moment.

One of the alcoves was at hand and, from the sounds of it, unoccupied. I sent a lingering admirer off to fetch some more wine, then, with a quick glance round, slid into the alcove.

It was furnished rather suggestively with a couch, a small table, and a pair of chairs—more suitable for laying aside garments than for sitting upon, I thought critically. I sat down nonetheless, pried my shoes off, and with a sigh of relief, propped my feet up on the other chair.

A faint jingling of curtain rings behind me announced the fact that my departure had not been unnoticed after all.

"Madame! At last we are alone!"

"Yes, more's the pity," I said, sighing. It was one of the countless Comtes, I thought. Or no, this one was a Vicomte; someone had introduced him to me earlier as the Vicomte de Rambeau. One of the short ones. I seemed to recall his beady little eyes gleaming up at me in appreciation from below the edge of my fan.

Wasting no time, he slid adroitly onto the other chair, lifting my feet into his lap. He clasped my silk-stockinged toes fervently against his crotch.

"Ah, *ma petite*! Such delicacy! Your beauty distracts me!"

I thought it must, if he was under the delusion that my feet were particularly delicate. Raising one to his lips, he nibbled at my toes.

"C'est un cochon qui vit dans la ville, c'est un cochon qui vit . . ."

I jerked my foot from his grasp and stood up hastily, rather impeded by my voluminous petticoats.

"Speaking of *cochons* who live in the city," I said, rather nervously, "I don't think my husband would be at all pleased to find you here."

"Your husband? Pah!" He dismissed Jamie with an airy wave of the hand. "He will be occupied for some time, I am sure. And while the cat's away. . . . come to me, *ma petite souris*; let me hear you squeak a bit."

Presumably intending to fortify himself for the fray, the Vicomte produced an enameled snuffbox from his pocket, deftly sprinkled a line of dark grains along the back of his hand, and wiped it delicately against his nostrils.

He took a deep breath, eyes glistening in anticipation, then jerked his head as the curtain was suddenly thrust aside with a jangling of brass rings. His aim distracted by the intrusion, the Vicomte sneezed directly into my bosom with considerable vigor.

I shrieked.

"You *disgusting* man!" I said, and walloped him across the face with my closed fan.

The Vicomte staggered back, eyes watering. He tripped over my size-nine shoes, which lay on the floor, and fell headfirst into the arms of Jamie, who was standing in the doorway.

"Well, you *did* attract a certain amount of notice," I said at last.

"Bah," he said. "The *salaud*'s lucky I didna tear off his head and make him swallow it."

"Well, that would have provided an interesting spectacle," I agreed dryly. "Sousing him in the fountain was nearly as good, though."

He looked up, his frown replaced with a reluctant grin.

"Aye, well. I didna drown the man, after all."

"I trust the Vicomte appreciates your restraint."

He snorted again. He was standing in the center of a sitting room, part of a small *appartement* in the palace, to which the King, once he had stopped laughing, had assigned us, insisting that we should not undertake the return journey to Paris tonight.

"After all, *mon chevalier*," he had said, eyeing Jamie's large, dripping form on the terrace, "we should dislike exceedingly for you to take a chill. I feel sure that the Court would be deprived of a great deal of entertainment in such a case, and Madame would never forgive me. Would you, sweetheart?" He reached out and pinched Madame de La Tourelle playfully on one nipple.

His mistress looked mildly annoyed, but smiled obediently. I noticed, though, that once the King's attention had been distracted, it was Jamie on whom her gaze lingered. Well, he was impressive, I had to admit, standing dripping in the torchlight with his clothes plastered to his body. That didn't mean I liked her doing it.

He peeled his wet shirt off and dropped it in a sodden heap. He looked even better without it.

"As for you," he said, eyeing me in a sinister manner, "did I not tell ye to stay away from those alcoves?"

"Yes. But aside from that, Mrs. Lincoln, how did you enjoy the play?" I asked politely.

"What?" He stared at me as though I had lost my mind on the spot.

"Never mind; it's a bit out of your frame of reference. I only meant, did you meet anyone useful before you came to defend your marital rights?"

He rubbed his hair vigorously with a towel plucked from the washstand. "Oh, aye. I played a game of chess with Monsieur Duverney. Beat him, too, and made him angry."

"Oh, that sounds promising. And who's Monsieur Duverney?"

He tossed me the towel, grinning. "The French Minister of Finance, Sassenach."

"Oh. And you're pleased because you made him angry?"

"He was angry at himself for losing, Sassenach," Jamie explained. "Now he won't rest until he's beaten me. He's coming round to the house on Sunday to play again."

"Oh, well done!" I said. "And in the process, you can assure him that the Stuarts' prospects are exceedingly dim, and convince him that Louis doesn't want to assist them financially, blood kin or not."

He nodded, combing back his wet hair with both hands. The fire had not yet been lit, and he shivered slightly.

"Where did you learn to play chess?" I asked curiously. "I didn't know you knew how."

"Colum MacKenzie taught me," he said. "When I was sixteen, and spent a year at Castle Leoch. I had tutors for French and German and mathematics and such, but I'd go up to Colum's room for an hour every evening to play chess. Not that it usually took him an hour to beat me," he added ruefully.

"No wonder you're good," I said. Jamie's uncle Colum, the victim of a deforming disease that had deprived him of most of his mobility, made up for it with a mind that would have put Machiavelli to shame.

Jamie stood up and unbuckled his swordbelt, narrowing his eyes at me. "Dinna think I don't know what you're up to, Sassenach. Changing the subject and flattering me like a courtesan. Did I not tell ye about those alcoves?"

"You said you didn't mean to beat me," I reminded him, sitting a bit farther back in my chair, just to be on the safe side.

He snorted again, tossing the swordbelt onto the chest of drawers and dropping his kilt next to the sodden shirt.

"Do I look the sort of man would beat a woman who's with child?" he demanded.

I eyed him doubtfully. Stark naked, with his hair in damp red snarls and the white scars still visible on his body, he looked as though he had just leaped off a Viking ship, rape and pillage on his mind.

"Actually, you look capable of just about anything," I told him. "As for the alcoves, yes, you told me. I suppose I should have gone outside to take my shoes off, but how was I to know that idiot would follow me in and begin nibbling on my toes? And if you don't mean to beat me, just what did you have in mind?" I took a firm grip on the arms of my chair.

He lay down on the bed and grinned at me.

"Take off that whore's dress, Sassenach, and come to bed."

"Why?"

"Well, I canna wallop you, or drench ye in the fountain." He shrugged. "I meant to give ye a terrible scolding, but I dinna think I can keep my eyes open long enough." He gave a terrific yawn, then blinked and grinned at me again. "Remind me to do it in the morning, eh?"

"Better, is it?" Jamie's dark-blue eyes were clouded with worry. "Is it right for ye to be sick so much, Sassenach?"

I pushed the hair back from my sweaty temples and dabbed a damp towel over my face.

"I don't know whether it's *right*," I said weakly, "but at least I believe it's normal. Some women are sick all through." Not a pleasant thought at the moment.

Jamie glanced, not at the gaily painted clock on the table, but as usual, out the window at the sun.

"Do ye feel well enough to go down to breakfast, Sassenach, or ought I to tell the chambermaid to bring up something on a tray?"

"No. I'm quite all right now." And I was. In the odd way of morning sickness, once the inexorable nausea had had its way with me, I felt perfectly fine within a moment or two. "Let me just rinse my mouth."

As I bent over the basin, sluicing cool water over my face, there was a rap at the door of the *appartement*. Likely the servant who had been dispatched to the house in Paris to bring us fresh clothes, I thought.

To my surprise, though, it was a courtier, with a written invitation to lunch.

"His Majesty is dining today with an English nobleman," the courtier explained, "newly arrived in Paris. His Majesty has summoned several of the prominent English merchants from the Cité to lunch, for the purpose of providing His Grace the Duke with the company of some of his countrymen. And someone pointed out to His Majesty that Madame your wife is an English lady, too, and thus should be invited to attend."

"All right," Jamie said, after a quick glance at me. "You may tell His Majesty that we will be honored to remain."

Soon thereafter, Murtagh had arrived, dour as ever, bearing a large bundle of fresh clothes, and my medicine box, which I had asked for. Jamie took him into the sitting room to give him instructions for the day, while I hastily struggled into my fresh gown, for the first time rather regretting my refusal to employ a lady's maid. Always unruly, the state of my hair had not been improved by sleeping in close embrace with a large, damp Scot; wild tangles shot off in several directions, resisting all attempts to tame them with brush and comb.

At length I emerged, pink and cross with effort, but with my hair in some semblance of order. Jamie looked at me and murmured something about hedgehogs under his breath, but caught a searing glance in return and had the good sense to shut up.

A stroll among the parterres and fountains of the palace gardens did a good bit to restore my equanimity. Most of the trees were still leafless, but the day was unexpectedly warm for late March, and the smell of the swelling buds on the twigs was green and pungent. You could almost feel the sap rising in the towering chestnuts and poplars that edged the paths and sheltered the hundreds of white marble statues.

I paused beside a statue of a half-draped man with grapes in his hair and a flute at his lips. A large, silky goat nibbled hungrily at more grapes that were cascading from the marble folds of the draperies.

"Who's this?" I asked, "Pan?"

Jamie shook his head, smiling. He was dressed in his old kilt and a worn, if comfortable coat, but he looked much better to me than did the luxuriously clad courtiers who passed us in chattering groups.

"No, I think there is a statue of Pan about, but it isna that one. That's one of the Four Humors of Man."

"Well, he looks fairly humorous," I said, glancing up at the goat's smiling friend.

Jamie laughed.

"And you a physician, Sassenach! Not that sort of humor. Do ye not know the four humors that make up the human body? That one's Blood"—he motioned at the flute-player, then pointed down the path—"and there's Melancholy." This was a tall man in a sort of toga, holding an open book.

Jamie pointed across the path. "And over there is Choler"—a nude and muscular young man, who certainly was scowling ferociously, without regard to the marble lion that was about to bite him smartly in the leg—"and that's Phlegm."

"Is it, by Jove?" Phlegm, a bearded gent with a folded hat, had both arms crossed on his chest, and a tortoise at his feet.

"Hum," I remarked.

"Do physicians not learn about humors in your time?" Jamie asked curiously.

"No," I said. "We have germs, instead."

"Really? Germs," he said to himself, trying the word over, rolling it on his tongue with a Scottish burr, which made it sound sinister in the extreme. "Gerrrms. And what do germs look like?"

I glanced up at a representation of "America," a nubile young maiden in a feathered skirt and headdress, with a crocodile at her feet.

"Well, they wouldn't make nearly such picturesque statues," I said.

The crocodile at America's feet reminded me of Master Raymond's shop.

"Did you mean it about not wanting me to go to Master Raymond's?" I asked. "Or do you just not want me to pierce my nipples?"

"I most definitely dinna want ye to pierce your nipples," he said firmly, taking me by the elbow and hurrying me onward, lest I derive any untoward inspiration from America's bare breasts. "But no, I dinna want ye to go to Master Raymond's, either. There are rumors about the man."

"There are rumors about everyone in Paris," I observed, "and I'd be willing to bet that Master Raymond knows all of them."

Jamie nodded, hair glinting in the pale spring sunshine.

"Oh, aye, I expect so. But I think I can learn what's needful in the taverns and drawing rooms. Master Raymond's said to be at the center of a particular circle, but it isna Jacobite sympathizers."

"Really? Who, then?"

"Cabalists and occultists. Witches, maybe."

"Jamie, you aren't seriously worried about witches and demons, are you?"

We had arrived at the part of the gardens known as the "Green Carpet."

This early in the spring, the green of the huge lawn was only a faint tinge, but people were lounging on it, taking advantage of the rare balmy day.

"Not witches, no," he said at last, finding a place near a hedge of forsythia and sitting down on the grass. "The Comte St. Germain, possibly."

I remembered the look in the Comte St. Germain's dark eyes at Le Havre, and shivered, in spite of the sunshine and the woolen shawl I wore.

"You think he's associated with Master Raymond?"

Jamie shrugged. "I don't know. But it was you told me the rumors about St. Germain, no? And if Master Raymond is part of that circle—then I think you should keep the hell away from him, Sassenach." He gave me a wry half-smile. "After all, I'd as soon not have to save ye from burning again."

The shadows under the trees reminded me of the cold gloom of the thieves' hole in Cranesmuir, and I shivered and moved closer to Jamie, farther into the sunlight.

"I'd as soon you didn't, either."

The pigeons were courting on the grass below a flowering forsythia bush. The ladies and gentlemen of the Court were performing similar activities on the paths that led through the sculpture gardens. The major difference was that the pigeons were quieter about it.

A vision in watered aqua silk hove abaft our resting place, in loud raptures over the divinity of the play the night before. The three ladies with him, while not so spectacular, echoed his opinions faithfully.

"Superb! Quite superb, the voice of La Couelle!"

"Oh, superb! Yes, wonderful!"

"Delightful, delightful! Superb is the only word for it!"

"Oh, yes, superb!"

The voices—all four of them—were shrill as nails being pulled from wood. By contrast, the gentleman pigeon doing his turn a few feet from my nose had a low and mellifluous coo, rising from a deep, amatory rumble to a breathy whistle as he puffed his breast and bowed repeatedly, laying his heart at the feet of his ladylove, who looked rather unimpressed so far.

I looked beyond the pigeon toward the aqua-satined courtier, who had hastened back to snatch up a lace-trimmed handkerchief, coyly dropped as bait by one of his erstwhile companions.

"The ladies call that one 'L'Andouille,' " I remarked. "I wonder why?"

Jamie grunted sleepily, and opened one eye to look after the departing courtier.

"Mm? Oh, 'The Sausage.' It means he canna keep his roger in his breeches. You know the sort . . . ladies, footmen, courtesans, pageboys. Lapdogs, too, if rumor is right," he added, squinting in the direction of the vanished aqua silk, where a lady of the court was now approaching, a fluffy white bundle clasped protectively to her ample bosom. "Reckless, that. I wouldna risk mine anywhere near one o' those wee yapping hairballs."

"Your roger?" I said, amused. "I used to hear it called peter, now and again. And the Yanks, for some peculiar reason, used to call theirs a dick. I once called a patient who was teasing me a 'Clever Dick,' and he nearly burst his stitches laughing."

Jamie laughed himself, stretching luxuriously in the warming spring sun. He blinked once or twice and rolled over, grinning at me upside down.

"You have much the same effect on me, Sassenach," he said. I stroked back the hair from his forehead, kissing him between the eyes.

"Why do men call it names?" I asked. "John Thomas, I mean. Or Roger, for that matter. Women don't do that."

"They don't?" Jamie asked, interested.

"No, of course not. I'd as soon call my nose Jane."

His chest moved up and down as he laughed. I rolled on top of him, enjoying the solid feel of him beneath me. I pressed my hips downward, but the layers of intervening petticoats rendered it more of a gesture than anything else.

"Well," Jamie said logically, "yours doesna go up and down by itself, after all, nor go carryin' on regardless of your own wishes in the matter. So far as I know, anyway," he added, cocking one eyebrow questioningly.

"No, it doesn't, thank God. I wonder if Frenchmen call theirs 'Pierre,' " I said, glancing at a passing dandy in green velvet-faced moiré.

Jamie burst into a laugh that startled the pigeons out of the forsythia bush. They flapped off in a ruffle of indignation, scattering wisps of gray down in their wake. The fluffy white lapdog, hitherto content to loll in its mistress's arms like a bundle of rags, awoke at once to an awareness of its responsibilities. It popped out of its warm nest like a Ping-Pong ball and galloped off in enthusiastic pursuit of the pigeons, barking dementedly, its mistress in similar cry behind it.

"I dinna ken, Sassenach," he said, recovering enough to wipe the tears from his eyes. "The only Frenchman I ever heard call it a name called his 'Georges.' "

"Georges!" I said, loudly enough to attract the attention of a small knot of passing courtiers. One, a short but vivacious specimen in dramatic black slashed with white satin, stopped alongside and bowed deeply, sweeping the ground at my feet with his hat. One eye was still swelled shut, and a livid welt showed across the bridge of his nose, but his style was unimpaired.

"A votre service, Madame," he said.

I might have managed if it weren't for the bloody nightingales. The dining salon was hot and crowded with courtiers and onlookers, one of the stays in my dress frame had come loose and was stabbing me viciously beneath the left kidney each time I drew breath, and I was suffering from that most ubiquitous plague of pregnancy, the urge to urinate every few minutes. Still, I might have managed. It was, after all, a serious breach of manners to leave the table before the King, even though luncheon was a casual affair, in comparison with the formal dinners customary at Versailles—or so I was given to understand. "Casual," however, is a relative term.

True, there were only three varieties of spiced pickle, not eight. And one soup, clear, not thick. The venison was merely roasted, not presented *en brochette,* and the fish, while tastily poached in wine, was served fileted, not whole and riding on a sea of aspic filled with shrimp.

As though frustrated by so much rustic simplicity, though, one of the chefs had provided a charming hors d'oeuvre—a nest, cunningly built from strips of pastry, ornamented with real sprigs of flowering apple, on the edge of which perched two nightingales, skinned and roasted, stuffed with apple and cinnamon, then redressed in their feathers. And in the nest was the entire family of baby birds, tiny stubs of outstretched wings brown and crispy, tender bare skins glazed with honey, blackened mouths agape to show the merest hint of the almond-paste stuffing within.

After a triumphal tour of the table to show it off—to the accompaniment of murmurs of admiration all round—the dainty dish was set before the King, who turned from his conversation with Madame de La Tourelle long enough to pluck one of the nestlings from its place and pop it into his mouth.

Crunch, crunch, crunch went Louis's teeth. Mesmerized, I watched the muscles of his throat ripple, and felt the rubble of small bones slide down my own gullet. Brown fingers reached casually for another baby.

At this point, I concluded that there were probably worse things than insulting His Majesty by leaving the table, and bolted.

Rising from my knees amid the shrubbery a few minutes later, I heard a sound behind me. Expecting to meet the eye of a justifiably irate gardener, I turned guiltily to meet the eye of an irate husband.

"Damn it, Claire, d'ye have to do this all the time?" he demanded.

"In a word—yes," I said, sinking exhaustedly onto the rim of an ornamental fountain. My hands were damp, and I smoothed them over my skirt. "Did you think I did it for fun?" I felt light-headed, and closed my eyes, trying to regain my internal balance before I fell into the fountain.

Suddenly there was a hand at the small of my back, and I half-leaned, half-fell into his arms as he sat beside me and gathered me in.

"Oh, God. I'm sorry, *mo duinne.* Are ye all right, Claire?"

I pushed away enough to look up at him and smile.

"I'm all right. Just a bit light-headed, is all." I reached up and tried to smooth away the deep line of concern on his forehead. He smiled back, but the line stayed, a thin vertical crease between the thick sandy curves of his eyebrows. He swished a hand in the fountain and smoothed it over my cheeks. I must have looked rather pale.

"I'm sorry," I added. "Really, Jamie, I couldn't help it."

His damp hand squeezed the back of my neck reassuringly, strong and steady. A fine spray of droplets from the mouth of a bug-eyed dolphin misted my hair.

"Och, dinna mind me, Sassenach. I didna mean to snap at ye. It's only . . ." He made a helpless gesture with one hand. ". . . only that I feel such a thick-heided clot. I see ye in a misery, and I know I've done it to ye, and there isna the slightest thing I can do to aid you. So I blame ye for it instead, and act cross and growl at you . . . why do ye no just tell me to go to the devil, Sassenach?" he burst out.

I laughed until my sides hurt under the tight corseting, holding on to his arm.

"Go to hell, Jamie," I said at last, wiping my eyes. "Go directly to hell. Do not pass Go. Do not collect two hundred dollars. There. Do you feel better now?"

"Aye, I do," he said, his expression lightening. "When ye start to talk daft, I know you're all right. Do *you* feel better, Sassenach?"

"Yes," I said, sitting up and beginning to take notice of my surroundings. The grounds of Versailles were open to the public, and small groups of merchants and laborers mingled oddly with the brightly colored nobles, all enjoying the good weather.

Suddenly the nearby door onto the terrace burst open, spilling the King's guests out into the garden in a tide of chatter. The exodus from luncheon had been augmented by a new deputation, apparently just decanted from the two large coaches I could see driving past the edge of the garden toward distant stables.

It was a large group of people, men and women, soberly clad by comparison with the bright colors of the courtiers around them. It was the sound of them, though, rather than the appearance, that had caught my attention. French, spoken by a number of people at a distance, strongly resembles the quacking conversation of ducks and geese, with its nasal elements. English, on the other hand, has a slower pace, and much less rise and fall in its intonations. Spoken at a distance where individual voices are impossible to distinguish, it has the gruff, friendly monotony of a sheepdog's barking. And the general effect of the mass exodus presently coming in our direction was of a gaggle of geese being driven to market by a pack of dogs.

The English party had arrived, somewhat belatedly. No doubt they were being tactfully shooed into the garden while the kitchen staff hastily prepared another dinner and reset the massive table for them.

I scanned the group curiously. The Duke of Sandringham I knew, of course, having met him once before in Scotland at Castle Leoch. His barrel-chested figure was easy to pick out, walking side by side with Louis, modish wig tilted in polite attention.

Most of the other people were strangers, though I thought the stylish lady of middle age just coming through the doors must be the Duchess of Claymore, whom I had heard was expected. The Queen, normally left behind at some country house to amuse herself as best she could, had been trotted out for the occasion. She was talking to the visitor, her sweet, anxious face flushed with the unaccustomed excitement of the occasion.

The young girl just behind the Duchess caught my eye. Quite plainly dressed, she had the sort of beauty that would make her stand out in any crowd. She was small, fine-boned but nicely rounded in figure, with dark, shiny, unpowdered hair and the most extraordinary white skin, flushed across the cheeks with a clear deep pink that made her look exactly like a flower petal.

Her coloring reminded me of a dress I'd once had in my own time, a light cotton frock decorated with red poppies. The thought for some reason struck me with a sudden unexpected wave of homesickness, and I gripped the edge of the marble bench, eyelids prickling with longing. It must be hearing plain bluff English spoken, I thought, after so many months among the lilt of Scotland and the quacking of France. The visitors sounded like home.

Then I saw him. I could feel all of the blood draining from my head as my eye traced disbelievingly over the elegant curve of the skull, dark-haired and bold amid the powdered wigs around it. Alarms rang in my head like air-raid sirens, as I fought to accept and repel the impressions that assaulted me. My subconscious saw the line of the nose, thought "Frank," and turned my body to fly toward him in welcome. "Not-Frank," came the slightly higher, rational center of my brain, freezing me in my tracks as I saw the familiar curve of a half-smiling mouth, repeating, "You *know* it's not Frank" as the muscles of my calves knotted. And then the lurch into panic and the clenching of hands and stomach, as the slower processes of logical thought came doggedly on the trail of instinct and knowledge, seeing the high brow and the arrogant tilt of the head, assuring me of the unthinkable. It could not be Frank. And if it were not, then it could only be . . .

"Jack Randall." It wasn't my voice that spoke, but Jamie's, sounding oddly calm and detached. Attention attracted by my peculiar behavior, he had looked where I was looking, and had seen what I had seen.

He didn't move. So far as I could tell through the increasing haze of panic, he didn't breathe. I was dimly aware of a nearby servant peering curiously upward at the towering form of the frozen Scottish warrior next to me, silent as a statue of Mars. But all my concern was for Jamie.

He was entirely still. Still as a lion is still, part of the grass of the plain, its stare hot and unblinking as the sun that burns the veldt. And I saw something move in the depths of his eyes. The telltale twitch of the stalking cat, the tiny jerk of the tuft at the end of the tail, precursor to carnage.

To draw arms in the presence of the King was death. Murtagh was on the far side of the garden, much too far away to help. Two more paces would bring

Randall within hearing distance. Within sword's reach. I laid a hand on his arm. It was rigid as the steel of the swordhilt under his hand. The blood roared in my ears.

"Jamie," I said. "Jamie!" And fainted.

10

A Lady, with Brown Hair Curling Luxuriantly

I swam up out of a flickering yellow haze composed of sunlight, dust, and fragmented memories, feeling completely disoriented.

Frank was leaning over me, face creased in concern. He was holding my hand, except that he wasn't. The hand I held was much larger than Frank's, and my fingers brushed the wiriness of coarse hairs on the wrist. Frank's hands were smooth as a girl's.

"Are you all right?" The voice was Frank's, low and cultured.

"Claire!" That voice, deeper and rougher, wasn't Frank's at all. Neither was it cultured. It was full of fright and anguish.

"Jamie." I found the name at last to match the mental image for which I had been seeking. "Jamie! Don't . . ." I sat bolt upright, staring wildly from one face to the other. I was surrounded by a circle of curious faces, courtiers two and three deep around me, with a small clear space left for His Majesty, who was leaning over, peering down at me with an expression of sympathetic interest.

Two men knelt in the dust beside me. Jamie on the right, eyes wide and face pale as the hawthorn blossoms above him. And on my left . . .

"Are you all right, Madame?" The light hazel eyes held only respectful concern, the fine dark brows arched over them in inquiry. It wasn't Frank, of course. Neither was it Jonathan Randall. This man was younger than the Captain by a good ten years, perhaps close to my own age, his face pale and unlined by exposure to weather. His lips had the same chiseled lines, but lacked the marks of ruthlessness that bracketed the Captain's mouth.

"You. . . ." I croaked, leaning away from him. "You're . . ."

"Alexander Randall, Esquire, Madame," he answered quickly, making an abortive gesture toward his head, as though to doff a hat he wasn't wearing. "I don't believe we have met?" he said, with a hint of doubt.

"I, er, that is, no, we haven't," I said, sagging back against Jamie's arm. The arm was steady as an iron railing, but the hand holding mine was trembling, and I pulled our clasped hands into the fold of my skirt to hide it.

"Rather an informal introduction, Mrs., er, no . . . it's Lady Broch Tuarach, is it not?" The high, piping voice pulled my attention back above me, to the flushed, cherubic countenance of the Duke of Sandringham peering interestedly over the shoulders of the Comte de Sévigny and the Duc d'Orléans. He pushed his ungainly body through the narrow opening afforded, and extended a hand to help me to my feet. Still holding my sweaty palm in his own, he bowed in the direction of Alexander Randall, Esquire, who was frowning in a puzzled sort of way.

"Mr. Randall is in my employ as secretary, Lady Broch Tuarach. Holy Orders is a noble calling, but unfortunately nobility of purpose does not pay the cobbler's bill, does it, Alex?" The young man flushed slightly at this barb, but he inclined his head civilly toward me, acknowledging his employer's introduction. Only then did I notice the sober dark suit and high white stock that marked him as a junior cleric of some sort.

"His Grace is correct, my lady. And that being so, I must hold his offer of employment in the deepest gratitude." A faint tightening of the lips at this speech seemed to indicate that the gratitude felt might not perhaps go so deep as all that, pleasant words notwithstanding. I glanced at the Duke, to find his small blue eyes creased against the sun, his expression blandly impenetrable.

This little tableau was broken by a clap of the King's hands summoning two footmen, who, at Louis's direction, grasped me by both arms and lifted me forcibly into a sedan chair, despite my protests.

"Certainly not, Madame," he said, graciously dismissing both protests and thanks. "Go home and rest; we do not wish you to be indisposed for the ball tomorrow, *non*?" His large brown eyes twinkled at me as he raised my hand to his lips. Not taking his eyes from my face, he bowed formally toward Jamie, who had gathered his wits sufficiently to be making a gracious speech of thanks, and said, "I shall perhaps accept your thanks, my lord, in the form of your permission to request a dance from your lovely wife."

Jamie's lips tightened at this, but he bowed in return and said, "My wife shares my honor at your attention, Your Majesty." He glanced in my direction. "If she is well enough to attend the ball tomorrow evening, I am sure she will look forward to dancing with Your Majesty." He turned without waiting for formal dismissal, and jerked his head toward the chair-bearers.

"Home," he said.

Home at last after a hot, jolting ride through streets that smelled of flowers and open sewers, I shed my heavy dress and its uncomfortable frame in favor of a silk dressing gown.

I found Jamie sitting by the empty hearth, eyes closed, hands on his knees as though thinking. He was pale as his linen shirt, glimmering in the shadow of the mantelpiece like a ghost.

"Holy Mother," he muttered, shaking his head. "Dear God and saints, so close. I came within a hairsbreadth of murdering that man. Do ye realize,

Claire, if ye hadna fainted . . . Jesus, *I meant to kill him,* with every last morsel of will I had." He broke off, shuddering again with reaction.

"Here, you'd better put your feet up," I urged, tugging at a heavy carved footstool.

"No, I'm all right now," he said, waving it away. "He's . . . Jack Randall's brother, then?"

"I should think it likely in the extreme," I said dryly. "He could scarcely be anyone else, after all."

"Mm. Did ye know he worked for Sandringham?"

I shook my head. "I didn't—don't—know anything about him other than his name and the fact that he's a curate. F-Frank wasn't particularly interested in him, as he wasn't a direct ancestor of his." The slight quaver of my voice as I spoke Frank's name gave me away.

Jamie put down the flask and came toward me. Stooping purposefully, he picked me up and cradled me against his chest. The smell of the gardens of Versailles rose sharp and fresh from the folds of his shirt. He kissed the top of my head and turned toward the bed.

"Come lay your head, Claire," he said quietly. "It's been a long day for us both."

I had been afraid that the encounter with Alexander Randall would set Jamie dreaming again. It did not happen often, but now and again, I would feel him wake beside me, body tensed in sudden battle. He would lurch out of bed then, and spend the night by the window as though it offered escape, refusing any form of solace or interference. And by the morning, Jack Randall and the other demons of the dark hours had been forced back into their box, battened down and held fast by the steel bands of Jamie's will, and all was well again.

But Jamie fell asleep quickly, and the stresses of the day had already fled from his face, leaving it peaceful and smooth by the time I put out the candle.

It was bliss to lie unmoving, with the warmth growing about my cold limbs, the myriad small aches of back and neck and knees fading into the softness of oncoming sleep. But my mind, released from watchfulness, replayed a thousand times that scene outside the palace—a quick glimpse of a dark head and a high brow, close-set ears and a fine-edged jaw—that first harsh flash of mistaken recognition, which struck my heart with a blow of joy and anguish. Frank, I had thought. Frank. And it was Frank's face I saw as I sank into sleep.

The lecture room was one of those at London University; ancient timbered ceiling and modern floors, lino scuffed by restless feet. The seats were the old smooth benches; new desks were saved for the science lectures. History could make do with sixty-year-old scarred wood; after all, the subject was fixed and would not change—why should its accommodation?

"Objects of *vertu,*" Frank's voice said, "and objects of use." His long fingers touched the rim of a silver candlestick, and the sun from the window sparked from the metal, as though his touch were electric.

The objects, all borrowed from the collections of the British Museum, were lined up along the edge of the table, close enough for the students in the front row to see the tiny cracks in the yellowed ivory of the French counter-box, and the stains of tobacco smoked long ago that browned the edges of the white clay pipe. An English gold-mounted scent bottle, a gilt-bronze inkstand with gadrooned lid, a cracked horn spoon, and a small marble clock topped with two swans drinking.

And behind the row of objects, a row of painted miniatures, laid flat on the table, features obscured by the light reflecting off their surfaces.

Frank's dark head bent over the objects, absorbed. The afternoon sun picked up a stray reddish gleam in his hair. He lifted the clay pipe, cupped one-handed like an eggshell.

"For some periods of history," he said, "we have history itself; the written testimony of the people who lived then. For others, we have only the objects of the period, to show us how men lived."

He put the pipe to his mouth and pursed his lips around the stem, puffing out his cheeks, brows raised comically. There was a muffled giggle from the audience, and he smiled and laid the pipe down.

"The art, and the objects of *vertu*"—he waved a hand over the glittering array—"these are what we most often see, the decorations of a society. And why not?" He picked an intelligent-looking brown-haired boy to address. An accomplished lecturer's trick; pick one member of the audience to talk to as though you were alone with him. A moment later, shift to another. And every-one in the room will feel the focus of your remarks.

"These are pretty things, after all." A finger's touch set the swans on the clock revolving, curved necks stately in twofold procession. "Worth preserving. But who'd bother keeping an old, patched tea cozy, or a worn-out automobile-tire?" A pretty blonde in glasses this time, who smiled and tittered briefly in response.

"But it's the useful objects, the things that aren't noted in documents, which are used and broken and discarded without a second thought, that tell you how the common man lived. The numbers of these pipes, for example, tell us something about the frequency and types of tobacco use among the classes of society, from high"—a finger tap on the lid of the enameled snuffbox—"to low." The finger moved to stroke the long, straight pipestem with affectionate familiarity.

Now a middle-aged woman, scribbling frantically to catch every word, hardly aware of the singular regard upon her. The lines creased beside smiling hazel eyes.

"You needn't take down *everything*, Miss Smith," he chided. "It's an hour's lecture, after all—your pencil will never last."

The woman blushed and dropped her pencil, but smiled shyly in answer to the friendly grin on Frank's lean, dark face. He had them now, everyone warmed by the glow of good humor, attention attracted by the small flashes of gilt and glitter. Now they would follow him without flagging or complaint, along the path of logic and into the thickets of discussion. A certain tenseness left his neck as he felt the students' attention settle and fix on him.

"The best witness to history is the man—or woman"—a nod to the pretty blonde—"who's lived it, right?" He smiled and picked up the cracked horn spoon. "Well, perhaps. After all, it's human nature to put the best face on things when you know someone will read what you've written. People tend to concentrate on the things they think important, and often enough, they tidy it up a bit for public consumption. It's rare to find a Pepys who records with equal interest the details of a Royal procession, and the number of times each night that he's obliged to use his chamber pot."

The laugh this time was general, and he relaxed, leaning casually back against the table, gesturing with the spoon.

"Similarly, the lovely objects, the artful artifacts, are the ones most often preserved. But the chamber pots and the spoons and the cheap clay pipes can tell us as much or more about the people who used them.

"And what about those people? We think of historical persons as something different than ourselves, sometimes halfway mythological. But someone played games with this"—the slender index finger stroked the counter-box—"a lady used this"—nudged the scent bottle—"dabbing scent behind her ears, on her wrists . . . where else do you ladies dab scent?" Lifting his head suddenly, he smiled at the plump blond girl in the front row, who blushed, giggled, and touched herself demurely just above the V of her blouse.

"Ah, yes. Just there. Well, so did the lady who owned this."

Still smiling at the girl, he unstoppered the scent bottle and passed it gently under his nose.

"What is it, Professor? Arpège?" Not so shy, this student; dark-haired, like Frank, with gray eyes that held more than a hint of flirtation.

He closed his eyes and inhaled deeply, nostrils flaring over the mouth of the bottle.

"No. It's L'Heure Bleu. My favorite."

He turned back to the table, hair falling over his brow in concentration as his hand hovered over the row of miniatures.

"And then there's a special class of objects—portraits. A bit of art, and at the same time, as much as we can see of the people themselves. But how real are they to us?"

He lifted a tiny oval and turned it to face the class, reading from the small gummed label affixed to its back.

"A Lady, by Nathaniel Plimer, signed with initials and dated 1786, with curled brown hair piled high, wearing a pink dress and a ruffle-collared che-mise, cloud and sky background." He held up a square beside it.

"A Gentleman, by Horace Hone, signed with monogram and dated 1780, with powdered hair *en queue,* wearing a brown coat, blue waistcoat, lawn jabot, and an Order, possibly the Most Honorable Order of the Bath."

The miniature showed a round-faced man, mouth rosily pursed in the formal pose of eighteenth-century portraits.

"The artists we know," he said, laying the portrait down. "They signed their work, or they left clues to their identity in the techniques and the subjects they used. But the people they painted? We see them, and yet we know nothing of them. The strange hairstyles, the odd clothes—they don't seem people that you'd know, do they? And the way so many artists painted them, the faces are all alike; pudding-faced and pale, most of them, and not a lot more you can say about them. Here and there, one stands out. . . ." Hand hovering over the row, he selected another oval.

"A Gentleman . . ."

He held up the miniature, and Jamie's blue eyes blazed out under the fiery thatch of his hair, combed for once, braided and ribboned into an unaccus-tomed formal order. The knife-edged nose was bold above the lace of his stock, and the long mouth seemed about to speak, half-curled at one corner.

"But they *were* real people," Frank's voice insisted. "They did much the same things you do—give or take a few small details like going to the pictures or driving down the motorway"—there were appreciative titters amongst the class—"but they cared about their children, they loved their husbands or wives . . . well, sometimes they did . . ." More laughter.

"A Lady," he said softly, cradling the last of the portraits in his palm, shielding it for the moment. "With brown hair curling luxuriantly to her shoul-ders, and a necklace of pearls. Undated. The artist unknown."

It was a mirror, not a miniature. My cheeks were flushed, and my lips trembled as Frank's finger gently traced the edge of my jaw, the graceful line of my neck. The tears welled in my eyes and spilled down my cheeks as I heard his voice, still lecturing, as he laid down the miniature, and I stared upward at the timbered ceiling.

"Undated. Unknown. But once . . . once, she was real."

I was having trouble breathing, and thought at first that I was being smothered by the glass over the miniature. But the material pressing on my nose was soft and damp, and I twisted my head away and came awake, feeling the linen pillow wet with tears beneath my cheek. Jamie's hand was large and warm on my shoulder, gently shaking me.

"Hush, lassie. Hush! You're but dreaming—I'm here."

I turned my face into the warmth of his naked shoulder, feeling the tears slick between cheek and skin. I clung tightly to his solidness, and the small night sounds of the Paris house came slowly to my ears, bringing me back to the life that was mine.

"I'm sorry," I whispered. "I was dreaming about . . . about . . ."

He patted my back, and reached under the pillow for a handkerchief.

"I know. Ye were calling his name." He sounded resigned.

I laid my head back on his shoulder. He smelled warm and rumpled, his own sleepy scent blending with the smell of the down-filled quilt and the clean linen sheets.

"I'm sorry," I said again.

He snorted briefly, not quite a laugh.

"Well, I'll no say I'm not wicked jealous of the man," he said ruefully, "because I am. But I can hardly grudge him your dreams. Or your tears." His finger gently traced the wet track down one cheek, then blotted it with the handkerchief.

"You don't?"

His smile in the dimness was lopsided.

"No. Ye loved him. I canna hold it against either of you that ye mourn him. And it gives me some comfort to know . . ." He hesitated, and I reached up to smooth the rumpled hair off his face.

"To know what?"

"That should the need come, you might mourn for me that way," he said softly.

I pressed my face fiercely into his chest, so my words were muffled.

"I *won't* mourn you, because I won't have to. I won't lose you, I won't!" A thought struck me, and I looked up at him, the faint roughness of his beard stubble a shadow on his face.

"You aren't afraid I would go back, are you? You don't think that because I . . . think of Frank. . . ."

"No." His voice was quick and soft, a response fast as the possessive tightening of his arms around me.

"No," he said again, more softly. "We are bound, you and I, and nothing on this earth shall part me from you." One large hand rose to stroke my hair. "D'ye mind the blood vow that I swore ye when we wed?"

"Yes, I think so. 'Blood of my blood, bone of my bone . . .' "

"I give ye my body, that we may be one," he finished. "Aye, and I have kept that vow, Sassenach, and so have you." He turned me slightly, and one hand cupped itself gently over the tiny swell of my stomach.

"Blood of my blood," he whispered, "and bone of my bone. You carry me within ye, Claire, and ye canna leave me now, no matter what happens. You are mine, always, if ye will it or no, if ye want me or nay. Mine, and I wilna let ye go."

I put a hand over his, pressing it against me.

"No," I said softly, "nor can you leave me."

"No," he said, half-smiling. "For I have kept the last of the vow as well." He clasped both hands about me, and bowed his head on my shoulder, so I could feel the warm breath of the words upon my ear, whispered to the dark.

"For I give ye my spirit, 'til our life shall be done."

11

Useful Occupations

"Who is that peculiar little man?" I asked Jamie curiously. The man in question was making his way slowly through the groups of guests gathered in the main salon of the de Rohans' house. He would pause a moment, scanning the group with a critical eye, then either shrug a bony shoulder and pass on, or suddenly step in close to a man or woman, hold something to their face and issue some sort of command. Whatever he was doing, his actions appeared to be the occasion of considerable hilarity.

Before Jamie could answer, the man, a small, wizened specimen in gray serge, spotted us, and his face lit up. He swooped down on Jamie like a tiny bird of prey suddenly descending upon a large and startled rabbit.

"Sing," he commanded.

"Eh?" Jamie blinked down at the little figure in astonishment.

"I said 'Sing,'" answered the man, patiently. He prodded Jamie admiringly in the chest. "With a resonating cavity like that, you should have a wonderful volume."

"Oh, he has volume," I said, amused. "You can hear him across three squares of the city when he's roused."

Jamie shot me a dirty look. The little man was circling him, measuring the breadth of his back and tapping on him like a woodpecker sampling a prime tree.

"I can't sing," he protested.

"Nonsense, nonsense. Of course you can. A nice, deep baritone, too," the little man murmured approvingly. "Excellent. Just what we need. Here, a bit of help for you. Try to match this tone."

Deftly whipping a small tuning fork from his pocket, he struck it smartly against a pillar and held it next to Jamie's left ear.

Jamie rolled his eyes heavenward, but shrugged and obligingly sang a note. The little man jerked back as though he'd been shot.

"No," he said disbelievingly.

"I'm afraid so," I said sympathetically. "He's right, you know. He really *can't* sing."

The little man squinted accusingly at Jamie, then struck his fork once more and held it out invitingly.

"Once more," he coaxed. "Just listen to it, and let the same sound come out."

Patient as ever, Jamie listened carefully to the "A" of the fork, and sang again, producing a sound wedged somewhere in the crack between E-flat and D-sharp.

"Not possible," said the little man, looking thoroughly disillusioned. "No one could be that dissonant, even on purpose."

"*I* can," said Jamie cheerfully, and bowed politely to the little man. We had by now begun to collect a small crowd of interested onlookers. Louise de Rohan was a great hostess, and her salons attracted the cream of Parisian society.

"Yes, he can," I assured our visitor. "He's tone-deaf, you see."

"Yes, I do see," the little man said, looking thoroughly depressed. Then he began to eye me speculatively.

"Not me!" I said, laughing.

"You surely aren't tone-deaf as well, Madame?" Eyes glittering like a snake slithering toward a paralyzed bird, the little man began to move toward me, tuning fork twitching like the flicking tongue of a viper.

"Wait a minute," I said, holding out a repressive hand. "Just who *are* you?"

"This is Herr Johannes Gerstmann, Sassenach." Looking amused, Jamie bowed again to the little man. "The King's singing-master. May I present you to my wife, Lady Broch Tuarach, Herr Gerstmann?" Trust Jamie to know every last member of the Court, no matter how insignificant.

Johannes Gerstmann. Well, that accounted for the faint accent I had detected under the formality of Court French. German, I wondered, or Austrian?

"I am assembling a small impromptu chorus," the little singing-master explained. "The voices need not be trained, but they must be strong and true." He cast a glance of disillusionment at Jamie, who merely grinned in response. He took the tuning fork from Herr Gerstmann and held it inquiringly in my direction.

"Oh, all right," I said, and sang.

Whatever he heard appeared to encourage Herr Gerstmann, for he put away the tuning fork and peered at me interestedly. His wig was a trifle too big, and tended to slide forward when he nodded. He did so now, then pushed the wig carelessly back, and said "Excellent tone, Madame! Really very nice, very nice indeed. Are you acquainted perhaps with *Le Papillon*?" He hummed a few bars.

"Well, I've heard it at least," I replied cautiously. "Um, the melody, I mean; I don't know the words."

"Ah! No difficulty, Madame. The chorus is simplicity; like this . . ."

My arm trapped in the singing-master's grip, I found myself being ineluctably drawn away toward the sound of harpsichord music in a distant room, Herr Gerstmann humming in my ear like a demented bumblebee.

I cast a helpless glance back at Jamie, who merely grinned and raised his cup of sorbet in a farewell salute before turning to take up a conversation with Monsieur Duverney the younger, the son of the Minister of Finance.

The Rohans' house—if you could use a mere word like "house" in description of such a place—was alight with lanterns strung through the back garden and edging the terrace. As Herr Gerstmann towed me through the corridors, I could see servants hurrying in and out of the supper rooms, laying linen and silver for the dining that would take place later. Most "salons" were small, intimate affairs, but the Princesse Louise de La Tour de Rohan was an expansive personality.

I had met the Princesse a week before, at another evening party, and had found her something of a surprise. Plump and rather plain, she had a round face with a small round chin, pale lashless blue eyes, and a star-shaped false beauty mark that did very little to fulfill its function in life. So this was the lady who enticed Prince Charles into ignoring the dictates of propriety? I thought, curtsying in the receiving line.

Still, she had an air of lively animation about her that was quite attractive, and a lovely soft pink mouth. Her mouth was the most animated part of her, in fact.

"But I am charmed!" she had exclaimed, grabbing my hand as I was presented to her. "How wonderful to meet you at last! My husband and my father have both sung the praises of milord Broch Tuarach unendingly, but of his delightful wife they have said nothing. I am enchanted beyond measure by your coming, my dear, sweet lady—must I really say Broch Tuarach, or won't it do if I only say Lady Tuarach? I'm not sure I could remember all of it, but one word, surely, even if such a strange-sounding word—is it Scottish? How enchanting!"

In fact, Broch Tuarach meant "the north-facing tower," but if she wanted to call me "Lady North-facing," it was all right with me. In the event, she quickly gave up trying to remember "Tuarach," and had since called me only *"ma chère Claire."*

Louise herself was with the group of singers in the music room, fluttering plumply from one to another, talking and laughing. When she saw me, she dashed across the room as fast as her draperies would allow, her plain face alight with animation.

"Ma chère Claire!" she exclaimed, ruthlessly commandeering me from Herr Gerstmann. "You are just in time! Come, you must talk to this silly English child for me."

The "silly English child" was in fact very young; a girl of not more than fifteen, with dark, shiny ringlets, and cheeks flushed so hotly with embarrassment that she reminded me of a brilliant poppy. In fact, it was the cheeks that recalled her to me; the girl I had glimpsed in the garden at Versailles, just before the unsettling appearance of Alexander Randall.

"Madame Fraser is English, too," Louise was explaining to the girl. "She will soon make you feel at home. She's shy," Louise explained, turning to me without pausing to draw breath. "Talk to her; persuade her to sing with us. She has a delightful voice, I am assured. There, *mes enfants,* enjoy yourselves!" And with a pat of benediction, she was off to the other side of the room, exclaiming, cajoling, marveling at a new arrival's gown, pausing to fondle the overweight youth who sat at the harpsichord, twisting ringlets of his hair around her finger as she chattered to the Duc di Castellotti.

"Makes you rather tired just to watch her, doesn't it?" I said in English, smiling at the girl. A tiny smile appeared on her own lips and she bobbed her head briefly, but didn't speak. I thought this must all be rather overwhelming; Louise's parties tended to make my own head spin, and the little poppy girl could scarcely be out of the schoolroom.

"I'm Claire Fraser," I said, "but Louise didn't remember to tell me your name." I paused invitingly, but she didn't reply. Her face got redder and redder, lips pressed tight together, and her fists clenched at her sides. I was a trifle alarmed at her appearance, but she finally summoned the will to speak. She took a deep breath, and raised her chin like one about to mount the scaffold.

"M-m-my-name is . . . M-M-M," she began, and at once I understood her silence and her painful shyness. She closed her eyes, biting her lip savagely, then opened her eyes and gamely had another try. "M-M-Mary Hawkins," she managed at last. "I d-d-don't sing," she added defiantly.

If I had found her interesting before, I was fascinated now. So this was Silas Hawkins's niece, the baronet's daughter, the intended fiancée of the Vicomte Marigny! It seemed a considerable weight of male expectation for such a young girl to bear. I glanced around to see whether the Vicomte was in evidence, and was relieved to find that he wasn't.

"Don't worry about it," I said, stepping in front of her, to shield her from the waves of people now filling the music room. "You needn't talk if you don't want to. Though perhaps you should try to sing," I said, struck by a thought. "I knew a physician once who specialized in the treatment of stammering; he said that people who stammer don't do it when they sing."

Mary Hawkins's eyes grew wide with astonishment at this. I looked around and saw a nearby alcove, curtained to hide a cozy bench.

"Here," I said, taking her by the hand. "You can sit in here, so you don't have to talk to people. If you want to sing, you can come out when we start; if not, just stay in here 'til the party's over." She stared at me for a minute, then gave me a sudden blinding smile of gratitude, and ducked into the alcove.

I loitered outside, to prevent any nosy servants from disturbing her hiding place, chatting with passersby.

"How lovely you look tonight, *ma chère!*" It was Madame de Ramage, one of the Queen's ladies. An older, dignified woman, she had come to supper in the Rue Tremoulins once or twice. She embraced me warmly, then looked around to be sure that we were unobserved.

"I had hoped to see you here, my dear," she said, leaning a bit closer and lowering her voice. "I wished to advise you to take care concerning the Comte St. Germain."

Half-turning in the direction of her gaze, I saw the lean-faced man from the docks of Le Havre, entering the music room with a younger, elegantly dressed woman on his arm. He hadn't seen me, apparently, and I hastily turned back to Madame de Remage.

"What . . . has he . . . I mean . . ." I could feel myself flushing still more deeply, rattled by the appearance of the saturnine Comte.

"Well, yes, he has been heard to speak of you," Madame de Ramage said, kindly helping me out of my confusion. "I gather that there was some small difficulty in Le Havre?"

"Something of the kind," I said. "All I did was to recognize a case of smallpox, but it resulted in the destruction of his ship, and . . . he wasn't pleased about it," I concluded weakly.

"Ah, so that was it." Madame de Ramage looked pleased. I imagined having the inside story, so to speak, would give her an advantage in the trade of gossip and information that was the commerce of Parisian social life.

"He has been going about telling people that he believes you to be a witch," she said, smiling and waving at a friend across the room. "A fine story! Oh, no one believes it," she assured me. "Everyone knows that if anyone is mixed up in such matters, it is Monsieur le Comte himself."

"Really?" I wanted to ask just what she meant by this, but just then Herr Gerstmann bustled up, clapping his hands as though shooing a flock of hens.

"Come, come, mesdames!" he said. "We are all complete; the singing commences!"

As the chorale hastily assembled near the harpsichord, I looked back toward the alcove where I had left Mary Hawkins. I thought I saw the curtain twitch, but wasn't sure. And as the music began, and the joined voices rose, I thought I heard a clear, high soprano from the direction of the alcove—but again, I wasn't sure.

"Verra nice, Sassenach," Jamie said when I rejoined him, flushed and breathless, after the singing. He grinned down at me and patted my shoulder.

"How would you know?" I said, accepting a glass of wine-punch from a passing servant. "You can't tell one song from another."

"Well, ye were loud, anyway," he said, unperturbed. "I could hear every word." I felt him stiffen slightly beside me, and turned to see what—or whom —he was looking at.

The woman who had just entered was tiny, scarcely as high as Jamie's lowest rib, with hands and feet like a doll's, and brows delicate as Chinese tracery, over eyes the deep black of sloes. She advanced with a step that mocked its own lightness, so she looked as though she were dancing just above the ground.

"There's Annalise de Marillac," I said, admiring her. "Doesn't she look lovely?"

"Oh, aye." Something in his voice made me glance sharply upward. A faint pink tinged the tips of his ears.

"And here I thought you spent your years in France fighting, not making romantic conquests," I said tartly.

To my surprise, he laughed at this. Catching the sound, the woman turned toward us. A brilliant smile lit her face as she saw Jamie looming among the crowd. She turned as though to come in our direction, but was distracted by a gentleman, wigged and resplendent in lavender satin, who laid an importuning hand on her fragile arm. She flicked her fan charmingly at Jamie in a gesture of regretful coquetry before devoting her attention to her new companion.

"What's so funny?" I asked, seeing him still grinning broadly after the lady's gently oscillating lace skirts.

He snapped suddenly back to an awareness of my presence, and smiled down at me.

"Oh, nothing, Sassenach. Only what ye said about fighting. I fought my first duel—well, the only one, in fact—over Annalise de Marillac. When I was eighteen."

His tone was mildly dreamy, watching the sleek, dark head bob away through the crowd, surrounded wherever it went by white clusters of wigs and powdered hair, with here and there a fashionably pink-tinged peruke for variety.

"A duel? With whom?" I asked, glancing around warily for any male attachments to the China doll who might feel inclined to follow up an old quarrel.

"Och, he isna here," Jamie said, catching and correctly interpreting my glance. "He's dead."

"You *killed* him?" Agitated, I spoke rather louder than intended. As a few nearby heads turned curiously in our direction, Jamie took me by the elbow and steered me hastily toward the nearest French doors.

"Mind your voice, Sassenach," he said, mildly enough. "No, I didna kill him. Wanted to," he added ruefully, "but didn't. He died two years ago, of the morbid sore throat. Jared told me."

He guided me down one of the garden paths, lit by lantern-bearing servants, who stood like bollards at five-yard intervals from the terrace to the

fountain at the bottom of the path. In the midst of a big reflecting pool, four
dolphins sprayed sheets of water over an annoyed-looking Triton in the center,
who brandished a trident rather ineffectually at them.

"Well, don't keep me in suspense," I urged as we passed out of hearing of
the groups on the terrace. "What happened?"

"All right, then," he said, resigned. "Well, ye will have observed that
Annalise is rather pretty?"

"Oh, really? Well, perhaps, now that you mention it, I can see something
of the kind," I answered sweetly, provoking a sudden sharp look, followed by a
lopsided smile.

"Aye. Well, I wasna the only young gallant in Paris to be of the same
opinion, nor the only one to lose his head over her, either. Went about in a
daze, tripping over my feet. Waited in the street, in hopes of seeing her come
out of her house to the carriage. Forgot to eat, even; Jared said my coat hung
on me like a scarecrow's, and the state of my hair didna much help the resemblance." His hand went absently to his head, patting the immaculate queue
that lay clubbed tight against his neck, bound with blue ribbon.

"Forgot to eat? Christ, you *did* have it bad," I remarked.

He chuckled. "Oh, aye. And still worse when she began to flirt wi' Charles
Gauloise. Mind ye," he added fairly, "she flirted with everyone—that was all
right—but she chose him for her supper partner ower-often for my taste, and
danced with him too much at the parties, and . . . well, the long and the
short of it, Sassenach, is that I caught him kissing her in the moonlight on her
father's terrace one night, and challenged him."

By this time, we had reached the fountain in our promenade. Jamie drew
to a stop and we sat on the rim of the fountain, upwind of the spray from the
puff-lipped dolphins. Jamie drew a hand through the dark water and lifted it
dripping, abstractedly watching the silver drops run down his fingers.

"Dueling was illegal in Paris then—as it is now. But there were places;
there always are. It was his to choose, and he picked a spot in the Bois de
Boulogne. Close by the road of the Seven Saints, but hidden by a screen of
oaks. The choice of weapon was his, too. I expected pistols, but he chose
swords."

"Why would he do that? You must have had a six-inch reach on him—or
more." I was no expert, but was perforce learning a small bit about the strategy
and tactics of swordfighting; Jamie and Murtagh took each other on every two
or three days to keep in practice, clashing and parrying and lunging up and
down the garden, to the untrammeled delight of the servants, male and female
alike, who all surged out onto the balconies to watch.

"Why did he choose smallswords? Because he was bloody good with one.
Also, I suspected he thought I might kill him accidentally with a pistol, while he
knew I'd be satisfied only to draw blood with a blade. I didna mean to kill him,

ye ken," he explained. "Only to humiliate him. And he knew it. No fool, was our Charles," he said, ruefully shaking his head.

The mist from the fountain was making ringlets escape from my coiffure, to curl around my face. I brushed back a wisp of hair, asking, "And did you humiliate him?"

"Well, I wounded him, at least." I was surprised to hear a small note of satisfaction in his voice, and raised an eyebrow at him. "He'd learnt his craft from LeJeune, one of the best swordmasters in France." Jamie explained. "Like fighting a damn flea, it was, and I fought him right-handed, too." He pushed a hand through his hair once more, as though checking the binding.

"My hair came loose, midway through," he said. "The thong holding it broke, and the wind was blowing it into my eyes, so all I could see was the wee white shape of Charles in his shirt, darting to and fro like a minnow. And that's how I got him, finally—the way ye spear a fish with a dirk." He snorted through his nose.

"He let out a skelloch as though I'd run him through, though I knew I'd but pinked him in one arm. I got the hair out of my face at last and looked beyond him to see Annalise standing there at the edge of the clearing, wi' her eyes wide and dark as yon pool." He gestured out over the silver-black surface beside us.

"So I sheathed my blade and smoothed back my hair, and stood there—half-expectin' her to come and throw herself into my arms, I suppose."

"Um," I said, delicately. "I gather she didn't?"

"Well, I didna ken anything about women then, did I?" he demanded. "No, she came and threw herself on *him,* of course." He made a Scottish noise deep in his throat, one of self-derision and humorous disgust. "Married him a month later, I heard."

"Aye, well." He shrugged suddenly, with a rueful smile. "So my heart was broken. Went home to Scotland and moped about for weeks, until my father lost patience wi' me." He laughed. "I even thought of turning monk over it. Said to my father over supper one night as I thought perhaps in the spring I'd go across to the Abbey and become a novice."

I laughed at the thought. "Well, you'd have no difficulty with the vow of poverty; chastity and obedience might come a bit harder. What did your father say?"

He grinned, teeth white in a dark face. "He was eating brose. He laid down the spoon and looked at me for a moment. Then he sighed and shook his head, and said, 'It's been a long day, Jamie.' Then he picked up the spoon again and went back to his supper, and I never said another word about it."

He looked up the slope to the terrace, where those not dancing strolled to and fro, cooling off between dances, sipping wine and flirting behind fans. He sighed nostalgically.

"Aye, a verra pretty lass, Annalise de Marillac. Graceful as the wind, and so small that ye wanted to tuck her inside your shirt and carry her like a kitten."

I was silent, listening to the faint music from the open doors above, as I contemplated the gleaming satin slipper that encased my size-nine foot.

After a moment, Jamie became aware of my silence.

"What is it, Sassenach?" he asked, laying a hand on my arm.

"Oh, nothing," I said with a sigh. "Only thinking that I rather doubt anyone will ever describe me as 'graceful as the wind.' "

"Ah." His head was half-turned, the long, straight nose and firm chin lighted from behind by the glow of the nearest lantern. I could see the half-smile on his lips as he turned back toward me.

"Well, I'll tell ye, Sassenach, 'graceful' is possibly not the first word that springs to mind at thought of you." He slipped an arm behind me, one hand large and warm around my silk-clad shoulder.

"But I talk to you as I talk to my own soul," he said, turning me to face him. He reached up and cupped my cheek, fingers light on my temple.

"And, Sassenach," he whispered, "your face is my heart."

It was the shifting of the wind, several minutes later, that parted us at last with a fine spray from the fountain. We broke apart and rose hastily, laughing at the sudden chill of the water. Jamie inclined his head inquiringly toward the terrace, and I took his arm, nodding.

"So," I observed, as we made our way slowly up the wide steps to the ballroom, "you've learnt a bit more about women now, I see."

He laughed, low and deep, tightening his grasp on my waist.

"The most important thing I've learned about women, Sassenach, is which one to choose." He stepped away, bowing to me, and gesturing through the open doors to the brilliant scene inside. "May I have this dance, milady?"

I spent the next afternoon at the d'Arbanvilles', where I met the King's singing-master once again. This time, we found time for a conversation, which I recounted to Jamie after supper.

"You what?" Jamie squinted at me, as though he suspected me of pulling some practical joke.

"I said, Herr Gerstmann suggested that I might be interested in meeting a friend of his. Mother Hildegarde is in charge of L'Hôpital des Anges—you know, the charity hospital down near the cathedral."

"I know where it is." His voice was marked by a general lack of enthusiasm.

"He had a sore throat, and that led to me telling him what to take for it, and a bit about medicines in general, and how I was interested in diseases and, well, you know how one thing leads to another."

"With you, it customarily does," he agreed, sounding distinctly cynical. I ignored his tone and went on.

"So, I'm going to go to the hospital tomorrow." I stretched on tiptoe to reach down my medicine box from its shelf. "Maybe I won't take it along with me the first time," I said, scanning the contents meditatively. "It might seem too pushing. Do you think?"

"Pushing?" He sounded stunned. "Are ye meaning to visit the place, or move into it?"

"Er, well," I said. I took a deep breath. "I, er, thought perhaps I could work there regularly. Herr Gerstmann says that all the physicians and healers who go there donate their time. Most of them don't turn up every day, but I have plenty of time, and I could—"

"Plenty of time?"

"Stop repeating everything I say," I said. "Yes, plenty of time. I know it's important to go to salons and supper parties and all that, but it doesn't take all day—at least it needn't. I could—"

"Sassenach, you're with child! Ye dinna mean to go out to nurse beggars and criminals?" He sounded rather helpless now, as though wondering how to deal with someone who had suddenly gone mad in front of him.

"I hadn't forgotten," I assured him. I pressed my hands against my belly, squinting down.

"It isn't really noticeable yet; with a loose gown I can get away with it for a time. And there's nothing wrong with me except the morning sickness; no reason why I shouldn't work for some months yet."

"No reason, except I wilna have ye doing it!" Expecting no company this evening, he had taken off his stock and opened his collar when he came home. I could see the tide of dusky red advancing up his throat.

"Jamie," I said, striving for reasonableness. "You know what I am."

"You're my wife!"

"Well, that, too." I flicked the idea aside with my fingers. "I'm a nurse, Jamie. A healer. You have reason to know it."

He flushed hotly. "Aye, I do. And because ye've mended me when I'm wounded, I should think it right for ye to tend beggars and prostitutes? Sassenach, do ye no ken the sort of people that L'Hôpital des Anges takes in?" He looked pleadingly at me, as though expecting me to return to my senses any minute.

"What difference does that make?"

He looked wildly around the room, imploring witness from the portrait over the mantelpiece as to my unreasonableness.

"You could catch a filthy disease, for God's sake! D'ye have no regard for your child, even if ye have none for me?"

Reasonableness was seeming a less desirable goal by the moment.

"Of course I have! What kind of careless, irresponsible person do you think I am?"

"The kind who would abandon her husband to go and play with scum in the gutter!" he snapped. "Since you ask." He ran a big hand through his hair, making it stick up at the crown.

"Abandon you? Since when is it abandoning you to suggest really doing something, instead of rotting away in the d'Arbanvilles' salon, watching Louise de Rohan stuff herself with pastry, and listening to bad poetry and worse music? I want to be useful!"

"Taking care of your own household isna useful? Being married to me isna useful?" The lacing round his hair broke under the stress, and the thick locks fluffed out like a flaming halo. He glared down his nose at me like an avenging angel.

"Sauce for the gander," I retorted coldly. "Is being married to *me* sufficient occupation for *you*? I don't notice you hanging round the house all day, adoring me. And as for the household, bosh."

"Bosh? What's bosh?" he demanded.

"Stuff and nonsense. Rot. Horsefeathers. In other words, don't be ridiculous. Madame Vionnet does everything, and does it several dozen times better than I could."

This was so patently true that it stopped him for a moment. He glared down at me, jaw working.

"Oh, aye? And if I forbid ye to go?"

This stopped me for a moment. I drew myself up and looked him up and down. His eyes were the color of rain-dark slate, the wide, generous mouth clamped in a straight line. Shoulders broad and back erect, arms folded across his chest like a cast-iron statue, "forbidding" was precisely the word that best described him.

"*Do* you forbid me?" The tension crackled between us. I wanted to blink, but wouldn't give him the satisfaction of breaking off my own steely gaze. What *would* I do if he forbade me to go? Alternatives raced through my mind, everything from planting the ivory letter-opener between his ribs to burning down the house with him in it. The only idea I rejected absolutely was that of giving in.

He paused, and drew a deep breath before speaking. His hands were curled into fists at his sides, and he uncurled them with conscious effort.

"No," he said. "No, I dinna forbid ye." His voice shook slightly with the effort to control it. "But if I asked you?"

I looked down then, and stared at his reflection in the polished tabletop. At first, the idea of visiting L'Hôpital des Anges had seemed merely an interesting idea, an attractive alternative to the endless gossip and petty intrigues of Parisian society. But now . . . I could feel the muscles of my arms swell as I clenched my own fists. I didn't just *want* to work again; I *needed* to.

"I don't know," I said at last.

He took a deep breath, and let it out slowly.

"Will ye think about it, Claire?" I could feel his eyes on me. After what seemed a long time, I nodded.

"I'll think about it."

"Good." His tension broken, he turned restlessly away. He wandered round the drawing room, picking up small objects and putting them down at random, finally coming to roost by the bookshelf, where he leaned, staring unseeingly at the leather-bound titles. I came tentatively up beside him, and laid a hand on his arm.

"Jamie, I didn't mean to upset you."

He glanced down at me and gave me a sidelong smile.

"Aye, well. I didna mean to fight wi' you, either, Sassenach. I'm short-tempered and ower-touchy, I expect." He patted my hand in apology, then moved aside, to stand looking down at his desk.

"You've been working hard," I said soothingly, following him.

"It's not that." He shook his head, and reached out to flip open the pages of the huge ledger that lay in the center of the desk.

"The wine business; that's all right. It's a great deal of work, aye, but I dinna mind it. It's the other." He gestured at a small stack of letters, held down by an alabaster paperweight. One of Jared's, it was carved in the shape of a white rose—the Stuarts' emblem. The letters it secured were from Abbot Alexander, from the Earl of Mar, from other prominent Jacobites. All filled with veiled inquiry, misty promises, contradictory expectations.

"I feel as though I'm fighting feathers!" Jamie said, violently. "A real fight, something I could get my hands on, that I could do. But this . . ." He snatched up the handful of letters from the desk, and tossed them into the air. The room was drafty, and the papers zigzagged wildly, sliding under furniture and fluttering on the carpet.

"There's nothing to get hold of," he said helplessly. "I can talk to a thousand people, write a hundred letters, drink wi' Charles 'til I'm blind, and never know if I'm getting on or not."

I let the scattered letters lie; one of the maids could retrieve them later.

"Jamie," I said softly. "We can't do anything but try."

He smiled faintly, hands braced on the desk. "Aye. I'm glad you said 'we,' Sassenach. I do feel verra much alone with it all sometimes."

I put my arms around his waist and laid my face against his back.

"You know I wouldn't leave you alone with it," I said. "I got you into it in the first place, after all."

I could feel the small vibration of a laugh under my cheek.

"Aye, you did. I wilna hold it against ye, Sassenach." He turned, leaned down, and kissed me lightly on the forehead. "You look tired, *mo duinne*. Go up to bed, now. I've a bit more work to do, but I'll join ye soon."

"All right." I *was* tired tonight, though the chronic sleepiness of early pregnancy was giving way to new energy; I was beginning to feel alert in the daytime, brimming with the urge to be active.

I paused at the door on my way out. He was still standing by the desk, staring down into the pages of the open ledger.

"Jamie?" I said.

"Aye?"

"The hospital—I said I'd think about it. You think, too, hm?"

He turned his head, one brow sharply arched. Then he smiled, and nodded briefly.

"I'll come to ye soon, Sassenach," he said.

It was still sleeting, and tiny particles of frozen rain rattled against the windows and hissed into the fire when the night wind turned to drive them down the flue. The wind was high, and it moaned and grumbled among the chimneys, making the bedroom seem all the cozier by contrast. The bed itself was an oasis of warmth and comfort, equipped with goose-down quilts, huge fluffy pillows, and Jamie, faithfully putting out British Thermal Units like an electric storage heater.

His large hand stroked lightly across my stomach, warm through the thin silk of my nightdress.

"No, there. You have to press a little harder." I took his hand and pressed the fingers downward, just above my pubic bone, where the uterus had begun to make itself obvious, a round, hard swelling a little larger than a grapefruit.

"Aye, I feel it," he murmured. "He's really there." A tiny smile of awed delight tugged at the corner of his mouth, and he looked up at me, eyes sparkling. "Can ye feel him move, yet?"

I shook my head. "Not yet. Another month or so, I think, from what your sister Jenny said."

"Mmm," he said, kissing the tiny bulge. "What d'ye think of 'Dalhousie,' Sassenach?"

"What do I think of 'Dalhousie' as *what*?" I inquired.

"Well, as a name," he said. He patted my stomach. "He'll need a name."

"True," I said. "Though what makes you think it's a boy? It might just as easily be a girl."

"Oh? Oh, aye, that's true," he admitted, as though the possibility had just occurred to him. "Still, why not start with the boys' names? We could name him for your uncle who raised you."

"Umm." I frowned at my midsection. Dearly as I had loved my uncle Lamb, I didn't know that I wanted to inflict either "Lambert" or "Quentin" on a helpless infant. "No, I don't think so. On the other hand, I don't think I'd want to name him for one of *your* uncles, either."

Jamie stroked my stomach absently, thinking.

"What was your father's name, Sassenach?" he asked.

I had to think for a moment to remember.

"Henry," I said. "Henry Montmorency Beauchamp. Jamie, I am *not* having a child named 'Montmorency Fraser,' no matter what. I'm not so keen on 'Henry,' either, though it's better than Lambert. How about William?" I suggested. "For your brother?" His older brother, William, had died in late childhood, but had lived long enough for Jamie to remember him with great affection.

His brow was furrowed in thought. "Hmm," he said. "Aye, maybe. Or we could call him . . ."

"James," said a hollow, sepulchral voice from the flue.

"What?" I said, sitting straight up in bed.

"James," said the fireplace, impatiently. "James, James!"

"Sweet bleeding Jesus," said Jamie, staring at the leaping flames on the hearth. I could feel the hair standing up on his forearm, stiff as wire. He sat frozen for a moment; then, a thought occurring to him, he jumped to his feet and went to the dormer window, not bothering to put anything on over his shirt.

He flung up the sash, admitting a blast of frigid air, and thrust his head out into the night. I heard a muffled shout, and then a scrabbling sound across the slates of the roof. Jamie leaned far out, rising on his toes to reach, then backed slowly into the room, rain-dampened and grunting with effort. He dragged with him, arms clasped about his neck, the form of a handsome boy in dark clothing, thoroughly soaked, with a bloodstained cloth wrapped around one hand.

The visitor caught his foot on the sill and landed clumsily, sprawling on the floor. He scrambled up at once, though, and bowed to me, snatching off his slouch hat.

"Madame," he said, in thickly accented French. "I must beg your pardon, I arrive so without ceremony. I intrude, but it is of necessity that I call upon my friend James at such an unsocial hour."

He was a sturdy, good-looking lad, with thick, light-brown hair curling loose upon his shoulders, and a fair face, cheeks flushed red with cold and exertion. His nose was running slightly, and he wiped it with the back of his wrapped hand, wincing slightly as he did so.

Jamie, both eyebrows raised, bowed politely to the visitor.

"My house is at your service, Your Highness," he said, with a glance that took in the general disorder of the visitor's attire. His stock was undone and hung loosely around his neck, half his buttons were done up awry, and the flies of his breeches flopped partially open. I saw Jamie frown slightly at this, and he moved unobtrusively in front of the boy, to screen me from the indelicate sight.

"If I may present my wife, Your Highness?" he said. "Claire, my lady Broch Tuarach. Claire, this is His Highness, Prince Charles, son of King James of Scotland."

"Um, yes," I said. "I'd rather gathered that. Er, good evening, Your Highness." I nodded graciously, pulling the bedclothes up around me. I supposed that under the circumstances, I could dispense with the usual curtsy.

The Prince had taken advantage of Jamie's long-winded introduction to fumble his trousers into better order, and now nodded back at me, full of Royal dignity.

"It is my pleasure, Madame," he said, and bowed once more, making a much more elegant production of it. He straightened and stood turning his hat in his hands, obviously trying to think what to say next. Jamie, standing barelegged in his shirt alongside, glanced from me to Charles, seemingly at an equal loss for words.

"Er . . ." I said, to break the silence. "Have you had an accident, Your Highness?" I nodded at the handkerchief wrapped around his hand, and he glanced down as though noticing it for the first time.

"Yes," he said, "ah . . . no. I mean . . . it is nothing, my lady." He flushed redder, staring at his hand. His manner was odd; something between embarrassment and anger. I could see the stain on the cloth spreading, though, and put my feet out of bed, groping for my dressing gown.

"You'd better let me have a look at it," I said.

The injury, exposed with some reluctance by the Prince, was not serious, but it was unusual.

"That looks like an animal bite," I said incredulously, dabbing at the small semicircle of puncture wounds in the webbing between thumb and forefinger. Prince Charles winced as I squeezed the flesh around it, meaning to cleanse the wound by bleeding before binding it.

"Yes," he said. "A monkey bite. Disgusting, flea-ridden beast!" he burst out. "I told her she must dispose of it. Undoubtedly the animal is diseased!"

I had found my medicine box, and now applied a thin layer of gentian ointment. "I don't think you need worry," I said, intent on my work. "So long as it isn't rabid, that is."

"Rabid?" The Prince went quite pale. "Do you think it could be?" Plainly he had no idea what "rabid" might mean, but wanted no part of it.

"Anything's possible," I said cheerfully. Surprised by his sudden appearance, it was just beginning to dawn on me that it would save everyone a great deal of trouble in the long run, if this young man would succumb gracefully to some quick and deadly disease. Still, I couldn't quite find it in my heart to wish him gangrene or rabies, and I tied up his hand neatly in a fresh linen bandage.

He smiled, bowed again, and thanked me very prettily in a mixture of French and Italian. Still apologizing effusively for his untimely visit, he was towed away by Jamie, now respectably kilted, for a drink downstairs.

Feeling the chill of the room seep through gown and robe, I crawled back into bed and drew the quilts up under my chin. So this was Prince Charles! Bonnie enough, to be sure; at least to look at. He seemed very young—much younger than Jamie, though I knew Jamie was only a year or two older. His Highness did have considerable charm of manner, though, and quite a bit of self-important dignity, despite his disordered dress. Was that really enough to take him to Scotland, at the head of an army of restoration? As I drifted off, I wondered exactly what the heir to the throne of Scotland had been doing, wandering over the Paris rooftops in the middle of the night, with a monkey bite on one hand.

The question was still on my mind when Jamie woke me sometime later by sliding into bed and planting his large, ice-cold feet directly behind my knees.

"Don't scream like that," he said, "you'll wake the servants."

"What in hell was Charles Stuart doing running about the rooftops with monkeys?" I demanded, taking evasive action. "Take those bloody ice cubes off me."

"Visiting his mistress," said Jamie succinctly. "All right, then; stop kicking me." He removed the feet and embraced me, shivering, as I turned to him.

"He has a mistress? Who?" Stimulated by whiffs of cold and scandal, I was quickly waking up.

It's Louise de La Tour," Jamie explained reluctantly, in response to my prodding. His nose looked longer and sharper than usual, with the thick brows drawn together above it. Having a mistress was bad enough, in his Scottish Catholic view, but it was well known that royalty had certain privileges in this regard. The Princesse Louise de La Tour was married, however. And royalty or not, taking a married woman as one's mistress was positively immoral, his cousin Jared's example notwithstanding.

"Ha," I said with satisfaction. "I knew it!"

"He says he's in love with her," he reported tersely, yanking the quilts up over his shoulders. "He insists she loves him too; says she's been faithful only to him for the last three months. Tcha!"

"Well, it's been known to happen," I said, amused. "So he was visiting her? How did he get out on the roof, though? Did he tell you that?"

"Oh, aye. He told me."

Charles, fortified against the night with several glasses of Jared's best aged port, had been quite forthcoming. The strength of true love had been tried severely this evening, according to Charles, by his inamorata's devotion to her pet, a rather ill-tempered monkey that reciprocated His Highness's dislike and had more concrete means of demonstrating its opinions. Snapping his fingers under the monkey's nose in derision, His Highness had suffered first a sharp bite in the hand, and then the sharper bite of his mistress's tongue, exercised in bitter reproach. The couple had quarreled hotly, to the point that Louise,

Princesse de Rohan, had ordered Charles from her presence. He had expressed himself only too willing to go—never, he emphasized dramatically, to return.

The Prince's departure, however, had been considerably hampered by the discovery that the Princesse's husband had returned early from his evening of gaming, and was comfortably ensconced in the anteroom with a bottle of brandy.

"So," said Jamie, smiling despite himself at the thought, "he wouldna stay with the lassie, but he couldna go out of the door—so he threw up the sash and jumped out on the roof. He got down almost to the street, he said, along the drainage pipes; but then the City guard came along, and he had to scramble back up to stay out of their sight. He had a rare time of it, he said, dodging about the chimneys and slipping on the wet slates, until it occurred to him that our house was only three houses down the row, and the rooftops close enough to hop them like lily pads."

"Mm," I said, feeling warmth reestablish itself around my toes. "Did you send him home in the coach?"

"No, he took one of the horses from the stable."

"If he's been drinking Jared's port, I hope they both make it to Montmartre," I remarked. "It's a good long way."

"Well, it will be a cold, wet journey, no doubt," said Jamie, with the smugness of a man virtuously tucked up in a warm bed with his lawfully wedded wife. He blew out the candle and pulled me close against his chest, spoon-fashion.

"Serve him right," he murmured. "A man ought to be married."

The servants were up before dawn, polishing and cleaning in preparation for entertaining Monsieur Duverney at a small, private supper in the evening.

"I don't know why they bother," I told Jamie, lying in bed with my eyes closed, listening to the bustle downstairs. "All they need do is dust off the chess set and put out a bottle of brandy; he won't notice anything else."

He laughed and bent to kiss me goodbye. "That's all right; I'll need a good supper if I'm to go on beating him." He patted my shoulder in farewell. "I'm going to the warehouse, Sassenach; I'll be home in time to dress, though."

In search of something to do that would take me out of the servants' way, I finally decided to have a footman escort me down to the Rohans'. Perhaps Louise could use a bit of solace, I thought, after her quarrel of the night before. Vulgar curiosity, I told myself primly, had nothing whatsoever to do with it.

When I returned in the late afternoon, I found Jamie slouched in a chair near the bedroom window with his feet propped on the table, collar undone and hair rumpled as he pored over a sheaf of scribbled papers. He looked up at the sound of the door closing, and the absorbed expression melted into a broad grin.

"Sassenach! There you are!" He swung his long legs down and came across to embrace me. He buried his face in my hair, nuzzling, then drew back and sneezed. He sneezed again, and let go of me to grope in his sleeve for the handkerchief he carried there, military style.

"What do ye smell like, Sassenach?" he demanded, pressing the linen square to his nose just in time to muffle the results of another explosive sneeze.

I reached into the bosom of my dress and plucked the small sachet from between my breasts.

"Jasmine, roses, hyacinth, and lily of the valley. . . . ragweed, too, apparently," I added as he snorted and wheezed into the capacious depths of the handkerchief. "Are you all right?" I looked around for some means of disposal, and settled for dropping the sachet into a stationery box on my desk at the far side of the room.

"Aye, I'll do. It's the hya . . . hya . . . hyaCHOO!"

"Goodness!" I hastily flung the window open, and motioned to him. He obligingly stuck his head and shoulders out into the wet drizzle of the morning, breathing in gusts of fresh, hyacinth-free air.

"Och, that's better," he said with relief, pulling in his head a few minutes later. His eyes widened. "What are ye doing now, Sassenach?"

"Washing," I explained, struggling with the back laces of my gown. "Or getting ready to, at least. I'm covered with oil of hyacinth," I explained, as he blinked. "If I don't wash it off, you're liable to explode."

He dabbed meditatively at his nose and nodded.

"You've a point there, Sassenach. Shall I have the footman fetch up some hot water?"

"No, don't bother. A quick rinse should take most of it off," I assured him, unbuttoning and unlacing as quickly as possible. I raised my arms, reaching behind my head to gather my hair into a bun. Suddenly Jamie leaned forward and grasped my wrist, pulling my arm into the air.

"What are you doing?" I said, startled.

"What have *you* done, Sassenach?" he demanded. He was staring under my arm.

"Shaved," I said proudly. "Or rather, waxed. Louise had her *servante aux petits soins*—you know, her personal groomer?—there this morning, and she did me, too."

"Waxed?" Jamie looked rather wildly at the candlestick by the ewer, then back at me. "You put wax in your oxters?"

"Not that kind of wax," I assured him. "Scented beeswax. The grooming lady heated it, then spread the warm wax on. Once it's cooled, you just jerk it off," I winced momentarily in recollection, "and Bob's your uncle."

"My uncle Bob wouldna countenance any such goings-on," said Jamie severely. "What in hell would ye do that for?" He peered closely at the site, still holding my wrist up. "Didn't it hur . . . hurt . . . choof!" He dropped my hand and backed up rapidly.

"Didn't it hurt?" he asked, handkerchief to nose once more.

"Well, a bit," I admitted. "Worth it, though, don't you think?" I asked, raising both arms like a ballerina and turning slightly to and fro. "First time I've felt entirely clean in months."

"Worth it?" he said, sounding a little dazed. "What's it to do wi' clean, that you've pulled all of the hairs out from under your arms?"

A little belatedly, I realized that none of the Scottish women I had encountered employed any form of depilation. Furthermore, Jamie had almost certainly never been in sufficiently close contact with an upper-class Parisienne to know that many of them *did*. "Well," I said, suddenly realizing the difficulty an anthropologist faces in trying to interpret the more singular customs of a primitive tribe. "It smells much less," I offered.

"And what's wrong wi' the way ye smell?" he said heatedly. "At least ye smelt like a woman, not a damn flower garden. What d'ye think I am, a man or a bumblebee? Would ye wash yourself, Sassenach, so I can get within less than ten feet of ye?"

I picked up a cloth and began sponging my torso. Madame Laserre, Louise's groomer, had applied scented oil all over my body; I rather hoped it would come off easily. It was disconcerting to have him hovering just outside sniffing range, glaring at me like a wolf circling its prey.

I turned my back to dip the cloth into the bowl, and said offhandedly over my shoulder, "Er, I did my legs, too."

I stole a quick glance over my shoulder. The original shock was fading into a look of total bewilderment.

"Your legs dinna smell like anything," he said. "Unless you've been walkin' knee-deep in the cow-byre."

I turned around and pulled my skirt up to my knees, pointing one toe forward to display the delicate curves of calf and shin.

"But they look so much nicer," I pointed out. "All nice and smooth; not like Harry the hairy ape."

He glanced down at his own fuzzy knees, offended.

"An ape, am I?"

"Not you, me!" I said, getting exasperated.

"My legs are any amount hairier than yours ever were!"

"Well, they're *supposed* to be; you're a man!"

He drew in breath as though about to reply, then let it out again, shaking his head and muttering something to himself in Gaelic. He flung himself back into the chair and sat back, watching me through narrowed eyes, every now and then muttering to himself again. I decided not to ask for a translation.

After most of my bath had been accomplished in what might best be described as a charged atmosphere, I decided to attempt conciliation.

"It might have been worse, you know," I said, sponging the inside of one thigh. "Louise had *all* her body hair removed."

That startled him back into English, at least temporarily.

"What, she's taken the hairs off her honeypot?" he said, horrified into uncharacteristic vulgarity.

"Mm-hm," I replied, pleased that this vision had at least distracted him from my own distressingly hairless condition. "Every hair. Madame Laserre plucked out the stray ones."

"Mary, Michael, and Bride!" He closed his eyes tightly, either in avoidance, or the better to contemplate the prospect I had described.

Evidently the latter, for he opened his eyes again and glared at me, demanding, "She's goin' about now bare as a wee lassie?"

"She says," I replied delicately, "that men find it erotic."

His eyebrows nearly met his hairline, a neat trick for someone with such a classically high brow.

"I do wish you would stop that muttering," I remarked, hanging the cloth over a chairback to dry. "I can't understand a word you say."

"On the whole, Sassenach," he replied, "that's as well."

12

L'Hôpital des Anges

"All right," Jamie said resignedly over breakfast. He pointed a spoon at me in warning. "Go ahead, then. But you'll take Murtagh as escort, besides the footman; it's a poor neighborhood near the cathedral."

"Escort?" I sat up straight, pushing back the bowl of parritch which I had been eyeing with something less than enthusiasm. "Jamie! Do you mean you don't mind if I visit L'Hôpital des Anges?"

"I don't know if I mean that, exactly," he said, spooning in his own parritch in a businesslike way. "But I expect I'll mind a lot more if ye don't. And if ye work at the Hôpital, at least it will keep ye from spending all your time with Louise de Rohan. I suppose there are worse things than associating wi' beggars and criminals," he said darkly. "At least I don't expect you'll come home from a hospital wi' your privates plucked bare."

"I'll try not," I assured him.

I had seen a number of good hospital matrons in my time, and a few of the really excellent ones, who had exalted a job into a vocation. With Mother Hildegarde, the process had been reversed, with impressive results.

Hildegarde de Gascogne was the most suitable person I could imagine to be in charge of a place like L'Hôpital des Anges. Nearly six feet tall, her gaunt, rawboned frame swathed in yards of black wool, she loomed over her nursing sisters like a broomstick scarecrow guarding a field of pumpkins. Porters, patients, sisters, orderlies, novices, visitors, apothecaries, all were swept up by the force of her presence, to be tidied away into neat heaps, wherever Mother Hildegarde might decree.

With that height, plus a face of an ugliness so transcendant as to be grotesquely beautiful, it was obvious why she had embraced a religious life—Christ was the only man from whom she might expect embrace in return.

Her voice was deep and resonant; with its nasal Gascony accent, it bonged through the corridors of the hospital like the echo of the church bells next door. I could hear her sometime before I saw her, the powerful voice increasing in volume as she came down the hall toward the office where six ladies of the Court and I huddled behind Herr Gerstmann, like island dwellers awaiting the arrival of a hurricane behind a flimsy barricade.

She filled the narrow doorway with a swoosh of batwings, and descended upon Herr Gerstmann with a cry of rapture, kissing him soundly on both cheeks.

"*Mon cher ami!* How unexpected a pleasure—and so much the more sweet for its unexpectedness. What brings you to me?"

Straightening, she turned a wide smile on the rest of us. The smile remained wide as Herr Gerstmann explained our mission, though a less experienced fortune-teller than I could have seen the tightening cheek muscles that turned it from a social grace to a rictus of necessity.

"We are most appreciative of your thoughts and your generosity, mesdames." The deep, bell-like voice went on with a gracious speech of gratitude. Meanwhile, I could see the small, intelligent eyes, set deep beneath bony brow ridges, darting back and forth, deciding how best to dispose of this nuisance in short order, while still extracting such money as these pious ladies might be induced to part with for the good of their souls.

Having come to a decision, she clapped her hands sharply. A short nun, on the general order of Cock-Robin, popped up in the doorway like a jack-in-the-box.

"Sister Angelique, be so kind as to take these ladies to the dispensary," she ordered. "Give them some suitable garments and then show them the wards. They may assist with the distribution of food to the patients—if they are so inclined." A slight twitch of the wide, thin mouth made it evident that Mother Hildegarde did not expect the ladies' pious inclination to survive the tour of the wards.

Mother Hildegarde was a shrewd judge of human nature. Three of the ladies made it through the first ward, with its cases of scrofula, scabies, eczema, defluxions, and stinking pyemia, before deciding that their charitable inclinations could be entirely satisfied by a donation to L'Hôpital, and fleeing back to the dispensary to shed the rough hopsacking gowns with which we had been furnished.

In the center of the next ward, a tall, gangly man in a dark frock coat was carrying out what appeared to be the skillful amputation of a leg; particularly skillful in that the patient was not sedated in any visible way, and was being restrained at the moment by the efforts of two husky orderlies and a solidly built nun who was sitting upon the patient's chest, her flowing draperies fortunately obscuring the man's face.

One of the ladies behind me made a small gagging sound; when I looked round, all I saw was the rather wide rear aspect of two of the would-be Samaritans, jammed hip to hip in the narrow doorway leading toward the dispensary and freedom. With a last desperate tug and the rending of silk, they burst through and fled precipitately down the dark hallway, nearly knocking over an orderly coming on the trot with a tray piled high with linens and surgical instruments.

I glanced to the side, and was amused to find Mary Hawkins still there. Somewhat whiter than the surgical linens—which were quite a disgraceful shade of gray, truth be told—and a bit green about the gills, but still there.

"*Vite! Dépêchez-vous!*" the surgeon uttered a peremptory shout, aimed presumably at the shaken orderly, who hastily reassembled his tray and came on the gallop to the spot where the tall, dark man was poised, bone saw in hand, ready to sever an exposed thigh bone. The orderly bent to tie a second tourniquet above the site of operation, the saw descended with an indescribable grating sound, and I took pity on Mary Hawkins, turning her in the other direction. Her arm trembled under my hand, and the peony lips were blanched and pinched as a frostbitten flower.

"Would you like to leave?" I asked politely. "I'm sure Mother Hildegarde could summon a carriage for you." I glanced over one shoulder to the vacant darkness of the hallway. "I'm afraid the Comtesse and Madame Lambert have left already."

Mary gulped audibly, but tightened an already firm jaw in determination. "N-no," she said. "If you stay, I'll stay."

I definitely intended staying; curiosity and the urge to worm my way into the operations of L'Hôpital des Anges were much too strong to weigh against any pity I might feel for Mary's sensibilities.

Sister Angelique had gone some distance before noticing that we had stopped. Returning, she stood patiently waiting, a small smile on her plump face, as though expecting that we, too, would turn and run. I bent over a pallet at the edge of the floor. A very thin woman lay listlessly under a single blanket, her eyes drifting dully over us without interest. It wasn't the woman who had attracted my attention, so much as the oddly shaped glass vessel standing on the floor alongside her pallet.

The vessel was brimming with a yellow fluid—urine, undoubtedly. I was mildly surprised; without chemical tests, or even litmus paper, what conceivable use could a urine sample be? Thinking over the various things one tested urine for, though, I had an idea.

I picked up the vessel carefully, ignoring Sister Angelique's exclamation of alarmed protest. I sniffed carefully. Sure enough; half-obscured by sour ammoniac fumes, the fluid smelled sickly sweet—rather like soured honey. I hesitated, but there was only one way to make sure. With a moue of distaste, I gingerly dipped the tip of one finger into the liquid and touched it delicately to my tongue.

Mary, watching bug-eyed at my side, choked slightly, but Sister Angelique was watching with sudden interest. I placed a hand on the woman's forehead; it was cool—no fever to account for the wasting.

"Are you thirsty, Madame?" I asked the patient. I knew the answer before she spoke, seeing the empty carafe near her head.

"Always, Madame," she replied. "And always hungry, as well. Yet no flesh gathers on my bones, no matter how much I eat." She raised a stick-thin arm, displaying a bony wrist, then let it fall as though the effort had exhausted her.

I patted the skinny hand gently, and murmured something in farewell, my exhilaration at having made a correct diagnosis substantially quenched by the knowledge that there was no possible cure for diabetes mellitus in this day; the woman before me was doomed.

In subdued spirits, I rose to follow Sister Angelique, who slowed her bustling steps to walk next to me.

"Could you tell from what she suffers, Madame?" the nun asked curiously. "Only from the urine?"

"Not only from that," I answered. "But yes, I know. She has—" Drat. What would they have called it now? "She has . . . um, sugar sickness. She gets no nourishment from the food she eats, and has a tremendous thirst. Consequently, she produces large quantities of urine."

Sister Angelique was nodding, a look of intense curiosity stamped on her pudgy features.

"And can you tell whether she will recover, Madame?"

"No, she won't," I said bluntly. "She's far gone already; she may not last out the month."

"Ah." The fair brows lifted, and the look of curiosity was replaced by one of respect. "That's what Monsieur Parnelle said."

"And who's he, when he's at home?" I asked flippantly.

The plump nun frowned in bewilderment. "Well, at his own establishment, I believe he is a maker of trusses, and a jeweler. When he comes here, though, he acts usually as a urinoscopist."

I felt my own brows rising. "A urinoscopist?" I said unbelievingly. "There actually are such things?"

"*Oui*, Madame. And he said just what you said, about the poor thin lady. I have never seen a woman who knew about the science of urinoscopy," Sister Angelique said, staring at me in frank fascination.

"Well, there are more things in heaven and on earth than are dreamt of in your philosophy, Sister," I said graciously. She nodded seriously, making me feel rather ashamed of my facetiousness.

"That is true, Madame. Will you have a look at the gentleman in the end bed? He has a complaint of the liver, we believe."

We continued, from one bed to another, making the complete circuit of the enormous hall. We saw examples of diseases I had seen only in textbooks, and every kind of traumatic injury, from head wounds inflicted in drunken brawls to a carter whose chest had been crushed by a rolling wine barrel.

I paused by some beds, asking questions of those patients who seemed able to answer. I could hear Mary breathing through her mouth behind my shoulder, but didn't check to see whether she was in fact holding her nose.

At the conclusion of the tour, Sister Angelique turned to me with an ironic smile.

"Well, Madame? Do you still desire to serve the Lord by helping his unfortunates?"

I was already rolling up the sleeves of my gown.

"Bring me a basin of hot water, Sister," I said, "and some soap."

"How was it, Sassenach?" Jamie asked.

"Horrible!" I answered, beaming broadly.

He raised one eyebrow, smiling down at me as I lay sprawled on the chaise.

"Oh, enjoyed yourself, did ye?"

"Oh, Jamie, it was so nice to be useful again! I mopped floors and I fed people gruel, and when Sister Angelique wasn't looking, I managed to change a couple of filthy dressings and lance an abscess."

"Oh, good," he said. "Did ye remember to eat, in the midst of all this frivolity?"

"Er, no, as a matter of fact, I didn't," I said guiltily. "On the other hand, I forgot to be sick, too." As though reminded of delinquency, the walls of my stomach took a sudden lurch inward. I pressed a fist under my breastbone. "Perhaps I should have a bite."

"Perhaps ye should," he agreed, a little grimly, reaching for the bell.

He watched as I obediently downed meat pie and cheese, describing L'Hôpital des Anges and its inmates in enthusiastic detail between bites as I ate.

"It's very crowded in some of the wards—two or three to a bed, which is awful, but—don't you want some of this?" I broke off to ask. "It's very good."

He eyed the piece of pastry I was holding out to him.

"If ye think ye can keep from telling me about gangrenous toenails long enough for a bite to make it from my gullet to my stomach, then yes."

Belatedly, I noticed the slight pallor on his cheeks, and the faint pinching of his nostrils. I poured a cup of wine and handed it to him before picking up my own plate again.

"And how was *your* day, my dear?" I asked demurely.

L'Hôpital des Anges became a refuge for me. The blunt and unsophisticated directness of nuns and patients was a wonderful refreshment from the continual chattering intrigues of the Court ladies and gentlemen. I was also positive that without the relief of allowing my facial muscles to relax into their normal expressions at the Hôpital, my face would quickly have frozen into an expression of permanent simpering vapidity.

Seeing that I appeared to know what I was doing, and required nothing of them beyond a few bandages and linens, the nuns quickly accepted my presence. And after an initial shock at my accent and title, so did the patients. Social prejudice is a strong force, but no match for simple competence when skill is in urgent demand and short supply.

Mother Hildegarde, busy as she was, took somewhat more time to make her own assessment of me. She never spoke to me at first, beyond a simple "*Bonjour,* Madame," in passing, but I often felt the weight of those small, shrewd eyes boring into my back as I stooped over the bed of an elderly man with shingles, or smeared aloe ointment on the blisters of a child burned in one of the frequent house fires that beset the poorer quarters of the city.

She never gave the appearance of hurrying, but covered an immense amount of ground during the day, pacing the flat gray stones of the Hôpital wards with a stride that covered a yard at a time, her small white dog Bouton hurrying at her heels to keep up.

A far cry from the fluffy lapdogs so popular with the ladies of the Court, he looked vaguely like a cross between a poodle and a dachshund, with a rough, kinky coat whose fringes fluttered along the edges of a wide belly and stumpy, bowed legs. His feet, splay-toed and black-nailed, clicked frantically over the stones of the floor as he trotted after Mother Hildegarde, pointed muzzle almost touching the sweeping black folds of her habit.

"Is that a *dog*?" I had asked one of the orderlies in amazement, when I first beheld Bouton, passing through the Hôpital at the heels of his mistress.

He paused in his floor-sweeping to look after the curly, plumed tail, disappearing into the next ward.

"Well," he said doubtfully, "Mother Hildegarde says he's a dog. I wouldn't like to be the one to say he isn't."

As I became more friendly with the nuns, orderlies, and visiting physicians of the Hôpital, I heard various other opinions of Bouton, ranging from the tolerant to the superstitious. No one knew quite where Mother Hildegarde had got him, nor why. He had been a member of the Hôpital staff for several years, with a rank—in Mother Hildegarde's opinion, which was the only one that counted—well above that of the nursing sisters, and equal to that of most of the visiting physicians and apothecaries.

Some of the latter regarded him with suspicious aversion, others with jocular affability. One chirurgeon referred to him routinely—out of Mother's hearing—as "that revolting rat," another as "the smelly rabbit," and one small, tubby truss-maker greeted him quite openly as "Monsieur le Dishcloth." The nuns considered him something between a mascot and a totem, while the junior priest from the cathedral next door, who had been bitten in the leg when he came to administer the sacraments to the patients, confided to me his own opinion that Bouton was one of the lesser demons, disguised as a dog for his own fell purposes.

In spite of the unflattering tone of the priest's remarks, I thought that he had perhaps come the closest to the truth. For after several weeks of observing the pair, I had come to the conclusion that Bouton was in fact Mother Hildegarde's familiar.

She spoke to him often, not in the tone one generally uses for dogs, but as one discussing important matters with an equal. As she paused beside this bed or that, often Bouton would spring onto the mattress, nuzzling and sniffing at the startled patient. He would sit down, often on the patient's legs, bark once, and glance up inquiringly at Mother, wagging his silky plumed tail as though asking her opinion of his diagnosis—which she always gave.

Though I was rather curious about this behavior, I had had no opportunity of closely observing the odd pair at work until one dark, rainy morning in March. I was standing by the bed of a middle-aged carter, making casual conversation with him while I tried to figure out what in bloody hell was wrong with the man.

It was a case that had come in the week before. He had had his lower leg caught in the wheel of a cart when he carelessly dismounted before the vehicle had stopped moving. It was a compound fracture, but a fairly uncomplicated one. I had reset the bone, and the wound seemed to be healing nicely. The tissue was a healthy pink, with good granulation, no bad smell, no telltale red streaks, no extreme tenderness, nothing at all to explain why the man still smoldered with fever and produced the dark, odorous urine of a lingering infection.

"*Bonjour,* Madame." The deep, rich voice spoke above me, and I glanced up at the towering form of Mother Hildegarde. There was a *whish* past my elbow, and Bouton landed on the mattress with a thump that made the patient groan slightly.

"What do you think?" said Mother Hildegarde. I wasn't at all sure whether she was addressing me or Bouton, but took the benefit of the doubt and explained my observations.

"So, there must be a secondary source of infection," I concluded, "but I can't find it. I'm wondering now whether perhaps he has an internal infection that's not related to the leg wound. A mild appendicitis, or a bladder infection, perhaps, though I don't find any abdominal tenderness, either."

Mother Hildegarde nodded. "A possibility, certainly. Bouton!" The dog cocked his head toward his mistress, who jerked an oblong chin in the direction of the patient. "*A la bouche,* Bouton," she ordered. With a mincing step, the dog pushed the round black nose that presumably gave him his name into the carter's face. The man's eyes, heavy-lidded with fever, sprang open at this intrusion, but a glance at the imposing presence of Mother Hildegarde stopped whatever complaint he might have been forming.

"Open your mouth," Mother Hildegarde instructed, and such was her force of character that he did so, even though his lips twitched at the nearness of Bouton's. Dog-kissing plainly wasn't on his agenda of desirable activities.

"No," said Mother Hildegarde thoughtfully, watching Bouton. "That isn't it. Have a look elsewhere, Bouton, but carefully. The man has a broken leg, remember."

As though he had in fact understood every word, the dog began to sniff curiously at the patient, nosing into his armpits, putting stubby feet on his chest in order to investigate, nudging gently along the crease of the groin. When it came to the injured leg, he stepped carefully over the limb before putting his nose to the surface of the bandages round it.

He returned to the groin area—well, what else, I thought impatiently, he's a dog, after all—nudged at the top of the thigh, then sat down and barked once, wagging triumphantly.

"There it is," said Mother Hildegarde, pointing to a small brown scab just below the inguinal crease.

"But that's almost healed," I protested. "It isn't infected."

"No?" The tall nun placed a hand on the man's thigh and pressed hard. Her muscular fingers dented the pale, clammy flesh, and the carter screamed like a banshee.

"Ah," she said in satisfaction, observing the deep prints left by her touch. "A pocket of putrefaction."

It was; the scab had loosened at one edge, and a thick ooze of yellow pus showed under it. A little probing, with Mother Hildegarde holding the man by leg and shoulder, revealed the problem. A long sliver of wood, flying free of the splintered cartwheel, had driven upward, deep into the thigh. Disregarded because of the apparently insignificant entrance wound, it had gone unnoticed by the patient himself, to whom the whole leg was one giant pain. While the tiny entrance wound had healed cleanly, the deeper wound had festered and formed a pocket of pus around the intrusion, buried in the muscle tissue where no surface symptoms were visible—to human senses, at least.

A little scalpel work to enlarge the entrance wound, a quick grip with a pair of long-nosed forceps, a smooth, forceful pull—and I held up a three-inch sliver of wood, coated with blood and slime.

"Not bad, Bouton," I said, with a nod of acknowledgment. A long pink tongue lolled happily, and the black nostrils sniffed in my direction.

"Yes, she's a good one," said Mother Hildegarde, and this time there was no doubt which of us she was speaking to, Bouton being male. Bouton leaned forward and sniffed politely at my hand, then licked my knuckles once in reciprocal acknowledgment of a fellow professional. I repressed the urge to wipe my hand on my gown.

"Amazing," I said, meaning it.

"Yes," said Mother Hildegarde, casually, but with an unmistakable note of pride. "He's very good at locating tumors beneath the skin, as well. And while I cannot always tell what he finds in the odors of breath and urine, he has a certain tone of bark that indicates unmistakably the presence of a derangement of the stomach."

Under the circumstances, I saw no reason to doubt it. I bowed to Bouton, and picked up a vial of powdered St.-John's-wort to dress the infection.

"Pleased to have your assistance, Bouton. You can work with me anytime."

"Very sensible of you," said Mother Hildegarde, with a flash of strong teeth. "Many of the physicians and *chirurgiens* who work here are less inclined to take advantage of his skills."

"Er, well. . . ." I didn't want to disparage anyone's reputation, but my glance across the hall at Monsieur Voleru must have been transparent.

Mother Hildegarde laughed. "Well, we take what God sends us, though occasionally I wonder whether He sends them to us only in order to keep them out of greater trouble elsewhere. Still, the bulk of our physicians are better than nothing—even if only marginally so. You"—and the teeth flashed once more, reminding me of a genial draft horse—"are a great deal better than nothing, Madame."

"Thanks."

"I have wondered, though," Mother Hildegarde went on, watching as I applied the medicated dressing, "why you see only the patients with wounds and broken bones? You avoid those with spots and coughs and fevers, yet it is more common for *les maîtresses* to deal with such things. I don't think I have ever seen a female *chirurgien* before." *Les maîtresses* were the unlicensed healers, mostly from the provinces, who dealt in herbals, poultices, and charms. *Les maîtresses sage-femme* were the midwives, the top of the heap so far as popular healers were concerned. Many were accorded more respect than the licensed practitioners, and were much preferred by the lower-class patients, as they were likely to be both more capable and much less expensive.

I wasn't surprised that she had observed my proclivities; I had gathered long since that very little about her Hôpital escaped Mother Hildegarde's notice.

"It isn't lack of interest," I assured her. "It's only that I'm with child, so I can't expose myself to anything contagious, for the child's sake. Broken bones aren't catching."

"Sometimes I wonder," said Mother Hildegarde, with a glance at an incoming stretcher. "We're having a plague of them this week. No, don't go." She motioned me back. "Sister Cecile will see to it. She'll call you if there's need."

The nun's small gray eyes regarded me with curiosity, mingled with appraisal.

"So, you are not only a milady, you are with child, but your husband does not object to your coming here? He must be a most unusual man."

"Well, he's Scottish," I said, by way of explanation, not wishing to go into the subject of my husband's objections.

"Oh, Scottish." Mother Hildegarde nodded understandingly. "Just so."

The bed trembled against my thigh as Bouton leaped off and trotted toward the door.

"He smells a stranger," Mother Hildegarde remarked. "Bouton assists the doorkeeper as well as the physicians—with no more gratitude for his efforts, I fear."

The sounds of peremptory barks and a high voice raised in terror came through the double doors of the entryway.

"Oh, it's Father Balmain again! Curse the man, can't he learn to stand still and let Bouton smell him?" Mother Hildegarde turned in haste to the succor of her companion, turning back at the last moment to smile engagingly at me. "Perhaps I will send him to assist you with your tasks, Madame, while I soothe Father Balmain. While no doubt a most holy man, he lacks true appreciation for the work of an artist."

She strode toward the doors with her long, unhurried stride, and with a last word for the carter, I turned to Sister Cecile and the latest stretcher case.

Jamie was lying on the carpet in the sitting room when I came back to the house, with a small boy sitting cross-legged on the floor beside him. Jamie was holding a bilboquet in one hand, and had the other poised over one eye.

"Of course I can," he was saying. "Anyday and twice on Sundays. Watch."

Placing the hand over his eye, he fixed the other piercingly on the bilboquet and gave the ivory cup a toss. The tethered ball leaped from its socket into an arc, and dropped as though guided by radar, landing back in its cup with a snug little plop.

"See?" he said, removing the hand from his eye. He sat up and handed the cup to the boy. "Here, you try it." He grinned at me, and slid a hand under the hem of my skirt, clasping my green silk ankle in greeting.

"Having fun?" I inquired.

"Not yet," he replied, giving the ankle a squeeze. "I was waiting for you, Sassenach." The long, warm fingers curled around my ankle slid higher, playfully stroking the curve of my calf, as a pair of limpid blue eyes gazed up at me, all innocence. His face had a streak of dried mud down one side, and there were dirty blotches on his shirt and kilt.

"Is that so?" I said, trying to pull my leg free of his grasp inconspicuously. "I should have thought your little playmate would have been all the company you needed."

The boy, understanding none of the English in which these exchanges were conducted, ignored them, intent on trying to work the bilboquet with one eye closed. The first two attempts having failed, he opened the second eye and glared at the toy, as though daring it not to work. The second eye closed again, but not all the way; a small slit remained, gleaming alertly below the thick fringe of dark lashes.

Jamie clicked his tongue disapprovingly, and the eye hastily snapped tight shut.

"Nah, then, Fergus, we'll have nay cheatin', if ye please," he said. "Fair's fair." The boy obviously caught the meaning, if not the words; he grinned sheepishly, displaying a pair of large, white, gleamingly perfect front teeth, square as a squirrel's.

Jamie's hand exerted an invisible pull, obliging me to move closer to him to avoid being toppled off my moroccan heels.

"Ah," he said. "Well, Fergus here is a man of many talents, and a boon companion for the idle hours when a man's wife has deserted him and left him to seek his own pursuits amidst the wickedness of the city"—the long fingers curled delicately into the hollow behind my knee, tickling suggestively—"but he isna qualified as a partner for the pastime I had in mind."

"Fergus?" I said, eyeing the boy, and trying to ignore the goings-on below. The lad was possibly nine or ten, but small for his age, and fine-boned as a ferret. Clad in clean, worn clothes several sizes too big for him, he was also as French as they come, with the pale, sallow skin and big, dark eyes of a Parisian street child.

"Well, his name is really Claudel, but we decided that didna sound verra manly, so he's to be called Fergus instead. A suitable warrior's name, that." Catching the sound of his name—or names—the boy glanced up and grinned shyly at me.

"This is Madame," Jamie explained to the boy, gesturing to me with his free hand. "You may call her milady. I dinna think he could manage 'Broch Tuarach,' " he added to me, "or even Fraser, for that matter."

" 'Milady' will be fine," I said, smiling. I wriggled my leg harder, trying to shake off the leechlike grip. "Er, *why,* if I may ask?"

"Why what? Oh, why Fergus, ye mean?"

"That's what I mean, all right." I wasn't sure just how far his arm would reach, but the hand was creeping slowly up the back of my thigh. "Jamie, take your hand away this minute!"

The fingers darted to one side, and deftly pulled loose the ribbon garter that held up my stocking. The stocking slithered down my leg to puddle round my ankle.

"You beast!" I kicked at him, but he dodged aside, laughing.

"Oh, beast, is it? What kind?"

"A cur!" I snapped, trying to bend over to pull up my stocking without falling off my heels. The child Fergus, after a brief, incurious glance at us, had resumed his trials with the bilboquet.

"As for the lad," he continued blithely, "Fergus is now in my employ."

"To do what?" I asked. "We already have a boy who cleans the knives and boots, and a stable-lad."

Jamie nodded. "Aye, that's true. We havena got a pickpocket, though. Or rather, we hadn't; we have, now."

I drew in my breath and blew it out again slowly.

"I see. I suppose it would be dense of me to ask exactly why we need to add a pickpocket to the household?"

"To steal letters, Sassenach," Jamie said calmly.

"Oh," I said, light beginning to dawn.

"I canna get anything sensible out of His Highness; when he's with me, he wilna do anything but moan about Louise de La Tour, or grind his teeth and curse because they've been quarreling again. In either case, all he wants to do is to get drunk as quickly as possible. Mar is losing all patience with him, for he's haughty and sullen by turns. And I canna get anything out of Sheridan."

The Earl of Mar was the most respected of the exiled Scottish Jacobites in Paris. A man whose long and illustrious prime was only now beginning to edge into elderliness, he had been the primary supporter of King James at the abortive Rising in 1715, and had followed his king into exile after the defeat at Sheriffsmuir. I had met the Earl and liked him; an elderly, courtly man with a personality as straight as his backbone. He was now doing his best—with little reward, it seemed—for his lord's son. I had met Thomas Sheridan, too; the Prince's tutor—an elderly man who handled His Highness's correspondence, translating impatience and illiteracy into courtly French and English.

I sat down and pulled my stocking back up. Fergus, apparently hardened to the sight of female limbs, ignored me altogether, concentrating grimly on the bilboquet.

"Letters, Sassenach," he said. "I need the letters. Letters from Rome, sealed with the Stuart crest. Letters from France, letters from England, letters from Spain. We can get them either from the Prince's house—Fergus can go with me, as a page—or possibly from the papal messenger who brings them; that would be a bit better, as we'd have the information in advance."

"So, we've made the bargain," Jamie said, nodding at his new servant. "Fergus will do his best to get what I need, and I will provide him with clothes and lodging and thirty écus a year. If he's caught while doing my service, I'll do my best to buy him off. If it canna be done, and he loses a hand or an ear, then I maintain him for the rest of his life, as he wilna be able to pursue his profession. And if he's hanged, then I guarantee to have Masses said for his soul for the space of a year. I think that's fair, no?"

I felt a cold hand pass down my spine.

"Jesus Christ, Jamie" was all I could find to say.

He shook his head, and reached out a hand for the bilboquet. "Not our Lord, Sassenach. Pray to St. Dismas. The patron saint of thieves and traitors."

Jamie reached over and took the bilboquet from the boy. He flicked his wrist sharply and the ivory ball rose in a perfect parabola, to descend into its cup with an inevitable plop.

"I see," I said. I eyed the new employee with interest as he took the toy Jamie offered him and started in on it once more, dark eyes gleaming with concentration. "Where did you get him?" I asked curiously.

"I found him in a brothel."

"Oh, of course," I said. "To be sure." I eyed the dirt and smears on his clothes. "Which you were visiting for some really excellent reason, I expect?"

"Oh, aye," he said. He sat back, arms wrapped about his knees, grinning as he watched me make repairs to my garter. "I thought you'd prefer me to be found in such an establishment, to the alternative of bein' found in a dark alleyway, wi' my head bashed in."

I saw the boy Fergus's eyes focus at a spot somewhat past the bilboquet, where a tray of iced cakes stood on a table near the wall. A small, pointed pink tongue darted out across his lower lip.

"I think your protégé is hungry," I said. "Why don't you feed him, and then you can tell me just what in bloody hell happened this afternoon."

"Well, I was on my way to the docks," he began, obediently rising to his feet, "and just past the Rue Eglantine, I began to have a queer feeling up the back of my neck."

Jamie Fraser had spent two years in the army of France, fought and stolen with a gang of Scottish "broken men," and been hunted as an outlaw through the moors and mountains of his native land. All of which had left him with an extreme sensitivity to the sensation of being followed.

He couldn't have said whether it was the sound of a footfall, too close behind, or the sight of a shadow that shouldn't be there, or something less tangible—the scent of evil on the air, perhaps—but he had learned that the prickle of warning among the short hairs of his neck was something to be ignored at his peril.

Promptly obeying the dictates of his cervical vertebrae, he turned left instead of right at the next corner, ducked around a whelk-seller's stall, cut between a barrow filled with steamed puddings and another of fresh vegetable marrows, and into a small charcuterie.

Pressed against the wall near the doorway, he peered out through a screen of hanging duck carcasses. Two men entered the street no more than a second later, walking close together, glancing quickly from side to side.

Every workingman in Paris carried the marks of his trade upon his person, and it didn't take much of a nose to detect the whiff of sea-salt on these two. If the small gold hoop in the shorter man's ear had not been a dead giveaway, the deep reddish-brown of their faces would have made it clear they were deep-water sailors.

Accustomed to the cramped quarters of shipboard and quay taverns, seamen seldom walked in a straight line. These two slid through the crowded alley like eels through rocks, eyes flicking past beggars, servingmaids, house-wives, merchants; sea wolves assessing potential prey.

"I let them get well past the shop," Jamie explained, "and I was just about to step out and go back the other way, when I saw another of them at the mouth of the alley."

This man wore the same uniform as the other two; sidelocks heavily coated with grease, a fish knife at his side and a marlinspike the length of a man's forearm thrust through his belt. Short and thickset, the man stood still at the end of the alley, holding his ground against the buffeting waves of commerce that ebbed and flowed through the narrow passage. Clearly he had been left on guard, while his fellows quested ahead.

"So I was left wondering what best to do," Jamie said, rubbing his nose. "I was safe enough where I was, but there was no back way from the shop, and the moment I stepped from the doorway, I'd be seen." He glanced down reflectively, smoothing the crimson fabric of his kilt across his thigh. An enor-mous red barbarian was going to be conspicuous, no matter how thick the crowd.

"So what did you do?" I asked. Fergus, ignoring the conversation, was stuffing his pockets methodically with cakes, pausing for a hasty bite every so often in the process. Jamie caught my glance at the boy and shrugged.

"He'll not have been in the habit of eating regularly," he said. "Let him be."

"All right," I said. "But go on—what did you do?"

"Bought a sausage," he said promptly.

A Dunedin, to be exact. Made of spiced duck, ham and venison, boiled, stuffed and sun-dried, a Dunedin sausage measured eighteen inches from end to end and was as hard as seasoned oakwood.

"I couldna step out wi' my sword drawn," Jamie explained, "but I didna like the idea of stepping past the fellow in the alleyway wi' no one at my back, and empty hands."

Bearing the Dunedin at port arms, and keeping a weather eye on the passing crowd, Jamie had stepped boldly down the alley, toward the watcher at its mouth.

The man had met his gaze quite calmly, showing no sign of any malign intent. Jamie might have thought his original premonition mistaken, had he not seen the watcher's eyes flick briefly to something over Jamie's shoulder. Obeying the instincts that had kept him alive thus far, he had dived forward, knocking the watcher down and sliding on his face across the filthy cobbles of the street.

The crowd scattered before him with shrieks of alarm, and he rolled to his feet to see the flung knife that had missed him, quivering in the boards of a ribbon stall.

"If I'd had a bit of doubt it was me they wanted, I didna fret about it longer," he said dryly.

He had kept hold of the sausage, and now found use for it, swinging it smartly across the face of one attacker.

"I broke his nose, I think," he said meditatively. "Anyway, he reeled back, and I shoved past and took off running, down the Rue Pelletier."

The inhabitants of the street scattered before him like geese, startled by the sight of a hurtling Scotsman, kilts flying around his churning knees. He didn't stop to look behind; by the shouts of indignant passersby, he could tell that the assailants were still in pursuit.

This part of the city was seldom patrolled by the King's Guard, and the crowd itself offered little protection other than a simple obstruction that might slow his pursuers. No one was likely to interfere in a matter of violence on a foreigner's behalf.

"There are no alleys off the Rue Pelletier. I needed at least to get to a place where I could draw my sword and have a wall at my back," Jamie explained. "So I pushed at the doors as I passed, 'til I hit one that opened."

Dashing into a gloomy hallway, past a startled porter, and through a hanging drape, he had shot into the center of a large, well-lighted room, and come to a screeching halt in the middle of one Madame Elise's salon, the scent of perfume heavy in his nostrils.

"I see," I said, biting my lip. "I, um, trust you didn't draw your sword in there?"

Jamie narrowed his eyes at me, but didn't deign to reply directly.

"I'll leave it to you, Sassenach," he said dryly, "to imagine what it feels like to arrive unexpectedly in the midst of a brothel, in possession of a verra large sausage."

My imagination proved fully equal to this task, and I burst out laughing.

"God, I wish I could have seen you!" I said.

"Thank God ye didn't!" he said fervently. A furious blush glowed on his cheekbones.

Ignoring remarks from the fascinated inmates, Jamie had made his way awkwardly through what he described, shuddering, as "tangles o' bare limbs," until he had spotted Fergus against one wall, regarding the intruder with a round-eyed astonishment.

Seizing upon this unexpected manifestation of maleness, Jamie had gripped the lad by the shoulder, and fervently implored him to show the way to the nearest exit, without loss of a moment.

"I could hear a hurly-burly breakin' out in the hallway," he explained, "and I kent they were in after me. I didna want to be having to fight for my life wi' a lot of naked women getting in the way."

"I can see that the prospect might be daunting," I agreed, rubbing my upper lip. "But obviously he got you out."

"Aye. He didna hesitate a moment, the dear lad. 'This way, Monsieur!' he says, and it was up the stair, and through a room, and out a window onto the roof, and awa' wi' us both." Jamie cast a fond glance at his new employee.

"You know," I observed, "there are *some* wives who wouldn't believe one word of a story like that."

Jamie's eyes opened wide in astonishment.

"They wouldna? Whyever not?"

"Possibly," I said dryly, "because they aren't married to *you*. I'm pleased that you escaped with your virtue intact, but for the moment, I'm rather more interested in the chaps who chased you in there."

"I didna have a great deal of leisure to think about it at the time," Jamie replied. "And now that I have, I still couldna say who they were, or why they were hunting me."

"Robbery, do you think?" The cash receipts of the wine business were conveyed between the Fraser warehouse, the Rue Tremoulins, and Jared's bank by strongbox, under heavy guard. Still, Jamie was very visible among the crowds near the river docks, and was undoubtedly known to be a wealthy foreign merchant—wealthy by contrast with most of the denizens of that neighborhood, at any rate.

He shook his head, flicking crumbs of dried mud off his shirtfront.

"It might be, I suppose. But they didna try to accost me; it was straight-out murder they meant."

His tone was quite matter-of-fact, but it gave me rather a wobbly feeling in the knees, and I sank down onto a settee. I licked my lips, gone suddenly dry.

"Who—who do you think . . . ?"

He shrugged, frowning as he scooped up a dab of icing from the plate and licked it off his finger.

"The only man I could think of who's threatened me is the Comte St. Germain. But I canna think what he'd gain from having me killed."

"He's Jared's business rival, you said."

"Oh, aye. But the Comte's no interest in German wines, and I canna see him going to the trouble of killing me, only to ruin Jared's new enterprise by bringing him back to Paris. That seems a trifle extreme," he said dryly, "even for a man wi' the Comte's temper."

"Well, do you think . . ." The idea made me mildly ill, and I swallowed twice before going on. "Do you think it might have been . . . revenge? For the *Patagonia* being burned?"

Jamie shook his head, baffled.

"I suppose it could be, but it seems a long time to wait. And why me, come to that?" he added. "It's you annoyed him, Sassenach. Why not kill you, if that's what he meant?"

The sick feeling got slightly worse.

"Do you have to be so bloody logical?" I said.

He saw the look on my face, and smiled suddenly, putting an arm around me for comfort.

"Nay, *mo duinne*. The Comte's a quick temper, but I canna see him going to the trouble and expense of killing either of us, only for revenge. If it might get him his ship back, then yes," he added, "but as it is, I expect he'd only think the price of three hired assassins throwing good money after bad."

He patted my shoulder and stood up.

"Nay, I expect it was only a try at robbery, after all. Dinna trouble yourself about it. I'll take Murtagh with me to the docks from now on, to be safe."

He stretched himself, and brushed the last of the crumbling dirt from his kilt. "Am I decent to go in to supper?" he asked, looking critically down his chest. "It must be nearly ready by now."

"What's ready?"

He opened the door, and a rich, spicy scent wafted up at once from the dining room below.

"Why, the sausage, of course," he said, with a grin over one shoulder. "Ye dinna think I'd let it go to waste?"

13

Deceptions

"barberry leaves, three handfuls in a decoction, steeped overnight,
poured over half a handful of black hellebore." I laid the list of
. . . ingredients down on the inlaid table as though it were slightly
slimy to the touch. "I got it from Madame Rouleaux. She's the best of the
angel-makers, but even she says it's dangerous. Louise, are you sure you want
to do this?"

Her round pink face was blotched, and the plump lower lip had a tendency
to quiver.

"What choice do I have?" She picked up the recipe for the abortifacient
and gazed at it in repulsed fascination.

"Black hellebore," she said, and shuddered. "The very name of it sounds
evil!"

"Well, it's bloody nasty stuff," I said bluntly. "It will make you feel as
though your insides are coming out. But the baby may come, too. It doesn't
always work." I remembered Master Raymond's warning—*It is dangerous to
wait too long*—and wondered how far gone she might be. Surely no more than
six weeks or so; she had told me the instant she suspected.

She glanced at me, startled, with red-rimmed eyes.

"You have used it yourself?"

"God, no!" I startled myself with the vehemence of my exclamation, and
took a deep breath.

"No. I've seen women who have, though—at L'Hôpital des Anges." The
abortionists—the angel-makers—practiced largely in the privacy of homes, their
own or their clients'. Their successes were not the ones that came to the hospital. I laid a hand unobtrusively over my own abdomen, as though for protection of its helpless occupant. Louise caught the gesture and hurled herself into
the sofa, burying her head in her hands.

"Oh, I wish I were dead!" she moaned. "Why, why couldn't I be as
fortunate as you—to be bearing the child of a husband I loved?" She clutched
her own plump stomach with both hands, staring down at it as though expecting the child to peek out between her fingers.

There were any number of answers to that particular question, but I didn't
think she really wanted to hear any of them. I took a deep breath and sat down
beside her, patting a heaving damask shoulder.

"Louise," I said. "Do you want the child?"

She lifted her head and stared at me in astonishment.

"But of course I want it!" she exclaimed. "It's his—it's Charles's! It's . . ." Her face crumpled, and she bowed her head once more over her hands, clasped so tightly over her belly. "It's mine," she whispered. After a long moment, she raised her streaming face, and with a pathetic attempt to pull herself together, wiped her nose on a trailing sleeve.

"But it's no good," she said. "If I don't . . ." She glanced at the recipe on the table and swallowed heavily. "Then Jules will divorce me—he'll cast me out. There would be the most terrible scandal. I might be excommunicated! Not even Father could protect me."

"Yes," I said. "But . . ." I hesitated, then cast caution to the winds. "Is there any chance Jules might be convinced the child is his?" I asked bluntly.

She looked blank for a moment, and I wanted to shake her.

"I don't see how, unless—oh!" Light dawned, and she looked at me, horrified.

"Sleep with Jules, you mean? But Charles would be furious!"

"Charles," I said through my teeth, "is not pregnant!"

"Well, but he's . . . that is . . . I couldn't!" The look of horror was fading, though, being slowly replaced with the growing realization of possibility.

I didn't want to push her; still, I saw no good reason for her to risk her life for the sake of Charles Stuart's pride, either.

"Do you suppose Charles would want you to endanger yourself?" I said. "For that matter—does he know about the child?"

She nodded, mouth slightly open as she thought about it, hands still clenched together over her stomach.

"Yes. That's what we quarreled about last time." She sniffed. "He was angry; he said it was all my fault, that I should have waited until he had reclaimed his father's throne. Then he would be king someday, and he could come and take me away from Jules, and have the Pope annul my marriage, and his sons could be heirs to England and Scotland . . ." She gave way once more, sniveling and wailing incoherently into a fold of her skirt.

I rolled my eyes in exasperation.

"Oh, do be quiet, Louise!" I snapped. It shocked her enough to make her stop weeping, at least momentarily, and I took advantage of the hiatus to press my point.

"Look," I said, as persuasively as possible, "you don't suppose Charles would want you to sacrifice his son, do you? Legitimate or not?" Actually, I rather thought Charles would be in favor of any step that removed inconvenience from his own path, regardless of the effects on Louise or his putative offspring. On the other hand, the Prince did have a marked streak of romanticism; perhaps he could be induced to view this as the sort of temporary adversity common to exiled monarchs. Obviously, I was going to need Jamie's help. I grimaced at the thought of what he was likely to say about it.

"Well. . . ." Louise was wavering, wanting desperately to be convinced. I had a momentary pang of pity for Jules, Prince de Rohan, but the vision of a young servant-girl, dying in protracted, blood-smeared agony on a pallet spread in the stone hallway of L'Hôpital des Anges was brutally clear in my mind.

It was nearly sunset when I left the de Rohans', footsteps dragging. Louise, palpitating with nervousness, was upstairs in her boudoir, her maid putting up her hair and arraying her in her most daring gown before she went down to a private supper with her husband. I felt completely drained, and hoped that Jamie hadn't brought anyone home for supper; I could use a spot of privacy, too.

He hadn't; when I entered the study, he was seated at the desk, poring over three or four sheets of close-written paper.

"Do you think 'the fur merchant' is more likely to be Louis of France, or his minister Duverney?" he asked, without looking up.

"Fine, thank you, darling, and how are *you*?" I said.

"All right," he said absently. The cowlicks on the top of his head were sticking up straight; he massaged his scalp vigorously as I watched, scowling down his long nose at the paper.

"I'm sure 'the tailor from Vendôme' must be Monsieur Geyer," he said, running a finger along the lines of the letter, "and 'our mutual friend'—that could be either the Earl of Mar, or possibly the papal envoy. I think the Earl, from the rest of it, but the—"

"What on earth is that?" I peered over his shoulder, and gasped when I saw the signature at the foot of the letter. James Stuart, by the grace of God King of England and Scotland.

"Bloody Christ! It worked, then!" Swinging around, I spotted Fergus, crouched on a stool in front of the fire, industriously stuffing pastries into his face. "Good lad," I said, smiling at him. He grinned back at me, cheeks puffed like a chipmunk's with chestnut tart.

"We got it from the papal messenger," Jamie explained, coming to the surface long enough to realize I was there. "Fergus took it from the bag while he was eating supper in a tavern. He'll spend the night there, so we'll have to put this back before morning. No difficulties there, Fergus?"

The boy swallowed and shook his head. "No, milord. He sleeps alone— not trusting his bedmates not to steal the contents of his bag." He grinned derisively at this. "The second window on the left, above the stables." He waved an airy hand, the deft, grubby fingers reaching for another pie. "It is nothing, milord."

I had a sudden vision of that fine-boned hand held squirming on a block, with an executioner's blade raised above the broomstick wrist. I gulped, forcing down the sudden lurch of my stomach. Fergus wore a small greenish copper medal on a string about his neck; the image of St. Dismas, I hoped.

"Well," I said, taking a deep breath to steady myself, "what's all this about fur merchants?"

There was no time then for leisurely inspection. In the end, I made a quick fair copy of the letter, and the original was carefully refolded and its original seal replaced with the aid of a knife blade heated in a candle flame.

Watching this operation critically, Fergus shook his head at Jamie. "You have the touch, milord. It is a pity that the one hand is crippled."

Jamie glanced dispassionately at his right hand. It really wasn't too bad; a couple of fingers set slightly askew, a thick scar down the length of the middle finger. The only major damage had been to the fourth finger, which stuck out stiffly, its second joint so badly crushed that the healing had fused two finger-bones together. The hand had been broken in Wentworth Prison, less than four months ago, by Jack Randall.

"Never mind," he said, smiling. He flexed the hand and flicked the fingers playfully at Fergus. "My great paws are too big to make a living picking pock-ets, anyway." He had regained an astounding degree of movement, I thought. He still carried the soft ball of rags I had made for him, squeezing it unobtru-sively hundreds of times a day as he went about his business. And if the knitting bones hurt him, he never complained.

"Off with ye, then," he told Fergus. "Come and find me when you're safe back, so I'll know ye havena been taken up by the police or the landlord of the tavern."

Fergus wrinkled his nose scornfully at such an idea, but nodded, tucking the letter carefully inside his smock before disappearing down the back stair toward the night that was both natural element and protection for him.

Jamie looked after him for a long minute, then turned to me. He truly looked at me for the first time, and his brows flew up.

"Christ, Sassenach!" he said. "You're pale as my sark! Are ye all right?"

"Just hungry," I said.

He rang at once for supper, and we ate it before the fire, while I told him about Louise. Rather to my surprise, while he knit his brows over the situation and muttered uncomplimentary things under his breath in Gaelic about both Louise and Charles Stuart, he agreed with my solution to the problem.

"I thought you'd be upset," I said, scooping up a mouthful of succulent cassoulet with a bit of bread. The warm, bacon-spiced beans soothed me, filling me with a sense of peaceful well-being. It was cold and dark outside, and loud with the rushing of the wind, but it was warm and quiet here by the fire together.

"Oh, about Louise de La Tour foisting a bastard on her husband?" Jamie frowned at his own dish, running a finger around the edge to pick up the last of the juice.

"Well, I'm no verra much in favor of it, I'll tell ye, Sassenach. It's a filthy trick to play on a man, but what's the poor bloody woman to do otherwise?" He shook his head, then glanced at the desk across the room and smiled wryly.

"Besides, it doesna become me to be takin' a high moral stand about other people's behavior. Stealing letters and spying and trying generally to subvert a man my family holds as King? I shouldna like to have someone judging me on the grounds of the things I'm doing, Sassenach."

"You have a damn good reason for what you're doing!" I objected.

He shrugged. The firelight flickering on his face hollowed his cheeks and threw shadows into the orbits of his eyes. It made him look older than he was; I tended to forget that he was not quite twenty-four.

"Aye, well. And Louise de La Tour has a reason, too," he said. "She wants to save one life, I want ten thousand. Does that excuse my risking wee Fergus— and Jared's business—and you?" He turned his head and smiled at me, the light gleaming from the long, straight bridge of his nose, glowing like sapphire in the one eye turned toward the fire.

"Nay, I think I wilna lose my sleep over the need for opening another man's letters," he said. "It may come to much worse than that before we've done, Claire, and I canna say ahead of time what my conscience will stand; it's best not to test it too soon."

There was nothing to be said to that; it was all true. I reached out and laid my hand against his cheek. He laid his own hand over mine, cradling it for a moment, then turned his head and gently kissed my palm.

"Well," he said, drawing a deep breath and returning to business. "Now that we've eaten, shall we have a look at this letter?"

The letter was coded; that much was obvious. To foil possible interceptors, Jamie explained.

"Who would want to intercept His Highness's mail?" I asked. "Besides us, I mean."

Jamie snorted with amusement at my naiveté.

"Almost anyone, Sassenach. Louis's spies, Duverney's spies, Philip of Spain's spies. The Jacobite lords and the ones who think they might turn Jacobite if the wind sets right. Dealers in information, who dinna care a fart in a breeze who lives or dies by it. The Pope himself; the Holy See's been support-ing the Stuarts in exile for fifty years—I imagine he keeps an eye on what they're doing." He tapped a finger on the copy I'd made of James's letter to his son.

"The seal on this letter had been removed maybe three times before I took it off myself," he said.

"I see," I said. "No wonder James codes his letters. Do you think you can make out what he says?"

Jamie picked up the sheets, frowning.

"I don't know; some, yes. Some other things, I've no idea. I think perhaps I can work it out, though, if I can see some other letters King James has sent. I'll see what Fergus can do for me there." He folded the copy and put it carefully away in a drawer, which he locked.

"Ye canna trust anyone, Sassenach," he explained, seeing my eyes widen. "We might easily have spies among the servants." He dropped the small key in the pocket of his coat, and held out his arm to me.

I took the candle in one hand and his arm in the other, and we turned toward the stairs. The rest of the house was dark, the servants—all but Fergus —virtuously asleep. I felt a trifle creepy, with the realization that one or more of the silent sleepers below or above might not be what they seemed.

"Doesn't it make you feel a bit nervous?" I asked as we went up the stairs. "Never being able to trust anyone?"

He laughed softly. "Well, I wouldna say *anyone*, Sassenach. There's you— and Murtagh, and my sister Jenny and her husband Ian. I'd trust the four of you wi' my life—I have, for that matter, more than once."

I shivered as he pulled back the drapes of the big bed. The fire had been banked for the night, and the room was growing cold.

"Four people you can trust doesn't seem like all that many," I said, un- lacing my gown.

He pulled his shirt over his head and tossed it on the chair. The scars on his back shone silver in the faint light from the night sky outside.

"Aye, well," he said matter-of-factly. "It's four more than Charles Stuart has."

There was a bird singing outside, though it was long before first light. A mockingbird, practicing his trills and runs over and over, perched on a rain gutter somewhere in the dark nearby.

Moving sleepily, Jamie rubbed his cheek against the smooth skin of my freshly waxed underarm, then turned his head and planted a soft kiss in the warm hollow that sent a small, delicious shudder down my side.

"Mm," he murmured, running a light hand over my ribs. "I like it when ye come out all gooseflesh like that, Sassenach."

"Like this?" I answered, running the nails of my right hand gently over the skin of his back, which obligingly rippled into goose bumps under the teasing of the touch.

"Ah."

"Ah, yourself, then," I answered softly, doing it some more.

"Mmmm." With a luxurious groan, he rolled to the side, wrapping his arms around me as I followed, enjoying the sudden contact of every inch of our naked skins, all down the front from head to toe. He was warm as a smothered fire, the heat of him safely banked for the night, to kindle again to a blaze in the black cold of dawn.

His lips fastened gently on one nipple, and I groaned myself, arching slightly to encourage him to take it deeper into the warmth of his mouth. My breasts were growing fuller, and more sensitive by the day; my nipples ached and tingled sometimes under the tight binding of my gowns, wanting to be suckled.

"Will ye let me do this later?" he murmured, with a soft bite. "When the child's come, and your breasts fill wi' milk? Will ye feed me, too, then, next to your heart?"

I clasped his head and cradled it, fingers deep in the baby-soft hair that grew thick at the base of his skull.

"Always," I whispered.

14

Meditations on the Flesh

Fergus was more than adept at his profession, and nearly every day brought in a new selection of His Highness's correspondence; sometimes I was hard pressed to copy everything before Fergus's next expedition, when he would replace the items abstracted, before stealing the new letters.

Some of these were further coded communications from King James in Rome; Jamie put aside the copies of these, to puzzle over at leisure. The bulk of His Highness's correspondence was innocuous—notes from friends in Italy, an increasing number of bills from local merchants—Charles had a taste for gaudy clothing and fine boots, as well as for brandywine—and the occasional note from Louise de La Tour de Rohan. These were fairly easy to pick out; aside from the tiny, mannered handwriting she employed, that made her letters look as though a small bird had been making tracks on them, she invariably saturated the paper with her trademark hyacinth scent. Jamie resolutely refused to read these.

"I willna be reading the man's love letters," he said firmly. "Even a plotter must scruple at *something*." He sneezed, and dropped the latest missive back into Fergus's pocket. "Besides," he added more practically, "Louise tells ye everything, anyway."

This was true; Louise had become a close friend, and spent nearly as much time in my drawing room as she did in her own, wringing her hands over Charles, then forgetting him in the fascination of discussing the marvels of pregnancy—*she* never had morning sickness, curse her! Scatterbrained as she was, I liked her very much; still, it was a great relief to escape from her company to L'Hôpital des Anges every afternoon.

While Louise was unlikely ever to set foot within L'Hôpital des Anges, I was not without company when I went there. Undaunted by her first exposure to the Hôpital, Mary Hawkins summoned up the courage to accompany me again. And yet again. While she couldn't quite bring herself to look directly at a wound yet, she was useful at spooning gruel into people and sweeping floors. Apparently she considered these activities a welcome change from either the gatherings of the Court or the life at her uncle's house.

While she was frequently shocked at some of the behavior she saw at Court —not that she saw much, but she was easily shocked—she didn't betray any particular distaste or horror at the sight of the Vicomte Marigny, which led me to conclude that her wretched family had not yet completed the negotiations for her marriage—and therefore hadn't told her about it.

This conclusion was borne out one day in late April, when, en route to L'Hôpital des Anges, she blushingly confided to me that she was in love.

"Oh, he's so handsome!" she enthused, her stammer entirely forgotten. "And so . . . well, so *spiritual,* as well."

"Spiritual?" I said. "Mm, yes, very nice." Privately I thought that that particular quality was not one which would have topped my own list of desirable attributes in a lover, but then tastes differed.

"And who is the favored gentleman, then?" I teased gently. "Anyone I know?"

The rosy blush deepened. "No, I shouldn't think so." She looked up then, eyes sparkling. "But—oh, I shouldn't tell you this, but I can't help myself. He wrote to my father. He's coming back to Paris next week!"

"Really?" This was interesting news. "I'd heard that the Comte de Palles is expected at Court next week," I said. "Is your, um, intended, one of his party?"

Mary looked aghast at the suggestion.

"A Frenchman! Oh, no, Claire; really, how could I marry a Frenchman?"

"Is there something wrong with Frenchmen?" I asked, rather surprised at her vehemence. "You do speak French, after all." Perhaps that was the trouble, though; while Mary did speak French very nicely, her shyness made her stammer even worse in that language than in English. I had come across a couple of kitchen-boys only the day before, entertaining each other with cruel imitations of *"la petite Anglaise maladroite."*

"You don't know about Frenchmen?" she whispered, eyes wide and horrified. "Oh, but of course, you wouldn't. Your husband is so gentle and so kind. . . . he wouldn't, I m-mean I know he d-doesn't trouble you that way . . ." Her face was suffused with a rich peony that reached from chin to hairline, and the stammer was about to strangle her.

"Do you mean . . ." I began, trying to think of some tactful way of extricating her without entangling myself in speculations about the habits of Frenchmen. However, considering what Mr. Hawkins had told me about Mary's father and his plans for her marriage, I rather thought perhaps I should try to disabuse her of the notions that she had clearly picked up from the gossip of salon and dressing room. I didn't want her to die of fright if she *did* end up married to a Frenchman.

"What they d-do . . . in . . . in *bed*!" she whispered hoarsely.

"Well," I said matter-of-factly, "there are only so many things you *can* do in bed with a man, after all. And since I see quite a large number of children about the city, I'd assume that even Frenchmen are fairly well versed in the orthodox methods."

"Oh! Children . . . well, yes, of course," she said vaguely, as though not seeing much connection. "B-b-but they said"—she cast her eyes down, embarrassed, and her voice sank even lower—"th-that he . . . a Frenchm-man's *thing*, you know. . . ."

"Yes, I know," I said, striving for patience. "So far as I know, they're much like any other man's. Englishmen and Scotsmen are quite similarly endowed."

"Yes, but they, they . . . p-p-put it between a lady's l-l-legs! I mean, right up *inside* her!" This bit of stop-press news finally out, she took a deep breath, which seemed to steady her, for the violent crimson of her face receded slightly. "An Englishman, or even a Scot . . . oh, I didn't m-mean it *that* way . . ." Her hand flew to her mouth in embarrassment. "But a decent man like your husband, surely he would n-never dream of forcing a wife to endure s-something like that!"

I placed a hand on my slightly bloated stomach and regarded her thoughtfully. I began to see why spirituality ranked so highly in Mary Hawkins's catalog of manly virtues.

"Mary," I said, "I think we must have a small talk."

<hr/>

I was still smiling privately to myself when I walked out into the Great Hall of the Hôpital, my own dress covered with the drab, sturdy fabric of a novice's habit.

A good many of the *chirurgiens,* urinoscopists, bonesetters, physicians, and other healers were donating their time and services as a charity; others came to learn or refine their skills. The hapless patients of L'Hôpital des Anges were in no position to protest being the subjects of assorted medical experiments.

Aside from the nuns themselves, the medical staff changed almost daily, depending upon who found themselves without paying patients that day, or who had a new technique that needed trial. Still, most of the free-lance medicos came often enough that I learned to recognize the regulars in short order.

One of the most interesting was the tall, gaunt man whom I had seen amputating a leg on my first visit to the Hôpital. Upon inquiry, I determined that his name was Monsieur Forez. Primarily a bonesetter, occasionally he would attempt the trickier types of amputation, particularly when a whole limb, rather than a joint, was involved. The nuns and orderlies seemed a bit in awe of Monsieur Forez; they never chaffed him or exchanged rude jokes, as they did with most of the other volunteer medical help.

Monsieur Forez was at work today. I approached quietly, to see what he was doing. The patient, a young workman, lay white-faced and gasping on a pallet. He had fallen from the scaffolding on the cathedral—always under construction—and broken both an arm and a leg. I could see that the arm was no particular challenge to a professional bonesetter—only a simple fracture of the radius. The leg, though, was something else; an impressive double compound fracture, involving both the mid-femur and the tibia. Sharp bone fragments protruded through the skin of both thigh and shin, and the lacerated flesh was blue with traumatic bruising over most of the upper aspect of the leg.

I didn't wish to distract the bonesetter's attention to his case, but Monsieur Forez appeared sunk in thought, slowly circling the patient, sidling back and forth like a large carrion crow, cautious lest the victim not be really dead yet. He did look rather like a crow, I thought, with that prominent beak of a nose, and the smooth black hair that he wore unpowdered, slicked back to a wispy knot at the nape of his neck. His clothes, too, were black and somber, though of good quality—evidently he had a profitable practice outside the Hôpital.

At last deciding on his course of action, Monsieur Forez lifted his chin from his hand and glanced around for assistance. His eye lighted on me, and he beckoned me forward. I was dressed in a coarse linen novice's gown, and lost in his concentration, he did not notice that I didn't wear the wimple and veil of a nursing sister.

"Here, *ma soeur,*" he directed, taking hold of the patient's ankle. "Grasp it tightly just behind the heel. Do not apply pressure until I tell you, but when I give the word, draw the foot directly toward you. Pull very slowly, but with force—it will take considerable strength, you understand."

"I understand." I grasped the foot as directed, while Monsieur Forez made his slow and gangling way toward the other end of the pallet, glancing contemplatively at the fractured leg.

"I have a stimulant here to assist," he said, drawing a small vial out of his coat pocket and setting it beside the patient's head. "It constricts the blood vessels of the surface skin, and drives the blood inward, where it may be of more use to our young friend." So speaking, he grasped the patient by the hair and thrust the vial into the young man's mouth, skillfully decanting the medicine down his throat without spilling a drop.

"Ah," he said approvingly as the man gulped and breathed deeply. "That will help. Now, as to the pain—yes, it is better if we can numb the leg, so he will be less inclined to resist our efforts as we straighten it."

He reached into his capacious pocket once more, this time coming out with a small brass pin, some three inches in length, with a wide, flat head. One bony, thick-jointed hand tenderly explored the inside of the patient's thigh near the groin, following the thin blue line of a large vein beneath the skin. The groping fingers hesitated, paused, palpated in a small circle, then settled on a point. Digging a sharp forefinger into the skin as though to mark his place, Monsieur Forez brought the point of the brass pin to bear in the same place. Another quick reach into the pocket of marvels produced a small brass hammer, with which he drove the pin straight into the leg with one blow.

The leg twitched violently, then seemed to relax into limpness. The vasoconstrictor administered earlier did in fact seem to be working; the ooze of blood from the severed tissues was markedly less.

"That's amazing!" I exclaimed. "What did you do?"

Monsieur Forez smiled shyly, a faint rosiness staining his blue-shadowed cheeks with pleasure at my admiration.

"Well, it does not always work quite so well," he admitted modestly. "Luck was with me this time." He pointed at the brass pin, explaining, "There is a large bundle of nerve endings there, Sister, what I have heard the anatomists call a *plexus*. If you are fortunate enough to pierce it directly, it numbs a great deal of the sensations in the lower extremity." He straightened abruptly, realizing that he was wasting time in talk that might better be spent in action.

"Come, *ma soeur*," he ordered. "Back to your post! The action of the stimulant is not long-lasting; we must work now, while the bleeding is suppressed."

Almost limp, the leg straightened easily, the splintered ends of bone drawing back through the skin. Following Monsieur Forez's orders, I now grasped the young man about the torso, while he maneuvered the foot and lower leg, so that we applied a constant traction while the final small adjustments were made.

"That will do, Sister. Now, if you will but hold the foot steady for a moment." A shout summoned an orderly with a couple of stout sticks and some rags for binding, and in no time we had the limb neatly splinted and the open wounds firmly dressed with pressure bandages.

Monsieur Forez and I exchanged a broad smile of congratulation over the body of our patient.

"Lovely work, that," I praised, shoving back a lock of hair that had come unbound during our exertions. I saw Monsieur Forez's face change suddenly, as he realized that I wore no veil, and just then the loud bonging of the Vespers bell rang from the adjacent church. I glanced openmouthed at the tall window at the end of the ward, left unglassed to allow unwholesome vapors to pass out. Sure enough, the oblong of sky was the deep half-indigo of early evening.

"Excuse me," I said, starting to wriggle out of the covering gown. "I must go at once; my husband will be worried about me coming home so late. I'm so glad to have had the chance of assisting you, Monsieur Forez." The tall bonesetter watched this disrobing act in patent astonishment.

"But you . . . well, no, of course you are not a nun, I should have realized that before . . . but you . . . who are you?" he asked curiously.

"My name's Fraser," I told him briefly. "Look, I *must* go, or my husband . . ."

He drew himself up to his full gawky height, and bowed with deep seriousness.

"I should esteem it a privilege if you would allow me to see you home, Madame Fraser."

"Oh . . . why, thank you," I said, touched at his thoughtfulness. "I have an escort, though," I said, looking vaguely around the hall for Fergus, who had taken over escort duty from Murtagh, when he was not needed to steal something. He was there, leaning against the doorjamb, twitching with impatience. I wondered how long he had been there—the sisters wouldn't allow him into the main hall or the wards, always insisting that he wait for me by the door.

Monsieur Forez eyed my escort dubiously, then took me firmly by the elbow.

"I will see you to your door, Madame," he declared. "This section of the city is much too dangerous in the evening hours for you to be abroad with no more than a child for protection."

I could see Fergus swelling with indignation at being called a child, and hastened to protest that he was an excellent escort, always taking care to guide me by the safest streets. Monsieur Forez paid no attention to either of us, merely nodding in a stately manner to Sister Angelique as he steered me through the huge double doors of the Hôpital.

Fergus trotted at my heels, plucking at my sleeve. "Madame!" he said in a urgent whisper. "Madame! I promised the master that I would see you safely home each day, that I would not allow you to associate with undesirable—"

"Ah, here we are. Madame, you sit here; your boy may have the other seat." Ignoring Fergus's yapping, Monsieur Forez picked him up and tossed him casually into the waiting carriage.

The carriage was a small open one, but elegantly equipped, with deep blue velvet seats and a small canopy to protect the passengers from sudden inclemencies of weather or slops flung from above. There was no coat of arms or other decoration on the equipage's door; Monsieur Forez was not of the nobility—must be a rich bourgeois, I thought.

We made polite conversation on the way home, discussing medical matters, while Fergus sulked in the corner, glowering under the ragged thatch of his hair. When we pulled up in the Rue Tremoulins, he leaped over the side without waiting for the coachman to open the door, and sprinted inside. I stared after him, wondering what ailed him, then turned to take my farewell of Monsieur Forez.

"Really, it is nothing," he assured me graciously, in response to my profuse thanks. "Your residence lies along the path I take to my own house, in any case. And I could not have trusted the person of such a gracious lady to the Paris streets at this hour." He handed me down from the carriage, and was opening his mouth to say more, when the gate slammed open behind us.

I turned in time to see Jamie's expression change from mild annoyance to startled surprise.

"Oh!" he said. "Good evening, Monsieur." He bowed to Monsieur Forez, who returned the salute with great solemnity.

"Your wife has allowed me the great pleasure of delivering her safely to your door, milord. As for her late arrival, I beg you will lay the blame for that on my own shoulders; she was most nobly assisting me in a small endeavor at L'Hôpital des Anges."

"I expect she was," said Jamie in a resigned tone. "After all," he added in English, raising an eyebrow at me, "ye couldna expect a mere husband to hold the same sort of appeal as an inflamed bowel or a case of bilious spots, could ye?" The corner of his mouth twitched, though, and I knew he wasn't really annoyed, only concerned that I hadn't come home; I felt a twinge of regret at having worried him.

Bowing once more to Monsieur Forez, he grasped me by the upper arm and hustled me through the gate.

"Where's Fergus?" I asked, as soon as the gate was closed behind us. Jamie snorted.

"In the kitchen, awaiting retribution, I expect."

"Retribution? What do you mean by that?" I demanded. Unexpectedly, he laughed.

"Well," he said, "I was sittin' in the study, wondering where in bloody hell you'd got to, and on the verge of going down to the Hôpital myself, when the door flew open, and young Fergus shot in and threw himself on the floor at my feet, begging me to kill him on the spot."

"Kill him? Whatever for?"

"Well, that's what I asked him myself, Sassenach. I thought perhaps you and he had been waylaid by footpads along the way—there are dangerous gangs of ruffians about the streets, ye ken, and I thought losin' you that way would be the only thing would make him behave so. But he said you were at the gate, so I came tearing along to see were ye all right, with Fergus at my heels, babbling about betraying my trust and being unworthy to call me master, and begging me to beat him to death. I found it a bit difficult to think, what wi' all that going on, so I told him I'd attend to him later, and sent him to the kitchen."

"Oh, bloody hell!" I said. "Does he really think he's betrayed your trust, just because I've come home a bit late?"

Jamie glanced aside at me.

"Aye, he does. And so he did, for that matter, letting ye ride in company with a stranger. He swears that he would ha' thrown himself in front of the horses before he would let ye enter the carriage, save that *you*," he added pointedly, "seemed on good terms wi' the man."

"Well, of course I was on good terms with him," I said indignantly. "I'd just been helping him set a leg."

"Mphm." This line of argument appeared to strike him as unconvincing.

"Oh, all right," I agreed reluctantly. "Perhaps it was a bit unwise. But he really did seem entirely respectable, and I *was* in a hurry to get home—I knew you'd be worried." Still, I was now wishing I had paid a little more attention to

Fergus's frantic mumblings and pluckings at my sleeve. At the time, I had been concerned only to reach home as soon as possible.

"You aren't really going to beat him, are you?" I asked in some alarm. "It wasn't his fault in the slightest—I insisted on going with Monsieur Forez. I mean, if anyone deserves beating, it's me."

Turning in the direction of the kitchen, Jamie cocked a sardonic eyebrow at me.

"Aye, it is," he agreed. "Having sworn to refrain from any such actions, though, I may have to settle for Fergus."

"Jamie! You wouldn't!" I stopped dead, yanking on his arm. "Jamie! Please!" Then I saw the smile hidden in the corner of his mouth, and sighed in relief.

"No," he said, letting the smile become visible. "I dinna mean to kill him —or even beat him, for that matter. I may have to go clout him over the ear a time or two, though, if only to save his honor," he added. "He thinks he's committed a major crime by not following my orders to guard ye—I can hardly let it pass without some sign of official displeasure."

He paused outside the baize door to the kitchens to fasten his cuffs and rewind the stock about his throat.

"Am I decent?" he inquired, smoothing back his thick, unruly hair. "Perhaps I should go and fetch my coat—I'm not sure what's proper for administering rebukes."

"You look fine," I said, suppressing a smile. "Very severe."

"Oh, that's good," he said, straightening his shoulders and compressing his lips. "I hope I don't laugh, that wouldna do at all," he muttered, pushing open the door to the kitchen stair.

The atmosphere in the kitchen was far from hilarious, though. At our entrance, the customary gabble ceased at once, and there was a hasty drawing up of the staff at one side of the room. Everyone stood stock-still for a moment, then there was a small stir between two kitchenmaids, and Fergus stepped out into the open space before us.

The boy's face was white and tracked with tears, but he was not weeping now. With considerable dignity, he bowed, first to me and then Jamie, in turn.

"Madame, Monsieur, I am ashamed," he said, low-voiced but distinct. "I am unworthy to be in your employment, but still I beg that you will not dismiss me." His high-pitched voice quavered a little at the thought, and I bit my lip. Fergus glanced aside at the ranks of the servants, as though for moral support, and received a nod of encouragement from Fernand the coachman. Drawing a deep breath for courage, he straightened up and addressed Jamie directly.

"I am ready to suffer my punishment now, milord," he said. As though this had been the signal, one of the footmen stepped out of the rigid crowd, led the boy to the scrubbed plank table, and passing on the other side, took hold of the lad's hands, pulling him half across the surface of the table and holding him so extended.

"But . . ." Jamie began, taken aback by the speed of events. He got no further before Magnus, the elderly butler, stepped gravely up and presented him with the leather strop used for sharpening the kitchen knives, laid ceremonially atop the meat platter.

"Er," Jamie said, looking helplessly at me.

"Um," I said, and took one step back. Eyes narrowed, he grabbed my hand, squeezing it tightly.

"No, ye don't, Sassenach," he muttered in English. "If I have to do it, you have to watch it!"

Glancing desperately back and forth between his would-be victim and the proffered instrument of execution, he hesitated for a moment longer, then gave up.

"Oh, bloody fucking hell," he muttered under his breath in English, grabbing the strop from Magnus. He flexed the broad strap dubiously between his hands; three inches wide and a quarter-inch thick, it was a formidable weapon. Clearly wishing himself anywhere else, he advanced upon the prone body of Fergus.

"All right, then," he said, glaring ferociously round the room. "Ten strokes, and I don't wish to hear a fuss about it." Several of the female servants blanched visibly at this, and clung to each other for support, but there was dead silence in the big room as he raised the strap.

The resultant crack at impact made me jump, and there were small squeaks of alarm from the kitchenmaids, but no sound from Fergus. The small body quivered, and Jamie closed his eyes briefly, then set his lips and proceeded to inflict the remainder of the sentence, strokes evenly spaced. I felt sick, and surreptitiously wiped my damp palms on my skirt. At the same time, I felt an unhinged urge to laugh at the terrible farce of the situation.

Fergus endured everything in total silence, and when Jamie had finished and stepped back, pale and sweating, the small body lay so still that I was afraid for a moment that he had died—of shock, if not from the actual effects of the beating. But then a deep shudder seemed to run over the small frame, and the boy slid backward and raised himself stiffly off the table.

Jamie leaped forward to grasp him by an arm, anxiously smoothing back the sweat-drenched hair from his forehead.

"Are ye all right, man?" he asked. "God, Fergus, tell me you're all right!"

The boy was white to the lips, and his eyes were the size of saucers, but he smiled at this evidence of goodwill on the part of his employer, buck teeth gleaming in the lamplight.

"Oh yes, milord," he gasped. "Am I forgiven?"

"Jesus Christ," Jamie muttered, and clasped the boy tightly against his chest. "Yes, of course ye are, fool." He held the boy at arm's length and shook him slightly. "I dinna want to do that ever again, d'ye hear me?"

Fergus nodded, eyes glowing, then broke away and fell to his knees before me.

"Do you forgive me also, Madame?" he asked, folding his hands formally in front of him, and looking trustfully up, like a chipmunk begging for nuts.

I thought I would expire on the spot of mortification, but mustered sufficient self-possession to reach down and raise the boy to his feet.

"There is nothing to forgive," I told him firmly, my cheeks burning. "You're a very courageous lad, Fergus. Why . . . er, why don't you go and have some supper now?"

At this, the atmosphere of the kitchen relaxed, as though everyone had drawn a massive sigh of relief at once. The other servants pushed forward, babbling concern and congratulations, and Fergus was swept off to a hero's reception, while Jamie and I beat a precipitous retreat back to our quarters abovestairs.

"Oh, God," Jamie said, collapsing into his chair as though completely drained. "Sweet bleeding Jesus. Mary, Michael, and Bride. Lord, I need a drink. Don't ring!" he exclaimed in alarm, though I hadn't made a move toward the bell rope. "I couldna bear to face one of the servants just now."

He got up and rummaged in the cupboard. "I think I've a bottle in here, though."

He had indeed, a nice aged Scotch. Removing the cork unceremoniously with his teeth, he lowered the level of the spirit by an inch or so, then handed the bottle to me. I followed his example without hesitation.

"Jesus Christ," I said, when I had recovered breath enough to speak.

"Yes," he said, taking the bottle back and taking another gulp. Setting the bottle down, he clutched his head, running his fingers through his hair until it stood on end in wild disarray. He laughed weakly.

"I've never felt so foolish in my entire life. God, I felt a clot-heid!"

"So did I," I said, taking my turn at the bottle. "Even more than you, I imagine. After all, it was all my fault. Jamie, I can't tell you how sorry I am; I never imagined . . ."

"Ah, dinna worry yourself." The tension of the last half-hour released, he squeezed my shoulder affectionately. "You couldna have any idea. Neither did I, for that matter," he added reflectively. "I suppose he thought I'd dismiss him, and he'd be back in the streets . . . poor little bugger. No wonder he thought himself lucky to take a beating instead."

I shuddered briefly, remembering the streets through which Monsieur Forez's carriage had traveled. Beggars dressed in rags and sores clung stubbornly to their territories, sleeping on the ground even on the coldest nights, lest some rival steal a profitable corner from them. Children much smaller than Fergus darted through the market crowds like hungry mice, eyes always watching for the dropped crumb, the unguarded pocket. And for those too un-healthy to work, too unattractive to sell to the brothels, or simply too unlucky —it would be a short life indeed, and far from merry. Little wonder if the prospect of being thrust from the luxury of three meals a day and clean clothes back into that sordid stew had been sufficient to send Fergus into paroxysms of needless guilt.

"I suppose so," I said. My manner of intake had declined from gulps to a more genteel sipping by this time. I sipped genteelly, then handed the bottle back, noting in a rather detached manner that it was more than half empty. "Still, I hope you didn't hurt him."

"Weel, nay doubt he'll be a bit sore." His Scots accent, usually faint, always grew more pronounced when he drank a lot. He shook his head, squint-ing through the bottle to judge the level of spirit remaining. "D'ye know, Sassenach, I never 'til tonight realized just how difficult it must ha' been for my father to beat me? I always thought it was me had the hardest part of that particular transaction." He tilted his head back and drank again, then set down the bottle and stared owl-eyed into the fire. "Being a father might be a bit more complicated than I'd thought. I'll have to think about it."

"Well, don't think too hard," I said. "You've had a lot to drink."

"Och, don't worry," he said cheerfully. "There's another bottle in the cupboard."

15

In Which Music Plays a Part

We stayed up late with the second bottle, going over and over the latest of the abstracted letters from the Chevalier de St. George —otherwise known as His Majesty, James III—and the letters to Prince Charles from Jacobite supporters.

"Fergus got a large packet, bound for His Highness," Jamie explained. "There was a lot of stuff in it, and we couldna copy it all quickly enough, so I kept some to go back the next time."

"See," he said, extracting one sheet from the pile and laying it on my knee, "the majority of the letters are in code, like this one—'I hear that the prospects for grouse seem most favorable this year in the hills above Salerno; hunters in that region should find themselves successful.' That's easy; it's a reference to Manzetti, the Italian banker; he's from Salerno. I found that Charles had been dining with him, and managed to borrow fifteen thousand livres—apparently James's advice was good. But here—" He shuffled through the stack, pulling out another sheet.

"Look at this," Jamie said, handing me a sheet covered with his lopsided scrawls.

I squinted obediently at the paper, from which I could pick out single letters, connected with a network of arrows and question marks.

"What language is that?" I asked, peering at it. "Polish?" Charles Stuart's mother, the late Clementina Sobieski, had been Polish, after all.

"No, it's in English," Jamie said, grinning. "You canna read it?"

"You can?"

"Oh, aye," he said smugly. "It's a cipher, Sassenach, and no a verra complicated one. See, all ye must do is break the letters up into groups of five, to start—only ye don't count the letters Q or X. The X's are meant as breaks between sentences, and the Q's are only stuck in here and there to make it more confusing."

"If you say so," I said, looking from the extremely confusing-looking letter, which began "Mrti ocruti dlopro qahstmin . . ." to the sheet in Jamie's hand, with a series of five-letter groups written on one line, single letters printed in carefully above them, one at a time.

"So, one letter is only substituted for another, but in the same order," Jamie was explaining, "so if you have a fair amount of text to work from, and you can guess a word here or there, then all ye need do is to translate from one alphabet to the other—see?" He waved a long strip of paper under my nose, with two alphabets printed one above the other, slightly offset.

"Well, more or less," I said. "I gather you do, though, which is what's important. What does it say?"

The expression of lively interest with which Jamie greeted all manner of puzzles faded a bit, and he let the sheet of paper fall to his knee. He looked at me, lower lip caught between his teeth in introspection.

"Well," he said, "that's what's odd. And yet I dinna see how I can be mistaken. The tone of James's letters overall tend one way, and this ciphered one spells it out clearly."

Blue eyes met mine under thick, ruddy brows.

"James wants Charles to find favor with Louis," he said slowly, "but he isna looking for support for an invasion of Scotland. James has no interest in seeking restoration to the throne."

"What?" I snatched the sheaf of letters from his hand, my eyes feverishly scanning the scribbled text.

Jamie was right; while the letters from supporters spoke hopefully of the impending restoration, James's letters to his son mentioned no such thing, but were all concerned with Charles's making a good impression upon Louis. Even the loan from Manzetti of Salerno had been sought to enable Charles to live with the appearance of a gentleman in Paris; not to support any military end.

"Well, I'm thinking James is a canny wee man," Jamie had said, tapping one of the letters. "For see, Sassenach, he's verra little money of his own; his wife had a great deal, but Uncle Alex told me that she left it all to the church when she died. The Pope has been maintaining James's establishment—after all, he's a Catholic monarch, and the Pope is bound to uphold his interests against those of the Elector of Hanover."

He clasped his hands around one knee, gazing meditatively at the pile of papers now laid between us on the sofa.

"Philip of Spain and Louis—the Old King, I mean—gave him a small number of troops and a few ships, thirty years ago, with which to try to regain his throne. But it all went wrong; bad weather sank some of the ships, and the rest had no pilots and landed in the wrong place—everything went awry, and in the end, the French simply sailed off again, with James not even setting foot upon the soil of Scotland. So perhaps in the years since, he gave up any thought of getting back his throne. But still, he had two sons coming to manhood, and no way to see them properly settled in life.

"So I ask myself, Sassenach"—he rocked backward a bit—"what would I do, in such a situation? The answer being, that I might try and see if my good cousin Louis—who's King of France, after all—might maybe see one son established in a good position; given a military appointment, maybe, and men to lead. A General of France is no bad position in life."

"Mm." I nodded, thinking. "Yes, but if I were a very smart man, I might not just come to Louis and beg, as a poor relation. I might send my son to Paris, and try to shame Louis into accepting him at Court. And meanwhile keep alive the illusion that I was actively seeking restoration."

"For once James admits openly that the Stuarts will never rule Scotland again," Jamie added softly, "then he has no more value to Louis."

And without the possibility of an armed Jacobite invasion to occupy the English, Louis would have little reason to give his young cousin Charles anything beyond the pittance that decency and public opinion would force him to provide.

It wasn't certain; the letters Jamie had been able to get, a few at a time, went back only as far as last January, when Charles had arrived in France. And, couched in code, cipher, and guarded language generally, the situation was far from clear. But taken all in all, the evidence did point in that direction.

And if Jamie's guess as to the Chevalier's motives was correct—then our task was accomplished already; had never in fact existed at all.

Thinking over the events of the night before, I was abstracted all the next day, through a visit to Marie d'Arbanville's morning salon to hear a Hungarian poet, through a visit to a neighborhood herbalist's to pick up some valerian and orris root, and through my rounds at L'Hôpital des Anges in the afternoon.

Finally, I abandoned my work, afraid that I might accidentally damage someone while wool-gathering. Neither Murtagh nor Fergus had yet arrived to escort me home, so I changed out of my covering gown and sat down in Mother Hildegarde's vacant office to wait, just inside the vestibule of the Hôpital.

I had been there for perhaps half an hour, idly pleating the stuff of my gown between my fingers, when I heard the dog outside.

The porter was absent, as he often was. Gone to buy food, no doubt, or run an errand for one of the nuns. As usual in his absence, the guardianship of the Hôpital's portals was given into the capable paws—and teeth—of Bouton.

The first warning yip was followed by a low, burring growl that warned the intruder to stay where he was, on pain of instant dismemberment. I rose and stuck my head out of the office door, to see whether Father Balmain might be braving the peril of the demon once more, in pursuit of his sacramental duties. But the figure outlined against the huge stained-glass window of the entry hall was not the spare form of the junior priest. It was a tall figure, whose silhouetted kilts swayed gracefully around his legs as he drew back from the small, toothed animal at his feet.

Jamie blinked, brought up short by the assault. Shading his eyes against the dazzle from the window, he peered down into the shadows.

"Oh, hallo there, wee dog," he said politely, and took a step forward, knuckles stretched out. Bouton raised the growl a few decibels, and he took a step back.

"Oh, like that, is it?" Jamie said. He eyed the dog narrowly.

"Think it over, laddie," he advised, squinting down his long, straight nose. "I'm a damn sight bigger than you. I wouldna undertake any rash ventures, if I were you."

Bouton shifted his ground slightly, still making a noise like a distant Fokker.

"Faster, too," said Jamie, making a feint to one side. Bouton's teeth snapped together a few inches from Jamie's calf, and he stepped back hastily. Leaning back against the wall, he folded his arms and nodded down at the dog.

"Well, you've a point there, I'll admit. When it comes to teeth, ye've the edge on me, and no mistake." Bouton cocked an ear suspiciously at this gracious speech, but went back to the low-pitched growl.

Jamie hooked one foot over the other, like one prepared to pass the time of day indefinitely. The multicolored light from the window washed his face with blue, making him look like one of the chilly marble statues in the cathedral next door.

"Surely you've better things to do than harry innocent visitors?" he asked, conversationally. "I've heard of you—you're the famous fellow that sniffs out sickness, no? Weel, then, why are they wastin' ye on silly things like door-guarding, when ye might be makin' yourself useful smelling gouty toes and pustulant arseholes? Answer me that, if ye will!"

A sharp bark in response to his uncrossing his feet was the only answer.

There was a stir of robes behind me as Mother Hildegarde entered from the inner office.

"What is it?" she asked, seeing me peering round the corner. "Have we visitors?"

"Bouton seems to be having a difference of opinion with my husband," I said.

"I don't have to put up wi' this, ye ken," Jamie was threatening. One hand was stealing toward the brooch that held his plaid at the shoulder. "One quick spring wi' my plaid, and I'll have ye trussed like a—oh, *bonjour,* Madame!" he said, changing swiftly to French at sight of Mother Hildegarde.

"*Bonjour,* Monsieur Fraser." She inclined her veil gracefully, more to hide the broad smile on her face than in greeting, I thought. "I see you have made the acquaintance of Bouton. Are you perhaps in search of your wife?"

This seeming to be my cue, I sidled out of the office behind her. My devoted spouse glanced from Bouton to the office door, plainly drawing conclusions.

"And just how long have ye been standin' there, Sassenach?" he asked dryly.

"Long enough," I said, with the smug self-assurance of one in Bouton's good books. "What would you have done with him, once you'd got him wrapped up in your plaid?"

"Thrown him out the window and run like hell," he answered, with a brief glance of awe at Mother Hildegarde's imposing form. "Does she by chance speak English?"

"No, luckily for you," I answered. I switched to French for the introductions. *"Ma mère, je vous présente mon mari, le seigneur de Broch Tuarach."*

"Milord." Mother Hildegarde had by now mastered her sense of humor, and greeted him with her usual expression of formidable geniality. "We shall miss your wife, but if you require her, of course—"

"I didn't come for my wife," Jamie interrupted. "I came to see you, *ma mère.*"

Seated in Mother Hildegarde's office, Jamie laid the bundle of papers he carried on the shining wood of her desk. Bouton, keeping a wary eye on the intruder, lay down at his mistress's feet. He laid his nose upon his feet, but kept his ears cocked, lip raised over one eyetooth in case he should be called upon to rend the visitor limb from limb.

Jamie narrowed his eyes at Bouton, pointedly pulling his feet away from the twitching black nose. "Herr Gerstmann recommended that I consult you, Mother, about these documents," he said, unrolling the thick sheaf and flattening it beneath his palms.

Mother Hildegarde regarded Jamie for a moment, one heavy brow raised quizzically. Then she turned her attention to the sheaf of papers, with that administrator's trick of seeming to focus entirely on the matter at hand, while still keeping her sensitive antennae tuned to catch the faintest vibration of emergency from the far-off reaches of the Hôpital.

"Yes?" she said. One blunt finger ran lightly over the lines of scribbled music, one by one, as though she heard the notes by touching them. A flick of the finger, and the sheet slid aside, half-exposing the next.

"What is it that you wish to know, Monsieur Fraser?" she asked.

"I don't know, Mother." Jamie was leaning forward, intent. He touched the black lines himself, dabbing gently at the smear where the writer's hand had carelessly brushed the staves before the ink had dried.

"There is something odd about this music, Mother."

The nun's wide mouth moved slightly in what might have been a smile.

"Really, Monsieur Fraser? And yet I understand—you will not be offended, I trust—that to you, music is . . . a lock to which you have no key?"

Jamie laughed, and a sister passing in the hallways turned, startled by such a sound in the confines of the Hôpital. It was a noisy place, but laughter was unusual.

"That is a very tactful description of my disability, Mother. And altogether true. Were you to sing one of these pieces"—his finger, longer and more slender, but nearly the same size as Mother Hildegarde's, tapped the parchment with a soft rustling noise—"I could not tell it from the Kyrie Eleison or from 'La Dame fait bien'—except by the words," he added, with a grin.

Now it was Mother Hildegarde's turn to laugh.

"Indeed, Monsieur Fraser," she said. "Well, at least you listen to the words!" She took the sheaf of papers into her hands, riffling the tops. I could see the faint swelling of her throat above the tight band of her wimple as she read, as though she was singing silently to herself, and one large foot twitched slightly, keeping time.

Jamie sat very still upon his stool, good hand folded over the crooked one on his knee, watching her. The slanted blue eyes were intent, and he paid no attention to the ongoing noise from the depths of the Hôpital behind him. Patients cried out, orderlies and nuns shouted back and forth, family members shrieked in sorrow or dismay, and the muted clang of metal instruments echoed off the ancient stones of the building, but neither Jamie nor Mother Hildegarde moved.

At last she lowered the pages, peering at him over the tops. Her eyes were sparkling, and she looked suddenly like a young girl.

"I think you are right!" she said. "I cannot take time to think it over carefully just now"—she glanced toward the doorway, momentarily darkened by the form of an orderly dashing past with a large sack of lint—"but there is something odd here." She tapped the pages on the desk, straightening them into an orderly stack.

"How extraordinary," she said.

"Be that as it may, Mother—can you, with your gift, discern what this particular pattern is? It would be difficult; I have reason to suppose that it is a cipher, and that the language of the message is English, though the text of the songs is in German."

Mother Hildegarde uttered a small grunt of surprise.

"English? You are sure?"

Jamie shook his head. "Not sure, no, but I think so. For one reason, there is the country of origin; the songs were sent from England."

"Well, Monsieur," she said, arching one eyebrow. "Your wife speaks English, does she not? And I imagine that you would be willing to sacrifice her company to assist me in performing this endeavor for you?"

Jamie eyed her, the half-smile on his face the mirror image of hers. He glanced down at his feet, where Bouton's whiskers quivered with the ghost of a growl.

"I'll make ye a bargain, Mother," he said. "If your wee dog doesna bite me in the arse on the way out, you can have my wife."

And so, that evening, instead of returning home to Jared's house in the Rue Tremoulins, I took supper with the sisters of the Couvent des Anges at their long refectory table, and then retired for the evening's work to Mother Hildegarde's private rooms.

There were three rooms in the Superior's suite. The outer one was furnished as a sitting room, with a fair degree of richness. This, after all, was where she must often receive official visitors. The second room was something of a shock, simply because I wasn't expecting it. At first, I had the impression that there was nothing in the small room but a large harpsichord, made of gleaming, polished walnut, and decorated with small, hand-painted flowers sprouting from a twisting vine that ran along the sounding board above glowing ebony keys.

On second look, I saw a few other bits of furniture in the room, including a set of bookshelves that ran the length of one wall, stuffed with works on musicology and hand-stitched manuscripts much like the one Mother Hildegarde now laid on the harpsichord's rack.

She motioned me to a chair placed before a small secretary against one wall.

"You will find blank paper and ink there, milady. Now, let us see what this little piece of music may tell us."

The music was written on heavy parchment, the lines of the staves cleanly ruled across the page. The notes themselves, the clef signs, rests, and accidentals, were all drawn with considerable care; this was plainly a final clean copy, not a draft or a hastily scribbled tune. Across the top of the page was the title "Lied des Landes." A Song of the Country.

"The title, you see, suggests something simple, like a *volkslied*," Mother Hildegarde said, pointing one long, bony forefinger at the page. "And yet the form of the composition is something quite different. Can you read music at sight?" The big right hand, large-knuckled and short-nailed, descended on the keys with an impossibly delicate touch.

Leaning over Mother Hildegarde's black-clad shoulder, I sang the first three lines of the piece, making the best I could of the German pronunciation. Then she stopped playing, and twisted to look up at me.

"That is the basic melody. It then repeats itself in variations—but *such* variations! You know, I have seen some things reminiscent of this. By a little old German named Bach; he sends me things now and again—" She waved carelessly at the shelf of manuscripts. "He calls them 'Inventions,' and they're really quite clever; playing off the variations in two or three melodic lines simultaneously. *This*"—she pursed her lips at the 'Lied' before us—"is like a clumsy imitation of one of his things. In fact, I would swear that. . . ." Muttering to herself, she pushed back the walnut bench and went to the shelf, running a finger rapidly down the rows of manuscripts.

She found what she was looking for, and returned to the bench with three bound pieces of music.

"Here are the Bach pieces. They're fairly old, I haven't looked at them in several years. Still, I'm almost sure . . ." She lapsed into silence, flipping quickly through the pages of the Bach scripts on her knee, one at a time, glancing back now and then at the "Lied" on the rack.

"Ha!" she let out a cry of triumph, and held out one of the Bach pieces to me. "See there?"

The paper was titled "Goldberg Variations," in a crabbed, smeared hand. I touched the paper with some awe, swallowed hard, and looked back at the "Lied." It took only a moment's comparison to see what she meant.

"You're right, it's the same!" I said. "A note different here and there, but basically it's exactly the same as the original theme of the Bach piece. How very peculiar!"

"Isn't it?" she said, in tones of deep satisfaction. "Now, why is this anonymous composer stealing melodies and treating them in such an odd fashion?"

This was clearly a rhetorical question, and I didn't bother with an answer, but asked one of my own.

"Is Bach's music much in vogue these days, Mother?" I certainly hadn't heard any at the musical salons I attended.

"No," she said, shaking her head as she peered at the music. "Herr Bach is not well known in France; I believe he had some small popularity in Germany and in Austria fifteen or twenty years ago, but even there his music is not performed much publicly. I am afraid his music is not the sort to endure; clever, but no heart. Hmph. Now, see here?" The blunt forefinger tapped here, and here, and here, turning pages rapidly.

"He has repeated the same melody—almost—but changed the key each time. I think this is perhaps what attracted your husband's notice; it is obvious even to someone who doesn't read music, because of the changing signatures— the *note tonique*."

It was; each key change was marked by a double vertical line followed by a new treble clef sign and the signature of sharps or flats.

"Five key changes in such a short piece," she said, tapping the last one again for emphasis. "And changes that make no sense at all, in terms of music. Look, the basic line is precisely the same, yet we move from the key of two flats, which is B-flat major, to A-major, with three sharps. Stranger yet, now he goes to a signature of two sharps, and yet he uses the G-sharp accidental!"

"How very peculiar," I said. Adding a G-sharp accidental to the section in D-major had the effect of making the musical line identical with the A-major section. In other words, there was no reason whatsoever to have changed the key signature.

"I don't know German," I said. "Can you read the words, Mother?"

She nodded, the folds of her black veil rustling with the movement, small eyes intent on the manuscript.

"What truly execrable lyrics!" she murmured to herself. "Not that one expects great poetry from Germans in general, but really . . . still—" She broke off with a shake of her veil. "We must assume that if your husband is correct in assuming this to be a cipher of some sort, that the message lies embedded in these words. They may therefore not be of great import in themselves."

"What does it say?" I asked.

" 'My shepherdess frolics with her lambs among the verdant hills,' " she read. "Horrible grammar, though of course liberties are often taken in writing songs, if the lyricist insists upon the lines rhyming, which they nearly always do if it is a love song."

"You know a lot about love songs?" I asked curiously. Full of surprises tonight, was Mother Hildegarde.

"Any piece of good music is in essence a love song," she replied matter-of-factly. "But as for what you mean—yes, I have seen a great many. When I was a young girl"—she flashed her large white teeth in a smile, acknowledging the difficulty of imagining her as a child—"I was something of a prodigy, you understand. I could play from memory anything I heard, and I wrote my first composition at the age of seven." She gestured at the harpsichord, the rich veneer shining with polish.

"My family has wealth; had I been a man, no doubt I would have been a musician." She spoke simply, with no trace of regret.

"Surely you could still have composed music, if you'd married?" I asked curiously.

Mother Hildegarde spread her hands, grotesque in the lamplight. I had seen those hands wrench loose a dagger embedded in bone, guide a displaced joint back into alignment, cup the blood-smeared head of a child emerging from between its mother's thighs. And I had seen those fingers linger on the ebony keys with the delicacy of moths' feet.

"Well," she said, after a moment's contemplation, "it is the fault of St. Anselm."

"It is?"

She grinned at my expression, her ugly face quite transformed from its stern public facade.

"Oh, yes. My godfather—the Old Sun King," she added casually, "gave to me a book of the Lives of the Saints for my own Saint's Day when I was eight. It was a beautiful book," she said reminiscently, "with gilded pages and a jeweled cover; intended more as a work of art than a work of literature. Still, I read it. And while I enjoyed all of the stories—particularly those of the martyrs—still there was one phrase in the story of St. Anselm that seemed to strike a response in my soul."

She closed her eyes and tilted back her head, recalling.

"St. Anselm was a man of great wisdom and great learning, a Doctor of the Church. But also a bishop, a man who cared for the people of his flock, and looked after their temporal needs as well as those of the spirit. The story detailed all of his works, and then concluded in these words—'And so he died, at the conclusion of an eminently useful life, and thus obtained his crown in Paradise.'" She paused, flexing her hands lightly on her knees.

"There was something about that that appealed most strongly to me. 'An eminently useful life.'" She smiled at me. "I could think of many worse epitaphs than that, milady." She spread her hands suddenly and shrugged, an oddly graceful gesture.

"I wished to be useful," she said. Then, dismissing idle conversation, she turned abruptly back to the music on the rack.

"So," she said. "Plainly the change in the key signatures—the *note tonique* —that is the oddity. Where can we go with that?"

My mouth dropped open with a small exclamation. Speaking in French as we had been, I hadn't noticed before. But observing Mother Hildegarde as she told her story, I had been thinking in English, and when I glanced back at the music it hit me.

"What is it?" the nun asked. "You have thought of something?"

"The key!" I said, half-laughing. "In French, a musical key is the *note tonique,* but the word for an object that unlocks . . ." I pointed to the large bunch of keys—normally carried on her girdle—that Mother Hildegarde had laid aside on the bookshelf when we came in. "That is a *passe-partout,* isn't it?"

"Yes," she said, watching me in puzzlement. She touched the skeleton key in turn. "*Une passe-partout.* That one," she said, pointing to a key with barrel and wards, "is more likely called a *clef.*"

"A clef!" I exclaimed joyously. "Perfect!" I stabbed a finger at the sheet of music before us. "See, *ma mère,* in English, the words are the same. A 'key' gives the basis of a piece of music, and a 'key' unlocks. In French, the *clef* is a key, and in English, the 'clef' is also part of the musical signature. And the key of the music is also the key to the cipher. Jamie *said* he thought it was an English cipher! Made by an Englishman with a really diabolical sense of humor, too," I added.

With that small insight, the cipher proved not too difficult to unravel. If the maker was English, the ciphered message likely was in English, too, which meant that the German words were provided only as a source of letters. And having seen Jamie's earlier efforts with alphabets and shifting letters, it took only a few tries to determine the pattern of the cipher.

"Two flats means you must take every second letter, starting from the beginning of the section," I said, frantically scribbling down the results. "And three sharps means to take every third letter, beginning at the end of the section. I suppose he used German both for concealment and because it's so bloody wordy; it takes nearly twice as many words to say the same thing as it would in English."

"You have got ink on your nose," Mother Hildegarde observed. She peered over my shoulder. "Does it make sense?"

"Yes," I said, my mouth gone suddenly dry. "Yes, it makes sense."

Deciphered, the message was brief and simple. Also deeply disturbing.

"His Majesty's loyal subjects of England await his lawful restoration. The sum of fifty thousand pounds is at your disposal. As an earnest of good faith, this will be paid only in person, upon His Highness's arrival on the soil of England," I read. "And there's a letter left over, an 'S.' I don't know if that's a signature of sorts, or only something the maker needed to make the German word come out right."

"Hmph." Mother Hildegarde glanced curiously at the scribbled message, then at me. "You will know already, of course," she said, with a nod, "but you may assure your husband that I will keep this in confidence."

"He wouldn't have asked your help if he didn't trust you," I protested.

The sketchy brows rose to the edge of her wimple, and she tapped the scribbled paper firmly.

"If this is the sort of endeavor in which your husband engages, he takes considerable risk in trusting anyone. Assure him that I am sensible of the honor," she added dryly.

"I'll do that," I said, smiling.

"Why, *chère Madame*," she said, catching sight of me, "you are looking quite pale! I myself often stay awake far into the night when I am working on a new piece, so I tend to pay little attention to the hour, but it must be late for you." She glanced at the hour-candle burning on the little table near the door.

"Gracious! It *is* growing late. Shall I summon Sister Madeleine to take you to your chamber?" Jamie had agreed, reluctantly, with Mother Hildegarde's suggestion that I spend the night at the Couvent des Anges, so that I need not return home through the dark streets late at night.

I shook my head. I was tired, and my back ached from sitting on the stool, but I didn't want to go to bed. The implications of the musical message were too disturbing to permit me to sleep right away, in any case.

"Well, then, let us take a little refreshment, in celebration of your accomplishment." Mother Hildegarde rose and went to the outer room, where I heard the ringing of a bell. Shortly one of the serving sisters came, bearing a tray of hot milk and small, iced cakes, and followed by Bouton. The serving sister placed a cake on a small china plate and set it on the floor before him as a matter of course, laying beside it a bowl of milk.

While I sipped my own hot milk, Mother Hildegarde set aside the source of our labors, laying it on the secretary, and instead placed a loose sheaf of music manuscript on the rack of the harpsichord.

"I shall play for you," she announced. "It will help to compose your mind for sleep."

The music was light and soothing, with a singing melody that wove back and forth from treble voice to bass in a pattern of pleasing complexity, but without the driving force of Bach.

"Is that yours?" I asked, choosing a pause as she lifted her hands at the conclusion of the piece.

She shook her head without turning around.

"No. A friend of mine, Jean Philippe Rameau. A good theorist, but he does not write with great passion."

I must have dozed, the music lulling my senses, for I woke suddenly to the murmur of Sister Madeleine's voice in my ear, and her warm, firm grip under my arm, lifting me to my feet and leading me away.

Looking back, I could see the broad span of Mother Hildegarde's black-swathed back, and the flex of powerful shoulders beneath the drape of her veil as she played, oblivious now to the world beyond the sanctum of her chamber. On the boards near her feet lay Bouton, nose on his paws, small body laid straight as the needle of a compass.

"So," Jamie said, "it's gone a little further than talk—maybe."

"Maybe?" I echoed. "An offer of fifty thousand pounds sounds fairly definite." Fifty thousand pounds, by current standards, was the yearly income of a good-sized duchy.

He raised one eyebrow cynically at the musical manuscript I had brought back with me from the convent.

"Aye, well. An offer like that is fairly safe, it it's contingent on either Charles or James setting foot in England. If Charles is in England, it means he's gotten sufficient backing from other places to get him to Scotland, first. No," he said, rubbing his chin thoughtfully, "what's interesting about this offer is that it's the first definite sign we've seen that the Stuarts—or one of them, at least—are actually making an effort at mounting a restoration attempt."

"One of them?" I caught the emphasis. "You mean you think James isn't in on this?" I looked at the coded message with even more interest.

"The message came to Charles," Jamie reminded me, "and it came from England—not through Rome. Fergus got it from a regular messenger, in a packet marked with English seals; not from a papal messenger. And everything I've seen in James's letters—" He shook his head, frowning. He hadn't yet shaved, and the morning light caught random sparks of copper among the auburn stubble of his beard.

"The packet had been opened; Charles has seen this manuscript. There was no date on it, so I dinna ken how long ago it came to him. And of course, we don't have the letters Charles has sent to his father. But there's no reference in any of James's letters to anyone who could possibly be the composer, let alone to any definite promises of support from England."

I could see the direction in which he was heading.

"And Louise de La Tour was babbling about how Charles meant to have her marriage annulled and claim her as his wife, once he was king. So you think perhaps Charles wasn't just talking through his hat to impress her?"

"Maybe not," he said. He poured water from the bedroom ewer into the basin and laved his face with water, preparatory to shaving.

"So it's possible that Charles is acting on his own?" I said, horrified and intrigued by the possibility. "That James has set him up for a masquerade of pretending to start a restoration attempt, in order to keep Louis impressed with the Stuarts' potential value, but—"

"But Charles isn't pretending?" Jamie interrupted. "Aye, that's how it seems. Is there a towel there, Sassenach?" Eyes screwed shut and face dripping, he was patting about on the surface of the table. I moved the manuscript to safety and found the towel, draped over the foot of the bed.

He examined his razor critically, decided it would do, and leaned over my dressing table to look in the mirror as he applied shaving soap to his cheeks.

"Why is it barbaric of me to take the hair off my legs and armpits, and it isn't barbaric for you to take it off your face?" I asked, watching him draw his upper lip down over his teeth as he scraped under his nose with tiny, delicate strokes.

"It is," he replied, squinting at himself in the mirror. "But it itches like a fiend if I don't."

"Have you ever grown a beard?" I asked curiously.

"Not on purpose," he replied, half-smiling as he scraped one cheek, "but I've had one now and then when I couldna help it—when I lived as an outlaw in Scotland. When it came to a choice between shaving in a cold burn with a dull razor every morning or itching, I chose to itch."

I laughed, watching him draw the razor along the edge of his jawbone with one long sweep.

"I can't imagine what you'd look like with a full beard. I've only seen you in the stubbly stage."

He smiled on one side of his mouth, drawing the other up as he scraped under the high, broad cheekbone on that side.

"Next time we're invited to Versailles, Sassenach, I'll ask if we may visit the Royal zoo. Louis has a creature there that one of his sea-captains brought him from Borneo, called an orang-utan. Ever seen one?"

"Yes," I said, "the zoo in London had a pair before the war."

"Then you'll know what I look like in a beard," he said, smiling at me as he finished his shave with a careful negotiation of the curve of his chin. "Scraggly and moth-eaten. Rather like the Vicomte Marigny," he added, "only red."

As though the name had reminded him, he returned to the main topic of discussion, wiping the remains of soap off his face with the linen towel.

"So I suppose what we must do now, Sassenach," he said, "is to keep a sharp eye out for Englishmen in Paris." He picked up the manuscript off the bed and riffled the pages thoughtfully. "If anyone is actually willing to contemplate support on this scale, I think they might be sending an envoy to Charles. If I were risking fifty thousand pounds, I might like to see what I was getting for my money, wouldn't you?"

"Yes, I would," I answered. "And speaking of Englishmen—does His Highness patriotically buy his brandywine from you and Jared, or does he by chance patronize the services of Mr. Silas Hawkins?"

"Mr. Silas Hawkins, who is so eager to know what the political climate is like in the Scottish Highlands?" Jamie shook his head at me admiringly. "And here I thought I married you because ye had a fair face and a fine fat arse. To think you've a brain as well!" He neatly dodged the blow I aimed at his ear, and grinned at me.

"I don't know, Sassenach, but I will before the day is out."

16

The Nature of Sulfur

P rince Charles *did* purchase his brandywine from Mr. Hawkins. Beyond that discovery, though, we made little progress over the course of the next four weeks. Things continued much as before. Louis of France continued to ignore Charles Stuart. Jamie continued to run the wine business and to visit Prince Charles. Fergus continued to steal letters. Louise, Princesse de Rohan, appeared in public on the arm of her husband, looking doleful, but blooming. I continued to throw up in the mornings, work at the Hôpital in the afternoons, and smile graciously over the supper table in the evenings.

Two things happened, though, that looked like being progress toward our goal. Charles, bored at confinement, began to invite Jamie to go to taverns with him in the evenings—often without the restraining and discretionary presence of his tutor, Mr. Sheridan, who professed himself much too old for such revels.

"God, the man drinks like a fish!" Jamie had exclaimed, returning from one of these jaunts reeking of cheap wine. He examined a large stain on the front of his shirt critically.

"I'll have to order a new shirt," he said.

"Worth it," I said, "if he tells you anything while he's drinking. What does he talk about?"

"Hunting and women," Jamie said succinctly, and declined firmly to elaborate further. Either politics did not weigh as heavily on Charles's mind as did Louise de La Tour, or else he was capable of discretion, even in the absence of his tutor Mr. Sheridan.

The second thing that happened was that Monsieur Duverney, the Minister of Finance, lost at chess to Jamie. Not once, but repeatedly. As Jamie had foreseen, the effect of losing was merely to make Monsieur Duverney more determined to win, and we were invited frequently to Versailles, where I circulated, collecting gossip and avoiding alcoves, and Jamie played chess, generally collecting an admiring crowd to watch, though I didn't myself consider it much of a spectator sport.

Jamie and the Minister of Finance, a small, round man with stooped shoulders, were bent over the chessboard, both apparently so intent on the game as to be oblivious to their surroundings, despite the murmur of voices and the clink of glasses just beyond their shoulders.

"I have seldom seen anything so wearisome as chess," murmured one of the ladies to another. "Amusement, they call it! I should be more amused watching my maid pick fleas off the black pageboys. At least they squeal and giggle a bit."

"I shouldn't mind making the red-haired lad squeal and giggle a bit," said her companion, smiling charmingly at Jamie, who had lifted his head and was gazing absently past Monsieur Duverney. Her companion caught sight of me, and dug the lady, a luscious blonde, in the ribs.

I smiled pleasantly at her, rather nastily enjoying the deep flush that rose from her low neckline, leaving her complexion in rosy blotches. As for Jamie, she could have twined her plump fingers in his hair for all the notice he would have paid, so abstracted did he seem.

I wondered just what was occupying his concentration. Surely it wasn't the game; Monsieur Duverney played a dogged game of cautious positioning, but used the same gambits repeatedly. The middle two fingers of Jamie's right hand moved slightly against his thigh, a brief flutter of quickly masked impatience, and I knew that whatever he was thinking of, it wasn't the game. It might take another half-hour, but he held Monsieur Duverney's king in the palm of his hand.

The Duc de Neve was standing next to me. I saw his dark little eyes fix on Jamie's fingers, then flick away. He paused meditatively for a moment, surveying the board, then glided away to increase his wager.

A footman paused by my shoulder and dipped obsequiously, offering me yet another glass of wine. I waved him away; I had had enough during the evening that my head was feeling light and my feet dangerously far away.

Turning to look for a place to sit down, I caught sight of the Comte St. Germain across the room. Perhaps he was what Jamie had been looking at. The Comte in turn was looking at me; staring at me, in fact, with a smile on his face. It wasn't his normal expression, and it didn't suit him. I didn't care for it at all, in fact, but bowed as graciously as I could in his direction, and then pushed off into the throng of ladies, chatting of this and that, but trying wherever possible to lead the conversation in the direction of Scotland and its exiled king.

By and large, the prospects for a Stuart restoration did not seem to be preoccupying the aristocracy of France. When I mentioned Charles Stuart now and then, the usual response was a rolling of the eyes or a shrug of dismissal. Despite the good offices of the Earl of Mar and the other Paris Jacobites, Louis was stubbornly refusing to receive Charles at Court. And a penniless exile who was not in the King's favor was not going to find himself invited out in society to make the acquaintance of wealthy bankers.

"The King is not particularly pleased that his cousin should have arrived in France without seeking his permission," the Comtesse de Brabant told me when I had introduced the topic. "He has been heard to say that England can stay Protestant, so far as he himself is concerned," she confided. "And if the English burn in hell with George of Hanover, so much the better." She pursed her lips in sympathy; she was a kindly sort. "I am sorry," she said. "I know that must be disappointing to you and your husband, but really . . ." She shrugged.

I thought we might be able to accommodate this sort of disappointment, and scouted eagerly for further bits of gossip along these lines, but met with little success this evening. Jacobites, I was given to understand, were a bore.

"Rook to queen's pawn five," Jamie mumbled later that evening as we prepared for bed. We were staying as guests in the palace once more. As the chess game had lasted well past midnight, and the Minister would not hear of our undertaking the journey back to Paris at such an hour, we had been accommodated in a small *appartement*—this one a notch or two above the first, I noted. It had a featherbed, and a window overlooking the south parterre.

"Rooks, eh?" I said, sliding into the bed and stretching out with a groan. "Are you going to dream about chess tonight?"

Jamie nodded, with a jaw-cracking yawn that made his eyes water.

"Aye, I'm sure I will. I hope it willna disturb ye, Sassenach, if I castle in my sleep."

My feet curled in the sheer joy of being unfettered and relieved of my increasing weight, and my lower spine sent out sharp jolts of a mildly pleasant pain as it readjusted to lying down.

"You can stand on your head in your sleep if you want," I said, yawning myself. "Nothing will bother me tonight."

I have seldom been more wrong.

I was dreaming of the baby. Grown almost to the birthing, it kicked and heaved in my swollen belly. My hands went to the mound, massaging the stretched skin, trying to quiet the turmoil within. But the squirming went on, and in the unexcited fashion of dreams, I realized that it was not a baby, but a snake that writhed in my belly. I doubled, drawing up my knees as I wrestled the serpent, my hands groping and pummeling, searching for the head of the beast that darted and thrust under my skin. My skin was hot to the touch, and my intestines coiled, turning into snakes themselves, biting and thrashing as they twined together.

"Claire! Wake up, lass! What's amiss?" The shaking and calling roused me at last to a fuzzy apprehension of my surroundings. I was in bed, and it was Jamie's hand on my shoulder, and the linen sheets over me. But the snakes continued to writhe in my belly, and I moaned loudly, the sound alarming me almost as much as it did Jamie.

He flung back the sheets and rolled me onto my back, trying to push my knees down. I stayed stubbornly rolled into a ball, clutching my stomach, trying to contain the pangs of sharp agony that stabbed through me.

He yanked the quilt back over me and rushed out of the room, barely pausing to snatch his kilt from the stool.

I had little attention to spare for anything other than my inner turmoil. My ears were ringing, and a cold sweat soaked my face.

"Madame? Madame!"

I opened my eyes enough to see the maid assigned to our *appartement,* eyes frantic and hair awry, bending over the bed. Jamie, half-naked and still more frantic, was behind her. I shut my eyes, groaning, but not before I saw him grab the maid by the shoulder, hard enough to shake her curls loose from her nightcap.

"Is she losing the child? Is she?"

It seemed extremely likely. I twisted on the bed, grunting, and doubled tighter, as though to protect the burden of pain I contained.

There was an increasing babble of voices in the room, mostly female, and a number of hands poked and prodded at me. I heard a male voice speaking amid the babble; not Jamie, someone French. At the voice's direction, a number of hands fastened themselves to my ankles and shoulders and stretched me flat upon the bed.

A hand reached under my nightdress and probed my belly. I opened my eyes, panting, and saw Monsieur Flèche, the Royal Physician, kneeling by the bed as he frowned in concentration. I should have felt flattered at this evidence of the King's favor, but had little attention to spare for it. The character of the pain seemed to be changing; while it grew stronger in spasms, it was more or less constant, and yet it seemed to be almost *moving,* traveling from somewhere high up in my abdomen to a lower spot.

"Not a miscarriage," Monsieur Flèche was assuring Jamie, who hovered anxiously over his shoulder. "There is no bleeding." I saw one of the attending ladies staring in rapt horror at the scars on his back. She grasped a companion by the sleeve, calling her attention to them.

"Perhaps an inflammation of the gallbladder," Monsieur Flèche was saying. "Or a sudden chill of the liver."

"Idiot," I said through clenched teeth.

Monsieur Flèche stared haughtily down his rather large nose at me, belatedly adding his gold-rimmed pince-nez to increase the effect. He laid a hand upon my clammy brow, incidentally covering my eyes so that I could no longer glare at him.

"Most likely the liver," he was saying to Jamie. "Impaction of the gallbladder causes this accumulation of bilious humors in the blood, which cause pain—and temporary derangement," he added authoritatively, pressing down harder as I thrashed to and fro. "She should be bled at once. Plato, the basin!"

I yanked one hand free and batted the restraining hand off my head.

"Get away from me, you bloody quack! Jamie! Don't let them touch me with that!" Plato, Monsieur Flèche's assistant, was advancing upon me with lancet and basin, while the ladies in the background gasped and fanned each other, lest they be overcome with excitement at this drama.

Jamie, white-faced, glanced helplessly between me and Monsieur Flèche. Coming to a sudden decision, he grabbed the hapless Plato and pulled him back from the bed, turned him and propelled him toward the door, lancet stabbing the air. The maids and ladies fell back shrieking before him.

"Monsieur! Monsieur *le chevalier!*" The physician was expostulating. He had clapped his wig professionally upon his head when called, but had not taken time to dress, and the sleeves of his bedgown flapped like wings as he followed Jamie across the room, waving his arms like a demented scarecrow.

The pain increased once more, a vise squeezing my insides, and I gasped and doubled up once more. As it eased a bit, I opened my eyes and saw one of the ladies, her eyes fixed alertly on my face. A look of dawning realization passed over her features, and still looking at me, she leaned over to whisper to one of her companions. There was too much noise in the room to hear, but I read her lips clearly.

"Poison," she said.

The pain shifted abruptly lower with an ominous interior gurgle, and I realized finally what it was. Not a miscarriage. Not appendicitis, still less a chilled liver. Nor was it poison, precisely. It was bitter cascara.

<hr />

"You," I said, advancing menacingly on Master Raymond, crouched defensively behind his worktable, beneath the protective aegis of his stuffed crocodile. "You! You bloody frog-faced little worm!"

"Me, madonna? I have done you no harm, have I?"

"Aside from causing me to have violent diarrhea in the presence of thirty-odd people, making me think I was having a miscarriage, and scaring my husband out of his skin, no harm at all!"

"Oh, your husband was present?" Master Raymond looked uneasy.

"He was," I assured him. It was in fact with considerable difficulty that I had succeeded in preventing Jamie from coming up to the apothecary's shop and extracting, by force, such information as Master Raymond possessed. I had finally persuaded him to wait with the coach outside, while I talked to the amphibious proprietor.

"But you aren't dead, madonna," the little herbalist pointed out. He had no brows to speak of, but one side of his wide, heavy forehead crinkled upward. "You could have been, you know."

In the stress of the evening and the physical shakiness that followed, I had rather overlooked this fact.

"So it wasn't just a practical joke?" I said, a little weakly. "Someone really meant to poison me, and I'm not dead only because you have scruples?"

"Perhaps my scruples are not entirely responsible for your survival, madonna; it is possible that it was a joke—I imagine there are other purveyors from whom one might obtain bitter cascara. But I have sold that substance to two persons within the last month—and neither of them asked for it."

"I see." I drew a long breath, and wiped the perspiration from my brow with my glove. So we had *two* potential poisoners loose; just what I needed.

"Will you tell me who?" I asked bluntly. "They might buy from someone else, next time. Someone without your scruples."

He nodded, his wide, froggy mouth twitching in thought.

"It is a possibility, madonna. As for the actual purchasers, I doubt that information would help you. They were servants; plainly acting on the orders of a master. One was maid to the Vicomtesse de Rambeau; the other a man I did not recognize."

I drummed my fingers on the counter. The only person who had made threats against me was the Comte St. Germain. Could he have hired an anonymous servant to procure what he thought was poison, and then slipped it into my glass himself? Casting my mind back to the gathering at Versailles, I thought it certainly possible. The goblets of wine had been passed around on trays by servants; while the Comte had not come within arm's length of me himself, it would have been no great problem to bribe a servant to give me a particular glass.

Raymond was eyeing me curiously. "I would ask you, madonna, have you done something to antagonize la Vicomtesse? She is a very jealous woman; this would not be the first time she has sought my aid in disposing of a rival, though fortunately her jealousies are short-lived. The Vicomte has a roving eye, you understand—there is always a new rival to displace her thoughts of the last one."

I sat down, uninvited.

"Rambeau?" I said, trying to attach the name to a face. Then the mists of memory cleared, revealing a stylishly dressed body and a homely round face, both liberally splashed with snuff.

"Rambeau!" I exclaimed. "Well, yes, I've met the man, but all I did was to smack him across the face with my fan when he bit my toes."

"In some moods, that would be sufficient provocation for la Vicomtesse," Master Raymond observed. "And if so, then I believe you are likely safe from further attacks."

"Thanks," I said dryly. "And if it wasn't the Vicomtesse?"

The little apothecary hesitated for a moment, his eyes narrowed against the glare of the morning sun that shone through the lozenged panes behind me. Then he made up his mind, and turned toward the stone table where his alembics simmered, jerking his head at me to follow.

"Come with me, madonna. I have something for you."

To my surprise, he ducked beneath the table and disappeared. As he didn't come back, I bent down and peered under the table myself. A bed of charcoal was glowing on the hearth, but there was space to either side of it. And in the wall beneath the table, concealed by the shadows, was the darker space of an opening.

With only a little hesitation, I kilted up my skirts and waddled under the table after him.

On the other side of the wall, there was room to stand up, though the room was quite small. The building's outer structure gave no hint of it.

Two walls of the hidden room were taken up by a honeycomb of shelves, each cell dustless and immaculate, each displaying the skull of a beast. The impact of the wall was enough to make me take a step backward; all the empty eyes seemed trained on me, teeth bared in gleaming welcome.

I blinked several times before I was able to locate Raymond, crouched cautiously at the foot of this ossuary like the resident acolyte. He held his arms raised nervously before him, eying me rather as though he expected me either to scream or to throw myself upon him. But I had seen sights a good deal more grisly than a mere rank of polished bone, and walked forward calmly to examine them more closely.

He had everything, it seemed. Tiny skulls, of bat, mouse and shrew, the bones transparent, little teeth spiked in pinpoints of carnivorous ferocity. Horses, from the huge Percherons, with massive scimitar-shaped jaws looking eminently suitable for flattening platoons of Philistines, down to the skulls of donkeys, as stubbornly enduring in their miniature curves as those of the enormous draft horses.

They had a certain appeal, so still and so beautiful, as though each object held still the essence of its owner, as if the lines of bone held the ghost of the flesh and fur that once they had borne.

I reached out and touched one of the skulls, the bone not cold as I would have expected, but strangely inert, as though the vanished warmth, long gone, hovered not far off.

I had seen human remains treated with far less reverence; the skulls of early Christian martyrs jammed cheek by bony jowl together in heaps in the catacombs, thigh bones tossed in a pile like jackstraws underneath.

"A bear?" I said, speaking softly. A big skull, this one, the canine teeth curved for ripping, but the molars oddly flattened.

"Yes, madonna." Seeing that I was not afraid, Raymond relaxed. His hand floated out, barely skimming the curves of the blunt, solid skull. "You see the teeth? An eater of fish, of meat"—a small finger traced the long, wicked curve of the canine, the flat serrations of molar—"but a grinder of berries, of grubs. They seldom starve, because they will eat anything."

I turned slowly from side to side, admiring, touching one here and there.

"They're lovely," I said. We spoke in quiet tones, as though to speak loudly might rouse the silent sleepers.

"Yes." Raymond's fingers touched them as mine did, stroking the long frontal bones, tracing the delicate squamosal arch of the cheek. "They hold the character of the animal, you see. You can tell much about what was, only from what is left."

He turned over one of the smaller skulls, pointing out the swelling bulges on the underside, like small, thin-walled balloons.

"Here—the canal of the ear enters into these, so that the sounds echo within the skull. Hence the sharp ears of the rat, madonna."

"Tympanic bullae," I said, nodding.

"Ah? I have but little Latin. My names for such things are . . . my own."

"Those . . ." I gestured upward. "Those are special, aren't they?"

"Ah. Yes, madonna. They are wolves. Very old wolves." He lifted down one of the skulls, handling it with reverent care. The snout was long and canid, with heavy canines and broad carnassial teeth. The sagittal crest rose stark and commanding from the back of the skull, testimony to the heavy muscles of the brawny neck that had once supported it.

Not a soft dull white like the other skulls, these were stained and streaked with brown, and shone glossy with much polishing.

"Such beasts are no more, madonna."

"No more? Extinct, you mean?" I touched it once more, fascinated. "Where on earth did you get them?"

"Not *on* the earth, madonna. Under it. They came from a peat bog, buried many feet down."

Looking closely, I could see the differences between these skulls and the newer, whiter ones on the opposite wall. These animals had been larger than ordinary wolves, with jaws that might have cracked the leg bones of a running elk or torn the throat from a fallen deer.

I shuddered slightly at the touch, reminded of the wolf I had killed outside Wentworth Prison, and its pack-mates who had stalked me in the icy twilight, barely six months ago.

"You do not care for wolves, madonna?" Raymond asked. "Yet the bears and the foxes do not trouble you? They also are hunters, eaters of flesh."

"Yes, but not mine," I said wryly, handing him back the age-dark skull. "I feel a good deal more sympathy with our friend the elk." I patted the high jutting nose with some affection.

"Sympathy?" The soft black eyes regarded me curiously. "It is an unusual emotion to feel for a bone, madonna."

"Well . . . yes," I said, slightly embarrassed, "but they don't really seem like just bones, you know. I mean, you can tell something about them, and get a feeling for what the animal was like, looking at these. They aren't just inanimate objects."

Raymond's toothless mouth stretched wide, as though I had inadvertently said something that pleased him, but he said nothing in reply.

"Why do you have all these?" I asked abruptly, suddenly realizing that racks of animal skulls were hardly the usual appurtenances of an apothecary's shop. Stuffed crocodiles, possibly, but not all this lot.

He shrugged good-naturedly.

"Well, they are company, of a sort, while I pursue my work." He gestured toward a cluttered workbench in one corner. "And while they may talk to me of many things, they are not so noisy as to attract the attention of the neighbors. Come here," he said, changing subjects abruptly. "I have something for you."

I followed him toward a tall cabinet at the end of the room, wondering.

He was not a naturalist, certainly not a scientist, as I understood the term. He kept no notes, made no drawings, no records that others might consult and learn from. And yet I had the odd conviction that he wanted very much to teach me the things that he knew—a sympathy for bones, perhaps?

The cabinet was painted with a number of odd signs, tailed and whorled, among what appeared to be pentagons and circles; Cabbalistic symbols. I recognized one or two, from some of Uncle Lamb's historical references.

"Interested in the Cabbala, are you?" I asked, eyeing the symbols with some amusement. That would account for the hidden workroom. While there was a strong interest in occult matters among some of the French literati and the aristocracy, it was an interest kept highly clandestine, for fear of the Church's cleansing wrath.

To my surprise, Raymond laughed. His blunt, short-nailed fingers pressed here and there on the front of the cabinet, touching the center of one symbol, the tail of another.

"Well, no, madonna. Most Cabbalists tend to be rather poor, so I do not seek their company often. But the symbols *do* keep curious people out of my cabinet. Which, if you think of it, is no small power for a bit of paint to exercise. So perhaps the Cabbalists are right, after all, when they say these signs hold power?"

He smiled mischievously at me, as the cabinet door swung open. I could see that it was in fact a double cabinet; if a nosy person ignored the warning of the symbols and merely opened the door, he or she would no doubt see only the harmless contents of an apothecary's closet. But if the proper sequence of hidden catches was pressed, then the inner shelves swung out as well, revealing a deep cavity behind them.

He pulled out one of the small drawers that lined the cavity, and upended it into his hand. Stirring the contents, he plucked out a single large white crystalline stone and handed it to me.

"For you," he said. "For protection."

"What? Magic?" I asked cynically, tilting the crystal from side to side in my palm.

Raymond laughed. He held his hand over the desk and let a handful of small colored stones trickle through his fingers, to bounce on the stained felt blotting-pad.

"I suppose you can call it so, madonna. Certainly I can charge more for it when I do." One fingertip nudged a pale greenish crystal free from the pile of colored stones.

"They have no more—and surely no less—magic than the skulls. Call them the bones of the earth. They hold the essence of the matrix in which they grew, and whatever powers that held, you may find here as well." He flicked a small yellowish nodule in my direction.

"Sulfur. Grind it with a few other small things, touch it with a match, and it will explode. Gunpowder. Is that magic? Or is it only the nature of sulfur?"

"I suppose it depends who you're talking to," I observed, and his face split in a delighted grin.

"If you ever seek to leave your husband, madonna," he said, chuckling, "be assured that you won't starve. I *said* you were a professional, did I not?"

"My husband!" I exclaimed, paling. My mind suddenly made sense of the muffled noises coming from the distant shop. There was a loud thump, as of a large fist brought down with considerable force on a countertop, and the deep rumble of a voice inclined to brook no interference made itself heard amid the babble of other sounds.

"Bloody Christ! I forgot Jamie!"

"Your husband is here?" Raymond's eyes went wider even than usual, and had he not already been so pale, I imagine he would have gone white, too.

"I left him outside," I explained, stooping to cross back through the secret opening. "He must have got tired of waiting."

"Wait, madonna!" Raymond's hand gripped my elbow, stopping me. He put his other hand over mine, the one that held the white crystal.

"That crystal, madonna. I said it is for your protection."

"Yes, yes," I said impatiently, hearing my name being shouted outside with increasing volume. "What does it do, then?"

"It is sensitive to poison, madonna. It will change color, in the presence of several harmful compounds."

That stopped me. I straightened up and stared at him.

"Poison?" I said, slowly. "Then . . ."

"Yes, madonna. You may be still in some danger." Raymond's froglike face was grim. "I cannot say for sure, or from which direction, for I do not know. If I find out, be assured I will tell you." His eyes flicked uneasily toward the entrance through the hearth. A thunder of blows sounded on the outer wall. "Assure your husband as well, please, madonna."

"Don't worry," I told him, ducking under the low lintel. "Jamie doesn't bite—I don't think."

"I was not worried about his *teeth*, madonna" came from behind me as I walked duckfooted over the ashes of the hearth.

Jamie, in the act of raising his dagger-hilt to hammer again on the paneling, caught sight of me emerging from the fireplace and lowered it.

"Och, there ye are," he observed mildly. He tilted his head to one side, watching me brush soot and ashes from the hem of my gown, then scowled at the sight of Raymond peeping cautiously out from under the drying table.

"Ah, and there's our wee toadling, as well. Has he some explanation, Sassenach, or had I best pin him up wi' the rest?" Not taking his eyes off Raymond, he nodded toward the wall of the outer workshop, where a number of dried toads and frogs were pinned to a long strip of hanging felt.

"No, no," I said hastily as Raymond made to duck back into his sanctuary. "He's told me everything. In fact, he's been *most* helpful."

With some reluctance, Jamie put up his dirk, and I reached down a hand to draw Raymond out of hiding. He flinched slightly at the sight of Jamie.

"This man is your husband, madonna?" he asked, in the tones of someone hoping the answer would be "no."

"Yes, of course," I answered. "My husband, James Fraser, my lord Broch Tuarach," I said, waving at Jamie, though I could scarcely have been referring to anyone else. I waved in the other direction. "Master Raymond."

"So I gathered," said Jamie dryly. He bowed and extended a hand toward Raymond, whose head reached a few inches past Jamie's waist. Raymond touched the outstretched hand briefly and yanked his own back, unable to repress a mild shiver. I stared at him in amazement.

Jamie merely raised one eyebrow, then leaned back and settled himself against the edge of the table. He crossed his arms across his chest.

"All right, then," he said. "What about it?"

I made most of the explanations, Raymond contributing only monosyllables of confirmation from time to time. The little apothecary seemed deprived of all his normal sly wit, and huddled on a stool near the fire, shoulders hunched in wariness. Only when I had finished with an explanation of the white crystal—and the presumed need for it—did he stir and seem to take on a little life once more.

"It is true, milord," he assured Jamie. "I do not know, in fact, whether it is your wife or yourself that may be in danger, or perhaps the two of you together. I have heard nothing specific; only the name 'Fraser,' spoken in a place where names are seldom named in blessing."

Jamie glanced sharply at him. "Aye? And you frequent such places, do you, Master Raymond? Are the people you speak of associates of yours?"

Raymond smiled, a little wanly. "I should be inclined to describe them more as a business rivals, milord."

Jamie grunted. "Mmmphm. Aye, well, and anyone who tries something may get a bit more of a blessing than he's bargained for." He touched the dirk at his belt, and straightened up.

"Still, I thank ye for the warning, Master Raymond." He bowed to the apothecary, but didn't offer his hand again. "As for the other"—he cocked an eyebrow at me—"if my wife is disposed to forgive your actions, then it isna my place to say more about it. Not," he added, "that I wouldna advise ye to pop back in your wee hole, the next time the Vicomtesse comes into your shop. Come along then, Sassenach."

As we rattled toward the Rue Tremoulins, Jamie was silent, staring out the window of the coach as the stiff fingers of his right hand tapped against his thigh.

"A place where names are seldom named in blessing," he murmured as the coach turned into the Rue Gamboge. "What might that be, I wonder?"

I remembered the Cabbalistic signs on Raymond's cabinet, and a small shiver raised the hairs on my forearms. I remembered Marguerite's gossip about the Comte St. Germain, and Madame de Ramage's warning. I told Jamie about them, and what Raymond had said.

"*He* may regard it as paint and window dressing," I finished, "but plainly he knows people who don't, or who is he looking to keep out of his cabinet?"

Jamie nodded. "Aye. I've heard a bit—only a bit—about such goings-on around the Court. I paid no attention at the time, thinking it only silliness, but now I'll find out a bit more." He laughed, suddenly, and drew me close to his side. "I'll set Murtagh to follow the Comte St. Germain. That'll give the Comte a *real* demon to play with."

17

Possession

Murtagh was duly set to watch the comings and goings of the Comte St. Germain, but beyond reporting that the Comte entertained a remarkable number of persons in his home— of both sexes and all classes—detected nothing particularly mysterious. The Comte did have one visitor of note, though—Charles Stuart, who came one afternoon, stayed for an hour, and left.

Charles had begun to require Jamie's company more frequently on his expeditions through the taverns and low places of the city. I personally thought this had more to do with Jules de La Tour de Rohan's party, held to celebrate the announcement of his wife's pregnancy, than it did with any sinister influence of the Comte's.

These expeditions sometimes lasted well into the night, and I became accustomed to going to bed without Jamie, waking when he crawled in beside me, his body chilled with walking through the evening fog, and the smell of tobacco smoke and liquor clinging to his hair and skin.

"He's so distraught about that woman that I dinna think he even remembers he's the heir to the thrones of Scotland and England," Jamie said, returning from one of these expeditions.

"Goodness, he *must* be upset," I said, sarcastically. "Let's hope he stays that way."

A week later, though, I woke to the cold gray light of dawn to find the bed beside me still vacant, the coverlet flat and undisturbed.

"Is milord Broch Tuarach in his study?" I leaned over the banister in my nightgown, startling Magnus, who was passing through the lower hall. Perhaps Jamie had chosen to sleep on the sofa in the study, so as not to disturb me.

"No, milady," he answered, staring up at me. "I came to unbolt the front door, and found that it had never been bolted. Milord did not come home last night."

I sat down heavily on the top step. I must have looked rather alarming, because the elderly butler nearly sprinted up the stairs to me.

"Madame," he said, anxiously chafing one of my hands. "Madame, are you all right?"

"I've been better, but it isn't important. Magnus, send one of the footmen to Prince Charles's house in Montmartre at once. Have him see if my husband is there."

"At once, milady. And I will send Marguerite up to attend you, as well." He turned and hurried down the stairs, the soft felt slippers he wore for his morning duties making a soft, shushing noise on the polished wood.

"And Murtagh!" I called after Magnus's departing back. "My husband's kinsman. Bring him to me, please!" The first thought that had sprung into my mind was that Jamie had perhaps stayed the night at Charles's villa; the second, that something had happened to him, whether by accident or by someone's deliberate intent.

"Where is he?" Murtagh's cracked voice spoke at the foot of the stair. He had obviously just awakened; his face was creased from whatever he had been lying on, and there were bits of straw in the folds of his ratty shirt.

"How should I know?" I snapped. Murtagh always looked as though he suspected everyone of something, and being rudely wakened had not improved his habitual scowl. The sight of him was nonetheless reassuring; if anything rough was in the offing, Murtagh looked the person to be dealing with it.

"He went out with Prince Charles last night, and didn't come back. That's all I know." I pulled myself up by the banister railing and smoothed down the silk folds of my nightgown. The fires had been lit, but hadn't had time to warm the house, and I was shivering.

Murtagh rubbed a hand over his face to assist thought.

"Mphm. Has someone gone to Montmartre?"

"Yes."

"Then I'll wait 'til they come back with word. If Jamie's there, well and good. If he isn't, mayhap they'll know when he parted company with His Highness, and where."

"And what if they're both gone? What if the Prince didn't come home either?" I asked. If there were Jacobites in Paris, there were also those who opposed the restoration of the Stuart line. And while assassinating Charles Stuart might not assure the failure of a potential Scottish Rising—he did, after all, have a younger brother, Henry—it might go some way toward damping James's enthusiasm for such a venture—if he had any to start with, I thought distractedly.

I remembered vividly the story Jamie had told me, of the attempt on his life during which he had met Fergus. Street assassinations were far from uncommon, and there were gangs of ruffians who hunted the Paris streets after dark.

"You'd best go dress yourself, lassie," Murtagh remarked. "I can see the gooseflesh from here."

"Oh! Yes, I suppose so." I glanced down at my arms; I had been hugging myself as suppositions raced through my mind, but to little effect; my teeth were beginning to chatter.

"Madame! You will give yourself a chill, surely!" Marguerite came stumping rapidly up the stairs, and I allowed her to shoo me into the bedroom, glancing back to see Murtagh below, carefully examining the point of his dirk before ramming it home in its sheath.

"You should be in bed, Madame!" Marguerite scolded. "It isn't good for the child, for you to let yourself be chilled like that. I will fetch a warming pan at once; where is your nightrobe? Get into it at once, yes, that's right . . ." I shrugged the heavy woolen nightrobe over the thin silk of my nightgown, but ignored Marguerite's clucking to go to the window and open the shutters.

The street outside was beginning to glow as the rising sun struck the upper facades of the stone houses along the Rue Tremoulins. There was a good deal of activity on the street, early as it was; maids and footmen engaged in scrubbing steps or polishing brass gate-fittings, barrowmen selling fruit, vegetables, and fresh seafood, crying their wares along the street, and the cooks of the great houses popping up from their basement doors like so many jinni, summoned by the cries of the barrowmen. A delivery cart loaded with coal clopped slowly along the street, pulled by an elderly horse who looked as though he would much rather be in his stable. But no sign of Jamie.

I at last allowed an anxious Marguerite to persuade me into bed, for the sake of warmth, but couldn't go back to sleep. Every sound from below brought me to the alert, hoping that each footstep on the pavement outside would be followed by Jamie's voice in the hall below. The face of the Comte St. Germain kept coming between me and sleep. Alone among the French nobility, he had some connection with Charles Stuart. He had, in all likelihood, been behind the earlier attempt on Jamie's life . . . and on mine. He was known to have unsavory associations. Was it possible that he had arranged to have both Charles and Jamie removed? Whether his purposes were political or personal made little difference, at this point.

When at last the sound of steps below did come, I was so occupied with visions of Jamie lying in a gutter with his throat cut, that I didn't realize he was home until the bedroom door opened.

"Jamie!" I sat up in bed with a cry of joy.

He smiled at me, then yawned immensely, making no effort to cover his mouth. I could see a goodly distance down his throat, and observed with relief that it wasn't cut. On the other hand, he looked distinctly the worse for wear. He lay down on the bed next to me and stretched, long and rackingly, then settled with a half-contented groan.

"What," I demanded, "happened to *you?*"

He opened one red-rimmed eye.

"I need a bath," he said, and closed it again.

I leaned toward him and sniffed delicately. The nose detected the usual smoky smell of closed rooms and damp wool, underlying a truly remarkable combination of alcoholic stenches—ale, wine, whisky, and brandy—which matched the variety of stains on his shirt. And forming a high note to the mixture, a horrible cheap cologne, of a particularly penetrating and noxious pungency.

"You do," I agreed. I scrambled out of bed and leaning out into the corridor, shouted for Marguerite, sending her on arrival for a hip bath and sufficient water to fill it. As a parting gift from Brother Ambrose, I had several cakes of a fine-milled hard soap, made with attar of roses, and told her to fetch those, as well.

As the maid set about the tedious business of bringing up the huge copper bath-cans, I turned my attention to the hulk on the bed.

I stripped off his shoes and stockings, then loosening the buckle of his kilt, I flipped it open. His hands went reflexively to his crotch, but my eyes were focused elsewhere.

"*What*," I said again, "happened to you?"

Several long scratches marked his thighs, angry red welts against the pale skin. And high on the inside of one leg was what could be nothing other than a bite; the toothmarks were plainly visible.

The maid, pouring hot water, cast an interested eye at the evidence and thought fit to put in her tuppence at this delicate moment.

"*Un petit chien?*" she asked. A little dog? Or something else. While I was far from fluent in the idiom of the times, I *had* learned that *les petits chiens* often walked the street on two legs with painted faces.

"Out," I said briefly in French, with a Head Matron intonation. The maid picked up the cans and left the room, pouting slightly. I turned back to Jamie, who opened one eye, and after a glance at my face, closed it again.

"Well?" I asked.

Instead of answering, he shuddered. After a moment, he sat up and rubbed his hands over his face, the stubble making a rasping noise. He cocked one ruddy eyebrow interrogatively. "I wouldna suppose a gently reared young lady such as yourself would be familiar wi' an alternate meaning for the term *soixante-neuf*?"

"I've heard the term," I said, folding my arms across my chest and regarding him with a certain amount of suspicion. "And may I ask just where *you* encountered that particular interesting number?"

"It was suggested to me—with some force—as a desirable activity by a lady I happened to meet last night."

"Was that by any chance the lady who bit you in the thigh?"

He glanced down and rubbed the mark meditatively.

"Mm, no. As a matter of fact, it wasn't. That lady seemed preoccupied wi' rather lower numbers. I think she meant to settle for the six, and the nine could go hang."

"Jamie," I said, tapping my foot in a marked manner, "*where* have you been all night?"

He scooped up a handful of water from the basin and splashed it over his face, letting the rivulets run down among the dark red hairs on his chest.

"Mm," he said, blinking drops from his thick lashes, "well, let me see. First there was supper at a tavern. We met Glengarry and Millefleurs there." Monsieur Millefleurs was a Parisian banker, while Glengarry was one of the younger Jacobites, chief of one sept of the MacDonell clan. A visitor in Paris, rather than a resident, he had been much in Charles's company lately, by Jamie's report. "And after supper, we went to the Duc di Castellotti's, for cards."

"And then?" I asked.

A tavern, apparently. And then another tavern. And then an establishment which appeared to share some of the characteristics of a tavern, but was embellished by the addition of several ladies of interesting appearance and even more interesting talents.

"Talents, eh?" I said, with a glance at the marks on his leg.

"God, they did it in public," he said, with a reminiscent shudder. "Two of them, on the table. Right between the saddle of mutton and the boiled potatoes. With the quince jelly."

"*Mon dieu,*" said the newly returned maid, setting down the fresh bathcan long enough to cross herself.

"You be quiet," I said, scowling at her. I turned my attention back to my husband. "And then what?"

Then, apparently, the action had become somewhat more general, though still accomplished in fairly public fashion. With due regard to Marguerite's sensibilities, Jamie waited until she had left for another round of water before elaborating further.

". . . and then Castellotti took the fat one with red hair and the small blond one off to a corner, and—"

"And what were *you* doing all this time?" I broke in on the fascinating recitative.

"Watching," he said, as though surprised. "It didna seem decent, but there wasna much choice about it, under the circumstances."

I had been groping in his sporran as he talked, and now fished out not only a small purse, but a wide metal ring, embellished with a coat of arms. I tried it curiously on a finger; it was much larger than any normal ring, and hung like a quoit on a stick.

"Whoever does this belong to?" I asked, holding it out. "It looks like the Duc di Castellotti's coat of arms, but whoever it belongs to must have fingers like sausages." Castellotti was an etiolated Italian stringbean, with the pinched face of a man with chronic dyspepsia—no wonder, judging from Jamie's story. Quince jelly, forsooth!

I glanced up to find Jamie blushing from navel to hairline.

"Er," he said, taking an exaggerated interest in a mud stain on one knee, "it . . . doesna go on a man's finger."

"Then what . . . oh." I looked at the circular object with renewed interest. "Goodness. I've heard of them before . . ."

"You have?" said Jamie, thoroughly scandalized.

"But I've never seen one. Does it fit you?" I reached out to try it. He clasped his hands reflexively over his private parts.

Marguerite, arriving with more water, assured him, "*Ne vous en faites pas, Monsieur. J'en ai déjà vu un.*" Don't worry yourself, monsieur; I've already seen one.

Dividing a glare between me and the maid, he pulled a quilt across his lap.

"Bad enough to spend all night defending my virtue," he remarked with some asperity, "without havin' it subjected to comment in the morning."

"Defending your virtue, hm?" I tossed the ring idly from hand to hand, catching it on opposing index fingers. "A gift, was it?" I asked, "or a loan?"

"A gift. Don't do that, Sassenach," he said, wincing. "It brings back memories."

"Ah yes," I said, eying him. "Now *about* those memories . . ."

"Not *me*!" he protested. "Surely ye dinna think I'd do such things? I'm a married man!"

"Monsieur Millefleurs isn't married?"

"He's not only married, he has two mistresses," Jamie said. "But he's French—that's different."

"The Duc di Castellotti isn't French—he's Italian."

"But he's a duke. That's different, too."

"Oh, it is, is it? I wonder if the Duchess thinks so."

"Considering a few things the Duc claimed he learnt from the Duchess, I would imagine so. Isn't that bath ready yet?"

Clutching the quilt about him, he lumbered from the bed to the steaming tub and stepped in. He dropped the quilt and lowered himself quickly, but not quite quickly enough.

"*Enorme!*" said the maid, crossing herself.

"*C'est tout,*" I said repressively. "*Merci bien.*" She dropped her eyes, blushed, and scuttled out.

As the door closed behind the maid, Jamie relaxed into the tub, high at the back to allow for lounging; the feeling of the times seemed to be that once having gone to the trouble of filling a bath, one might as well enjoy it. His stubbled face assumed an expression of bliss as he sank gradually lower into the steaming water, a flush of heat reddening his fair skin. His eyes were closed, and a faint mist of moisture gleamed across the high, broad cheekbones and shone in the hollows beneath his eyesockets.

"Soap?" he asked hopefully, opening his eyes.

"Yes, indeed." I fetched a cake and handed it to him, then sat down on a stool alongside the bath. I watched for some time as he scrubbed industriously, fetching him a cloth and a pumice stone, with which he painstakingly rasped the soles of his feet and his elbows.

"Jamie," I said at last.

"Aye?"

"I don't mean to quarrel with your methods," I said, "and we agreed that you might have to go to some lengths, but . . . did you *really* have to . . ."

"To what, Sassenach?" He had stopped washing and was watching me intently, head on one side.

"To . . . to . . ." To my annoyance, I was flushing as deeply as he was, but without the excuse of hot water.

A large hand rose dripping out of the water and rested on my arm. The wet heat burned through the thin fabric of my sleeve.

"Sassenach," he said, "what do ye think I've been doing?"

"Er, well," I said, trying and failing to keep my eyes away from the marks on his thigh. He laughed, though he didn't sound truly amused.

"O ye of little faith!" he said sardonically.

I withdrew beyond his reach.

"Well," I said, "when one's husband comes home covered with bites and scratches and reeking with perfume, admits he's spent the night in a bawdy house, and . . ."

"And tells ye flat-out he's spent the night watching, not doing?"

"You didn't get those marks on your leg from watching!" I snapped suddenly, then clamped my lips together. I felt like a jealous biddy, and I didn't care for it. I had vowed to take it all calmly, like a woman of the world, telling myself that I had complete faith in Jamie and—just in case—that you can't make omelets without breaking eggs. Even if something *had* happened . . .

I smoothed the wet spot on my sleeve, feeling the air chill through the cooling silk. I struggled to regain my former light tone.

"Or are those the scars of honorable combat, gained in defending your virtue?" Somehow the light tone didn't quite come off. Listening to myself, I had to admit that the overall tone was really quite nasty. I was rapidly ceasing to care.

No slouch at reading tones of voice, Jamie narrowed his eyes at me and seemed about to reply. He drew in his breath, then apparently thought better of whatever he had been going to say and let it out again.

"Yes," he said calmly. He fished about in the tub between his legs, coming up at length with the cake of soap, a roughly shaped ball of white slickness. He held it out on his palm.

"Will ye help me to wash my hair? His Highness vomited on me in the coach coming home, and I reek a bit, all things considered."

I hesitated a moment, but accepted the olive branch, temporarily at least.

I could feel the solid curve of his skull under the thick, soapy hair, and the welt of the healed scar across the back of his head. I dug my thumbs firmly into his neck muscles, and he relaxed slightly under my hands.

The soap bubbles ran down across the wet, gleaming curves of his shoulders, and my hands followed them, spreading the slickness so that my fingers seemed to float on the surface of his skin.

He *was* big, I thought. Near him so much, I tended to forget his size, until I saw him suddenly from a distance, towering among smaller men, and I would be struck anew by his grace and the beauty of his body. But he sat now with his knees nearly underneath his chin, and his shoulders filled the tub from one side to the other. He leaned forward slightly to assist my ministrations, exposing the hideous scars on his back. The thick red welts of Jack Randall's Christmas gift lay heavily over the thin white lines of the earlier floggings.

I touched the scars gently, my heart squeezed by the sight. I had seen those wounds when they were fresh, seen him driven to the edge of madness by torture and abuse. But I had healed him, and he had fought with all the power of a gallant heart to be whole once more, to come back to me. Moved by tenderness, I brushed the trailing ends of his hair aside, and bent to kiss the back of his neck.

I straightened abruptly. He felt my movement and turned his head slightly.

"What is it, Sassenach?" he asked, voice slow with drowsy contentment.

"Not a thing," I said, staring at the dark-red blotches on the side of his neck. The nurses in the quarters at Pembroke used to conceal them with jaunty scarves tied about their necks the morning after their dates with soldiers from the nearby base. I always thought the scarves were really meant as a means of advertisement, rather than concealment.

"No, not a thing," I said again, reaching for the ewer on the stand. Placed near the window, it was ice-cold to the touch. I stepped behind Jamie and upended it on his head.

I lifted the silk skirts of my nightdress to avoid the sudden wave that spilled over the side of the bath. He was sputtering from the cold, but too shocked yet to form any of the words I could see gathering force on his lips. I beat him to it.

"Just watched, did you?" I asked coldly. "I wouldn't suppose you enjoyed it a bit, did you, poor thing?"

He thrust himself back in the tub with a violence that made the water slosh over the sides, splattering on the stone floor, and twisted around to look up at me.

"What d'ye want me to say?" he demanded. "Did I want to rut with them? Aye, I did! Enough to make my balls ache with not doing it. And enough to make me feel sick wi' the thought of touching one of the sluts."

He shoved the sopping mass of his hair out of his eyes, glaring at me.

"Is that what ye wanted to know? Are ye satisfied now?"

"Not really," I said. My face was hot, and I pressed my cheek against the icy pane of the window, hands clenched on the sill.

"Who looks on a woman with lust in his heart hath committed adultery with her already. Is that how ye see it?"

"Is it how *you* see it?"

"No," he said shortly. "I don't. And what would ye do if I *had* lain wi' a whore, Sassenach? Slap my face? Order me out of your chamber? Keep yourself from my bed?"

I turned and looked at him.

"I'd kill you," I said through my teeth.

Both eyebrows shot up, and his mouth dropped slightly with incredulity.

"Kill *me*? God, if I found you wi' another man, I'd kill *him*." He paused, and one corner of his mouth quirked wryly.

"Mind ye," he said, "I'd no be verra pleased wi' *you*, either, but still, it's him I'd kill."

"Typical man," I said. "Always missing the point."

He snorted with a bitter humor.

"Am I, then? So you dinna believe me. Want me to prove it to ye, Sassenach, that I've lain wi' no one in the last few hours?" He stood up, water cascading down the stretches of his long legs. The light from the window highlighted the reddish-gold hairs of his body and the steam rose off his flesh in wisps. He looked like a figure of freshly molten gold. I glanced briefly down.

"Ha," I said, with the maximum of scorn it was possible to infuse into one syllable.

"Hot water," he said briefly, stepping out of the tub. "Dinna worry yourself, it won't take long."

"That," I said, with delicate precision, "is what *you* think."

His face flushed still more deeply, and his hands curled involuntarily into fists.

"No reasoning wi' you, is there?" he demanded. "God, I spend the night torn between disgust and agony, bein' tormented by my companions for being unmanly, then come home to be tormented for being unchaste! *Mallaichte bàs!*"

Looking wildly about, he spotted his discarded clothing on the floor near the bed and lunged for it.

"Here, then!" he said, scrabbling for his belt. "Here! If lusting is adultery and you'll kill me for adultery, then ye'd best do it, hadn't ye!" He came up with his dirk, a ten-inch piece of dark steel, and thrust it at me, haft first. He squared his shoulders, presenting the broad expanse of his chest to me, and glared belligerently.

"Go ahead," he insisted. "Ye dinna mean to be forsworn, I hope? Being so sensitive to your honor as a wife and all?"

It was a real temptation. My clenched hands quivered at my sides with the longing to take the dagger and plant it firmly between his ribs. Only the knowledge that, all his dramatizing aside, he certainly wouldn't allow me to stab him, stopped me from trying. I felt sufficiently ridiculous, without humiliating myself further. I whirled away from him in a flurry of silk.

After a moment, I heard the clank of the dirk on the floorboards. I stood without moving, staring out of the window at the back courtyard below. I heard faint rustling sounds behind me, and glanced into the faint reflections of the window. My face showed in the windowpane as a smudged oval in a nimbus of sleep-snarled brown hair. Jamie's naked figure moved dimly in the glass like someone seen underwater, searching for a towel.

"The towel is on the bottom shelf of the ewer-stand," I said, turning around.

"Thank you." He dropped the dirty shirt with which he had begun gingerly dabbing himself and reached for the towel, not looking at me.

He wiped his face, then seemed to make some decision. He lowered the towel and looked directly at me. I could see the emotions struggling for mastery on his face, and felt as though I were still looking into the mirror of the window. Sense triumphed in both of us at once.

"I'm sorry," we said, in unison. And laughed.

The damp of his skin soaked through the thin silk, but I didn't care.

Minutes later, he mumbled something into my hair.

"What?"

"Too close," he repeated, moving back a bit. "It was too damn close, Sassenach, and it scared me."

I glanced down at the dirk, lying forgotten on the floor.

"Scared? I've never seen anyone less scared in my life. You knew damned well I wouldn't do it."

"Oh, that." He grinned. "No, I didna think you'd kill me, much as ye might like to." He sobered quickly. "No, it was . . . well, those women. What I felt like with them. I didna want them, truly not . . ."

"Yes, I know," I said, reaching for him, but he wasn't stopping there. He held back from me, looking troubled.

"But the . . . the lusting, I suppose ye'd call it . . . that was . . . too close to what I feel sometimes for you, and it . . . well, it doesna seem right to me."

He turned away, rubbing at his hair with the linen towel, so his voice came half-muffled.

"I always thought it would be a simple matter to lie wi' a woman," he said softly. "And yet . . . I want to fall on my face at your feet and worship you" —he dropped the towel and reached out, taking me by the shoulders—"and still I want to force ye to your knees before me, and hold ye there wi' my hands tangled in your hair, and your mouth at my service . . . and I want both things *at the same time,* Sassenach." He ran his hands up under my hair and gripped my face between them, hard.

"I dinna understand myself at all, Sassenach! Or maybe I do." He released me and turned away. His face had long since dried, but he picked up the fallen towel and wiped the skin of his jaw with it, over and over. The stubble made a faint rasping sound against the fine linen. His voice was still quiet, barely audible from a few feet away.

"Such things—the knowledge of them, I mean—it came to me soon after . . . after Wentworth." Wentworth. Where he had given his soul to save my life, and suffered the tortures of the damned in retrieving it.

"I thought at the first that Jack Randall had stolen a bit of my soul, and then I knew it was worse than that. All of it was my own, and had been all along; it was only he'd shown it to me, and made me know it for myself. That's what he did that I canna forgive, and may his own soul rot for it!"

He lowered the towel and looked at me, face worn with the strains of the night, but eyes bright with urgency.

"Claire. To feel the small bones of your neck beneath my hands, and that fine, thin skin on your breasts and your arms . . . Lord, you are my wife, whom I cherish and I love wi' all my life, and still I want to kiss ye hard enough to bruise your tender lips, and see the marks of my fingers on your skin."

He dropped the towel. He raised his hands and held them trembling in the air before his face, then very slowly brought them down to rest on my head as though in benediction.

"I want to hold you like a kitten in my shirt, *mo duinne,* and still I want to spread your thighs and plow ye like a rutting bull." His fingers tightened in my hair. "I dinna understand myself!"

I pulled my head back, freeing myself, and took a half-step backward. The blood seemed all to be on the surface of my skin, and a chill ran down my body at the brief separation.

"Do you think it's different for me? Do you think I don't feel the same?" I demanded. "That I don't sometimes want to bite you hard enough to taste blood, or claw you 'til you cry out?"

I reached out slowly to touch him. The skin of his breast was damp and warm. Only the nail of my forefinger touched him, just below the nipple. Lightly, barely touching, I drew the nail upward, downward, circling round, watching the tiny nub rise hard amid the curling ruddy hairs.

The nail pressed slightly harder, sliding down, leaving a faint red streak on the fair skin of his chest. I was trembling all over by this time, but did not turn away.

"Sometimes I want to ride you like a wild horse, and bring you to the taming—did you know that? I can do it, you know I can. Drag you over the edge and drain you to a gasping husk. I can drive you to the edge of collapse and sometimes I delight in it, Jamie, I do! And yet so often I want"—my voice broke suddenly and I had to swallow hard before continuing—"I want . . . to hold your head against my breast and cradle you like a child and comfort you to sleep."

My eyes were so full of tears that I couldn't see his face clearly; couldn't see if he wept as well. His arms went tight around me and the damp heat of him engulfed me like the breath of a monsoon.

"Claire, ye do kill me, knife or no," he whispered, face buried in my hair. He bent and picked me up, carrying me to the bed. He sank to his knees, laying me amid the rumpled quilts.

"You'll lie wi' me now," he said quietly. "And I shall use ye as I must. And if you'll have your revenge for it, then take it and welcome, for my soul is yours, in all the black corners of it."

The skin of his shoulders was warm with the heat of the bath, but he shivered as with cold as my hands traveled up to his neck, and I pulled him down to me.

And when I had at length taken my last revenge of him, I did cradle him, stroking back the roughened, half-dry locks.

"And sometimes," I whispered to him, "I wish it could be you inside me. That I could take you into me and keep you safe always."

His hand, large and warm, lifted slowly from the bed and cupped the small round swell of my belly, sheltering and caressing.

"You do, my own," he said. "You do."

I felt it for the first time while lying in bed the next morning, watching Jamie dress for the day. A tiny fluttering sensation, at once entirely familiar and completely new. Jamie had his back turned to me, as he wriggled into his knee-length shirt and stretched his arms, settling the folds of white linen across the breadth of his shoulders.

I lay quite still, waiting, hoping for it to come again. It did, this time as a series of infinitesimal quick movements, like the bursting of bubbles rising to the surface of a carbonated liquid.

I had a sudden memory of Coca-Cola; that odd, dark, fizzy American drink. I had tasted it once, while having supper with an American colonel, who served it as a delicacy—which it was, in wartime. It came in thick greenish bottles, smooth-ribbed and tapered, with a high-waisted nip to the glass, so that the bottle was roughly woman-shaped, with a rounded bulge just below the neck, swelling to a broader one farther down.

I remembered how the millions of tiny bubbles had rushed into the narrow neck when the bottle was opened, smaller and finer than the bubbles of champagne, bursting joyous in the air. I laid one hand very gently on my abdomen, just above the womb.

There it was. There was no sense of him, or her, as I had thought there might be—but there was certainly a sense of Someone. I wondered whether perhaps babies had no gender—physical characteristics aside—until birth, when the act of exposure to the outside world set them forever as one or the other.

"Jamie," I said. He was tying back his hair, gathering it into a thick handful at the base of his neck and winding a leather lace about it. Head bent in the task, he looked up at me from under his brows and smiled.

"Awake, are ye? It's early yet, *mo duinne.* Go back to sleep for a bit."

I had been going to tell him, but something stopped me. He couldn't feel it, of course, not yet. It wasn't that I thought he wouldn't care, but there was something about that first awareness that seemed suddenly private; the second shared secret between me and the child—the first being our knowledge of its existence, mine a conscious knowing, the embryo's a simple being. The sharing of that knowledge linked us close as did the blood that passed through both of us.

"Do you want me to braid your hair for you?" I asked. When he went to the docks, sometimes he would ask me to plait his ruddy mane in a tight queue, proof against the tugging winds on deck and quay. He always teased that he would have it dipped in tar, as the sailors did, to solve the problem permanently.

He shook his head, and reached for his kilt.

"No, I'm going to call on His Highness Prince Charles today. And drafty as his house is, I think it wilna be blowing my hair in my eyes." He smiled at me, coming to stand by the bed. He saw my hand lying on my stomach, and put his own lightly over it.

"Feeling all right, are ye, Sassenach? The sickness is better?"

"Much." The morning sickness had in fact abated, though waves of nausea still assailed me at odd moments. I found I could not bear the smell of frying tripe with onions, and had had to ban this popular dish from the servants' menu, since the smell crept from the basement kitchen like a ghost up the back stairs, to pop out at me unexpectedly when I opened the door of my sitting room.

"Good." He raised my hand, and bent over to kiss my knuckles in farewell. "Go back to sleep, *mo duinne,*" he repeated.

He closed the door gently behind him, as though I were already sleeping, leaving me to the early morning silence of the chamber, with the small busy noises of the household safely barred by paneled oak.

Squares of pale sunlight from the casement window lay bright on the opposite wall. It would be a beautiful day, I could tell, the spring air ripening with warmth, and the plum blossoms bursting pink and white and bee-rich in the gardens of Versailles. The courtiers would be outside in the gardens today, rejoicing in the weather as much as the barrowmen who wheeled their wares through the streets.

So did I rejoice, alone and not alone, in my peaceful cocoon of warmth and quiet.

"Hello," I said softly, one hand over the butterfly wings that beat inside me.

PART THREE

Malchance

18

Rape in Paris

There was an explosion at the Royal Armory, near the beginning of May. I heard later that a careless porter had put down a torch in the wrong place, and a minute later, the largest assortment of gunpowder and firearms in Paris had gone up with a noise that startled the pigeons off Notre Dame.

At work in L'Hôpital des Anges, I didn't hear the explosion itself, but I certainly noticed the echoes. Though the Hôpital was on the opposite side of the city from the Armory, there were sufficient victims of the explosion that a good many of them overflowed the other hospitals and were brought to us, mangled, burned, and moaning in the backs of wagons, or supported on pallets by friends who carried them through the streets.

It was full dark before the last of the victims had been attended to, and the last bandage-swathed body laid gently down among the grubby, anonymous ranks of the Hôpital's patients.

I had dispatched Fergus home with word that I would be late, when I saw the magnitude of the task awaiting the sisters of des Anges. He had come back with Murtagh, and the two of them were lounging on the steps outside, waiting to escort us home.

Mary and I emerged wearily from the double doors, to find Murtagh demonstrating the art of knife-throwing to Fergus.

"Go on then," he was saying, back turned to us. "Straight as ye can, on the count of three. One . . . two . . . three!" At "three," Fergus bowled the large white onion he was holding, letting it bounce and hop over the uneven ground.

Murtagh stood relaxed, arm drawn back at a negligent cock, dirk held by the tip between his fingers. As the onion spun past, his wrist flicked once, quick and sharp. Nothing else moved, not so much as a stir of his kilts, but the onion leaped sideways, transfixed by the dirk, and fell mortally wounded, rolling feebly in the dirt at his feet.

"B-bravo, Mr. Murtagh!" Mary called, smiling. Startled, Murtagh turned, and I could see the flush rising on his lean cheeks in the light from the double doors behind us.

"Mmmphm," he said.

"Sorry to take so long," I said apologetically. "It took rather a time to get everyone squared away."

"Och, aye," the little clansman answered laconically. He turned to Fergus. "We'll do best to find a coach, lad; it's late for the ladies to be walking."

"There aren't any here," Fergus said, shrugging. "I've been up and down the street for the last hour; every spare coach in the Cité has gone to the Armory. We might get something in the Rue du Faubourg St.-Honoré, though." He pointed down the street, at a dark, narrow gap between buildings that betrayed the presence of a passageway through to the next street. "It's quick through there."

After a short, frowning pause for thought, Murtagh nodded agreement. "All right, lad. Let's go, then."

It was cold in the alleyway, and I could see my breath in small white puffs, despite the moonless night. No matter how dark it got in Paris, there was always light somewhere; the glow of lamps and candles seeped through shutters and chinks in the walls of wooden buildings, and light pooled around the stalls of the street vendors and scattered from the small horn and metal lanterns that swung from cart tails and coach trees.

The next street was one of merchants, and here and there the proprietors of the various businesses had hung lanterns of pierced metal above their doors and shopyard entrances. Not content to rely upon the police to protect their property, often several businessmen would join together and hire a watchman to guard their premises at night. When I saw one such figure in front of the sailmaker's shop, sitting hunched in the shadows atop a pile of folded canvas, I nodded in response to his gruff "*Bonsoir,* Monsieur, mesdames."

As we passed the sailmaker's shop, though, I heard a sudden cry of alarm from the watchman.

"Monsieur! Madame!"

Murtagh swung round at once to meet the challenge, sword already hissing from its scabbard. Slower in my reflexes, I was only halfway turned as he stepped forward, and my eye caught the flicker of movement from the doorway behind him. The blow took Murtagh from behind before I could shout a warning, and he went sprawling facedown in the street, arms and legs gone loose and nerveless, sword and dirk flying from his hands to clatter on the stones.

I stooped quickly for the dirk as it slid past my foot, but a pair of hands seized my arms from behind.

"Take care of the man," ordered a voice behind me. "Quickly!"

I wrenched at my captor's grip; the hands dropped to my wrists and twisted them sharply, making me cry out. There was a billow of white, ghost-like in the dim street, and the "watchman" bent over Murtagh's prone body, a length of white fabric trailing from his hands.

"Help!" I shrieked. "Leave him alone! Help! Brigands! Assassins! HELP!"

"Be still!" A quick clout over the ear made my head spin for a moment. When my eyes stopped watering, I could make out a long, white sausage-shape in the gutter; Murtagh, shrouded and neatly secured in a canvas sail-bag. The false watchman was crouched over him; he rose, grinning, and I could see that he was masked, a dark strip of fabric extending from forehead to upper lip.

A thin strip of light from the nearby chandler's fell across his body as he rose. In spite of the cold evening, he was wearing no more than a shirt that glowed momentarily emerald green in the passing light. A pair of breeches, buckled at the knee, and what amazingly appeared to be silk hose and leather shoes, not the bare feet or sabots I had expected. Not ordinary bandits, then.

I caught a quick glimpse of Mary, at one side. One of the masked figures had her in a tight grip from behind, one arm clasped across her midriff, the other rummaging its way under her skirts like a burrowing animal.

The one in front of me put a hand ingratiatingly behind my head and pulled me close. The mask covered him from forehead to upper lip, leaving his mouth free for obvious reasons. His tongue thrust into my mouth, tasting strongly of drink and onions. I gagged, bit it, and spat as it was removed. He cuffed me heavily, knocking me to my knees in the gutter.

Mary's silver-buckled shoes were kicking dangerously near my nose as the ruffian holding her unceremoniously yanked her skirt above her waist. There was a tearing of satin, and a loud screech from above as his fingers plunged between her struggling thighs.

"A virgin! I've got a virgin!" he crowed. One of the men bowed mockingly to Mary.

"Mademoiselle, my congratulations! Your husband will have cause to thank us on his wedding night, as he will encounter no awkward obstructions to hinder his pleasure. But we are selfless—we ask for no thanks for the performance of our duties. The doing of service is pleasure in itself."

If I had needed anything beyond the silk hose to tell me that our assailants were not street ruffians, this speech—greeted with howls of laughter—would have done it. Fitting names to the masked faces was something else again.

The hands that grasped my arm to haul me to my feet were manicured, with a small beauty mark just above the fork of the thumb. I must remember that, I thought grimly. If they let us live afterward, it might be useful.

Someone else grabbed my arms from behind, yanking them back so strongly that I cried out. The posture thus induced made my breasts stand out in the low-cut bodice as though they were being offered on a platter.

The man who seemed in charge of operations wore a loose shirt of some pale color, decorated with darker spots—embroidery perhaps. It gave him an imprecise outline in the shadows, making it difficult to look at him closely. As he leaned forward and ran a finger appraisingly over the tops of my breasts, though, I could see the dark hair greased flat to his head and smell the heavy pomade. He had large ears, the better to hold up the strings of his mask.

"Do not worry yourselves, mesdames," Spotted-shirt said. "We mean you no harm; we intend only to give you a little gentle exercise—your husbands or fiancés need never know—and then we shall release you."

"Firstly, you may honor us with your sweet lips, mesdames," he announced, stepping back and tugging at the lacings of his breeches.

"Not that one," protested Green-shirt, pointing at me. "She bites."

"Not if she wants to keep her teeth," replied his companion. "On your knees, Madame, if you please." He shoved down strongly on my shoulders, and I jerked back, stumbling. He grabbed me to keep me from getting away, and the full hood of my cloak fell back, freeing my hair. Pins loosened in the struggle, it fell over my shoulders, strands flying like banners in the night wind, blinding me as they whipped across my face.

I staggered backward, pulling away from my assailant, shaking my head to clear my eyes. The street was dark, but I could see a few things in the faint gleam of lanterns through the shuttered shop windows, or in the glow of starlight that struck through the shadows to the street.

Mary's silver shoe buckles caught the light, kicking. She was on her back, struggling, with one of the men on top of her, swearing as he fought to get his breeches down and to control her at the same time. There was the sound of tearing cloth, and his buttocks gleamed white in a shaft of light from a courtyard gate.

Someone's arms seized me round the waist and dragged me backward, raising my feet off the ground. I scraped my heel down the length of his shin, and he squealed in outrage.

"Hold her!" ordered Spotted-shirt, coming out of the shadows.

"You hold her!" My captor thrust me unceremoniously into the arms of his friend, and the light from the courtyard shone into my eyes, temporarily blinding me.

"Mother of God!" The hands clutching my arms slackened their grip, and I yanked loose, to see Spotted-shirt, mouth hanging open in horrified amazement below the mask. He backed away from me, crossing himself as he went.

"In nomine Patris, et Filii, et Spiritus Sancti," he babbled, crossing and recrossing. "La Dame Blanche!"

"La Dame Blanche!" The man behind me echoed the cry, in tones of terror.

Spotted-shirt was still backing away, now making signs in the air which were considerably less Christian than the sign of the Cross, but which presumably had the same intent. Pointing index and little fingers at me in the ancient horned sign against evil, he was working his way steadily down a list of spiritual authorities, from the Trinity to powers on a considerably lower level, muttering the Latin names so fast that the syllables blurred together.

I stood in the street, shaken and dazed, until a terrible shriek from the ground near my feet recalled me to my senses. Too occupied with his own business to pay any attention to matters above him, the man on top of Mary made a gutteral sound of satisfaction and began to move his hips rhythmically, to the accompaniment of throat-tearing screams from Mary.

Acting purely from instinct, I took a step toward them, drew back my leg, and kicked him as hard as I could in the ribs. The breath exploded from his lungs in a startled "Oof!" and he rocked to one side.

One of his friends darted forward and seized him by the arm, shouting urgently, "Up! Up! It's La Dame Blanche! Run!"

Still sunk in the frenzy of rape, the man stared stupidly and tried to turn back to Mary, who was frantically writhing and twisting, trying to free the folds of her skirts from the weight that held her trapped. Both Green-shirt and Spotted-shirt were now pulling on her assailant's arms, and succeeded in getting him to his feet. His torn breeches drooped about his thighs, the blood-smeared rod of his erection trembling with mindless eagerness between the dangling shirttails.

The clatter of running feet approaching seemed finally to rouse him. His two helpers, hearing the sound, dropped his arms and fled precipitately, leaving him to his fate. With a muffled curse, he made his way down the nearest alley, hopping and hobbling as he tried to yank his breeches up around his waist.

"Au secours! Au secours! Gendarmes!" A breathless voice was shouting down the alleyway for help, as its owner fumbled his way in our direction, stumbling over rubbish in the dark. I hardly thought a footpad or other miscreant would be staggering down an alleyway shouting for the gendarmerie, though in my present state of shock, almost nothing would have surprised me.

I *was* surprised, though, when the black shape that flapped out of the alley proved to be Alexander Randall, swathed in black cape and slouch hat. He glanced wildly around the small cul-de-sac, from Murtagh, masquerading as a bag of rubbish, to me, standing frozen and gasping against a wall, to the huddled shape of Mary, nearly invisible among the other shadows. He stood helpless for a moment, then whirled and clambered up the iron gate from which our assailants had emerged. From the top of this, he could just reach the lantern suspended from the rafter above.

The light was a comfort; pitiful as was the sight it revealed, at least it banished the lurking shadows that threatened at any moment to turn into new dangers.

Mary was on her knees, curled into herself. Head buried in her arms, she was shaking, in total silence. One shoe lay on its side on the cobbles, silver buckle winking in the swaying light of the lantern.

Like a bird of ill omen, Alex swooped down beside her.

"Miss Hawkins! Mary! Miss Hawkins! Are you all right?"

"Of all the damn-fool questions," I said with some asperity as she moaned and shrank away from him. "Naturally she isn't all right. She's just been raped." With a considerable effort, I pried myself from the comforting wall at my back, and started toward them, noting with clinical detachment that my knees were wobbling.

They gave way altogether in the next moment as a huge, batlike shape swooped down a foot in front of me, landing on the cobbles with a substantial thud.

"Well, well, look who's dropped in!" I said, and started to laugh in an unhinged sort of way. A large pair of hands grabbed me by the shoulders and administered a good shake.

"Be quiet, Sassenach," said Jamie, blue eyes gleaming black and dangerous in the lanternlight. He straightened up, the folds of his blue velvet cloak falling back over his shoulders as he stretched his arms toward the roof from which he had jumped. He could just grasp the edge of it, standing on his toes.

"Well, come down, then!" he said impatiently, looking up. "Put your feet over the edge onto my shoulders, and ye can slide down my back." With a grating of loose roof slates, a small black figure wriggled its way cautiously backward, then swarmed down the tall figure like a monkey on a stick.

"Good man, Fergus." Jamie clapped the boy casually on the shoulder, and even in the dim light I could see the glow of pleasure that rose in his cheeks. Jamie surveyed the landscape with a tactician's eye, and with a muttered word, sent the lad down the alley to keep watch for approaching gendarmes. The essentials taken care of, he squatted down before me once more.

"Are ye all right, Sassenach?" he inquired.

"Nice of you to ask," I said politely. "Yes, thanks. She's not so well, though." I waved vaguely in Mary's direction. She was still rolled into a ball, shuddering and quaking like a jelly, oozing away from Alex's fumbling efforts to pat her.

Jamie spared no more than a glance at her. "So I see. Where in hell is Murtagh?"

"Over there," I answered. "Help me up."

I staggered over to the gutter, where the sack that held Murtagh was heaving to and fro like an agitated caterpillar, emitting a startling mixture of muffled profanities in three languages.

Jamie drew his dirk, and with what seemed to be a rather callous disregard for the contents, slit the sack from end to end. Murtagh popped out of the opening like a Jack out of its box. Half his spiky black hair was pasted to his head by whatever noisome liquid the bag had rested in. The rest stood on end, lending a fiercer cast to a face rendered already sufficiently warlike by a large purple knot on the forehead and a rapidly darkening eye.

"Who hit me?" he barked.

"Well, it wasn't me," answered Jamie, raising one eyebrow. "Come along, man, we havena got all night."

"This is never going to work," I muttered, stabbing pins decorated with brilliants at random through my hair. "She ought to have medical care, for one thing. She needs a doctor!"

"She has one," Jamie pointed out, lifting his chin and peering down his nose into the mirror as he tied his stock. "You." Stock tied, he grabbed a comb and pulled it hurriedly through the thick, ruddy waves of his hair.

"No time to braid it," he muttered, holding a thick tail behind his head as he rummaged in a drawer. "Have ye a bit of ribbon, Sassenach?"

"Let me." I moved swiftly behind him, folding under the ends of the hair and wrapping the club in a length of green ribbon. "Of all the bloody nights to have a dinner party on!"

And not just any dinner party, either. The Duke of Sandringham was to be guest of honor, with a small but select party to greet him. Monsieur Duverney was coming, with his eldest son, a prominent banker. Louise and Jules de La Tour were coming, and the d'Arbanvilles. Just to make things interesting, the Comte St. Germain had also been invited.

"St. Germain!" I had said in astonishment, when Jamie had told me the week before. "Whatever for?"

"I do business with the man," Jamie had pointed out. "He's been to dinner here before, with Jared. But what I want is to have the opportunity of watching him talk to you over dinner. From what I've seen of him in business, he's not the man to hide his thoughts." He picked up the white crystal that Master Raymond had given me and weighed it thoughtfully in his palm.

"It's pretty enough," he had said. "I'll have it set in a gold mounting, so you can wear it about your neck. Toy with it at dinner until someone asks ye about it, Sassenach. Then tell them what it's for, and make sure to watch St. Germain's face when ye do. If it was him gave ye the poison at Versailles, I think we'll see some sign of it."

What I wanted at the moment was peace, quiet, and total privacy in which to shake like a rabbit. What I had was a dinner party with a duke who might be a Jacobite or an English agent, a Comte who might be a poisoner, and a rape victim hidden upstairs. My hands shook so that I couldn't fasten the chain that held the mounted crystal; Jamie stepped behind me and snicked the catch with one flick of his thumb.

"Haven't you got any nerves?" I demanded of him. He grimaced at me in the mirror and put his hands over his stomach.

"Aye, I have. But it takes me in the belly, not the hands. Have ye some of that stuff for cramp?"

"Over there." I waved at the medicine box on the table, left open from my dosing of Mary. "The little green bottle. One spoonful."

Ignoring the spoon, he tilted the bottle and took several healthy gulps. He lowered it and squinted at the liquid within.

"God, that's foul stuff! Are ye nearly ready, Sassenach? The guests will be here any minute."

Mary was concealed for the moment in a spare room on the second floor. I had checked her carefully for injuries, which seemed limited to bruises and shock, then dosed her quickly with as large a slug of poppy syrup as seemed feasible.

Alex Randall had resisted all Jamie's attempts to send him home, and instead had been left to stand guard over Mary, with strict instructions to fetch me if she woke.

"How on earth did that idiot happen to be there?" I asked, scrabbling in the drawer for a box of powder.

"I asked him that," Jamie replied. "Seems the poor fool's in love with Mary Hawkins. He's been following her to and fro about the town, drooping like a wilted flower because he knows she's to wed Marigny."

I dropped the box of powder.

"*H-h-he's* in love with *her*?" I wheezed, waving away the cloud of floating particles.

"So he says, and I see nay reason to doubt it," Jamie said, brushing powder briskly off the bosom of my dress. "He was a bit distraught when he told me."

"I should imagine so." To the conflicting welter of emotions that filled me, I now added pity for Alex Randall. Of course he wouldn't have spoken to Mary, thinking the devotion of an impoverished secretary nothing compared to the wealth and position of a match with the House of Gascogne. And now what must he feel, seeing her subjected to brutal attack, virtually under his nose?

"Why in hell didn't he speak up? She would have run off with him in a moment." For the pale English curate, of course, must be the "spiritual" object of Mary's speechless devotion.

"Randall's a gentleman," Jamie replied, handing me a feather and the pot of rouge.

"You mean he's a silly ass," I said uncharitably.

Jamie's lip twitched. "Well, perhaps," he agreed. "He's also a poor one; he hasna the income to support a wife, should her family cast her off—which they certainly would, if she eloped with him. And his health is feeble; he'd find it hard to find another position, for the Duke would likely dismiss him without a character."

"One of the servants is bound to find her," I said, returning to an earlier worry in order to avoid thinking about this latest manifestation of tragedy.

"No, they won't. They'll all be busy serving. And by the morning, she may be recovered enough to go back to her uncle's house. I sent round a note," he added, "to tell them she was staying the night with a friend, as it was late. Didna want them searching for her."

"Yes, but—"

"Sassenach." His hands on my shoulders stopped me, and he peered over my shoulder to meet my eyes in the mirror. "We canna let her be seen by anyone, until she's able to speak and to act as usual. Let it be known what's happened to her, and her reputation will be ruined entirely."

"Her reputation! It's hardly her fault she was raped!" My voice shook slightly, and his grip on my shoulders tightened.

"It isna right, Sassenach, but it's how it is. Let it be known that she's a maid no more, and no man will take her—she'll be disgraced, and live a spinster to the end of her days." His hand squeezed my shoulder, left it, and returned to help guide a pin into the precariously anchored hair.

"It's all we can do for her, Claire," he said. "Keep her from harm, heal her as best we can—and find the filthy bastards who did it." He turned away and groped in my casket for his stick pin. "Christ," he added softly, speaking into the green velvet lining, "d'ye think I don't know what it is to her? Or to him?"

I laid my hand on his groping fingers and squeezed. He squeezed back, then lifted my hand and kissed it briefly.

"Lord, Sassenach! Your fingers are cold as snow." He turned me around to look earnestly into my face. "Are *you* all right, lass?"

Whatever he saw in my face made him mutter "Christ" again, sink to his knees, and pull me against his ruffled shirtfront. I gave up the pretense of courage, and clung to him, burying my face in the starchy warmth.

"Oh, God, Jamie. I was so scared. I *am* so scared. Oh, God, I wish you could make love to me now."

His chest vibrated under my cheek with his laugh, but he hugged me closer.

"You think that would help?"

"Yes."

In fact, I thought that I would not feel safe again, until I lay in the security of our bed, with the sheltering silence of the house all about us, feeling the strength and the heat of him around and within me, buttressing my courage with the joy of our joining, wiping out the horror of helplessness and near-rape with the sureness of mutual possession.

He held my face between his hands and kissed me, and for a moment, the fear of the future and the terror of the night fell away. Then he drew back and smiled. I could see his own worry etched in the lines of his face, but there was nothing in his eyes but the small reflection of my face.

"On account, then," he said softly.

We had reached the second course without incident, and I was beginning to relax slightly, though my hand still had a tendency to tremble over the consommé.

"How perfectly fascinating!" I said, in response to a story of the younger Monsieur Duverney's, to which I wasn't listening, my ears being tuned for any suspicious noises abovestairs. "Do tell me more."

I caught Magnus's eye as he served the Comte St. Germain, seated across from me, and beamed congratulations at him as well as I could with a mouthful of fish. Too well trained to smile in public, he inclined his head a respectful quarter-inch and went on with the service. My hand went to the crystal at my neck, and I stroked it ostentatiously as the Comte, with no sign of perturbation on his saturnine features, dug into the trout with almonds.

Jamie and the elder Duverney were close in conversation at the other end of the table, food ignored as Jamie scribbled left-handed figures on a scrap of paper with a stub of chalk. Chess, or business? I wondered.

As guest of honor, the Duke sat at the center of the table. He had enjoyed the first courses with the gusto of a natural-born trencherman, and was now engaged in animated conversation with Madame d'Arbanville, on his right. As the Duke was the most obviously prominent Englishman in Paris at the time, Jamie had thought it worthwhile cultivating his acquaintance, in hopes of uncovering any rumors that might lead to the sender of the musical message to Charles Stuart. My attention, though, kept straying from the Duke to the gentleman seated across from him—Silas Hawkins.

I had thought I might just die on the spot and save trouble all round when the Duke had walked through the door, gesturing casually over his shoulder, and saying, "I say, Mrs. Fraser, you do know Hawkins here, don't you?"

The Duke's small, merry blue eyes had met mine with a look of guileless confidence that his whims would be accommodated, and I had had no choice but to smile and nod, and tell Magnus to be sure another place was set. Jamie, seeing Mr. Hawkins as he came through the door of the drawing room, had looked as though he were in need of another dose of stomach medicine, but had pulled himself together enough to extend a hand to Mr. Hawkins and start a conversation about the quality of the inns on the road to Calais.

I glanced at the carriage clock over the mantelpiece. How long before they would all be gone? I mentally tallied the courses already served, and those to come. Nearly to the sweet course. Then the salad and cheese. Brandy and coffee, port for the men, liqueurs for the ladies. An hour or two for stimulating conversation. Not too stimulating, please God, or they would linger 'til dawn.

Now they were talking of the menace of street gangs. I abandoned the fish and picked up a roll.

"And I have heard that some of these roving bands are composed not of rabble, as you would expect, but of some of the younger members of the nobility!" General d'Arbanville puffed out his lips at the monstrousness of the idea. "They do it for sport—sport! As though the robbery of decent men and the outraging of ladies were nothing more than a cockfight!"

"How extraordinary," said the Duke, with the indifference of a man who never went anywhere without a substantial escort. The platter of savouries hovered near his chin, and he scooped half a dozen onto his plate.

Jamie glanced at me, and rose from the table.

"If you'll excuse me, mesdames, messieurs," he said with a bow, "I have something rather special in the way of port that I would like to have His Grace taste. I'll fetch it from the cellar."

"It must be the Belle Rouge," said Jules de La Tour, licking his lips in anticipation. "You have a rare treat in store, Your Grace. I have never tasted such a wine anywhere else."

"Ah? Well, you soon will, Monsieur le Prince," the Comte St. Germain broke in. "Something even better."

"Surely there is nothing better than Belle Rouge!" General d'Arbanville exclaimed.

"Yes, there is," the Comte declared, looking smug. "I have found a new port, made and bottled on the island of Gostos, off the coast of Portugal. A color rich as rubies, and a flavor that makes Belle Rouge taste like colored water. I have a contract for delivery of the entire vintage in August."

"Indeed, Monsieur le Comte?" Silas Hawkins raised thick, graying brows toward our end of the table. "Have you found a new partner for investment, then? I understood that your own resources were. . . . depleted, shall we say? following the sad destruction of the *Patagonia*." He took a cheese savoury from the plate and popped it delicately into his mouth.

The Comte's jaw muscles bulged, and a sudden chill descended on our end of the table. From Mr. Hawkins's sidelong glance at me, and the tiny smile that lurked about his busily chewing mouth, it was clear that he knew all about my role in the destruction of the unfortunate *Patagonia*.

My hand went again to the crystal at my neck, but the Comte didn't look at me. A hot flush had risen from his lacy stock, and he glared at Mr. Hawkins with open dislike. Jamie was right; not a man to hide his emotions.

"Fortunately, Monsieur," he said, mastering his choler with an apparent effort, "I *have* found a partner who wishes to invest in this venture. A fellow countryman, in fact, of our gracious host." He nodded sardonically toward the doorway, where Jamie had just appeared, followed by Magnus, who bore an enormous decanter of the Belle Rouge port.

Hawkins stopped chewing for a moment, his mouth unattractively open with interest. "A Scotsman? Who? I didn't think there were any Scots in the wine business in Paris besides the house of Fraser."

A definite gleam of amusement lit the Comte's eyes as he glanced from Mr. Hawkins to Jamie. "I suppose it is debatable whether the investor in question could be considered Scottish at the moment; nonetheless, he is milord Broch Tuarach's fellow countryman. Charles Stuart is his name."

This bit of news had all the impact the Comte might have hoped for. Silas Hawkins sat bolt upright with an exclamation that made him choke on the remnants of his mouthful. Jamie, who had been about to speak, closed his mouth and sat down, regarding the Comte thoughtfully. Jules de La Tour began to spray exclamations and globules of spit, and both d'Arbanvilles made ejaculations of amazement. Even the Duke took his eyes off his plate and blinked at the Comte in interest.

"Really?" he said. "I understood the Stuarts were poor as church mice. You're sure he's not gulling you?"

"I have no wish to cast aspersions, or arouse suspicions," chipped in Jules de La Tour, "but it is well known at Court that the Stuarts have no money. It is true that several of the Jacobite supporters have been seeking funds lately, but without luck, so far as I have heard."

"That's true," interjected the younger Duverney, leaning forward with interest. "Charles Stuart himself has spoken privately with two bankers of my acquaintance, but no one is willing to advance him any substantial sum in his present circumstances."

I shot a quick glance at Jamie, who answered with an almost imperceptible nod. This came under the heading of good news. But then what about the Comte's story of an investment?

"It is true," he said belligerently. "His Highness has secured a loan of fifteen thousand livres from an Italian bank, and has placed the entire sum at my disposal, to be used in commissioning a ship and purchasing the bottling of the Gostos vineyard. I have the signed letter right here." He tapped the breast of his coat with satisfaction, then sat back and looked triumphantly around the table, stopping at Jamie.

"Well, milord," he said, with a wave at the decanter that sat on the white cloth in front of Jamie, "are you going to allow us to taste this famous wine?"

"Yes, of course," Jamie murmured. He reached mechanically for the first glass.

Louise, who had sat quietly eating through most of the dinner, noted Jamie's discomfort. A kind friend, she turned to me in an obvious effort to change the course of the conversation to a neutral topic.

"That is a beautiful stone you wear about your neck, *ma chère*," she said, gesturing at my crystal. "Where did you get it?"

"Oh, this?" I said. "Well, in fact—"

I was interrupted by a piercing scream. It stopped all conversation, and the brittle echoes of it chimed in the crystals of the chandelier overhead.

"Mon Dieu," said the Comte St. Germain, into the silence. "What—"

The scream was repeated, and then repeated again. The noise spilled down the wide stairway and into the foyer.

The guests, rising from the dinner table like a covey of flushed quail, also spilled into the foyer, in time to see Mary Hawkins, clad in the shredded remnants of her shift, lurch into view at the top of the stair. There she stood, as though for maximum effect, mouth stretched wide, hands splayed across her bosom, where the ripped fabric all too clearly displayed the bruises left by grappling hands on her breasts and arms.

Her pupils shrunk to pinpoints in the light of the candelabra, her eyes seemed blank pools in which horror was reflected. She looked down, but plainly saw neither stairway nor crowd of gaping onlookers.

"No!" she shrieked. "No! Let me go! Please, I beg you! DON'T TOUCH ME!" Blinded by the drug as she was, apparently she sensed some movement behind her, for she turned and flailed wildly, hands clawing at the figure of Alex Randall, who was trying vainly to get hold of her, to calm her.

Unfortunately, from below, his attempts looked rather like those of a rejected seducer bent on further attack.

"Nom de Dieu," burst out General d'Arbanville. *"Racaille!* Let her go at once!" The old soldier leaped for the stair with an agility belying his years, hand reaching instinctively for his sword—which, luckily, he had laid aside at the door.

I hastily thrust myself and my voluminous skirts in front of the Comte and the younger Duverney, who showed symptoms of following the General to the rescue, but I could do nothing about Mary's uncle, Silas Hawkins. Eyes popping from his head, the wine merchant stood stunned for a moment, then lowered his head and charged like a bull, forcing his way through the onlookers.

I looked wildly about for Jamie, and found him on the edge of the crowd. I caught his eye and raised my brows in silent question; in any case, nothing I said could have been heard above the hubbub in the foyer, punctuated by Mary's steam-whistle shrieks from above.

Jamie shrugged at me, then glanced around him. I saw his eyes light for a moment on a three-legged table near the wall, holding a tall vase of chrysanthemums. He glanced up, measuring the distance, closed his eyes briefly as though commending his soul to God, then moved with decision.

He sprang from the floor to the table, grasped the banister railing and vaulted over it, onto the stairway, a few feet in advance of the General. It was such an acrobatic feat that one or two ladies gasped, little cries of admiration intermingled with their exclamations of horror.

The exclamations grew louder as Jamie bounded up the remaining stairs, elbowed his way between Mary and Alex, and seizing the latter by the shoulder, took careful aim and hit him solidly on the point of the jaw.

Alex, who had been staring at his employer below in openmouthed amazement, folded gently at the knees and crumpled into a heap, eyes still wide, but gone suddenly blank and empty as Mary's.

19

An Oath Is Sworn

The clock on the mantelpiece had an annoyingly loud tick. It was the only sound in the house, other than the creakings of the boards, and the far-off thumps of servants working late in the kitchens below. I had had enough noise to last me some time, though, and wanted only silence to mend my frazzled nerves. I opened the clock's case and removed the counterweight, and the tick ceased at once.

It had undeniably been the dinner party of the season. People not fortunate enough to have been present would be claiming for months that they had been, bolstering their case with bits of repeated gossip and distorted description.

I had finally got my hands on Mary long enough to force another strong dose of poppy juice down her throat. She collapsed in a pitiful heap of blood-stained clothes, leaving me free to turn my attention to the three-sided argument going on among Jamie, the General, and Mr. Hawkins. Alex had the good sense to stay unconscious, and I arranged his limp form neatly alongside Mary's on the landing, like a couple of dead mackerel. They looked like Romeo and Juliet laid out in the public square as a reproach to their relatives, but the resemblance was lost on Mr. Hawkins.

"Ruined!" he kept shrieking. "You've ruined my niece! The Vicomte will never have her now! Filthy Scottish prick! You and your strumpet"—he swung on me—"whore! Procuress! Seducing innocent young girls into your vile clutches for the pleasure of bastardly scum! You—" Jamie, with a certain long-suffering grimness, put a hand on Mr. Hawkins's shoulders, turned him about, and hit him, just under the fleshy jaw. Then he stood abstractedly rubbing his abused knuckles, watching as the stout wine merchant's eyes rolled upward. Mr. Hawkins fell back against the paneling and slid gently down the wall into a sitting position.

Jamie turned a cold blue gaze on General d'Arbanville, who, observing the fate of the fallen, wisely put down the wine bottle he had been waving, and took a step back.

"Oh, go ahead," urged a voice behind my shoulder. "Why stop now, Tuarach? Hit all three of them! Make a clean sweep of it!" The General and Jamie focused a glance of united dislike on the dapper form behind me.

"Go away, St. Germain," Jamie said. "This is none of your affair." He sounded weary, but raised his voice in order to be heard above the uproar below. The shoulder seams of his coat had been split, and folds of his linen shirt showed white through the rents.

St. Germain's thin lips curved upward in a charming smile. Plainly the Comte was having the time of his life.

"Not my affair? How can such happenings not be the affair of every public-spirited man?" His amused gaze swept the landing, littered with bodies. "After all, if a guest of His Majesty has so perverted the meaning of hospitality as to maintain a brothel in his house, is that not the—no, you don't!" he said, as Jamie took a step toward him. A blade gleamed suddenly in his hand, appearing as though by magic from the ruffled lace cascading over his wrist. I saw Jamie's lip curl slightly, and he shifted his shoulders inside the ruins of his coat, settling himself for battle.

"Stop it at once!" said an imperious voice, and the two Duverneys, older and younger, pushed their way onto the already overcrowded landing. Duverney the younger turned and waved his arms commandingly at the herd of people on the stairs, who were sufficiently cowed by his scowl to move back a step.

"You," said the elder Duverney, pointing at St. Germain. "If you have any feeling of public spirit, as you suggest, you will employ yourself usefully in removing some of those below."

St. Germain locked eyes with the banker, but after a moment, the noble shrugged, and the dagger disappeared. St. Germain turned without comment and made his way downstairs, pushing those before him and loudly urging them to leave.

Despite his exhortations, and those of Gérard, the younger Duverney, behind him, the bulk of the dinner guests departed, brimming with scandal, only upon the arrival of the King's Guard.

Mr. Hawkins, recovered by this time, at once lodged a charge of kidnapping and pandering against Jamie. For a moment, I really thought Jamie was going to hit him again; his muscles bunched under the azure velvet, but then relaxed as he thought better of it.

After a considerable amount of confused argument and explanation, Jamie agreed to go to the Guard's headquarters in the Bastille, there—perhaps—to explain himself.

Alex Randall, white-faced, sweating, and clearly having no idea what was going on, was taken, too—the Duke had not waited to see the fate of his secretary, but had discreetly summoned his coach and left before the arrival of the Guard. Whatever his diplomatic mission, being involved in a scandal wouldn't help it. Mary Hawkins, still insensible, was removed to her uncle's house, wrapped in a blanket.

I had narrowly avoided being included in the roundup when Jamie flatly refused to allow it, insisting that I was in a delicate condition and could on no account be removed to a prison. At last, seeing that Jamie was more than willing to start hitting people again in order to prove his point, the Guard Captain relented, on condition that I agreed not to leave the city. While the thought of fleeing Paris had its attractions, I could hardly leave without Jamie, and gave my *parole d'honneur* with no reservations.

As the group milled confusedly about the foyer, lighting lanterns and gathering hats and cloaks, I saw Murtagh, bruised face set grimly, hovering on the outskirts of the mob. Plainly he intended to accompany Jamie, wherever he was going, and I felt a quick stab of relief. At least my husband wouldn't be alone.

"Dinna worry yourself, Sassenach." He hugged me briefly, whispering in my ear. "I'll be back in no time. If anything goes wrong . . ." He hesitated, then said firmly, "It wilna be necessary, but if ye need a friend, go to Louise de La Tour."

"I will." I had no time for more than a glancing kiss, before the Guardsmen closed in about him.

The doors of the house swung open, and I saw Jamie glance behind him, catch sight of Murtagh, and open his mouth as though to say something. Murtagh, setting hands to his swordbelt, glared fiercely and pushed his way toward Jamie, nearly shoving the younger Duverney into the street. A short, silent battle of wills ensued, conducted entirely by means of ferocious glares, and then Jamie shrugged and tossed up his hands in resignation.

He stepped out into the street, ignoring the Guardsmen who pressed close on all sides, but stopped at sight of a small figure standing near the gate. He stooped and said something, then straightened, turned toward the house and gave me a smile, clearly visible in the lanternlight. Then, with a nod to the elder Monsieur Duverney, he stepped into the waiting coach and was borne away, Murtagh clinging to the rear of the carriage.

Fergus stood in the street, looking after the coach as long as it was in sight. Then, mounting the steps with a firm tread, he took me by the hand and led me inside.

"Come, milady," he said. "Milord has said I am to care for you, 'til his return."

Now Fergus slipped into the salon, the door closing silently behind him.

"I have made the rounds of the house, milady," he whispered. "All buttoned up." Despite the worry, I smiled at his tone, so obviously an imitation of Jamie's. His idol had entrusted him with a responsibility, and he plainly took his duties seriously.

Having escorted me to the sitting room, he had gone to make the rounds of the house as Jamie did each night, checking the fastenings of the shutters, the bars on the outer doors—which I knew he could barely lift—and the banking of the fires. He had a smudge of soot from forehead to cheekbone on one side, but had rubbed his eye with a fist at one point, so his eye blinked out of a clear white ring, like a small raccoon.

"You should rest, milady," he said. "Don't worry, I'll be here."

I didn't laugh, but smiled at him. "I couldn't sleep, Fergus. I'll just sit here for a bit. Perhaps you should go to bed, though; you've had an awfully long night of it." I was reluctant to order him to bed, not wanting to impair his new dignity as temporary man of the house, but he was clearly exhausted. The small, bony shoulders drooped, and dark smudges showed beneath his eyes, darker even than the coating of soot.

He yawned unashamedly, but shook his head.

"No, milady. I will stay with you . . . if you do not mind?" he added hastily.

"I don't mind." In fact, he was too tired either to talk or to fidget in his usual manner, and his sleepy presence on the hassock was comforting, like that of a cat or a dog.

I sat gazing into the low-burning flames, trying to conjure up some semblance of serenity. I tried summoning images of still pools, forest glades, even the dark peace of the Abbey chapel, but nothing seemed to be working; over all the images of peace lay those of the evening: hard hands and gleaming teeth, coming out of a darkness filled with fear; Mary's white and stricken face, a twin to Alex Randall's; the flare of hatred in Mr. Hawkins's piggy eyes; the sudden mistrust on the faces of the General and the Duverneys; St. Germain's ill-concealed delight in scandal, shimmering with malice like the crystal drops of the chandeliers. And last of all, Jamie's smile, reassurance and uncertainty mingled in the shifting light of jostling lanterns.

What if he didn't come back? That was the thought I had been trying to suppress, ever since they took him away. If he was unable to clear himself of the charge? If the magistrate was one of those suspicious of foreigners—well, more suspicious than usual, I amended—he could easily be imprisoned indefinitely. And above and beyond the fear that this unlooked-for crisis could undo all the careful work of the last weeks, was the image of Jamie in a cell like the one where I had found him at Wentworth. In light of the present crisis, the news that Charles Stuart was investing in wine seemed trivial.

Left alone, I now had plenty of time to think, but my thoughts didn't seem to be getting me anywhere. Who or what was "La Dame Blanche"? What sort of "white lady," and why had the mention of that name made the attackers run off?

Thinking back over the subsequent events of the dinner party, I remembered the General's remarks about the criminal gangs that roamed the streets of Paris, and how some of them included members of the nobility. That was consistent with the speech and the dress of the leader of the men who had attacked me and Mary, though his companions seemed a good deal rougher in aspect. I tried to think whether the man reminded me of anyone I knew, but the memory of him was indistinct, clouded by darkness and the receding haze of shock.

In general form, he had been not unlike the Comte St. Germain, though surely the voice was different. But then, if the Comte was involved, surely he would take pains to disguise his voice as well as his face? At the same time, I found it almost impossible to believe that the Comte could have taken part in such an attack, and then sat calmly across the table from me two hours later, sipping soup.

I ran my fingers through my hair in frustration. There was nothing that could be done before morning. If morning came, and Jamie didn't, then I could begin to make the rounds of acquaintances and presumed friends, one of whom might have news or help to offer. But for the hours of the night, I was helpless; powerless to move as a dragonfly in amber.

My fingers jammed against one of the decorated hairpins, and I yanked at it impatiently. Tangled in my hair, it stuck.

"Ouch!"

"Here, milady. I'll get it."

I hadn't heard him pass behind me, but I felt Fergus's small, clever fingers in my hair, disentangling the tiny ornament. He laid it aside, then, hesitating, said, "The others, milady?"

"Oh, thank you, Fergus," I said, grateful. "If you wouldn't mind."

His pickpocket's touch was light and sure, and the thick locks began to fall around my face, released from their moorings. Little by little, my breathing slowed as my hair came down.

"You are worried, milady?" said the small, soft voice behind me.

"Yes," I said, too tired to keep up a false bravado.

"Me, too," he said simply.

The last of the hairpins clinked on the table, and I slumped in the chair, eyes closed. Then I felt a touch again, and realized that he was brushing my hair, gently combing out the tangles.

"You permit, milady?" he said, feeling it as I tensed in surprise. "The ladies used to say it helped them, if they were feeling worried or upset."

I relaxed again under the soothing touch.

"I permit," I said. "Thank you." After a moment, I said, "What ladies, Fergus?"

There was a momentary hesitation, as of a spider disturbed in the building of a web, and then the delicate ordering of strands resumed.

"At the place where I used to sleep, milady. I couldn't come out because of the customers, but Madame Elise would let me sleep in a closet under the stairs, if I was quiet. And after all the men had gone, near morning, then I would come out and sometimes the ladies would share their breakfast with me. I would help them with the fastening of their underthings—they said I had the best touch of anyone," he added, with some pride, "and I would comb their hair, if they liked."

"Mm." The soft whisper of the brush through my hair was hypnotic. Without the clock on the mantel, there was no telling time, but the silence of the street outside meant it was very late indeed.

"How did you come to sleep at Madame Elise's, Fergus?" I asked, barely suppressing a yawn.

"I was born there, milady," he answered. The strokes of the brush grew slower, and his voice was growing drowsy. "I used to wonder which of the ladies was my mother, but I never found out."

The opening of the sitting-room door woke me. Jamie stood there, red-eyed and white-faced with fatigue, but smiling in the first gray light of the day.

"I was afraid you weren't coming back," I said, a moment later, into the top of his head. His hair had the faint acrid scent of stale smoke and tallow, and his coat had completed its descent into total disreputability, but he was warm and solid, and I wasn't disposed to be critical about the smell of the head I was cradling next my bosom.

"So was I," he said, somewhat muffled, and I could feel his smile. The arms around my waist tightened and released, and he sat back, smoothing my hair out of my eyes.

"God, you are so beautiful," he said softly. "Unkempt and unslept, wi' the waves of your hair all about your face. Bonny love. Have ye sat here all night long, then?"

"I wasn't the only one." I motioned toward the floor, where Fergus lay curled up on the carpet, head on a cushion by my feet. He shifted slightly in his sleep, mouth open a bit, soft pink and full-lipped as the baby he so nearly was.

Jamie laid a big hand gently on his shoulder.

"Come on, then, laddie. Ye've done well to guard your mistress." He scooped the boy up and laid him against his shoulder, mumbling and sleepy-eyed. "You're a good man, Fergus, and ye've earned your rest. Come on to your bed." I saw Fergus's eyes flare wide in surprise, then half-close as he relaxed, nodding in Jamie's arms.

I had opened the shutters and rekindled the fire by the time Jamie returned to the sitting room. He had shed his ruined coat, but still wore the rest of last night's finery.

"Here." I handed him a glass of wine, and he drank it standing, in three gulps, shuddered, then collapsed onto the small sofa, and held out the cup for more.

"Not a drop," I said, "until you tell me what's going on. You aren't in prison, so I assume everything's all right, but—"

"Not all right, Sassenach," he interrupted, "but it could be worse."

After a great deal of argument to and fro—a good deal of it Mr. Hawkins's reiterations of his original impressions—the judge-magistrate who had been hustled out of his cozy bed to preside over this impromptu investigation had ruled grumpily that since Alex Randall was one of the accused, he could hardly be considered an impartial witness. Nor could I, as the wife and possible accomplice of the other accused. Murtagh had been, by his own testimony, insensible during the alleged attack, and the child Claudel was not legally capable of bearing witness.

Clearly, Monsieur le Juge had said, aiming a vicious glare at the Guard Captain, the only person capable of providing the truth of the matter was Mary Hawkins, who was by all accounts incapable of doing so at the present time. Therefore, all the accused should be locked up in the Bastille until such time as Mademoiselle Hawkins could be interviewed, and surely Monsieur le Capitaine should have been able to think that out for himself?

"Then why aren't you locked up in the Bastille?" I asked.

"Monsieur Duverney the elder offered security for me," Jamie replied, pulling me down onto the sofa beside him. "He sat rolled up in the corner like a hedgehog, all through the clishmaclaver. Then when the judge made his decision, he stood up and said that, having had the opportunity to play chess with me on several occasions, he didna feel that I was of a moral character so dissolute as to permit of my having conspired in the commission of an act so depraved—" He broke off and shrugged.

"Well, ye ken what he talks like, once he's got going. The general idea was that a man who could take him at chess six times in seven wouldna lure innocent young lasses to his house to be defiled."

"Very logical," I said dryly. "I imagine what he really meant was, if they locked you up, you wouldn't be able to play with him anymore."

"I expect so," he agreed. He stretched, yawned, and blinked at me, smiling.

"But I'm home, and right now, I don't greatly care why. Come here to me, Sassenach." Grasping my waist with both hands, he boosted me onto his lap, wrapped his arms around me, and sighed with pleasure.

"All I want to do," he murmured in my ear, "is to shed these filthy clouts, and lie wi' you on the hearthrug, go to sleep straight after, with my head on your shoulder, and stay that way 'til tomorrow."

"Rather an inconvenience to the servants," I remarked. "They'll have to sweep round us."

"Damn the servants," he said comfortably. "What are doors for?"

"To be knocked on, evidently," I said as a soft rap sounded outside.

Jamie paused a moment, nose buried in my hair, then sighed, and raised his head, sliding me off his lap onto the sofa.

"Thirty seconds," he promised me in an undertone, then said, *"Entrez!"* in a louder voice.

The door swung open and Murtagh stepped into the room. I had rather overlooked Murtagh in the bustles and confusion of the night before, and now thought to myself that his appearance had not been improved by neglect.

He lacked as much sleep as Jamie; the one eye that was open was red-rimmed and bloodshot. The other had darkened to the color of a rotten banana, a slit of glittering black visible in the puffed flesh. The knot on his forehead had now achieved full prominence: a purple goose-egg just over one brow, with a nasty split through it.

The little clansman had said barely a word since his release from the bag the night before. Beyond a brief inquiry as to the whereabouts of his knives—retrieved by Fergus, who, questing in his usual rat-terrier fashion, had found both dirk and *sgian dhu* behind a pile of rubbish—he had preserved a grim silence through the exigencies of our getaway, guarding the rear as we hurried on foot through the dim Paris alleys. And once arrived at the house, a piercing glance from his operating eye had been sufficient to quell any injudicious questions from the kitchen servants.

I supposed he must have said something at the *commissariat de police* if only to bear witness to the good character of his employer—though I did wonder just how much credibility I would be inclined to place in Murtagh, were I a French judge. But now he was silent as the gargoyles on Notre Dame, one of which he strongly resembled.

However disreputable his appearance, though, Murtagh never seemed to lack for dignity, nor did he now. Back straight as a ramrod, he advanced across the carpet, and knelt formally before Jamie, who looked nonplussed at this behavior.

The wiry little man drew the dirk from his belt, without flourishes, but with a good deal of deliberateness, and held it out, haft first. The bony, seamed face was expressionless, but the one black eye rested unwaveringly on Jamie's face.

"I've failed ye," the little man said quietly. "And I'll ask ye, as my chief, to take my life now, so I needna live longer wi' the shame of it."

Jamie drew himself slowly upright, and I felt him push away his own tiredness as he brought his gaze to bear on his retainer. He was quite still for a moment, hands resting on his knees. Then he reached out and placed one hand gently over the purple knot on Murtagh's head.

"There's nay shame to ha' fallen in battle, *mo caraidh*," he said softly. "The greatest of warriors may be overcome."

But the little man shook his head stubbornly, black eye unwinking.

"Nay," he said. "I didna fall in battle. Ye gave me your trust; your own lady and your child unborn to guard, and the wee English lassie as well. And I gave the task sae little heed that I had nay chance to strike a blow when the danger came. Truth to tell, I didna even see the hand that struck me down." He did blink then, once.

"Treachery—" Jamie began.

"And now see what's come of it," Murtagh interrupted. I had never heard him speak so many words in a row in all the time I had known him. "Your good name smirched, your wife attacked, and the wee lass . . ." The thin line of his mouth clamped tight for a moment, and his stringy throat bobbed once as he swallowed. "For that alone, the bitter sorrow chokes me."

"Aye." Jamie spoke softly, nodding. "Aye, I do see, man. I feel it, too." He touched his chest briefly, over his heart. The two men might have been alone together, their heads inches apart as Jamie bent toward the older man. Hands folded in my lap, I neither moved nor spoke; it was not my affair.

"But I'm no your chief, man," Jamie went on, in a firmer tone. "Ye've sworn me no vow, and I hold nay power ower ye."

"Aye, that ye do." Murtagh's voice was firm as well, and the haft of the dirk never trembled.

"But—"

"I swore ye my oath, Jamie Fraser, when ye were no more than a week old, and a bonny lad at your mother's breast."

I could feel the tiny start of astonishment as Jamie's eyes opened wide.

"I knelt at Ellen's feet, as I kneel now by yours," the little clansman went on, narrow chin held high. "And I swore to her by the name o' the threefold God, that I would follow ye always, to do your bidding, and guard your back, when ye became a man grown, and needing such service." The harsh voice softened then, and the eyelid drooped over the one tired eye.

"Aye, lad. I do cherish ye as the son of my own loins. But I have betrayed your service."

"That ye havena and never could." Jamie's hands rested on Murtagh's shoulders, squeezing firmly. "Nay, I wilna have your life from ye, for I've need of ye still. But I will lay an oath on ye, and you'll take it."

There was a long moment's hesitation, then the spiky black head nodded imperceptibly.

Jamie's voice dropped still further, but it was not a whisper. Holding the middle three fingers of his right hand stiff, he laid them together over the hilt of the dirk, at the juncture of haft and tang.

"I charge ye, then, by your oath to me and your word to my mother—find the men. Hunt them, and when they be found, I do charge ye wi' the vengeance due my wife's honor—and the blood of Mary Hawkins's innocence."

He paused a moment, then took his hand from the knife. The clansman raised it, holding it upright by the blade. Acknowledging my presence for the first time, he bowed his head toward me and said, "As the laird has spoken, lady, so I will do. I will lay vengeance at your feet."

I licked dry lips, not knowing what to say. No response seemed necessary, though; he brought the dirk to his lips and kissed it, then straightened with decision and thrust it home in its sheath.

20

La Dame Blanche

The dawn had broadened into day by the time we had changed our clothes, and breakfast was on its way up the stairs from the kitchen.

"What I want to know," I said, pouring out the chocolate, "is who in bloody hell is La Dame Blanche?"

"La Dame Blanche?" Magnus, leaning over my shoulder with a basket of hot bread, started so abruptly that one of the rolls fell out of the basket. I fielded it neatly and turned round to look up at the butler, who was looking rather shaken.

"Yes, that's right," I said. "You've heard the name, Magnus?"

"Why, yes, milady," the old man answered. "La Dame Blanche is *une sorcière.*"

"A sorceress?" I said incredulously.

Magnus shrugged, tucking in the napkin around the rolls with excessive care, not looking at me.

"The White Lady," he murmured. "She is called a wisewoman, a healer. And yet . . . she sees to the center of a man, and can turn his soul to ashes, if evil be found there." He bobbed his head, turned, and shuffled off hastily in the direction of the kitchen. I saw his elbow bob, and realized that he was crossing himself as he went.

"Jesus H. Christ," I said, turning back to Jamie. "Did you ever hear of La Dame Blanche?"

"Um? Oh? Oh, aye, I've . . . heard the stories." Jamie's eyes were hidden by long auburn lashes as he buried his nose in his cup of chocolate, but the blush on his cheeks was too deep to be put down to the heat of the rising steam.

I leaned back in my chair, crossed my arms, and regarded him narrowly.

"Oh, you have?" I said. "Would it surprise you to hear that the men who attacked Mary and me last night referred to me as La Dame Blanche?"

"They did?" He looked up quickly at that, startled.

I nodded. "They took one look at me in the light, shouted 'La Dame Blanche,' and then ran off as though they'd just noticed I had plague."

Jamie took a deep breath and let it out slowly. The red color was fading from his face, leaving it pale as the white china plate before him.

"God in heaven," he said, half to himself. "God . . . in . . . heaven!"

I leaned across the table and took the cup from his hand.

"Would you like to tell me just what you know about La Dame Blanche?" I suggested gently.

"Well . . ." He hesitated, but then looked at me sheepishly. "It's only . . . I told Glengarry that you were La Dame Blanche."

"You told Glengarry *what*?" I choked on the bite of roll I had taken. Jamie pounded me helpfully on the back.

"Well, it was Glengarry and Castellotti, was what it was," he said defensively. "I mean, playing at cards and dice is one thing, but they wouldna leave it at that. And they thought it verra funny that I'd wish to be faithful to my wife. They said . . . well, they said a number of things, and I . . . I got rather tired of it." He looked away, the tips of his ears burning.

"Mm," I said, sipping tea. Having heard Castellotti's tongue in action, I could imagine the sort of merciless teasing Jamie had taken.

He drained his own cup at one swallow, then occupied himself with carefully refilling it, keeping his eyes fixed on the pot to avoid meeting mine. "But I couldna just walk out and leave them, either, could I?" he demanded. "I had to stay with His Highness through the evening, and it would do no good to have him thinkin' me unmanly."

"So you told them I was La Dame Blanche," I said, trying hard to keep any hint of laughter out of my voice. "And if you tried any funny business with ladies of the evening, I'd shrivel your private parts."

"Er, well . . ."

"My God, they *believed* it?" I could feel my own face flushing as hotly as Jamie's, with the effort to control myself.

"I was verra convincing about it," he said, one corner of his mouth beginning to twitch. "Swore them all to secrecy on their mothers' lives."

"And how much did you all have to drink before this?"

"Oh, a fair bit. I waited 'til the fourth bottle."

I gave up the struggle and burst out laughing.

"Oh, Jamie!" I said. "You darling!" I leaned over and kissed his furiously blushing cheek.

"Well," he said awkwardly, slathering butter over a chunk of bread. "It was the best I could think of. And they did stop pushing trollops into my arms."

"Good," I said. I took the bread from him, added honey, and gave it back.

"I can hardly complain about it," I observed. "Since in addition to guarding your virtue, it seems to have kept me from being raped."

"Aye, thank God." He set down the roll and grasped my hand. "Christ, if anything had happened to you, Sassenach, I'd—"

"Yes," I interrupted, "but if the men who attacked us knew I was supposed to be La Dame Blanche . . ."

"Aye, Sassenach." He nodded down at me. "It canna have been either

Glengarry nor Castellotti, for they were with me at the house where Fergus came to fetch me when you were attacked. But it must have been someone they told of it."

I couldn't repress a slight shiver at the memory of the white mask and the mocking voice behind it.

With a sigh, he let go of my hand. "Which means, I suppose, that I'd best go and see Glengarry, and find out just how many people he's been regaling wi' tales of my married life." He rubbed a hand through his hair in exasperation. "And then I must go call on His Highness, and find out what in hell he means by this arrangement with the Comte St. Germain."

"I suppose so," I said thoughtfully, "though knowing Glengarry, he's probably told half of Paris by now. I have some calls to make this afternoon, myself."

"Oh, aye? And who are you going to call upon, Sassenach?" he asked, eyeing me narrowly. I took a deep breath, bracing myself at the thought of the ordeal that lay ahead.

"First, on Master Raymond," I said. "And then, on Mary Hawkins."

"Lavender, perhaps?" Raymond stood on tiptoe to take a jar from the shelf. "Not for application, but the aroma is soothing; it calms the nerves."

"Well, that depends on whose nerves are involved," I said, recalling Jamie's reaction to the scent of lavender. It was the scent Jack Randall had favored, and Jamie found exposure to the herb's perfume anything but soothing. "In this case, though, it might help. Do no harm, at any rate."

"Do no harm," he quoted thoughtfully. "A very sound principle."

"That's the first bit of the Hippocratic Oath, you know," I said, watching him as he bent to rummage in his drawers and bins. "The oath a physician swears. 'First, do no harm.'"

"Ah? And have you sworn this oath yourself, madonna?" The bright, amphibious eyes blinked at me over the edge of the high counter.

I felt myself flushing before that unblinking gaze.

"Er, well, no. Not actually. I'm not a real physician. Not yet." I couldn't have said what made me add that last sentence.

"No? Yet you are seeking to mend that which a 'real' physician would never try, knowing that a lost maidenhead is not restorable." His irony was evident.

"Oh, isn't it?" I answered dryly. Fergus had, with encouragement, told me quite a bit about the "ladies" at Madame Elise's house. "What's that bit with the shoat's bladder full of chicken blood, hm? Or do you claim that things like that fall into an apothecary's realm of competence, but not a physician's?"

He had no eyebrows to speak of, but the heavy shelf of his forehead lifted slightly when he was amused.

"And who is harmed by that, madonna? Surely not the seller. Not the buyer, either—he is likely to get more enjoyment for his money than the purchaser of the genuine article. Not even the maidenhead itself is harmed! Surely a very moral and Hippocratic endeavor, which any physician might be pleased to assist?"

I laughed. "And I expect you know more than a few who do?" I said. "I'll take the matter up with the next Medical Review Board I see. In the meantime, short of manufactured miracles, what can we do in the present case?"

"Mm." He laid out a gauze square on the counter and poured a handful of finely shredded dried leaves into the center of it. A sharp, pleasant tang rose from the small heap of grayish-green vegetation.

"This is Saracen's consound," he said, skilfully folding the gauze into a tidy square with the ends tucked in. "Good for soothing irritated skin, minor lacerations, and sores of the privy parts. Useful, I think?"

"Yes, indeed," I said, a little grimly. "As an infusion or a decoction?"

"Infusion. Warm, probably, under the circumstances." He turned to another shelf and abstracted one of the large white jars of painted porcelain. This one said CHELIDONIUM on the side.

"For the inducement of sleep," he explained. His lipless mouth stretched back at the corners. "I think perhaps you had better avoid the use of the opium-poppy derivatives; this particular patient appears to have an unpredictable response to them."

"Heard all about it already, have you?" I said resignedly. I could hardly have hoped he hadn't. I was well aware that information was one of the more important commodities he sold; consequently the little shop was a nexus for gossip from dozens of sources, from street vendors to gentlemen of the Royal Bedchamber.

"From three separate sources," Raymond replied. He glanced out the window, craning his neck to see the huge *horloge* that hung from the wall of the building near the corner. "And it's barely two o'clock. I expect I will hear several more versions of the events at your dinner before nightfall." The wide, gummy mouth opened, and a soft chuckle emerged. "I particularly liked the version in which your husband challenged General d'Arbanville to a duel in the street, while you more pragmatically offered Monsieur le Comte the enjoyment of the unconscious girl's body, if he would refrain from calling the King's Guard."

"Mmphm," I said, sounding self-consciously Scottish. "Have you any particular interest in knowing what actually *did* happen?"

The horned-poppy tonic, a pale amber in the afternoon sunlight, sparkled as he poured it into a small vial.

"The truth is always of use, madonna," he answered, eyes fixed on the slender stream. "It has the value of rarity, you know." He set the porcelain jar on the counter with a soft thump. "And thus is worth a fair price in exchange," he added. The money for the medicines I had bought was lying on the counter, the coins gleaming in the sun. I narrowed my eyes at him, but he merely smiled blandly, as though he had never heard of froglegs in garlic butter.

The *horloge* outside struck two. I calculated the distance to the Hawkins's house in Rue Malory. Barely half an hour, if I could get a carriage. Plenty of time.

"In that case," I said, "shall we step into your private room for a bit?"

"And that's it," I said, taking a long sip of cherry brandy. The fumes in the workroom were nearly as strong as those rising from my glass, and I could feel my head expanding under their influence, rather like a large, cheerful red balloon. "They let Jamie go, but we're still under suspicion. I can't imagine that will last long, though, do you?"

Raymond shook his head. A draft stirred the crocodile overhead, and he rose to shut the window.

"No. A nuisance, nothing more. Monsieur Hawkins has money and friends, and of course he is distraught, but still. Plainly you and your husband were guilty of nothing more than excessive kindness, in trying to keep the girl's misfortune a secret." He took a deep swallow from his own glass.

"And that is your concern at present, of course. The girl?"

I nodded. "One of them. There's nothing I can do about her reputation at this point. All I can do is try to help her to heal."

A sardonic black eye peered over the rim of the metal goblet he was holding.

"Most physicians of my acquaintance would say, 'All I can do is try to heal her.' You will help her to heal? It's interesting that you perceive the difference, madonna. I thought you would."

I set down the cup, feeling that I had had enough. Heat was radiating from my cheeks, and I had the distinct feeling that the tip of my nose was pink.

"I told you I'm not a real physician." I closed my eyes briefly, determined that I could still tell which way was up, and opened them again. "Besides, I've . . . er, dealt with a case of rape once before. There isn't a great deal you can do, externally. Maybe there isn't a great deal you can do, period," I added. I changed my mind and picked up the cup again.

"Perhaps not," Raymond agreed. "But if anyone is capable of reaching the patient's center, surely it would be La Dame Blanche?"

I set the cup down, staring at him. My mouth was unbecomingly open, and I closed it. Thoughts, suspicions, and realizations were rioting through my head, colliding with each other in tangles of conjecture. Temporarily sidestepping the traffic jam, I seized on the other half of his remark, to give me time to think.

"The patient's center?"

He reached into an open jar on the table, withdrew a pinch of white powder, and dropped it into his goblet. The deep amber of the brandy immediately turned the color of blood, and began to boil.

"Dragon's blood," he remarked, casually waving at the bubbling liquid. "It only works in a vessel lined with silver. It ruins the cup, of course, but it's most effective, done under the proper circumstances."

I made a small, gurgling noise.

"Oh, the patient's center," he said, as though recalling something we had talked about many days ago. "Yes, of course. All healing is done essentially by reaching the . . . what shall we call it? the soul? the essence? say, the center. By reaching the patient's center, from which they can heal themselves. Surely you have seen it, madonna. The cases so ill or so wounded that plainly they will die—but they don't. Or those who suffer from something so slight that surely they must recover, with the proper care. But they slip away, despite all you can do for them."

"Everyone who minds the sick has seen things like that," I replied cautiously.

"Yes," he agreed. "And the pride of the physician being what it is, most often he blames himself for those that die, and congratulates himself upon the triumph of his skill for those that live. But La Dame Blanche sees the essence of a man, and turns it to healing—or to death. So an evildoer may well fear to look upon her face." He picked up the cup, raised it in a toast to me, and drained the bubbling liquid. It left a faint pink stain on his lips.

"Thanks," I said dryly. "I think. So it wasn't just Glengarry's gullibility?"

Raymond shrugged, looking pleased with himself. "The inspiration was your husband's," he said modestly. "And a really excellent idea, too. But of course, while your husband has the respect of men for his own natural gifts, he would not be considered an authority on supernatural manifestations."

"You, of course, *would*."

The massive shoulders lifted slightly under the gray velvet robe. There were several small holes in one sleeve, charred around the edges, as though a number of tiny coals had burned their way through. Carelessness while conjuring, I supposed.

"You have been seen in my shop," he pointed out. "Your background is a mystery. And as your husband noted, my own reputation is somewhat suspect. I do move in . . . circles, shall we say?"—the lipless mouth broadened in a grin—"where a speculation as to your true identity may be taken with undue seriousness. And you know how people talk," he added with an air of prim disapproval that made me burst out laughing.

He set down the cup and leaned forward.

"You said that Mademoiselle Hawkins's health was *one* concern, madonna. Have you others?"

"I have." I took a small sip of brandy. "I'd guess that you hear a great deal about what goes on in Paris, don't you?"

He smiled, black eyes sharp and genial. "Oh, yes, madonna. What is it that you want to know?"

"Have you heard anything about Charles Stuart? Do you know who he is, for that matter?"

That surprised him; the shelf of his forehead lifted briefly. Then he picked up a small glass bottle from the table in front of him, rolling it meditatively between his palms.

"Yes, madonna," he said. "His father is—or should be—King of Scotland, is he not?"

"Well, that depends on your perspective," I said, stifling a small belch. "He's either the King of Scotland in exile, or the Pretender to the throne, but that's of no great concern to me. What I want to know is . . . is Charles Stuart doing anything that would make one think he might be planning an armed invasion of Scotland or England?"

He laughed out loud.

"Goodness, madonna! You are a most uncommon woman. Have you any idea how rare such directness is?"

"Yes," I admitted, "but there isn't really any help for it. I'm not good at beating round bushes." I reached out and took the bottle from him. "*Have* you heard anything?"

He glanced instinctively toward the half-door, but the shopgirl was occupied in mixing perfume for a voluble customer.

"Something small, madonna, only a casual mention in a letter from a friend—but the answer is most definitely yes."

I could see him hesitating in how much to tell me. I kept my eyes on the bottle in my hand, to give him time to make up his mind. The contents rolled with a pleasant sensation as the little vial twisted in my palm. It was oddly heavy for its size, and had a strange, dense, fluid feel to it, as though it was filled with liquid metal.

"It's quicksilver," Master Raymond said, answering my unspoken question. Apparently whatever mind-reading he had been doing had decided him in my favor, for he took back the bottle, poured it out in a shimmering silver puddle on the table before us, and sat back to tell me what he knew.

"One of His Highness's agents has made inquiries in Holland," he said. "A man named O'Brien—and a man more inept at his job I hope never to employ," he added. "A secret agent who drinks to excess?"

"Everyone around Charles Stuart drinks to excess," I said. "What was O'Brien doing?"

"He wished to open negotiations for a shipment of broadswords. Two thousand broadswords, to be purchased in Spain, and sent through Holland, so as to conceal their place of origin."

"Why would he do that?" I asked. I wasn't sure whether I was naturally stupid, or merely fuddled with cherry brandy, but it seemed a pointless undertaking, even for Charles Stuart.

Raymond shrugged, prodding the puddle of quicksilver with a blunt forefinger.

"One can guess, madonna. The Spanish king is a cousin of the Scottish king, is he not? As well as of our good King Louis?"

"Yes, but . . ."

"Might it not be that he is willing to help the cause of the Stuarts, but not openly?"

The brandy haze was receding from my brain.

"It might."

Raymond tapped his finger sharply downward, making the puddle of quicksilver shiver into several small round globules, that shimmied wildly over the tabletop.

"One hears," he said mildly, eyes still on the droplets of mercury, "that King Louis entertains an English duke at Versailles. One hears also that the Duke is there to seek some arrangements of trade. But then it is rare to hear *everything*, madonna."

I stared at the rippling drops of mercury, fitting all this together. Jamie, too, had heard the rumor that Sandringham's embassage concerned more than trade rights. What if the Duke's visit really concerned the possibilities of an agreement between France and England—perhaps with regard to the future of Brussels? And if Louis was negotiating secretly with England for support for his invasion of Brussels—then what might Philip of Spain be inclined to do, if approached by an impecunious cousin with the power to distract the English most thoroughly from any attention to foreign ventures?

"Three Bourbon cousins," Raymond murmured to himself. He shepherded one of the drops toward another; as the droplets touched, they merged at once, a single shining drop springing into rounded life as though by magic. The prodding finger urged another droplet inward, and the single drop grew larger. "One blood. But one interest?"

The finger struck down again, and glittering fragments ran over the tabletop in every direction.

"I think not, madonna," Raymond said calmly.

"I see," I said, with a deep breath. "And what do you think about Charles Stuart's new partnership with the Comte St. Germain?"

The wide amphibian smile grew broader.

"I have heard that His Highness goes often to the docks these days—to talk with his new partner, of course. And he looks at the ships at anchor—so fine and quick, so . . . expensive. The land of Scotland *does* lie across the water, does it not?"

"It does indeed," I said. A ray of light hit the quicksilver with a flash, attracting my attention to the lowering sun. I would have to go.

"Thank you," I said. "Will you send word? If you hear anything more?"

He inclined his massive head graciously, the swinging hair the color of mercury in the sun, then jerked it up abruptly.

"Ah! Do not touch the quicksilver, madonna!" he warned as I reached toward a droplet that had rolled toward my edge of the table. "It bonds at once with any metal it touches." He reached across and tenderly scooped the tiny pellet toward him. "You do not wish to spoil your lovely rings."

"Right," I said. "Well, I'll admit you've been helpful so far. No one's tried to poison me lately. I don't suppose you and Jamie between you are likely to get me burnt for witchcraft in the Place de la Bastille, do you?" I spoke lightly, but my memories of the thieves' hole and the trial at Cranesmuir were still fresh.

"Certainly not," he said, with dignity. "No one's been burnt for witch-craft in Paris in . . . oh, twenty years, at least. You're perfectly safe. As long as you don't kill anyone," he added.

"I'll do my best," I said, and rose to go.

Fergus found me a carriage with no difficulty, and I spent the short trip to the Hawkins house musing over recent developments. I supposed that Ray-mond had in fact done me a service by expanding on Jamie's original wild story to his more superstitious clients, though the thought of having my name ban-died about in séances or Black Masses left me with some misgivings.

It also occurred to me that, rushed for time, and beset with speculations of kings and swords and ships, I had not had time to ask Master Raymond where —if anywhere—the Comte St. Germain entered into his own realm of influ-ence.

Public opinion seemed to place the Comte firmly in the center of the mysterious "circles" to which Raymond referred. But as a participant—or a rival? And did the ripples of these circles spread as far as the King's chamber? Louis was rumored to take interest in astrology; could there be some connec-tion, through the dark channels of Cabbalism and sorcery, among Louis, the Comte, and Charles Stuart?

I shook my head impatiently, to clear it of brandy fumes and pointless questions. The only thing that could be said for certain was that he had entered into a dangerous partnership with Charles Stuart, and that was concern enough for the present.

The Hawkins residence on the Rue Malory was a solid, respectable-look-ing house of three stories, but its internal disruption was apparent even to the casual observer. The day was warm, but all the shutters were still sealed tight against any intrusion of prying eyes. The steps had not been scrubbed this morning, and the marks of dirty feet smeared the white stone. No sign of cook or housemaid out front to bargain for fresh meat and gossip with the bar-rowmen. It was a house battened down against the coming of disaster.

Feeling not a little like a harbinger of doom myself, despite my relatively cheerful yellow gown, I sent Fergus up the steps to knock for me. There was some give-and-take between Fergus and whoever opened the door, but one of Fergus's better character traits was an inability to take "no" for an answer, and shortly I found myself face-to-face with a woman who appeared to be the lady of the house, and therefore Mrs. Hawkins, Mary's aunt.

I was forced to draw my own conclusions, as the woman seemed much too distraught to assist me by offering any sort of tangible information, such as her name.

"But we can't see anybody!" she kept exclaiming, glancing furtively over her shoulder, as though expecting the bulky form of Mr. Hawkins suddenly to materialize accusingly behind her. "We're . . . we have . . . that is . . ."

"I don't want to see you," I said firmly. "I want to see your niece, Mary."

The name seemed to throw her into fresh paroxysms of alarm.

"She . . . but . . . Mary? No! She's . . . she's not well!"

"I don't suppose she is," I said patiently. I lifted my basket into view. "I've brought some medicines for her."

"Oh! But . . . but . . . she . . . you . . . aren't you . . . ?"

"Havers, woman," said Fergus in his best Scots accent. He viewed this spectacle of derangement disapprovingly. "The maid says the young mistress is upstairs in her room."

"Just so," I said. "Lead on, Fergus." Waiting for no further encourage-ment, he ducked under the outstretched forearm that barred our way, and made off into the gloomy depths of the house. Mrs. Hawkins turned after him with an incoherent cry, allowing me to slip past her.

There was a maid on duty outside Mary's door, a stout party in a striped apron, but she offered no resistance to my statement that I intended to go in. She shook her head mournfully. "I can do nothing with her, Madame. Perhaps you will have better luck."

This didn't sound at all promising, but there was little choice. At least I wasn't likely to do further harm. I straightened my gown and pushed open the door.

It was like walking into a cave. The windows were covered with heavy brown velvet draperies, drawn tight against the daylight, and what chinks of light seeped through were immediately quenched in the hovering layer of smoke from the hearth.

I took a deep breath and let it out again at once, coughing. There was no stir from the figure on the bed; a pathetically small, hunched shape under a goose-feather duvet. Surely the drug had worn off by now, and she couldn't be asleep, after all the racket there had been in the hallway. Probably playing possum, in case it was her aunt come back for further blithering harangues. I would have done the same, in her place.

I turned and shut the door firmly in Mrs. Hawkins's wretched face, then walked over to the bed.

"It's me," I said. "Why don't you come out, before you suffocate in there?"

There was a sudden upheaval of bedclothes, and Mary shot out of the quilts like a dolphin rising from the sea waves, and clutched me round the neck.

"Claire! Oh, Claire! Thank God! I thought I'd n-never see you again! Uncle said you were in prison! He s-said you—"

"Let go!" I managed to detach her grip, and force her back enough to get a look at her. She was red-faced, sweaty, and disheveled from hiding beneath the covers, but otherwise looked fine. Her brown eyes were wide and bright, with no sign of opium intoxication, and while she looked excited and alarmed, apparently a night's rest, coupled with the resilience of youth, had taken care of most of her physical injuries. The others were what worried me.

"No, I'm not in prison," I said, trying to stem her eager questions. "Obviously not, though it isn't for any lack of trying on your uncle's part."

"B-but I *told* him—" she began, then stammered and let her eyes fall. "—at least I *t-t-tried* to tell him, but he—but I . . ."

"Don't worry about it," I assured her. "He's so upset he wouldn't listen to anything you said, no matter how you said it. It doesn't matter, anyway. The important thing is you. How do you feel?" I pushed the heavy dark hair back from her forehead and looked her over searchingly.

"All right," she answered, and gulped. "I . . . bled a little bit, but it stopped." The blood rose still higher in her fair cheeks, but she didn't drop her eyes. "I . . . it's . . . sore. D-does that go away?"

"Yes, it does," I said gently. "I brought some herbs for you. They're to be brewed in hot water, and as the infusion cools, you can apply it with a cloth, or sit in it in a tub, if one's handy. It will help." I got the bundles of herbs from my reticule and laid them on her side table.

She nodded, biting her lip. Plainly there was something more she wanted to say, her native shyness battling her need for confidence.

"What is it?" I asked, as matter-of-factly as I could.

"Am I going to have a baby?" she blurted out, looking up fearfully. "You said . . ."

"No," I said, as firmly as I could. "You aren't. He wasn't able to . . . finish." In the folds of my skirt, I crossed both pairs of fingers, hoping fervently that I was right. The chances were very small indeed, but such freaks had been known to happen. Still, there was no point in alarming her further over the faint possibility. The thought made me faintly ill. Could such an accident be the possible answer to the riddle of Frank's existence? I put the notion aside; a month's wait would prove or dispel it.

"It's hot as a bloody oven in here," I said, loosening the ties at my throat in order to breathe. "And smoky as hell's vestibule, as my old uncle used to say." Unsure what on earth to say to her next, I rose and went round the room throwing back drapes and opening windows.

"Aunt Helen said I mustn't let anyone see me," Mary said, kneeling up in bed as she watched me. "She says I'm d-disgraced, and people will point at me in the street if I go out."

"They might, the ghouls." I finished my airing and came back to her. "That doesn't mean you need bury yourself alive and suffocate in the process." I sat down beside her, and leaned back in my chair, feeling the cool fresh air blow through my hair as it swept the smoke from the room.

She was silent for a long time, toying with the bundles of herbs on the table. Finally she looked up at me, smiling bravely, though her lower lip trembled slightly.

"At least I won't have to m-marry the Vicomte. Uncle says he'll n-never have me now."

"No, I don't suppose so."

She nodded, looking down at the gauze wrapped square on her knee. Her fingers fiddled restlessly with the string, so that one end came loose and a few crumbs of goldenrod fell out onto the coverlet.

"I . . . used to th-think about it; what you told me, about how a m-man . . ." She stopped and swallowed, and I saw a single tear fall onto the gauze. "I didn't think I could stand to let the Vicomte do that to me. N-now it's been done . . . and n-nobody can undo it and I'll never have to d-do it again . . . and . . . and . . . oh, Claire, Alex will never speak to me again! I'll never see him again, never!"

She collapsed into my arms, weeping hysterically and scattering herbs. I clutched her against my shoulder and patted her, making small shushing noises, though I shed a few tears myself that fell unnoticed into the dark shininess of her hair.

"You'll see him again," I whispered. "Of course you will. It won't make a difference to him. He's a good man."

But I knew it would. I had seen the anguish on Alex Randall's face the night before, and at the time thought it only the same helpless pity for suffering that I saw in Jamie and Murtagh. But since I had learned of Alex Randall's professed love for Mary, I had realized how much deeper his own pain must go —and his fear.

He seemed a good man. But he was also a poor, younger son, in ill health and with little chance of advancement; what position he did have was entirely dependent on the Duke of Sandringham's goodwill. And I had little hope that the Duke would look kindly on the idea of his secretary's union with a disgraced and ruined girl, who had now neither social connections nor dowry to bless herself with.

And if Alex found somewhere the courage to wed her in spite of every-thing—what chance would they have, penniless, cast out of polite society, and with the hideous fact of the rape overshadowing their knowledge of each other?

There was nothing I could do but hold her, and weep with her for what was lost.

It was twilight by the time I left, with the first stars coming out in faint speckles over the chimneypots. In my pocket was a letter written by Mary, properly witnessed, containing her statement of the events of the night before. Once this was delivered to the proper authorities, we should at least have no further trouble from the law. Just as well; there was plenty of trouble pending from other quarters.

Mindful, this time, of danger, I made no objection to Mrs. Hawkins's unwilling offer to have me and Fergus transported home in the family carriage.

I tossed my hat on the card table in the vestibule, observing the large number of notes and small nosegays that overflowed the salver there. Apparently we weren't yet pariahs, though the news of the scandal must long since have spread through the social strata of Paris.

I waved away the anxious inquiries of the servants, and drifted upward toward the bedchamber, shedding my outer garments carelessly along the way. I felt too drained to care about anything.

But when I pushed open the bedchamber door and saw Jamie, lying back in a chair by the fire, my apathy was at once supplanted by a surge of tender-ness. His eyes were closed and his hair sticking up in all directions, sure sign of mental turmoil at some point. But he opened his eyes at the slight noise of my entrance and smiled at me, eyes clear and blue in the warm light of the candela-brum.

"It's all right" was all he whispered to me as he gathered me into his arms. "You're home." Then we were silent, as we undressed each other and went finally to earth, each finding delayed and wordless sanctuary in the other's embrace.

21

Untimely Resurrection

My mind was still on bankers when our coach pulled up to the Duke's rented residence on the Rue St. Anne. It was a large, handsome house, with a long, curving drive lined with poplar trees, and extensive grounds. A wealthy man, the Duke.

"Do you suppose it was the loan Charles got from Manzetti that he's investing with St. Germain?" I asked.

"It must be," Jamie replied. He pulled on the pigskin gloves suitable for a formal call, grimacing slightly as he smoothed the tight leather over the stiff fourth finger of his right hand. "The money his father thinks he's spending to maintain himself in Paris."

"So Charles really is trying to raise money for an army," I said, feeling a reluctant admiration for Charles Stuart. The coach came to a halt, and the footman hopped down to open the door.

"Well, he's trying to raise money, at least," Jamie corrected, handing me out of the coach. "For all I ken, he wants it to elope with Louise de La Tour and his bastard."

I shook my head. "I don't think so. Not from what Master Raymond told me yesterday. Besides, Louise says she hasn't seen him since she and Jules . . . well . . ."

Jamie snorted briefly. "At least she's got some sense of honor, then."

"I don't know whether that's it," I observed, taking his arm as we climbed the steps to the door. "She said Charles was so furious at her for sleeping with her husband that he stormed off, and she hasn't seen him since. He writes her passionate letters from time to time, swearing to come and take her and the child away with him as soon as he comes into his rightful place in the world, but she won't let him come to see her; she's too afraid of Jules finding out the truth."

Jamie made a disapproving Scottish noise.

"God, is there any man safe from cuckoldry?"

I touched his arm lightly. "Likely some more than others."

"Ye think so?" he said, but smiled down at me.

The door swung open to reveal a short, tubby butler, with a bald head, a spotless uniform, and immense dignity.

"Milord," he said, bowing to Jamie, "and milady. You are expected. Please come in."

The Duke was charm itself as he received us in the main drawing room.

"Nonsense, nonsense," he said, dismissing Jamie's apologies for the contretemps of the dinner party. "Damned excitable fellows, the French. Make an ungodly fuss over everything. Now, do let us look over all these fascinating propositions, shall we? And perhaps your good lady would like to . . . um, amuse herself with a perusal of . . . eh?" He waved an arm vaguely in the direction of the wall, leaving it open to question whether I might amuse myself by looking at the several large paintings, the well-furnished bookshelf, or the several glass cases in which the Duke's collection of snuffboxes resided.

"Thank you," I murmured, with a charming smile, and wandered over to the wall, pretending to be absorbed in a large Boucher, featuring the backview of an amply endowed nude woman seated on a rock in the wilderness. If this was a reflection of current tastes in female anatomy, it was no wonder that Jamie appeared to think so highly of my bottom.

"Ha," I said. "What price foundation garments, eh?"

"Eh?" Jamie and the Duke, startled, looked up from the portfolio of investment papers that formed the ostensible reason for our visit.

"Never mind me," I said, waving a gracious hand. "Just enjoying the art."

"I'm deeply gratified, ma'am," said the Duke politely, and at once reimmersed himself in the papers, as Jamie began the tedious and painstaking real business of the visit—the inconspicuous extraction of such information as the Duke might be willing to part with regarding his own sympathies—or otherwise—toward the Stuart cause.

I had my own agenda for this visit, as well. As the men became more immersed in their discussions, I edged my way toward the door, pretending to look through the well-furnished shelves. As soon as the coast looked clear, I meant to slip out into the hallway and try to find Alex Randall. I had done what I could to repair the damage done to Mary Hawkins; anything further would have to come from him. Under the rules of social etiquette, he couldn't call upon her at her uncle's house, nor could she contact him. But I could easily make an opportunity for them to meet at the Rue Tremoulins.

The conversation behind me had dropped to a confidential murmur. I stuck my head into the hall, but didn't see a footman immediately. Still, one couldn't be far away; a house of this size must have a staff numbering in the dozens. As large as it was, I would need directions in order to locate Alexander Randall. I chose a direction at random and walked along the hallway, looking for a servant of whom to inquire.

I saw a flicker of motion at the end of the hall, and called out. Whoever it was made no answer, but I heard a surreptitious scuttle of feet on polished boards.

That seemed curious behavior for a servant. I stopped at the end of the hall and looked around. Another hall extended at right angles to the one I stood in, lined on one side with doors, on the other with long windows that opened on the drive and the garden. Most of the doors were closed, but the one closest to me was slightly ajar.

Moving quietly, I stepped up to it and put my ear next to the paneling. Hearing nothing, I took hold of the handle and boldly pushed the door open.

"What in the name of God are *you* doing here?" I exclaimed in astonishment.

"Oh, you scared me! Gracious, I thought I was g-going to die." Mary Hawkins pressed both hands against her bodice. Her face was blanched white, and her eyes dark and wide with terror.

"You're not," I said. "Unless your uncle finds out you're here; then he'll probably kill you. Or does he know?"

She shook her head. "No. I didn't t-tell anyone. I took a public fiacre."

"*Why*, for God's sake?"

She glanced around like a frightened rabbit looking for a bolthole, but failing to find one, instead drew herself up and tightened her jaw.

"I had to find Alex. I had to t-talk to him. To see if he—if he . . ." Her hands were wringing together, and I could see the effort it cost her to get the words out.

"Never mind," I said, resigned. "I understand. Your uncle won't, though, and neither will the Duke. His Grace doesn't know you're here, either?"

She shook her head, mute.

"All right," I said, thinking. "Well, the first thing we must do is—"

"Madame? May I assist you?"

Mary started like a hare, and I felt my own heart leap uncomfortably into the back of my throat. Bloody footmen; never in the right place at the right time.

There was nothing to do now but brazen it out. I turned to the footman, who was standing stiff as a ramrod in the doorway, looking dignified and suspicious.

"Yes," I said, with as much hauteur as I could summon on short notice. "Will you please tell Mr. Alexander Randall that he has visitors."

"I regret that I cannot do so, Madame," said the footman, with remote formality.

"And why not?" I demanded.

"Because, Madame," he answered, "Mr. Alexander Randall is no longer in His Grace's employ. He was dismissed." The footman glanced at Mary, then lowered his nose an inch and unbent sufficiently to say, "I understand that Monsieur Randall has taken ship back to England."

"No! He can't be gone, he can't!"

Mary darted toward the door, and nearly cannoned into Jamie as he entered. She drew up short with a startled gasp, and he stared at her in astonishment.

"What—" he began, then saw me behind her. "Oh, there ye are, Sassenach. I made an excuse to come and find ye—His Grace just told me that Alex Randall—"

"I know," I interrupted. "He's gone."

"No!" Mary moaned. "No!" She darted toward the door, and was through it before either of us could stop her, her heels clattering on the polished parquet.

"Bloody fool!" I kicked off my own shoes, picked up my skirts, and whizzed after her. Stocking-footed, I was much faster than she in her high-heeled slippers. Maybe I could catch her before she ran into someone else and was caught, with the concomitant scandal *that* would involve.

I followed the whisk of her disappearing skirts round the bend of the hall. The floor here was carpeted; if I didn't hurry, I might lose her at an intersection, unable to hear from the footsteps which way she had gone. I put my head down, charged round the last corner, and crashed head-on into a man coming the other way.

He let out a startled "Whoof!" as I struck him amidships, and clutched me by the arms to keep upright as we swayed and staggered together.

"I'm sorry," I began, breathlessly. "I thought you were—oh, Jesus H. fucking Christ!"

My initial impression—that I had encountered Alexander Randall—had lasted no more than the split second necessary to see the eyes above that finely chiseled mouth. The mouth was much like Alex's, bar the deep lines around it. But those cold eyes could belong to only one man.

The shock was so great that for a moment everything seemed paradoxically normal; I had an impulse to apologize, dust him off, and continue my pursuit, leaving him forgotten in the corridor, as just a chance encounter. My adrenal glands hastened to remedy this impression, dumping such a dose of adrenaline into my bloodstream that my heart contracted like a squeezed fist.

He was recovering his own breath by now, along with his momentarily shattered self-possession.

"I am inclined to concur with your sentiments, Madam, if not precisely with their manner of expression." Still clutching me by the elbows, he held me slightly away from him, squinting to see my face in the shadowed hall. I saw the shock of recognition blanch his features as my face came into the light. "Bloody hell, it's you!" he exclaimed.

"I thought you were dead!" I wrenched at my arms, trying to free them from the iron-tight grip of Jonathan Randall.

He let go of one arm, in order to rub his middle, surveying me coldly. The thin, fine-cut features were bronzed and healthy; he gave no outward sign of having been trampled five months before by thirty quarter-ton beasts. Not so much as a hoofprint on his forehead.

"Once more, Madam, I find myself sharing your sentiments. I was under a very similar misapprehension concerning *your* state of health. Possibly you are a witch, after all—what did you do, turn yourself into a wolf?" The wary dislike stamped on his face was mingled with a touch of superstitious awe. After all, when you turn someone out into the midst of a pack of wolves on a cold winter evening, you rather expect them to cooperate by being eaten forthwith. The sweatiness of my own palms and the drumlike beating of my heart were testimony to the unsettling effect of having someone you thought safely dead suddenly rise up in front of you. I supposed he must be feeling a trifle queasy as well.

"Wouldn't *you* like to know?" The urge to annoy him—to disturb that icy calm—was the first emotion to surface from the seething mass of feelings that had erupted within me at sight of his face. His fingers tightened on my arm, and his lips thinned. I could see his mind working, starting to tick off possibilities.

"If it wasn't yours, whose body did Sir Fletcher's men take out of the dungeon?" I demanded, trying to take advantage of any break in his composure. An eyewitness had described to me the removal of "a rag doll, rolled in blood"—presumably Randall—from the scene of the cattle stampede that had masked Jamie's escape from that same dungeon.

Randall smiled, without much humor. If he was as rattled as I, he didn't show it. His breathing was a trifle faster than usual, and the lines that edged mouth and eyes cut deeper than I remembered, but he wasn't gasping like a landed fish. I was. I took in as much oxygen as my lungs would allow and tried to breathe through my nose.

"It was my orderly, Marley. Though if you aren't answering my questions, why should I answer yours?" He looked me up and down, carefully evaluating my appearance: silk gown, hair ornaments, jewelry, and stockinged feet.

"Married a Frenchman, did you?" he asked. "I always did think you were a French spy. I trust your new husband keeps you in better order than . . ."

The words died in his throat as he looked up to see the source of the footsteps that had just turned into the hall behind me. If I had wanted to discompose him, that urge was now fully gratified. No Hamlet on the stage had ever reacted to the appearance of a ghost with more convincing terror than I saw stamped on that aristocratic face. The hand still holding my arm clawed deep into my flesh, and I felt the jolt of shock that surged through him like an electric charge.

I knew what he saw behind me, and was afraid to turn. There was a deep silence in the hall; even the wash of the cypress branches against the windows seemed part of the quiet, like the ear-roaring silence that waves make, at the bottom of the sea. Very slowly, I disengaged my arm from his grasp, and his hand fell nerveless to his side. There was no sound behind me, though I could hear voices start up from the room at the end of the hall. I prayed that the door would stay closed, and tried desperately to remember how Jamie was armed.

My mind went blank, then blazed with the reassuring vision of his small-sword, hung by its belt from a hook on the wardrobe, sun glowing on the enameled hilt. But he still had his dirk, of course, and the small knife he habitually carried in his stocking. Come to that, I was entirely sure that in a pinch, he would consider his bare hands perfectly adequate. And if you cared to describe my present situation, standing between the two of them, as a pinch . . . I swallowed once and slowly turned around.

He was standing quite still, no more than a yard behind me. One of the tall, paned casements opened near him, and the dark shadows of the cypress needles rippled over him like water over a sunken rock. He showed no more expression than a rock, either. Whatever lived behind those eyes was hidden; they were wide and blank as windowpanes, as though the soul they mirrored were long since flown.

He didn't speak, but after a moment, reached out one hand to me. It floated open in the air, and I finally summoned the presence of mind to take it. It was cool and hard, and I clung to it like the wood of a raft.

He drew me in, close to his side, took my arm and turned me, all without speaking or changing expression. As we reached the turning of the hall, Randall spoke behind us.

"Jamie," he said. The voice was hoarse with shock, and held a note half-way between disbelief and pleading.

Jamie stopped then, and turned to look at him. Randall's face was a ghastly white, with a small red patch livid on each cheekbone. He had taken off his wig, clenched in his hands, and sweat pasted the fine dark hair to his temples.

"No." The voice that spoke above me was soft, almost expressionless. Looking up, I could see that the face still matched it, but a quick, hot pulse beat in his neck, and the small, triangular scar above his collar flushed red with heat.

"I am called Lord Broch Tuarach for formality's sake," the soft Scottish voice above me said. "And beyond the requirements of formality, you will never speak to me again—until you beg for your life at the point of my sword. Then, you may use my name, for it will be the last word you ever speak."

With sudden violence, he swept around, and his flaring plaid swung wide, blocking my view of Randall as we turned the corner of the hall.

The carriage was still waiting by the gate. Afraid to look at Jamie, I climbed in and absorbed myself in tucking the folds of yellow silk around my legs. The click of the carriage door shutting made me look up abruptly, but before I could reach the handle, the carriage started with a jerk that threw me back in my seat.

Struggling and swearing, I fought my way to my knees and peered out of the back window. He was gone. Nothing moved on the drive but the swaying shadows of cypress and poplar.

I hammered frenziedly on the roof of the carriage, but the coachman merely shouted to the horses and urged them on faster. There was little traffic at this hour, and we hurtled through the narrow streets as though the devil were after us.

When we drew up in the Rue Tremoulins, I sprang out of the coach, at once panicked and furious.

"Why didn't you stop?" I demanded of the coachman. He shrugged, safely impervious atop his perch.

"The master ordered me to drive you home without delay, Madame." He picked up the whip and touched it lightly to the off-horse's rump.

"Wait!" I shouted. "I want to go back!" But he only hunched himself turtle-like into his shoulders, pretending not to hear me, as the coach rattled off.

Fuming with impotence, I turned toward the door, where the small figure of Fergus appeared, thin brows raised questioningly at my appearance.

"Where's Murtagh?" I snapped. The little clansman was the only person I could think of who might be able first, to find Jamie, and secondly, to stop him.

"I don't know, Madame. Maybe down there." The boy nodded in the direction of the Rue Gamboge, where there were several taverns, ranging in respectability from those where a traveling lady might dine with her husband, to the dens near the river, which even an armed man might hesitate to enter alone.

I laid a hand on Fergus's shoulder, as much for support as in exhortation. "Run and find him, Fergus. Quickly as you can!"

Alarmed by my tone, he leaped off the step and was gone, before I could add "Be careful!" Still, he knew the lower levels of Paris life much better than I did; no one was better adapted to eeling through a tavern crowd than an ex-pickpocket. At least I hoped he was an ex-pickpocket.

But I could worry effectively about only one thing at a time, and visions of Fergus being captured and hanged for his activities receded before the vision Jamie's final words to Randall had evoked.

Surely, *surely* he would not have gone back into the Duke's house? No, I reassured myself. He had no sword. Whatever he might be feeling—and my soul sank within me to think of what he felt—he wouldn't act precipitously. I had seen him in battle before, mind working in an icy calm, severed from the emotions that could cloud his judgment. And for this, above all things, surely he would adhere to the formalities. He would seek the rigid prescriptions, the formulae for the satisfaction of honor, as a refuge—something to cling to against the tides that shook him, the bone-deep surge of bloodlust and revenge.

I stopped in the hallway, mechanically shedding my cloak and pausing by the mirror to straighten my hair. *Think, Beauchamp,* I silently urged my pale reflection. If he's going to fight a duel, what's the first thing he'll need?

A sword? No, couldn't be. His own was upstairs, hanging on the armoire. While he might easily borrow one, I couldn't imagine his setting out to fight the most important duel of his life armed with any but his own. His uncle, Dougal MacKenzie, had given it to him at seventeen, seen him schooled in its use, taught him the tricks and the strengths of a left-handed swordsman, using that sword. Dougal had made him practice, left hand against left hand, for hours on end, until, he told me, he felt the length of Spanish metal come alive, an extension of his arm, hilt welded to his palm. Jamie had said he felt naked without it. And this was not a fight to which he would go naked.

No, if he had needed the sword at once, he would have come home to fetch it. I ran my hand impatiently through my hair, trying to think. Damn it, what was the protocol of dueling? Before it came to swords, what happened? A challenge, of course. Had Jamie's words in the hallway constituted that? I had vague ideas of people being slapped across the face with gloves, but had no idea whether that was really the custom, or merely an artifact of memory, born of a film-maker's imagination.

Then it came to me. First the challenge, then a place must be arranged—a suitably circumspect place, unlikely to come to the notice of the police or the King's Guard. And to deliver the challenge, to arrange the place, a second was required. Ah. That was where he had gone, then; to find his second. Murtagh.

Even if Jamie found Murtagh before Fergus did, still there would be the formalities to arrange. I began to breathe a little easier, though my heart was still pounding, and my laces still seemed too tight. None of the servants was visible; I yanked the laces loose and drew a deep, expanding breath.

"I didna know ye were in the habit of undressing in the hallways, or I would ha' stayed in the drawing room," said an ironic Scots voice behind me.

I whirled, my heart leaping high enough to choke me. The man standing stretched in the drawing room doorway, arms outspread to brace him casually against the frame, was big, nearly as large as Jamie, with the same taut grace of movement, the same air of cool self-possession. The hair was dark, though, and the deep-set eyes a cloudy green. Dougal MacKenzie, appearing suddenly in my home as though called by my thought. Speak of the devil.

"What in God's name are you doing here?" The shock of seeing him was subsiding, though my heart still pounded. I hadn't eaten since breakfast, and a sudden wave of queasiness washed over me. He stepped forward and grasped me by the arm, pulling me toward a chair.

"Sit ye down, lass," he said. "Ye'll no be feeling just the thing, it looks like."

"Very observant of you," I said. Black spots floated at the edge of my vision, and small bright flashes danced before my eyes. "Excuse me," I said politely, and put my head between my knees.

Jamie. Frank. Randall. Dougal. The faces flickered in my mind, the names seemed to ring in my ears. My palms were sweating, and I pressed them under my arms, hugging myself to try to stop the tremblings of shock. Jamie wouldn't be facing Randall immediately; that was the important thing. There was a little time, in which to think, to take preventive action. But what action? Leaving my subconscious to wrestle with this question, I forced my breathing to slow and turned my attention to matters closer to hand.

"I repeat," I said, sitting up and smoothing back my hair, "what are you doing here?"

The dark brows flickered upward.

"Do I need a reason to visit a kinsman?"

I could still taste the bile at the back of my throat, but my hands had stopped trembling, at least.

"Under the circumstances, yes," I said. I drew myself up, grandly ignoring my untied laces, and reached for the brandy decanter. Anticipating me, Dougal took a glass from the tray and poured out a teaspoonful. Then, after a considering glance at me, he doubled the dose.

"Thanks," I said dryly, accepting the glass.

"Circumstances, eh? And which circumstances would those be?" Not waiting for answer or permission, he calmly poured out another glass for himself and lifted it in a casual toast. "To His Majesty."

I felt my mouth twist sideways. "King James, I suppose?" I took a small sip of my own drink, and felt the hot aromatic fumes sear the membranes behind my eyes. "And does the fact that you're in Paris mean that you've converted Colum to your way of thinking?" For while Dougal MacKenzie might be a Jacobite, it was his brother Colum who led the MacKenzies of Leoch as chieftain. Legs crippled and twisted by a deforming disease, Colum no longer led his clan into battle; Dougal was the war chieftain. But while Dougal might lead men into battle, it was Colum who held the power to say whether the battle would take place.

Dougal ignored my question, and having drained his glass, immediately poured out another drink. He savored the first sip of this one, rolling it visibly around his mouth and licking a final drop from his lips as he swallowed.

"Not bad," he said. "I must take some back for Colum. He needs something a bit stronger than the wine, to help him sleep nights."

This was indeed an oblique answer to my question. Colum's condition was degenerating, then. Always in some pain from the disease that eroded his body, Colum had taken fortified wine in the evenings, to help him to sleep. Now he needed straight brandy. I wondered how long it would be before he might be forced to resort to opium for relief.

For when he did, that would be the end of his reign as chieftain of his clan. Deprived of physical resources, still he commanded by sheer force of character. But if the strength of Colum's mind were lost to pain and drugs, the clan would have a new leader—Dougal.

I gazed at him over the rim of my glass. He returned my stare with no sign of abashment, a slight smile on that wide MacKenzie mouth. His face was much like his brother's—and his nephew's—strong and boldly modeled, with broad, high cheekbones and a long, straight nose like the blade of a knife.

Sworn as a boy of eighteen to support his brother's chieftainship, he had kept that vow for nearly thirty years. And would keep it, I knew, until the day that Colum died or could lead no longer. But on that day, the mantle of chief would descend on his shoulders, and the men of clan MacKenzie would follow where he led—after the saltire of Scotland, and the banner of King James, in the vanguard of Bonnie Prince Charlie.

"Circumstances?" I said, turning to his earlier question. "Well, I don't suppose one would consider it in the best of taste to come calling on a man whom you'd left for dead and whose wife you'd tried to seduce."

Being Dougal MacKenzie, he laughed. I didn't know quite what it would take to disconcert the man, but I certainly hoped I was there to see it when it finally happened.

"Seduction?" he said, lips quirked in amusement. "I offered ye marriage."

"You offered to rape me, as I recall," I snapped. He had, in fact, offered to marry me—by force—after declining to help me in rescuing Jamie from Wentworth Prison the winter before. While his principal motive had been the possession of Jamie's estate of Lallybroch—which would belong to me upon Jamie's death—he hadn't been at all averse to the thought of the minor emoluments of marriage, such as the regular enjoyment of my body.

"As for leaving Jamie in the prison," he went on, ignoring me as usual, "there seemed no way to get him out, and no sense in risking good men in a vain attempt. He'd be the first to understand that. And it was my duty as his kinsman to offer his wife my protection, if he died. I was the lad's foster father, no?" He tilted back his head and drained his glass.

I took a good gulp of my own, and swallowed quickly so as not to choke. The spirit burned down my throat and gullet, matching the heat that was rising in my cheeks. He was right; Jamie hadn't blamed him for his reluctance to break into Wentworth Prison—he hadn't expected *me* to do it, either, and it was only by a miracle that I had succeeded. But while I had told Jamie, briefly, of Dougal's intention of marrying me, I hadn't tried to convey the carnal aspects of that intention. I had, after all, never expected to see Dougal Mac-Kenzie again.

I knew from past experience that he was a seizer of opportunities; with Jamie about to be hanged, he had not even waited for execution of the sentence before trying to secure me and my about-to-be-inherited property. If—

no, I corrected myself, *when*—Colum died or became incompetent, Dougal would be in full command of clan MacKenzie within a week. And if Charles Stuart found the backing he was seeking, Dougal would be there. He had some experience in being a power behind the throne, after all.

I tipped up the glass, considering. Colum had business interests in France; wine and timber, mostly. These undoubtedly were the pretext for Dougal's visit to Paris, might even be his major ostensible reason. But he had other reasons, I was sure. And the presence in the city of Prince Charles Edward Stuart was almost certainly one of them.

One thing to be said for Dougal MacKenzie was that an encounter with him stimulated the mental processes, out of the sheer necessity of trying to figure out what he was actually up to at any given moment. Under the inspiration of his presence and a good slug of Portuguese brandy, my subconscious was stirring with the birth of an idea.

"Well, be that as it may, I'm glad you're here now," I said, replacing my empty glass on the tray.

"You are?" The thick dark brows rose incredulously.

"Yes." I rose and gestured toward the hall. "Fetch my cloak while I do up my laces. I need you to come to the *commissariat de police* with me."

Seeing his jaw drop, I felt the first tiny upsurge of hope. If I had managed to take Dougal MacKenzie by surprise, surely I could stop a duel?

"D'ye want to tell me what you think you're doing?" Dougal inquired, as the coach bumped around the Cirque du Mireille, narrowly avoiding an oncoming barouche and a cart full of vegetable marrows.

"No," I said briefly, "but I suppose I'll have to. Did you know that Jack Randall is still alive?"

"I'd not heard he was dead," Dougal said reasonably.

That took me up short for a moment. But of course he was right; we had thought Randall dead only because Sir Marcus MacRannoch had mistaken the trampled body of Randall's orderly for the officer himself, during Jamie's rescue from Wentworth Prison. Naturally no news of Randall's death would have gone round the Highlands, since it hadn't occurred. I tried to gather my scattered thoughts.

"He *isn't* dead," I said. "But he is in Paris."

"In Paris?" That got his attention; his brows went up, and then his eyes widened with the next thought.

"Where's Jamie?" he asked sharply.

I was glad to see he appreciated the main point. While he didn't know what had passed between Jamie and Randall in Wentworth Prison—no one was ever going to know that, save Jamie, Randall, and, to some extent, me—he knew more than enough about Randall's previous actions to realize exactly what Jamie's first impulse would be on meeting the man here, away from the sanctuary of England.

"I don't know," I said, looking out the window. We were passing Les Halles, and the smell of fish was ripe in my nostrils. I pulled out a scented handkerchief and covered my nose and mouth. The strong, sharp tang of the wintergreen with which I scented it was no match for the reek of a dozen eel-sellers' stalls, but it helped a bit. I spoke through the spicy linen folds.

"We met Randall unexpectedly at the Duke of Sandringham's today. Jamie sent me home in the coach, and I haven't seen him since."

Dougal ignored both the stench and the raucous cries of fishwives calling their wares. He frowned at me.

"He'll mean to kill the man, surely?"

I shook my head, and explained my reasoning about the sword.

"I can't let a duel happen," I said, dropping the handkerchief in order to speak more clearly. "I won't!"

Dougal nodded abstractedly.

"Aye, that would be dangerous. Not that the lad couldna take Randall with ease—I taught him, ye ken," he added with some boastfulness, "but the sentence for dueling . . ."

"Got it in one," I said.

"All right," he said slowly. "But why the police? You dinna mean to have the lad locked up beforehand, do ye? Your own husband?"

"Not Jamie," I said. "Randall."

A broad grin broke out on his face, not unmixed with skepticism.

"Oh, aye? And how d'ye mean to work that one?"

"A friend and I were . . . attacked on the street a few nights ago," I said, swallowing at the memory. "The men were masked; I couldn't tell who they were. But one of them was about the same height and build as Jonathan Randall. I mean to say that I met Randall at a house today and recognized him as one of the men who attacked us."

Dougal's brows shot up and then drew together. His cool gaze flickered over me. Suddenly there was a new speculation in his appraisal.

"Christ, you've the devil's own nerve. Robbery, was it?" he asked softly. Against my will, I could feel the rage rising in my cheeks.

"No," I said, clipping the word between my teeth.

"Ah." He sat back against the coach's squabs, still looking at me. "Ye'll have taken no harm, though?" I glanced aside, at the passing street, but could feel his eyes, prying at the neck of my gown, sliding over the curve of my hips.

"Not me," I said. "But my friend . . ."

"I see." He was quiet for a moment, then said meditatively, "Ever heard of 'Les Disciples,' have you?"

I jerked my head back around to him. He lounged in the corner like a crouching cat, watching me through eyes narrowed against the sun.

"No. What are they?" I demanded.

He shrugged and sat upright, peering past me at the approaching bulk of the Quai des Orfèvres, hovering gray and dreary above the glitter of the Seine.

"A society—of a sort. Young men of family, with an interest in things . . . unwholesome, shall we say?"

"Let's," I said. "And just what do you know about Les Disciples?"

"Only what I heard in a tavern in the Cité," he said. "That the society demands a good deal from its members, and the price of initiation is high . . . by some standards."

"That being?" I dared him with my eyes. He smiled rather grimly before replying.

"A maidenhead, for one thing. The nipples of a married woman, for another." He shot a quick glance at my bosom. "Your friend's a virgin, is she? Or was?"

I felt hot and cold by turns. I wiped my face with the handkerchief and tucked it into the pocket of my cloak. I had to try twice, for my hand trembled.

"She was. What else have you heard? Do you know who's involved with Les Disciples?"

Dougal shook his head. There were threads of silver in the russet hair over his temples, that caught the light of the afternoon.

"Only rumors. The Vicomte de Busca, the youngest of the Charmisse sons —perhaps. The Comte St. Germain. Eh! Are ye all right, lass?"

He leaned forward in some consternation, peering at me.

"Fine," I said, breathing deeply through my nose. "Bloody fine." I pulled out the handkerchief and wiped the cold sweat off my brow.

"We mean you no harm, mesdames." The ironic voice echoed in the dark of my memory. The green-shirted man was medium-height and dark, slim and narrow-shouldered. If that description fit Jonathan Randall, it also fit the Comte St. Germain. Would I have recognized his voice, though? Could any normal man conceivably have sat across from me at dinner, eating salmon mousse and making genteel conversation, barely two hours after the incident in the Rue du Faubourg St.-Honoré?

Considered logically, though, why not? *I* had, after all. And I had no particular reason for supposing the Comte to be a normal man—by my standards—if rumor were true.

The coach was drawing to a halt, and there was little time for contemplation. Was I about to ensure that the man responsible for Mary's violation went free, while I also ensured the safety of Jamie's most loathed enemy? I took a deep, quivering breath. Damn little choice about it, I thought. Life was paramount; justice would just have to wait its turn.

The coachman had alighted and was reaching for the door handle. I bit my lip and glanced at Dougal MacKenzie. He met my gaze with a slight shrug. What did I want of him?

"Will you back my story?" I asked abruptly.

He looked up at the towering bulk of the Quai des Orfèvres. Brilliant afternoon light blazed through the open door.

"You're sure?" he asked.

"Yes." My mouth was dry.

He slid across the seat and extended a hand to me.

"Pray God we dinna both end in a cell, then," he said.

An hour later, we stepped into the empty street outside the *commissariat de police*. I had sent the coach home, lest anyone who knew us should see it standing outside the Quai des Orfèvres. Dougal offered me an arm, and I took it perforce. The ground here was muddy underfoot, and the cobbles in the street made uncertain going in high-heeled slippers.

"Les Disciples," I said as we made our way slowly along the banks of the Seine toward the towers of Notre Dame. "Do you really think the Comte St. Germain might have been one of the men who . . . who stopped us in the Rue du Faubourg St.-Honoré?" I was beginning to tremble with reaction and fatigue—and with hunger; I had had nothing since breakfast, and the lack was making itself felt. Sheer nerve had kept me going through the interview with the police. Now the need to think was passing, and with it, the ability to do so.

Dougal's arm was hard under my hand, but I couldn't look up at him; I needed all my attention to keep my footing. We had turned into the Rue Elise and the cobbles were shiny with damp and smeared with various kinds of filth. A porter lugging a crate paused in our path to clear his throat and hawk noisily into the street at my feet. The greenish glob clung to the curve of a stone, finally slipping off to float sluggishly onto the surface of a small mud puddle that lay in the hollow of a missing cobble.

"Mphm." Dougal was looking up and down the street for a carriage, brow creased in thought. "I canna say; I've heard worse than that of the man, but I havena had the honor of meeting him." He glanced down at me.

"You've managed brawly so far," he said. "They'll have Jack Randall in the Bastille within the hour. But they'll have to let the man go sooner or later, and I wouldna wager much on the chances of Jamie's temper cooling in the meantime. D'ye want me to speak to him—convince him to do nothing foolish?"

"No! For God's sake, stay out of it!" The thunder of carriage wheels was loud on the cobbles, but my voice was rose high enough to make Dougal brows lift in surprise.

"All right, then," he said, mildly. "I'll leave it to you to manage him. He's stubborn as a stone . . . but I suppose you have your ways, no?" This was said with a sidelong glance and knowing smirk.

"I'll manage." I would. I would have to. For everything I had told Dougal was true. All true. And yet so far from the truth. For I would send Charles Stuart and his father's cause to the devil gladly, sacrifice any hope of stopping his headlong dash to folly, even risk the chance of Jamie's imprisonment, for the sake of healing the breach Randall's resurrection had opened in Jamie's mind. I would help him to kill Randall, and feel only joy in the doing of it, except for the one thing. The one consideration strong enough to outweigh Jamie's pride, loom larger than his sense of manhood, than his threatened soul's peace. Frank.

That was the single idea that had driven me through this day, sustained me well past the point where I would have welcomed collapse. For months I had thought Randall dead and childless, and feared for Frank's life. But for those same months I had been comforted by the presence of the plain gold ring on the fourth finger of my left hand.

The twin of Jamie's silver ring upon my right, it was a talisman in the dark hours of the night, when doubts came on the heels of dreams. If I wore his ring still, then the man who had given it to me would live. I had told myself that a thousand times. No matter that I didn't know how a man dead without issue could sire a line of descent that led to Frank; the ring was there, and Frank would live.

Now I knew why the ring still shone on my hand, metal chilly as my own cold finger. Randall was alive, could still marry, could still father the child who would pass life on to Frank. Unless Jamie killed him first.

I had taken what steps I could for the moment, but the fact I had faced in the Duke's corridor remained. The price of Frank's life was Jamie's soul, and how was I to choose between them?

The oncoming fiacre, ignoring Dougal's hail, barreled past without stopping, wheels passing close enough to splash muddy water on Dougal's silk hose and the hem of my gown.

Desisting from a volley of heartfelt Gaelic, Dougal shook a fist after the retreating coach.

"Well, and now what?" he demanded rhetorically.

The blob of mucus-streaked spittle floated on the puddle at my feet, reflecting gray light. I could feel its cold slime viscid on my tongue. I put out a hand and grasped Dougal's arm, hard as a smooth-skinned sycamore branch. Hard, but it seemed to be swaying dizzily, swinging me far out over the cold and glittering, fish-smelling, slimy water nearby. Black spots floated before my eyes.

"Now," I said, "I'm going to be sick."

<hr/>

It was nearly sunset when I returned to the Rue Tremoulins. My knees trembled, and it was an effort to put one foot in front of the other on the stairs.

I went directly to the bedroom to shed my cloak, wondering whether Jamie had returned yet.

He had. I stopped dead in the doorway, surveying the room. My medicine box lay open on the table. The scissors I used for cutting bandages lay half-open on my dressing table. They were fanciful things, given to me by a knifemaker who worked now and then at L'Hôpital des Anges; the handles were gilt, worked in the shape of storks' heads, with the long bills forming the silver blades of the scissors. They gleamed in the rays of the setting sun, lying amid a cloud of reddish gold silk threads.

I took several steps toward the dressing table, and the silky, shimmering strands lifted in the disturbed air of my movement, drifting across the tabletop.

"Jesus bloody Christ," I breathed. He had been here, all right, and now he was gone. So was his sword.

The hair lay in thick, gleaming strands where it had fallen, littering dressing table, stool and floor. I plucked a shorn lock from the table and held it, feeling the fine, soft hairs separate between my fingers like the threads of embroidery silk. I felt a cold panic that started somewhere between my shoulder blades and prickled down my spine. I remembered Jamie, sitting on the fountain behind the Rohans' house, telling me how he had fought his first duel in Paris.

"The lace that held my hair back broke, and the wind whipped it into my face so I could scarcely see what I was doing."

He was taking no chance of that happening again. Seeing the evidence left behind, feeling the lock of hair in my hand, soft and alive-feeling still, I could imagine the cold deliberation with which he had done it; the snick of metal blades against his skull as he cut away all softness that might obscure his vision. Nothing would stand between him and the killing of Jonathan Randall.

Nothing but me. Still holding the lock of his hair, I went to the window and stared out, as though hoping to see him in the street. But the Rue Tremoulins was quiet, nothing moving but the flickering shadows of the poplar trees by the gates and the small movement of a servant, standing at the gate of the house to the left, talking to a watchman who brandished his pipe to emphasize a point.

The house hummed quietly around me, with dinner preparations taking place belowstairs. No company was expected tonight, so the usual bustle was subdued; we ate simply when alone.

I sat down on the bed and closed my eyes, folding my hands across my swelling stomach, the lock of hair gripped tight, as though I could keep him safe, so long as I didn't let go.

Had I been in time? Had the police found Jack Randall before Jamie did? What if they had arrived concurrently, or just in time to find Jamie challenging Randall to a formal duel? I rubbed the lock of hair between thumb and forefinger, splaying the cut ends in a small spray of roan and amber. Well, if so, at least they would both be safe. In prison, perhaps, but that was a minor consideration by contrast to other dangers.

And if Jamie had found Randall first? I glanced outside; the light was fading fast. Duels were traditionally fought at dawn, but I didn't know whether Jamie would have waited for morning. They might at this moment be facing each other, somewhere in seclusion, where the clash of steel and the cry of mortal wounding would attract no attention.

For a mortal fight it would be. What lay between those two men would be settled only by death. And whose death would it be? Jamie's? Or Randall's— and with him, Frank's? Jamie was likely the better swordsman, but as the challenged, Randall would have the choice of weapons. And success with pistols lay less with the skill of the user than with his fortune; only the best-made pistols aimed true, and even those were prone to misfire or other accidents. I had a sudden vision of Jamie, limp and quiet on the grass, blood welling from an empty eye socket, and the smell of black powder strong among the scents of spring in the Bois de Boulogne.

"What in hell are you doing, Claire?"

My head snapped up, so hard I bit my tongue. Both his eyes were present and in their correct positions, staring at me from either side of the knife-edged nose. I had never seen him with his hair so close-clipped before. It made him look like a stranger, the strong bones of his face stark beneath the skin and the dome of his skull visible under the short, thick turf of his hair.

"What am I doing?" I echoed. I swallowed, working some moisture back into my dry mouth. "What am I doing? I'm sitting here with a lock of your hair in my hand, wondering whether you were dead or not! That's what I'm doing!"

"I'm not dead." He crossed to the armoire and opened it. He wore his sword, but had changed clothes since our visit to Sandringham's house; now he was dressed in his old coat—the one that allowed him free movement of his arms.

"Yes, I noticed," I said. "Thoughtful of you to come tell me."

"I came to fetch my clothes." He pulled out two shirts and his full-length cloak and laid them across a stool while he went to rummage in the chest of drawers for clean linen.

"Your clothes? Where on earth are you going?" I hadn't known what to expect when I saw him again, but I certainly hadn't expected this.

"To an inn." He glanced at me, then apparently decided I deserved more than a three-word explanation. He turned and looked at me, his eyes blue and opaque as azurite.

"When I sent ye home in the coach, I walked for a bit, until I had a grip on myself once more. Then I came home to fetch my sword, and returned to the Duke's house to give Randall a formal challenge. The butler told me Randall had been arrested."

His gaze rested on me, remote as the ocean depths. I swallowed once more.

"I went to the Bastille. They told me you'd sworn to an accusation against Randall, saying he'd attacked you and Mary Hawkins the other night. Why, Claire?"

My hands were shaking, and I dropped the lock of hair I had been holding. Its cohesion disturbed by handling, it disintegrated, and the fine red hairs spilled loose across my lap.

"Jamie," I said, and my voice was shaking, too, "Jamie, you can't kill Jack Randall."

One corner of his mouth twitched, very slightly.

"I dinna ken whether to be touched at your concern for my safety, or to be offended at your lack of confidence. But in either case, you needna worry. I can kill him. Easily." The last word was spoken quietly, with an underlying tone that mingled venom with satisfaction.

"That isn't what I mean! Jamie—"

"Fortunately," he went on, as though not hearing me, "Randall has proof that he was at the Duke's residence all during the evening of the rape. As soon as the police finish interviewing the guests who were present, and satisfy themselves that Randall is innocent—of *that* charge, at least—then he'll be let go. I shall stay at the inn until he's free. And then I shall find him." His eyes were fixed on the wardrobe, but plainly he was seeing something else. "He'll be waiting for me," he said softly.

He stuffed the shirts and linen into a traveling-bag and slung his cloak over his arm. He was turning to go through the door when I sprang up from the bed and caught him by the sleeve.

"Jamie! For God's sake, Jamie, listen to me! You can't kill Jack Randall because I won't let you!"

He stared down at me in utter astonishment.

"Because of Frank," I said. I let go of his sleeve and stepped back.

"Frank," he repeated, shaking his head slightly as though to clear a buzzing in his ears. "Frank."

"Yes," I said. "If you kill Jack Randall now, then Frank . . . he won't exist. He won't be born. Jamie, you can't kill an innocent man!"

His face, normally a pale, ruddy bronze, had faded to a blotchy white as I spoke. Now the red began to rise again, burning the tips of his ears and flaming in his cheeks.

"An innocent man?"

"Frank is an innocent man! I don't care about Jack Randall—"

"Well, I do!" He snatched up the bag and strode toward the door, cloak streaming over one arm. "Jesus God, Claire! You'd try to stop me taking my vengeance on the man who made me play whore to him? Who forced me to my knees and made me suck his cock, smeared with my own blood? *Christ,*

Claire!" He flung the door open with a crash and was in the hallway by the time I could reach him.

It had grown dark by now, but the servants had lit the candles, and the hallway was aglow with soft light. I grasped him by the arm and yanked at him.

"Jamie! Please!"

He jerked his arm impatiently out of my grasp. I was almost crying, but held back the tears. I caught the bag and pulled it out of his hand.

"Please, Jamie! Wait, just for a year! The child—Randall's—it will be conceived next December. After that, it won't matter. But please—for my sake, Jamie—wait that long!"

The candelabra on the gilt-edged table threw his shadow huge and wavering against the far wall. He stared up at it, hands clenched, as though facing a giant, blank-faced and menacing, that towered above him.

"Aye," he whispered, as though to himself, "I'm a big chap. Big and strong. I can stand a lot. Yes, I can stand it." He whirled on me, shouting.

"I can stand a lot! But just because I can, does that mean I must? Do I have to bear everyone's weakness? Can I not have my own?"

He began to pace up and down the hall, the shadow following in silent frenzy.

"You cannot ask it of me! You, you of all people! You, who know what . . . what . . ." He choked, speechless with rage.

He hit the stone wall of the passage repeatedly as he walked, smashing the side of his fist viciously into the limestone wall. The stone swallowed each blow in soundless violence.

He turned back and came to a halt facing me, breathing heavily. I stood stock-still, afraid to move or speak. He nodded once or twice, rapidly, as though making up his mind about something, then drew the dirk from his belt with a hiss and held it in front of my nose. With a visible effort, he spoke calmly.

"You may have your choice, Claire. Him, or me." The candle flames danced in the polished metal as he turned the knife slowly. "I cannot live while he lives. If ye wilna have me kill him, then kill me now, yourself!" He grabbed my hand and forced my fingers around the handle of the dirk. Ripping the lacy jabot open, he bared his throat and yanked my hand upward, fingers hard around my own.

I pulled back with all my strength, but he forced the tip of the blade against the soft hollow above the collarbone, just below the livid cicatrice that Randall's own knife had left there years before.

"Jamie! Stop it! Stop it right now!" I brought my other hand down on his wrist as hard as I could, jarring his grip enough to jerk my fingers free. The knife clattered to the floor, bouncing from the stones to a quiet landing on a corner of the leafy Aubusson carpet. With that clarity of vision for small details that afflicts life's most awful moments, I saw that the blade lay stark across the curling stem of a bunch of fat green grapes, as though about to sever it and cut them free of the weft to roll at our feet.

He stood frozen before me, face white as bone, eyes burning. I gripped his arm, hard as wood beneath my fingers.

"Please believe me, please. I wouldn't do this if there were any other way." I took a deep, quivering breath to quell the leaping pulse beneath my ribs.

"You owe me your life, Jamie. Not once, twice over. I saved you from hanging at Wentworth, and when you had fever at the Abbey. You owe me a life, Jamie!"

He stared down at me for a long moment before answering. When he did, his voice was quiet again, with an edge of bitterness.

"I see. And ye'll claim your debt now?" His eyes burned with the clear, deep blue that burns in the heart of a flame.

"I have to! I can't make you see reason any other way!"

"Reason. Ah, reason. No, I canna say that reason is anything I see just now." He folded his arms behind his back, gripping the stiff fingers of his right hand with the curled ones of his left. He walked slowly away from me, down the endless hall, head bowed.

The passage was lined with paintings, some lighted from below by torchere or candelabra, some from above by the gilded sconces; a few less favored, skulked in the darkness between. Jamie walked slowly between them, glancing up now and again as though in converse with the wigged and painted gallery.

The hall ran the length of the second floor, carpeted and tapestried, with enormous stained-glass windows set into the walls at either end of the corridor. He walked all the way to the far end, then, wheeling with the precision of a soldier on parade, all the way back, still at a slow and formal pace. Down and back, down and back, again and again.

My legs trembling, I subsided into a fauteuil near the end of the passage. Once one of the omnipresent servants approached obsequiously to ask if Madame required wine, or perhaps a biscuit? I waved him away with what politeness I could muster, and waited.

At last he came to a halt before me, feet planted wide apart in silver-buckled shoes, hands still clasped behind his back. He waited for me to look up at him before he spoke. His face was set, with no twitch of agitation to betray him, though the lines near his eyes were deep with strain.

"A year, then" was all he said. He turned at once and was several feet away by the time I struggled out of the deep green-velvet chair. I had barely gained my feet when he suddenly whirled back past me, reached the huge stained-glass window in three strides, and smashed his right hand through it.

The window was made up of thousands of tiny colored panes, held in place by strips of melted lead. Though the entire window, a mythological scene of the Judgment of Paris, shuddered in its frame, the leading held most of the panes intact; in spite of the crash and tinkle, only a jagged hole at the feet of Aphrodite let in the soft spring air.

Jamie stood a moment, pressing both hands tight into his midriff. A dark red stain grew on the frilled cuff, lacy as a bridal shirt. He brushed past me once again as I moved toward him, and stalked away unspeaking.

I collapsed once more into the armchair, hard enough to make a small puff of dust rise from the plush. I lay there limp, eyes closed, feeling the cool night breeze wash over me. The hair was damp at my temples, and I could feel my pulse, quick as a bird's, racing at the base of my throat.

Would he ever forgive me? My heart clenched like a fist at the memory of the knowledge of betrayal in his eyes. *"How could you ask it?"* he had said. *"You, you who know . . ."* Yes, I knew, and I thought the knowing might tear me from Jamie as I had been torn from Frank.

But whether Jamie could forgive me or not, I could never forgive myself, if I condemned an innocent man—and one I had once loved.

"The sins of the fathers," I murmured to myself. "The sins of the fathers shall not be visited upon the children."

"Madame?"

I jumped, opening my eyes to find an equally startled chambermaid backing away. I put a hand to my pounding heart, gasping for air.

"Madame, you are unwell? Shall I fetch—"

"No," I said, as firmly as I could. "I am quite well. I wish to sit here for a time. Please go away."

The girl seemed only too anxious to oblige. "*Oui*, Madame!" she said, and vanished down the corridor, leaving me gazing blankly at a scene of amorous love in a garden, hanging on the opposite wall. Suddenly cold, I drew up the folds of the cloak I had had no time to shed, and closed my eyes again.

It was past midnight when I went at last to our bedroom. Jamie was there, seated before a small table, apparently watching a pair of lacewings fluttering dangerously around the single candlestick which was all the light there was in the room. I dropped my cape on the floor and went toward him.

"Don't touch me," he said. "Go to bed." He spoke almost abstractedly, but I halted in my tracks.

"But your hand—" I started.

"It doesn't matter. Go to bed," he repeated.

The knuckles of his right hand were laced with blood, and the cuff of his shirt was stiff with it, but I would not have dared touch him then had he had a knife stuck in his belly. I left him staring at the death-dance of the lacewings and went to bed.

I woke sometime near dawn, with the first light of the coming day fuzzing the outlines of the furniture in the room. Through the double doors to the anteroom, I could see Jamie as I had left him, still seated at the table. Now the candle was burnt out, the lacewings gone, and he sat with his head in his hands, fingers furrowed in the brutally cropped hair. The light stole all color from the room; even the hair spiking up like flames between his fingers was quenched to the color of ashes.

I slid out of bed, cold in the thin embroidered nightdress. He didn't turn as I came up behind him, but he knew I was there. When I touched his hand he let it drop to the table, and allowed his head to fall back until it rested just below my breasts. He sighed deeply as I rubbed it, and I felt the tension begin to go out of him. My hands worked their way down over neck and shoulders, feeling the chill of his flesh through the thin linen. Finally I came around in front of him. He reached up and grasped me around the waist, pulling me to him and burying his head in my nightdress, just above the round swell of the unborn child.

"I'm cold," I said at last, very softly. "Will you come and warm me?"

After a moment, he nodded, and stumbled blindly to his feet. I led him to bed, stripped him as he sat unresisting, and tucked him under the quilts. I lay in the curve of his arm, pressed tight against him, until the chill of his skin had faded and we lay ensconced in a pocket of soft warmth.

Tentatively, I laid a hand on his chest, stroking lightly back and forth until the nipple stood up, a tiny nub of desire. He laid his hand over mine, stilling it. I was afraid he would push me away, and he did, but only so that he could roll toward me.

The light was growing stronger, and he spent a long time just looking down at my face, stroking it from temple to chin, drawing his thumb down the line of my throat and out along the wing of my collarbone.

"God, I do love you," he whispered, as though to himself. He kissed me, preventing response, and circling one breast with his maimed right hand, prepared to take me.

"But your hand—" I said, for the second time that night.

"It doesn't matter," he said, for the second time that night.

PART FOUR

Scandale

22

The Royal Stud

The coach bumped slowly over a particularly bad stretch of road, one left pitted and holed by the winter freeze and the beating of spring rains. It had been a wet year; even now, in early summer, there were moist, boggy patches under the lush growth of gooseberry bushes by the sides of the road.

Jamie sat beside me on the narrow, padded bench that formed one seat of the coach. Fergus sprawled in the corner of the other bench, asleep, and the motion of the coach made his head rock and sway like the head of a mechanical doll with a spring for its neck. The air in the coach was warm, and dust came through the windows in small golden spurts whenever we hit a patch of dry earth.

We had talked desultorily at first of the surrounding countryside, of the Royal stables at Argentan for which we were headed, of the small bits of gossip that composed the daily fare of conversation in Court and business circles. I might have slept, too, lulled by the coach's rhythm and the warmth of the day, but the changing contours of my body made sitting in one position uncomfortable, and my back ached from the jolting. The baby was becoming increasingly active, too, and the small flutters of the first movements had developed into definite small pokes and proddings; pleasant in their own fashion, but distracting.

"Perhaps ye should have stayed at home, Sassenach," Jamie said, frowning slightly as I twisted, adjusting my position yet again.

"I'm all right," I said with a smile. "Just twitchy. And it would have been a shame to miss all this." I waved at the coach window, where the broad sweep of fields shone green as emeralds between the windbreak rows of dark, straight poplars. Dusty or not, the fresh air of the countryside was rich and intoxicating after the close, fetid smells of the city and the medicinal stenches of L'Hôpital des Anges.

Louis had agreed, as a gesture of cautious amity toward the English diplomatic overtures, to allow the Duke of Sandringham to purchase four Percheron broodmares from the Royal stud at Argentan, with which to improve the bloodlines of the small herd of draft horses which His Grace maintained in England. His Grace was therefore visiting Argentan today, and had invited Jamie along to give advice on which mares should be chosen. The invitation was given at an evening party, and one thing leading to another, the visit had ended up as a full-scale picnic expedition, involving four coaches and several of the ladies and gentlemen of the Court.

"It's a good sign, don't you think?" I asked, with a cautious glance to be sure our companions were indeed fast asleep. "Louis giving the Duke permission to buy horses, I mean. If he's making gestures toward the English, then he's presumably not inclined to be sympathetic to James Stuart—at least not openly."

Jamie shook his head. He declined absolutely to wear a wig, and the bold, clean shape of his polled head had occasioned no little excitement at Court. It had its advantages at the present moment; while a faint sheen of perspiration glowed on the bridge of his long, straight nose, he wasn't nearly as wilted as I.

"No, I'm fairly sure now that Louis means to have nothing to do with the Stuarts—at least so far as any move toward restoration goes. Monsieur Duverney assures me that the Council is entirely opposed to any such thing; while Louis may eventually yield to the Pope's urgings so far as to make Charles a small allowance, he isna disposed to bring the Stuarts into any kind of prominence in France, wi' Geordie of England looking over his shoulder." He wore his plaid today pinned with a brooch at the shoulder—a beautiful thing his sister had sent him from Scotland, made in the shape of two running stags, bodies bent so that they joined in a circle, heads and tails touching. He pulled up a fold of the plaid and wiped his face with it.

"I think I've spoken with every banker in Paris of any substance over the last months, and they're united in basic disinterest." He smiled wryly. "Money's none so plentiful that anyone wants to back a dicey proposition like the Stuart restoration."

"And that," I said, stretching my back with a groan, "leaves Spain."

Jamie nodded. "It does. And Dougal MacKenzie." He looked smug, and I sat up, intrigued.

"Have you heard from him?" Despite an initial wariness, Dougal had accepted Jamie as a devoted fellow Jacobite, and the usual crop of coded letters had been augmented by a series of discreet communications sent by Dougal from Spain, meant to be read by Jamie and passed on to Charles Stuart.

"I have indeed." I could tell from his expression that it was good news, and it was—though not for the Stuarts.

"Philip has declined to lend any assistance to the Stuarts," Jamie said. "He's had word from the papal office, ye ken; he's to keep awa' from the whole question of the Scottish throne."

"Do we know why?" The latest interception from a papal messenger had contained several letters, but as these were all addressed to James or Charles Stuart, they might well contain no reference to His Holiness's conversations with Spain.

"Dougal thinks he knows." Jamie laughed. "He's fair disgusted, is Dougal. Said he'd been kept cooling his heels in Toledo for nearly a month, and sent awa' at last with no more than a vague promise of aid 'in the fullness of time, *Deo volente.*' " His deep voice captured a pious intonation perfectly, and I laughed myself.

"Benedict wants to avoid friction between Spain and France; he doesna want Philip and Louis wasting money that he might have a use for, ye ken," he added cynically. "It's hardly fitting for a pope to say so, but Benedict has his doubts as to whether a Catholic king could hold England anymore. Scotland's got its Catholic chiefs among the Highland clans, but it's some time since England owned a Catholic king—likely to be the hell of a lot longer before they do again—*Deo volente*," he added, grinning.

He scratched his head, ruffling the short red-gold hair above his temple. "It looks verra dim for the Stuarts, Sassenach, and that's good news. No, there'll be no aid from the Bourbon monarchs. The only thing that concerns me now is this investment Charles Stuart's made with the Comte St. Germain."

"You don't think it's just a business arrangement, then?"

"Well, it is," he said, frowning, "and yet there's more behind it. I've heard talk, aye?"

While the banking families of Paris were not inclined to take the Young Pretender to the throne of Scotland with any seriousness, that situation might easily change, were Charles Stuart suddenly to have money to invest.

"His Highness tells me he's been talking to the Gobelins," Jamie said. "St. Germain introduced him; otherwise they'd not give him the time o' day. And old Gobelin thinks him a wastrel and a fool, and so does one of the Gobelin sons. The other, though—he says that he'll wait and see; if Charles succeeds with this venture, then perhaps he can put other opportunities in his way."

"Not at all good," I observed.

Jamie shook his head. "No. Money breeds money, ye ken. Let him succeed at one or two large ventures, and the bankers will begin to listen to him. The man's no great thinker," he said, with a wry twist of his mouth, "but he's verra charming in person; he can persuade people into things against their better judgment. Even so, he'll make no headway without a small bit of capital to his name—but he'll have that, if this investment succeeds."

"Mm." I shifted my position once more, wriggling my toes in their hot leather prison. The shoes had fit when made for me, but my feet were beginning to swell a bit, and my silk stockings were damp with sweat. "Is there anything we can do about it?"

Jamie shrugged, with a lopsided smile. "Pray for bad weather off Portugal, I suppose. Beyond the ship sinking, I dinna see much way for the venture to fail, truth be told. St. Germain has contracts already for the sale of the entire cargo. Both he and Charles Stuart stand to triple their money."

I shivered briefly at the mention of the Comte. I couldn't help recalling

Dougal's speculations. I had not told Jamie about Dougal's visit, nor about his speculations as to the Comte's nocturnal activities. I didn't like keeping secrets from him, but Dougal had demanded my silence as his price for helping me in the matter of Jonathan Randall, and I had had little choice but to agree.

Jamie smiled suddenly at me, and stretched out a hand.

"I'll think of something, Sassenach. For now, give me your feet. Jenny said it helped to have me rub her feet when she was wi' child."

I didn't argue, but slipped my feet out of the hot shoes and swung them up onto his lap with a sigh of relief as the air from the window cooled the damp silk over my toes.

His hands were big, and his fingers at once strong and gentle. He rubbed his knuckles down the arch of my foot and I leaned back with a soft moan. We rode silently for several minutes, while I relaxed into a state of mindless bliss.

Head bent over my green silk toes, Jamie remarked casually, "It wasna really a debt, ye ken."

"What wasn't?" Fogged as I was by warm sun and foot massage, I hadn't any idea what he meant.

Not stopping his rubbing, he looked up at me. His expression was serious, though the hint of a smile lit his eyes.

"You said that I owed ye a life, Sassenach, because you'd saved mine for me." He took hold of one big toe and wiggled it. "But I've been reckoning, and I'm none so sure that's true. Seems to me that it's nearly even, taken all in all."

"What you do mean, even?" I tried to pull my foot loose, but he held tight.

"If you've saved my life—and ye have—well, I've saved yours as well, and at least as often. I saved ye from Jack Randall at Fort William, you'll recall—and I took ye from the mob at Cranesmuir, no?"

"Yes," I said cautiously. I had no idea where he was going, but he wasn't just making idle conversation. "I'm grateful for it, of course."

He made a small Scottish noise of dismissal, deep in his throat. "It isna a matter for gratitude, Sassenach, on your part *or* mine—my point is only that it's no a matter of obligation, either." The smile had vanished from his eyes, and he was entirely serious.

"I didna give ye Randall's life as an exchange for my own—it wouldna be a fair trade, for one thing. Close your mouth, Sassenach," he added practically, "flies will get in." There were in fact a number of the insects present; three were resting on the Fergus's shirtfront, undisturbed by its constant rise and fall.

"Why did you agree, then?" I stopped struggling, and he wrapped both hands around my feet, running his thumbs slowly over the curves of my heels.

"Well, it wasna for any of the reasons you tried to make me see. As for Frank," he said, "well, it's true enough that I've taken his wife, and I do pity him for it—more sometimes than others," he added, with an impudent quirk of one eyebrow. "Still, is it any different than if he were my rival here? You had free choice between us, and you chose me—even with such luxuries as hot baths thrown in on his side. Oof!" I jerked one foot loose and drove it into his ribs. He straightened up and grabbed it, in time to prevent me repeating the blow.

"Regretting your choice, are you?"

"Not yet," I said, struggling to repossess my foot, "but I may any minute. Keep talking."

"Well then. I couldna see that the fact that you picked me entitled Frank Randall to particular consideration. Besides," he said frankly, "I'll admit to bein' just a wee bit jealous of the man."

I kicked with my other foot, aiming lower. He caught that one before it landed, twisting my ankle skillfully.

"As for owing him his life, on general principles," he continued, ignoring my attempts to escape, "that's an argument Brother Anselm at the Abbey could answer better than I. Certainly I wouldna kill an innocent man in cold blood. But there again, I've killed men in battle, and is this different?"

I remembered the soldier, and the boy in the snow that I had killed in our escape from Wentworth. I no longer tormented myself with memories of them, but I knew they would never leave me.

He shook his head. "No, there are a good many arguments ye might make about that, but in the end, such choices come down to one: You kill when ye must, and ye live with it after. I remember the face of every man I've killed, and always will. But the fact remains, I am alive and they are not, and that is my only justification, whether it be right or no."

"But that's not true in this case," I pointed out. "It isn't a case of kill or be killed."

He shook his head, dislodging a fly that had settled on his hair. "Now there you're wrong, Sassenach. What it is that lies between Jack Randall and me will be settled only when one of us is dead—and maybe not then. There are ways of killing other than with a knife or a gun, and there are things worse than physical death." His tone softened. "In Ste. Anne, you pulled me back from more than one kind of death, *mo duinne,* and never think I don't know it." He shook his head. "Perhaps I do owe you more than you owe me, after all."

He let go my feet and rearranged his long legs. "And that leads me to consider your conscience as well as mine. After all, you had no idea what would happen when ye made your choice, and it's one thing to abandon a man, and another to condemn him to death."

I did not at all like this manner of describing my actions, but I couldn't shirk the facts. I had in fact abandoned Frank, and while I could not regret the choice I had made, still I did and always would regret its necessity. Jamie's next words echoed my thoughts eerily.

He continued, "If ye had known it might mean Frank's—well, his death, shall we say—perhaps you would have chosen differently. Given that ye did choose me, have I the right to make your actions of more consequence than you intended?"

Absorbed in his argument, he had been oblivious of its effect on me. Catching sight of my face now, he stopped suddenly, watching me in silence as we jostled our way through the greens of the countryside.

"I dinna see how it can have been a sin for you to do as ye did, Claire," he said at last, reaching out to lay a hand on my stockinged foot. "I am your lawful husband, as much as he ever was—or will be. You do not even know that ye could have returned to him; *mo duinne,* ye might have gone still further back, or gone forward to a different time altogether. You acted as ye thought ye must, and no one can do better than that." He looked up, and the look in his eyes pierced my soul.

"I'm honest enough to say that I dinna care what the right and wrong of it may be, so long as you are here wi' me, Claire," he said softly. "If it was a sin for you to choose me . . . then I would go to the Devil himself and bless him for tempting ye to it." He lifted my foot and gently kissed the tip of my big toe.

I laid my hand on his head; the short hair felt bristly but soft, like a very young hedgehog.

"I don't think it was wrong," I said softly. "But if it was . . . then I'll go to the Devil with you, Jamie Fraser."

He closed his eyes and bowed his head over my foot. He held it so tightly that I could feel the long, slender metatarsals pressed together; still, I didn't pull back. I dug my fingers into his scalp and tugged his hair gently.

"Why then, Jamie? Why did you decide to let Jack Randall live?"

He still gripped my foot, but opened his eyes and smiled at me.

"Well, I thought a number of things, Sassenach, as I walked up and down that evening. For one thing, I thought that you would suffer, if I did kill the filthy scut. I would do, or not do, quite a few things to spare you distress, Sassenach, but—how heavily does your conscience weigh, against my honor?

"No." He shook his head again, disposing of another point. "Each one of us can be responsible only for his own actions and his own conscience. What I do canna be laid to your account, no matter what the effects." He blinked, eyes watering from the dusty wind, and passed a hand across his hair in a vain attempt to smooth the disheveled ends. Clipped short, the spikes of a cowlick stood up on the crest of his skull in a defiant spray.

"Why, then?" I demanded, leaning forward. "You've told me all the reasons why not; what's left?"

He hesitated for a moment, but then met my eyes squarely.

"Because of Charles Stuart, Sassenach. So far we have stopped all the earths, but with this investment of his—well, he might yet succeed in leading an army in Scotland. And if so . . . well, ye ken better than I do what may come, Sassenach."

I did, and the thought turned me cold. I could not help remembering one historian's description of the Highlanders' fate at Culloden—"the dead lay four deep, soaking in rain and their own blood."

The Highlanders, mismanaged and starving, but ferocious to the end, would be wasted in one decisive half-hour. They would be left to lie in heaps, bleeding in a cold April rain, the cause they had cherished for a hundred years dead along with them.

Jamie reached forward suddenly and took my hands.

"I think it will not happen, Claire; I think we will stop him. And if not, then still I dinna expect anything to happen to me. But if it should . . ." He was in deadly earnest now, speaking soft and urgently. "If it does, then I want there to be a place for you; I want someone for you to go to if I am . . . not there to care for you. If it canna be me, then I would have it be a man who loves you." His grasp on my fingers grew tighter; I could feel both rings digging into my flesh, and felt the urgency in his hands.

"Claire, ye know what it cost me to do this for you—to spare Randall's life. Promise me that if the time should come, you'll go back to Frank." His eyes searched my face, deep blue as the sky in the window behind him. "I tried to send ye back twice before. And I thank God ye wouldna go. But if it comes to a third time—then promise me you will go back to him—back to Frank. For that is why I spare Jack Randall for a year—for your sake. Promise me, Claire?"

"*Allez! Allez! Montez!*" the coachman shouted from above, encouraging the team up a slope. We were nearly there.

"All right," I said at last. "I promise."

The stables at Argentan were clean and airy, redolent of summer and the smell of horses. In an open box stall, Jamie circled a Percheron mare, enamored as a horsefly.

"Ooh, what a bonnie wee lass ye are! Come here, sweetheart, let me see that beautiful fat rump. Mm, aye, that's grand!"

"I wish my husband would talk that way to *me*," remarked the Duchesse de Neve, provoking giggles from the other ladies of the party, who stood in the straw of the central aisle, watching.

"Perhaps he would, Madame, if your own back view provided such stimulation. But then, perhaps your husband does not share my lord Broch Tuarach's appreciation for a finely shaped rump." The Comte St. Germain allowed his eyes to drift over me with a hint of contemptuous amusement. I tried to imagine those black eyes gleaming through the slits of a mask, and succeeded only too well. Unfortunately, the lace of his wrist frills fell well past his knuckles; I couldn't see the fork of his thumb.

Catching the byplay, Jamie leaned comfortably on the mare's broad back, only his head, shoulders and forearms showing above the bulk of the Percheron.

"My lord Broch Tuarach appreciates beauty wherever it may be encountered, Monsieur le Comte; in animal or woman. Unlike some I might name, though, I am capable of telling the difference between the two." He grinned maliciously at St. Germain, then patted the mare's neck in farewell as the party broke out laughing.

Jamie took my arm to lead me toward the next stable, followed more slowly by the rest of the party.

"Ah," he said, inhaling the mixture of horse, harness, manure, and hay as though it were incense. "I do miss the smell of a stable. And the country makes me sick for Scotland."

"Doesn't look a lot like Scotland," I said, squinting in the bright sun as we emerged from the dimness of the stable.

"No, but it's country," he said, "it's clean, and it's green, and there's nay smoke in the air, or sewage underfoot—unless ye count horse dung, which I don't."

The sun of early summer shone on the roofs of Argentan, nestled among gently rolling green hills. The Royal stud was just outside the town, much more solidly constructed than the houses of the King's subjects nearby. The barns and stables were of quarried stone, stone-floored, slate-roofed, and maintained in a condition of cleanliness that surpassed that of L'Hôpital des Anges by a fair degree.

A loud whooping came from behind the corner of the stable, and Jamie stopped short, just in time to avoid Fergus, who shot out in front of us as though fired from a slingshot, hotly pursued by two stable-lads, both a good deal bigger. A dirty green streak of fresh manure down the side of the first boy's face gave some clue as to the cause of the altercation.

With considerable presence of mind, Fergus doubled on his tracks, shot past his pursuers, and whizzed into the middle of the party, whence he took refuge behind the bulwark of Jamie's kilted hips. Seeing their prey thus safely gone to earth, his pursuers glanced fearfully at the oncoming phalanx of courtiers and gowns, exchanged a look of decision, and, as one, turned and loped off.

Seeing them go, Fergus stuck his head out from behind my skirt and yelled something in gutter French that earned him a sharp cuff on the ear from Jamie.

"Off wi' ye," he said brusquely. "And for God's sake, dinna be throwin' horse apples at people bigger than you are. Now, go and keep out of trouble." He followed up this advice with a healthy smack on the seat of the breeches that sent Fergus staggering off in the opposite direction to that taken by his erstwhile assailants.

I had been of two minds as to the wisdom of taking Fergus with us on this expedition, but most of the ladies were bringing pageboys with them, to run errands and carry the baskets of food and other paraphernalia deemed essential to a day's outing. And Jamie had wanted to show the lad a bit of country, feeling that he'd earned a holiday. All well and good, except that Fergus, who had never been outside Paris in his life, had got the exhilaration of air, light, and beautiful huge animals right up his nose, and, demented with excitement, had been in constant trouble since our arrival.

"God knows what he'll do next," I said darkly, looking after Fergus's retreating form. "Set one of the hayricks on fire, I expect."

Jamie was unperturbed at the suggestion.

"He'll be all right. All lads get into manure fights."

"They do?" I turned around, scrutinizing St. Germain, immaculate in white linen, white serge, and white silk, bending courteously to listen to the Duchesse, as she minced slowly across the straw-strewn yard.

"Maybe *you* did," I said. "Not him. Not the Bishop, either, I don't think." I was wondering whether this excursion had been a good idea, at least on my part. Jamie was in his element with the giant Percherons, and the Duke was clearly impressed with him, which was all to the good. On the other hand, my back ached miserably from the carriage ride, and my feet felt hot and swollen, pressing painfully against the tight leather of my shoes.

Jamie looked down at me and smiled, pressing my hand where it lay on his arm.

"None so long now, Sassenach. The guide wants to show us the breeding sheds, and then you and the other ladies can go and sit down wi' the food, while the men stand about makin' crude jests about the size of each other's cock."

"Is that the general effect of watching horses bred?" I asked, fascinated.

"Well, on men it is; I dinna ken what it does to ladies. Keep an ear out, and ye can tell me later."

There was in fact an air of suppressed excitement among the members of the party as we all pressed into the rather cramped quarters of a breeding shed. Stone, like the other buildings, this one was equipped not with partitioned stalls down both sides, but with a small fenced pen, with holding stalls at either side, and a sort of chute or runway along the back, with several gates that could be opened or closed to control a horse's movement.

The building itself was light and airy, owing to huge, unglazed windows that opened at either end, giving a view of a grassy paddock outside. I could see several of the enormous Percheron mares grazing near the edge of this; one or two seemed restless, breaking into a rocking gallop for a few paces, then dropping back to a trot or a walk, shaking heads and manes with a high, whinnying noise. Once, when this happened, there was a loud, nasal scream from one of the holding stalls at the end of the shed, and the paneling shook with the thud of a mighty kick from its inhabitant.

"*He's* ready," a voice murmured appreciatively behind me. "I wonder which is the lucky mademoiselle?"

"The one nearest the gate," the Duchesse suggested, always ready to wager. "Five livres on that one."

"Ah, no! You're wrong, Madame, she's too calm. It will be the little one, under the apple tree, rolling her eyes like a coquette. See how she tosses her head? That one's my choice."

The mares had all stopped at the sound of the stallion's cry, lifting inquiring noses and flicking their ears nervously. The restless ones tossed their heads and whickered; one stretched her neck and let out a long, high call.

"That one," Jamie said quietly, nodding at her. "Hear her call him?"

"And what is she saying, my lord?" the Bishop asked, a glint in his eye. Jamie shook his head solemnly.

"It is a song, my lord, but one that a man of the cloth is deaf to—or should be," he added, to gales of laughter.

Sure enough, it was the mare who had called who was chosen. Once inside, she stopped dead, head up, and stood testing the air with flaring nostrils. The stallion could smell her; his cries echoed eerily off the timbered roof, so loud that conversation was impossible.

No one wanted to talk now, anyway. Uncomfortable as I was, I could feel the quick tingle of arousal through my breasts, and a tightening of my swollen belly as the mare once more answered the stallion's call.

Percherons are very large horses. A big one stands over five feet at the shoulder, and the rump of a well-fed mare is almost a yard across, a pale, dappled gray or shining black, adorned with a waterfall of black hair, thick as my arm at the root of it.

The stallion burst from his stall toward the tethered mare with a suddenness that made everyone fall back from the fence. Puffs of dust flew up in clouds as the huge hooves struck the packed dirt of the pen, and drops of saliva flew from his open mouth. The groom who had opened his stall door jumped aside, tiny and insignificant next to the magnicent fury let loose in the pen.

The mare curvetted and squealed in alarm, but then he was on her, and his teeth closed on the sturdy arch of her neck, forcing her head down into submission. The great swathe of her tail swept high, leaving her naked, exposed to his lust.

"*Jésus,*" whispered Monsieur Prudhomme.

It took very little time, but it seemed a lot longer, watching the heaving of sweat-darkened flanks, and the play of light on swirling hair and the sheen of great muscles, tense and straining in the flexible agony of mating.

Everyone was very quiet as we left the shed. Finally the Duke laughed, nudged Jamie, and said, "You are accustomed to such sights, my lord Broch Tuarach?"

"Aye," Jamie answered. "I've seen it a good many times."

"Ah?" the Duke said. "And tell me, my lord, how does the sight make you feel, after so many times?"

One corner of Jamie's mouth twitched as he replied, but he remained otherwise straight-faced.

"Verra modest, Your Grace," he said.

"What a sight!" the Duchesse de Neve said. She broke a biscuit, dreamy-eyed, and munched it slowly. "So arousing, was it not?"

"What a prick, you mean," said Madame Prudhomme, rather coarsely. "I wish Philibert had one like that. As it is . . ." She cocked an eyebrow toward a plate of tiny sausages, each perhaps two inches long, and the ladies seated on the picnic cloth broke into giggles.

"A bit of chicken, please, Paul," said the Comtesse St. Germain to her pageboy. She was young, and the bawdy conversation of the older ladies was making her blush. I wondered just what sort of marriage she had with St. Germain; he never took her out in public, save on occasions like this, where the presence of the Bishop prevented his appearing with one of his mistresses.

"Bah," said Madame Montresor, one of the ladies-in-waiting, whose husband was a friend of the Bishop's. "Size isn't everything. What difference if it's the size of a stallion's, if he lasts no longer than one? Less than two minutes? I ask you, what good is that?" She held up a cornichon between two fingers and delicately licked the tiny pale-green pickle, the pink tip of her tongue pointed and dainty. "It isn't what they have in their breeches, I say; it's what they do with it."

Madame Prudhomme snorted. "Well, if you find one who knows how to do anything with it but poke it into the nearest hole, tell me. I would be interested to see what else can be done with a thing like that."

"At least you have one who's interested," broke in the Duchesse de Neve. She cast a glance of disgust at her husband, huddled with the other men near one of the paddocks, watching a harnessed mare being put through her paces.

"Not tonight, my dearest," she imitated the sonorous, nasal tones of her husband to perfection. "I am *fatigued*." She put a hand to her brow and rolled her eyes up. "The press of business is so wearing." Encouraged by the giggles, she went on with her imitation, now widening her eyes in horror and crossing her hands protectively over her lap. "What, *again*? Do you not know that to expend the male essence gratuitously is to court ill-health? Is it not enough that your demands have worn me to a nubbin, Mathilde? Do you wish me to have an *attack*?"

The ladies cackled and screeched with laughter, loud enough to attract the attention of the Bishop, who waved at us and smiled indulgently, provoking further gales of hilarity.

"Well, at least he is not expending all his male essence in brothels—or elsewhere," said Madame Prudhomme, with an eloquently pitying glance at the Comtesse St. Germain.

"No," said Mathilde gloomily. "He hoards it as though it were gold. You'd think there was no more to be had, the way he . . . oh, Your Grace! Will you not have a cup of wine?" She smiled charmingly up at the Duke, who had approached quietly from behind. He stood smiling at the ladies, one fair brow slightly arched. If he had heard the subject of our conversation, he gave no sign of it.

Seating himself beside me on the cloth, His Grace made casual, witty conversation with the ladies, his oddly high-pitched voice forming no contrast to theirs. While he seemed to pay close attention to the conversation, I noticed that his eyes strayed periodically to the small cluster of men who stood by the paddock fence. Jamie's kilt was bright even amid the gorgeous cut velvets and stiffened silk.

I had had some hesitation in meeting the Duke again. After all, our last visit had ended in the arrest of Jonathan Randall, upon my accusation of attempted rape. But the Duke had been all charming urbanity on this outing, with no mention of either of the Randall brothers. Neither had there been any public mention of the arrest; whatever the Duke's diplomatic activities, they seemed to rank highly enough to merit a Royal seal of silence.

On the whole, I welcomed the Duke's appearance at the picnic cloth. For one thing, his presence kept the ladies from asking me—as some bold souls did every so often, at parties—whether it was true about what Scotsmen wore beneath their kilts. Given the mood of the present party, I didn't think my customary reply of "Oh, the usual" would suffice.

"Your husband has a fine eye for horses," the Duke observed to me, freed for a moment when the Duchesse de Neve, on his other side, leaned across the cloth to talk to Madame Prudhomme. "He tells me that both his father and his uncle kept small but quite fine stables in the Highlands."

"Yes, that's true." I sipped my wine. "But you've visited Colum MacKenzie at Castle Leoch; surely you've seen his stable for yourself." I had in fact first met the Duke at Leoch the year before, though the meeting had been brief; he had left on a hunting expedition shortly before I was arrested for witchcraft. I thought surely he must have known about that, but if so, he gave no sign of it.

"Of course." The Duke's small, shrewd blue eyes darted left, then right, to see whether he was observed, then shifted into English. "At the time, your husband informed me that he did not reside upon his own estates, owing to an unfortunate—and mistaken—charge of murder laid against him by the English Crown. I wondered, my lady, whether that charge of outlawry still holds?"

"There's still a price on his head," I said bluntly.

The Duke's expression of polite interest didn't change. He reached absently for one of the small sausages on the platter.

"That is not an irremediable matter," he said quietly. "After my encounter with your husband at Leoch, I made some inquiries—oh, suitably discreet, I assure you, my dear lady. And I think that the matter might be arranged without undue difficulty, given a word in the right ear—from the right sources."

This was interesting. Jamie had first told the Duke of Sandringham about his outlawry at Colum MacKenzie's suggestion, in the hopes that the Duke might be persuaded to intervene in the case. As Jamie had not in fact committed the crime in question, there could be little evidence against him; it was quite possible that the Duke, a powerful voice among the nobles of England, could indeed arrange to have the charges dismissed.

"Why?" I said. "What do you want in return?"

The sketchy blond brows shot upward, and he smiled, showing small white even teeth.

"My word, you *are* direct, are you not? Might it not be only that I appreciate your husband's expertise and assistance in the selection of horses, and would like to see him restored to a place where that skill might once again be profitably exercised?"

"It might be, but it isn't," I said. I caught Madame Prudhomme's sharp eyes on us, and smiled pleasantly at him. "Why?"

He popped the sausage whole into his mouth and chewed it slowly, his bland round face reflecting nothing more than enjoyment of the day and the meal. At last he swallowed and patted his mouth delicately with one of the linen napkins.

"Well," he said, "as a matter of supposition only, you understand—"

I nodded, and he went on. "*As* a matter of supposition, then, perhaps we may suppose that your husband's recent friendship with—a certain personage recently arrived from Rome? Ah, I see you understand me. Yes. Let us suppose that that friendship has become a matter of some concern to certain parties who would prefer this personage to return peaceably to Rome—or alternatively, to settle in France, though Rome would be better—safer, you know?"

"I see." I took a sausage myself. They were richly spiced, and little bursts of garlic wafted up my nose at each bite. "And these parties take a sufficiently serious view of this friendship to offer a dismissal of the charges against my husband in return for its severance? Again, why? My husband is no one of great importance."

"Not now," the Duke agreed. "But he may be in future. He has linkages to several powerful interests among the French banking families, and more among the merchants. He is also received at Court, and has some access to Louis's ear. In short, if he does not at present hold the power to command substantial sums of money and influence, he is likely to do so soon. He is also a member of not one but *two* of the more powerful Highland clans. And the parties who wish the personage in question to return to Rome harbor a not unreasonable fear that this influence might be exerted in undesirable directions.

So much better if your husband were to return—his good name restored—to his lands in Scotland, do you not think?"

"It's a thought," I said. It was also a bribe, and an attractive one. Sever all connection with Charles Stuart, and be free to return to Scotland and Lallybroch, without the risk of being hanged. The removal of a possibly troublesome supporter of the Stuarts, at no expense to the Crown, was an attractive proposition from the English side, too.

I eyed the Duke, trying to figure out just where he fitted into the scheme of things. Ostensibly an envoy from George II, Elector of Hanover and King—so long as James Stuart remained in Rome—of England, he could well have a dual purpose in his visit to France. To engage with Louis in the delicate exchange of civility and threat that constituted diplomacy, and simultaneously to quash the specter of a fresh Jacobite rising? Several of Charles's usual coterie had disappeared of late, pleading the press of urgent business abroad. Bought off or scared away? I wondered.

The bland countenance gave no clue to his thoughts. He pushed back the wig from a balding brow and scratched his head unselfconsciously.

"Do think about it, my dear," he urged. "And when you have thought—speak to your husband."

"Why don't you speak to him yourself?"

He shrugged and took more sausages, three this time. "I find that so often men are more amenable to a word spoken from the home quarter, from one they trust, rather than to what they may perceive as pressure from an outside source." He smiled. "There is the matter of pride to be considered; that must be handled delicately. And for delicate handling—well, they do talk of 'the woman's touch,' do they not?"

I hadn't time to respond to this, when a shout from the main stable jerked all heads in that direction.

A horse was coming toward us, up the narrow alley between the main stable and the long, open shed that held the forge. A Percheron colt, and a young one, no more than two or three, judging from the dappling of his hide. Even young Percherons are big, and the colt seemed huge, as he blundered to and fro at a slow trot, tail lashing from side to side. Plainly the colt was not yet broken to a saddle; the massive shoulders twitched in an effort to dislodge the small form that straddled his neck, both hands buried deep in the thick black mane.

"Bloody hell, it's Fergus!" The ladies, disturbed by the shouting, had all gotten to their feet by now, and were peering interestedly at the sight.

I didn't realize that the men had joined us until one woman said, "But how dangerous it seems! Surely the boy will be injured if he falls!"

"Well, if he doesna hurt himself falling off, I'll attend to it directly, once I've got my hands on the wee bugger," said a grim voice behind me. I turned to see Jamie peering over my head at the rapidly approaching horse.

"Should you get him off?" I asked.

He shook his head. "No, let the horse take care of it."

In fact, the horse seemed more bewildered than frightened by the strange weight on his back. The dappled gray skin twitched and shivered as though beset by hordes of flies, and the colt shook its head confusedly, as though wondering what was going on.

As for Fergus, his legs were stretched nearly at right angles across the Percheron's broad back; clearly the only hold he had on the horse was his death-grip on the mane. At that, he might have managed to slide down or at least tumble off unscathed, had the victims of the manure fight not completed their plan to exact a measure of revenge.

Two or three grooms were following the horse at a cautious distance, blocking the alleyway behind it. Another had succeeded in running ahead, and opening the gate to an empty paddock that stood near us. The gate was between the group of visiting picnickers and the end of the alleyway between the buildings; clearly the intention was to nudge the horse quietly into the paddock, where it could trample Fergus or not as it chose, but at least would itself be safe from escape or injury.

Before this could be accomplished, though, a lithe form popped its head through a small loft window, high above the alleyway. The spectators intent on the horse, no one noticed but me. The boy in the loft observed, withdrew, and reappeared almost at once, holding a large flake of hay in both hands. Judging the moment to a nicety, he dropped it as Fergus and his mount passed directly beneath.

The effect was much like a bomb going off. There was an explosion of hay where Fergus had been, and the colt gave a panicked whinny, got its hindquarters under it, and took off like a Derby winner, heading straight for the little knot of courtiers, who scattered to the four winds, screeching like geese.

Jamie had flung himself on me, pushing me out of the way and knocking me to the ground in the process. Now he rose off my supine form, cursing fluently in Gaelic. Without pausing to inquire after my welfare, he raced off in the direction taken by Fergus.

The horse was rearing and twisting, altogether spooked, churning forelegs keeping at bay a small gang of grooms and stable-lads, all of whom were rapidly losing their professional calm at the thought of one of the King's valuable horses damaging itself before their eyes.

By some miracle of stubbornness or fear, Fergus was still in place, skinny legs flailing as he slithered and bounced on the heaving back. The grooms were all shouting at him to let go, but he ignored this advice, eyes squeezed tight shut as he clung to the two handfuls of horsehair like a lifeline. One of the grooms was carrying a pitchfork; he waved this menacingly in the air, causing a shriek of dismay from Madame Montresor, who plainly thought he meant to skewer the child.

The shriek didn't ease the colt's nerves to any marked extent. It danced and skittered, backing away from the people who were beginning to surround it. While I didn't think the groom actually intended to stab Fergus off the horse's back, there was a real danger that the child would be trampled if he fell off—and I didn't see how he was going to avoid that fate for much longer. The horse made a sudden dash for a small clump of trees that grew near the paddock, either seeking shelter from the mob, or possibly having concluded that the incubus on its back might be scraped off on a branch.

As it passed beneath the first branches, I caught a glimpse of red tartan among the greenery, and then there was a flash of red as Jamie launched himself from the shelter of a tree. His body struck the colt a glancing blow and he tumbled to the ground in a flurry of plaid and bare legs that would have revealed to a discerning observer that this particular Scotsman wasn't wearing anything under his kilt at the moment.

The party of courtiers rushed up as one, concentrating on the fallen Lord Broch Tuarach, as the grooms pursued the disappearing horse on the other side of the trees.

Jamie lay flat on his back under the beech trees, his face a dead greenish-white, both eyes and mouth wide open. Both arms were locked tight around Fergus, who clung to his chest like a leech. Jamie blinked at me as I dashed up to him, and made a faint effort at a smile. The faint wheezings from his open mouth deepened into a shallow panting, and I relaxed in relief; he'd only had his wind knocked out.

Finally realizing that he was no longer moving, Fergus raised a cautious head. Then he sat bolt upright on his employer's stomach and said enthusiastically, "That was fun, milord! Can we do it again?"

Jamie had pulled a muscle in his thigh during the rescue at Argentan, and was limping badly by the time we returned to Paris. He sent Fergus—none the worse either for the escapade or the scolding that followed it—down to the kitchen to seek his supper, and sank into a chair by the hearth, rubbing the swollen leg.

"Hurt much?" I asked sympathetically.

"A bit. All it needs is rest, though." He stood up and stretched luxuriously, long arms nearly reaching the blackened oak beams above the mantel. "Cramped in that coach; I'd've sooner ridden."

"Mmm. So would I." I rubbed the small of my back, aching with the strain of the trip. The ache seemed to press downward through my pelvis to my legs—joints loosening from pregnancy, I supposed.

I ran an exploratory hand over Jamie's leg, then gestured to the chaise.

"Come and lie on your side. I've some nice ointment I can rub your leg with; it might ease the ache a bit."

"Well, if ye dinna mind." He rose stiffly and lay down on his left side, kilt pulled above his knee.

I opened my medicine box and rummaged through the boxes and jars. Agrimony, slippery elm, pellitory-of-the-wall . . . ah, there it was. I pulled out the small blue glass jar Monsieur Forez had given me and unscrewed the lid. I sniffed cautiously; salves went rancid easily, but this one appeared to have a good proportion of salt mixed in for preservation. It had a nice mellow scent, and was a beautiful color—the rich yellow-white of fresh cream.

I scooped out a good bit of the salve and spread it down the long muscle of the thigh, pushing Jamie's kilt above his hip to keep out of the way. The flesh of his leg was warm; not the heat of infection, only the normal heat of a young male body, flushed with exercise and the glowing pulse of health. I massaged the cream gently into the skin, feeling the swell of the hard muscle, probing the divisions of quadriceps and hamstring. Jamie made a small grunting sound as I rubbed harder.

"Hurt?" I asked.

"Aye, a bit, but don't stop," he answered. "Feels as though it's doing me good." He chuckled. "I wouldna admit it to any but you, Sassenach, but it *was* fun. I havena moved like that in months."

"Glad you enjoyed yourself," I said dryly, taking another dab of cream. "I had an interesting time myself." Not pausing in the massage, I told him of Sandringham's offer.

He grunted in response, wincing slightly as I hit a tender spot. "So Colum was right, when he thought the man might be able to help with the charges against me."

"So it would seem. I suppose the question is—do you want to take him up on it?" I tried not to hold my breath, as I waited for his answer. For one thing, I knew what it would be; the Frasers as a family were renowned for stubbornness, and despite his mother's having been a MacKenzie, Jamie was a Fraser through and through. Having made up his mind to stopping Charles Stuart, he was hardly likely to abandon the effort. Still, it was tempting bait—to me, as well as to him. To be able to go back to Scotland, to his home; to live in peace.

But there was another rub, of course. If we did go back, leaving Charles's plans to run their course into the future I knew, then any peace in Scotland would be short-lived indeed.

Jamie gave a small snort, apparently having followed my own thought processes. "Well, I'll tell ye, Sassenach. If I thought that Charles Stuart might succeed—might free Scotland from English rule—then I would give my lands, my liberty, and life itself to help him. Fool he might be, but a royal fool, and not an ungallant one, I think." He sighed.

"But I know the man, and I've talked with him—and with all the Jacobites that fought with his father. And given what you tell me will happen if it comes to a Rising again . . . I dinna see that I've any choice but to stay, Sassenach.

Once he is stopped, then there may be a chance to go back—or there may not. But for now, I must decline His Grace's offer wi' thanks."

I patted his thigh gently. "That's what I thought you'd say."

He smiled at me, then glanced down at the yellowish cream that coated my fingers. "What's that stuff?"

"Something Monsieur Forez gave me. He didn't say what it's called. I don't think it's got any active ingredients, but it's a nice, greasy sort of cream."

The body under my hands stiffened and Jamie glanced over his shoulder at the blue jar.

"Monsieur Forez gave it ye?" he said uneasily.

"Yes," I answered, surprised. "What's the matter?" For he had put aside my cream-smeared hands and, swinging his legs over the side of the chaise longue, was reaching for a towel.

"Has that jar a fleur-de-lys on the lid, Sassenach?" he asked, wiping the ointment from his leg.

"Yes, it has," I said. "Jamie, what's wrong with that salve?" The look on his face was peculiar in the extreme; it kept vacillating between dismay and amusement.

"Oh, I wouldna say there's anything *wrong* about it, Sassenach," he answered finally. Having rubbed his leg hard enough to leave the curly red-gold hair bristling above reddened skin, he tossed the towel aside and looked thoughtfully at the jar.

"Monsieur Forez must think rather highly of ye, Sassenach," he said. "It's expensive stuff, that."

"But—"

"It's not that I dinna appreciate it," he assured me hastily. "It's only that havin' come within a day's length of being one of the ingredients myself, it makes me feel a bit queer."

"Jamie!" I felt my voice rising. "*What* is that stuff?" I grabbed the towel, hastily swabbing my salve-coated hands.

"Hanged-men's grease," he answered reluctantly.

"H-h-h . . ." I couldn't even get the word out, and started over. "You mean . . ." Goose bumps rippled up my arms, raising the fine hairs like pins in a cushion.

"Er, aye. Rendered fat from hanged criminals." He spoke cheerfully, regaining his composure as quickly as I was losing mine. "Verra good for the rheumatism and joint-ill, they say."

I recalled the tidy way in which Monsieur Forez had gathered up the results of his operations in L'Hôpital des Anges, and the odd look on Jamie's face when he had seen the tall *chirurgien* escort me home. My knees were watery, and I felt my stomach flip like a pancake.

"Jamie! Who in bloody fucking hell is Monsieur Forez?" I nearly screamed.

Amusement was definitely getting the upper hand in his expression.

"He's the public hangman for the Fifth Arondissement, Sassenach. I thought ye knew."

Jamie returned damp and chilled from the stableyard, where he had gone to scrub himself, the required ablutions being on a scale greater than the bedroom basin could provide.

"Don't worry, it's all off," he assured me, skinning out of his shirt and sliding naked beneath the covers. His flesh was rough and chilly with gooseflesh, and he shivered briefly as he took me in his arms.

"What is it, Sassenach? I don't still smell of it, do I?" he asked, as I huddled stiff under the bedclothes, hugging myself with my arms.

"No," I said. "I'm scared. Jamie, I'm bleeding."

"Jesus," he said softly. I could feel the sudden thrill of fear that ran through him at my words, identical to the one that ran through me. He held me close to him, smoothing my hair and stroking my back, but both of us felt the awful helplessness in the face of physical disaster that made his actions futile. Strong as he was, he couldn't protect me; willing he might be, but he couldn't help. For the first time, I wasn't safe in his arms, and the knowledge terrified both of us.

"D'ye think—" he began, then broke off and swallowed. I could feel the tremor run down his throat and hear the gulp as he swallowed his fear. "Is it bad, Sassenach? Can ye tell?"

"No," I said. I held him tighter, trying to find an anchorage. "I don't know. It isn't heavy bleeding; not yet, anyway."

The candle was still alight. He looked down at me, eyes dark with worry.

"Had I better fetch someone to ye, Claire? A healer, one of the women from the Hôpital?"

I shook my head and licked dry lips.

"No. I don't . . . I don't think there's anything they could do." It was the last thing I wanted to say; more than anything, I wanted there to be someone we could find who knew how to make it all right. But I remembered my early nurse's training, the few days I had spent on the obstetrical ward, and the words of one of the doctors, shrugging as he left the bed of a patient who'd had a miscarriage. "There's really nothing you can do," he'd said. "If they're going to lose a child, they generally do, no matter what you try. Bed rest is really the only thing, and even that often won't do it."

"It may be nothing," I said, trying to hearten both of us. "It isn't unusual for women to have slight bleeding sometimes during pregnancy." It wasn't unusual—during the first three months. I was more than five months along, and this was by no means usual. Still, there were many things that could cause bleeding, and not all of them were serious.

"It may be all right," I said. I laid a hand on my stomach, pressing gently.

I felt an immediate response from the occupant, a lazy, stretching push that at once made me feel better. I felt a rush of passionate gratitude that made tears come to my eyes.

"Sassenach, what can I do?" Jamie whispered. His hand came around me and lay over mine, cupping my threatened abdomen.

I put my other hand on top of his, and held on.

"Just pray," I said. "Pray for us, Jamie."

23

The Best-laid Plans of Mice and Men . . .

The bleeding had stopped by the morning. I rose very cautiously, but all remained well. Still, it was obvious that the time had come for me to stop working at L'Hôpital des Anges, and I sent Fergus with a note of explanation and apology to Mother Hildegarde. He returned with her prayers and good wishes, and a bottle of a brownish elixir much esteemed—according to the accompanying note—by *les maîtresses sage-femme* for the prevention of miscarriage. After Monsieur Forez's salve, I was more than a little dubious about using any medication I hadn't prepared myself, but a careful sniff reassured me that at least the ingredients were purely botanical.

After considerable hesitation, I drank a spoonful. The liquid was bitter and left a nasty taste in my mouth, but the simple act of doing something—even something I thought likely to be useless—made me feel better. I spent the greater part of each day now lying on the chaise longue in my room, reading, dozing, sewing, or simply staring into space with my hands over my belly.

When I was alone, that is. When he was home, Jamie spent most of his time with me, talking over the day's business, or discussing the most recent Jacobite letters. King James had apparently been told of his son's proposed investment in port wine, and approved it wholeheartedly as ". . . a very sounde scheme, which I cannot but feel will go a great way in providing for you as I should wish to see you established in France."

"So James thinks the money's intended merely to establish Charles as a gentleman, and give him some position here," I said. "Do you think that could be all he has in mind? Louise was here this afternoon; she says Charles came to see her last week—insisted on seeing her, though she refused to receive him at first. She says he was very excited and puffed up about something, but he wouldn't tell her what; just kept hinting mysteriously about something great he was about to do. 'A great adventure' is what she says he said. That doesn't sound like a simple investment in port, does it?"

"It doesn't." Jamie looked grim at the thought.

"Hm," I said. "Well, all things taken together, it seems a good bet that Charles isn't meaning just to settle down upon the profits of his venture and become an upstanding Paris merchant."

"If I were a wagering man, I'd lay my last garter on it," Jamie said. "The question now is, how do we stop him?"

The answer came several days later, after any amount of discussion and useless suggestions. Murtagh was with us in my bedroom, having brought up several bolts of cloth from the docks for me.

"They say there's been an outbreak of pox in Portugal," he observed, dumping the expensive watered silk on the bed as though it were a load of used burlap. "There was a ship carrying iron from Lisbon came in this morning, and the harbor master was over it with a toothcomb, him and three assistants. Found naught, though." Spotting the brandy bottle on my table, he poured a tumbler half-full and drank it like water, in large, healthy swallows. I watched this performance openmouthed, pulled from the spectacle only by Jamie's exclamation.

"Pox?"

"Aye," said Murtagh, pausing between swallows. "Smallpox." He lifted the glass again and resumed his systematic refreshment.

"Pox," Jamie muttered to himself. "Pox."

Slowly, the frown left his face and the vertical crease between his eyebrows disappeared. A deeply contemplative look came over him, and he lay back in his chair, hands linked behind his neck, staring fixedly at Murtagh. The hint of a smile twitched his wide mouth sideways.

Murtagh observed this process with considerable skeptical resignation. He drained his cup and sat stolidly hunched on his stool as Jamie sprang to his feet and began circling the little clansman, whistling tunelessly through his teeth.

"I take it you have an idea?" I said.

"Oh, aye," he said, and began to laugh softly to himself. "Oh, aye, that I have."

He turned to me, eyes alight with mischief and inspiration.

"Have ye anything in your box of medicines that would make a man feverish? Or give him flux? Or spots?"

"Well, yes," I said slowly, thinking. "There's rosemary. Or cayenne. And cascara, of course, for diarrhea. Why?"

He looked at Murtagh, grinning widely, then, overcome with his idea, cackled and ruffled his kinsman's hair, so it stuck up in black spikes. Murtagh glared at him, exhibiting a strong resemblance to Louise's pet monkey.

"Listen," Jamie said, bending toward us conspiratorially. "What if the Comte St. Germain's ship comes back from Portugal wi' pox aboard?"

I stared at him. "Have you lost your mind?" I inquired politely. "What if it did?"

"If it did," Murtagh interrupted, "they'd lose the cargo. It would be burnt or dumped in the harbor, by law." A gleam of interest showed in the small black eyes. "And how d'ye mean to manage that, lad?"

Jamie's exhilaration dropped slightly, though the light in his eyes remained.

"Well," he admitted, "I havena got it thought out all the way as yet, but for a start . . ."

The plan took several days of discussion and research to refine, but was at last settled. Cascara to cause flux had been rejected as being too debilitating in action. However, I'd found some good substitutes in one of the herbals Master Raymond had lent me.

Murtagh, armed with a pouch full of rosemary essence, nettle juice, and madder root, would set out at the end of the week for Lisbon, where he would gossip among the sailors' taverns, find out the ship chartered by the Comte St. Germain, and arrange to take passage on it, meanwhile sending back word of the ship's name and sailing date to Paris.

"No, that's common," said Jamie, in answer to my question as to whether the captain might not find this behavior fishy. "Almost all cargo ships carry a few passengers; however many they can squeeze between decks. And Murtagh will have enough money to make him a welcome addition, even if they have to give him the captain's cabin." He wagged an admonitory finger at Murtagh.

"And get a cabin, d'ye hear? I don't care what it costs; ye'll need privacy for taking the herbs, and we dinna want the chance of someone seeing ye, if you've naught but a hammock slung in the bilges." He surveyed his godfather with a critical eye. "Have ye a decent coat? If you go aboard looking like a beggar, they're like to hurl ye off into the harbor before they find out what ye've got in your sporran."

"Mmphm," said Murtagh. The little clansman usually contributed little to the discussion, but what he did say was cogent and to the point. "And when do I take the stuff?" he asked.

I pulled out the sheet of paper on which I had written the instructions and dosages.

"Two spoonfuls of the rose madder—that's this one"—I tapped the small clear-glass bottle, filled with a dark pinkish fluid—"to be taken four hours before you plan to demonstrate your symptoms. Take another spoonful every two hours after the first dose—we don't know how long you'll have to keep it up."

I handed him the second bottle, this one of green glass filled with a purplish-black liquor. "This is concentrated essence of rosemary leaves. This one acts faster. Drink about one-quarter of the bottle half an hour before you mean to show yourself; you should start flushing within half an hour. It wears off quickly, so you'll need to take more when you can manage inconspicuously." I took another, smaller vial from my medicine box. "And once you're well advanced with the 'fever,' then you can rub the nettle juice on your arms and face, to raise blisters. Do you want to keep these instructions?"

He shook his head decidedly. "Nay, I'll remember. There's more risk to being found wi' the paper than there is to forgetting how much to take." He turned to Jamie.

"And you'll meet the ship at Orvieto, lad?"

Jamie nodded. "Aye. She's bound to make port there; all the wine haulers do, to take on fresh water. If by chance she doesna do so, then—" He shrugged. "I shall hire a boat and try to catch her up. So long as I board her before we reach Le Havre, it should be all right, but best if we can do it while we're still close off the coast of Spain. I dinna mean to spend longer at sea than I must." He pointed with his chin at the bottle in Murtagh's hand.

"Ye'd best wait to take the stuff 'til ye see me come on board. With no witnesses, the captain might take the easy way out and just put ye astern in the night."

Murtagh grunted. "Aye, he might try." He touched the hilt of his dirk, and there was the faintest ironic emphasis on the word "try."

Jamie frowned at him. "Dinna forget yourself. You're meant to be suffering from the pox. With luck, they'll be afraid to touch ye, but just in case . . . wait 'til I'm within call and we're well offshore."

"Mmphm."

I looked from one to the other of the two men. Farfetched as it was, it might conceivably work. If the captain of the ship could be convinced that one of his passengers was infected with smallpox, he would under no circumstances take his ship into the harbor at Le Havre, where the French health restrictions would require its destruction. And, faced with the necessity of sailing back with his cargo to Lisbon and losing all profit on the voyage, or losing two weeks at Orvieto while word was sent to Paris, he might very well instead consent to sell the cargo to the wealthy Scottish merchant who had just come aboard.

The impersonation of a smallpox victim was the crucial role in this masquerade. Jamie had volunteered to be the guinea pig for testing the herbs, and they had worked magnificently on him. His fair skin had flushed dark red within minutes, and the nettle juice raised immediate blisters that could easily be mistaken for those of pox by a ship's doctor or a panicked captain. And should any doubt remain, the madder-stained urine gave an absolutely perfect illusion of a man pissing blood as the smallpox attacked his kidneys.

"Christ!" Jamie had exclaimed, startled despite himself at the first demonstration of the herb's efficacy.

"Oh, jolly good!" I said, peering over his shoulder at the white porcelain chamber pot and its crimson contents. "That's better than I expected."

"Oh, aye? How long does it take to wear off, then?" Jamie had asked, looking down rather nervously.

"A few hours, I think," I told him. "Why? Does it feel odd?"

"Not odd, exactly," he said, rubbing. "It itches a bit."

"That's no the herb," Murtagh interjected dourly. "It's just the natural condition for a lad of your age."

Jamie grinned at his godfather. "Remember back that far, do ye?"

"Farther back than you were born or thought of, laddie," Murtagh had said, shaking his head.

The little clansman now stowed the vials in his sporran, methodically wrapping each one in a bit of soft leather to prevent breakage.

"I'll send word of the ship and her sailing so soon as I may. And I'll see ye within the month off Spain. You'll have the money before then?"

Jamie nodded. "Oh, aye. By next week, I imagine." Jared's business had prospered under Jamie's stewardship, but the cash reserves were not sufficient to purchase entire shiploads of port, while still fulfilling the other commitments of the House of Fraser. The chess games had borne fruit in more than one regard, though, and Monsieur Duverney the younger, a prominent banker, had willingly guaranteed a sizable loan for his father's friend.

"It's a pity we can't bring the stuff into Paris," Jamie had remarked during the planning, "but St. Germain would be sure to find out. I expect we'll do best to sell it through a broker in Spain—I know a good man in Bilbao. The profit will be much smaller than it would be in France, and the taxes are higher, but ye canna have everything, can ye?"

"I'll settle for paying back Duverney's loan," I said. "And speaking of loans, what's Signore Manzetti going to do about the money he's loaned Charles Stuart?"

"Whistle for it, I expect," said Jamie cheerfully. "And ruin the Stuarts' reputation with every banker on the Continent while he's about it."

"Seems a bit hard on poor old Manzetti," I observed.

"Aye well. Ye canna make an omelet wi'out breakin' eggs, as my auld grannie says."

"You haven't got an auld grannie," I pointed out.

"No," he admitted, "but if I had, that's what she'd say." He had dropped the playfulness then, momentarily. "It's no verra fair to the Stuarts, forbye. In fact, should any of the Jacobite lords come to know what I've been doing, I expect they'd call it treason, and they'd be right." He rubbed a hand over his brow, and shook his head, and I saw the deadly seriousness that his playfulness covered.

"It canna be helped, Sassenach. If you're right—and I've staked my life so far on it—then it's a choice between the aspirations of Charles Stuart and the lives of a hell of a lot of Scotsmen. I've no love for King Geordie—me, wi' a price on my head?—but I dinna see that I can do otherwise."

He frowned, running a hand through his hair, as he always did when thinking or upset. "If there were a chance of Charles succeeding . . . aye, well, that might be different. To take a risk in an honorable cause—but your history says he willna succeed, and I must say, all I know of the man makes it seem likely that you're right. They're my folk and my family at stake, and if the cost of their lives is a banker's gold . . . well, it doesna seem more a sacrifice than that of my own honor."

He shrugged in half-humorous despair. "So now I've gone from stealing His Highness's mail to bank robbery and piracy on the high seas, and it seems there's nay help for it."

He was silent for a moment, looking down at his hands, clenched together on the desk. Then he turned his head to me and smiled.

"I always wanted to be a pirate, when I was a bairn," he said. "Pity I canna wear a cutlass."

I lay in bed, head and shoulders propped on pillows, hands clasped lightly over my stomach, thinking. Since the first alarm, there had been very little bleeding, and I felt well. Still, any sort of bleeding at this stage was cause for alarm. I wondered privately what would happen if any emergency arose while Jamie was gone to Spain, but there was little to be gained by worrying. He had to go; there was too much riding on that particular shipload of wine for any private concerns to intrude. And if everything went all right, he should be back well before the baby was due.

As it was, all personal concerns would have to be put aside, danger or no. Charles, unable to contain his own excitement, had confided to Jamie that he would shortly require two ships—possibly more—and had asked his advice on hull design and the mounting of deck cannon. His father's most recent letters from Rome had betrayed a slight tone of questioning—with his acute Bourbon nose for politics, James Stuart smelled a rat, but plainly hadn't yet been informed of what his son was up to. Jamie, hip-deep in decoded letters, thought it likely that Philip of Spain had not yet mentioned Charles's overtures or the Pope's interest, but James Stuart had his spies, as well.

After a little while, I became aware of some slight change in Jamie's attitude. Glancing toward him, I saw that while he was still holding a book open on his knee, he had ceased to turn the pages—or to look at them, for that matter. His eyes were fixed on me instead; or, to be specific, on the spot where my nightrobe parted, several inches lower than strict modesty might dictate, strict modesty hardly seeming necessary in bed with one's husband.

His gaze was abstracted, dark blue with longing, and I realized that if not socially required, modesty in bed with one's husband might be at least considerate, under the circumstances. There were alternatives, of course.

Catching me looking at him, Jamie blushed slightly and hastily returned to an exaggerated interest in his book. I rolled onto my side and rested a hand on his thigh.

"Interesting book?" I asked, idly caressing him.

"Mphm. Oh, aye." The blush deepened, but he didn't take his eyes from the page.

Grinning to myself, I slipped my hand under the bedclothes. He dropped the book.

"Sassenach!" he said. "Ye know you canna . . ."

"No," I said, "but you can. Or rather, I can for you."

He firmly detached my hand and gave it back to me.

"No, Sassenach. It wouldna be right."

"It wouldn't?" I said, surprised. "Whyever not?"

He squirmed uncomfortably, avoiding my eyes.

"Well, I . . . I wouldna feel right, Sassenach. To take my pleasure from ye, and not be able to give ye . . . well, I wouldna feel right about it, is all."

I burst into laughter, laying my head on his thigh.

"Jamie, you are too sweet for words!"

"I am not sweet," he said indignantly. "But I'm no such a selfish—Claire, stop that!"

"You were planning to wait several more months?" I asked, not stopping.

"I could," he said, with what dignity was possible under the circumstances. "I waited tw-twenty-two years, and I can . . ."

"No, you can't," I said, pulling back the bedclothes and admiring the shape so clearly visible beneath his nightshirt. I touched it, and it moved slightly, eager against my hand. "Whatever God meant you to be, Jamie Fraser, it wasn't a monk."

With a sure hand, I pulled up his nightshirt.

"But . . ." he began.

"Two against one," I said, leaning down. "You lose."

———

Jamie worked hard for the next few days, readying the wine business to look after itself during his absence. Still, he found time to come up and sit with me for a short time after lunch most days, and so it was that he was with me when a visitor was announced. Visitors were not uncommon; Louise came every other day or so, to chatter about pregnancy or to moan over her lost love —though I privately thought she enjoyed Charles a great deal more as the object of noble renunciation than she did as a present lover. She had promised to bring me some Turkish sweetmeats, and I rather expected her plump pink face to peek through the door.

To my surprise, though, the visitor was Monsieur Forez. Magnus himself showed him into my sitting room, taking his hat and cloak with an almost superstitious reverence.

Jamie looked surprised at this visitation, but rose to his feet to greet the hangman politely and offer him refreshment.

"As a general rule, I take no spirits," Monsieur Forez said with a smile.

"But I would not insult the hospitality of my esteemed colleague." He bowed ceremoniously in the direction of the chaise where I reclined. "You are well, I trust, Madame Fraser?"

"Yes," I said cautiously. "Thank you." I wondered to what we owed the honor of the visit. For while Monsieur Forez enjoyed considerable prestige and a fair amount of wealth in return for his official duties, I didn't think his job got him many dinner invitations. I wondered suddenly whether hangmen had any social life to speak of.

He crossed the room and laid a small package on the chaise beside me, rather like a fatherly vulture bringing home dinner for his chicks. Keeping in mind the hanged-men's grease, I picked the package up gingerly and weighed it in my hand; light for its size, and smelling faintly astringent.

"A small remembrance from Mother Hildegarde," he explained. "I understand it is a favorite remedy of *les maîtresses sage-femme*. She has written directions for its use, as well." He withdrew a folded, sealed note from his inner pocket and handed it over.

I sniffed the package. Raspberry leaves and saxifrage; something else I didn't recognize. I hoped Mother Hildegarde had included a list of the ingredients as well.

"Please thank Mother Hildegarde for me," I said. "And how is everyone at the Hôpital?" I greatly missed my work there, as well as the nuns and the odd assortment of medical practitioners. We gossiped for some time about the Hôpital and its personnel, with Jamie contributing the occasional comment, but usually just listening with a polite smile, or—when the subject turned to the clinical—burying his nose in his glass of wine.

"What a pity," I said regretfully, as Monsieur Forez finished his description of the repair of a crushed shoulder blade. "I've never seen that done. I do miss the surgical work."

"Yes, I will miss it as well," Monsieur Forez nodded, taking a small sip from his wineglass. It was still more than half-full; apparently he hadn't been joking about his abstention from spirits.

"You're leaving Paris?" Jamie said in some surprise.

Monsieur Forez shrugged, the folds of his long coat rustling like feathers.

"Only for a time," he said. "Still, I will be gone for at least two months. In fact, Madame," he bowed his head toward me again, "that is the main reason for my visit today."

"It is?"

"Yes. I am going to England, you understand, and it occurred to me that if you wished it, Madame, it would be a matter of the greatest simplicity for me to carry any message that you desired. Should there be anyone with whom you wished to communicate, that is," he added, with his usual precision.

I glanced at Jamie, whose face had suddenly altered, from an open expression of polite interest to that pleasantly smiling mask that hid all thoughts. A stranger wouldn't have noticed the difference, but I did.

"No," I said hesitantly. "I have no friends or relatives in England; I'm afraid I have no connections there at all, since I was—widowed." I felt the usual small stab at this reference to Frank, but suppressed it.

If this seemed odd to Monsieur Forez, he didn't show it. He merely nodded, and set down his half-drunk glass of wine.

"I see. It is fortunate indeed that you have friends here, then." His voice seemed to hold a warning of some kind, but he didn't look at me as he bent to straighten his stocking before rising. "I shall call upon you on my return, then, and hope to find you again in good health."

"What is the business that takes you to England, Monsieur?" Jamie said bluntly.

Monsieur Forez turned to him with a faint smile. He cocked his head, eyes bright, and I was struck once more by his resemblance to a large bird. Not a carrion crow at the moment, though, but a raptor, a bird of prey.

"And what business should a man of my profession travel on, Monsieur Fraser?" he asked. "I have been hired to perform my usual duties, at Smithfield."

"An important occasion, I take it," said Jamie. "To justify the summoning of a man of your skill, I mean." His eyes were watchful, though his expression showed nothing beyond polite inquiry.

Monsieur Forez's eyes grew brighter. He rose slowly to his feet, looking down at Jamie where he sat near the window.

"That is true, Monsieur Fraser," he said softly. "For it is a matter of skill, make no mistake. To choke a man to death at the end of a rope—pah! Anyone can do that. To break a neck cleanly, with one quick fall, that requires some calculation in terms of weight and drop, and a certain amount of practice in the placing of the rope, as well. But to walk the line between these methods, to properly execute the sentence of a traitor's death; that requires great skill indeed."

My mouth felt suddenly dry, and I reached for my own glass. "A traitor's death?" I said, feeling as though I really didn't want to hear the answer.

"Hanging, drawing, and quartering," Jamie said briefly. "That's what you mean, of course, Monsieur Forez?"

The hangman nodded. Jamie rose to his feet, as though against his will, facing the gaunt, black-clad visitor. They were much of a height, and could look each other in the face without difficulty. Monsieur Forez took a step toward Jamie, expression suddenly abstracted, as though he were about to make a demonstration of some medical point.

"Oh, yes," he said. "Yes, that is the traitor's death. First, the man must be hanged, as you say, but with a nice judgment, so that the neck is not broken, nor the windpipe crushed—suffocation is not the desired result, you understand."

"Oh, I understand." Jamie's voice was soft, with an almost mocking edge, and I glanced at him in bewilderment.

"Do you, Monsieur?" Monsieur Forez smiled faintly, but went on without waiting for an answer. "It is a matter of timing then; you judge by the eyes. The face will darken with blood almost immediately—more quickly if the subject is of fair complexion—and as choking proceeds, the tongue is forced from the mouth. That is what delights the crowds, of course, as well as the popping eyes. But you watch for the signs of redness at the corners of the eyes, as the small blood vessels burst. When that happens, you must give at once the signal for the subject to be cut down—a dependable assistant is indispensable, you understand," he half-turned, to include me in this macabre conversation, and I nodded, despite myself.

"Then," he continued, turning back to Jamie, "you must administer at once a stimulant, to revive the subject while the shirt is being removed—you must insist that a shirt opening down the front is provided; often it is difficult to get them off over the head." One long, slender finger reached out, pointing at the middle button of Jamie's shirt, but not quite touching the fresh-starched linen.

"I would suppose so," Jamie said.

Monsieur Forez retracted the finger, nodding in approval at this evidence of comprehension.

"Just so. The assistant will have kindled the fire beforehand; this is beneath the dignity of the executioner. And then the time of the knife is at hand."

There was a dead silence in the room. Jamie's face was still set in inscrutability, but a slight moisture gleamed on the side of his neck.

"It is here that the utmost of skill is required," Monsieur Forez explained, raising a finger in admonition. "You must work quickly, lest the subject expire before you have finished. Mixing a dose with the stimulant which constricts the blood vessels will give you a few moments' grace, but not much."

Spotting a silver letter-opener on the table, he crossed to it and picked it up. He held it with his hand wrapped about the hilt, forefinger braced on top of the blade, pointed down at the shining walnut of the tabletop.

"Just there," he said, almost dreamily. "At the base of the breastbone. And quickly, to the crest of the groin. You can see the bone easily in most cases. Again"—and the letter opener flashed to one side and then the other, quick and delicate as the zigzag flight of a hummingbird—"following the arch of the ribs. You must not cut deeply, for you do not wish to puncture the sac which encloses the entrails. Still, you must get through skin, fat, and muscle, and do it with one stroke. This," he said with satisfaction, gazing down at his own reflection in the tabletop, "is artistry."

He laid the knife gently on the table, and turned back to Jamie. He shrugged pleasantly.

"After that, it is a matter of speed and some dexterity, but if you have been exact in your methods, it will present little difficulty. The entrails are sealed within a membrane, you see, resembling a bag. If you have not severed this by accident, it is a simple matter, needing only a little strength, to force your hands beneath the muscular layer and pull free the entire mass. A quick cut at stomach and anus"—he glanced disparagingly at the letter opener—"and then the entrails may be thrown upon the fire."

"Now"—he raised an admonitory finger—"if you have been swift and delicate in your work, there is now a moment's leisure, for mark you, as yet no large vessels will have been severed."

I felt quite faint, although I was sitting down, and I was sure that my face was as white as Jamie's. Pale as he was, Jamie smiled, as though humoring a guest in conversation.

"So the . . . subject . . . can live a bit longer?"

"*Mais oui,* Monsieur." The hangman's bright black eyes swept over Jamie's powerful frame, taking in the width of shoulder and the muscular legs. "The effects of such shock are unpredictable, but I have seen a strong man live for more than a quarter of an hour in this state."

"I imagine it seems a lot longer to the subject," Jamie said dryly.

Monsieur Forez appeared not to hear this, picking up the letter opener again and flourishing it as he spoke.

"As death approaches, then, you must reach up into the cavity of the body to grasp the heart. Here skill is called upon again. The heart retracts, you see, without the downward anchorage of the viscera, and often it is surprisingly far up. In addition, it is most slippery." He wiped one hand on the skirt of his coat in pantomime. "But the major difficulty lies in severing the large vessels above very quickly, so that the organ may be pulled forth while still beating. You wish to please the crowd," he explained. "It makes a great difference to the remuneration. As to the rest—" He shrugged a lean, disdainful shoulder. "Mere butchery. Once life is extinct, there is no further need of skill."

"No, I suppose not," I said faintly.

"But you are pale, Madame! I have detained you far too long in tedious conversation!" he exclaimed. He reached for my hand, and I resisted the very strong urge to yank it back. His own hand was cool, but the warmth of his lips as he brushed his mouth lightly across my hand was so unexpected that I tightened my own grasp in surprise. He gave my hand a slight, invisible squeeze, and turned to bow formally to Jamie.

"I must take my leave, Monsieur Fraser. I shall hope to meet you and your charming wife again . . . under such pleasant circumstances as we have enjoyed today." The eyes of the two men met for a second. Then Monsieur Forez appeared to recall the letter opener he was still holding in one hand. With an exclamation of surprise, he held it out on his open palm. Jamie arched one brow, and picked the knife up delicately by the point.

"*Bon voyage,* Monsieur Forez," he said. "And I thank you"—his mouth twisted wryly—"for your most instructive visit."

He insisted upon seeing our visitor to the door himself. Left alone, I got up and went to the window, where I stood practicing deep-breathing exercises until the dark-blue carriage disappeared around the corner of the Rue Gamboge.

The door opened behind me, and Jamie stepped in. He still held the letter opener. He crossed deliberately to the large famille rose jar that stood by the hearth and dropped the paper knife into it with a clang, then turned to me, doing his best to smile.

"Well, as warnings go," he said, "that one was verra effective."

I shuddered briefly.

"Wasn't it, though?"

"Who do you think sent him?" Jamie asked. "Mother Hildegarde?"

"I expect so. She warned me, when we decoded the music. She said what you were doing was dangerous." The fact of just *how* dangerous had been lost upon me, until the hangman's visit. I hadn't suffered from morning nausea for some time, but I felt my gorge rising now. *If the Jacobite lords knew what I was doing, they'd call it treason.* And what steps might they take, if they did find out?

To all outward intents, Jamie was an avowed Jacobite supporter; in that guise, he visited Charles, entertained the Earl Marischal to dinner, and attended court. And so far, he had been skillful enough, in his chess games, his tavern visits, and his drinking parties, to undercut the Stuart cause while seeming outwardly to support it. Besides the two of us, only Murtagh knew that we sought to thwart a Stuart rising—and even he didn't know why, merely accepting his chief's word that it was right. That pretense was necessary, while operating in France. But the same pretense would brand Jamie a traitor, should he ever set foot on English soil.

I had known that, of course, but in my ignorance, had thought that there was little difference between being hanged as an outlaw, and executed as a traitor. Monsieur Forez's visit had taken care of *that* bit of naiveté.

"You're bloody calm about it," I said. My own heart was still thumping erratically, and my palms were cold, but sweaty. I wiped them on my gown, and tucked them between my knees to warm them.

Jamie shrugged slightly and gave me a lopsided smile.

"Well, there's the hell of a lot of unpleasant ways to die, Sassenach. And if one of them should fall to my lot, I wouldna like it much. But the question is: Am I scairt enough of the possibility that I would stop what I'm doing to avoid it?" He sat down on the chaise beside me, and took one of my hands between his own. His palms were warm, and the solid bulk of him next to me was reassuring.

"I thought that over for some time, Sassenach, in those weeks at the Abbey while I healed. And again, when we came to Paris. And again, when I met Charles Stuart." He shook his head, bent over our linked hands.

"Aye, I can see myself standing on a scaffold. I saw the gallows at Wentworth—did I tell ye that?"

"No. No, you didn't."

He nodded, eyes gone blank in remembrance.

"They marched us down to the courtyard; those of us in the condemned cell. And made us stand in rows on the stones, to watch an execution. They hanged six men that day, men I knew. I watched each man mount the steps—twelve steps, there were—and stand, hands bound behind his back, looking down at the yard as they put the rope around his neck. And I wondered then, how I would manage come my turn to mount those steps. Would I weep and pray, like John Sutter, or could I stand straight like Willie MacLeod, and smile at a friend in the yard below?"

He shook his head suddenly, like a dog flinging off drops of water, and smiled at me a little grimly. "Anyway, Monsieur Forez didna tell me anything I hadna thought of before. But it's too late, *mo duinne*." He laid a hand over mine. "Aye, I'm afraid. But if I would not turn back for the chance of home and freedom, I shallna do it for fear. No, *mo duinne*. It's too late."

24

The Bois de Boulogne

onsieur Forez's visit proved merely to be the first of a series of unusual disruptions.

"There is an Italian person downstairs, Madame," Magnus informed me. "He would not give me his name." There was a pinched look about the butler's mouth; I gathered that if the visitor would not give his name, he had been more than willing to give the butler a number of other words.

That, coupled with the "Italian person" designation, was enough to give me a clue as to the visitor's identity, and it was with relatively little surprise that I entered the drawing room to find Charles Stuart standing by the window.

He swung about at my entrance, hat in his hands. He was plainly surprised to see *me;* his mouth dropped open for a second, then he caught himself and gave me a quick, brief bow of acknowledgment.

"Milord Broch Tuarach is not at home?" he inquired. His brows drew together in displeasure.

"No, he isn't," I said. "Will you take a little refreshment, Your Highness?"

He looked around the richly appointed drawing-room with interest, but shook his head. So far as I knew, he had been in the house only once before, when he had come over the rooftops from his rendezvous with Louise. Neither he nor Jamie had thought it appropriate for him to be invited to the dinners here; without official recognition by Louis, the French nobility scorned him.

"No. I thank you, Madame Fraser. I shall not stay; my servant waits outside, and it is a long ride to return to my lodgings. I wished only to make a request of my friend James."

"Er . . . well, I'm sure that my husband would be happy to oblige Your Highness—if he can," I answered cautiously, wondering just what the request was. A loan, probably; Fergus's gleanings of late had included quite a number of impatient letters from tailors, bootmakers, and other creditors.

Charles smiled, his expression altering to one of surprising sweetness.

"I know; I cannot tell you, Madame, how greatly I esteem the devotion and service of your husband; the sight of his loyal face warms my heart amid the loneliness of my present surroundings."

"Oh?" I said.

"It is not a difficult thing I ask," he assured me. "It is only that I have made a small investment; a cargo of bottled port."

"Really?" I said. "How interesting." Murtagh had left for Lisbon that morning, vials of nettle juice and madder root in his pouch.

"It is a small thing," Charles flipped a lordly hand, disdaining the investment of every cent he had been able to borrow. "But I wish that my friend James shall accomplish the task of disposing of the cargo, once it shall arrive. It is not appropriate, you know"—and here he straightened his shoulders and elevated his nose just a trifle, quite unconsciously—"for a—a person such as myself, to be seen to engage in trade."

"Yes, I quite see, Your Highness," I said, biting my lip. I wondered whether he had expressed this point of view to his business partner, St. Germain—who undoubtedly regarded the young pretender to the Scottish throne as a person of less consequence than any of the French nobles—who engaged in "trade" with both hands, whenever the chance of profit offered.

"Is Your Highness quite alone in this enterprise?" I inquired innocently.

He frowned slightly. "No, I have a partner; but he is a Frenchman. I should much prefer to entrust the proceeds of my venture to the hands of a countryman. Besides," he added thoughtfully, "I have heard that my dear James is a most astute and capable merchant; it is possible that he might be able to increase the value of my investment by means of judicious sale."

I supposed whoever had told him of Jamie's capability hadn't bothered to add the information that there was probably no wine merchant in Paris whom St. Germain more disliked. Still, if everything worked out as planned, that shouldn't matter. And if it didn't, it was possible that St. Germain would solve all of our problems by strangling Charles Stuart, once he found out that the latter had contracted delivery of half his exclusive Gostos port to his most hated rival.

"I'm sure that my husband will do his utmost to dispose of Your Highness's merchandise to the maximum benefit of all concerned," I said, with complete truth.

His Highness thanked me graciously, as befitting a prince accepting the service of a loyal subject. He bowed, kissed my hand with great formality, and departed with continuing protestations of gratitude to Jamie. Magnus, looking dourly unimpressed by the Royal visit, closed the door upon him.

In the event, Jamie didn't come home until after I had fallen asleep, but I told him over breakfast of Charles's visit, and his request.

"God, I wonder if His Highness will tell the Comte?" he said. Having ensured the health of his bowels by disposing of his parritch in short order, he proceeded to add a French breakfast of buttered rolls and steaming chocolate on top of it. A broad grin spread across his face in contemplation of the Comte's reaction, as he sipped his cocoa.

"I wonder is it *lèse-majesté* to hammer an exiled prince? For if it's not, I hope His Highness has Sheridan or Balhaldy close by when St. Germain hears about it."

Further speculation along these lines was curtailed by the sudden sound of voices in the hallway. A moment later, Magnus appeared in the door, a note borne on his silver tray.

"Your pardon, milord," he said, bowing. "The messenger who brought this desired most urgently that it be brought to your attention at once."

Brows raised, Jamie took the note from the tray, opened and read it.

"Oh, bloody hell!" he said in disgust.

"What is it?" I asked. "Not word from Murtagh already?"

He shook his head. "No. It's from the foreman of the warehouse."

"Trouble at the docks?"

An odd mixture of emotions was visible on Jamie's face; impatience struggling with amusement.

"Well, not precisely. The man's got himself into a coil at a brothel, it seems. He humbly begs my pardon"—he waved ironically at the note—"but hopes I'll see fit to come round and assist him. In other words," he translated, crumpling his napkin as he rose, "will I pay his bill?"

"Will you?" I said, amused.

He snorted briefly and dusted crumbs from his lap.

"I suppose I'll have to, unless I want to supervise the warehouse myself—and I havena time for that." His brow creased as he mentally reviewed the duties of the day. This was a task that might take some little time, and there were orders waiting on his desk, ship's captains waiting on the docks, and casks waiting in the warehouse.

"I'd best take Fergus wi' me to carry messages," he said, resigned. "He can maybe go to Montmartre wi' a letter, if I'm too short of time."

"Kind hearts are more than coronets," I told Jamie as he stood by his desk, ruefully flipping through the impressive pile of waiting paperwork.

"Oh, aye?" he said. "And whose opinion is that?"

"Alfred, Lord Tennyson, I think," I said. "I don't believe he's come along yet, but he's a poet. Uncle Lamb had a book of famous British poets. There was a bit from Burns in there, too, I recall—he's a Scot," I explained. "He said, 'Freedom and Whisky gang teither.' "

Jamie snorted. "I canna say if he's a poet, but he's a Scot, at least." He smiled then, and bent to kiss me on the forehead. "I'll be home to my supper, *mo duinne*. Keep ye well."

I finished my own breakfast, and thriftily polished off Jamie's toast as well, then waddled upstairs for my morning nap. I had had small episodes of bleeding since the first alarm, though no more than a spot or two, and nothing at all for several weeks. Still, I kept to my bed or the chaise as much as possible, only venturing down to the salon to receive visitors, or to the dining room for meals with Jamie. When I descended for lunch, though, I found the table laid for one.

"Milord has not come back yet?" I asked in some surprise. The elderly butler shook his head.

"No, milady."

"Well, I imagine he'll be back soon; make sure there's food waiting for him when he arrives." I was too hungry to wait for Jamie; the nausea tended to return if I went too long without eating.

After lunch, I lay down to rest again. Conjugal relations being temporarily in abeyance, there wasn't that much one could do in bed, other than read or sleep, which meant I did quite a lot of both. Sleeping on my stomach was impossible, sleeping on my back uncomfortable, as it tended to make the baby squirm. Consequently, I lay on my side, curling around my growing abdomen like a cocktail shrimp round a caper. I seldom slept deeply, but tended rather to doze, letting my mind drift to the gentle random movements of the child.

Somewhere in my dreams, I thought I felt Jamie near me, but when I opened my eyes the room was empty, and I closed them again, lulled as though I, too, floated weightless in a blood-warm sea.

I was wakened at length, somewhere in the late afternoon, by a soft tap on the bedroom door.

"*Entrez,*" I said, blinking as I came awake. It was the butler, Magnus, apologetically announcing more visitors.

"It is the Princesse de Rohan, Madame," he said. "The Princesse wished to wait until you awakened, but when Madame d'Arbanville also arrived, I thought perhaps . . ."

"That's all right, Magnus," I said, struggling upright and swinging my feet over the side of the bed. "I'll come down."

I looked forward to the visitors. We had stopped entertaining during the last month, and I rather missed the bustle and conversation, silly as much of it was. Louise came frequently to sit with me and regale me with the latest doings of the Court, but I hadn't seen Marie d'Arbanville in some time. I wondered what brought her here today.

I was ungainly enough to take the stairs slowly, my increased weight jarring upward from the soles of my feet on each step. The paneled door of the drawing room was closed, but I heard the voice inside clearly.

"Do you think she *knows?*"

The question, asked in the lowered tones that portended the juiciest of gossip, reached me just as I was about to enter the drawing room. Instead, I paused at the threshold, just out of sight.

It was Marie d'Arbanville who had spoken. Welcome everywhere because of her elderly husband's position, and gregarious even by French standards, Marie heard everything worth hearing within the environs of Paris.

"Does she know what?" The reply was Louise's; her high, carrying voice had the perfect self-confidence of the born aristocrat, who doesn't care who hears what.

"Oh, you haven't heard!" Marie pounced on the opening like a kitten, delighted to find a new mouse to play with. "Goodness! Of course, I only heard myself an hour ago."

And raced directly over here to tell me about it, I thought. Whatever "it" was. I thought I stood a better chance of hearing the unexpurgated version from my position in the hallway.

"It is my lord Broch Tuarach," Marie said, and I didn't need to see her, to imagine her leaning forward, green eyes darting back and forth, snapping with enjoyment of her news. "Only this morning, he challenged an Englishman to a duel—over a whore!"

"What!" Louise's cry of astonishment drowned out my own gasp. I grabbed hold of a small table and held on, black spots whirling before my eyes as the world came apart at the seams.

"Oh, yes!" Marie was saying. "Jacques Vincennes was there; he told my husband all about it! It was in that brothel down near the fish market—imagine going to a brothel at that hour of the morning! Men are so odd. Anyway, Jacques was having a drink with Madame Elise, who runs the place, when all of a sudden there was the most frightful outcry upstairs, and all kinds of thumping and shouting."

She paused for breath—and dramatic effect—and I heard the sound of liquid being poured.

"So, Jacques of course raced to the stairs—well, that's what he *says,* anyway; I expect he actually hid behind the sofa, he's such a coward—and after more shouting and thumping, there was a terrible crash, and an English officer came hurtling down the stairs, half-undressed, with his wig off, staggering and smashing into the walls. And who should appear at the top of the stairs, looking like the vengeance of God, but our own *petit* James!"

"No! And I would have sworn he was the last . . . but go on! What happened then?"

A teacup chimed softly against its saucer, followed by Marie's voice, released by excitement from the modulations of secrecy.

"Well—the man reached the foot of the stairs still on his feet, by some miracle, and he turned at once, and looked up at Lord Tuarach. Jacques says the man was very self-possessed, for someone who'd just been kicked downstairs with his breeches undone. He smiled—not a real smile, you know, the nasty sort—and said, 'There's no need for violence, Fraser; you could have waited for your turn, surely? I should have thought you get enough at home. But then, some men derive pleasure from paying for it.' "

Louise made shocked noises. "How awful! The *canaille*! But of course, it is no reproach to milord Tuarach—" I could hear the strain in her voice as friendship warred with the urge to gossip. Not surprisingly, gossip won.

"Milord Tuarach cannot enjoy his wife's favors at the moment; she carries a child, and the pregnancy is dangerous. So of course he would relieve his needs at a brothel; what gentleman would do otherwise? But go on, Marie! What happened then?"

"Well." Marie drew breath as she approached the high point of the story. "Milord Tuarach rushed down the stairs, seized the Englishman by the throat, and shook him like a rat!"

"Non! Ce n'est pas vrai!"

"Oh, yes! It took three of Madame's servants to restrain him—such a wonderful big man, isn't he? So fierce-looking!"

"Yes, but then what?"

"Oh—well, Jacques said the Englishman gasped for a bit, then straightened up and said to milord Tuarach, 'That's twice you've come near killing me, Fraser. Someday you may succeed.' And then milord Tuarach cursed in that terrible Scottish tongue—I don't understand a word, do you?—and then he wrenched himself free from the men holding him, struck the Englishman across the face with his bare hand"—Louise gasped at the insult—"and said, 'Tomorrow's dawn will see you dead!' Then he turned about and ran up the stairs, and the Englishman left. John said he looked quite white—and no wonder! Just imagine!"

I imagined, all right.

"Are you well, Madame?" Magnus's anxious voice drowned out Louise's further exclamations. I put out a hand, groping, and he took it at once, putting his other hand under my elbow in support.

"No. I'm not well. Please . . . tell the ladies?" I waved weakly toward the drawing room.

"Of course, Madame. In a moment; but now let me see you to your chamber. This way, *chère Madame* . . ." He led me up the stairs, murmuring consolingly as he supported me. He escorted me to the bedroom chaise, where he left me, promising to send up a maid at once to attend me.

I didn't wait for assistance; the first shock passing, I could navigate well enough, and I stood and made my way across the room to where my small medicine box sat on the dressing table. I didn't think I was going to faint now, but there was a bottle of spirits of ammonia in there that I wanted handy, just in case.

I turned back the lid and stood still, staring into the box. For a moment, my mind refused to register what my eyes saw; the folded white square of paper, carefully wedged upright between the multicolored bottles. I noted rather abstractedly that my fingers shook as I took the paper out; it took several tries to unfold it.

I am sorry. The words were bold and black, the letters carefully formed in the center of the sheet, the single letter "J" written with equal care below. And below that, two more words, these scrawled hastily, done as a postscript of desperation: *I must!*

"You must," I murmured to myself, and then my knees buckled. Lying on the floor, with the carved panels of the ceiling flickering dimly above, I found myself thinking that I had always heretofore assumed that the tendency of eighteenth-century ladies to swoon was due to tight stays; now I rather thought it might be due to the idiocy of eighteenth-century men.

There was a cry of dismay from somewhere nearby, and then helpful hands were lifting me, and I felt the yielding softness of the wool-stuffed mattress under me, and cool cloths on my brow and wrists, smelling of vinegar.

I was soon restored to what senses I had, but strongly disinclined to talk. I reassured the maids that I was in fact all right, shooed them out of the room, and lay back on the pillows, trying to think.

It was Jack Randall, of course, and Jamie had gone to kill him. That was the only clear thought in the morass of whirling horror and speculation that filled my mind. Why, though? What could have made him break the promise he had made me?

Trying to consider carefully the events Marie had related—third-hand as they were—I thought there had to have been something more than just the shock of an unexpected encounter. I knew the Captain, knew him a great deal better than I wanted to. And if there was one thing of which I was reasonably sure, it was that he would not have been purchasing the usual services of a brothel—the simple enjoyment of a woman was not in his nature. What he enjoyed—needed—was pain, fear, humiliation.

These commodities, of course, could also be purchased, if at a somewhat higher price. I had seen enough, in my work at L'Hôpital des Anges, to know that there were *les putains* whose chief stock in trade lay not between their legs, but in strong bones overlaid with expensive fragile skin that bruised at once, and showed the marks of whips and blows.

And if Jamie, his own fair skin scarred with the marks of Randall's favor, had come upon the Captain, enjoying himself in similar fashion with one of the ladies of the establishment— That, I thought, could have carried him past any thought of promises or restraint. There was a small mark on his left breast, just below the nipple; a tiny whitish pucker, where he had cut from his skin the branded mark of Jonathan Randall's heated signet ring. The rage that had led him to suffer mutilation rather than bear that shameful mark could easily break forth again, to destroy its inflictor—and his hapless progeny.

"Frank," I said, and my left hand curled involuntarily over the shimmer of my gold wedding ring. "Oh, dear God. Frank." For Jamie, Frank was no more than a ghost, the dim possibility of a refuge for me, in the unlikely event of necessity. For me, Frank was the man I had lived with, had shared my bed and body with—had abandoned, at the last, to stay with Jamie Fraser.

"I can't," I whispered, to the empty air, to the small companion who stretched and twisted lazily within me, undisturbed by my own distress. "I can't let him do it!"

The afternoon light had faded into the gray shades of dusk, and the room seemed filled with all the despair of the world's ending. *Tomorrow's dawn will see you dead.* There was no hope of finding Jamie tonight. I knew he would not return to the Rue Tremoulins; he wouldn't have left that note if he were coming back. He could never lie beside me through the night, knowing what he intended doing in the morning. No, he had undoubtedly sought refuge in some inn or tavern, there to ready himself in solitude for the execution of justice that he had sworn.

I thought I knew where the place of execution would be. With the memory of his first duel strong in his mind, Jamie had shorn his hair in preparation. The memory would have come to him again, I was sure, when choosing a spot to meet his enemy. The Bois de Boulogne, near the path of the Seven Saints. The Bois was a popular place for illicit duels, its dense growth sheltering the participants from detection. Tomorrow, one of its shady clearings would see the meeting of Jamie Fraser and Jack Randall. And me.

I lay on the bed, not bothering to undress or cover myself, hands clasped across my belly. I watched the twilight fade to black, and knew I would not sleep tonight. I took what comfort I could in the small movements of my unseen inhabitant, with the echo of Jamie's words ringing in my ears: *Tomorrow's dawn will see you dead.*

The Bois de Boulogne was a small patch of almost-virgin forest, perched incongruously on the edge of Paris. It was said that wolves as well as foxes and badgers were still to be found lurking in its depths, but this story did nothing to discourage the amorous couples that dallied under the branches on the grassy earth of the forest. It was an escape from the noise and dirt of the city, and only its location kept it from becoming a playground for the nobility. As it was, it was patronized largely by those who lived nearby, who found a moment's respite in the shade of the large oaks and pale birches of the Bois, and by those from farther away who sought privacy.

It was a small wood, but still too large to quarter on foot, looking for a clearing large enough to hold a pair of duelists. It had begun to rain during the night, and the dawn had come reluctantly, glowing sullen through a cloud-dark sky. The forest whispered to itself, the faint patter of rain on the leaves blending with the subdued rustle and rub of leaf and branches.

The carriage pulled to a stop on the road that led through the Bois, near the last small cluster of ramshackle buildings. I had told the coachman what to do; he swung down from his seat, tethered the horses, and disappeared among the buildings. The folk who lived near the Bois knew what went on there.

There could not be that many spots suitable for dueling; those there were would be known.

I sat back and pulled the heavy cloak tighter around me, shivering in the cold of the early dawn. I felt terrible, with the fatigue of a sleepless night dragging at me, and the leaden weight of fear and grief resting in the pit of my stomach. Overlying everything was a seething anger that I tried to push away, lest it interfere with the job at hand.

It kept creeping back, though, bubbling up whenever my guard was down, as it was now. How could he do this? my mind kept muttering, in a cold fury. I shouldn't be here; I should be home, resting quietly by Jamie's side. I shouldn't have to be pursuing him, preventing him, fighting both anger and illness. A nagging pain from the coach ride knotted at the base of my spine. Yes, he might well be upset; I could understand that. But it was a man's *life* at stake, for God's sake. How could his bloody pride be more important than that? And to leave me, with no word of explanation! To leave me to find out from the gossip of neighbors what had happened.

"You promised me, Jamie, damn you, you *promised* me!" I whispered, under my breath. The wood was quiet, dripping and mist-shrouded. Were they here already? Would they be here? Was I wrong in my guess about the place?

The coachman reappeared, accompanied by a young lad, perhaps fourteen, who hopped nimbly up on the seat beside the coachman, and waved his hand, gesturing ahead and to the left. With a brief crack of the whip and a click of the tongue, the coachman urged the horses into a slow trot, and we turned down the road into the shadows of the wakening wood.

We stopped twice, pausing while the lad hopped down and darted into the undergrowth, each time reappearing within a moment or two, shaking his head in negation. The third time, he came tearing back, the excitement on his face so evident that I had the carriage door open before he got near enough to call out to the coachman.

I had money ready in my hand; I thrust it at him, simultaneously clutching at his sleeve, saying, "Show me where! Quickly, quickly!"

I scarcely noticed either the clutching branches that laced across the path, nor the sudden wetness that soaked my clothing as I brushed them. The path was soft with fallen leaves, and neither my shoes nor those of my guide made any sound as I followed the shadow of his ragged, damp-spotted shirt.

I heard them before I saw them; they had started. The clash of metal was muffled by the wet shrubbery, but clear enough, nonetheless. No birds sang in the wet dawn, but the deadly voice of battle rang in my ears.

It was a large clearing, deep in the Bois, but accessible by path and road. Large enough to accommodate the footwork needed for a serious duel. They were stripped to their shirts, fighting in the rain, the wet fabric clinging, showing the outline of shoulder and backbone.

Jamie had said he was the better fighter; he might be, but Jonathan Randall was no mean swordsman, either. He wove and dodged, lithe as a snake, sword striking like a silver fang. Jamie was just as fast, amazing grace in such a tall man, light-footed and sure-handed. I watched, rooted to the ground, afraid to cry out for fear of distracting Jamie's attention. They spun in a tight circle of stroke and parry, feet touching lightly as a dance on the turf.

I stood stock-still, watching. I had come through the fading night to find this, to stop them. And having found them, now I could not intervene, for fear of causing a fatal interruption. All I could do was wait, to see which of my men would die.

Randall had his blade up and in place to deflect the stroke, but not quickly enough to brace it against the savagery that sent his sword flying.

I opened my mouth to scream. I had meant to call Jamie's name, to stop him now, in that moment's grace between the disarming of his opponent and the killing stroke that must come next. I did scream, in fact, but the sound emerged weak and strangled. As I had stood there, watching, the nagging pain in my back had deepened, clenching like a fist. Now I felt a sudden breaking somewhere, as though the fist had torn loose what it held.

I groped wildly, clutching at a nearby branch. I saw Jamie's face, set in a sort of calm exultance, and realized that he could hear nothing through the haze of violence that enveloped him. He would see nothing but his goal, until the fight was ended. Randall, retreating before the inexorable blade, slipped on the wet grass and went down. He arched his back, attempting to rise, but the grass was slippery. The fabric of his stock was torn, and his head was thrown back, dark hair rain-soaked, throat exposed like that of a wolf begging mercy. But vengeance knows no mercy, and it was not the exposed throat that the descending blade sought.

Through a blackening mist, I saw Jamie's sword come down, graceful and deadly, cold as death. The point touched the waist of the doeskin breeches, pierced and cut down in a twisting wrench that darkened the fawn with a sudden flood of black-red blood.

The blood was a hot rush down my thighs, and the chill of my skin moved inward, toward the bone. The bone where my pelvis joined my back was breaking; I could feel the strain as each pain came on, a stroke of lightning flashing down my backbone to explode and flame in the basin of my hips, a stroke of destruction, leaving burnt and blackened fields behind.

My body as well as my senses seemed to fragment. I saw nothing, but could not tell whether my eyes were open or closed; everything was spinning dark, patched now and then with the shifting patterns you see at night as a child, when you press your fists against shut eyelids.

The raindrops beat on my face, on my throat and shoulders. Each heavy drop struck cold, then dissolved into a tiny warm stream, coursing across my chilled skin. The sensation was quite distinct, apart from the wrenching agony that advanced and retreated, lower down. I tried to focus my mind on that, to force my attention from the small, detached voice in the center of my brain, the one saying, as though making notes on a clinical record: "You're having a hemorrhage, of course. Probably a ruptured placenta, judging from the amount of blood. Generally fatal. The loss of blood accounts for the numbness in hands and feet, and the darkened vision. They say that the sense of hearing is the last to go; that seems to be true."

Whether it were the last of my senses to be left to me or not, hearing I still had. And it was voices I heard, most agitated, some striving for calmness, all speaking in French. There was one word I could hear and understand—my own name, shouted over and over, but at a distance. "Claire! Claire!"

"Jamie," I tried to say, but my lips were stiff and numb with cold. Movement of any kind was beyond me. The commotion near me was settling to a steadier level; someone had arrived who was at least willing to act as though they knew what to do.

Perhaps they did. The soaked wad of my skirt was lifted gently from between my thighs, and a thick pad of cloth thrust firmly into place instead. Helpful hands turned me onto my left side, and drew my knees up toward my chest.

"Take her to the Hôpital," suggested one voice near my ear.

"She won't live that long," said another, pessimistically. "Might as well wait a few minutes, then send for the meat wagon."

"No," insisted another. "The bleeding is slowing; she may live. Besides, I know her; I've seen her at L'Hôpital des Anges. Take her to Mother Hildegarde."

I summoned all the strength I had left, and managed to whisper, "Mother." Then I gave up the struggle, and let the darkness take me.

25

Raymond the Heretic

The high, vaulted ceiling over me was supported by ogives, those four-teenth-century architectural features in which four ribs rise from the tops of pillars, to join in double crossing arches.

My bed was set under one of these, gauze curtains drawn around me for privacy. The central point of the ogive was not directly above me, though; my bed had been placed a few feet off-center. This bothered me whenever I glanced upward; I kept wanting to move the bed by force of will, as though being centered beneath the roof would help to center me within myself.

If I had a center any longer. My body felt bruised and tender, as though I had been beaten. My joints ached and felt loose, like teeth undermined by scurvy. Several thick blankets covered me, but they could do no more than trap heat, and I had none to save. The chill of the rainy dawn had settled in my bones.

All these physical symptoms I noted objectively, as though they belonged to someone else; otherwise I felt nothing. The small, cold, logical center of my brain was still there, but the envelope of feeling through which its utterances were usually filtered was gone; dead, or paralyzed, or simply no longer there. I neither knew nor cared. I had been in L'Hôpital des Anges for five days.

Mother Hildegarde's long fingers probed in relentless gentleness through the cotton of the bedgown I wore, probing the depths of my belly, seeking the hard edges of a contracting uterus. The flesh was soft as ripe fruit, though, and tender beneath her fingers. I winced as her fingers sank deep, and she frowned, muttering something under her breath that might have been a prayer.

I caught a name in the murmurings, and asked, "Raymond? You know Master Raymond?" I could think of few less likely pairings than this redoubt-able nun and the little gnome of the cavern of skulls.

Mother Hildegarde's thick brows shot up, astonished.

"Master Raymond, you say? That heretical charlatan? *Que Dieu nous en garde!*" May God protect us.

"Oh. I thought I heard you say 'Raymond.'"

"Ah." The fingers had returned to their work, probing the crease of my groin in search of the lumps of enlarged lymph nodes that would signal infec-tion. They were there, I knew; I had felt them myself, moving my hands in restless misery over my empty body. I could feel the fever, an ache and a chill deep in my bones, that would burst into flame when it reached the surface of my skin.

"I was invoking the aid of St. Raymond Nonnatus," Mother Hildegarde explained, wringing out a cloth in cold water. "He is an aid most invaluable in the assistance of expectant mothers."

"Of which I am no longer one." I noticed remotely the brief stab of pain that creased her brows; it disappeared almost at once as she busied herself in mopping my brow, smoothing the cold water briskly over the rounds of my cheeks and down into the hot, damp creases of my neck.

I shivered suddenly at the touch of the cold water, and she stopped at once, laying a considering hand on my forehead.

"St. Raymond is not one to be picky," she said, absently reproving. "I myself take help where it can be found; a course I would recommend to you."

"Mmm." I shut my eyes, retreating into the haven of gray fog. Now there seemed to be faint lights in the fog, brief cracklings like the scatter of sheet lightning on a summer horizon.

I heard the clicking of jet rosary beads as Mother Hildegarde straightened up, and the soft voice of one of the sisters in the doorway, summoning her to another in the day's string of emergencies. She had almost reached the door when a thought struck her. She turned with a swish of heavy skirts, pointing at the foot of my bed with an authoritative finger.

"Bouton!" she said. *"Au pied, reste!"*

The dog, as unhesitating as his mistress, whirled smartly in mid-step and leaped to the foot of the bed. Once there, he took a moment to knead the bedclothes with his paws and turn three times widdershins, as though taking the curse off his resting place, before lying down at my feet, resting his nose on his paws with a deep sigh.

Satisfied, Mother Hildegarde murmured, *"Que Dieu vous bénisse, mon enfant,"* in farewell, and disappeared.

Through the gathering fog and the icy numbness that wrapped me, I dimly appreciated her gesture. With no child to lay in my arms, she had given me her own best substitute.

The shaggy weight on my feet was in fact a small bodily comfort. Bouton lay still as the dogs beneath the feet of the kings carved on the lids of their tombs at St. Denis, his warmth denying the marble chill of my feet, his presence an improvement on either solitude or the company of humans, as he required nothing of me. Nothing was precisely what I felt, and all I had to give.

Bouton emitted a small, popping dog-fart and settled into sleep. I drew the covers over my nose and tried to do likewise.

I slept, eventually. And I dreamed. Fever dreams of weariness and desolation, of an impossible task done endlessly. Unceasing painful effort, carried out in a stony, barren place. Of thick gray fog, through which loss pursued me like a demon in the mist.

I woke, quite suddenly, to find that Bouton was gone, but I was not alone.

Raymond's hairline was completely level, a flat line drawn across the wide brow as though with a rule. He wore his thick, graying hair swept back and hanging straight to the shoulder, so the massive forehead protruded like a block of stone, completely overshadowing the rest of his face. It hovered over me now, looking to my fevered eyes like the slab of a tombstone.

The lines and furrows moved slightly as he spoke to the sisters, and I thought they seemed like letters, written just below the surface of the stone, trying to burrow their way to the surface so that the name of the dead could be read. I was convinced that in another moment, my name would be legible on that white slab, and at that moment, I would truly die. I arched my back and screamed.

"Now, see there! She doesn't want you, you disgusting old creature—you're disturbing her rest. Come away at once!" Mother Hildegarde clutched Raymond imperatively by the arm, tugging him away from the bed. He resisted, standing rooted like a stone gnome in a lawn, but Sister Celeste added her not inconsiderable efforts to Mother Hildegarde's, and they lifted him clean off his feet and bore him away between them, the clog dropping from one frantically kicking foot as they went.

The clog lay where it had fallen, on its side, square in the center of a scrubbed flagstone. With the intense fixation of fever, I was unable to take my eyes off it. I traced the impossibly smooth curve of the worn edge over and over, each time pulling back my gaze from the impenetrable darkness of the inside. If I let myself enter that blackness, my soul would be sucked out into chaos. As my eyes rested on it, I could hear again the sounds of the time passage through the circle of stones, and I flung out my arms, clutching frantically at the wadded bedding, seeking some anchorage against confusion.

Suddenly an arm shot through the draperies, and a work-reddened hand snatched up the shoe and disappeared. Deprived of focus, my heat-addled mind spun round the grooves of the flags for a time, then, soothed by the geometric regularity, turned inward and wobbled into sleep like a dying top.

There was no stillness in my dreams, though, and I stumbled wearily through mazes of repeating figures, endless loopings and whorls. It was with a sense of profound relief that I saw at last the irregularities of a human face.

And an irregular face it was, to be sure, screwed up as it was in a ferocious frown, lips pursed in adjuration. It was only as I felt the pressure of the hand over my mouth that I realized I was no longer asleep.

The long, lipless mouth of the gargoyle hovered next to my ear.

"Be still, *ma chère*! If they find me here again, I'm done for!" The large, dark eyes darted from side to side, keeping watch for any movement of the drapes.

I nodded slowly, and he released my mouth, his fingers leaving a faint whiff of ammonium and sulfur behind. He had somewhere found—or stolen, I thought dimly—a ragged gray friar's gown to cover the grimy velvet of his apothecary's robe, and the depths of the hood concealed both the telltale silver hair and that monstrous forehead.

The fevered delusions receded slightly, displaced by what remnants of curiosity remained to me. I was too weak to say more than "What . . ." when he placed a finger once more across my lips, and threw back the sheet covering me.

I watched in some bemusement as he rapidly unknotted the strings of my shift and opened the garment to the waist. His movements were swift and businesslike, completely lacking in lechery. Not that I could imagine anyone capable of trying to ravish a fever-wracked carcass like mine, particularly not within hearing of Mother Hildegarde. But still . . .

I watched with remote fascination as he placed his cupped hands on my breasts. They were broad and almost square, the fingers all of a length, with unusually long and supple thumbs that curved around my breasts with amazing delicacy. Watching them, I had an unusually vivid memory of Marian Jenkinson, a girl with whom I had trained at Pembroke Hospital, telling the rapt inmates of the nurses' quarters that the size and shape of a man's thumbs were a sure indication of the quality of his more intimate appendage.

"And it's true, I swear it," Marian would declare, shaking back her blond hair dramatically. But when pressed for examples, she would only giggle and dimple, rolling her eyes toward Lieutenant Hanley, who strongly resembled a gorilla, opposable—and sizable—thumbs notwithstanding.

The large thumbs were pressing gently but firmly into my flesh, and I could feel my swollen nipples rising against the hard palms, cold by comparison with my own heated skin.

"Jamie," I said, and a shiver passed over me.

"Hush, madonna," said Raymond. His voice was low, kind but somehow abstracted, as though he were paying no attention to me, in spite of what he was doing.

The shiver came back; it was as though the heat passed from me to him, but his hands did not warm. His fingers stayed cool, and I chilled and shook as the fever ebbed and flowed, draining from my bones.

The afternoon light was dim through the thick gauze of the drapes around my bed, and Raymond's hands were dark on the white flesh of my breasts. The shadows between the thick, grimy fingers were not black, though. They were . . . blue, I thought.

I closed my eyes, looking at the particolored swirl of patterns that immediately appeared behind my lids. When I opened them again, it was as though something of the color remained behind, coating Raymond's hands.

As the fever ebbed, leaving my mind clearer, I blinked, trying to raise my head for a better look. Raymond pressed slightly harder, urging me to lie back, and I let my head fall on the pillow, peering slantwise over my chest.

I wasn't imagining it after all—or was I? While Raymond's hands weren't moving themselves, a faint flicker of colored light seemed to move over them, shedding a glow of rose and a pallor of blue across my own white skin.

My breasts were warming now, but warming with the natural heat of health, not the gnawing burn of fever. The draft from the open archway outside found a way through the drapes and lifted the damp hair at my temples, but I wasn't chilled now.

Raymond's head was bent, face hidden by the cowl of his borrowed robe. After what seemed a long time, he moved his hands from my breasts, very slowly over my arms, pausing and squeezing gently at the joints of shoulder and elbow, wrists and fingers. The soreness eased, and I thought I could see briefly a faint blue line within my upper arm, the glowing ghost of the bone.

Always touching, never hurrying, he brought his hands back over the shallow curve of my collarbone and down the meridian of my body, splaying his palms across my ribs.

The oddest thing about all this was that I was not at all astonished. It seemed an infinitely natural thing, and my tortured body relaxed gratefully into the hard mold of his hands, melting and reforming like molded wax. Only the lines of my skeleton held firm.

An odd feeling of warmth now emanated from those broad, square, work-man's hands. They moved with painstaking slowness over my body, and I could *feel* the tiny deaths of the bacteria that inhabited my blood, small explosions as each scintilla of infection disappeared. I could feel each interior organ, com-plete and three-dimensional, and see it as well, as though it sat on a table before me. There the hollow-walled stomach, here the lobed solidness of my liver, and each convolution and twist of intestine, turned in and on and around itself, neatly packed in the shining web of its mesentery membrane. The warmth glowed and spread within each organ, illuminating it like a small sun within me, then died and moved on.

Raymond paused, hands pressed side by side on my swollen belly. I thought he frowned, but it was hard to tell. The cowled head turned, listening, but the usual noises of the hospital continued in the distance, with no warning heeltaps coming our way.

I gasped and moved involuntarily, as one hand moved lower, cupped briefly between my legs. An increase in pressure from the other hand warned me to be silent, and the blunt fingers eased their way inside me.

I closed my eyes and waited, feeling my inner walls adjust to this odd intrusion, the inflammation subsiding bit by bit as he probed gently deeper.

Now he touched the center of my loss, and a spasm of pain contracted the heavy walls of my inflamed uterus. I breathed a small moan, then clamped my lips as he shook his head.

The other hand slid down to rest comfortingly on my belly as the groping fingers of the other touched my womb. He was still then, holding the source of my pain between his two hands as though it were a sphere of crystal, heavy and fragile.

"Now," he said softly. "Call him. Call the red man. Call him."

The pressure of the fingers within and the palm without grew harder, and I pressed my legs against the the bed, fighting it. But there was no strength left in me to resist, and the inexorable pressure went on, cracking the crystal sphere, freeing the chaos within.

My mind filled with images, worse than the misery of the fever-dreams, because more real. Grief and loss and fear racked me, and the dusty scent of death and white chalk filled my nostrils. Casting about in the random patterns of my mind for help, I heard the voice still muttering, patiently but firmly, "Call him," and I sought my anchor.

"Jamie! JAMIE!"

A bolt of heat shot through my belly, from one hand to the other, like an arrow through the center of the basin of my bones. The pressing grip relaxed, slid free, and the lightness of harmony filled me.

The bedframe quivered as he ducked beneath it, barely in time.

"Milady! Are you all right?" Sister Angelique shoved through the drapes, round face creased with worry beneath her wimple. The concern in her eyes was underlaid with resignation; the sisters knew I would die soon—if this looked to be my last struggle, she was prepared to summon the priest.

Her small, hard hand rested briefly against my cheek, moved quickly to my brow, then back. The sheet still lay crumpled around my thighs, and my gown lay open. Her hands slid inside it, into my armpits, where they remained for a moment before withdrawing.

"God be praised!" she cried, eyes moistening. "The fever is gone!" She bent close, peering in sudden alarm, to be sure that the disappearance of the fever was not due to the fact that I was dead. I smiled at her weakly.

"I'm all right," I said. "Tell Mother."

She nodded eagerly, and pausing only long enough to draw the sheet modestly over me, she hurried from the room. The drapes had hardly swung closed behind her when Raymond emerged from under the bed.

"I must go," he said. He laid a hand upon my head. "Be well, madonna."

Weak as I was, I rose up, grasping his arm. I slid my hand up the length of forge-tough muscle, seeking, but not finding. The smoothness of his skin was unblemished, clear to the crest of the shoulder. He stared down at me in astonishment.

"What are you doing, madonna?"

"Nothing." I sank back, disappointed. I was too weak and too light-headed to be careful of my words.

"I wanted to see whether you had a vaccination scar."

"Vaccination?" Skilled as I was at reading faces by now, I would have seen the slightest twitch of comprehension, no matter how swiftly it was concealed. But there was none.

"Why do you call me madonna still?" I asked. My hands rested on the slight concavity of my stomach, gently as though not to disturb the shattering emptiness. "I've lost my child."

He looked mildly surprised.

"Ah. I did not call you madonna because you were with child, my lady."

"Why, then?" I didn't really expect him to answer, but he did. Tired and drained as we both were, it was as though we were suspended together in a place where neither time nor consequence existed; there was room for nothing but truth between us.

He sighed.

"Everyone has a color about them," he said simply. "All around them, like a cloud. Yours is blue, madonna. Like the Virgin's cloak. Like my own."

The gauze curtain fluttered briefly and he was gone.

26

Fontainebleau

For several days, I slept. Whether this was a necessary part of physical recovery, or a stubborn retreat from waking reality, I do not know, but I woke only reluctantly to take a little food, falling at once back into a stupor of oblivion, as though the small, warm weight of broth in my stomach were an anchor that pulled me after it, down through the murky fathoms of sleep.

A few days later I woke to the sound of insistent voices near my ear, and the touch of hands lifting me from the bed. The arms that held me were strong and masculine, and for a moment, I felt afloat in joy. Then I woke all the way, struggling feebly against a wave of tobacco and cheap wine, to find myself in the grasp of Hugo, Louise de La Tour's enormous footman.

"Put me down!" I said, batting at him weakly. He looked startled at this sudden resurrection from the dead, and nearly dropped me, but a high, commanding voice stopped both of us.

"Claire, my dear friend! Do not be afraid, *ma chère,* it's all right. I am taking you to Fontainebleau. The air, and good food—it's what you need. And rest, you need rest . . ."

I blinked against the light like a newborn lamb. Louise's face, round, pink, and anxious, floated nearby like a cherub on a cloud. Mother Hildegarde stood behind her, tall and stern as the angel at the gates of Eden, the heavenly illusion enhanced by the fact that they were both standing in front of the stained-glass window in the vestibule of the Hôpital.

"Yes," she said, her deep voice making the simplest word more emphatic than all Louise's twittering. "It will be good for you. *Au revoir,* my dear."

And with that, I was borne down the steps of the Hôpital and stuffed willy-nilly into Louise's coach, with neither strength nor will to protest.

The bumping of the coach over potholes and ruts kept me awake on the journey to Fontainebleau. That, and Louise's constant conversation, aimed at reassurance. At first I made some dazed attempt to respond, but soon realized that she required no answers, and in fact, talked more easily without them.

After days in the cool gray stone vault of the Hôpital, I felt like a freshly unwrapped mummy, and shrank from the assault of so much brightness and color. I found it easier to deal with if I drew back a bit, and let it all wash past me without trying to distinguish its elements.

This strategy worked until we reached a small wood just outside Fontaine-bleau. The trunks of the oaks were dark and thick, with low, spreading canopies that shadowed the ground beneath with shifting light, so that the whole wood seemed to be moving slightly in the wind. I was vaguely admiring the effect, when I noticed that some of what I had assumed to be tree trunks *were* in fact moving, turning very slowly to and fro.

"Louise!" My exclamation and my grip on her arm stopped her chatter in mid-word.

She lunged heavily across me to see what I was looking at, then flopped back to her side of the carriage and thrust her head out of the window, shouting at the coachman.

We came to a slithering, dusty halt just opposite the wood. There were three of them, two men and a woman. Louise's high, agitated voice went on, expostulating and questioning, punctuated by the coachman's attempts to explain or apologize, but I paid no attention.

In spite of their turning and the small fluttering of their clothing, they were very still, more inert than the trees that held them. The faces were black with suffocation; Monsieur Forez wouldn't have approved at all, I thought, through the haze of shock. An amateur execution, but effective, for all that. The wind shifted, and a faint, gassy stink blew over us.

Louise shrieked and pounded on the window frame in a frenzy of indignation, and the carriage started with a jerk that rocked her back in the seat.

"Merde!" she said, rapidly fanning her flushed face. "The idiocy of that fool, stopping like that right there! What recklessness! The shock of it is bad for the baby, I am sure, and you, my poor dear. . . . oh, dear, my poor Claire! I'm so sorry, I didn't mean to remind you . . . how can you forgive me, I'm so tactless . . ."

Luckily her agitation at possibly having upset me made her forget her own upset at sight of the bodies, but it was very wearying, trying to stem her apologies. At last, in desperation, I changed the subject back to the hanged ones.

"Who?" The distraction worked; she blinked, and remembering the shock to her *système*, pulled out a bottle of ammoniac spirits and took a hearty sniff that made her sneeze in reflex.

"Hugue . . . choo! Huguenots," she got out, snorting and wheezing. "Protestant heretics. That's what the coachman says."

"They hang them? Still?" Somehow, I had thought such religious persecution a relic of earlier times.

"Well, not just for being Protestants usually, though that's enough," Louise said, sniffing. She dabbed her nose delicately with an embroidered handkerchief, examined the results critically, then reapplied the cloth to her nose and blew it with a satisfying honk.

"Ah, that's better." She tucked the handkerchief back in her pocket and leaned back with a sigh. "Now I am restored. What a shock! If they have to hang them, that's all well, but must they do so by a public thoroughfare, where ladies must be exposed to such disgustingness? Did you *smell* them? Pheew! This is the Comte Medard's land; I'll send him a very nasty letter about it, see if I don't."

"But why did they hang these people?" I asked, interrupting in the brutal manner that was the only possible way of actually conversing with Louise.

"Oh, witchcraft, most likely. There was a woman, you saw. Usually it's witchcraft when the women are involved. If it's only men, most often it's just preaching sedition and heresy, but the women don't preach. Did you see the ugly dark clothes she had on? Horrible! So depressing only to wear dark colors all the time; what kind of religion would make its followers wear such plain clothes all the time? Obviously the Devil's work, anyone can see that. They are afraid of women, that's what it is, so they . . ."

I closed my eyes and leaned back in the seat. I hoped it wasn't very far to Louise's country house.

In addition to the monkey, from whom she would not be parted, Louise's country house contained a number of other decorations of dubious taste. In Paris, her husband's taste and her father's must be consulted, and the rooms of the house there were consequently done richly, but in subdued tones. But Jules seldom came to the country house, being too busy in the city, and so Louise's taste was allowed free rein.

"This is my newest toy; is it not lovely?" she cooed, running her hand lovingly over the carved dark wood of a tiny house that sprouted incongruously from the wall next to a gilt-bronze sconce in the shape of Eurydice.

"That looks like a cuckoo clock," I said disbelievingly.

"You have seen one before? I didn't think there were any to be found anywhere in Paris!" Louise pouted slightly at the thought that her toy might not be unique, but brightened as she twisted the hands of the clock to the next hour. She stood back, beaming proudly as the tiny clockwork bird stuck its head out and emitted several shrill *Cuckoo!*s in succession.

"Isn't it precious?" She touched the bird's head briefly as it disappeared back into its hidey-hole. "Berta, the housekeeper here, got it for me; her brother brought it all the way from Switzerland. Whatever you want to say about the Swiss, they are clever woodcarvers, no?"

I wanted to say no, but instead merely murmured something tactfully admiring.

Louise's grasshopper mind leaped nimbly to a new topic, possibly triggered by thoughts of Swiss servants.

"You know, Claire," she said, with a touch of reproof, "you ought really to come to Mass in the chapel each morning."

"Why?"

She tossed her head in the direction of the doorway, where one of the maids was passing with a tray.

"I don't care at all, myself, but the servants—they're very superstitious out here in the countryside, you know. And one of the footmen from the Paris house was foolish enough to tell the cook all about that silly story of your being La Dame Blanche. I have told them that's all nonsense, of course, and threatened to dismiss anyone I catch spreading such gossip, but . . . well, it might help if you came to Mass. Or at least prayed out loud now and then, so they could hear you."

Unbeliever that I was, I thought daily Mass in the house's chapel might be going a bit far, but with vague amusement, agreed to do what I could to allay the servants' fears; consequently, Louise and I spent the next hour reading psalms aloud to each other, and reciting the Lord's Prayer in unison—loudly. I had no idea what effect this performance might have on the servants, but it did at least exhaust me sufficiently that I went up to my room for a nap, and slept without dreaming until the next morning.

I often had difficulty sleeping, possibly because my waking state was little different from an uneasy doze. I lay awake at night, gazing at the white-gesso ceiling with its furbishes of fruit and flowers. It hung above me like a dim gray shape in the darkness, the personification of the depression that clouded my mind by day. When I did close my eyes at night, I dreamed. I couldn't block the dreams with grayness; they came in vivid colors to assault me in the dark. And so I seldom slept.

There was no word from Jamie—or of him. Whether it was guilt or injury that had kept him from coming to me at the Hôpital, I didn't know. But he hadn't come, nor did he come to Fontainebleau. By now he likely had left for Orvieto.

Sometimes I found myself wondering when—or whether—I would see him again, and what—if anything—we might say to each other. But for the most part, I preferred not to think about it, letting the days come and go, one by one, avoiding thoughts of both the future and the past by living only in the present.

Deprived of his idol, Fergus drooped. Again and again, I saw him from my window, sitting disconsolately beneath a hawthorn bush in the garden, hugging his knees and looking down the road toward Paris. At last, I stirred myself to go out to him, making my way heavily downstairs and down the garden path.

"Can't you find anything to do, Fergus?" I asked him. "Surely one of the stable-lads could use a hand, or something."

"Yes, milady," he agreed doubtfully. He scratched absentmindedly at his buttocks. I observed this behavior with deep suspicion.

"Fergus," I said, folding my arms, "have you got lice?" He snatched his hand back as though burned.

"Oh, no, milady!"

I reached down and pulled him to his feet, sniffed delicately in his general vicinity, and put a finger inside his collar, far enough to reveal the grimy ring around his neck.

"Bath," I said succinctly.

"No!" He jerked away, but I grabbed him by the shoulder. I was surprised by his vehemence; while no fonder of bathing than the normal Parisian—who regarded the prospect of immersion with a repugnance akin to horror—still, I could scarcely reconcile the usually obliging child I knew with the little fury that suddenly squirmed and twisted under my hand.

There was a ripping noise, and he was free, bounding through the black-berry bushes like a rabbit pursued by a weasel. There was a rustle of leaves and a scrabble of stones, and he was gone, over the wall and headed for the outbuild-ings at the back of the estate.

I made my way through the maze of rickety outbuildings behind the châ-teau, cursing under my breath as I skirted mud puddles and heaps of filth. Suddenly, there was a high-pitched whining buzz and a cloud of flies rose from the pile a few feet ahead of me, bodies sparking blue in the sunlight.

I wasn't close enough to have disturbed them; there must have been some movement from the darkened doorway beside the dungheap.

"Aha!" I said out loud. "Got you, you filthy little son of a whatnot! Come out of there this instant!"

No one emerged, but there was an audible stir inside the shed, and I thought I caught a glimpse of white in the shadowed interior. Holding my nose, I stepped over the manure pile into the shed.

There were two gasps of horror; mine, at beholding something that looked like the Wild Man of Borneo flattened against the back wall, and his, at beholding me.

The sunlight trickled through the cracks between the boards, giving enough light for us to see each other clearly, once my eyes had adapted to the relative dark. He wasn't, after all, quite as awful-looking as I'd thought at first, but he wasn't a lot better, either. His beard was as filthy and matted as his hair, flowing past his shoulders onto a shirt ragged as any beggar's. He was barefoot, and if the term *sans-culottes* wasn't yet in common use, it wasn't for lack of trying on his part.

I wasn't afraid of him, because he was so obviously afraid of *me*. He was pressing himself against the wall as though trying to get through it by osmosis.

"It's all right," I said soothingly. "I won't hurt you."

Instead of being soothed, he drew himself abruptly upright, reached into the bosom of his shirt and pulled out a wooden crucifix on a leather thong. He held this out toward me and started praying, in a voice shaking with terror.

"Oh, bother," I said crossly. "Not another one!" I took a deep breath. *"Pater-Noster-qui-es-in-coeliset-in-terra . . ."* His eyes bugged out, and he kept holding the crucifix, but at least he stopped his own praying in response to this performance.

". . . Amen!" I concluded with a gasp. I held up both hands and waggled them in front of his face. "See? Not a word backward, not a single *quotidianus da nobis hodie* out of place, right? Didn't even have my fingers crossed. So I can't be a witch, can I?"

The man slowly lowered his crucifix and stood gaping at me. "A witch?" he said. He looked as though he thought *I* were crazy, which I felt was a bit thick under the circumstances.

"You didn't think I was a witch?" I said, beginning to feel a trifle foolish.

Something that looked like a smile twitched into existence and out again among the tangles of his beard.

"No, Madame," he said. "I am accustomed to people saying such things of *me.*"

"You are?" I eyed him closely. Besides the rags and filth, the man was obviously starving; the wrists that stuck out of his shirt were scrawny as a child's. At the same time, his French was graceful and educated, if oddly accented.

"If you're a witch," I said, "you aren't very successful at it. Who the hell are you?"

At this, the fright came back into his eyes again. He looked from side to side, seeking escape, but the shed was solidly built, if old, with no entrance other than the one in which I was standing. At last, calling on some hidden reserve of courage, he drew himself up to his full height—some three inches below my own—and with great dignity, said "I am the Reverend Walter Laurent, of Geneva."

"You're a *priest?*" I was thunderstruck. I couldn't imagine what might have brought a priest—Swiss or not—to this state.

Father Laurent looked nearly as horror-struck as I.

"A priest?" he echoed. "A papist? Never!"

Suddenly the truth struck me.

"A Huguenot!" I said. "That's it—you're a Protestant, aren't you?" I remembered the bodies I had seen hanging in the forest. That, I thought, explained rather a lot.

His lips quivered, but he pressed them tightly together for a moment before opening them to reply.

"Yes, Madame. I am a pastor; I have been preaching in this district for a month." He licked his lips briefly, eyeing me. "Your pardon, Madame—I think you are not French?"

"I'm English," I said, and he relaxed suddenly, as though someone had taken all the stiffening out of his spine.

"Great Father in Heaven," he said, prayerfully. "You are then a Protestant also?"

"No, I'm a Catholic," I answered. "But I'm not at all vicious about it," I added hastily, seeing the look of alarm spring back into his light-brown eyes. "Don't worry, I won't tell anyone you're here. I suppose you came to try to steal a little food?" I asked sympathetically.

"To steal is a sin!" he said, horrified. "No, Madame. But . . ." He clamped his lips shut, but his glance in the direction of the château gave him away.

"So one of the servants brings you food," I said. "So you let them do the stealing for you. But then I suppose you can absolve them from the sin, so it all works out. Rather thin moral ice you're on, if you ask me," I said reprovingly, "but then it isn't any of my business, I suppose."

A light of hope shone in his eyes. "You mean—you will not have me arrested, Madame?"

"No, of course not. I've a sort of fellow-feeling for fugitives from the law, having come rather close to being burnt at the stake once myself." I didn't know quite why I was being so chatty; the relief of meeting someone who seemed intelligent, I supposed. Louise was sweet, devoted and kind, and had precisely as much brain as the cuckoo clock in her drawing room. Thinking of the Swiss clock, I suddenly realized who Pastor Laurent's secret parishioners must be.

"Look," I said, "if you want to stay here, I'll go up to the château and tell Berta or Maurice that you're here."

The poor man was nothing but skin, bones, and eyes. Everything he thought was reflected in those large, gentle brown orbs. Right now, he was plainly thinking that whoever had tried to burn me at the stake had been on the right track.

"I have heard," he began slowly, reaching for a fresh grip on his crucifix, "of an Englishwoman whom the Parisians call 'La Dame Blanche.' An associate of Raymond the Heretic."

I sighed. "That's me. Though I'm not an associate of Master Raymond's, I don't think. He's just a friend." Seeing him squint doubtfully at me, I inhaled again. *"Pater Noster . . ."*

"No, no, Madame, please." To my surprise, he had lowered the crucifix, and was smiling.

"I also am an acquaintance of Master Raymond's, whom I knew in Geneva. There he was a reputable physician and herbalist. Now, alas, I fear that he has turned to darker pursuits, though of course nothing was proved."

"Proved? About what? And what's all this about Raymond the Heretic?"

"You did not know?" Thin brows lifted over the brown eyes. "Ah. Then you are not associated with Master Raymond's . . . activities." He relaxed noticeably.

"Activity" seemed like a poor description for the way in which Raymond had healed me, so I shook my head.

"No, but I wish you'd tell me. Oh, but I shouldn't be standing here talking; I should go and send Berta with food."

He waved a hand, with some dignity.

"It is of no urgency, Madame. The appetites of the body are of no importance when weighed against the appetites of the soul. And Catholic or not, you have been kind to me. If you are not now associated with Master Raymond's occult activities, then it is right that you should be warned in time."

And ignoring the dirt and the splintered boards of the floor, he folded his legs and sat down against the wall of the shed, gracefully motioning me also to sit. Intrigued, I collapsed opposite him, tucking up the folds of my skirt to keep them from dragging in the manure.

"Have you heard of a man named du Carrefours, Madame?" the Pastor said. "No? Well, his name is well known in Paris, I assure you, but you would do well not to speak it. This man was the organizer and the leader of a ring of unspeakable vice and depravity, in association with the most debased occult practices. I cannot bring myself to mention to you some of the ceremonies that were performed in secret among the nobility. And they call *me* a witch!" he muttered, almost under his breath.

He raised one bony forefinger, as though to forestall my unspoken objection.

"I am aware, Madame, of the sort of gossip that is commonly spread, without reference to fact—who should know it better than we? But the activities of du Carrefours and his followers—these are a matter of common knowledge, for he was tried for them, imprisoned, and eventually burned in the Place de la Bastille as punishment for his crimes."

I remembered Raymond's light remark, "No one's been burned in Paris in —oh, twenty years at least," and shuddered, in spite of the warm weather.

"And you say that Master Raymond was associated with this du Carrefours?"

The Pastor frowned, scratching absently at his matted beard. He likely had both lice and fleas, I thought, and tried to move back imperceptibly.

"Well, it is difficult to say. No one knows where Master Raymond came from; he speaks several tongues, all without noticeable accent. A very mysterious man, Master Raymond, but—I would swear by the name of my God—a good one."

I smiled at him. "I think so, too."

He nodded, smiling, but then grew serious as he resumed his story. "Just so, Madame. Still, he corresponded with du Carrefours from Geneva; I know this, for he told me so himself—he supplied various substances to order: plants, elixirs, the dried skins of animals. Even a sort of fish—a most peculiar and frightening thing, which he told me was brought up from the darkest depths of the sea; a horrible thing, all teeth, with almost no flesh—but with the most horrifying small . . . *lights* . . . like tiny lanterns, beneath its eyes."

"Really," I said, fascinated.

Pastor Laurent shrugged. "All this may be quite innocent, of course, a mere matter of business. But he disappeared from Geneva at the same time that du Carrefours came at first under suspicion—and within weeks of du Carrefours's execution, I had begun to hear stories that Master Raymond had established his business in Paris, and that he had taken over a number of du Carrefours's clandestine activities as well."

"Hmm," I said. I was thinking of Raymond's inner room, and the cabinet painted with Cabbalistic signs. To keep out those who believed in them. "Anything else?"

The Reverend Laurent's eyebrows arched skyward.

"No, Madame," he said, rather weakly. "Nothing else, to my knowledge."

"Well, I'm really not given to that sort of thing myself," I assured him.

"Oh? Good," he said, hesitantly. He sat silently for a moment, as though making up his mind about something, then inclined his head courteously toward me.

"You will pardon me if I intrude, Madame? Berta and Maurice have told me something of your loss. I am sorry, Madame."

"Thank you," I said, staring at the stripes of sunlight on the floor.

There was another silence, then Pastor Laurent said delicately, "Your husband, Madame? He is not here with you?"

"No," I said, still keeping my eyes on the floor. Flies lighted momentarily, then zoomed off, finding no nourishment. "I don't know where he is."

I didn't mean to say any more, but something made me look up at the ragged little preacher.

"He cared more for his honor than he did for me or his child or an innocent man," I said bitterly. "I don't *care* where he is; I never want to see him again!"

I stopped abruptly, shaken. I had not put it into words before, even to myself. But it was true. There had been a great trust between us, and Jamie had broken it, for the sake of revenge. I understood; I had seen the power of the thing that drove him, and knew it couldn't be denied forever. But I had asked for a few months' grace, which he had promised me. And then, unable to wait, he had broken his word, and by so doing, sacrificed everything that lay between him and me. Not only that: He had jeopardized the undertaking in which we were engaged. I could understand, but I would not forgive.

Pastor Laurent laid a hand on mine. It was grimy with crusted dirt, and his nails were broken and black-edged, but I didn't draw away. I expected platitudes or a homily, but he didn't speak, either; just held my hand, very gently, for a long time, as the sun moved across the floor and the flies buzzed slow and heavy past our heads.

"You had better go," he said at last, releasing my hand. "You will be missed."

"I suppose so." I drew a deep breath, feeling at least steadier, if not better. I felt in the pocket of my gown; I had a small purse with me.

I hesitated, not wanting to offend him. After all, by his lights I was a heretic, even if not a witch.

"Will you let me give you some money?" I asked carefully.

He thought for a moment, then smiled, the light-brown eyes glowing.

"On one condition, Madame. If you will allow me to pray for you?"

"A bargain," I said, and gave him the purse.

27

An Audience with
His Majesty

s the days passed at Fontainebleau, I gradually regained my bodily
strength, though my mind continued to drift, my thoughts shying
away from any sort of memory or action.

There were few visitors; the country house was a refuge, where the frenetic
social life of Paris seemed like one more of the uneasy dreams that haunted me.
I was surprised, then, to have a maid summon me to the drawing room to meet
a visitor. The thought crossed my mind that it might be Jamie, and I felt a
surge of dizzy sickness. But then reason reasserted itself; Jamie must have left
for Spain by now; he could not possibly return before late August. And when
he did?

I couldn't think of it. I pushed the idea into the back of my mind, but my
hands shook as I fastened my laces to go downstairs.

Much to my surprise, the "visitor" was Magnus, the butler from Jared's
Paris house.

"Your pardon, Madame," he said, bowing deeply when he saw me. "I did
not wish to presume . . . but I could not tell whether perhaps the matter was
of importance . . . and with the master gone . . ." Lordly in his own sphere
of influence, the old man was badly discomposed by being so far afield. It took
some time to extract a coherent story from him, but at length a note was
produced, folded and sealed, addressed to me.

"The hand is that of Monsieur Murtagh," Magnus said, in a tone of half-
repugnant awe. That explained his hesitance, I thought. The servants in the
Paris house all regarded Murtagh with a sort of respectful horror, which had
been exaggerated by reports of the events in the Rue du Faubourg St.-Honoré.

It had come to the Paris house two weeks earlier, Magnus explained.
Unsure what to do with it, the servants had dithered and conferred, but at
length, he had decided that it must be brought to my attention.

"The master being gone," he repeated. This time I paid attention to what
he was saying.

"Gone?" I said. The note was crumpled and stained from its journey, light
as a leaf in my hand. "You mean Jamie left *before* this note arrived?" I could
make no sense of this; this must be Murtagh's note giving the name and sailing
date of the ship that would bear Charles Stuart's port from Lisbon. Jamie could
not have left for Spain before receiving the information.

As though to verify this, I broke the seal and unfolded the note. It was addressed to me, because Jamie had thought there was less chance of my mail being intercepted than his. From Lisbon, dated nearly a month before, the letter boasted no signature, but didn't need one.

"The *Scalamandre* sails from Lisbon on the 18th of July" was all the note said. I was surprised to see what a small, neat hand Murtagh wrote; somehow I had been expecting a formless scrawl.

I looked up from the paper to see Magnus and Louise exchanging a very odd kind of look.

"What is it?" I said abruptly. "Where's Jamie?" I had put down his absence from L'Hôpital des Anges after the miscarriage to his guilt at the knowledge that his reckless action had killed our child, had killed Frank, and had nearly cost me my life. At that point, I didn't care; I didn't want to see him, either. Now I began to think of another, more sinister explanation for his absence.

It was Louise who spoke at last, squaring her plump shoulders to the task. "He's in the Bastille," she said, taking a deep breath. "For dueling."

My knees felt watery, and I sat down on the nearest available surface.

"Why in hell didn't you tell me?" I wasn't sure what I felt at this news; shock, or horror—fear? or a small sense of satisfaction?

"I—I didn't want to upset you, *chérie*," Louise stammered, taken aback at my apparent distress. "You were so weak . . . and there was nothing you could do, after all. And you didn't ask," she pointed out.

"But what . . . how . . . how long is the sentence?" I demanded. Whatever my initial emotion, it was superseded by a sudden rush of urgency. Murtagh's note had arrived at the Rue Tremoulins two weeks ago. Jamie should have left upon its receipt—but he hadn't.

Louise was summoning servants and ordering wine and ammoniac spirits and burnt feathers, all at once; I must look rather alarming.

"It is a contravention of the King's order," she said, pausing in her flutter. "He will remain in prison at the King's pleasure."

"Jesus H. Roosevelt Christ," I muttered, wishing I had something stronger to say.

"It is fortunate that *le petit* James did not kill his opponent," Louise hastened to add. "In that case, the penalty would have been much more . . . eek!" She twitched her striped skirts aside just in time to avoid the cascade of chocolate and biscuits as I knocked over the newly arrived refreshments. The tray clanged to the floor unregarded as I stared down at her. My hands were clasped tightly against my ribs, the right protectively curled over the gold ring on my left hand. The thin metal seemed to burn against my skin.

"He isn't dead, then?" I asked, like one in a dream. "Captain Randall . . . he's alive?"

"Why, yes," she said, peering curiously up at me. "You did not know? He is badly wounded, but it is said that he recovers. Are you quite well, Claire? You look . . ." But the rest of what she was saying was lost in the roaring that filled my ears.

"You did too much, too soon," Louise said severely, pulling back the curtains. "I said so, didn't I?"

"I imagine so," I said. I sat up and swung my legs out of bed, checking cautiously for any residual signs of faintness. No swimming of head, ringing of ears, double vision, or inclination to fall on the floor. Vital signs all right.

"I need my yellow gown, and then would you send for the carriage, Louise?" I asked.

Louise looked at me in horror. "You are not meaning to go out? Nonsense! Monsieur Clouseau is coming to attend you! I have sent a messenger to fetch him here at once!"

The news that Monsieur Clouseau, a prominent society physician, was coming from Paris to examine me, would have been sufficient grounds to get me on my feet, had I needed them.

The eighteenth of July was ten days away. With a fast horse, good weather, and a disregard for bodily comfort, the journey from Paris to Orvieto could be made in six. That left me four days to contrive Jamie's release from the Bastille; no time to fiddle about with Monsieur Clouseau.

"Hmm," I said, looking round the room thoughtfully. "Well, call the maid to dress me, at any rate. I don't want Monsieur Clouseau to find me in my shift."

Though she still looked suspicious, this sounded plausible; most ladies of the Court would rise from a deathbed in order to make sure they were dressed appropriately for the occasion.

"All right," she agreed, turning to go. "But you stay in bed until Yvonne arrives, you hear?"

The yellow gown was one of my best, a loose, graceful thing made in the modish sacque style, with a wide rolled collar, full sleeves, and a beaded closure down the front. Powdered, combed, stockinged, and perfumed at last, I surveyed the pair of shoes Yvonne had laid out for me to step into. I turned my head this way and that, frowning appraisingly.

"Mm, no," I said at last. "I don't think so. I'll wear the others, the ones with the red morocco heels, instead."

The maid looked dubiously at my dress, as though mentally assessing the effect of red morocco with yellow moiré silk, but obediently turned to rummage in the foot of the huge armoire.

Tiptoeing silently up behind her in my stockinged feet, I shoved her head-first into the armoire, and slammed the door on the heaving, shrieking mass beneath the pile of fallen dresses within. Turning the key in the door, I dropped it neatly into my pocket, mentally shaking hands with myself. Neat job, Beauchamp, I thought. All this political intrigue is teaching you things they never dreamt of in nursing school, no doubt about it.

"Don't worry," I told the shaking armoire soothingly. "Someone will be along to let you out soon, I imagine. And you can tell La Princesse that you didn't *let* me go anywhere."

A despairing wail from inside the armoire seemed to be mentioning Monsieur Clouseau's name.

"Tell him to have a look at the monkey," I called over my shoulder, "It's got mange."

The success of my encounter with Yvonne buoyed my mood. Once ensconced in the carriage, rattling back toward Paris, though, my spirits sank appreciably.

While I was no longer quite so angry at Jamie, I still did not wish to see him. My feelings were in complete turmoil, and I had no intention of examining them closely; it hurt too much. Grief was there, and a horrible sense of failure, and over all, the sense of betrayal; his and mine. He should never have gone to the Bois de Boulogne; I should never have gone after him.

But we both did as our natures and our feelings dictated, and together we had—perhaps—caused the death of our child. I had no wish to meet my partner in the crime, still less to expose my grief to him, to match my guilt with his. I fled from anything that reminded me of the dripping morning in the Bois; certainly I fled from any memory of Jamie, caught as I had last seen him, rising from the body of his victim, face glowing with the vengeance that would shortly claim his own family.

I could not think of it even in passing, without a terrible clenching in my stomach, that brought back the ghost of the pain of premature labor. I pressed my fists into the blue velvet of the carriage seat, raising myself to ease the imagined pressure on my back.

I turned to look out the window, hoping to distract myself, but the sights went blindly by, as my mind returned, unbidden, to thoughts of my journey. Whatever my feelings for Jamie, whether we would ever see each other again, what we might be, or not be, to one another—still the fact remained that he was in prison. And I rather thought I knew just what imprisonment might mean to him, with the memories of Wentworth that he carried; the groping hands that fondled him in dreams, the stone walls he hammered in his sleep.

More importantly, there was the matter of Charles and the ship from Portugal; the loan from Monsieur Duverney, and Murtagh, about to take ship from Lisbon for a rendezvous off Orvieto. The stakes were too high to allow my own emotions any play. For the sake of the Scottish clans, and the Highlands themselves, for Jamie's family and tenants at Lallybroch, for the thousands who would die at Culloden and in its aftermath—it had to be tried. And to try, Jamie would have to be free; it wasn't something I could undertake myself.

No, there was no question. I would have to do whatever I must to have him released from the Bastille.

And just what could I do?

I watched the beggars scramble and gesture toward the windows as we entered the Rue du Faubourg St.-Honoré. When in doubt, I thought, seek the assistance of a Higher Authority.

I rapped on the panel beside the driver's seat. It slid back with a grating noise, and the mustached face of Louise's coachman peered down at me.

"Madame?"

"Left," I said. "To L'Hôpital des Anges."

Mother Hildegarde tapped her blunt fingers thoughtfully on a sheet of music paper, as though drumming out a troublesome sequence. She sat at the mosaic table in her private office, across from Herr Gerstmann, summoned to join us in urgent council.

"Well, yes," said Herr Gerstmann doubtfully. "Yes, I believe I can arrange a private audience with His Majesty, but . . . you are certain that your husband . . . um . . ." The music master seemed to be having unusual trouble in expressing himself, which made me suspect that petitioning the King for Jamie's release might be just a trifle more complicated than I had thought. Mother Hildegarde verified this suspicion with her own reaction.

"Johannes!" she exclaimed, so agitated as to drop her usual formal manner of address. "She cannot do that! After all, Madame Fraser is not one of the Court ladies—she is a person of virtue!"

"Er, thank you," I said politely. "If you don't mind, though . . . what, precisely, would my state of virtue have to do with my seeing the King to ask for Jamie's release?"

The nun and the singing-master exchanged looks in which horror at my naiveté was mingled with a general reluctance to remedy it. At last Mother Hildegarde, braver of the two, bit the bullet.

"If you go alone to ask such a favor from the King, he will expect to lie with you," she said bluntly. After all the carry-on over telling me, I was hardly surprised, but I glanced at Herr Gerstmann for confirmation, which he gave in the form of a reluctant nod.

"His Majesty is susceptible to requests from ladies of a certain personal charm," he said delicately, taking a sudden interest in one of the ornaments on the desk.

"But there is a price to such requests," added Mother Hildegarde, not nearly so delicate. "Most of the courtiers are only too pleased when their wives find Royal favor; the gain to them is well worth the sacrifice of their wives' virtue." The wide mouth curled with scorn at the thought, then straightened into its usual grimly humorous line.

"But your husband," she said, "does not appear to me to be the sort who makes a complaisant cuckold." The heavy arched brows supplied the question mark at the end of the sentence, and I shook my head in response.

"I shouldn't think so." In fact, this was one of the grosser understatements I had ever heard. If "complaisant" was not the very last word that came to mind at the thought of Jamie Fraser, it was certainly well down toward the bottom of the list. I tried to imagine just what Jamie would think, say, or do, if he ever learned that I had lain with another man, up to and including the King of France.

The thought made me remember the trust that had existed between us, almost since the day of our marriage, and a sudden feeling of desolation swept over me. I shut my eyes for a moment, fighting illness, but the prospect had to be faced.

"Well," I said, taking a deep breath, "is there another way?"

Mother Hildegarde knitted her brows, frowning at Herr Gerstmann, as though expecting him to produce the answer. The little music master shrugged, though, frowning in his turn.

"If there were a friend of some importance, who might intercede for your husband with His Majesty?" he asked tentatively.

"Not likely." I had examined all such alternatives myself, in the coach from Fontainebleau, and been forced to conclude that there was no one whom I could reasonably ask to undertake such an ambassage. Owing to the illegal and scandalous nature of the duel—for of course Marie d'Arbanville had spread her gossip all over Paris—none of the Frenchmen of our acquaintance could very well afford to take an interest in it. Monsieur Duverney, who had agreed to see me, had been kind, but discouraging. Wait, had been his advice. In a few months, when the scandal has died down a bit, then His Majesty might be approached. But now . . .

Likewise the Duke of Sandringham, so bound by the delicate proprieties of diplomacy that he had dismissed his private secretary for only the appearance of involvement in scandal, was in no position to petition Louis for a favor of this sort.

I stared down at the inlaid tabletop, scarcely seeing the complex curves of enamel that swept through abstractions of geometry and color. My forefinger traced the loops and whorls before me, providing a precarious anchor for my racing thoughts. If it was indeed necessary for Jamie to be released from prison, in order to prevent the Jacobite invasion of Scotland, then it seemed that I would have to do the releasing, whatever the method, and whatever its consequences.

At last I looked up, meeting the music master's eyes. "I'll have to," I said softly. "There's no other way."

There was a moment of silence. Then Herr Gerstmann glanced at Mother Hildegarde.

"She will stay here," Mother Hildegarde declared firmly. "You may send to tell her the time of the audience, Johannes, once you have arranged it."

She turned to me. "After all, if you are really set upon this course, my dear friend . . ." Her lips pressed tightly together, then opened to say, "It may be a sin to assist you in committing immorality. Still, I will do it. I know that your reasons seem good to you, whatever they may be. And perhaps the sin will be outweighed by the grace of your friendship."

"Oh, Mother." I thought I might cry if I said more, so contented myself with merely squeezing the big, work-roughened hand that rested on my shoulder. I had a sudden longing to fling myself into her arms and bury my face against the comforting black serge bosom, but her hand left my shoulder and went to the long jet rosary that clicked among the folds of her skirt as she walked.

"I will pray for you," she said, smiling what would have been a tremulous smile on a face less solidly carved. Her expression changed suddenly to one of deep consideration. "Though I do wonder," she added meditatively, "exactly *who* would be the proper patron saint to invoke in the circumstances?"

Mary Magdalene was the name that came to mind as I raised my hands overhead in a simulation of prayer, to allow the small wicker dress frame to slip over my shoulders and settle onto my hips. Or Mata Hari, but I was quite sure *she'd* never make the Calendar of Saints. I wasn't sure about the Magdalene, for that matter, but a reformed prostitute seemed the most likely among the heavenly host to be sympathetic to the venture being now undertaken.

I reflected that the Convent of the Angels had probably never before seen a robing such as this. While the postulants about to take their final vows were most splendidly arrayed as brides of Christ, red silk and rice powder probably didn't figure heavily in the ceremonies.

Very symbolic, I thought, as the rich scarlet folds slithered over my upturned face. White for purity, and red for . . . whatever this was. Sister Minèrve, a young sister from a wealthy noble family, had been selected to assist me in my toilette; with considerable skill and aplomb, she dressed my hair, tucking in the merest scrap of ostrich feather trimmed with seed pearls. She combed my brows carefully, darkening them with the small lead combs, and painted my lips with a feather dipped in a pot of rouge. The feel of it on my lips tickled unbearably, exaggerating my tendency to break into unhinged giggles. Not hilarity; hysteria.

Sister Minèrve reached for the hand mirror. I stopped her with a gesture; I didn't want to look myself in the eye. I took a deep breath, and nodded.

"I'm ready," I said. "Send for the coach."

I had never been in this part of the palace before. In fact, after the multiple twists and turnings through the candle-lit corridors of mirrors, I was no longer sure exactly how many of me there were, let alone where any of them were going.

The discreet and anonymous Gentleman of the Bedchamber led me to a small paneled door in an alcove. He rapped once, then bowed to me, whirled, and left without waiting for an answer. The door swung inward, and I entered.

The King still had his breeches on. The realization slowed my heartbeat to something like a tolerable rate, and I ceased feeling as though I might throw up any minute.

I didn't know quite what I had been expecting, but the reality was mildly reassuring. He was informally dressed, in shirt and breeches, with a dressing gown of brown silk draped across his shoulders for warmth. His Majesty smiled, and urged me to rise with a hand under my arm. His palm was warm—I had subconsciously expected his touch to be clammy—and I smiled back, as best I could.

The attempt must not have been altogether successful, for he patted my arm kindly, and said "Don't be afraid of me, *chère* Madame. I don't bite."

"No," I said. "Of course not."

He was a lot more poised than I was. Well, of course he is, I thought to myself, he does this all the time. I took a deep breath and tried to relax.

"You will have a little wine, Madame?" he asked. We were alone; there were no servants, but the wine was already poured, in a pair of goblets that stood on the table, glowing like rubies in the candlelight. The chamber was ornate, but very small, and aside from the table and a pair of oval-backed chairs, held only a luxuriously padded green-velvet chaise longue. I tried to avoid looking at it as I took my goblet, with a murmur of thanks.

"Sit, please." Louis sank down upon one of the chairs, gesturing to me to take the other. "Now please," he said, smiling at me, "tell me what it is that I may do for you."

"M-my husband," I began, stammering a little from nervousness. "He's in the Bastille."

"Of course," the King murmured. "For dueling. I recall." He took my free hand in his own, fingers resting lightly on my pulse. "What would you have me do, *chère* Madame? You know it is a serious offense; your husband has broken my own decree." One finger stroked the underside of my wrist, sending small tickling sensations up my arm.

"Y-yes, I understand that. But he was . . . provoked." I had an idea.

"You know he's a Scot; men of that country are"—I tried to think of a good synonym for "berserk"—"most fierce where questions of their honor are concerned."

Louis nodded, head bent in apparent absorption over the hand he held. I could see the faint greasy shine to his skin, and smell his perfume. Violets. A strong, sweet smell, but not enough to completely mask his own acrid maleness.

He drained his wine in two long swallows and discarded the goblet, the better to clasp my hand in both his own. One short-nailed finger traced the lines of my wedding ring, with its interlaced links and thistle blossoms.

"Quite so," he said, bringing my hand closer, as though to examine the ring. "Quite so, Madame. However . . ."

"I'd be . . . most grateful, Your Majesty," I interrupted. His head rose and I met his eyes, dark and quizzical. My heart was going like a trip-hammer. "Most . . . grateful."

He had thin lips and bad teeth; I could smell his breath, thick with onion and decay. I tried holding my own breath, but this could hardly be more than a temporary expedient.

"Well . . ." he said slowly, as though thinking it over. "I would myself be inclined toward mercy, Madame . . ."

I released my breath in a short gasp, and his fingers tightened on mine in warning. "But you see, there are complications."

"There are?" I said faintly.

He nodded, eyes still fixed on my face. His fingers wandered lightly over the back of my hand, tracing the veins.

"The Englishman who was so unfortunate as to have offended milord Broch Tuarach," he said. "He was in the employ of . . . a certain man—an English noble of some importance."

Sandringham. My heart lurched at the mention of him, indirect as it was.

"This noble is engaged in—shall we say, certain negotiations which entitle him to consideration?" The thin lips smiled, emphasizing the imperious prow of the nose above. "And this nobleman has interested himself in the matter of the duel between your husband and the English Captain Randall. I am afraid that he was most exigent in demanding that your husband suffer the full penalty of his indiscretion, Madame."

Bloody tub of lard, I thought. Of course—since Jamie had refused the bribe of a pardon, what better way to prevent his "involving himself" in the Stuarts' affairs than to ensure Jamie's staying safely jugged in the Bastille for the next few years? Sure, discreet, and inexpensive; a method bound to appeal to the Duke.

On the other hand, Louis was still breathing heavily on my hand, which I took as a sign that all was not necessarily lost. If he wasn't going to grant my request, he could scarcely expect me to go to bed with him—or if he did, he was in for a rude surprise.

I girded my loins for another try.

"And does Your Majesty take orders from the English?" I asked boldly.

Louis's eyes flew open with momentary shock. Then he smiled wryly, seeing what I intended. Still, I had touched a nerve; I saw the small twitch of his shoulders as he resettled his conviction of power like an invisible mantle.

"No, Madame, I do not," he said with some dryness. "I do, however, take account of . . . various factors." The heavy lids drooped over his eyes for a moment, but he still held my hand.

"I have heard that your husband interests himself in the affairs of my cousin," he said.

"Your Majesty is well informed," I said politely. "But since that is so, you will know that my husband does not support the restoration of the Stuarts to the throne of Scotland." I prayed that this was what he wanted to hear.

Apparently it was; he smiled, raised my hand to his lips, and kissed it briefly.

"Ah? I had heard . . . conflicting stories about your husband."

I took a deep breath and resisted the impulse to snatch my hand back.

"Well, it's a matter of business," I said, trying to sound as matter-of-fact as possible. "My husband's cousin, Jared Fraser, is an avowed Jacobite; Jamie— my husband—can't very well go about letting his real views be made public, when he's in partnership with Jared." Seeing the doubt begin to fade from his face, I hurried it along. "Ask Monsieur Duverney," I suggested. "He's well acquainted with my husband's true sympathies."

"I have." Louis paused for a long moment, watching his own fingers, dark and stubby, tracing delicate circles over the back of my hand.

"So very pale," he murmured. "So fine. I believe I could see the blood flow beneath your skin."

He let go of my hand then and sat regarding me. I was extremely good at reading faces, but Louis's was quite impenetrable at the moment. I realized suddenly that he'd been a king since the age of five; the ability to hide his thoughts was as much a part of him as his Bourbon nose or the sleepy black eyes.

This thought brought another in its wake, with a chill that struck me deep in the pit of the stomach. He was the King. The Citizens of Paris would not rise for forty years or more; until that day, his rule within France was absolute. He could free Jamie with a word—or kill him. He could do with me as he liked; there was no recourse. One nod of his head, and the coffers of France could spill the gold that would launch Charles Stuart, loosing him like a deadly bolt of lightning to strike through the heart of Scotland.

He was the King. He would do as he wished. And I watched his dark eyes, clouded with thought, and waited, trembling, to see what the Royal pleasure might be.

"Tell me, *ma chère* Madame," he said at last, stirring from his introspection. "If I were to grant your request, to free your husband . . ." he paused, considering.

"Yes?"

"He would have to leave France," Louis said, one thick brow raised in warning. "That would be a condition of his release."

"I understand." My heart was pounding so hard that it nearly drowned out his words. Jamie leaving France was, after all, precisely the point. "But he's exiled from Scotland . . ."

"I think that might be arranged."

I hesitated, but there seemed little choice but to agree on Jamie's behalf. "All right."

"Good." The King nodded, pleased. Then his eyes returned to me, rested on my face, glided down my neck, my breasts, my body. "I would ask a small service of you in return, Madame," he said softly.

I met his eyes squarely for one second. Then I bowed my head. "I am at Your Majesty's complete disposal," I said.

"Ah." He rose and threw off the dressing gown, leaving it flung carelessly over the back of his armchair. He smiled and held out a hand to me. "*Très bien, ma chère.* Come with me, then."

I closed my eyes briefly, willing my knees to work. You've been married twice, for heaven's sake, I thought to myself. Quit making such a bloody fuss about it.

I rose to my feet and took his hand. To my surprise, he didn't turn toward the velvet chaise, but instead led me toward the door at the far side of the room.

I had one moment of ice-cold clarity as he let go my hand to open the door.

Damn you, Jamie Fraser, I thought. *Damn you to hell!*

———————

I stood quite still on the threshold, blinking. My meditations on the protocol of Royal disrobing faded into sheer astonishment.

The room was quite dark, lit only by numerous tiny oil-lamps, set in groups of five in alcoves in the wall of the chamber. The room itself was round, and so was the huge table that stood in its center, the dark wood gleaming with pinpoint reflections. There were people sitting at the table, no more than hunched dark blurs against the blackness of the room.

There was a murmur at my entrance, quickly stilled at the King's appearance. As my eyes grew more accustomed to the murk, I realized with a sense of shock that the people seated at the table wore hoods; the nearest man turned toward me, and I caught the faint gleam of eyes through holes in the velvet. It looked like a convention of hangmen.

Apparently I was the guest of honor. I wondered for a nervous moment just what might be expected of me. From Raymond's hints, and Marguerite's, I had nightmare visions of occult ceremonies involving infant sacrifice, ceremonial rape, and general-purpose satanic rites. It is, however, quite rare for the supernatural actually to live up to its billing, and I hoped this occasion would be no exception.

"We have heard of your great skill, Madame, and your . . . reputation." Louis smiled, but there was a tinge of caution in his eyes as he looked at me, as though not quite certain what I might do. "We should be most obliged, my dear Madame, should you be willing to give us the benefits of such skill this evening."

I nodded. Most obliged, eh? Well, that was all to the good; I wanted him obliged to me. What was he expecting me to do, though? A servant placed a huge wax candle on the table and lighted it, shedding a pool of mellow light on the polished wood. The candle was decorated with symbols like those I had seen in Master Raymond's secret chamber.

"*Regardez*, Madame." The King's hand was under my elbow, directing my attention beyond the table. Now that the candle was lighted, I could see the two figures who stood silently among the flickering shadows. I started at the sight, and the King's hand tightened on my arm.

The Comte St. Germain and Master Raymond stood there, side by side, separated by a distance of six feet or so. Raymond gave no sign of acknowledgment, but stood quietly, staring off to one side with the pupil-less black eyes of a frog in a bottomless well.

The Comte saw me, and his eyes widened in disbelief; then he scowled at me. He was dressed in his finest, all in white, as usual; a white stiffened satin coat over cream-colored silk vest and breeches. A tracery of seed pearls decorated his cuffs and lapels, gleaming in the candlelight. Sartorial splendor aside, the Comte looked rather the worse for wear, I thought—his face was drawn with strain, and the lace of his stock was wilted, his collar darkened with sweat.

Raymond, conversely, looked calm as a turbot on ice, standing stolidly with both hands folded into the sleeves of his usual scruffy velvet robe, broad, flat face placid and inscrutable.

"These two men stand accused, Madame," said Louis, with a gesture at Raymond and the Comte. "Of sorcery, of witchcraft, of the perversion of the legitimate search for knowledge into an exploration of arcane arts." His voice was cold and grim. "Such practices flourished during the reign of my grandfather; but we shall not suffer such wickedness in our realm."

The King flicked his fingers at one of the hooded figures, who sat with pen and ink before a sheaf of papers. "Read the indictments, if you please," he said.

The hooded man rose obediently to his feet and began to read from one of the papers: charges of bestiality and foul sacrifice, of the spilling of the blood of innocents, the profanation of the most holy rite of the Mass by desecration of the Host, the performance of amatory rites upon the altar of God—I had a quick flash of just what the healing Raymond had performed on me at L'Hôpital des Anges must have looked like, and felt profoundly grateful that no one had discovered him.

I heard the name "du Carrefours" mentioned, and swallowed a sudden rising of bile. What had Pastor Laurent said? The sorcerer du Carrefours had been burned in Paris, only twenty years before, on just such charges as those I was hearing: "—the summoning of demons and powers of darkness, the procurement of illness and death for payment"—I put a hand to my stomach, in vivid memory of bitter cascara —"the ill-wishing of members of the Court, the defilement of virgins—" I shot a quick look at the Comte, but his face was stony, lips pressed tight as he listened.

Raymond stood quite still, silver hair brushing his shoulders, as though listening to something as inconsequential as the song of a thrush in the bushes. I had seen the Cabbalistic symbols on his cabinet, but I could hardly reconcile the man I knew—the compassionate poisoner, the practical apothecary—with the list of vileness being read.

At last the indictments ceased. The hooded man glanced at the King, and at a signal, sank back into his chair.

"Extensive inquiry has been made," the King said, turning to me. "Evidence has been presented, and the testimony of many witnesses taken. It seems clear"—he turned a cold gaze on the two accused magi—"that both men have undertaken investigations into the writings of ancient philosophers, and have employed the art of divinations, using calculation of the movements of heavenly bodies. Still . . ." He shrugged. "This is not of itself a crime. I am given to understand"—he glanced at a heavyset man in a hood, whom I suspected of being the Bishop of Paris—"that this is not necessarily at variance with the teachings of the Church; even the blessed St. Augustine was known to have made inquiries into the mysteries of astrology."

I rather dimly recalled that St. Augustine had indeed looked into astrology, and had rather scornfully dismissed it as a load of rubbish. Still, I doubted that Louis had read Augustine's *Confessions,* and this line of argument was undoubtedly a good one for an accused sorcerer; star-gazing seemed fairly harmless, by comparison with infant sacrifice and nameless orgies.

I was beginning to wonder, with considerable apprehension, just what I was doing in this assemblage. Had someone seen Master Raymond with me in the Hôpital after all?

"We have no quarrel with the proper use of knowledge, nor the search for wisdom," the King went on in measured tones. "There is much that can be learned from the writings of the ancient philosophers, if they are approached with proper caution and humility of spirit. But it is true that while much good may be found in such writings, so, too, may evil be discovered, and the pure search for wisdom be perverted into the desire for power and wealth—the things of this world."

He glanced back and forth between the two accused sorcerers once more, obviously drawing conclusions as to who might be more inclined to *that* sort of perversion. The Comte was still sweating, damp patches showing dark on the white silk of his coat.

"No, Your Majesty!" he said, shaking back his dark hair and fixing burning eyes on Master Raymond. "It is true that there are dark forces at work in the land—the vileness of which you speak walks among us! But such wickedness does not dwell in the breast of your most loyal subject"—he smote himself on the breast, lest we have missed the point—"no, Your Majesty! For the perversion of knowledge and the use of forbidden arts, you must look beyond your own Court." He didn't accuse Master Raymond directly, but the direction of his pointed gaze was obvious.

The King was unmoved by this outburst. "Such abominations flourished during the reign of my grandfather," he said softly. "We have rooted them out wherever they have been found; destroyed the threat of such evil where it shall exist in our realm. Sorcerers, witches, those who pervert the teachings of the Church . . . Monsieurs, we shall not suffer such wickedness to arise again."

"So." He slapped both palms lightly against the table and straightened himself. Still staring at the Raymond and the Comte, he held out a hand in my direction.

"We have brought here a witness," he declared. "An infallible judge of truth, of purity of heart."

I made a small, gurgling noise, which made the King turn to look at me.

"A White Lady," he said softly. "La Dame Blanche cannot lie; she sees the heart and the soul of a man, and may turn that truth to good . . . or to destruction."

The air of unreality that had hung over the evening vanished in a pop. The faint wine-buzz was gone, and I was suddenly stone-cold sober. I opened my mouth, and then shut it, realizing that there was precisely nothing I could say.

Horror snaked down my backbone and coiled in my belly as the King made his dispositions. Two pentagrams were to be drawn on the floor, within which the two sorcerers would stand. Each would then bear witness to his own activities and motives. And the White Lady would judge the truth of what was said.

"Jesus H. Christ," I said, under my breath.

"Monsieur le Comte?" The King gestured to the first pentagram, chalked on the carpet. Only a king would treat a genuine Aubusson with that kind of cavalier disregard.

The Comte brushed close to me as he went to take his place. As he passed me, I caught the faintest whisper: "Be warned, Madame. I do not work alone."

He took up his spot and turned to face me with an ironic bow, outwardly composed.

The implication was reasonably clear; I condemned him, and his minions would be round promptly to cut off my nipples and burn Jared's warehouse. I licked dry lips, cursing Louis. Why couldn't he just have wanted my body?

Raymond stepped casually into his own chalk-limned space, and nodded cordially in my direction. No hint of guidance in those round black eyes.

I hadn't the faintest idea what to do next. The King motioned to me to stand opposite him, between the two pentagrams. The hooded men rose to stand behind the King; a blank-faced crowd of menace.

Everything was extremely quiet. Candle smoke hung in a pall near the gilded ceiling, wisps drifting the languid air currents. All eyes were trained on me. Finally, out of desperation, I turned to the Comte and nodded.

"You may begin, Monsieur le Comte," I said.

He smiled—at least I assumed it was meant to be a smile—and began, starting out with an explication of the foundation of the Cabbala and moving right along to an exegesis on the twenty-three letters of the Hebrew alphabet, and the profound symbolism of it all. It sounded thoroughly scholarly, completely innocuous, and terribly dull. The King yawned, not bothering to cover his mouth.

Meanwhile, I was turning over alternatives in my mind. This man had threatened and attacked me, and tried to have Jamie assassinated—whether for personal or political reasons, it made little difference. He had in all likelihood been the ringleader of the gang of rapists who had waylaid me and Mary. Beyond all this, and beyond the rumors I had heard of his other activities, he was a major threat to the success of our attempt at stopping Charles Stuart. Was I going to let him get away? Let him go on to exert his influence with the King on the Stuarts' behalf, and to go on roaming the darkened streets of Paris with his band of masked bullies?

I could see my nipples, erect with fright, standing out boldly against the silk of my dress. But I drew myself up and glared at him anyway.

"Just one minute," I said. "All that you say so far is true, Monsieur le Comte, but I see a shadow behind your words."

The Comte's mouth fell open. Louis, suddenly interested, ceased slouching against the table and stood upright. I closed my eyes and laid my fingers against my lids, as though looking inward.

"I see a name in your mind, Monsieur le Comte," I said. I sounded breathless and half-choked with fright, but there was no help for it. I dropped my hands and looked straight at him. "Les Disciples du Mal," I said. "What have you to do with Les Disciples, Monsieur le Comte?"

He really wasn't good at hiding his emotions. His eyes bulged and his face went white, and I felt a small fierce surge of satisfaction under my fear.

The name of Les Disciples du Mal was familiar to the King as well; the sleepy dark eyes narrowed suddenly to slits.

The Comte may have been a crook and a charlatan, but he wasn't a coward. Summoning his resources, he glared at me and flung back his head.

"This woman lies," he said, sounding as definite as he had when informing the audience that the letter aleph was symbolic of the font of Christ's blood. "She is no true White Lady, but the servant of Satan! In league with her master, the notorious sorcerer, du Carrefours's apprentice!" He pointed dramatically at Raymond, who looked mildly surprised.

One of the hooded men crossed himself, and I heard the soft whisper of a brief prayer among the shadows.

"I can prove what I say," the Comte declared, not letting anyone else get a word in edgewise. He reached into the breast of his coat. I remembered the dagger he had produced from his sleeve on the night of the dinner party, and tensed myself to duck. It wasn't a knife that he brought out, though.

"The Holy Bible says, 'They shall handle serpents unharmed,'" he thundered. "'And by such signs shall ye know the servants of the true God!'"

I thought it was probably a small python. It was nearly three feet long, a smooth, gleaming length of gold and brown, slick and sinuous as oiled rope, with a pair of disconcerting golden eyes.

There was a concerted gasp at its appearance, and two of the hooded judges took a quick step back. Louis himself was more than slightly taken aback, and looked hastily about for his bodyguard, who stood goggle-eyed by the door of the chamber.

The snake flicked its tongue once or twice, tasting the air. Apparently deciding that the mix of candle wax and incense wasn't edible, it turned and made an attempt to burrow back into the warm pocket from which it had been so rudely removed. The Comte caught it expertly behind the head, and shoved it toward me.

"You see?" he said triumphantly. "The woman shrinks away in fear! She is a witch!"

Actually, compared to one judge, who was huddling against the far wall, I was a monument of fortitude, but I must admit that I had taken an involuntary step backward when the snake appeared. Now I stepped forward again, intending to take it away from him. The bloody thing wasn't poisonous, after all. Maybe we'd see how harmless it was if I wrapped it round his neck.

Before I could reach him, though, Master Raymond spoke behind me. What with all the commotion, I'd rather forgotten him.

"That is not all the Bible says, Monsieur le Comte," Raymond observed. He didn't raise his voice, and the wide amphibian face was bland as pudding. Still, the buzz of voices stopped, and the King turned to listen.

"Yes, Monsieur?" he said.

Raymond nodded in polite acknowledgment of having the floor, and reached into his robe with both hands. From one pocket he produced a flask, from the other a small cup.

" 'They shall handle serpents unharmed,' " he quoted, " 'and if they drink any deadly poison, they shall not die.' " He held the cup out on the palm of his hand, its silver lining gleaming in the candlelight. The flask was poised above it, ready to pour.

"Since both milady Broch Tuarach and myself have been accused," Raymond said, with a quick glance at me, "I would suggest that all three of us partake of this test. With your permission, Your Majesty?"

Louis looked rather stunned by the rapid progress of events, but he nodded, and a thin stream of amber liquid splashed into the cup, which at once turned red and began to bubble, as though the contents were boiling.

"Dragon's blood," Raymond said informatively, waving at the cup. "Entirely harmless to the pure of heart." He smiled a toothless, encouraging smile, and handed me the cup.

There didn't seem much to do but drink it. Dragon's blood appeared to be some form of sodium bicarbonate; it tasted like brandy with seltzer. I took two or three medium-sized swallows and handed it back.

With due ceremony, Raymond drank as well. He lowered the cup, exhibiting pink-stained lips, and turned to the King.

"If La Dame Blanche may be asked to give the cup to Monsieur le Comte?" he said. He gestured to the chalk lines at his feet, to indicate that he might not step outside the protection of the pentagram.

At the King's nod, I took the cup and turned mechanically toward the Comte. Perhaps six feet of carpeting to cross. I took the first step, and then another, knees trembling more violently than they had in the small anteroom, alone with the King.

The White Lady sees a man's true nature. Did I? Did I really know about either of them, Raymond or the Comte?

Could I have stopped it? I asked myself that a hundred times, a thousand times—later. Could I have done otherwise?

I remembered my errant thought on meeting Charles Stuart; how convenient for everyone if he should die. But one cannot kill a man for his beliefs, even if the exercise of those beliefs means the death of innocents—or can one?

I didn't know. I didn't know that the Comte was guilty, I didn't know that Raymond was innocent. I didn't know whether the pursuit of an honorable cause justified the use of dishonorable means. I didn't know what one life was worth—or a thousand. I didn't know the true cost of revenge.

I did know that the cup I held in my hands was death. The white crystal hung around my neck, its weight a reminder of poison. I hadn't seen Raymond add anything to it; no one had, I was sure. But I didn't need to dip the crystal into the bloodred liquid to know what it now contained.

The Comte saw the knowledge in my face; La Dame Blanche cannot lie. He hesitated, looking at the bubbling cup.

"Drink, Monsieur," said the King. The dark eyes were hooded once more, showing nothing. "Or are you afraid?"

The Comte might have a number of things to his discredit, but cowardice wasn't one of them. His face was pale and set, but he met the King's eyes squarely, with a slight smile.

"No, Majesty," he said.

He took the cup from my hand and drained it, his eyes fixed on mine. They stayed fixed, staring into my face, even as they glazed with the knowledge of death. The White Lady may turn a man's nature to good, or to destruction.

The Comte's body hit the floor, writhing, and a chorus of shouts and cries rose from the hooded watchers, drowning any sound he might have made. His heels drummed briefly, silent on the flowered carpet; his body arched, then subsided into limpness. The snake, thoroughly disgruntled, struggled free of the disordered folds of white satin and slithered rapidly away, heading for the sanctuary of Louis's feet.

All was pandemonium.

28

The Coming of the Light

I returned from Paris to Louise's house at Fontainebleau. I didn't want to go to the Rue Tremoulins—or anywhere else that Jamie might find me. He would have little time to look; he would have to leave for Spain virtually at once, or risk the failure of his scheme.

Louise, good friend that she was, forgave my subterfuge, and—to her credit—forbore to ask me where I had gone, or what I had done there. I didn't speak much to anyone, but stayed in my room, eating little, and staring at the fat, naked *putti* that decorated the white ceiling. The sheer necessity of the trip to Paris had roused me for a time, but now there was nothing I must do, no daily routine to support me. Rudderless, I began to drift again.

Still, I tried sometimes to make an effort. Prodded by Louise, I would come down to a social dinner, or join her for tea with a visiting friend. And I tried to pay attention to Fergus, the only person in the world for whom I had still some sense of responsibility.

So, when I heard his voice raised in altercation on the other side of an outbuilding as I dutifully took my afternoon walk, I felt obliged to go and see what was the matter.

He was face to face with one of the stable-lads, a bigger boy with a sullen expression and broad shoulders.

"Shut your mouth, ignorant toad," the stable-lad was saying. "You don't know what you're talking about!"

"I know better than you—you, whose mother mated with a pig!" Fergus put two fingers in his nostrils, pushed his nose up and danced to and fro, shouting "Oink, oink!" repeatedly.

The stable-lad, who did have a rather noticeably upturned proboscis, wasted no time in idle repartee, but waded in with both fists clenched and swinging. Within seconds, the two were rolling on the muddy ground, squalling like cats and ripping at each other's clothes.

While I was still debating whether to interfere, the stable-lad rolled on top of Fergus, got his neck in both hands, and began to bang his head on the ground. On the one hand, I rather considered that Fergus had been inviting some such attention. On the other, his face was turning a dark, dusky red, and I had some reservations about seeing him cut off in his prime. With a certain amount of deliberation, I walked up behind the struggling pair.

The stable-lad was kneeling astride Fergus's body, choking him, and the seat of his breeches was stretched tight before me. I drew back my foot and booted him smartly in the trouser seam. Precariously balanced, he fell forward with a startled cry, atop the body of his erstwhile victim. He rolled to the side and bounced to his feet, fists clenched. Then he saw me, and fled without a word.

"What do you think you're playing at?" I demanded. I yanked Fergus, gasping and spluttering, to his feet, and began to beat his clothes, knocking the worst of the mud clumps and hay wisps off of him.

"Look at that," I said accusingly. "You've torn not only your shirt, but your breeches as well. We'll have to ask Berta to mend them." I turned him around and fingered the torn flap of fabric. The stable-lad had apparently gotten a hand in the waistband of the breeches, and ripped them down the side seam; the buckram fabric drooped from his slender hips, all but baring one buttock.

I stopped talking suddenly, and stared. It wasn't the disgraceful expanse of bare flesh that riveted me, but a small red mark that adorned it. About the size of a halfpenny piece, it was the dark, purplish-red color of a freshly healed burn. Disbelievingly, I touched it, making Fergus start in alarm. The edges of the mark were incised; whatever had made it had sunk into the flesh. I grabbed the boy by the arm to stop him running away, and bent to examine the mark more closely.

At a distance of six inches, the shape of the mark was clear; it was an oval, carrying within it smudged shapes that must have been letters.

"Who did this to you, Fergus?" I asked. My voice sounded queer to my own ears; preternaturally calm and detached.

Fergus yanked, trying to pull away, but I held on.

"Who, Fergus?" I demanded, giving him a little shake.

"It's nothing, Madame; I hurt myself sliding off the fence. It's just a splinter." His large black eyes darted to and fro, seeking a refuge.

"That's not a splinter. I know what it is, Fergus. But I want to know who did it." I had seen something like it only once before, and that wound freshly inflicted, while this had had some time to heal. But the mark of a brand is unmistakable.

Seeing that I meant it, he quit struggling. He licked his lips, hesitating, but his shoulders slumped, and I knew I had him now.

"It was . . . an Englishman, milady. With a ring."

"When?"

"A long time ago, Madame! In May."

I drew a deep breath, calculating. Three months. Three months earlier when Jamie had left the house to visit a brothel, in search of his warehouse foreman. In Fergus's company. Three months since Jamie had encountered Jack Randall in Madame Elise's establishment, and seen something that made all promises null and void, that had formed in him the determination to kill Jack Randall. Three months since he had left—never to return.

It took considerable patience, supplemented by a firm grip on Fergus's upper arm, but I succeeded at last in extracting the story from him.

When they arrived at Madame Elise's establishment, Jamie had told Fergus to wait for him while he went upstairs to make the financial arrangements. Judging from prior experience that this might take some time, Fergus had wandered into the large salon, where a number of young ladies that he knew were "resting," chattering together and fixing each other's hair in anticipation of customers.

"Business is sometimes slow in the mornings," he explained to me. "But on Tuesdays and Fridays, the fishermen come up the Seine to sell their catch at the morning market. Then they have money, and Madame Elise does a fine business, so *les jeunes filles* must be ready right after breakfast."

Most of the "girls" were in fact the older inhabitants of the establishment; fishermen were not considered the choicest of clients, and so went by default to the less desirable prostitutes. Among these were most of Fergus's former friends, though, and he passed an agreeable quarter of an hour in the salon, being petted and teased. A few early clients appeared, made their choice, and departed for the upstairs rooms—Madame Elise's house boasted four narrow stories—without disturbing the conversation of the remaining ladies.

"And then the Englishman came in, with Madame Elise." Fergus stopped and swallowed, the large Adam's apple bobbing uneasily in his skinny throat.

It was obvious to Fergus, who had seen men in every state of inebriation and arousal, that the Captain had been making a night of it. He was flushed and untidy, and his eyes were bloodshot. Ignoring Madame Elise's attempts to guide him toward one of the prostitutes, he had broken away and wandered through the room, restlessly scanning the wares on display. Then his eye had lighted on Fergus.

"He said, 'You. Come along,' and took me by the arm. I held back, Madame—I told him my employer was above, and that I couldn't—but he wouldn't listen. Madame Elise whispered in my ear that I should go with him, and she would split the money with me afterward." Fergus shrugged, and looked at me helplessly. "I knew the ones who like little boys don't usually take very long; I thought he would be finished long before milord was ready to leave."

"Jesus bloody Christ," I said. My fingers relaxed their grip and slid nervelessly down his sleeve. "Do you mean—Fergus, had you done it before?"

He looked as though he wanted to cry. So did I.

"Not very often, Madame," he said, and it was almost a plea for understanding. "There are houses where that is the specialty, and usually the men who like that go there. But sometimes a customer would see me and take a fancy . . ." His nose was starting to run and he wiped it with the back of his hand.

I rummaged in my pocket for a handkerchief and gave it to him. He was beginning to sniffle as he recalled that Friday morning.

"He was much bigger than I thought. I asked him if I could take it in my mouth, but he . . . but he wanted to . . ."

I pulled him to me and pressed his head tight against my shoulder, muffling his voice in the cloth of my gown. The frail blades of his shoulder bones were like a bird's wings under my hand.

"Don't tell me any more," I said. "Don't. It's all right, Fergus; I'm not angry. But don't tell me any more."

This was a futile order; he couldn't stop talking, after so many days of fear and silence.

"But it's all my fault, Madame!" he burst out, pulling away. His lip was trembling, and tears welled in his eyes. "I should have kept quiet; I shouldn't have cried out! But I couldn't help it, and milord heard me, and . . . and he burst in . . . and . . . oh, Madame, I shouldn't have, but I was so glad to see him, and I ran to him, and he put me behind him and hit the Englishman in the face. And then the Englishman came up from the floor with the stool in his hand, and threw it, and I was so afraid, I ran out of the room and hid in the closet at the end of the hall. Then there was so much shouting and banging, and a terrible crash, and more shouting. And then it stopped, and soon milord opened the door of the closet and took me out. He had my clothes, and he dressed me himself, because I couldn't fasten the buttons—my fingers shook."

He grabbed my skirt with both hands, the necessity of making me believe him tightening his face into a monkey mask of grief.

"It's my fault, Madame, but I didn't know! I didn't know he would go to fight the Englishman. And now milord is gone, and he'll never come back, and it's all my fault!"

Wailing now, he fell facedown on the ground at my feet. He was crying so loudly that I didn't think he heard me as I bent to lift him up, but I said it anyway.

"It isn't your fault, Fergus. It isn't mine, either—but you're right; he's gone."

Following Fergus's revelation, I sank ever deeper into apathy. The gray cloud that had surrounded me since the miscarriage seemed to draw closer, wrapping me in swaddling folds that dimmed the light of the brightest day. Sounds seemed to reach me faintly, like the far-off ringing of a buoy through fog at sea.

Louise stood in front of me, frowning worriedly as she looked down at me.

"You're much too thin," she scolded. "And white as a plate of tripes. Yvonne said you didn't eat any breakfast again!"

I couldn't remember when I had last been hungry. It hardly seemed important. Long before the Bois de Boulogne, long before my trip to Paris. I fixed my gaze on the mantelpiece and drifted off into the curlicues of the rococo carving. Louise's voice went on, but I didn't pay attention; it was only a noise in the room, like the brushing of a tree branch against the stone wall of the château, or the humming of the flies that had been drawn in by the smell of my discarded breakfast.

I watched one of them, rising off the eggs in sudden motion as Louise clapped her hands. It buzzed in short, irritable circles before settling back to its feeding spot. The sound of hurrying footsteps came behind me, there was a sharp order from Louise, a submissive "*Oui,* Madame," and the sudden *thwap!* of a flywhisk as the maid set about removing the flies, one by one. She dropped each small black corpse into her pocket, plucking it off the table and polishing the smear left behind with a corner of her apron.

Louise bent down, thrusting her face suddenly into my field of view.

"I can see all the bones in your face! If you won't eat, at least go outside for a bit!" she said impatiently. "The rain's stopped; come along, and we'll see if there are any muscats left in the arbor. Maybe you'll eat some of those."

Outside or inside was much the same to me; the soft, numbing grayness was still with me, blurring outlines and making every place seem like every other. But it seemed to matter to Louise, so I rose obediently to go with her.

Near the garden door, though, she was waylaid by the cook, with a list of questions and complaints about the menu for dinner. Guests had been invited, with the intention of distracting me, and the bustle of preparation had been causing small explosions of domestic discord all morning.

Louise emitted a martyred sigh, then patted me on the back.

"You go on," she said, urging me toward the door. "I'll send a footman with your cloak."

It was a cool day for August because of the rain that had been coming down since the night before. Pools of water lay in the graveled paths, and the dripping from the drenched trees was nearly as incessant as the rain itself.

The sky was still filled with gray, but it had faded from the angry black of water-logged cloud. I folded my arms around my elbows; it looked as though the sun might come out soon, but it was still cold enough to want a cloak.

When I heard steps behind me on the path, I turned to find François, the second footman, but he carried nothing. He looked oddly hesitant, peering as though to make sure I was the person he was looking for.

"Madame," he said, "there is a visitor for you."

I sighed internally; I didn't want to be bothered with the effort of rousing myself to be civil to company.

"Tell them I'm indisposed, please," I said, turning to continue my walk. "And when they've gone, bring me my cloak."

"But Madame," he said behind me, "it is le seigneur Broch Tuarach—your husband."

Startled, I whirled to look at the house. It was true; I could see Jamie's tall figure, already coming around the corner of the house. I turned, pretending I hadn't seen him, and walked off toward the arbor. The shrubbery was thick down there; perhaps I could hide.

"Claire!" Pretending was useless; he had seen me as well, and was coming down the path after me. I walked faster, but I was no match for those long legs. I was puffing before I had covered half the distance to the arbor, and had to slow down; I was in no condition for strenuous exercise.

"Wait, Claire!"

I half-turned; he was almost upon me. The soft gray numbness around me quivered, and I felt a sort of frozen panic at the thought that the sight of him might rip it away from me. If it did, I would die, I thought, like a grub dug up from the soil and tossed onto a rock to shrivel, naked and defenseless in the sun.

"No!" I said. "I don't want to talk to you. Go away." He hesitated for a moment, and I turned away from him and began to walk rapidly down the path toward the arbor. I heard his steps on the gravel of the path behind me, but kept my back turned, and walked faster, almost running.

As I paused to duck under the arbor, he made a sudden lunge forward and grasped my wrist. I tried to pull away from him, but he held on tight.

"Claire!" he said again. I struggled, but kept my face turned away; if I didn't look at him, I could pretend he wasn't there. I could stay safe.

He let go of my wrist, but grabbed me by both shoulders instead, so that I had to lift my head to keep my balance. His face was sunburned and thin, with harsh lines cut beside his mouth, and his eyes above were dark with pain. "Claire," he said more softly, now that he could see me looking at him. "Claire—it was my child, too."

"Yes, it was—and you killed it!" I ripped away from him, flinging myself through the narrow arch. I stopped inside, panting like a terrified dog. I hadn't realized that the arch led into a tiny vine-covered folly. Latticed walls surrounded me on all sides—I was trapped. The light behind me failed as his body blocked the arch.

"Don't touch me." I backed away, staring at the ground. *Go away!* I thought frantically. *Please, for God's sake, leave me in peace!* I could feel my gray wrappings being inexorably stripped away, and small, bright streaks of pain shot through me like lightning bolts piercing cloud.

He stopped, a few feet away. I stumbled blindly toward the latticed wall and half-sat, half-fell onto a wooden bench. I closed my eyes and sat shivering.

While it was no longer raining, there was a cold, damp wind coming through the lattice to chill my neck.

He didn't come closer. I could feel him, standing there, looking down at me. I could hear the raggedness of his breathing.

"Claire," he said once more, with something like despair in his voice, "Claire, do ye not see . . . Claire, you must speak to me! For God's sake, Claire, I don't know even was it a girl or a boy!"

I sat frozen, hands gripping the rough wood of the bench. After a moment, there was a heavy, crunching noise on the ground in front of me. I cracked my eyes open, and saw that he had sat down, just as he was, on the wet gravel at my feet. He sat with bowed head, and the rain had left spangles in his damp-darkened hair.

"Will ye make me beg?" he said.

"It was a girl," I said after a moment. My voice sounded funny; hoarse and husky. "Mother Hildegarde baptized her. Faith. Faith Fraser. Mother Hildegarde has a very odd sense of humor."

The bowed head didn't move. After a moment, he said quietly, "Did you see the child?"

My eyes were open all the way now. I stared at my knees, where blown drops of water from the vines behind me were making wet spots on the silk.

"Yes. The *maîtresse sage-femme* said I ought, so they made me." I could hear in memory the low, matter-of-fact tones of Madame Bonheur, most senior and respected of the midwives who gave of their time at L'Hôpital des Anges.

"Give her the child; it's always better if they see. Then they don't imagine things."

So I didn't imagine. I remembered.

"She was perfect," I said softly, as though to myself. "So small. I could cup her head in the palm of my hand. Her ears stuck out just a little—I could see the light shine through them.

The light had shone through her skin as well, glowing in the roundness of cheek and buttock with the light that pearls have; still and cool, with the strange touch of the water world still on them.

"Mother Hildegarde wrapped her in a length of white satin," I said, looking down at my fists, clenched in my lap. "Her eyes were closed. She hadn't any lashes yet, but her eyes were slanted. I said they were like yours, but they said all babies' eyes are like that."

Ten fingers, and ten toes. No nails, but the gleam of tiny joints, kneecaps and fingerbones like opals, like the jeweled bones of the earth itself. Remember man, that thou art dust. . . .

I remembered the far-off clatter of the Hôpital, where life still went on, and the subdued murmur of Mother Hildegarde and Madame Bonheur, closer by, talking of the priest who would say a special Mass at Mother Hildegarde's request. I remembered the look of calm appraisal in Madame Bonheur's eyes as she turned to look me over, seeing my weakness. Perhaps she saw also the telltale brightness of the approaching fever; she had turned again to Mother Hildegarde and her voice had dropped further—perhaps suggesting that they wait; two funerals might be needed.

And unto dust thou shalt return.

But I had come back from the dead. Only Jamie's hold on my body had been strong enough to pull me back from that final barrier, and Master Raymond had known it. I knew that only Jamie himself could pull me back the rest of the way, into the land of the living. That was why I had run from him, done all I could to keep him away, to make sure he would never come near me again. I had no wish to come back, no desire to feel again. I didn't want to know love, only to have it ripped away once more.

But it was too late. I knew that, even as I fought to hold the gray shroud around me. Fighting only hastened its dissolution; it was like grasping shreds of cloud, that vanished in cold mist between my fingers. I could feel the light coming, blinding and searing.

He had risen, was standing over me. His shadow fell across my knees; surely that meant the cloud had broken; a shadow doesn't fall without light.

"Claire," he whispered. "Please. Let me give ye comfort."

"Comfort?" I said. "And how will you do that? Can you give me back my child?"

He sank to his knees before me, but I kept my head down, staring into my upturned hands, laid empty on my lap. I felt his movement as he reached to touch me, hesitated, drew back, reached again.

"No," he said, his voice scarcely audible. "No, I canna do that. But . . . with the grace of God . . . I might give ye another?"

His hand hovered over mine, close enough that I felt the warmth of his skin. I felt other things as well: the grief that he held tight under rein, the anger and the fear that choked him, and the courage that made him speak in spite of it. I gathered my own courage around me, a flimsy substitute for the thick gray shroud. Then I took his hand and lifted my head, and looked full into the face of the sun.

We sat, hands clasped and pressed together on the bench, unmoving, unspeaking, for what seemed like hours, with the cool rain-breeze whispering our thoughts in the grape leaves above. Water drops scattered over us with the passing of the wind, weeping for loss and separation.

"You're cold," Jamie murmured at last, and pulled a fold of his cloak around me, bringing with it the warmth of his skin. I came slowly against him under its shelter, shivering more at the startling solidness, the sudden heat of him, than from the cold.

I laid my hand on his chest, tentative as though the touch of him might burn me in truth, and so we sat for a good while longer, letting the grape leaves talk for us.

"Jamie," I said softly, at last. "Oh, Jamie. Where were you?"

His arm tightened about me, but it was some time before he answered.

"I thought ye were dead, *mo duinne*," he said, so softly I could hardly hear him above the rustling of the arbor.

"I saw ye there—on the ground, at the last. God! Ye were so white, and your skirts all soaked wi' blood . . . I tried to go to ye, Claire, so soon as I saw —I ran to ye, but it was then the Guard took me."

He swallowed hard; I could feel the tremor pass down him, through the long curve of his backbone.

"I fought them . . . I fought, and aye I pleaded . . . but they wouldna stay, and they carried me awa' wi' them. And they put me in a cell, and left me there . . . thinking ye were dead, Claire; knowing that I'd killed you."

The fine tremor went on, and I knew he was weeping, though I could not see his face above me. How long had he sat alone in the dark of the Bastille, alone but for the scent of blood and the empty husk of vengeance?

"It's all right," I said, and pressed my hand harder against his chest, as though to still the hasty beating of his heart. "Jamie, it's all right. It . . . it wasn't your fault."

"I tried to bash my head against the wall—only to stop thinking," he said, nearly in a whisper. "So they tied me, hand and foot. And next day, de Rohan found me, and told me that ye lived, though likely not for long."

He was silent then, but I could feel the pain inside him, sharp as crystal spears of ice.

"Claire," he murmured at last. "I am sorry."

I am sorry. The words were those of the note he had left me, before the world shattered. But now I understood them.

"I know," I said. "Jamie, I *know*. Fergus told me. I know why you went."

He drew a deep, shuddering breath.

"Aye, well . . ." he said, and stopped.

I let my hand fall to his thigh; chilled and damp from the rain, his riding breeches were rough under my palm.

"Did they tell you—when they let you go—why you were released?" I tried to keep my own breathing steady, but failed.

His thigh tensed under my hand, but his voice was under better control now.

"No," he said. "Only that it was . . . His Majesty's pleasure." The word "pleasure" was ever so faintly underlined, spoken with a delicate ferocity that made it abundantly clear that he did indeed know the means of his release, whether the warders had told him or not.

I bit my lower lip hard, trying to make up my mind what to tell him now.

"It was Mother Hildegarde," he went on, voice steady. "I went at once to

L'Hôpital des Anges, in search of you. And found Mother Hildegarde, and the wee note ye'd left for me. She . . . told me."

"Yes," I said, swallowing. "I went to see the King . . ."

"I know!" His hand tightened on mine, and from the sound of his breathing, I could tell that his teeth were clenched together.

"But Jamie . . . when I went . . ."

"Christ!" he said, and sat up suddenly, turning to face me. "Do ye not know what I . . . Claire." He closed his eyes briefly, and took a deep breath. "I rode all the way to Orvieto, seeing it; seeing his hands on the white of your skin, his lips on your neck, his—his cock—I saw it at the *lever*—I saw the damn filthy, stubby thing sliding up . . . God, Claire! I sat in prison thinking ye dead, and then I rode to Spain, wishing to Christ ye were!"

The knuckles of the hand holding mine were white, and I could feel the small bones of my fingers crackle in his grip.

I jerked my hand free.

"Jamie, listen to me!"

"No!" he said. "No, I dinna want to hear . . ."

"Listen, damn you!"

There was enough force in my voice to shut him up for an instant, and while he was mute, I began rapidly to tell him the story of the King's chamber; the hooded men, and the shadowed room, the sorcerers' duel, and the death of the Comte St. Germain.

As I talked, the high color faded from his wind-brisked cheeks, and his expression softened from anguish and fury to bewilderment, and gradually, to astonished belief.

"Jesus," he breathed at last. "Oh, holy God."

"Didn't know what you were starting with that silly story, did you?" I felt exhausted, but managed a smile. "So . . . so the Comte . . . it's all right, Jamie. He's . . . gone."

He didn't say anything in reply, but drew me gently to him, so my forehead rested on his shoulder, and my tears soaked into the fabric of his shirt. After a minute, though, I sat up, and stared at him, wiping my nose.

"I just thought, Jamie! The port—Charles Stuart's investment! If the Comte is dead . . ."

He shook his head, smiling faintly.

"No, *mo duinne*. It's safe."

I felt a flood of relief.

"Oh, thank God. You managed, then? Did the medicines work on Murtagh?"

"Well, no," he said, the smile broadening, "but they did on me."

Relieved at once of fear and anger, I felt light-headed, and half-giddy. The smell of the rain-swept grapes was strong and sweet, and it was a blessed relief to lean against him, feeling his warmth as comfort, not as threat, as I listened to the story of the port-wine piracy.

"There are men that are born to the sea, Sassenach," he began, "but I'm afraid I'm no one of them."

"I know," I said. "Were you sick?"

"I have seldom been sicker," he assured me wryly.

The seas off Orvieto had been rough, and within an hour it became clear that Jamie was not going to be able to carry out his original part in the plan.

"I couldna do anything but lie in my hammock and groan, in any case," he said, shrugging, "so it seemed I might as well have pox, too."

He and Murtagh had hastily changed roles, and twenty-four hours off the coast of Spain, the master of the *Scalamandre* had discovered to his horror that plague had broken out below.

Jamie scratched his neck reflectively, as though still feeling the effects of the nettle juice.

"They thought of throwing me overboard when they found out," he said, "and I must say it seemed a verra fine idea to me." He gave me a lopsided grin. "Have ye ever had seasickness while covered wi' nettle rash, Sassenach?"

"No, thank God." I shuddered at the thought. "Did Murtagh stop them?"

"Oh, aye. He's verra fierce, is Murtagh. He slept across the threshold wi' his hand on his dirk, until we came safe to port at Bilbao."

True to forecast, the *Scalamandre*'s captain, faced with the unprofitable choice of proceeding to Le Havre and forfeiting his cargo, or returning to Spain and cooling his heels while word was sent to Paris, had leaped at the opportunity to dispose of his hold's worth of port to the new purchaser chance had thrown in his way.

"Not that he didna drive a hard bargain," Jamie observed, scratching his forearm. "He haggled for half a day—and me dying in my hammock, pissing blood and puking my guts out!"

But the bargain had been concluded, both port and smallpox patient unloaded with dispatch at Bilbao, and—aside from a lingering tendency to urinate vermilion—Jamie's recovery had been rapid.

"We sold the port to a broker there in Bilbao," he said. "I sent Murtagh at once to Paris, to repay Monsieur Duverney's loan—and then . . . I came here."

He looked down at his hands, lying quiet in his lap. "I couldna decide," he said softly. "To come or no. I walked, ye ken, to give myself time to think. I walked all the way from Paris to Fontainebleau. And nearly all the way back. I turned back half a dozen times, thinking myself a murderer and a fool, not knowing if I would rather kill myself or you . . ."

He sighed then, and looked up at me, eyes dark with reflections of the fluttering leaves.

"I had to come," he said simply.

I didn't say anything, but laid my hand over his and sat beside him. Fallen grapes littered the ground under the arbor, the pungent scent of their fermentation promising the forgetfulness of wine.

The cloud-streaked sun was setting, and a blur of gold silhouetted the respectful form of Hugo, looming black in the entrance to the arbor.

"Your pardon, Madame," he said. "My mistress wishes to know—will *le seigneur* be staying for supper?"

I looked at Jamie. He sat still, waiting, the sun through the grape leaves streaking his hair with a tiger's blaze, shadows falling across his face.

"I think you'd better," I said. "You're awfully thin."

He looked me over with a half-smile. "So are you, Sassenach."

He rose and offered me his arm. I took it and we went in together to supper, leaving the grape leaves to their muted conversation.

<hr />

I lay next to Jamie, close against him, his hand resting on my thigh as he slept. I stared upward into the darkness of the bedroom, listening to the peaceful sigh of his sleeping breath, breathing myself the fresh-washed scent of the damp night air, tinged with the smell of wisteria.

The collapse of the Comte St. Germain had been the end of the evening, so far as all were concerned save Louis. As the company made to depart, murmuring excitedly among themselves, he took my arm, and led me out through the same small door by which I had entered. Good with words when required, he had no need of them here.

I was led to the green silk chaise, laid on my back and my skirts gently lifted before I could speak. He did not kiss me; he did not desire me. This was the ritual claiming of the payment agreed upon. Louis was a shrewd bargainer, and not one to forgive a debt he thought owed to him, whether the payment had value to him or not. And perhaps it did, after all; there was more than a hint of half-fearful excitement in his preparations—who but a king would dare to take La Dame Blanche in his embrace?

I was closed and dry, unready. Impatient, he seized a flagon of rose-scented oil from the table, and massaged it briefly between my legs. I lay unmoving, soundless, as the hastily probing finger withdrew, replaced at once by a member little larger, and—"suffered" is the wrong word, there was neither pain nor humiliation involved; it was a transaction—I waited, then, through the quick thrusting, and then he was on his feet, face flushed with excitement, hands fumbling to refasten his breeches over the small swelling within. He would not risk the possibility of a half-Royal, half-magic bastard; not with Madame de La Tourelle ready—a good deal readier than I, I hoped—and waiting in her own chambers down the hall.

I had given what was implicitly promised; now he could with honor accede to my request, feeling no *virtu* had gone forth from him. As for me, I met his courteous bow with my own, took my elbow from the grip with which he had gallantly escorted me to the door, and left the audience chamber only a few minutes after entering it, with the King's assurance that the order for Jamie's freedom would be given in the morning.

The Gentleman of the Bedchamber was standing in the hall, waiting. He bowed to me, and I bowed back, then followed him down the Hall of Mirrors, feeling the slipperiness of my oily thighs as they brushed each other, and smelling the strong scent of roses between my legs.

Hearing the gate of the palace shut behind me, I had closed my eyes and thought that I would never see Jamie again. And if by chance I did, I would rub his nose in the scent of roses, until his soul sickened and died.

But now instead I held his hand on my thigh, listening to his breathing, deep and even in the dark beside me. And I let the door close forever on His Majesty's audience.

29

To Grasp the Nettle

"Scotland." I sighed, thinking of the cool brown streams and dark pines of Lallybroch, Jamie's estate. "Can we really go home?"

"I expect we'll have to," he answered wryly. "The King's pardon says I leave France by mid-September, or I'm back in the Bastille. Presumably, His Majesty has arranged a pardon as well from the English Crown, so I willna be hanged directly I get off the ship in Inverness."

"I suppose we could go to Rome, or to Germany," I suggested, tentatively. I wanted nothing more than to go home to Lallybroch, and heal in the quiet peace of the Scottish Highlands. My heart sank at the thought of royal courts and intrigue, the constant press of danger and insecurity. But if Jamie felt we must . . .

He shook his head, red hair falling over his face as he stooped to pull on his stockings.

"Nay, it's Scotland or the Bastille," he said. "Our passage is already booked, just to make sure." He straightened and brushed the hair out of his eyes with a wry smile. "I imagine the Duke of Sandringham—and possibly King George—want me safe at home, where they can keep an eye on me. Not spying in Rome, or raising money in Germany. The three weeks' grace, I gather, is a courtesy to Jared, giving him time to come home before I leave."

I was sitting in the window seat of my bedroom, looking out over the tumbled green sea of the Fontainebleau woods. The hot, languid air of summer seemed to press down, sapping all energy.

"I can't say I'm not glad." I sighed, pressing my cheek against the glass in search of a moment's coolness. The legacy of yesterday's chill rain was a blanketing humidity that made hair and clothes cling to my skin, itching and damp. "Do you think it's safe, though? I mean, will Charles give up, now that the Comte is dead, and the money from Manzetti lost?"

Jamie frowned, rubbing his hand along the edge of his jaw to judge the growth of the stubble.

"I wish I knew whether he'd had a letter from Rome in the last two weeks," he said, "and if so, what was in it. But aye, I think we've managed. No banker in Europe will advance anyone of the name of Stuart a brass centime, that's for sure. Philip of Spain has other fish to fry, and Louis—" He shrugged, his mouth twisting wryly. "Between Monsieur Duverney and the Duke of

Sandringham, I'd say Charles's expectations in that direction are somewhat less than poor. Shall I shave, d'ye think?"

"Not on my account," I said. The casual intimacy of the question made me suddenly shy. We had shared a bed the night before, but we had both been exhausted, and the delicate web woven between us in the arbor had seemed too fragile to support the stress of attempting to make love. I had spent the night in a terrible consciousness of his warm proximity, but thought I must, under the circumstances, leave the first move to him.

Now I caught the play of light across his shoulders as he turned to find his shirt, and was seized with the desire to touch him; to feel him, smooth and hard and eager against me once more.

His head popped through the neck of his shirt, and his eyes met mine, suddenly and unguarded. He paused for a moment, looking at me, but not speaking. The morning sounds of the château were clearly audible, outside the bubble of silence that surrounded us; the bustling of servants, the high thin sound of Louise's voice, raised in some sort of altercation.

Not here, Jamie's eyes said. *Not in the midst of so many people.*

He looked down, carefully fastening his shirt buttons. "Does Louise keep horses for riding?" he asked, eyes on his task. "There are some cliffs a few miles away; I thought perhaps we might ride there—the air may be cooler."

"I think she does," I said. "I'll ask."

We reached the cliffs just before noon. Not cliffs so much as jutting pillars and ridges of limestone that sat among the yellowing grass of the surrounding hills like the ruins of an ancient city. The pale ridges were split and fissured from time and weather, spattered with thousands of strange, tiny plants that had found a foothold in the merest scrape of eroded soil.

We left the horses hobbled in the grass, and climbed on foot to a wide, flat shelf of limestone covered with tufts of rough grass, just below the highest tumble of stone. There was little shade from the scruffy bushes, but up this high, there was a small breeze.

"God, it's hot!" Jamie said. He flipped loose the buckle of his kilt, so it fell around his feet, and started to wriggle out of his shirt.

"What are you doing, Jamie?" I said, half-laughing.

"Stripping," he replied, matter-of-factly. "Why don't ye do the same, Sassenach? You're more soaked than I am, and there's none here to see."

After a moment's hesitation, I did as he suggested. It was entirely isolated here; too craggy and rocky for sheep, the chance of even a stray shepherd coming upon us was remote. And alone, naked together, away from Louise and her throngs of intrusive servants . . . Jamie spread his plaid on the rough ground as I peeled out of my sweat-clinging garments.

He stretched lazily and settled back, arms behind his head, completely oblivious to curious ants, stray bits of gravel and the stubs of prickly vegetation.

"You must have the hide of a goat," I remarked. "How can you lie on the bare ground like that?" As bare as he, I reposed more comfortably on a thick fold of the plaid he had thoughtfully spread out for me.

He shrugged, eyes closed against the warm afternoon sun. The light gilded him in the hollow where he lay, making him glow red-gold against the dark of the rough grass beneath him.

"I'll do," he said comfortably, and lapsed into silence, the sound of his breathing near enough to reach me over the faint whine of the wind that crossed the ridges above us.

I rolled onto my belly and laid my chin on my crossed forearms, watching him. He was wide at the shoulder and narrow at the hip, with long, powerful haunches slightly dented by muscles held taut even as he relaxed. The small, warm breeze stirred the drying tufts of soft cinnamon hair beneath his arms, and ruffled the copper and gold that waved gently over his wrists, where they braced his head. The slight breeze was welcome, for the early autumn sun was still hot on my shoulders and calves.

"I love you," I said softly, not meaning him to hear me, but only for the pleasure of saying it.

He did hear, though, for the hint of a smile curved the wide mouth. After a moment, he rolled over onto his belly on the plaid beside me. A few blades of grass clung to his back and buttocks. I brushed one lightly away, and his skin shivered briefly at my touch.

I leaned to kiss his shoulder, enjoying the warm scent of his skin and the faint salty taste of him.

Instead of kissing me back, though, he pulled away a bit, and lay propped on one elbow, looking at me. There was something in his expression that I didn't understand, and it made me faintly uneasy.

"Penny for your thoughts," I said, running a finger down the deep groove of his backbone. He moved just far enough to avoid my touch, and took a deep breath.

"Well, I was wondering—" he began, and then stopped. He was looking down, fiddling with a tiny flower that sprang out of the grass.

"You were wondering what?"

"What it was like . . . with Louis."

I thought my heart had stopped for a moment. I knew all the blood had left my face, because I could feel the numbness of my lips as I forced the words out.

"What . . . it . . . was like?"

He looked up then, making only a passing-fair attempt at a lopsided smile.

"Well," he said. "He *is* a king. You'd think it would be . . . different, somehow. You know . . . special, maybe?"

The smile was slipping, and his face had gone as white as my own. He looked down again, avoiding my stricken gaze.

"I suppose all I was wondering," he murmured, "was . . . was he . . . was he different from me?" I saw him bite his lip as though wishing the words unsaid, but it was far too late for that.

"How in hell did you know?" I said. I felt dizzy and exposed, and rolled onto my stomach, pressing myself hard to the short turf.

He shook his head, teeth still clenched in his lower lip. When he finally released it, a deep red mark showed where he had bitten it.

"Claire," he said softly. "Oh, Claire. You gave me all yourself from the first time, and held nothing back from me. You never did. When I asked ye for honesty, I told ye then that it isna in you to lie. When I touched ye so—" His hand moved, cupping my buttock, and I flinched, not expecting it.

"How long have I loved you?" he asked, very quietly. "A year? Since the moment I saw you. And loved your body how often—half a thousand times or more?" One finger touched me then, gently as a moth's foot, tracing the line of arm and shoulder, gliding down my rib cage 'til I shivered at the touch and rolled away, facing him now.

"You never shrank from my touch," he said, eyes intent on the path his finger took, dipping down to follow the curve of my breast. "Not even at the first, when ye might have done so, and no surprise to me if ye had. But you didn't. You gave me everything from the very first time; held nothing back, denied me no part of you."

"But now . . ." he said, drawing back his hand. "I thought at first it was only that you'd lost the child, and maybe were shy of me, or feeling strange after so long apart. But then I knew that wasn't it."

There was a very long silence, then. I could feel the steady, painful thudding of my heart against the cold ground, and hear the conversation of the wind in the pines down below. Small birds called, far away. I wished I were one. Or far away, at any rate.

"Why?" he asked softly. "Why lie to me? When I had come to you thinking I knew, anyway?"

I stared down at my hands, linked beneath my chin, and swallowed.

"If . . ." I began, and swallowed again. "If I told you that I had let Louis . . . you would have asked about it. I thought you couldn't forget . . . maybe you could forgive me, but you'd never forget, and it would always be there between us." I swallowed once more, hard. My hands were cold despite the heat, and I felt a ball of ice in my stomach. But if I was telling him the truth now, I must tell him all of it.

"If you'd asked—and you did, Jamie, you did! I would have had to talk about it, live it over, and I was afraid . . ." I trailed off, unable to speak, but he wasn't going to let me off.

"Afraid of what?" he prodded.

I turned my head slightly, not meeting his eye, but enough to see his outline dark against the sun, looming through the sun-sparked curtain of my hair.

"Afraid I'd tell you why I did it," I said softly. "Jamie . . . I had to, to get you freed from the Bastille—I would have done worse, if I'd had to. But then . . . and afterward . . . I half-hoped someone would tell you, that you'd find out. I was so angry, Jamie—for the duel, and the baby. And because you'd forced me to do it . . . to go to Louis. I wanted to do something to drive you away, to make sure I never saw you again. I did it . . . partly . . . because I wanted to hurt you," I whispered.

A muscle contracted near the corner of his mouth, but he went on staring downward at his clasped hands. The chasm between us, so perilously bridged, gaped yawning and impassable once more.

"Aye. Well, you did."

His mouth clamped shut in a tight line, and he didn't speak for some time. Finally he turned his head and looked directly at me. I would have liked to avoid his eyes, but couldn't.

"Claire," he said softly. "What did ye feel—when I gave my body to Jack Randall? When I let him take me, at Wentworth?"

A tiny shock ran through me, from scalp to toenails. It was the last question I had expected to hear. I opened and closed my mouth several times before finding an answer.

"I . . . don't know," I said weakly. "I hadn't thought. Angry, of course. I was furious—outraged. And sick. And frightened for you. And . . . sorry for you."

"Were ye jealous? When I told you about it later—that he'd roused me, though I didna want it?"

I drew a deep breath, feeling the grass tickle my breasts.

"No. At least I don't think so; I didn't think so then. After all, it wasn't as though you'd . . . wanted to do it." I bit my lip, looking down. His voice was quiet and matter-of-fact at my shoulder.

"I dinna think you wanted to bed Louis—did you?"

"No!"

"Aye, well," he said. He put his thumbs together on either side of a blade of grass, and concentrated on pulling it up slowly by the roots. "I was angry, too. And sick and sorry." The grass blade came free of its sheath with a tiny squeaking sound.

"When it was me," he went on, almost whispering, "I thought you could not bear the thought of it, and I would not have blamed you. I knew ye must turn from me, and I tried to send you away, so I wouldna have to see the disgust and the hurt in your face." He closed his eyes and raised the grass blade between his thumbs, barely brushing his lips.

"But you wouldna go. You took me to your breast and cherished me. You healed me, instead. You loved me, in spite of it." He took a deep, unsteady breath and turned his head to me again. His eyes were bright with tears, but no wetness escaped to slide down his cheeks.

"I thought, maybe, that I could bring myself to do that for you, as you did it for me. And that is why I came to Fontainebleau, at last."

He blinked once, hard, and his eyes cleared.

"Then when ye told me that nothing had happened—for a bit, I believed you, because I wanted to so much. But then . . . I could tell, Claire. I couldna hide it from myself, and I knew you had lied to me. I thought you wouldna trust me to love you, or . . . that you *had* wanted him, and were afraid to let me see it."

He dropped the grass, and his head sank forward to rest on his knuckles.

"Ye said you wanted to hurt me. Well, the thought of you lying with the King hurt worse than the brand on my breast, or the cut of the lash on my naked back. But the knowledge that ye thought ye couldna trust me to love you is like waking from the hangman's noose to feel the gutting knife sunk in my belly. Claire—" His mouth opened soundlessly, then closed tight for a moment, until he found the strength to go on.

"I do not know if the wound is mortal, but Claire—I do feel my heart's blood leave me, when I look at you."

The silence between us grew and deepened. The small buzz of an insect calling in the rocks vibrated in the air.

Jamie was still as a rock, his face blank as he stared down at the ground below him. I couldn't bear that blank face, and the thought of what must lie concealed behind it. I had seen a hint of his despairing fury in the arbor, and my heart felt hollow at the thought of that rage, mastered at such fearful cost, now held under an iron control that kept in not only rage, but trust and joy.

I wished desperately for some way to break the silence that parted us; some act that could restore the lost truth between us. Jamie sat up then, arms folded tight about his thighs, and turned away as he gazed out over the peaceful valley.

Better violence, I thought, than silence. I reached across the chasm between us and laid a hand on his arm. It was warm from the sun, live to my touch.

"Jamie," I whispered. "Please."

His head turned slowly toward me. His face seemed still calm, though the cat-eyes narrowed further as he looked at me in silence. He reached out, finally, and one hand gripped me by the wrist.

"Do ye wish me to beat you, then?" he said softly. His grasp tightened hard, so that I jerked unconsciously, trying to pull away from him. He pulled back, yanking me across the rough grass, bringing my body against him.

I felt myself trembling, and gooseflesh lifted the hairs on my forearms, but I managed to speak.

"Yes," I said.

His expression was unfathomable. Still holding my eyes with his own, he reached out his free hand, fumbling over the rocks until he touched a bunch of nettles. He drew in his breath as his fingers touched the prickly stems, but his jaw clenched; he closed his fist and ripped the plants up by the roots.

"The peasants of Gascony beat a faithless wife wi' nettles," he said. He lowered the spiky bunch of leaves and brushed the flower heads lightly across one breast. I gasped from the sudden sting, and a faint red blotch appeared as though by magic on my skin.

"Will ye have me do so?" he asked. "Shall I punish you that way?"

"If you . . . if you like." My lips were trembling so hard I could barely get out the words. A few crumbs of earth from the nettles' roots had fallen between my breasts; one rolled down the slope of my ribs, dislodged by my pounding heart, I imagined. The welt on my breast burned like fire. I closed my eyes, imagining in vivid detail exactly what being thrashed with a bunch of nettles would feel like.

Suddenly the viselike grip on my wrist relaxed. I opened my eyes to find Jamie sitting cross-legged by me, the plants thrown aside and scattered on the ground. He had a faint, rueful smile on his lips.

"I beat you once in justice, Sassenach, and ye threatened to disembowel me with my own dirk. Now you'll ask me to whip ye wi' nettles?" He shook his head slowly, wondering, and his hand reached as though by its own volition to cup my cheek. "Is my pride worth so much to you, then?"

"Yes! Yes, it bloody is!" I sat up myself, and grasped him by the shoulders, taking both of us by surprise as I kissed him hard and awkwardly.

I felt his first involuntary start, and then he pulled me to him, arm tight around my back, mouth answering mine. Then he had me pressed flat to the earth, his weight holding me immobile beneath him. His shoulders darkened the bright sky above, and his hands held my arms against my sides, keeping me prisoner.

"All right," he whispered. His eyes bored into mine, daring me to close them, forcing me to hold his gaze. "All right. And ye wish it, I shall punish you." He moved his hips against me in imperious command, and I felt my legs open for him, my gates thrown wide to welcome ravishment.

"Never," he whispered to me. "*Never*. Never another but me! Look at me! Tell me! *Look at me, Claire*!" He moved in me, strongly, and I moaned and would have turned my head, but he held my face between his hands, forcing me to meet his eyes, to see his wide, sweet mouth, twisted in pain.

"Never," he said, more softly. "For you are mine. My wife, my heart, my soul." The weight of him held me still, like a boulder on my chest, but the friction of our flesh made me thrust against him, wanting more. And more.

"My body," he said, gasping for breath as he gave me what I sought. I bucked beneath him as though I wanted to escape, my back arching like a bow, pressing me into him. He lay then at full length on me, scarcely moving, so that our most intimate connection seemed barely closer than the marriage of our skins.

The grass was harsh and prickly under me, the pungence of crushed stems sharp as the smell of the man who took me. My breasts were flattened under him, and I felt the small tickle of the hairs on his chest as we rubbed together, back and forth. I squirmed, urging him to violence, feeling the swell of his thighs as he pressed me down.

"Never," he whispered to me, face only inches from mine.

"Never," I said, and turned my head, closing my eyes to escape the intensity of his gaze.

A gentle, inexorable pressure turned me back to face him, as the small, rhythmic movements went on.

"No, my Sassenach," he said softly. "Open your eyes. Look at me. For that is your punishment, as it is mine. See what you have done to me, as I know what I have done to you. Look at me."

And I looked, held prisoner, bound to him. Looked, as he dropped the last of his masks, and showed me the depths of himself, and the wounds of his soul. I would have wept for his hurt, and for mine, had I been able. But his eyes held mine, tearless and open, boundless as the salt sea. His body held mine captive, driving me before his strength, like the west wind in the sails of a bark.

And I voyaged into him, as he into me, so that when the last small storms of love began to shake me, he cried out, and we rode the waves together as one flesh, and saw ourselves in each other's eyes.

The afternoon sun was hot on the white limestone rocks, casting deep shadows into the clefts and hollows. I found what I was looking for at last, growing from a narrow crack in a giant boulder, in gay defiance of the lack of soil. I broke a stalk of aloe from its clump, split the fleshy leaf, and spread the cool green gel inside across the welts on Jamie's palm.

"Better?" I said.

"Much." Jamie flexed his hand, grimacing. "Christ, those nettles sting!"

"They do." I pulled down the neck of my bodice and spread a little aloe juice on my breast with a gingerly touch. The coolness brought relief at once.

"I'm rather glad you didn't take me up on my offer," I said wryly, with a glance at a nearby bunch of blooming nettle.

He grinned and patted me on the bottom with his good hand.

"Well, it was a near thing, Sassenach. Ye shouldna tempt me like that." Then, sobering, he bent and kissed me gently.

"No, *mo duinne*. I swore to ye the once, and I was meaning it. I shallna raise a hand to you in anger, ever. After all," he added softly, turning away, "I have done enough to hurt you."

I shrank from the pain of memory, but I owed him justice as well.

"Jamie," I said, lips trembling a bit. "The . . . baby. It wasn't your fault. I felt as though it was, but it wasn't. I think . . . I think it would have happened anyway, whether you'd fought Jack Randall or not."

"Aye? Ah . . . well." His arm was warm and comforting about me, and he pressed my head into the curve of his shoulder. "It eases me a bit to hear ye say so. It wasna the child so much as Frank that I meant, though. D'ye think you can forgive me for that?" The blue eyes were troubled as he looked down at me.

"Frank?" I felt a shock of surprise. "But . . . there's nothing to forgive." Then a thought struck me; perhaps he really didn't know that Jack Randall was still alive—after all, he had been arrested immediately after the duel. But if he didn't know. . . . I took a deep breath. He would have to find it out in any case; perhaps better from me.

"You didn't kill Jack Randall, Jamie," I said.

To my puzzlement, he didn't seem shocked or surprised. He shook his head, the afternoon sun striking sparks from his hair. Not yet long enough to lace back again, it had grown considerably in prison, and he had to brush it out of his eyes continuously.

"I know that, Sassenach," he said.

"You do? But . . . what . . ." I was at a loss.

"You . . . dinna know about it?" he said hesitantly.

A cold feeling crept up my arms, despite the heat of the sun.

"Know what?"

He chewed his lower lip, eyeing me reluctantly. At last he took a deep breath and let it out with a sigh.

"No, I didna kill him. But I wounded him."

"Yes, Louise said you wounded him badly. But she said he was recovering." Suddenly, I saw again in memory that last scene in the Bois de Boulogne; the last thing I had seen before the blackness took me. The sharp tip of Jamie's sword, slicing through the rain-spattered doeskin. The sudden red stain that darkened the fabric . . . and the angle of the blade, glinting with the force that drove it downward.

"Jamie!" I said, eyes widening with horror. "You didn't . . . Jamie, what have you done!"

He looked down, rubbing his welted palm against the side of his kilt. He shook his head, wondering at himself.

"I was such a fool, Sassenach. I couldna think myself a man and let him go unpunished for what he'd done to the wee lad, and yet . . . all the time, I kept thinking to myself, 'Ye canna kill the bastard outright, you've promised. Ye canna kill him.' " He smiled faintly, without humor, looking down at the marks on his palm.

"My mind was boiling over like a pot of parritch on the flame, yet I held to that thought. 'Ye canna kill him.' And I didn't. But I was half-mad wi' the fury of the fighting, and the blood singing in my ears—and I didna stop a moment to remember why it was I must not kill him, beyond that I had promised you. And when I had him there on the ground before me, and the memory of Wentworth and Fergus, and the blade live in my hand—" He broke off suddenly.

I felt the blood draining from my head and sat down heavily on a rock outcropping.

"Jamie," I said. He shrugged helplessly.

"Well, Sassenach," he said, still avoiding my gaze, "all I can say is, it's a hell of a place to be wounded."

"Jesus." I sat still, stunned by this revelation. Jamie sat quiet beside me, studying the broad backs of his hands. There was still a small pink mark on the back of the right one. Jack Randall had driven a nail through it, in Wentworth.

"D'ye hate me for it, Claire?" His voice was soft, almost tentative.

I shook my head, eyes closed.

"No." I opened them, and saw his face close by, wearing a troubled frown. "I don't know *what* I think now, Jamie. I really don't. But I don't hate you." I put a hand on his, and squeezed it gently. "Just . . . let me be by myself for a minute, all right?"

Clad once more in my now-dry gown, I spread my hands flat on my thighs. One silver, one gold. Both my wedding rings were still there, and I had no idea what that meant.

Jack Randall would never father a child. Jamie seemed sure of it, and I wasn't inclined to question him. And yet I still wore Frank's ring, I still remembered the man who had been my first husband, could summon at will thoughts and memories of who he had been, what he would do. How was it possible, then, that he would not exist?

I shook my head, thrusting back the wind-dried curls behind my ears. I didn't know. Chances were, I never *would* know. But whether one could change the future or not—and it seemed we had—I was certain that I couldn't change the immediate past. What had been done had been done, and nothing I could do now would alter it. Jack Randall would sire no children.

A stone rolled down the slope behind me, bouncing and setting off small slides of gravel. I turned and glanced up, to where Jamie, dressed once more, was exploring.

The rockfall above was recent. Fresh white surfaces showed where the stained brown of the weathered limestone had fractured, and only the smallest of plants had yet gained a foothold in this tumbled pile of rock, unlike the thick growth of shrubs that blanketed the rest of the hillside.

Jamie inched to one side, absorbed in finding handholds through the intricacies of the fall. I saw him edge around a giant boulder, hugging the rock, and the faint scrape of his dirk against the stone came to me through the still afternoon air.

Then he disappeared. Expecting him to reappear round the other side of the rock, I waited, enjoying the sun on my shoulders. But he didn't come back into sight, and after a few moments, I grew worried. He might have slipped and fallen or banged his head on a rock.

I took what seemed forever to undo the fastenings of my heeled boots again, and still he had not come back. I rucked up my skirts, and started up the hill, bare toes cautious on the rough warm rocks.

"Jamie!"

"Here, Sassenach." He spoke behind me, startling me, and I nearly lost my balance. He caught me by the arm and lifted me down to a small clear space between the jagged fallen stones.

He turned me toward the limestone wall, stained with water rust, and smoke. And something more.

"Look," he said softly.

I looked where he pointed, up across the smooth expanse of the cave wall, and gasped at the sight.

Painted beasts galloped across the rock face above me, hooves spurning the air as they leaped toward the light above. There were bison, and deer, grouped together in tail-raised flight, and at the end of the rock shelf, a tracing of delicate birds, wings spread as they hovered above the charge of the earth-bound beasts.

Done in red and black and ochre with a delicate grace that used the lines of the rock itself for emphasis, they thundered soundlessly, haunches rounded with effort, wings taking flight through the crevices of stone. They had lived once in the dark of a cave, lit only by the flames of those who made them. Exposed to the sun by the fall of their sheltering roof, they seemed alive as anything that walked upon the earth.

Lost in contemplation of the massive shoulders that thrust their way from the rock, I didn't miss Jamie until he called me.

"Sassenach! Come here, will ye?" There was something odd about his voice, and I hurried toward him. He stood at the entrance of a small side-cave, looking down.

They lay behind an outcrop of the rock, as though they had sought shelter from the wind that chased the bison.

There were two of them, lying together on the packed earth of the cave floor. Sealed in the dry air of the cave, the bones had endured, though flesh had long since dried to dust. A tiny remnant of brown-parchment skin clung to the round curve of one skull, a strand of hair gone red with age stirring softly in the draft of our presence.

"My God," I said, softly, as though I might disturb them. I moved closer to Jamie, and his hand slid around my waist.

"Do you think . . . were they . . . killed here? A sacrifice, perhaps?"

Jamie shook his head, staring pensively down at the small heap of delicate, friable bones.

"No," he said. He, too, spoke softly, as though in the sanctuary of a church. He turned and lifted a hand to the wall behind us, where the deer leaped and the cranes soared into space beyond the stone.

"No," he said again. "The folk that made such beasts . . . they couldna do such things." He turned again then to the two skeletons, entwined at our feet. He crouched over them, tracing the line of the bones with a gentle finger, careful not to touch the ivory surface.

"See how they lie," he said. "They didna fall here, and no one laid out their bodies. They lay down themselves." His hand glided above the long arm-bones of the larger skeleton, a dark shadow fluttering like a large moth as it crossed the jackstraw pile of ribs.

"He had his arms around her," he said. "He cupped his thighs behind her own, and held her tight to him, and his head is resting on her shoulder."

His hand made passes over the bones, illuminating, indicating, clothing them once more with the flesh of imagination, so I could see them as they had been, embraced for the last time, for always. The small bones of the fingers had fallen apart, but a vestige of gristle still joined the metacarpals of the hands. The tiny phalanges overlay each other; they had linked hands in their last waiting.

Jamie had risen and was surveying the interior of the cavern, the late afternoon sun painting the walls with splashes of crimson and ochre.

"There." He pointed to a spot near the cavern entrance. The rocks there were brown with dust and age, but not rusty with water and erosion, like those deeper in the cave.

"That was the entrance, once," he said. "The rocks fell once before, and sealed this place." He turned back and rested a hand on the rocky outcrop that shielded the lovers from the light.

"They must have felt their way around the cave, hand in hand," I said. "Looking for a way out, in the dust and the dark."

"Aye." He rested his forehead against the stone, eyes closed. "And the light was gone, and the air failed them. And so they lay down in the dark to die." The tears made wet tracks through the dust on his cheeks. I brushed a hand beneath my own eyes, and took his free hand, carefully weaving my fingers with his.

He turned to me, wordless, and the breath rushed from him as he pulled me hard against him. Our hands groped in the dying light of the setting sun, urgent in the touch of warmth, the reassurance of flesh, reminded by the hardness of the invisible bone beneath the skin, how short life is.

PART FIVE

"I Am Come Home"

30

Lallybroch

I t was called Broch Tuarach, for the ancient cylinder of stone, built some hundreds of years before, that poked up from the hillside behind the manor. The people who lived on the estate called it "Lallybroch." Insofar as I could gather, this meant "lazy tower," which made at least as much sense as applying the term "North-facing Tower" to a cylindrical structure.

"How can something that's round face north?" I asked as we made our way slowly down a long slope of heather and granite, leading the horses in single file down the narrow, twisting path the red deer had trampled through the springy growth. "It hasn't *got* a face."

"It has a door," Jamie said reasonably. "The door faces north." He dug in his feet as the slope dropped sharply, hissing through his teeth in signal to the horse he led behind him. The muscular hindquarters in front of me bunched suddenly, as the cautious stride altered to a tentative mincing, each hoof sliding a few inches in the damp earth before another step was risked. The horses, purchased in Inverness, were good-sized, handsome beasts. The wiry little Highland ponies would have made much better work of the steep slope, but these horses, all mares, were meant for breeding, not work.

"All right," I said, stepping carefully over a tiny runnel of water that crossed the deer path. "Good enough. What about 'Lallybroch,' though? Why is it a lazy tower?"

"It leans a bit," Jamie replied. I could see the back of his head, bent in concentration on the footing, a few tendrils of red-gold hair lifting from the crown in the afternoon breeze that blew up the slope. "Ye canna see it much from the house, but if you stand on the west side, you'll see it leans to the north a bit. And if ye look from one of the slits on the top floor over the door, ye canna see the wall beneath you because of the slant."

"Well, I suppose no one had heard of plumb lines in the thirteenth century," I observed. "It's a wonder it hasn't fallen down by now."

"Oh, it's fallen down a number of times," Jamie said, raising his voice slightly as the wind freshened. "The folk who lived there just put it back up again; that's likely why it leans."

"I see it! I see it!" Fergus's voice, shrill with excitement, came from behind me. He had been allowed to stay on his mount, as his negligible weight was unlikely to cause the horse any great difficulty, bad footing notwithstanding. Glancing back, I could see him kneeling on his saddle, bouncing up and down with excitement. His horse, a patient, good-natured bay mare, gave a grunt at this, but kindly refrained from flinging him off into the heather. Ever since his adventure with the Percheron colt at Argentan, Fergus had seized every chance to get on a horse, and Jamie, amused and sympathetic to a fellow horse-lover, had indulged him, taking him up behind his own saddle when he rode through the Paris streets, allowing him now and then to get up alone on one of Jared's coach horses, large stolid creatures that merely flicked their ears in a puzzled sort of way at Fergus's kicks and shouts.

I shaded my eyes, looking in the direction where he pointed. He was right; from his higher vantage point, he had spotted the dark form of the old stone broch, perched on its hill. The modern manor-house below was harder to see; it was built of white-harled stone, and the sun reflected from its walls as from the surrounding fields. Set in a hollow of sloping barley fields, it was still partly obscured to our view by a row of trees that formed the windbreak at the foot of a field.

I saw Jamie's head rise, and fix as he saw the home farm of Lallybroch below. He stood quite still for a minute, not speaking, but I saw his shoulders lift and set themselves square. The wind caught his hair and the folds of his plaid and lifted them, as though he might rise in the air, joyous as a kite.

It reminded me of the way the sails of the ships had filled, turning past the headland into the shipping roads as they left the harbor of Le Havre. I had stood on the end of the quay, watching the bustle and the comings and goings of shipping and commerce. The gulls dived and shrieked among the masts, their voices raucous as the shouting of the seamen.

Jared Munro Fraser had stood by me, watching benignly the flow of passing seaborne wealth, some of it his. It was one of his ships, the *Portia,* that would carry us to Scotland. Jamie had told me that all Jared's ships were named for his mistresses, the figureheads carved in the likenesses of the ladies in question. I squinted against the wind at the prow of the ship, trying to decide whether Jamie had been teasing me. If not, I concluded, Jared preferred his women well endowed.

"I shall miss you both," Jared said, for the fourth time in half an hour. He looked truly regretful, even his cheerful nose seeming less upturned and optimistic than usual. The trip to Germany had been a success; he sported a large diamond in his stock, and the coat he wore was a rich bottle-green velvet with silver buttons.

"Ah, well," he said, shaking his head. "Much as I should like to keep the laddie with me, I canna grudge him joy of his homecoming. Perhaps I shall come to visit ye someday, my dear; it's been long since I set foot in Scotland."

"We'll miss you, too," I told him, truthfully. There were other people I would miss—Louise, Mother Hildegarde, Herr Gerstmann. Master Raymond most of all. Yet I looked forward to returning to Scotland, to Lallybroch. I had no wish to go back to Paris, and there were people there I most certainly had no desire to see again—Louis of France, for one.

Charles Stuart, for another. Cautious probing amongst the Jacobites in Paris had confirmed Jamie's initial impression; the small burst of optimism fired by Charles's boasting of his "grand venture" had faded, and while the loyal supporters of King James held true to their sovereign, there seemed no chance that this stolid loyalty of stubborn endurance would lead to action.

Let Charles make his own peace with exile, then, I thought. Our own was over. We were going home.

"The baggage is aboard," said a dour Scots voice in my ear. "The master of the ship says come ye along now; we sail wi' the tide."

Jared turned to Murtagh, then glanced right and left down the quay. "Where's the laddie, then?" he asked.

Murtagh jerked his head down the pier. "In the tavern yon. Gettin' stinkin' drunk."

I had wondered just how Jamie had planned to weather the Channel crossing. He had taken one look at the lowering red sky of dawn that threatened later storms, excused himself to Jared, and disappeared. Looking in the direction of Murtagh's nod, I saw Fergus, sitting on a piling near the entrance to one grogshop, plainly doing sentry duty.

Jared, who had exhibited first disbelief and then hilarity when informed of his nephew's disability, grinned widely at this news.

"Oh, aye?" he said. "Well, I hope he's left the last quart 'til we come for him. He'll be hell to carry up the gangplank, if he hasn't."

"What did he do that for?" I demanded of Murtagh, in some exasperation. "I told him I had some laudanum for him." I patted the silk reticule I carried. "It would knock him out a good deal faster."

Murtagh merely blinked once. "Aye. He said if he was goin' to have a headache, he'd as soon enjoy the gettin' of it. And the whisky tastes a good bit better goin' down than yon filthy black stuff." He nodded at my reticule, then at Jared. "Come on, then, if ye mean to help me wi' him."

In the forward cabin of the *Portia*, I had sat on the captain's bunk, watching the steady rise and fall of the receding shoreline, my husband's head cradled on my knees.

One eye opened a slit and looked up at me. I stroked the heavy damp hair off his brow. The scent of ale and whisky hung about him like perfume.

"You are going to feel exactly like hell when you wake up in Scotland," I told him.

The other eye opened, and regarded the dancing waves of light reflected across the timbered ceiling. Then they fixed on me, deep pools of limpid blue.

"Between hell now, and hell later, Sassenach," he said, his speech measured and precise, "I will take later, every time." His eyes closed. He belched softly, once, and the long body relaxed, rocked at ease on the cradle of the deep.

The horses seemed as eager as we; sensing the nearness of stables and food, they began to push the pace a bit, heads up and ears cocked forward in anticipation.

I was just reflecting that I could do with a wash and a bite to eat, myself, when my horse, slightly in the lead, dug in its feet and came to a slithering halt, hooves buried fetlock deep in the reddish dust. The mare shook her head violently from side to side, snorting and whooshing.

"Hey, lass, what's amiss? Got a bee up your nose?" Jamie swung down from his own mount and hurried to grab the gray mare's bridle. Feeling the broad back shiver and twitch beneath me, I slid down as well.

"Whatever is the matter with her?" I gazed curiously at the horse, which was pulling backward against Jamie's grip on the bridle, shaking her mane, with eyes bugging. The other horses, as though infected by her unease, began to stamp and shift as well.

Jamie glanced briefly over his shoulder at the empty road.

"She sees something."

Fergus raised himself in his shortened stirrups and shaded his eyes, staring over the mare's back. Lowering his hand, he looked at me and shrugged.

I shrugged back; there seemed to be nothing whatever to cause the mare's distress—the road and the fields lay vacant all around us, grain-heads ripening and drying in the late summer sun. The nearest grove of trees was more than a hundred yards away, beyond a small heap of stones that might have been the remnants of a tumbled chimneystack. Wolves were almost unheard of in cleared land like this, and surely no fox or badger would disturb a horse at this distance.

Giving up the attempt to coax the mare forward, Jamie led her in a half-circle; she went willingly enough, back in the direction we had come.

He motioned to Murtagh to lead the other horses out of the way, then swung himself into the saddle, and leaning forward, one hand clutched in the mare's mane, urged her slowly forward, speaking softly in her ear. She came hesitantly, but without resistance, until she reached the point of her previous stopping. There she halted again and stood shivering, and nothing would persuade her to move a step farther.

"All right, then," said Jamie, resigned. "Have it your way." He turned the horse's head and led her into the field, the yellow grain-heads brushing the shaggy hairs of her belly. We rustled after them, the horses bending their necks to snatch a mouthful of grain here and there as we passed through the field.

As we rounded a small granite outcrop just below the crest of the hill, I heard a brief warning bark just ahead. We emerged onto the road to find a black and white shepherd dog on guard, head up and tail stiff as he kept a wary eye on us.

He uttered another short yap, and a matching black and white figure shot out of a clump of alders, followed more slowly by a tall, slender figure wrapped in a brown hunting plaid.

"Ian!"

"Jamie!"

Jamie tossed the mare's reins back to me, and met his brother-in-law in the middle of the road, where the two men clutched each other round the shoulders, laughing and pounding each other on the back. Released from suspicion, the dogs frolicked happily around them, tails wagging, darting aside now and then to sniff at the legs of the horses.

"We didna expect ye 'til tomorrow at the earliest," Ian was saying, his long, homely face beaming.

"We had a good wind crossing," Jamie explained. "Or at least Claire tells me we did; I wasna taking much notice, myself." He cast a glance back at me, grinning, and Ian came up to grasp my hand.

"Good-sister," he said in formal greeting. Then he smiled, the warmth of it lighting his soft brown eyes. "Claire." Impulsively, he kissed my fingers, and I squeezed his hand.

"Jenny's gone daft wi' cleaning and cooking," he said, still smiling at me. "You'll be lucky to have a bed to sleep in tonight; she's got all the mattresses outside, being beaten."

"After three nights in the heather, I wouldn't mind sleeping on the floor," I assured him. "Are Jenny and the children all well?"

"Oh, aye. She's breeding again," he added. "Due in February."

"Again?" Jamie and I spoke together, and a rich blush rose in Ian's lean cheeks.

"God, man, wee Maggie's less than a year old," Jamie said, with a censorious cock of one brow. "Have ye no sense of restraint?"

"Me?" Ian said indignantly. "Ye think I had anything to do with it?"

"Well, if ye didn't, I should think ye'd be interested in who did," Jamie said, the corner of his mouth twitching.

The blush deepened to a rich rose color, contrasting nicely with Ian's smooth brown hair. "Ye know damn well what I mean," he said. "I slept on the trundle bed wi' Young Jamie for two months, but then Jenny . . ."

"Oh, you're saying my sister's a wanton, eh?"

"I'm saying she's as stubborn as her brother when it comes to getting what she wants," Ian said. He feinted to one side, dodged neatly back and landed a blow in the pit of Jamie's stomach. Jamie doubled over, laughing.

"Just as well I've come home, then," he said. "I'll help ye keep her under control."

"Oh, aye?" Ian said skeptically. "I'll call all the tenants to watch."

"Lost a few sheep, have ye?" Jamie changed the subject with a gesture that took in the dogs and Ian's long crook, dropped in the dust of the roadway.

"Fifteen yows and a ram," Ian said, nodding. "Jenny's own flock of merinos, that she keeps for the special wool. The ram's a right bastard; broke down the gate. I thought they might have been in the grain up here, but nay sign o' them."

"We didn't see them up above," I said.

"Oh, they wouldna be up there," Ian said, waving a dismissive hand. "None o' the beasts will go past the cottage."

"Cottage?" Fergus, growing impatient with this exchange of civilities, had kicked his mount up alongside mine. "I saw no cottage, milord. Only a pile of stones."

"That's all that's left of MacNab's cottage, laddie," said Ian. He squinted up at Fergus, silhouetted against the late afternoon sun. "And ye'd be well-advised to keep away from there yourself."

The hair prickled on the back of my neck, despite the heat of the day. Ronald MacNab was the tenant who had betrayed Jamie to the men of the Watch a year before, the man who had died for his treachery within a day of its being found out. Died, I remembered, among the ashes of his home, burned over his head by the men of Lallybroch. The pile of chimneystones, so innocent when we had passed them a moment ago, had now the grim look of a cairn. I swallowed, forcing back the bitter taste that rose at the back of my throat.

"MacNab?" Jamie said softly. His expression was at once alert. "Ronnie MacNab?"

I had told Jamie of MacNab's betrayal, and his death, but I hadn't told him the means of it.

Ian nodded. "Aye. He died there, the night the English took ye, Jamie. The thatch must ha' caught from a spark, and him too far gone in drink to get out in time." He met Jamie's eyes straight on, all teasing gone.

"Ah? And his wife and child?" Jamie's look was the same as Ian's; cool and inscrutable.

"Safe. Mary MacNab's kitchen-maid at the house, and Rabbie works in the stables." Ian glanced involuntarily over his shoulder in the direction of the ruined cottage. "Mary comes up here now and again; she's the only one on the place will go there."

"Was she fond of him, then?" Jamie had turned to look in the direction of the cottage, so his face was hidden from me, but there was tension in the line of his back.

Ian shrugged. "I shouldna think so. A drunkard, and vicious with it, was Ronnie; not even his auld mother had much use for him. No, I think Mary feels it her duty to pray for his soul—much good it'll do him," he added.

"Ah." Jamie paused a moment as though in thought, then tossed his horse's reins over its neck and turned up the hill.

"Jamie," I said, but he was already walking back up the road, toward the small clearing beside the grove. I handed the reins I was holding to a surprised Fergus.

"Stay here with the horses," I said. "I have to go with him." Ian moved to come with me, but Murtagh stopped him with a shake of the head, and I went on alone, following Jamie up over the crest of the hill.

He had the long, tireless stride of a hill-walker, and had reached the small clearing before I caught him up. He stood at the edge of what had been the outer wall. The square shape of the cottage's earth floor was still barely visible, the new growth that covered it sparser than the nearby barley, greener and wild in the shade of the trees.

There was little trace of the fire left; a few chunks of charred wood poked through the grass near the stone hearth that lay open now, flat and exposed as a tombstone. Careful not to step within the outlines of the vanished walls, Jamie began to walk around the clearing. He circled the hearthstone three times, walking always widdershins, left, and left, and left again, to confound any evil that might follow.

I stood to one side and watched. This was a private confrontation, but I couldn't leave him to face it alone, and though he didn't glance at me, still I knew he was glad of my presence.

At last he stopped by the fallen pile of stones. Reaching out, he laid a hand gingerly on it and closed his eyes for a moment, as though in prayer. Then, stooping, he picked up a stone the size of his fist, and placed it carefully on the pile, as though it might weigh down the uneasy soul of the ghost. He crossed himself, turned and came toward me with a firm, unhurried step.

"Don't look back," he said quietly, taking me by the arm as we turned toward the road.

I didn't.

Jamie, Fergus, and Murtagh went with Ian and the dogs in search of the sheep, leaving me to take the string of horses down to the house alone. I was far from being an accomplished horse-handler, but thought I could manage half a mile, so long as nothing popped out at me unexpectedly.

This was very different from our first homecoming to Lallybroch; then, we had been in flight, both of us. Me from the future, Jamie from his past. Our residence then had been happy, but tenuous and insecure; always there was the chance of discovery, of Jamie's arrest. Now, thanks to the Duke of Sandringham's intervention, Jamie had come to take possession of his birthright, and I, my lawful place beside him as his wife.

Then, we had arrived disheveled, unexpected, a violent disruption in the household. This time, we had come announced, with due ceremony, bearing presents from France. While I was sure our reception would be cordial, I did wonder how Ian and Jamie's sister Jenny would take our permanent return. After all, they had lived as master and mistress of the estate for the last several years, ever since the death of Jamie's father, and the disastrous events that had precipitated him into a life of outlawry and exile.

I topped the last hill without incident, and the manor house and its out-buildings lay below me, slate roofs darkening as the first banks of rain clouds rolled in. Suddenly, my mare started, and so did I, struggling to keep a hold on the reins as she curvetted and plunged in alarm.

Not that I could blame her; from around the corner of the house had emerged two huge, puffy objects, rolling along the ground like overweight clouds.

"Stop that!" I shouted. "Whoa!" All the horses were now swerving and pulling, and I was inches away from a stampede. Fine homecoming, I thought, if I let all Jamie's new breeding stock break their collective legs.

One of the clouds rose slightly, then sank flat to the ground, and Jenny Fraser Murray, released from the burden of the feather mattress she had been carrying, raced for the road, dark curls flying.

Without a moment's hesitation, she leaped for the bridle of the nearest animal, and jerked down, hard.

"Whoa!" she said. The horse, obviously recognizing the voice of author-ity, did whoa. With a little effort, the other horses were calmed, and by the time I could slide down from my saddle, we had been joined by another woman and a boy of nine or ten, who lent an experienced hand with the remaining beasts.

I recognized young Rabbie MacNab, and deduced that the woman must be his mother, Mary. The bustle and shuffle of horses, bundles and mattresses precluded much conversation, but I had time for a quick hug of greeting with Jenny. She smelled of cinnamon and honey and the clean sweat of exertion, with an undertone of baby-scent, that paradoxical smell composed of spit-up milk, soft feces, and the ultimate cleanliness of fresh, smooth skin.

We clung together for a moment, hugging tight, remembering our last embrace, when we had parted on the edge of a night-dark wood—me to go in search of Jamie, she to return to a newborn daughter.

"How's little Maggie?" I asked, breaking away at last.

Jenny made a face, wryness mingled with pride. "She's just walking, and the terror o' the house." She glanced up the empty road. "Met Ian, did ye?"

"Yes, Jamie, Murtagh, and Fergus went with him to find the sheep."

"Better them than us," she said, with a quick gesture toward the sky. "It's coming on to rain any minute. Let Rabbie stable the horses and you come lend a hand wi' the mattresses, or we'll all sleep wet tonight."

A frenzy of activity ensued, but when the rain came, Jenny and I were snug in the parlor, undoing the parcels we had brought from France, and admiring the size and precocity of wee Maggie, a sprightly miss of some ten months, with round blue eyes and a head of strawberry fuzz, and her elder brother, Young

Jamie, a sturdy almost-four-year-old. The impending arrival was no more than a tiny bulge beneath their mother's apron, but I saw her hand rest tenderly there from time to time, and felt a small pang to see it.

"You mentioned Fergus," Jenny said, as we talked. "Who's that?"

"Oh, Fergus? He's—well, he's—" I hesitated, not sure quite how to describe Fergus. A pickpocket's prospects for employment on a farm seemed limited. "He's Jamie's," I said at last.

"Oh, aye? Well, I suppose he can sleep in the stable," said Jenny, resigned. "Speaking of Jamie"—she glanced at the window, where the rain was streaming down—"I hope they find those sheep soon. I've a good dinner planned, and I dinna want it to spoil with keeping."

In fact, darkness had fallen, and Mary MacNab had laid the table before the men returned. I watched her at her work; a small, fine-boned woman with dark-brown hair and a faintly worried look that faded into a smile when Rabbie returned from the stables and went to the kitchen, hungrily asking when dinner would be.

"When the men are back, *mo luaidh*," she said, "Ye know that. Go and wash, so you'll be ready."

When the men finally did appear, they seemed a good deal more in need of a wash than did Rabbie. Rain-soaked, draggled, and muddy to the knees, they trailed slowly into the parlor. Ian unwound the wet plaid from his shoulders and hung it over the firescreen, where it dripped and steamed in the heat of the fire. Fergus, worn out by his abrupt introduction to farm life, simply sat down where he was and stared numbly at the floor between his legs.

Jenny looked up at the brother she had not seen for nearly a year. Glancing from his rain-drenched hair to his mud-crusted feet, she pointed to the door.

"Outside, and off wi' your boots," she said firmly. "And if ye've been in the high field, remember to piss on the doorposts on your way back in. That's how ye keep a ghost from comin' in the house," she explained to me in a lowered tone, with a quick look at the door through which Mary MacNab had disappeared to fetch the dinner.

Jamie, slumped into a chair, opened one eye and gave his sister a dark-blue look.

"I land in Scotland near dead wi' the crossing, ride for four days over the hills to get here, and when I arrive, I canna even come in the house for a drop to wet my parched throat; instead I'm off through the mud, huntin' lost sheep. And once I *do* get here, ye want to send me out in the dark again to piss on doorposts. Tcha!" He closed the eye again, crossed his hands across his stomach, and sank lower in his chair, a study in stubborn negation.

"Jamie, my dearie," his sister said sweetly. "D'ye want your dinner, or shall I feed it to the dogs?"

He remained motionless for a long moment, eyes closed. Then, with a hissing sigh of resignation, he got laboriously to his feet. With a moody twitch of his shoulder, he summoned Ian and the two of them turned, following Murtagh, who was already out the door. As he passed, Jamie reached down a long arm, hauled Fergus to his feet, and dragged the boy sleepily along.

"Welcome home," Jamie said morosely, and with a last wistful glance at fire and whisky, trudged out into the night once more.

31

Mail Call

fter this inauspicious homecoming, matters rapidly improved. Lallybroch absorbed Jamie at once, as though he had never left, and I found myself pulled effortlessly into the current of farm life as well. It was an unsettled autumn, with frequent rain, but with fair, bright days that made the blood sing, too. The place bustled with life, everyone hurrying through the harvest time and the preparations that must be made for the coming winter.

Lallybroch was remote, even for a Highland farm. No real roads led there, but the post still reached us by messenger, over the crags and the heather-clad slopes, a connection with the world outside. It was a world that sometimes seemed unreal in memory, as though I had never danced among the mirrors of Versailles. But the letters brought back France, and reading them, I could see the poplar trees along the Rue Tremoulins, or hear the reverberating bong of the cathedral bell that hung above L'Hôpital des Anges.

Louise's child was born safely; a son. Her letters, rife with exclamations and underlinings, overflowed with besotted descriptions of the angelic Henri. Of his father, putative or real, there was no mention.

Charles Stuart's letter, arriving a month later, made no mention of the child, but according to Jamie, was even more incoherent than usual, seething with vague plans and grandiosities.

The Earl of Mar wrote soberly and circumspectly, but his general annoyance with Charles was clear. The Bonnie Prince was not behaving. He was rude and overbearing to his most loyal followers, ignored those who might be of help to him, insulted whom he should not, talked wildly, and—reading between the lines—drank to excess. Given the attitude of the times regarding alcoholic intake on the part of gentlemen, I thought Charles's performance must have been fairly spectacular, to occasion such comment. I supposed the birth of his son had not, in fact, escaped his notice.

Mother Hildegarde wrote from time to time, brief, informative notes squeezed into a few minutes that could be snatched from her daily schedule. Each letter ended with the same words; "Bouton also sends his regards."

Master Raymond did not write, but every so often, a parcel would come addressed to me, unsigned and unmarked, but containing odd things: rare herbs and small, faceted crystals; a collection of stones, each the size of Jamie's thumbnail, smooth and disc-shaped. Each one had a tiny figure carved into one side, some with lettering above or on the reverse. And then there were the bones—a bear's digit, with the great curved claw still attached; the complete vertebrae of a small snake, articulated and strung on a leather thong, so the whole string flexed in a lifelike manner; an assortment of teeth, ranging from a string of round, peglike things that Jamie said came from a seal, through the high-crowned, scythe-cusped teeth of deer, to something that looked suspiciously like a human molar.

From time to time, I carried some of the smooth, carved stones in my pocket, enjoying the feel of them between my fingers. They were old; I knew that much. From Roman times at least; perhaps even earlier. And from the look of some of the creatures on them, whoever had carved them had meant them to be magic. Whether they were like the herbs—having some actual virtue—or only a symbol, like the signs of the Cabbala, I didn't know. They seemed benign, though, and I kept them.

While I enjoyed the daily round of domestic tasks, what I liked best were the long walks to the various cottages on the estate. I always carried a large basket with me on these visits, containing an assortment of things, from small treats for the children to the most commonly needed medicines. These were called for frequently, for poverty and poor hygiene made illness common, and there were no physicians north of Fort William or south of Inverness.

Some ailments I could treat readily, like the bleeding gums and skin eruptions characteristic of mild scurvy. Other things were beyond my power to heal.

◄━━━━━►

I laid a hand on Rabbie MacNab's head. The shaggy hair was damp at his temples, but his jaw hung open, slack, relaxed, and the pulse in his neck beat slowly.

"He's all right now," I said. His mother could see that as well as I could; he lay sprawled in the peaceful abandon of sleep, cheeks flushed from the heat of the nearby fire. Still, she stayed tense and watchful, hovering over the bedstead until I spoke. Once I had given absolution to the evidence of her own eyes, she was willing to believe, though; her bunched shoulders slumped under her shawl.

"Thank the Blessed Mother," Mary MacNab murmured, crossing herself briefly, "and you, my lady."

"I didn't do anything," I protested. This was quite literally true; the only service I had been able to render young Rabbie was to make his mother let him alone. It had, in fact, taken a certain amount of forcefulness to discourage her efforts to feed him bran mixed with cock's blood, wave burning feathers under his nose, or dash cold water over him—none of these remedies being of marked use to someone suffering an epileptic seizure. When I arrived, his mother had

been volubly regretting her inability to administer the most effective of remedies: spring water drunk from the skull of a suicide.

"It frichts me so when he's taen like that," Mary MacNab said, gazing
longingly at the bed where her son lay. "I had Father MacMurtry to him the
last time, and he prayed a terrible long time, and sprinkled holy water on the
lad to drive the de'ils out. But noo they've come back." She clasped her hands
tight together, as though she wished to touch her son, but couldn't bring
herself to do so.

"It isn't devils," I said. "It's only a sickness, and not all that bad a one, at
that."

"Aye, my lady, an' ye say so," she murmured, unwilling to contradict me,
but plainly unconvinced.

"He'll be all right." I tried to reassure the woman, without raising hopes
that couldn't be met. "He always recovers from these fits, doesn't he?" The fits
had come on two years ago—probably the result of head injury from beatings
administered by his late father, I thought—and while the seizures were infre-
quent, they were undeniably terrifying to his mother when they occurred.

She nodded reluctantly, plainly unconvinced.

"Aye . . . though he bangs his heid something fearful now and then,
thrashin' as he does."

"Yes, that's a risk," I said patiently. "If he does it again, just pull him away
from anything hard, and let him alone. I know it looks bad, but really, he'll be
quite all right. Just let the fit run its course, and when it's over, put him to bed
and let him sleep." I knew that words were of limited value, no matter how
true they might be. Something more concrete was needed for reassurance.

As I turned to go, I heard a small click in the deep pocket of my skirt, and
had a sudden inspiration. Reaching in, I pulled out two or three of the small
smooth charmstones Raymond had sent me. I selected the milky white one—
chalcedony, perhaps—with the tiny figure of a writhing man carved into one
side. So that's what it's for, I thought.

"Sew this into his pocket," I said, laying the tiny charm ceremoniously in
the woman's hand. "It will protect him from . . . from devils." I cleared my
throat. "You needn't worry about him, then, even if he has another fit; he'll
come out of it all right."

I left then, feeling at once extremely foolish and halfway pleased, amidst an
eager flood of relieved thanks. I wasn't sure whether I was becoming a better
physician or merely a more practiced charlatan. Still, if I couldn't do much for
Rabbie, I could help his mother—or let her help herself, at least. Healing
comes from the healed; not from the physician. That much, Raymond had
taught me.

I left the house then, to do my errands for the day, calling on two of the cottages near the west end of the farm. All was well at the Kirbys and the Weston Frasers, and I was soon on my way back to the house. At the top of a slope, I sat down under a large beech tree to rest for a moment before the long walk back. The sun was coming down the sky, but hadn't yet reached the row of pines that topped the ridge on the west side of Lallybroch. It was still late afternoon, and the world glowed with the colors of late autumn.

The fallen beechmast was cool and slippery under me, but a good many leaves still clung, yellowed and curling, to the tree above. I leaned back against the smooth-barked trunk and closed my eyes, dimming the bright glare of ripe barley fields to a dark red glow behind my eyelids.

The stifling confines of the crofters' cottages had given me a headache. I leaned my head against the birch's smooth bark and began to breathe slowly and deeply, letting the fresh outdoor air fill my lungs, beginning what I always thought of as "turning in."

This was my own imperfect attempt to duplicate the feeling of the process Master Raymond had shown me in L'Hôpital des Anges; a summoning of the look and feel of each bit of myself, imagining exactly what the various organs and systems looked and felt like when they were functioning properly.

I sat quietly, hands loose in my lap, and listened to the beat of my heart. Beating fast from the exertion of the climb, it slowed quickly to a resting pace. The autumn breeze lifted the tendrils of hair from my neck and cooled my fire-flushed cheeks.

I sat, eyes closed, and traced the path of my blood, from the secret, thick-walled chambers of my heart, blue-purple through the pulmonary artery, reddening swiftly as the sacs of the lungs dumped their burden of oxygen. Then out in a bursting surge through the arch of the aorta, and the tumbling race upward and down and out, through carotids, renals, subclavians. To the smallest capillaries, blooming beneath the surface of the skin, I traced the path of my blood through the systems of my body, remembering the feel of perfection, of health. Of peace.

I sat still, breathing slowly, feeling languorous and heavy as though I had just risen from the act of love. My skin felt thin, my lips slightly swollen, and the pressure of my clothes was like the touch of Jamie's hands. It was no random choice that had invoked his name to cure me. Whether it was health of mind or body, the love of him was necessary to me as breath or blood. My mind reached out for him, sleeping or waking, and finding him, was satisfied. My body flushed and glowed, and as it came to full life, it hungered for his.

The headache was gone. I sat a moment longer, breathing. Then I got to my feet and walked down the hill toward home.

I had never actually had a home. Orphaned at five, I had lived the life of a academic vagabond with my uncle Lamb for the next thirteen years. In tents on a dusty plain, in caves in the hills, in the swept and garnished chambers of an empty pyramid, Quentin Lambert Beauchamp, M.S., Ph.D., F.R.A.S., etc., had set up the series of temporary camps in which he did the archaeological work that would make him famous long before a car crash ended his brother's life and threw me into his. Not one to dither over petty details like an orphaned niece, Uncle Lamb had promptly enrolled me in a boarding school.

Not one to accept the vagaries of fate without a fight, I declined absolutely to go there. And, recognizing something in me that he had himself in abundant measure, Uncle Lamb had shrugged, and on the decision of a heartbeat, had taken me forever from the world of order and routine, of sums, clean sheets, and daily baths, to follow him into vagabondage.

The roving life had continued with Frank, though with a shift from field to universities, as the digging of a historian is usually conducted within walls. So, when the war came in 1939, it was less a disruption to me than to most.

I had moved from our latest hired flat into the junior nurses' quarters at Pembroke Hospital, and from there to a field station in France, and back again to Pembroke before war's end. And then, those few brief months with Frank, before we came to Scotland, seeking to find each other again. Only to lose each other once and for all, when I had walked into a stone circle, through madness, and out the other side, into the past that was my present.

It was strange, then, and rather wonderful, to wake in the upper bedroom at Lallybroch, next to Jamie, and realize, as I watched the dawn touch his sleeping face, that he had been born in this bed. All the sounds of the house, from the creak of the back stair under an early-rising maid's foot, to the drumming rain on the roofslates, were sounds he had heard a thousand times before; heard so often, he didn't hear them anymore. I did.

His mother, Ellen, had planted the late-blooming rosebush by the door. Its faint, rich scent still wafted up the walls of the house to the bedroom window. It was as though she reached in herself, to touch him lightly in passing. To touch me, too, in welcome.

Beyond the house itself lay Lallybroch; fields and barns and village and crofts. He had fished in the stream that ran down from the hills, climbed the oaks and towering larches, eaten by the hearthstone of every croft. It was his place.

But he, too, had lived with disruption and change. Arrest, and the flight of outlawry; the rootless life of a mercenary soldier. Arrest again, imprisonment and torture, and the flight into exile so recently ended. But he had lived in one place for his first fourteen years. And even at that age, when he had been sent, as was the custom, to foster for two years with his mother's brother, Dougal MacKenzie, it was part and parcel of the life expected for a man who would return to live forever on his land, to care for his tenants and estate, to be a part of a larger organism. Permanence was his destiny.

But there had been that space of absence, and the experience of things beyond the boundaries of Lallybroch, even beyond the rocky coasts of Scotland. Jamie had spoken with kings, had touched law, and commerce, seen adventure and violence and magic. Once the boundaries of home had been transgressed, could destiny be enough to hold him? I wondered.

As I came down from the crest of the hill, I saw him below, heaving boulders into place as he repaired a rift in a drystone dike that bordered one of the smaller fields. Near him on the ground lay a pair of rabbits, neatly gutted but not yet skinned.

" 'Home is the sailor, home from the sea, and the hunter home from the hill,' " I quoted, smiling at him as I came up beside him.

He grinned back, wiped the sweat from his brow, then pretended to shudder.

"Dinna mention the sea to me, Sassenach. I saw two wee laddies sailing a bit of wood in the millpond this morning and nearly heaved up my breakfast at the sight."

I laughed. "You haven't any urge to go back to France, then?"

"God, no. Not even for the brandy." He heaved one last stone to the top of the wall and settled it into place. "Going back to the house?"

"Yes. Do you want me to take the rabbits?"

He shook his head, and bent to pick them up. "No need; I'm going back myself. Ian needs a hand wi' the new storage cellar for the potatoes."

The first potato crop ever planted on Lallybroch was due for harvest within a few days, and—on my timorous and inexpert advice—a small rootcellar was being dug to house them. I had distinctly mixed feelings, whenever I looked at the potato field. On the one hand, I felt considerable pride in the sprawling, leafy vines that covered it. On the other, I felt complete panic at the thought that sixty families might depend on what lay under those vines for sustenance through the winter. It was on my advice—given hastily a year ago— that a prime barley field had been planted in potatoes, a crop hitherto unknown in the Highlands.

I knew that in the fullness of time, potatoes would become an important staple of life in the Highlands, less susceptible to blight and failure than the crops of oats and barley. Knowing that from a paragraph read in a geography book long ago was a far cry from deliberately taking responsibility for the lives of the people who would eat the crop.

I wondered if the taking of risks for other people got easier with practice. Jamie did it routinely, managing the affairs of the estate and the tenants as though he had been born to it. But, of course, he *had* been born to it.

"Is the cellar nearly ready?" I asked.

"Oh, aye. Ian's got the doors built, and the pit's nearly dug. It's only there's a soft bit of earth near the back, and his peg gets stuck in when he stands there." While Ian managed very well on the wooden peg he wore in substitute for his lower right leg, there were the occasional awkwardnesses such as this.

Jamie glanced thoughtfully up the hill behind us. "We'll need the cellar finished and covered by tonight; it's going to rain again before dawn."

I turned to look in the direction of his gaze. Nothing showed on the slope but grass and heather, a few trees, and the rocky seams of granite that poked bony ridges through the scruffy overgrowth.

"How in hell can you tell that?"

He smiled, pointing uphill with his chin. "See the small oak tree? And the ash nearby?"

I glanced at the trees, baffled. "Yes. What about them?"

"The leaves, Sassenach. See how both trees look lighter than usual? When there's damp in the air, the leaves of an oak or an ash will turn, so ye see the underside. The whole tree looks several shades lighter."

"I suppose it does," I agreed doubtfully. "If you happen to know what color the tree is normally."

Jamie laughed and took my arm. "I may not have an ear for music, Sassenach, but I've eyes in my head. And I've seen those trees maybe ten thousand times, in every weather there is."

It was some way from the field to the farmhouse, and we walked in silence for the most part, enjoying the brief warmth of the afternoon sun on our backs. I sniffed the air, and thought that Jamie was probably right about the coming rain; all the normal autumn smells seemed intensified, from the sharp pine resins to the dusty smell of ripe grain. I thought that I must be learning, myself; becoming attuned to the rhythms and sights and smells of Lallybroch. Maybe in time, I would come to know it as well as Jamie did. I squeezed his arm briefly, and felt the pressure of his hand on mine in response.

"D'ye miss France, Sassenach?" he said suddenly.

"No," I said, startled. "Why?"

He shrugged, not looking at me. "Well, it's only I was thinking, seeing ye come down the hill wi' the basket on your arm, how bonny ye looked wi' the sun on your brown hair. I thought you looked as though ye grew there, like one of the saplings—like ye'd always been a part of this place. And then it struck me, that to you, Lallybroch's maybe a poor wee spot. There's no grand life, like there was in France; not even interesting work, as ye had at the Hôpital." He glanced down at me shyly.

"I suppose I worry you'll grow bored wi' it here—in time."

I paused before answering, though it wasn't something I hadn't thought about.

"In time," I said carefully. "Jamie—I've seen a lot of things in my life, and been in a lot of places. Where I came from—there were things there that I miss sometimes. I'd like to ride a London omnibus again, or pick up a telephone and talk to someone far away. I'd like to turn a tap, and have hot water, not carry it from the well and heat it in a cauldron. I'd like all that—but I don't need it. As for a grand life, I didn't want it when I had it. Nice clothes are all very well, but if gossip and scheming and worry and silly parties and tiny rules of etiquette go with them . . . no. I'd as soon live in my shift and say what I like."

He laughed at that, and I squeezed his arm once more.

"As for the work . . . there's work for me here." I glanced down into the basket of herbs and medicines on my arm. "I can be useful. And if I miss Mother Hildegarde, or my other friends—well, it isn't as fast as a telephone, but there are always letters."

I stopped, holding his arm, and looked up at him. The sun was setting, and the light gilded one side of his face, throwing the strong bones into relief.

"Jamie . . . I only want to be where you are. Nothing else."

He stood still for a moment, then leaned forward and kissed me very gently on the forehead.

———

"It's funny," I said as we came over the crest of the last small hill that led down to the house. "I had just been wondering the same kinds of things about *you*. Whether you'd be happy here, after the things you did in France."

He smiled, half-ruefully, and looked toward the house, its three stories of white-harled stone glowing gold and umber in the sunset.

"Well, it's home, Sassenach. It's my place."

I touched him gently on the arm. "And you were born to it, you mean?"

He drew a deep breath, and reached out to rest a hand on the wooden fence-rail that separated this lower field from the grounds near the house.

"Well, in fact I wasna born to it, Sassenach. By rights, it should have been Willie was lairdie here. Had he lived, I expect I would have been a soldier—or maybe a merchant, like Jared."

Willie, Jamie's elder brother, had died of the smallpox at the age of eleven, leaving his small brother, aged six, as the heir to Lallybroch.

He made an odd half-shrugging gesture, as though seeking to ease the pressure of his shirt across his shoulders. It was something he did when feeling awkward or unsure; I hadn't seen him do it in months.

"But Willie died. And so I am laird." He glanced at me, a little shyly, then reached into his sporran and pulled something out. A little cherrywood snake that Willie had carved for him as a birthday gift lay on his palm, head twisted as though surprised to see the tail following it.

Jamie stroked the little snake gently; the wood was shiny and seasoned with handling, the curves of the body gleaming like scales in early twilight.

"I talk to Willie, sometimes, in my mind," Jamie said. He tilted the snake on his palm. "If you'd lived, Brother, if ye'd been laird as you were meant to be, would ye do what I've done? or would ye find a better way?" He glanced down at me, flushing slightly. "Does that sound daft?"

"No." I touched the snake's smooth head with a fingertip. The high clear call of a meadowlark came from the far field, thin as crystal in the evening air.

"I do the same," I said softly, after a moment. "With Uncle Lamb. And my parents. My mother especially. I—I didn't think of her often, when I was young, just every now and then I'd dream about someone soft and warm, with a lovely singing voice. But when I was sick, after . . . Faith—sometimes I imagined she was there. With me." A sudden wave of grief swept over me, remembrance of losses recent and long past.

Jamie touched my face gently, wiping away the tear that had formed at the corner of one eye but not quite fallen.

"I think sometimes the dead cherish us, as we do them," he said softly. "Come on, Sassenach. Let's walk a bit; there's time before dinner."

He linked my arm in his, tight against his side, and we turned along the fence, walking slowly, the dry grass rustling against my skirt.

"I ken what ye mean, Sassenach," Jamie said. "I hear my father's voice sometimes, in the barn, or in the field. When I'm not even thinkin' of him, usually. But all at once I'll turn my head, as though I'd just heard him outside, laughing wi' one of the tenants, or behind me, gentling a horse."

He laughed suddenly, and nodded toward a corner of the pasture before us.

"It's a wonder I dinna hear him here, but I never have."

It was a thoroughly unremarkable spot, a wood-railed gate in the stone fence that paralleled the road.

"Really? What did he used to say here?"

"Usually it was 'If ye're through talkin', Jamie, turn about and bend ower.' "

We laughed, pausing to lean on the fence. I bent closer, squinting at the wood.

"So this is where you got smacked? I don't see any toothmarks," I said.

"No, it wasna all that bad," he said, laughing. He ran a hand affectionately along the worn ash fence rail.

"We used to get splinters in our fingers, sometimes, Ian and me. We'd go up to the house after, and Mrs. Crook or Jenny would pick them out for us—scolding all the time."

He glanced toward the manor, where all the first-floor windows glowed with light against the gathering night. Dark forms moved briefly past the windows; small, quick-moving shadows in the kitchen windows, where Mrs. Crook and the maids were at the dinner preparations. A larger form, tall and slender as a fence rail, loomed suddenly in one of the drawing room windows. Ian stood a moment, silhouetted in the light as though called by Jamie's reminiscence. Then he drew the curtains and the window dulled to a softer, shrouded glow.

"I was always glad when Ian was with me," Jamie said, still looking toward the house. "When we got caught at some devilry and got thrashed for it, I mean."

"Misery loves company?" I said, smiling.

"A bit. I didna feel quite so wicked when there were the two of us to share the guilt between. But it was more that I could always count on him to make a lot of noise."

"What, to cry out, you mean?"

"Aye. He'd always howl and carry on something awful, and I knew he would do it, so I didna feel so ashamed of my own noise, if I had to cry out." It was too dark to see his face anymore, but I could still see the half-shrugging gesture he made when embarrassed or uncomfortable.

"I always tried not to, of course, but I couldna always manage. If my da thought it worth thrashing me over, he thought it worth doing a proper job. And Ian's father had a right arm like a tree bole."

"You know," I said, glancing down at the house, "I never thought of it particularly before, but why on earth did your father thrash you out here, Jamie? Surely there's enough room in the house—or the barn."

Jamie was silent for a moment, then shrugged again.

"I didna ever ask. But I reckon it was something like the King of France."

"The King of France?" This apparent non sequitur took me aback a bit.

"Aye. I dinna ken," he said dryly, "quite what it's like to have to wash and dress and move your bowels in public, but I can tell ye that it's a verra humbling experience to have to stand there and explain to one of your father's tenants just what ye did that's about to get your arse scalded for ye."

"I imagine it must be," I said, sympathy mingled with the urge to laugh. "Because you were going to be laird, you mean? That's why he made you do it here?"

"I expect so. The tenants would know I understood justice—at least, from the receiving end."

32

Field of Dreams

T he field had been plowed in the usual "rigs," high ridges of piled earth, with deep furrows drawn between them. The rigs rose knee-high, so a man walking down the furrows could sow his seed easily by hand along the top of the rig beside him. Designed for the planting of barley or oats, no reason had been seen to alter them for the planting of potatoes.

"It said 'hills,' " Ian said, peering over the leafy expanse of the potato field, "but I thought the rigs would do as well. The point of the hills seemed to be to keep the things from rotting wi' too much water, and an old field wi' high rigs seemed like to do that as well."

"That seems sensible," Jamie agreed. "The top parts seem to be flourishing, anyway. Does the man say how ye ken when to dig the things up, though?"

Charged with the planting of potatoes in a land where no potato had ever been seen, Ian had proceeded with method and logic, sending to Edinburgh both for seed potatoes, and for a book on the subject of planting. In due course, *A Scientific Treatise on Methods of Farming,* by Sir Walter O'Bannion Reilly had made its appearance, with a small section on potato planting as presently practiced in Ireland.

Ian was carrying this substantial volume under one arm—Jenny had told me that he wouldn't go near the potato field without it, lest some knotty question of philosophy or technique occur to him while there—and now flipped it open, bracing it on one forearm as he groped in his sporran for the spectacles he wore when reading. These had belonged to his late father; small circles of glass, set in wire rims, and customarily worn on the end of his nose, they made him look like a very earnest young stork.

"Harvesting of the crop should be undertaken simultaneously with the appearance of the first winter goose," he read, then looked up, squinting accusingly over his spectacles at the potato field, as though expecting an indicative goose to stick its head up among the furrowed rigs.

"Winter goose?" Jamie peered frowning at the book over Ian's shoulder. "What sort of goose does he mean? Greylags? But ye see those all year. That canna be right."

Ian shrugged. "Maybe ye only see them in the winter in Ireland. Or maybe it's some kind of Irish goose he means, and not greylags at all."

Jamie snorted. "Well, the fat lot of good that does us. Does he say anything useful?"

Ian ran a finger down the lines of type, moving his lips silently. We had by now collected a small crowd of cottars, all fascinated by this novel approach to agriculture.

"Ye dinna dig potatoes when it's wet," Ian informed us, eliciting a louder snort from Jamie.

"Hmm," Ian murmured to himself. "Potato rot, potato bugs—we didna ha' any potato bugs, I suppose that's lucky—potato vines . . . umm, no, that's only what to do if the vines wilt. Potato blight—we canna tell if we have that until we see the potatoes. Seed potatoes, potato storage—"

Impatient, Jamie turned away from Ian, hands on his hips.

"Scientific farming, eh?" he demanded. He glared at the field of dark-green, leafy vines. "I suppose it's too damn scientific to explain how ye tell when the bloody things are ready to eat!"

Fergus, who had been tagging along behind Jamie as usual, looked up from a caterpillar, inching its slow and fuzzy way along his forefinger.

"Why don't you just dig one up and see?" he asked.

Jamie stared at Fergus for a moment. His mouth opened, but no sound emerged. He shut it, patted Fergus gently on the head, and went to fetch a pitchfork from its place against the fence.

The cottars, all men who had helped to plant and tend the field under Ian's direction—assisted by Sir Walter—clustered round to see the results of their labor.

Jamie chose a large and flourishing vine near the edge of the field and poised the fork carefully near its roots. Visibly holding his breath, he put a foot on the heel of the fork and pushed. The tines slid slowly into the damp brown dirt.

I was holding my own breath. There was a good deal more depending on this experiment than the reputation of Sir Walter O'Bannion Reilly. Or my own, for that matter.

Jamie and Ian had confirmed that the barley crop this year was smaller than normal, though still sufficient for the needs of the Lallybroch tenants. Another bad year would exhaust the meager reserves of grain, though. For a Highland estate, Lallybroch was prosperous; but that was saying something only by comparison with other Highland farms. Successful potato planting could well make the difference between hunger and plenty for the folk of Lallybroch over the next two years.

Jamie's heel pressed down and he leaned back on the handle of the fork. The earth crumbled and cracked around the vine, and with a sudden, rending *pop* the potato vine lifted up and the earth revealed its bounty.

A collective "Ah!" went up from the spectators, at sight of the myriad brown globules clinging to the roots of the uprooted vine. Ian and I both fell to our knees in the dirt, scrabbling in the loosened soil for potatoes severed from the parent vine.

"It worked!" Ian kept saying as he pulled potato after potato out of the ground. "Look at that! See the size of it?"

"Yes, look at this one!" I exclaimed in delight, brandishing one the size of my two fists held together.

At length, we had the produce of our sample vine laid in a basket; perhaps ten good-sized potatoes, twenty-five or so fist-size specimens, and a number of small things the size of golf balls.

"What d'ye think?" Jamie scrutinized our collection quizzically. "Ought we to leave the rest, so the little ones will grow more? Or take them now, before the cold comes?"

Ian groped absently for his spectacles, then remembered that Sir Walter was over by the fence, and abandoned the effort. He shook his head.

"No, I think this is right," he said. "The book says ye keep the bittie ones for the seed potatoes for next year. We'll want a lot of those." He gave me a grin of relieved delight, his hank of thick, straight brown hair dropping across his forehead. There was a smudge of dirt down the side of his face.

One of the cottars' wives was bending over the basket, peering at its contents. She reached out a tentative finger and prodded one of the potatoes.

"Ye eat them, ye say?" Her brow creased skeptically. "I dinna see how ye'd ever grind them in a quern for bread or parritch."

"Well, I dinna believe ye grind them, Mistress Murray," Jamie explained courteously.

"Och, aye?" The woman squinted censoriously at the basket. "Well, what d'ye do wi' them, then?"

"Well, you . . ." Jamie started, and then stopped. It occurred to me, as it no doubt had to him, that while he had eaten potatoes in France, he had never seen one prepared for eating. I hid a smile as he stared helplessly at the dirt-crusted potato in his hand. Ian also stared at it; apparently Sir Walter was mute on the subject of potato cooking.

"You roast them." Fergus came to the rescue once more, bobbing up under Jamie's arm. He smacked his lips at the sight of the potatoes. "Put them in the coals of the fire. You eat them with salt. Butter's good, if you have it."

"We have it," said Jamie, with an air of relief. He thrust the potato at Mrs. Murray, as though anxious to be rid of it. "You roast them," he informed her firmly.

"You can boil them, too," I contributed. "Or mash them with milk. Or fry them. Or chop them up and put them in soup. A very versatile vegetable, the potato."

"That's what the book says," Ian murmured, with satisfaction.

Jamie looked at me, the corner of his mouth curling in a smile.

"Ye never told me you could cook, Sassenach."

"I wouldn't call it cooking, exactly," I said, "but I probably can boil a potato."

"Good." Jamie cast an eye at the group of tenants and their wives, who were passing the potatoes from hand to hand, looking them over rather dubiously. He clapped his hands loudly to attract attention.

"We'll be having supper here by the field," he told them. "Let's be fetching a bit of wood for a fire, Tom and Willie, and Mrs. Willie, if ye'd be so kind as to bring your big kettle? Aye, that's good, one of the men will help ye to bring it down. You, Kincaid—" He turned to one of the younger men, and waved off in the direction of the small cluster of cottages under the trees. "Go and tell everyone—it's potatoes for supper!"

And so, with the assistance of Jenny, ten pails of milk from the dairy shed, three chickens caught from the coop, and four dozen large leeks from the kailyard, I presided over the preparation of cock-a-leekie soup and roasted potatoes for the laird and tenants of Lallybroch.

The sun was below the horizon by the time the food was ready, but the sky was still alight, with streaks of red and gold that lanced through the dark branches of the pine grove on the hill. There was a little hesitation when the tenants came face-to-face with the proposed addition to their diet, but the party-like atmosphere—helped along by a judicious keg of home-brewed whisky—overcame any misgivings, and soon the ground near the potato field was littered with the forms of impromptu diners, hunched over bowls held on their knees.

"What d'ye think, Dorcas?" I overheard one woman say to her neighbor. "It's a wee bit queer-tasting, no?"

Dorcas, so addressed, nodded and swallowed before replying.

"Aye, it is. But the laird's eaten six o' the things so far, and they havena kilt him yet."

The response from the men and children was a good deal more enthusiastic, likely owing to the generous quantities of butter supplied with the potatoes.

"Men would eat horse droppings, if ye served them wi' butter," Jenny said, in answer to an observation along these lines. "Men! A full belly, and a place to lie down when they're drunk, and that's all they ask o' life."

"A wonder ye put up wi' Jamie and me," Ian teased, hearing her, "seein' ye've such a low opinion of men."

Jenny waved her soup ladle dismissively at husband and brother, seated side by side on the ground near the kettle.

"Och, you two aren't 'men.' "

Ian's feathery brows shot upward, and Jamie's thicker red ones matched them.

"Oh, we're not? Well, what are we, then?" Ian demanded.

Jenny turned toward him with a smile, white teeth flashing in the firelight. She patted Jamie on the head, and dropped a kiss on Ian's forehead.

"You're mine," she said.

After supper, one of the men began to sing. Another brought out a wooden flute and accompanied him, the sound thin but piercing in the cold autumn night. The air was chilly, but there was no wind, and it was cozy enough, wrapped in shawls and blankets, huddled in small family clusters round the fire. The blaze had been built up after the cooking, and now made a substantial dent in the darkness.

It was warm, if a trifle active, in our own family huddle. Ian had gone to fetch another armload of wood, and baby Maggie clung to her mother, forcing her elder brother to seek refuge and body warmth elsewhere.

"I'm going to stick ye upside down in yonder kettle, an' ye dinna leave off pokin' me in the balls," Jamie informed his nephew, who was squirming vigorously on his uncle's lap. "What's the matter, then—have ye got ants in your drawers?"

This query was greeted with a gale of giggles and a marked effort to burrow into his host's midsection. Jamie groped in the dark, making deliberately clumsy grabs at his namesake's arms and legs, then wrapped his arms around the boy and rolled suddenly over on top of him, forcing a startled whoop of delight from small Jamie.

Jamie pinned his nephew forcibly to the ground and held him there with one hand while he groped blindly on the ground in the dark. Seizing a handful of wet grass with a grunt of satisfaction, he raised himself enough to jam the grass down the neck of small Jamie's shirt, changing the giggling to a high-pitched squeal, no less delighted.

"There, then," Jamie said, rolling off the small form. "Go plague your auntie for a bit."

Small Jamie obligingly scrambled over to me on hands and knees, still giggling, and nestled on my lap among the folds of my cloak. He sat as still as is possible for an almost four-year-old boy—which is not very still, all things considered—and let me remove the bulk of the grass from his shirt.

"You smell nice, Auntie," he said, buffing my chin affectionately with his mop of black curls. "Like food."

"Well, thank you," I said. "Ought I to take that to mean you're hungry again?"

"Aye. Is there milk?"

"There is." I could just reach the stoneware jug by stretching out my fingers. I shook the bottle, decided there was not enough left to make it worthwhile to fetch a cup, and tilted the jug, holding it for the little boy to drink from.

Temporarily absorbed in the taking of nourishment, he was still, the small, sturdy body heavy on my thigh, back braced against my arm as he wrapped his own pudgy hands around the jug.

The last drops of milk gurgled from the jug. Small Jamie relaxed all at once, and emitted a soft burp of repletion. I could feel the heat glowing from him, with that sudden rise of temperature which presages falling asleep in very young children. I wrapped a fold of the cloak around him, and rocked him slowly back and forth, humming softly to the tune of the song beyond the fire. The small bumps of his vertebrae were round and hard as marbles under my fingers.

"Gone to sleep, has he?" The larger Jamie's bulk loomed near my shoulder, the firelight picking out the hilt of his dirk, and the gleam of copper in his hair.

"Yes," I said. "At least he's not squirming, so he must have. It's rather like holding a large ham."

Jamie laughed, then was still himself. I could feel the hardness of his arm just brushing mine, and the warmth of his body through the folds of plaid and arisaid.

A night breeze brushed a strand of hair across my face. I brushed it back, and discovered that small Jamie was right; my hands smelled of leeks and butter, and the starchy smell of cut potatoes. Asleep, he was a dead weight, and while holding him was comforting, he was cutting off the circulation in my left leg. I twisted a bit, intending to lay him across my lap.

"Don't move, Sassenach," Jamie's voice came softly, next to me. "Just for a moment, *mo duinne*—be still."

I obligingly froze, until he touched me on the shoulder.

"That's all right, Sassenach," he said, with a smile in his voice. "It's only that ye looked so beautiful, wi' the fire on your face, and your hair waving in the wind. I wanted to remember it."

I turned to face him, then, and smiled at him, across the body of the child. The night was dark and cold, alive with people all around, but there was nothing where we sat but light and warmth—and each other.

33

Thy Brother's Keeper

Fergus, after an initial period of silent watchfulness from corners, had become a part of the household, taking on the official position of stable-lad, along with young Rabbie MacNab.

While Rabbie was a year or two younger than Fergus, he was as big as the slight French lad, and they quickly became inseparable friends, except on the occasions when they argued—which was two or three times a day —and then attempted to kill each other. After a fight one morning had escalated into a punching, kicking, fist-swinging brawl that rolled through the dairy shed and spilled two pannikins of cream set out to sour, Jamie took a hand.

With an air of long-suffering grimness, he had taken each miscreant by the scruff of a skinny neck, and removed them to the privacy of the barn, where, I assumed, he overcame any lingering scruples he might have had about the administration of physical retribution. He strode out of the barn, shaking his head and buckling his belt back on, and left with Ian to ride up the valley to Broch Mordha. The boys had emerged some time later, substantially subdued and—united in tribulation—once more the best of friends.

Sufficiently subdued, in fact, to allow young Jamie to tag along with them as they did their chores. As I glanced out the window later in the morning, I saw the three of them playing in the dooryard with a ball made of rags. It was a cold, misty day, and the boys' breath rose in soft clouds as they galloped and shouted.

"Nice sturdy little lad you've got there," I remarked to Jenny, who was sorting through her mending basket in search of a button. She glanced up, saw what I was looking at, and smiled.

"Oh, aye, wee Jamie's a dear lad." She came to join me by the window, peering out at the game below.

"He's the spit of his da," she remarked fondly, "but he's going to be a good bit wider through the shoulder, I think. He'll maybe be the size of his uncle; see those legs?" I thought she was probably right; while small Jamie, nearly four, still had the chunky roundness of a toddler, his legs were long, and the small back was wide and flat with muscle. He had the long, graceful bones of his uncle, and the same air his larger namesake projected, of being composed of something altogether tougher and springier than mere flesh.

I watched the little boy pounce on the ball, scoop it up with a deft snatch, and throw it hard enough to sail past the head of Rabbie MacNab, who raced off, shouting, to retrieve it.

"Something else is like his uncle," I said. "I think he's maybe going to be left-handed, too."

"Oh, God!" said Jenny, brow furrowed as she peered at her offspring. "I hope not, but you're maybe right." She shook her head, sighing.

"Lord, when I think of the trouble poor Jamie had, from being caurry-fisted! Everybody tried to break him of it, from my parents to the schoolmaster, but he always was stubborn as a log, and wouldna budge. Everybody but Ian's father, at least," she added, as an afterthought.

"He didn't think being left-handed was wrong?" I asked curiously, aware that the general opinion of the times was that left-handedness was at the best unlucky, and at the worst, a symptom of demonic possession. Jamie wrote—with difficulty—with his right hand, because he had been beaten regularly at school for picking up the quill with his left.

Jenny shook her head, black curls bobbing under her kertch.

"No, he was a queer man, auld John Murray. He said if the Lord had chosen to strengthen Jamie's left arm so, then 'twould be a sin to spurn the gift. And he was a rare man wi' a sword, auld John, so my father listened, and he let Jamie learn to fight left-handed."

"I thought Dougal MacKenzie taught Jamie to fight left-handed," I said. I rather wondered what Jenny thought of her uncle Dougal.

She nodded, licking the end of a thread before putting it through the eye of her needle with one quick poke.

"Aye, it was, but that was later, when Jamie was grown, and went to foster wi' Dougal. It was Ian's father taught him his first strokes." She smiled, eyes on the shirt in her lap.

"I remember, when they were young, auld John told Ian it was his job to stand to Jamie's right, for he must guard his chief's weaker side in a fight. And he did—they took it verra seriously, the two of them. And I suppose auld John was right, at that," she added, snipping off the excess thread. "After a time, nobody would fight them, not even the MacNab lads. Jamie and Ian were both fair-sized, and bonny fighters, and when they stood shoulder to shoulder, there was no one could take the pair o' them down, even if they were outnumbered."

She laughed suddenly, and smoothed back a lock of hair behind her ear.

"Watch them sometime, when they're walking the fields together. I dinna suppose they even realize they do it still, but they do. Jamie always moves to the left, so Ian can take up his place on the right, guardin' the weak side."

Jenny gazed out the window, the shirt momentarily forgotten in her lap, and laid a hand over the small swelling of her stomach.

"I hope it's a boy," she said, looking at her black-haired son below. "Left-handed or no, it's good for a man to have a brother to help him." I caught her glance at the picture on the wall—a very young Jamie, standing between the knees of his elder brother, Willie. Both young faces were snub-nosed and solemn; Willie's hand rested protectively on his little brother's shoulder.

"Jamie's lucky to have Ian," I said.

Jenny looked away from the picture, and blinked once. She was two years older than Jamie; she would have been three years younger than William.

"Aye, he is. And so am I," she said softly, picking up the shirt once more.

I took a child's smock from the mending basket and turned it inside out, to get at the ripped seam beneath the armhole. It was too cold out for anyone but small boys at play or men at work, but it was warm and cozy in the parlor; the windows fogged over quickly as we worked, isolating us from the icy world outside.

"Speaking of brothers," I said, squinting as I threaded my own needle, "did you see Dougal and Colum MacKenzie much, as you were growing up?"

Jenny shook her head. "I've never met Colum. Dougal came here a time or two, bringing Jamie home for Hogmanay or such, but I canna say I know him well." She looked up from her mending, slanted eyes bright with interest. "You'll know them, though. Tell me, what's Colum MacKenzie like? I always wondered, from the bits of things I'd hear from visitors, but my parents never would speak of him." She paused a moment, a crease between her brows.

"No, I'm wrong; my da did say something about him, once. 'Twas just after Dougal had left, to go back to Beannachd wi' Jamie. Da was leaning on the fence outside, watching them ride out o' sight, and I came up to wave to Jamie—it always grieved me sore when he left, for I didna ken how long he'd be gone. Anyway, we watched them over the crest of the hill, and then Da stirred a bit, and grunted, and said, 'God help Dougal MacKenzie when his brother Colum dies.' Then he seemed to remember I was there, for he turned round and smiled at me, and said, 'Well, lassie, what's for our dinner, then?' and wouldna say more about it." The black brows, fine and bold as the strokes of calligraphy, lifted in puzzled inquiry.

"I thought that odd, for I'd heard—who hasn't?—that Colum is sore crippled, and Dougal does the chief's work for him, collecting rents and settling claims—and leading the clan to battle, when needs be."

"He does. But—" I hesitated, unsure how to describe that odd symbiotic relationship. "Well," I said with a smile, "the closest I can come is to tell you that once I overheard them arguing, and Colum said to Dougal, 'I'll tell ye, if the brothers MacKenzie have but one cock and one brain between them, then I'm glad of my half of the bargain!' "

Jenny gave a sudden laugh of surprise, then stared at me, a speculative gleam deep in her blue eyes, so like her brother's.

"Och, so that's the way of it, is it? I did wonder once, hearing Dougal talk about Colum's son, wee Hamish; he seemed a bit fonder than an uncle might be."

"You're quick, Jenny," I said, staring back at her. "Very quick. It took me a long time to work that out, and I saw them every day for months."

She shrugged modestly, but a small smile played about her lips.

"I listen," she said simply. "To what folk say—and what they don't. And people do gossip something terrible here in the Highlands. So"—she bit off a thread and spat the ends neatly into the palm of her hand—"tell me about Leoch. Folk say it's big, but not so grand as Beauly or Kilravock."

We worked and talked through the morning, moving from mending to winding wool for knitting, to laying out the pattern for a new baby dress for Maggie. The shouts from the boys outside ceased, to be replaced by murmurous noises and banging from the back of the house, suggesting that the younger male element had gotten cold and come to infest the kitchens, instead.

"I wonder will it snow soon?" Jenny said, with a glance at the window. "There's wetness in the air; did ye see the haze over the loch this morning?"

I shook my head. "I hope not. That will make it hard for Jamie and Ian, coming back." The village of Broch Mordha was less than ten miles from Lallybroch, but the way lay over steadily rising hills, with steep and rocky slopes, and the road was little more than a deer track.

In the event, it did snow, soon after noon, and the flakes kept swirling down long past nightfall.

"They'll have stayed in Broch Mordha," Jenny said, pulling her nightcapped head in from an inspection of the cloudy sky, with its snow-pink glow. "Dinna worry for them; they'll be tucked up cozy in someone's cottage for the night." She smiled reassuringly at me as she pulled the shutters to. A sudden wail came from down the hall, and she picked up the skirts of her nightrobe with a muffled exclamation.

"Good night, Claire," she called, already hurrying off on her maternal errand of mercy. "Sleep well."

I usually did sleep well; in spite of the cold, damp climate, the house was tightly constructed, and the goosefeather bed was plentifully supplied with quilts. Tonight, though, I found myself restless without Jamie. The bed seemed vast and clammy, my legs twitchy, and my feet cold.

I tried lying on my back, hands lightly clasped across my ribs, eyes closed, breathing deep, to summon up a picture of Jamie; if I could imagine him there, breathing deeply in the dark beside me, perhaps I could fall asleep.

The sound of a cock crowing at full blast lifted me off the pillow, as though a stick of dynamite had been touched off beneath the bed.

"Idiot!" I said, every nerve in my body twanging from the shock. I got up and cracked the shutter. It had stopped snowing, but the sky was still pale with cloud, a uniform color from horizon to horizon. The rooster let loose another bellow in the hen-coop below.

"Shut up!" I said. "It's the middle of the night, you feathered bastard!" The avian equivalent of a raspberry echoed through the still night, and down the hall, a child began to cry, followed by a rich but muffled Gaelic expletive in Jenny's voice.

"You," I said to the invisible rooster, "are living on borrowed time." There was no response to this, and after a pause to make certain that the rooster had in fact called it a night, I closed the shutters and did the same.

The commotion had derailed any coherent train of thought. Instead of trying to start another, I decided to try turning inward, in the hopes that physical contemplation would relax me enough to sleep.

It worked. As I began to hover on the edge of sleep, my mind fixed somewhere around my pancreas, I could dimly hear the sounds of small Jamie pattering down the hall to his mother's bedroom—roused from sleep by a full bladder, he seldom had the presence of mind to take the obvious step, and would frequently blunder down the stair from the nursery in search of assistance instead.

I had wondered, coming to Lallybroch, whether I might find it difficult to be near Jenny; if I would be envious of her easy fruitfulness. And I might have been, had I not seen that abundant motherhood had its price as well.

"There's a pot right by your bed, clot-heid," Jenny's exasperated voice came outside my door as she steered small Jamie back to his bed. "Ye must have stepped in it on your way out; why can ye no get it through your heid to use that one? Why have ye got to come use mine, every night in creation?" Her voice faded as she turned up the stair, and I smiled, visualization moving down the sweeping curve of my intestines.

There was another reason I did not envy Jenny. I had at first feared that the birth of Faith had done me some internal damage, but that fear had disappeared with Raymond's touch. As I completed the inventory of my body, and felt my spine go slack on the edge of sleep, I could feel that all was well there. It had happened once, it could happen again. All that was needed was time. And Jamie.

Jenny's footsteps sounded on the boards of the hallway, quickening in response to a sleepy squawk from Maggie, at the far end of the house.

"Bairns are certain joy, but nay sma' care," I murmured to myself, and fell asleep.

Through the next day, we waited, doing our chores and going through the daily routine with one ear cocked for the sound of horses in the dooryard.

"They'll have stayed to do some business," Jenny said, outwardly confident. But I saw her pause every time she passed the window that overlooked the lane leading to the house.

As for me, I had a hard time controlling my imagination. The letter, signed by King George, confirming Jamie's pardon, was locked in the drawer of the desk in the laird's study. Jamie regarded it as a humiliation, and would have burned it, but I had insisted it be kept, just in case. Now, listening for sounds through the rush of winter wind, I kept having visions of it having all been a mistake, or a hoax of some kind—of Jamie once more arrested by red-coated dragoons, taken away again to the misery of prison, and the impending danger of the hangman's noose.

The men returned at last just before nightfall, horses laden with bags containing the salt, needles, pickling spice, and other small items that Lallybroch could not produce for itself.

I heard one of the horses whinny as it came into the stableyard, and ran downstairs, meeting Jenny on her way out through the kitchens.

Relief swept through me as I saw Jamie's tall figure, shadowed against the barn. I ran through the yard, disregarding the light covering of snow that lingered on the ground, and flung myself into his arms.

"Where the hell have you been?" I demanded.

He took time to kiss me before replying. His face was cold against mine, and his lips tasted faintly and pleasantly of whisky.

"Mm, sausage for supper?" he said approvingly, sniffing at my hair, which smelled of kitchen smoke. "Good, I'm fair starved."

"Bangers and mash," I said. "Where have you been?"

He laughed, shaking out his plaid to get the blown snow off. "Bangers and mash? That's food, is it?"

"Sausages with mashed potatoes," I translated. "A nice traditional English dish, hitherto unknown in the benighted reaches of Scotland. Now, you bloody Scot, where in hell have you been for the last two days? Jenny and I were worried!"

"Well, we had a wee accident—" Jamie began, when he spotted the small figure of Fergus, bearing a lantern. "Och, ye've brought a light, then, Fergus? Good lad. Set it there, where ye won't set fire to the straw, and then take this poor beast into her stall. When ye've got her settled, come along to your own supper. You'll be able to sit to it by now, I expect?" He aimed a friendly cuff at Fergus's ear. The boy dodged and grinned back; apparently whatever had happened in the barn yesterday had left no hard feelings.

"Jamie," I said, in measured tones. "If you don't stop talking about horses and sausages and tell me what sort of accident you had, I am going to kick you in the shins. Which will be very hard on my toes, because I'm only wearing slippers, but I warn you, I'll do it anyway."

"That's a threat, is it?" he said, laughing. "It wasna serious, Sassenach, only that—"

"Ian!" Jenny, delayed momentarily by Maggie, had just arrived, in time to see her husband step into the circle of lanternlight. Startled by the shock in her voice, I turned to see her dart forward and put a hand to Ian's face.

"Whatever happened to ye, man?" she said. Plainly, whatever the accident had been, Ian had borne the brunt of it. One eye was blackened and swollen half-shut, and there was a long, raw scrape down the slope of one cheekbone.

"I'm all right, *mi dhu*," he said, patting Jenny gently as she embraced him, little Maggie squeezed uncomfortably between them. "Only a bit bruised here and there."

"We were comin' down the slope of the hill two miles outside the village, leading the horses because the footing was bad, and Ian stepped in a molehole and broke his leg," Jamie explained.

"The wooden one," Ian amplified. He grinned, a little sheepishly. "The mole had a bit the best o' that encounter."

"So we stayed at a cottage nearby long enough to carve him a new one," Jamie ended the story. "Can we eat? The sides of my belly are flapping together."

We went in without further ado, and Mrs. Crook and I served the supper while Jenny bathed Ian's face with witch hazel and made anxious inquiries about other injuries.

"It's nothing," he assured her. "Only bruises here and there." I had watched him coming into the house, though, and seen that his normal limp was badly exaggerated. I had a few quiet words with Jenny as we cleared away the supper plates, and once we were settled in the parlor, the contents of the saddlebags safely disposed of, she knelt on the rug beside Ian and took hold of the new leg.

"Let's have it off, then," she said firmly. "You've hurt yourself, and I want Claire to look it over. She can maybe help ye more than I can."

The original amputation had been done with some skill, and greater luck; the army surgeon who had taken the lower leg off had been able to save the knee joint. This gave Ian a great deal more flexibility of movement than he might otherwise have had. For the moment, though, the knee joint was more a liability than an advantage.

The fall had twisted his leg cruelly; the end of the stump was blue with bruising, and lacerated where the sharp edge of the cuff had pressed through the skin. It must have been agony to set any weight on it, even had all else been normal. As it was, the knee had twisted, too, and the flesh on the inside of the joint was swollen, red and hot.

Ian's long, good-natured face was nearly as red as the injured joint. While perfectly matter-of-fact about his disability, I knew he hated the occasional helplessness it imposed. His embarrassment at being so exposed now was likely as painful to him as my touching of his leg.

"You've torn a ligament through here," I told him, tracing the swelling inside his knee with a gentle finger. "I can't tell how bad it is, but bad enough. You've got fluid inside the joint; that's why it's swollen."

"Can ye help it, Sassenach?" Jamie was leaning over my shoulder, frowning worriedly at the angry-looking limb.

I shook my head. "Not a lot I can do for it, beyond cold compresses to reduce the swelling." I looked up at Ian, fixing him with my best approximation of a Mother Hildegarde look.

"What *you* can do," I said, "is stay in bed. You can have whisky for the pain tomorrow; tonight, I'll give you laudanum so you can sleep. Keep off it for a week, at least, and we'll see how it does."

"I canna do that!" Ian protested. "There's the stable wall needs mending, two dikes down in the upper field, and the ploughshares to be sharpened, and—"

"And a leg to mend, too," said Jamie, firmly. He gave Ian what I privately called his "laird's look," a piercing blue glare that caused most people to leap to his bidding. Ian, who had shared meals, toys, hunting expeditions, fights, and thrashings with Jamie, was a good deal less susceptible than most people.

"The hell I will," he said flatly. His hot brown eyes met Jamie's with a look in which pain and anger mingled with resentment—and something else I didn't recognize. "D'ye think ye can order me?"

Jamie sat back on his heels, flushing as though he'd been slapped. He bit back several obvious retorts, finally saying quietly, "No. I wilna try to order ye. May I ask ye, though—to care for yourself?"

A long look passed between the men, containing some message I couldn't read. At last, Ian's shoulders slumped as he relaxed, and he nodded, with a crooked smile.

"You can ask." He sighed, and rubbed at the scrape on his cheekbone, wincing as he touched the abraded skin. He took a deep breath, steeling himself, then held out a hand to Jamie. "Help me up, then?"

It was an awkward job, getting a man with one leg up two flights of stairs, but it was managed at last. At the bedroom door, Jamie left Ian to Jenny. As he stepped back, Ian said something soft and quick to Jamie in Gaelic. I still was not proficient in the tongue, but I thought he had said, "Be well, brother."

Jamie paused, looking back, and smiled, the candle lighting his eyes with warmth.

"You, too, *mo brathair*."

I followed Jamie down the hall to our own room. I could tell from the slump of his shoulders that he was tired, but I had a few questions I wanted to ask before he fell asleep.

"It's only bruises here and there," Ian had said, reassuring Jenny. It was. Here and there. Besides the bruises on his face and leg, I had seen the darkened marks that lay half-hidden under the collar of his shirt. No matter how much Ian's intrusion had been resented, I couldn't imagine a mole trying to strangle him in retaliation.

In the event, Jamie didn't want to sleep at once.

"Oh, absence makes the heart grow fonder, does it?" I said. The bed, so vast the night before, now seemed scarcely big enough.

"Mm?" he said, eyes half-closed in content. "Oh, the heart? Aye, that, too. Oh, God, don't stop; that feels wonderful."

"Don't worry, I'll do it some more," I assured him. "Let me put out the candle, though." I rose and blew it out; with the shutters left open, there was plenty of light reflected into the room from the snowy sky, even without the candle's flame. I could see Jamie clearly, the long shape of his body relaxed beneath the quilts, hands curled half-open at his side. I crawled in beside him and took up his right hand, resuming my slow massage of his fingers and palm.

He gave a long sigh, almost a groan, as I rubbed a thumb in firm circles over the pads at the base of his fingers. Stiffened by hours of clenching around his horse's reins, the fingers warmed and relaxed slowly under my touch. The house was quiet, and the room cold, outside the sanctuary of the bed. It was pleasant to feel the length of his body warming the space beside me, and enjoy the intimacy of touch, with no immediate feeling of demand. In time, this touch might token more; it was winter, and the nights were long. He was there; so was I, and content with things as they were for the moment.

"Jamie," I said, after a time, "who hurt Ian?"

He didn't open his eyes, but gave a long sigh before answering. He didn't stiffen in resistance, though; he had been expecting the question.

"I did," he said.

"What?" I dropped his hand in shock. He closed his fist and opened it, testing the movement of his fingers. Then he laid his left hand on the counter-pane beside it, showing me the knuckles, slightly puffed by contact with the protuberances of Ian's bony countenance.

"Why?" I said, appalled. I could tell that there was something new and edgy between Jamie and Ian, though it didn't look exactly like hostility. I couldn't imagine what might have made Jamie strike Ian; his brother-in-law was nearly as close to him as was his sister, Jenny.

Jamie's eyes were open now, but not looking at me. He rubbed his knuckles restlessly, looking down at them. Aside from the mild bruising of his knuckles, there were no marks on Jamie; apparently Ian hadn't fought back.

"Well, Ian's been married too long," he said defensively.

"I'd say you'd been out in the sun too long," I remarked, staring at him, "except that there isn't any. Have you got a fever?"

"No," he said, evading my attempts to feel his forehead. "No, it's only— stop that, Sassenach, I'm all right." He pressed his lips together, but then gave up and told me the whole story.

Ian had in fact broken his wooden leg by stepping into a molehole near Broch Mordha.

"It was near evening—we'd had a lot to do in the village—and snowing.

And I could see Ian's leg was paining him a lot, even though he kept insisting he could ride. Anyway, there were two or three cottages near, so I got him up on one of the ponies, and brought him up the slope to beg shelter for the night."

With characteristic Highland hospitality, both shelter and supper were offered with alacrity, and after a warm bowl of brose and fresh oatcake, both visitors had been accommodated with a pallet before the fire.

"There was scarce room to lay a quilt by the hearth, and we were squeezed a bit, but we lay down side by side and made ourselves as comfortable as might be." He drew a deep breath, and looked at me half-shyly.

"Well, I was worn out by the journey, and slept deep, and I suppose Ian did the same. But he's slept every night wi' Jenny for the last five years, and I suppose, havin' a warm body next to him in the bed—well, somewhere in the night, he rolled toward me, put his arm about me and kissed me on the back o' the neck. And I"—he hesitated, and I could see the deep color flood his face, even in the grayish light of the snow-lit room—"I woke from a sound sleep, thinking he was Jack Randall."

I had been holding my breath through this story; now I let it out slowly.

"That must have been the hell of a shock," I said.

One side of Jamie's mouth twitched. "It was the hell of a shock to Ian, I'll tell ye," he said. "I rolled over and punched him in the face, and by the time I came all the way to myself, I was on top of him, throttling him, wi' his tongue sticking out of his head. Hell of a shock to the Murrays in the bed, too," he added reflectively. "I told them I'd had a nightmare—well, I had, in a way— but it caused the hell of a stramash, what wi' the bairns shriekin', and Ian choking in the corner, and Mrs. Murray sittin' bolt upright in bed, sayin' 'Who, who?' like a wee fat owl."

I laughed despite myself at the image.

"Oh God, Jamie. Was Ian all right?"

Jamie shrugged a little. "Well, ye saw him. Everyone went back to sleep, after a time, and I just lay before the fire for the rest of the night, staring at the roof beams." He didn't resist as I picked up his left hand, gently stroking the bruised knuckles. His fingers closed over mine, holding them.

"So when we left the next morning," he went on, "I waited 'til we'd come to a spot where ye can sit and look over the valley below. And then"—he swallowed, and his hand tightened slightly on mine—"I told him. About Randall. And everything that happened."

I began to understand the ambiguity of the look Ian had given Jamie. And I now understood the look of strain on Jamie's face, and the smudges under his eyes. Not knowing what to say, I just squeezed his hands.

"I hadna thought I'd ever tell anyone—anyone but you," he added, returning the squeeze. He smiled briefly, then pulled one hand away to rub his face.

011000000

"But Ian . . . well, he's . . ." He groped for the right word. "He *knows* me, d'ye see?"

"I think so. You've known him all your life, haven't you?"

He nodded, looking sightlessly out the window. The swirling snow had begun to fall again, small flakes dancing against the pane, whiter than the sky.

"He's only a year older than me. When I was growing, he was always there. Until I was fourteen, there wasna a day went by when I didna see Ian. And even later, after I'd gone to foster wi' Dougal, and to Leoch, and then later still to Paris, to university—when I'd come back, I'd walk round a corner and there he would be, and it would be like I'd never left. He'd just smile when he saw me, like he always did, and then we'd be walkin' away together, side by side, ower the fields and the streams, talkin' of everything." He sighed deeply, and rubbed a hand through his hair.

"Ian . . . he's the part of me that belongs here, that never left," he said, struggling to explain. "I thought . . . I must tell him; I didna want to feel . . . apart. From Ian. From here." He gestured toward the window, then turned toward me, eyes dark in the dim light. "D'ye see why?"

"I think so," I said again, softly. "Did Ian?"

He made that small, uncomfortable shrugging motion, as though easing a shirt too tight across his back. "Well, I couldna tell. At first, when I began to tell him, he just kept shaking his head, as though he couldna believe me, and then when he did—" He paused and licked his lips, and I had some idea of just how much that confession in the snow had cost him. "I could see he wanted to jump to his feet and stamp back and forth, but he couldn't, because of his leg. His fists were knotted up, and his face was white, and he kept saying 'How? Damn ye, Jamie, *how* could ye let him do it?' "

He shook his head. "I dinna remember what I said. Or what he said. We shouted at each other, I know that much. And I wanted to hit him, but I couldn't, because of his leg. And he wanted to hit me, but couldn't—because of his leg." He gave a brief snort of laughter. "Christ, we must ha' looked a rare pair of fools, wavin' our arms and shouting at each other. But I shouted longer, and finally he shut up and listened to the end of it.

"Then all of a sudden, I couldna go on talking; it just seemed like no use. And I sat down all at once on a rock, and put my head in my hands. Then after a time, Ian said we'd best be going on. And I nodded, and got up, and helped him on his horse, and we started off again, not speakin' to each other."

Jamie seemed suddenly to realize how tightly he was holding my hand. He released his grip, but continued to hold my hand, turning my wedding ring between his thumb and forefinger.

"We rode for a long time," he said softly. "And then I heard a small sound behind me, and reined up so Ian's horse came alongside, and I could see he'd been weeping—still was, wi' the tears streaming down his face. And he saw me look at him, and shook his head hard, as if he was still angry, but then he held out his hand to me. I took it, and he gave me a squeeze, hard enough to break the bones. Then he let go, and we came on home."

I could feel the tension go out of him, with the ending of the story. "Be well, brother," Ian had said, balanced on his one leg in the bedroom door.

"It's all right, then?" I asked.

"It will be." He relaxed completely now, sinking back into the goose-down pillows. I slid down under the quilts beside him, and lay close, fitted against his side. We watched the snow fall, hissing softly against the glass.

"I'm glad you're safe home," I said.

I woke to the same gray light in the morning. Jamie, already dressed for the day, was standing by the window.

"Oh, you're awake, Sassenach?" he said, seeing me lift my head from the pillow. "That's good. I brought ye a present."

He reached into his sporran and pulled out several copper doits, two or three small rocks, a short stick wrapped with fishline, a crumpled letter, and a tangle of hair ribbons.

"Hair ribbons?" I said. "Thank you; they're lovely."

"No, those aren't for you," he said, frowning as he disentangled the blue strands from the mole's foot he carried as a charm against rheumatism. "They're for wee Maggie." He squinted dubiously at the rocks remaining in his palm. To my astonishment, he picked one up and licked it.

"No, not that one," he muttered, and dived back into his sporran.

"What on earth do you think you're doing?" I inquired with interest, watching this performance. He didn't answer, but came out with another handful of rocks, which he sniffed at, discarding them one by one until he came to a nodule that struck his fancy. This one he licked once, for certainty, then dropped it into my hand, beaming.

"Amber," he said, with satisfaction, as I turned the irregular lump over with a forefinger. It seemed warm to the touch, and I closed my hand over it, almost unconsciously.

"It needs polishing, of course," he explained. "But I thought it would make ye a bonny necklace." He flushed slightly, watching me. "It's . . . it's a gift for our first year of marriage. When I saw it, I was minded of the bit of amber Hugh Munro gave ye, when we wed."

"I still have that," I said softly, caressing the odd little lump of petrified tree sap. Hugh's chunk of amber, one side sheared off and polished into a small window, had a dragonfly embedded in the matrix, suspended in eternal flight. I kept it in my medicine box, the most powerful of my charms.

A gift for our first anniversary. We had married in June, of course, not in December. But on the date of our first anniversary, Jamie had been in the

Bastille, and I . . . I had been in the arms of the King of France. No time for a celebration of wedded bliss, that.

"It's nearly Hogmanay," Jamie said, looking out the window at the soft snowfall that blanketed the fields of Lallybroch. "It seems a good time for beginnings, I thought."

"I think so, too." I got out of bed and came to him at the window, putting my arms around his waist. We stayed locked together, not speaking, until my eye suddenly fell on the other small, yellowish lumps that Jamie had removed from his sporran.

"What on earth are those things, Jamie?" I asked, letting go of him long enough to point.

"Och, those? They're honey balls, Sassenach." He picked up one of the objects, dusting at it with his fingers. "Mrs. Gibson in the village gave them to me. Verra good, though they got a bit dusty in my sporran, I'm afraid." He held out his open hand to me, smiling. "Want one?"

34

The Postman Always Rings Twice

I didn't know what—or how much—Ian had told Jenny of his conversation in the snow with Jamie. She behaved toward her brother just as always, matter-of-fact and acerbic, with a slight touch of affectionate teasing. I had known her long enough, though, to realize that one of Jenny's greatest gifts was her ability to see something with utter clarity—and then to look straight through it, as though it wasn't there.

The dynamics of feeling and behavior shifted among the four of us during the months, and settled into a pattern of solid strength, based on friendship and founded in work. Mutual respect and trust were simply a necessity; there was so much to be done.

As Jenny's pregnancy progressed, I took on more and more of the domestic duties, and she deferred to me more often. I would never try to usurp her place; she had been the axis of the household since the death of her mother, and it was to her that the servants or tenants most frequently came. Still, they grew used to me, treating me with a friendly respect which bordered sometimes on acceptance, and sometimes on awe.

The spring was marked first by the planting of an enormous crop of potatoes; over half the available land was given to the new crop—a decision justified within weeks by a hailstorm that flattened the new-sprung barley. The potato vines, creeping low and stolid over the ground, survived.

The second event of the spring was the birth of a second daughter, Katherine Mary, to Jenny and Ian. She arrived with a suddenness that startled everyone, including Jenny. One day Jenny complained of an aching back and went to lie down. Very shortly it became clear what was really happening, and Jamie went posthaste for Mrs. Martins, the midwife. The two of them arrived back just in time to share in a celebratory glass of wine as the thin, high squalls of the new arrival echoed through the halls of the house.

And so the year burgeoned and greened, and I bloomed, the last of my hurts healing in the heart of love and work.

Letters arrived irregularly; sometimes there would be mail once a week, sometimes nothing would come for a month or more. Considering the lengths to which messengers had to go to deliver mail in the Highlands, I thought it incredible that anything ever arrived.

Today, though, there was a large packet of letters and books, wrapped against the weather in a sheet of oiled parchment, tied with twine. Sending the postal messenger to the kitchen for refreshment, Jenny untied the string carefully and thriftily stowed it in her pocket. She thumbed through the small pile of letters, putting aside for the moment an enticing-looking package addressed from Paris.

"A letter for Ian—that'll be the bill for the seed, I expect, and one from Auntie Jocasta—oh, good, we've not heard from her in months, I thought she might be ill, but I see her hand is firm on the pen—"

A letter addressed with bold black strokes fell onto Jenny's pile, followed by a note from one of Jocasta's married daughters. Then another for Ian from Edinburgh, one for Jamie from Jared—I recognized the spidery, half-legible writing—and another, a thick, creamy sheet, sealed with the Royal crest of the House of Stuart. Another of Charles's complaints about the rigors of life in Paris, and the pains of intermittently requited love, I imagined. At least this one looked short; usually he went on for several pages, unburdening his soul to "*cher* James," in a misspelled quadrilingual patois that at least made it clear he sought no secretarial help for his personal letters.

"Ooh, three French novels and a book of poetry from Paris!" Jenny said in excitement, opening the paper-wrapped package. "*C'est un embarras de richesse,* hm? Which shall we read tonight?" She lifted the small stack of books from their wrappings, stroking the soft leather cover of the top one with a forefinger that trembled with delight. Jenny loved books with the same passion her brother reserved for horses. The manor boasted a small library, in fact, and if the evening leisure between work and bed was short, still it usually included at least a few minutes' reading.

"It gives ye something to think on as ye go about your work," Jenny explained, when I found her one night swaying with weariness, and urged her to go to bed, rather than stay up to read aloud to Ian, Jamie, and myself. She yawned, fist to her mouth. "Even if I'm sae tired I hardly see the words on the page, they'll come back to me next day, churning or spinning or waulkin' wool, and I can turn them over in my mind."

I hid a smile at the mention of wool waulking. Alone among the Highland farms, I was sure, the women of Lallybroch waulked their wool not only to the old traditional chants but also to the rhythms of Molière and Piron.

I had a sudden memory of the waulking shed, where the women sat in two facing rows, barefooted and bare-armed in their oldest clothes, bracing themselves against the walls as they thrust with their feet against the long, sodden worm of woolen cloth, battering it into the tight, felted weave that would repel Highland mists and even light rain, keeping the wearer safe from the chill.

Every so often one woman would rise and go outside, to fetch the kettle of steaming urine from the fire. Skirts kilted high, she would walk spraddle-legged down the center of the shed, drenching the cloth between her legs, and the hot fumes rose fresh and suffocating from the soaking wool, while the waulkers pulled back their feet from random splashes, and made crude jokes.

"Hot piss sets the dye fast," one of the women had explained to me as I blinked, eyes watering, on my first entrance to the shed. The other women had watched at first, to see if I would shrink back from the work, but wool-waulking was no great shock, after the things I had seen and done in France, both in the war of 1944 and the hospital of 1744. Time makes very little difference to the basic realities of life. And smell aside, the waulking shed was a warm, cozy place, where the women of Lallybroch visited and joked between bolts of cloth, and sang together in the working, hands moving rhythmically across a table, or bare feet sinking deep into the steaming fabric as we sat on the floor, thrusting against a partner thrusting back.

I was pulled back from my memories of wool-waulking by the noise of heavy boots in the hallway, and a gust of cool, rainy air as the door opened. Jamie, and Ian with him, talking together in Gaelic, in the comfortable, unemphatic manner that meant they were discussing farm matters.

"That field's going to need draining next year," Jamie was saying as he came past the door. Jenny, seeing them, had put down the mail and gone to fetch fresh linen towels from the chest in the hallway.

"Dry yourselves before ye come drip on the rug," she ordered, handing one to each of the men. "And tak' off your filthy boots, too. The post's come, Ian—there's a letter for ye from that man in Perth, the one ye wrote to about the seed potatoes."

"Oh, aye? I'll come read it, then, but is there aught to eat while I do it?" Ian asked, rubbing his wet head with the towel until the thick brown hair stood up in spikes. "I'm famished, and I can hear Jamie's belly garbeling from here."

Jamie shook himself like a wet dog, making his sister emit a small screech as the cold drops flew about the hall. His shirt was pasted to his shoulders and loose strands of rain-soaked hair hung in his eyes, the color of rusted iron.

I draped a towel around his neck. "Finish drying off, and I'll go fetch you something."

I was in the kitchen when I heard him cry out. I had never heard such a sound from him before. Shock and horror were in it, and something else—a note of finality, like the cry of a man who finds himself seized in a tiger's jaws. I was down the hall and running for the drawing room without conscious thought, a tray of oatcakes still clutched in my hands.

When I burst through the door, I saw him standing by the table where Jenny had laid the mail. His face was dead white, and he swayed slightly where he stood, like a tree cut through, waiting for someone to shout "Timber" before falling.

"What?" I said, scared to death by the look on his face. "Jamie, what? What is it?!"

With a visible effort, he picked up one of the letters on the table and handed it to me.

I set down the oatcakes and took the sheet of paper, scanning it rapidly. It was from Jared; I recognized the thin, scrawly handwriting at once. " 'Dear Nephew,' " I read to myself, " '. . . so pleased . . . words cannot express my admiration . . . your boldness and courage will be an inspiration . . . cannot fail of success . . . my prayers shall be with you . . .' " I looked up from the paper, bewildered. "What on earth is he talking about? What have you done, Jamie?"

The skin was stretched tight across the bones of his face, and he grinned, mirthless as a death's-head, as he picked up another sheet of paper, this one a cheaply printed handbill.

"It's not what *I've* done, Sassenach," he said. The broadsheet was headed by the crest of the Royal House of Stuart. The message beneath was brief, couched in stately language.

It stated that by the ordination of Almighty God, King James, VIII of Scotland and III of England and Ireland asserted herewith his just rights to claim the throne of three kingdoms. And herewith acknowledged the support of these divine rights by the chieftains of the Highland clans, the Jacobite lords, and "various other such loyal subjects of His Majesty, King James, as have subscribed their names upon this Bill of Association in token thereof."

My fingers grew icy as I read, and I was conscious of a feeling of terror so acute that it was a real effort to keep on breathing. My ears rang with pounding blood, and there were dark spots before my eyes.

At the bottom of the sheet were signed the names of the Scottish chieftains who had declared their loyalty to the world, and staked their lives and reputations on the success of Charles Stuart. Clanranald was there, and Glengarry. Stewart of Appin, Alexander MacDonald of Keppoch, Angus MacDonald of Scotus.

And at the bottom of the list was written, "James Alexander Malcolm MacKenzie Fraser, of Broch Tuarach."

"Jesus bloody fucking Christ," I whispered, wishing there were something stronger I could say, as a form of relief. "The filthy bastard's signed your name to it!"

Jamie, still pale and tight-faced, was beginning to recover.

"Aye, he has," he said briefly. His hand snaked out for the unopened letter remaining on the table—a heavy vellum, with the Stuart crest showing plainly in the wax seal. Jamie ripped the letter open impatiently, tearing the paper. He read it quickly, then dropped it on the table as though it burned his hands.

"An apology," he said hoarsely. "For lacking the time to send me the document, in order that I might sign it myself. And his gratitude, for my loyal support. Jesus, Claire! What am I going to do?"

It was a cry from the heart, and one to which I had no answer. I watched helplessly as he sank onto a hassock and sat staring, rigid, at the fire.

Jenny, transfixed by all this drama, moved now to take up the letters and the broadsheet. She read them over carefully, her lips moving slightly as she did so, then set them gently down on the polished tabletop. She looked at them, frowning, then crossed to her brother, and laid a hand on his shoulder.

"Jamie," she said. Her face was very pale. "There's only the one thing ye *can* do, my dearie. Ye must go and fight for Charles Stuart. Ye must help him win."

The truth of her words penetrated slowly through the layers of shock that wrapped me. The publication of this Bond of Association branded those who signed it as rebels, and as traitors to the English crown. It didn't matter now how Charles had managed, or where he had gotten the funds to begin; he was well and truly launched on the seas of rebellion, and Jamie—and I—were launched with him, willy-nilly. There was, as Jenny had said, no choice.

My eye caught Charles's letter, where it had fallen from Jamie's hand. ". . . Though there be manie who tell me I am foolish to embark in this werk without the support of Louis—or at least of his bankes!—I will entertain no notion at all of returning to that place from whence I come," it read. "Rejoice with me, my deare frend, for I am come Home."

35

Moonlight

A s the preparations for leaving went forward, a current of excitement and speculation ran all through the estate. Weapons hoarded since the Rising of the '15 were excavated from thatch and hayrick and hearth, burnished and sharpened. Men met in passing and paused to talk in earnest groups, heads together under the hot August sun. And the women grew quiet, watching them.

Jenny shared with her brother the capacity to be opaque, to give no clue of what she was thinking. Transparent as a pane of glass myself, I rather envied this ability. So, when she asked me one morning if I would fetch Jamie to her in the brewhouse, I had no notion of what she might want with him.

Jamie stepped in behind me and stood just within the door of the brewhouse, waiting as his eyes adjusted to the dimness. He took a deep breath, inhaling the bitter, damp pungency with evident enjoyment.

"Ahh," he said, sighing dreamily. "I could get drunk in here just by breathing."

"Weel, hold your breath, then, for a moment, for I need ye sober," his sister advised.

He obligingly inflated his lungs and puffed out his cheeks, waiting. Jenny poked him briskly in the stomach with the handle of her masher, making him double over in an explosion of breath.

"Clown," she said, without rancor. "I wanted to talk to ye about Ian."

Jamie took an empty bucket from the shelf, and upturning it, sat down on it. A faint glow from the oiled-paper window above him lit his hair with a deep copper gleam.

"What about Ian?" he asked.

Now it was Jenny's turn to take a deep breath. The wide bran tub before her gave off a damp warmth of fermentation, filled with the yeasty aroma of grain, hops, and alcohol.

"I want ye to take Ian with you, when ye go."

Jamie's eyebrows flew up, but he didn't say anything immediately. Jenny's eyes were fixed on the motions of the masher, watching the smooth roil of the mixture. He looked at her thoughtfully, big hands hanging loose between his thighs.

"Tired of marriage, are ye?" he asked conversationally. "Likely it would be easier just for me to take him out in the wood and shoot him for ye." There was a quick flash of blue eyes over the mash tub.

"If I want anyone shot, Jamie Fraser, I'll do it myself. And Ian wouldna be my first choice as target, either."

He snorted briefly, and one corner of his mouth quirked up.

"Oh, aye? Why, then?"

Her shoulders moved in a seamless rhythm, one motion fading into the next.

"Because I'm asking ye."

Jamie spread his right hand out on his knee, absently stroking the jagged scar that zigzagged its way down his middle finger.

"It's dangerous, Jenny," he said quietly.

"I know that."

He shook his head slowly, still gazing down at his hand. It had healed well, and he had good use of it, but the stiff fourth finger and the roughened patch of scar tissue on the back gave it an odd, crooked appearance.

"You think ye know."

"I know, Jamie."

His head came up, then. He looked impatient, but was striving to stay reasonable.

"Aye, I know Ian will ha' told ye stories, about fighting in France, and all. But you've no notion how it really is, Jenny. *Mo cridh,* it isna a matter of a cattle raid. It's a war, and likely to be a damn bloody shambles of one, too. It's—"

The masher struck the side of the tub with a clack and fell back into the mash.

"Don't tell me I dinna ken what it's like!" Jenny blazed at him. "Stories, is it? Who d'ye think nursed Ian when he came home from France wi' half a leg and a fever that nearly killed him?"

She slapped her hand flat on the bench. The stretched nerves had snapped.

"Don't know? *I* don't know? *I* picked the maggots out of the raw flesh of his stump, because his own mother couldna bring herself to do it! *I* held the hot knife against his leg to seal the wound! *I* smelled his flesh searing like a roasted pig and listened to him scream while I did it! D'ye dare to stand there and tell me I . . . don't . . . KNOW how it is!"

Angry tears ran down her cheeks. She brushed at them, groping in her pocket for a handkerchief.

Lips pressed tight together, Jamie rose, pulled a handkerchief from his sleeve, and handed it to her. He knew better than to touch or try to comfort her. He stood staring at her for a moment as she wiped furiously at her eyes and dripping nose.

"Aye, well, ye know, then," he said. "And yet you want me to take him?"

"I do." She blew her nose and wiped it briskly, then tucked the handkerchief in her pocket.

"He kens well enough that he's crippled, Jamie. Kens it a good bit too well. But he could manage with ye. There's a horse for him; he wouldna have to walk."

He made an impatient gesture with one hand.

"Could he manage is no the question, is it? A man can do what he thinks he must—why do *you* think he must?"

Composed once more, she fished the tool out of the mash and shook it. Brown droplets spattered into the tub.

"He hasna asked ye, has he? Whether ye'll need him or no?"

"No."

She stabbed the masher back into the tub and resumed her work.

"He thinks ye wilna want him because he's lame, and that he'd be no use to ye." She looked up then, troubled dark-blue eyes the twins of her brother's. "Ye knew Ian before, Jamie. He's different now."

He nodded reluctantly, resuming his seat on the bucket.

"Aye. Well, but ye'd expect it, no? And he seems well enough." He looked up at his sister and smiled.

"He's happy wi' ye, Jenny. You and the bairns."

She nodded, black curls bobbing.

"Aye, he is," she said softly. "But that's because he's a whole man to me, and always will be." She looked directly at her brother. "But if he thinks he's of no use to you, he wilna be whole to himself. And that's why I'll have ye take him."

Jamie laced his hands together, elbows braced on his knees, and rested his chin on his linked knuckles.

"This wilna be like France," he said quietly. "Fighting there, ye risk no more than your life in battle. Here . . ." He hesitated, then went on. "Jenny, this is treason. If it goes wrong, those that follow the Stuarts are like to end on a scaffold."

Her normally pale complexion went a shade whiter, but her motions didn't slow.

"There's nay choice for me," he went on, eyes steady on her. "But will ye risk us both? Will ye have Ian look down from the gallows on the fire waiting for his entrails? You'll chance raising your bairns wi'out their father—to save his pride?" His face was nearly as pale as hers, glimmering in the darkness of the brewhouse.

The strokes of the masher were slower now, without the fierce velocity of her earlier movements, but her voice held all the conviction of her slow, inexorable mashing.

"I'll have a whole man," she said steadily. "Or none."

Jamie sat without moving for a long moment, watching his sister's dark head bent over her work.

"All right," he said at last, quietly. She didn't look up or vary her movements, but the white kertch seemed to incline slightly toward him.

He sighed explosively, then rose and turned abruptly to me.

"Come on out of here, Sassenach," he said. "Christ, I *must* be drunk."

"What makes ye think you can order me about?" The vein in Ian's temple throbbed fiercely. Jenny's hand squeezed mine tighter.

Jamie's assertion that Ian would accompany him to join the Stuart army had been met first with incredulity, then with suspicion, and—as Jamie persisted—anger.

"You're a fool," Ian declared flatly. "I'm a cripple, and ye ken it well enough."

"I ken you're a bonny fighter, and there's none I'd rather have by my side in a battle," Jamie said firmly. His face gave no sign of doubts or hesitation; he had agreed to Jenny's request, and would carry it out, no matter what. "You've fought there often enough; will ye desert me now?"

Ian waved an impatient hand, dismissing this flattery. "That's as may be. If my leg comes off or gives way, there's precious little fighting I'll do—I'll be lyin' on the ground like a worm, waiting for the first Redcoat who comes by to spit me. And beyond that"—he scowled at his brother-in-law—"who d'ye think will mind this place for ye until you come back, and I'm off to the wars with ye?"

"Jenny," Jamie replied promptly. "I shall leave enough men behind that they can be seeing to the work; she can manage the accounts well enough."

Ian's brows shot up, and he said something very rude in Gaelic.

"*Pog ma mahon!* You'll ha' me leave her to run the place alone, wi' three small bairns at her apron, and but half the men needed? Man, ye've taken leave o' your senses!" Flinging up both hands, Ian swung around to the sideboard where the whisky was kept.

Jenny, seated next to me on the sofa with Katherine on her lap, made a small sound under her breath. Her hand sought mine under cover of our mingled skirts, and I squeezed her fingers.

"What makes ye think ye can order me about?"

Jamie eyed his brother-in-law's tense back for a moment, scowling. Suddenly, a muscle at the corner of his mouth twitched.

"Because I'm bigger than you are," he said belligerently, still scowling.

Ian rounded on him, incredulity stamped on his face. Indecision played in his eyes for less than a second. His shoulders squared up and his chin lifted.

"I'm older than you," he answered, with an identical scowl.

"I'm stronger."

"No, you're not!"

"Aye, I am!"

"No, *I* am!"

A vein of dead seriousness underlay the laughter in their voices; while this little confrontation might be passed off as all in fun, they were as intent on each other as they had ever been in youth or childhood, and the echoes of challenge rang in Jamie's voice as he ripped loose his cuff and jerked back the sleeve of his shirt.

"Prove it," he said. He cleared the chess table with a careless sweep of the hand, sat down and braced his elbow on the inlaid surface, fingers flexed for an offensive. Deep blue eyes glared up into Ian's dark-brown ones, hot with the same anger.

Ian took half a second to appraise the situation, then jerked his head in a brief nod of acceptance, making his heavy sheaf of dark hair flop into his eyes.

With calm deliberation, he brushed it back, unfastened his cuff, and rolled his sleeve to the shoulder, turn by turn, never taking his eyes from his brother-in-law.

From where I stood, I could see Ian's face, a little flushed under his tan, long, narrow chin set in determination. I couldn't see Jamie's face, but the determination was eloquently expressed by the line of back and shoulders.

The two men set their elbows carefully, maneuvering to find a good spot, rubbing back and forth with the point of the elbow to be sure the surface was not slippery.

With due ritual, Jamie spread his fingers, palm toward Ian. Ian carefully placed his own palm against it. The fingers matched, touching for a moment in a mirror image, then shifted, one to the right and one to the left, linked and clasping.

"Ready?" Jamie asked.

"Ready." Ian's voice was calm, but his eyes gleamed under the feathery brows.

The muscles tensed at once, all along the length of the two arms, springing into sharp definition as they shifted in their seats, seeking leverage.

Jenny caught my eye and rolled her eyes heavenward. Whatever she had been expecting of Jamie, it wasn't this.

Both men were focused on the straining knot of fingers, to the exclusion of everything else. Both faces were deep red with exertion, sweat damping the hair on their temples, eyes bulging slightly with effort. Suddenly I saw Jamie's gaze break from its concentration on the clenched fists as he saw Ian's lips clamp tighter. Ian felt the shift, looked up, met Jamie's eyes . . . and the two men burst into laughter.

The hands clung for a moment longer, locked in spasm, then fell apart.

"A draw, then," said Jamie, pushing back a strand of sweat-damp hair. He shook his head good-naturedly at Ian.

"All right, man. If I could order ye, I wouldna do it. But I can ask, no? Will ye come with me?"

Ian dabbed at the side of his neck, where a runnel of sweat dampened his collar. His gaze roamed about the room, resting for a moment on Jenny. Her face was no paler than usual, but I could see the hasty pulse, beating just below the angle of her jaw. Ian stared at her intently as he rolled his sleeve down again, in careful turns. I could see a deep pink flush begin to rise from the neck of her gown.

Ian rubbed his jaw as though thinking, then turned toward Jamie and shook his head.

"No, my jo," he said softly. "Ye need me here, and here I shall stay." His eyes rested on Jenny, with Katherine held against her shoulder, and on small Maggie, clutching her mother's skirt with grubby hands. And on me. Ian's long mouth curled in a slight smile. "I shall stay here," he repeated. "Guardin' your weak side, man."

"Jamie?"

"Aye?" The answer came at once; I knew he hadn't been asleep, though he lay still as a figure carved on a tomb. It was moon-bright in the room, and I could see his face when I rose on my elbow; he was staring upward, as though he could see beyond the heavy beams to the open night and the stars beyond.

"You aren't going to try to leave me behind, are you?" I wouldn't have thought of asking were it not for the scene with Ian, earlier in the evening. For once it was settled that Ian would stay, Jamie had sat down with him to issue orders—choosing who would march with the laird to the aid of the Prince, who would stay behind to tend to animals and pasture and the maintenance of Lallybroch.

I knew it had been a wrenching process of decision, though he gave no sign of it, calmly discussing with Ian whether Ross the smith could be spared to go and deciding that he could, though the ploughshares needed for the spring must all be in good repair before leaving. Whether Joseph Fraser Kirby might go, and deciding that he should not, as he was the main support not only of his own family but that of his widowed sister. Brendan was the oldest boy of both families, and at nine, ill-prepared to replace his father, should Joseph not come home.

It was a matter for the most delicate planning. How many men should go, to have some impact on the course of the war? For Jenny was right, Jamie had no choice now—no choice but to help Charles Stuart win. And to that end, as many men and arms as could possibly be summoned should be thrown into the cause.

But on the other side was me, and my deadly knowledge—and lack of it. We had succeeded in preventing Charles Stuart from getting money to finance his rebellion; and still the Bonnie Prince, reckless, feckless, and determined to claim his legacy, had landed to rally the clans at Glenfinnan. From a further letter from Jared, we had learned that Charles had crossed the Channel with two small frigates, provided by one Antoine Walsh, a sometime-slaver with an eye for opportunity. Apparently, he saw Charles's venture as less risky than a slaving expedition, a gamble in which he might or might not be justified. One frigate had been waylaid by the English; the other had landed Charles safe on the isle of Eriskay.

Charles had landed with only seven companions, including the owner of a small bank named Aeneas MacDonald. Unable to finance an entire expedition, MacDonald had provided the funds for a small stock of broadswords, which constituted Charles's entire armament. Jared sounded simultaneously admiring and horrified by the recklessness of the venture, but, loyal Jacobite that he was, did his best to swallow his misgivings.

And so far, Charles had succeeded. From the Highland grapevine, we learned that he had landed at Eriskay, crossed to Glenfinnan, and there waited, accompanied only by several large casks of brandywine, to see whether the clans would answer the call to his standard. And after what must have been several nerve-racking hours, three hundred men of clan Cameron had come down the defiles of the steep green hills, led not by their chieftain, who was away from his home—but by his sister, Jenny Cameron.

The Camerons had been the first, but they had been joined by others, as the Bill of Association showed.

If Charles should now proceed to disaster, despite all efforts, then how many men of Lallybroch could be spared, left at home to save something from the wreck?

Ian himself would be safe; that much was sure, and some balm to Jamie's spirit. But the others—the sixty families who lived on Lallybroch? Choosing who would go and who would stay must seem in some lights like choosing men for sacrifice. I had seen commanders before; the men whom war forced to make such choices—and I knew what it cost them.

Jamie had done it—he had no choice—but on two matters he had held firm; no women would accompany his troop, and no lads under eighteen years of age would go. Ian had looked mildly surprised at this—while most women with young children would normally stay behind, it was far from unusual for Highland wives to follow their men to battle, cooking and caring for them, and sharing the army's rations. And the lads, who considered themselves men at fourteen, would be grossly humiliated at being omitted from the tally. But Jamie had given his orders in a tone that brooked no argument, and Ian, after a moment's hesitation, had merely nodded and written them down.

I hadn't wanted to ask him, in the presence of Ian and Jenny, whether his ban on womenfolk was intended to include me. Because, whether it was or not, I was going with him, and that, I thought, was bloody all about it.

"Leave you behind?" he said now, and I saw his mouth curl into a sideways grin. "D'ye think I'd stand a chance of it?"

"No," I said, snuggling next to him in sudden relief. "You wouldn't. But I thought you might think about it."

He gave a small snort, and drew me down, head on his shoulder. "Oh, aye. And if I thought I could leave ye, I'd chain ye to the banister; not much else would stop ye." I could feel his head shake above me, in negation. "No. I must take ye wi' me, Sassenach, whether I will or no. There are things you'll maybe know along the way—even if they dinna seem like anything now, they may later. And you're a rare fine healer, Sassenach—I canna deny the men your skill, and it be needed."

His hand patted my shoulder, and he sighed. "I would give anything, *mo duinne,* could I leave ye here safe, but I cannot. So you will go with me—you and Fergus."

"Fergus?" I was surprised by this. "But I thought you wouldn't take any of the younger lads!"

He sighed again, and I put my hand flat on the center of his chest, where his heart beat beneath the small hollow, slow and steady.

"Well, Fergus is a bit different. The other lads—I willna take them, because they belong here; if it all goes to smash, they'll be left to keep their families from starving, to work the fields and tend beasts. They'll likely need to grow up fast, if it happens, but at least they'll be here to do it. But Fergus . . . this isna his place, Sassenach. Nor is France, or I would send him back. But he has no place there, either."

"His place is with you," I said softly, understanding. "Like mine."

He was silent for a long time, then his hand squeezed me gently.

"Aye, that's so," he said quietly. "Sleep now, *mo duinne,* it's late."

The fretful wail pulled me toward the surface of wakefulness for the third time. Baby Katherine was teething, and didn't care who knew it. From their room down the hall, I heard Ian's sleepy mumble, and Jenny's higher voice, resigned, as she got out of bed and went to soothe the infant.

Then I heard the soft, heavy footfalls in the corridor, and realized that Jamie, still wakeful, was walking barefoot through the house.

"Jenny?" His voice, low-pitched to avoid disturbance, was still plainly audible in the creaking silence of the manor house,

"I heard the wee lassie greetin'," he said. "If she canna sleep, neither can I, but you can. If she's fed and dry, perhaps we can bear each other company for a bit, while you go back to your bed."

Jenny smothered a yawn, and I could hear the smile in her voice.

"Jamie dear, you're a mother's blessing. Aye, she's full as a drum, and a dry clout on her this minute. Take her, and I wish ye joy of each other." A door closed, and I heard the heavy footfall again, heading back toward our room, and the low murmur of Jamie's voice as he muttered soothingly to the baby.

I snuggled deeper into the comfort of the goose-down bed and turned toward sleep again, hearing with half an ear the baby's whining, interspersed with hiccuping sobs, and Jamie's deep, tuneless humming, the sound as comforting as the thought of beehives in the sun.

"Eh, wee Kitty, *ciamar a tha thu? Much, mo naoidheachan, much.*"

The sound of them went up and down the passage, and I dropped further toward sleep, but kept half-wakeful on purpose to hear them. One day perhaps he would hold his own child so, small round head cradled in the big hands, small solid body cupped and held firm against his shoulder. And thus he would sing to his own daughter, a tuneless song, a warm, soft chant in the dark.

The constant small ache in my heart was submerged in a flood of tenderness. I had conceived once; I could do so again. Faith had given me the gift of that knowledge, Jamie the courage and means to use it. My hands rested lightly on my breasts, cupping the deep swell of them, knowing beyond doubt that one day they would nourish the child of my heart. I drifted into sleep with the sound of Jamie's singing in my ears.

Sometime later I drifted near the surface again, and opened my eyes to the light-filled room. The moon had risen, full and beaming, and all the objects in the room were plainly visible, in that flat, two-dimensional way of things seen without shadow.

The baby had quieted, but I could hear Jamie's voice in the hall, still speaking, but much more quietly, hardly more than a murmur. And the tone of it had changed; it wasn't the rhythmic, half-nonsense way one talks to babies, but the broken, halting speech of a man seeking the way through the wilderness of his own heart.

Curious, I slipped out of bed and crept quietly to the door. I could see them there at the end of the hall. Jamie sat leaning back against the side of the window seat, wearing only his shirt. His bare legs were raised, forming a back against which small Katherine Mary rested as she sat facing him in his lap, her own chubby legs kicking restlessly over his stomach.

The baby's face was blank and light as the moon's, her eyes dark pools absorbing his words. He traced the curve of her cheek with one finger, again and again, whispering with heartbreaking gentleness.

He spoke in Gaelic, and so low that I could not have told what he said, even had I known the words. But the whispering voice was thick, and the moonlight from the casement behind him showed the tracks of the tears that slid unregarded down his own cheeks.

It was not a scene that bore intrusion. I came back to the still-warm bed, holding in my mind the picture of the laird of Lallybroch, half-naked in the moonlight, pouring out his heart to an unknown future, holding in his lap the promise of his blood.

When I woke in the morning, there was a warm, unfamiliar scent next to me, and something tangled in my hair. I opened my eyes to find Katherine Mary's rosebud lips smacking dreamily an inch from my nose, her fat fingers clutched in the hair above my left ear. I cautiously disengaged myself, and she stirred, but flopped over onto her stomach, drew her knees up and went back to sleep.

Jamie was lying on the other side of the child, face half-buried in his pillow. He opened one eye, clear blue as the morning sky.

"Good morning, Sassenach," he said, speaking quietly so as not to disturb the small sleeper. He smiled at me as I sat up in bed. "Ye looked verra sweet, the two of you, asleep face-to-face like that."

I ran a hand through my tangled hair, and smiled myself at Kitty's up-turned bottom, jutting absurdly into the air.

"That doesn't look at all comfortable," I observed. "But she's still asleep, so it can't be that bad. How late were you up with her last night? I didn't hear you come to bed."

He yawned and ran a hand through his hair, smoothing it away from his face. There were shadows under his eyes, but he seemed peacefully content.

"Oh, some time. Before moonset, at least. I didna want to wake Jenny by taking the wean back to her, so I laid her in the bed between us, and she didna twitch once, the rest of the night."

The baby was kneading the mattress with elbows and knees, rooting in the bedclothes with a low grunting noise. It must be close to time for her morning feed. This supposition was borne out in the next moment, when she raised her head, eyes still tight shut, and let out a healthy howl. I reached hastily for her and picked her up.

"There-there-there," I soothed, patting the straining little back. I swung my legs out of bed, then reached back and patted Jamie on the head. The rough bright hair was warm under my hand.

"I'll take her to Jenny," I said. "It's early yet; you sleep some more."

"I may do that, Sassenach," Jamie said, flinching at the noise. "I'll see ye at breakfast, shall I?" He rolled onto his back, crossed his hands on his chest in his favorite sleeping posture, and was breathing deeply again by the time Katherine Mary and I had reached the door.

The baby squirmed vigorously, rooting for a nipple and squawking in frustration when none was immediately forthcoming. Hurrying along the hall, I met Jenny, hurrying out of her bedroom in response to her offspring's cries, pulling on a green dressing gown as she came. I held out the baby, waving little fists in urgent demand.

"There, *mo mùirninn,* hush now, hush," Jenny soothed. With a cock of the eyebrow in invitation, she took the child from me and turned back into her room.

I followed her in and sat on the rumpled bed as she sat down on a nursing stool by the hearth and hastily bared one breast. The yowling little mouth clamped at once on to a nipple and we all relaxed in relief as sudden silence descended.

"Ah," Jenny sighed. Her shoulders slumped a fraction as the flow of milk started. "That's better, my wee piggie, no?" She opened her eyes and smiled at me, eyes clear and blue as her brother's.

" 'Twas kind of ye to keep the lassie all night; I slept like the dead."

I shrugged, smiling at the picture of mother and child, relaxed together in total content. The curve of the baby's head exactly echoed the high, round curve of Jenny's breast and small, slurping noises came from the little bundle as her body sagged against her mother's, fitting easily into the curve of Jenny's lap.

"It was Jamie, not me," I said. "He and his niece seem to have got on well together." The picture of them came back to me, Jamie talking in earnest, low tones to the child, tears slipping down his face.

Jenny nodded, watching my face.

"Aye. I thought perhaps they'd comfort each other a bit. He doesna sleep well these days?" Her voice held a question.

"No," I answered softly. "He has a lot on his mind."

"Well he might," she said, glancing at the bed behind me. Ian was gone already, risen at dawn to see to the stock in the barn. The horses that could be spared from the farming—and some that couldn't—needed shoeing, needed harness, in preparation for their journey to rebellion.

"You can talk to a babe, ye ken," she said suddenly, breaking into my thought. "Really talk, I mean. Ye can tell them anything, no matter how foolish it would sound did ye say it to a soul could understand ye."

"Oh. You heard him, then?" I asked. She nodded, eyes on the curve of Katherine's cheek, where the tiny dark lashes lay against the fair skin, eyes closed in ecstasy.

"Aye. Ye shouldna worrit yourself," she added, smiling gently at me. "It isna that he feels he canna talk to you; he knows he can. But it's different to talk to a babe that way. It's a person; ye ken that you're not alone. But they dinna ken your words, and ye don't worry a bit what they'll think of ye, or what they may feel they must do. You can pour out your heart to them wi'out choosing your words, or keeping anything back at all—and that's a comfort to the soul."

She spoke matter-of-factly, as though this were something that everyone knew. I wondered whether she spoke that way often to her child. The generous wide mouth, so like her brother's, lifted slightly at one side.

"It's the way ye talk to them before they're born," she said softly. "You'll know?"

I placed my hands gently over my belly, one atop the other, remembering. "Yes, I know."

She pressed a thumb against the baby's cheek, breaking the suction, and with a deft movement, shifted the small body to bring the full breast within reach.

"I've thought that perhaps that's why women are so often sad, once the child's born," she said meditatively, as though thinking aloud. "Ye think of them while ye talk, and you have a knowledge of them as they are inside ye, the way you think they are. And then they're born, and they're different—not the way ye thought of them inside, at all. And ye love them, o' course, and get to know them the way they are . . . but still, there's the thought of the child ye once talked to in your heart, and that child is gone. So I think it's the grievin' for the child unborn that ye feel, even as ye hold the born one in your arms." She dipped her head and kissed her daughter's downy skull.

"Yes," I said. "Before . . . it's all possibility. It might be a son, or a daughter. A plain child, a bonny one. And then it's born, and all the things it might have been are gone, because now it *is*."

She rocked gently back and forth, and the small clutching hand that seized the folds of green silk over her breast began to loose its grip.

"And a daughter is born, and the son that she might have been is dead," she said quietly. "And the bonny lad at your breast has killed the wee lassie ye thought ye carried. And ye weep for what you didn't know, that's gone for good, until you know the child you have, and then at last it's as though they could never have been other than they are, and ye feel naught but joy in them. But 'til then, ye weep easy."

"And men . . ." I said, thinking of Jamie, whispering secrets to the un-hearing ears of the child.

"Aye. They hold their bairns, and they feel all the things that might be, and the things that will never be. But it isna so easy for a man to weep for the things he doesna ken."

PART SIX

The Flames of Rebellion

36

Prestonpans

F our days' march found us on the crest of a hill near Calder. A sizable moor stretched out at the foot of the hill, but we set up camp within the shelter of the trees above. There were two small streams cutting through the moss-covered rock of the hillside, and the crisp weather of early fall made it seem much more like picnicking than a march to war.

But it was the seventeenth of September, and if my sketchy knowledge of Jacobite history was correct, war it would be, in a matter of days.

"Tell it to me again, Sassenach," Jamie had said, for the dozenth time, as we made our way along the winding trails and dirt roads. I rode Donas, while Jamie walked alongside, but now slid down to walk beside him, to make conversation easier. While Donas and I had reached an understanding of sorts, he was the kind of horse that demanded your full concentration to ride; he was all too fond of scraping an unwary rider off by walking under low branches, for example.

"I told you before, I don't know that much," I said. "There was very little written about it in the history books, and I didn't pay a great deal of attention at the time. All I can tell you is that the battle was fought—er, *will* be fought— near the town of Preston, and so it's called the Battle of Prestonpans, though the Scots called—call—it the Battle of Gladsmuir, because of an old prophecy that the returning king will be victorious at Gladsmuir. Heaven knows where the real Gladsmuir is, if there is one."

"Aye. And?"

I furrowed my brow, trying to recall every last scrap of information. I could conjure a mental picture of the small, tattered brown copy of *A Child's History of England,* read by the flickering light of a kerosene lantern in a mud hut somewhere in Persia. Mentally flicking the pages, I could just recall the two-page section that was all the author had seen fit to devote to the second Jacobite Rising, known to historians as "the '45." And within that two-page section, the single paragraph dealing with the battle we were about to fight.

"The Scots win," I said helpfully.

"Well, that's the important point," he agreed, a bit sarcastically, "but it would be a bit of help to know a little more."

"If you wanted prophecy, you should have gotten a seer," I snapped, then relented. "I'm sorry. It's only that I don't *know* much, and it's very frustrating."

"Aye, it is." He reached down and took my hand, squeezing it as he smiled at me. "Dinna fash yourself, Sassenach. Ye canna say more than ye know, but tell me it all, just once more."

"All right." I squeezed back, and we walked on, hand in hand. "It was a remarkable victory," I began, reading from my mental page, "because the Jacobites were so greatly outnumbered. They surprised General Cope's army at dawn—they charged out of the rising sun, I remember that—and it was a rout. There were hundreds of casualties on the English side, and only a few from the Jacobite side—thirty men, that was it. Only thirty men killed."

Jamie glanced behind us, at the straggling tail of the Lallybroch men, strung out as they walked along the road, chatting and singing in small groups. Thirty men was what we had brought from Lallybroch. It didn't seem that small a number, looking at them. But I had seen the battlefields of Alsace-Lorraine, and the acres of meadowland converted to muddy boneyards by the burial of the thousands slain.

"Taken all in all," I said, feeling faintly apologetic, "I'm afraid it was really rather . . . unimportant, historically speaking."

Jamie blew out his breath through pursed lips, and looked down at me rather bleakly.

"Unimportant. Aye, well."

"I'm sorry," I said.

"Not your fault, Sassenach."

But I couldn't help feeling that it was, somehow.

The men sat around the fire after their supper, lazily enjoying the feeling of full stomachs, exchanging stories and scratching. The scratching was endemic; close quarters and lack of hygiene made body lice so common as to excite no remark when one man detached a representative specimen from a fold of his plaid and tossed it into the fire. The louse flamed for an instant, one among the sparks of the fire, and then was gone.

The young man they called Kincaid—his name was Alexander, but there were so many Alexanders that most of them ended up being called by nicknames or middle names—seemed particularly afflicted with the scourge this evening. He dug viciously under one arm, into his curly brown hair, then—with a quick glance to see whether I was looking in his direction—at his crotch.

"Got 'em bad, have ye, lad?" Ross the smith observed sympathetically.

"Aye," he answered, "the wee buggers are eatin' me alive."

"Bloody hell to get out of your cock hairs," Wallace Fraser observed, scratching himself in sympathy. "Gives me the yeuk to watch ye, laddie."

"D'ye ken the best way to rid yourself o' the wee beasties?" Sorley Mc-

Clure asked helpfully, and at Kincaid's negative shake of the head, leaned forward and carefully pulled a flaming stick from the fire.

"Lift your kilt a moment, laddie, and I'll smoke 'em out for ye," he offered, to catcalls and jeers of laughter from the men.

"Bloody farmer," Murtagh grumbled. "And what would ye know about it?"

"You know a better way?" Wallace raised thick brows skeptically, wrinkling the tanned skin of his balding forehead.

"O' course." He drew his dirk with a flourish. "The laddie's a soldier now; let him do it like a soldier does."

Kincaid's open face was guileless and eager. "How's that?"

"Weel, verra simple. Ye take your dirk, lift your plaidie, and shave off half the hairs on your crutch." He raised the dirk warningly. "Only half, mind."

"Half? Aye, well . . ." Kincaid looked doubtful, but was paying close attention. I could see the grins of anticipation broadening on the faces of the men around the fire, but no one was laughing yet.

"Then . . ." Murtagh gestured at Sorley and his stick. "*Then,* laddie, ye set the other half on fire, and when the beasties rush out, ye spear them wi' your dirk."

Kincaid blushed hotly enough to be seen even by firelight as the circle of men erupted in hoots and roars. There was a good deal of rude shoving as a couple of the men pretended to try the fire cure on each other, brandishing flaming billets of wood. Just as it seemed that the horseplay was getting out of hand, and likely to lead to blows in earnest, Jamie returned from hobbling the animals. He stepped into the circle, and tossed a stone bottle from under one arm to Kincaid. Another went to Murtagh, and the shoving died down.

"Ye're fools, the lot o' ye," he declared. "The second best way to rid yourself of lice is to pour whisky on them and get them drunk. When they've fallen down snoring, then ye stand up and they'll drop straight off."

"Second best, eh?" said Ross. "And what's the best way, sir, and I might ask?"

Jamie smiled indulgently round the circle, like a parent amused by the antics of his children.

"Why, let your wife pick them off ye, one by one." He cocked an elbow and bowed to me, one eyebrow raised. "If you'd oblige me, my lady?"

While put forward as a joke, individual removal was in fact the only effective method of ridding oneself of lice. I fine-combed my own hair—all of it—morning and evening, washed it with yarrow whenever we paused near water deep enough to bathe in, and had so far avoided any serious infestations. Aware that I would remain louseless only so long as Jamie did, I administered the same treatment to him, whenever I could get him to sit still long enough.

"Baboons do this all the time," I remarked, delicately disentangling a foxtail from his thick red mane. "But I believe they eat the fruits of their labors."

"Dinna let me prevent ye, Sassenach, and ye feel so inclined," he responded. He hunched his shoulders slightly in pleasure as the comb slid through the thick, glossy strands. The firelight filled my hands with a cascade of sparks and golden streaks of fire. "Mm. Ye wouldna think it felt so nice to have someone comb your hair for ye."

"Wait 'til I get to the rest of it," I said, tweaking him familiarly and making him giggle. "Tempted though I am to try Murtagh's suggestion instead."

"Touch my cock hairs wi' a torch, and you'll get the same treatment," he threatened. "What was it Louise de La Tour says bald lassies are?"

"Erotic." I leaned forward and nipped the upper flange of one ear between my teeth.

"Mmmphm."

"Well, tastes differ," I said. "*Chacun à son gout,* and all that."

"A bloody French sentiment, and I ever heard one."

"Isn't it, though?"

A loud, rolling growl interrupted my labors. I laid down the comb and peered ostentatiously into the tree-filled shadows.

"Either," I said, "there are bears in this wood, or . . . why haven't you eaten?"

"I was busy wi' the beasts," he answered. "One of the ponies has a cracked hoof and I had to bind it with a poultice. Not that I've so much appetite, what wi' all this talk of eating lice."

"What sort of poultice do you use on a horse's hoof?" I asked, ignoring this remark.

"Different things; fresh dung will do in a pinch. I used chewed vetch leaves mixed wi' honey this time."

The saddlebags had been dumped by our private fire, near the edge of the small clearing where the men had erected my tent. While I would have been willing to sleep under the stars, as they did, I admitted to a certain thankfulness for the small privacy afforded me by the sheet of canvas. And, as Murtagh had pointed out with his customary bluntness, when I thanked him for his assistance in erecting the shelter, the arrangement was not solely for *my* benefit.

"And if he takes his ease between your thighs of a night, there's none will grudge it to him," the little clansman had said, with a jerk of the head toward Jamie, deep in conversation with several of the other men. "But there's nay need to make the lads think ower-much o' things they canna have, now is there?"

"Quite," I said, with an edge to my voice. "Very thoughtful of you."

One of his rare smiles curled the corner of the thin-lipped mouth.

"Och, quite," he said.

A quick rummage through the saddlebags turned up a heel of cheese and several apples. I gave these to Jamie, who examined them dubiously.

"No bread?" he asked.

"There may be some in the other bag. Eat those first, though; they're good for you." He shared the Highlanders' innate suspicion of fresh fruit and vegetables, though his great appetite made him willing to eat almost anything in extremity.

"Mm," he said, taking a bite of one apple. "If ye say so, Sassenach."

"I do say so. Look." I pulled my lips back, baring my teeth. "How many women of my age do you know who still have all their teeth?"

A grin bared his own excellent teeth.

"Well, I'll admit you're verra well preserved, Sassenach, for such an auld crone."

"Well nourished, is what I am," I retorted. "Half the people on your estate are suffering from mild scurvy, and from what I've seen on the road, it's even worse elsewhere. It's vitamin C that prevents scurvy, and apples are full of it."

He took the apple away from his mouth and frowned at it suspiciously.

"They are?"

"Yes, they are," I said firmly. "So are most other kinds of plants—oranges and lemons are best, but of course you can't get those here—but onions, cabbage, apples . . . eat something like that every day, and you won't get scurvy. Even green herbs and meadow grass have vitamin C."

"Mmphm. And that's why deer dinna lose their teeth as they get old?"

"I daresay."

He turned the apple to and fro, examining it critically, then shrugged.

"Aye, well," he said, and took another bite.

I had just turned to fetch the bread when a faint crackling sound drew my attention. I caught sight from the corner of my eye of shadowy movement in the darkness and the firelight flashed from something near Jamie's head. I whirled toward him, shouting, just in time to see him topple backward off the log and disappear into the void of the night.

There was no moon, and the only clue to what was happening was a tremendous scuffling sound in the dry alder leaves, and the noise of men locked in effortful but silent conflict, with grunts, gasps, and the occasional muffled curse. There was a short, sharp cry, and then complete quiet. It lasted, I suppose, only a few seconds, though it seemed to go on forever.

I was still standing by the fire, frozen in my original position, when Jamie reemerged from the Stygian dark of the forest, a captive before him, one arm twisted behind its back. Loosing his grip, he whirled the dark figure around and gave it an abrupt shove that sent it crashing backward into a tree. The man hit the trunk hard, loosing a shower of leaves and acorns, and slid slowly down to lie dazed in the leaf-meal.

Attracted by the noise, Murtagh, Ross, and a couple of the other Fraser men materialized by the fire. Hauling the intruder to his feet, they pulled him roughly into the circle of firelight. Murtagh grabbed the captive by the hair and jerked his head backward, bringing his face into view.

It was a small, fine-boned face, with big, long-lashed eyes that blinked dazedly at the crowding faces.

"But he's only a boy!" I exclaimed. "He can't be more than fifteen!"

"Sixteen!" said the boy. He shook his head, senses returning. "Not that that makes any difference," he added haughtily, in an English accent. Hampshire, I thought. He was a long way from home.

"It doesn't," Jamie grimly agreed. "Sixteen or sixty, he's just made a verra creditable attempt at cutting my throat." I noticed then the reddened handkerchief pressed against the side of his neck.

"I shan't tell you anything," the boy said. His eyes were dark pools in the pale face, though the firelight shone on the gleam of fair hair. He was clutching one arm tightly in front of him; I thought perhaps it was injured. The boy was clearly making a major effort to stand upright among the men, lips compressed against any wayward expression of fear or pain.

"Some things you don't need to tell me," said Jamie, looking the lad over carefully. "One, you're an Englishman, so likely you've come with troops nearby. And two, you're alone."

The boy seemed startled. "How do you know that?"

Jamie raised his eyebrows. "I suppose that ye'd not have attacked me unless you thought that the lady and I were alone. If you were with someone else who also thought that, they would presumably have come to your assistance just now—is your arm broken, by the way? I thought I felt something snap. If you were with someone else who knew we were not alone, they would ha' stopped ye from trying anything so foolish." Despite this diagnosis, I noticed three of the men fade discreetly into the forest in response to a signal from Jamie, presumably to check for other intruders.

The boy's expression hardened at hearing his act described as foolish. Jamie dabbed at his neck, then inspected the handkerchief critically.

"If you're tryin' to kill someone from behind, laddie, pick a man who's not sitting in a pile of dry leaves," he advised. "And if you're using a knife on someone larger than you, pick a surer spot; throat-cutting's chancy unless your victim will sit still for ye."

"Thank you for the valuable advice," the boy sneered. He was doing a fair job at maintaining his bravado, though his eyes flicked nervously from one threatening, whiskered face to another. None of the Highlanders would have won any beauty prizes in broad daylight; by night, they weren't the sort of thing you wanted to meet in a dark place.

Jamie answered courteously, "You're quite welcome. It's unfortunate that ye won't get the chance to apply it in future. Why *did* you attack me, since I think to ask?"

Men, attracted by the noise, had begun filtering in from the surrounding campsites, sliding wraithlike out of the woods. The boy's glance flickered around the growing circle of men, resting at length on me. He hesitated for a moment, but answered, "I was hoping to release the lady from your custody."

A small stir of suppressed amusement ran around the circle, only to be quelled by a brief gesture from Jamie. "I see," he said noncommittally. "You heard us talking and determined that the lady is English and well-born. Whereas I—"

"Whereas you, sir, are a conscienceless outlaw, with a reputation for thievery and violence! Your face and description are on broadsheets throughout Hampshire and Sussex! I recognized you at once; you're a rebel and an unprincipled voluptuary!" the boy burst out hotly, face stained a deeper red even than the firelight.

I bit my lip and looked down at my shoes, so as not to meet Jamie's eye.

"Aye, well. Just as ye say," Jamie agreed cordially. "That being the case, perhaps you can advance some reason why I shouldna kill ye immediately?" Drawing the dirk smoothly from its sheath, he twisted it delicately, making the fire jump from the blade.

The blood had faded from the young man's face, leaving him ghostly in the shadows, but he drew himself upright at this, pulling against the captors on either side. "I expected that. I am quite prepared to die," he said, stiffening his shoulders.

Jamie nodded thoughtfully, then, stooping, laid the blade of his dirk in the fire. A plume of smoke rose around the blackening metal, smelling strongly of the forge. We all watched in silent fascination as the flame, spectral blue where it touched the blade, seemed to bring the deadly iron to life in a flush of deep red heat.

Wrapping his hand in the bloodstained cloth, Jamie cautiously pulled the dirk from the fire. He advanced slowly toward the boy, letting the blade fall, as though of its own volition, until it touched the lad's jerkin. There was a strong smell of singed cloth from the handkerchief wrapped around the haft of the knife, which grew stronger as a narrow burnt line traced its way up the front of the jerkin in the dagger's path. The point, darkening as it cooled, stopped just short of the upwardly straining chin. I could see thin lines of sweat shining in the stretched hollows of the slender neck.

"Aye, well, I'm afraid that I'm no prepared to kill ye—just yet." Jamie's voice was soft, filled with a quiet menace all the more frightening for its control.

"Who d'ye march with?" The question snapped like a whip, making its hearers flinch. The knife point hovered slightly nearer, smoking in the night wind.

"I'll—I'll not tell you!" The boy's lips closed tight on the stammered answer, and a tremor ran down the delicate throat.

"Nor how far away your comrades lie? Nor their number? Nor their direction of march?" The questions were put lightly again, with a finicking touch of the blade along the edge of the boy's jaw. His eyes showed white all around, like a panicked horse, but he shook his head violently, making the golden hair fly. Ross and Kincaid tightened their grip against the pull of the boy's arms.

The darkened blade pressed suddenly flat along its length, hard under the angle of the jaw. There was a thin and breathy scream, and the stink of burning skin.

"Jamie!" I said, shocked beyond bearing. He did not turn to look at me, but kept his eyes fixed on his prisoner, who, released from the grip on his arms, had sunk to his knees in the drift of dead leaves, hand clutched to his neck.

"This is no concern of yours, Madam," he said between his teeth. Reaching down, he grabbed the boy by the shirtfront and jerked him to his feet. Wavering, the knife blade rose between them, and poised itself just under the lad's left eye. Jamie tilted his head in silent question, to receive a minimal but definite negative shake in return.

The boy's voice was no more than a shaky whisper; he had to clear his throat to make himself heard. "N-no," he said. "No. There is nothing you can do to me that will make me tell you anything."

Jamie held him for a moment longer, eye to eye, then let go of the bunched fabric and stepped back. "No," he said slowly, "I dinna suppose there is. Not to you. But what about the lady?"

I didn't at first realize that he meant me, until he grabbed me by the wrist and yanked me to him, making me stumble slightly on the rough ground. I fell toward him, and he twisted my arm roughly behind my back.

"You may be indifferent to your own welfare, but ye might perhaps have some concern for the lady's honor, since you were at such pains to rescue her." Turning me toward himself, he twined his fingers in my hair, forced my head back and kissed me with a deliberate brutality that made me squirm involuntarily in protest.

Freeing my hair, he pulled me hard against him, facing the boy on the other side of the fire. The boy's eyes were enormous, aghast with reflections of flame in the wide dark pupils.

"Let her go!" he demanded hoarsely. "What are you proposing to do with her?"

Jamie's hands reached to the neck of my gown. With a sudden jerk, he tore the fabric of gown and shift, baring most of my bosom. Reacting instinctively, I kicked him in the shin. The boy made an inarticulate sound and jerked forward, but was stopped short once more by Ross and Kincaid.

"Since you ask," said Jamie's voice pleasantly behind me, "I am proposing to ravish this lady before your eyes. I shall then give her to my men, to do what they will with. Perhaps ye would like to have a turn before I kill you? A man should no die a virgin, do ye think?"

I was struggling in good earnest now, my arm held in an iron grip behind my back, my protests muffled by Jamie's large, warm palm clapped over my mouth. I sank my teeth hard into the heel of his hand, tasting blood. He took his hand sharply away with a smothered exclamation, but returned it almost immediately, forcing a wadded piece of cloth past my teeth. I made strangled sounds around the gag as Jamie's hands darted to my shoulders, forcing the torn pieces of my gown farther apart. With a rending of linen and fustian, he bared me to the waist, pinning my arms at my sides. I saw Ross glance at me and quickly away, fixing his gaze with dogged intent on the prisoner, a slow flush staining his cheekbones. Kincaid, himself no more than nineteen, stared in shock, his mouth open as a flytrap.

"Stop it!" The boy's voice was trembling, but with outrage now rather than fear. "You—you unspeakable poltroon! How dare you dishonor a lady, you Scottish jackal!" He stood for a moment, chest heaving with emotion, then made up his mind. He raised his jaw and thrust out his chin.

"Very well. I do not see that in honor I have any choice. Release the lady and I will tell you what you want to know."

One of Jamie's hands left my shoulder momentarily. I didn't see his gesture, but Ross released the boy's injured arm and went quickly to fetch my cloak, which had fallen unheeded to the ground during the excitement of the boy's capture. Jamie pulled both my hands behind me, and, yanking off my belt, used it to bind them securely behind my back. Taking the cloak from Ross, he swirled it around my shoulders and fastened it carefully. Stepping back, he bowed ironically to me, then turned to face his captive.

"You have my word that the lady will be safe from my advances," he said. The note in his voice could have been due to the strain of anger and frustrated lust; I recognized it as the agonized restraint of an overwhelming impulse to laugh, and could cheerfully have killed him.

Face like stone, the boy gave the required information, speaking in brief syllables.

His name was William Grey, second son of Viscount Melton. He accompanied a troop of two hundred men, traveling to Dunbar, intending to join there with General Cope's army. His fellows were presently encamped some three miles to the west. He, William, out walking through the forest, had seen the light of our fire, and come to investigate. No, he had no companion with him. Yes, the troop carried heavy armament, sixteen carriage-mounted "galloper" cannon, and two sixteen-inch mortars. Most of the troop were armed with muskets, and there was one company of thirty horse.

The boy was beginning to wilt under the combined strain of the questioning and his injured arm, but refused an offer to be seated. Instead, he leaned against the tree, cradling his elbow in his left palm.

The questions went on for nearly an hour, covering the same ground over and over, pinpointing discrepancies, enlarging details, searching out the telltale omission, the point evaded. Satisfied at last, Jamie sighed deeply and turned from the boy, who slumped in the wavering shadows of the oak. He held out a hand without speaking; Murtagh, as usual divining his intent, handed him a pistol.

He turned back to the prisoner, busying himself in checking the priming and loading of the pistol. The twelve inches of heart-butted metal gleamed dark, the firelight picking out sparks of silver at trigger and priming pin. "Head or heart?" Jamie asked casually, raising his head at last.

"Eh?" The boy's mouth hung open in blank incomprehension.

"I am going to shoot you," Jamie explained patiently. "Spies are usually hanged, but in consideration of your gallantry, I am willing to give you a quick, clean death. Do ye prefer to take the ball in the head, or the heart?"

The boy straightened quickly, squaring his shoulders. "Oh, ah, yes, of course." He licked his lips and swallowed. "I think . . . in the—in the heart. Thank you," he added, as an obvious afterthought. He raised his chin, compressing lips that still held a suggestion of their soft, childish curve.

Nodding, Jamie cocked the pistol with a click that echoed in the silence under the oak trees.

"Wait!" said the prisoner. Jamie looked at him inquiringly, pistol leveled at the thin chest.

"What assurance have I that the lady will remain unmolested after I am— after I have gone?" the boy demanded, looking belligerently around the circle of men. His single working hand was clenched hard, but shook nonetheless. Ross made a sound which he skillfully converted into a sneeze.

Jamie lowered the pistol, and with an iron control, kept his face carefully composed in an expression of solemn gravity.

"Weel," he said, the Scots accent growing broader under the strain, "ye ha' my own word, of course, though I quite see that ye might have some hesitation in accepting the word of a . . ."—his lip twitched despite himself— "of a Scottish poltroon. Perhaps ye would accept the assurances of the lady herself?" He raised an eyebrow in my direction and Kincaid sprang at once to free me, fumbling awkwardly with the gag.

"Jamie!" I exclaimed furiously, mouth freed at last. "This is unconscionable! How could you do such a thing? You—you—"

"Poltroon," he supplied helpfully. "Or jackal, if ye like that better. What d'ye say, Murtagh," turning to his lieutenant, "am I a poltroon or a jackal?"

Murtagh's seam of a mouth twisted sourly. "I'd say ye're dogsmeat, if you untie yon lass wi'out a dirk in yer hand."

Jamie turned apologetically to his prisoner. "I must apologize to my wife for forcing her to take part in this deception. I assure you that her participation was entirely unwilling." He ruefully examined his bitten hand in the light from the fire.

"Your wife!" The boy stared wildly from me to Jamie.

"I'll assure ye likewise that while the lady on occasion honors my bed with her presence, she has never done so under duress. And won't now," he added pointedly, "but let's no untie her just yet, Kincaid."

"James Fraser," I hissed between clenched teeth. "If you touch that boy, you'll certainly never share my bed again!"

Jamie raised one eyebrow. His canines gleamed briefly in the firelight. "Well, that's a serious threat, to an unprincipled voluptuary such as myself, but I dinna suppose I can consider my own interests in such a situation. War's war, after all." The pistol, which had been allowed to fall, began to rise once more.

"Jamie!" I screamed.

He lowered the pistol again, and turned to me with an expression of exaggerated patience. "Yes?"

I took a deep breath, to keep my voice from shaking with rage. I could only guess what he was up to, and hoped I was doing the right thing. Right or not, when this was over . . . I choked off an intensely pleasing vision of Jamie writhing on the ground with my foot on his Adam's apple, in order to concentrate on my present role.

"You haven't any evidence whatever that he's a spy," I said. "He says he stumbled on you by accident. Who wouldn't be curious if they saw a fire out in the woods?"

Jamie nodded, following the argument. "Aye, and what about attempted murder? Spy or no, he tried to kill me, and admits as much." He tenderly fingered the raw scratch at the side of his throat.

"Well, of course he did," I said hotly. "He says he knew you were an outlaw. There's a bloody price on your head, for heaven's sake!"

Jamie rubbed his chin dubiously, at last turning to the prisoner. "Well, it's a point," he said. "William Grey, your advocate makes a good case for ye. It's no the policy either of His Highness Prince Charles or myself to execute persons unlawfully, enemy or no." He summoned Kincaid with a wave of the hand.

"Kincaid, you and Ross take this man in the direction he says his camp lies. If the information he gave us proves to be true, tie him to a tree a mile from the camp in the line of march. His friends will find him there tomorrow. If what he told us is *not* true . . . "—he paused, cold eyes bent on the prisoner—"cut his throat."

He looked the boy in the face and said, without a shadow of mockery, "I give you your life. I hope ye'll use it well."

Moving behind me, he cut the cloth binding my wrists. As I turned furiously, he motioned toward the boy, who had sat down suddenly on the ground beneath the oak. "Perhaps ye'd be good enough to tend the boy's arm before he goes?" The scowl of pretended ferocity had left his face, leaving it blank as a wall. His eyelids were lowered, preventing me from meeting his gaze.

Without a word, I went to the boy and sank to my knees beside him. He seemed dazed, and didn't protest my examination, or the subsequent manipulations, though the handling must have been painful.

The split bodice of my gown kept sliding off my shoulders, and I muttered beneath my breath as I irritably hitched up one side or the other for the dozenth time. The bones of the boy's forearm were light and angular under the skin, hardly thicker than my own. I splinted the arm and slung it, using my own kerchief. "It's a clean break," I told him, keeping my voice impersonal. "Try to keep it still for two weeks, at least." He nodded, not looking at me.

Jamie had been sitting quietly on a log watching my ministrations. My breath coming unevenly, I walked up to him and slapped him as hard as I could. The blow left a white patch on one cheek and made his eyes water, but he didn't move or change expression.

Kincaid pulled the boy to his feet and propelled him to the edge of the clearing with a hand at his back. At the edge of the shadows he halted and turned back. Avoiding looking at me, he spoke only to Jamie.

"I owe you my life," he said formally. "I should greatly prefer not to, but since you have forced the gift upon me, I must regard it as a debt of honor. I shall hope to discharge that debt in the future, and once it is discharged . . ." The boy's voice shook slightly with suppressed hatred, losing all its assumed formality in the utter sincerity of his feelings. ". . . I'll kill you!"

Jamie rose from the log to his full height. His face was calm, free of any taint of amusement. He inclined his head gravely to his departing prisoner. "In that case, sir, I must hope that we do not meet again."

The boy straightened his shoulders and returned the bow stiffly. "A Grey does not forget an obligation, sir," he said, and vanished into the darkness, Kincaid at his elbow.

There was a discreet interval of breathless waiting, as the leaf-shuffling sounds of feet moved off through the darkness. Then the laughter started, first with a soft, fizzing noise through the nostrils of one man, then a tentative chuckle from another. Never raucous, still it gathered volume, spiraling round the circle of men.

Jamie took one step into the circle, face turned toward his men. The laughter stopped abruptly. Glancing down at me, he said briefly, "Go to the tent."

Warned by my expression, he gripped my wrist before I could raise my hand.

"If you're going to slap me again, at least let me turn the other cheek," he said dryly. "Besides, I think I can save ye the trouble. But I'd advise you to go to the tent, just the same."

Dropping my hand, he strode out to the edge of the fire, and with one peremptory jerk of the head, gathered the scattered men into a reluctant, half-wary clump before him. Their faces were big-eyed, orbits scooped with darkness by the shadows.

I didn't understand everything he said, as he spoke in an odd mixture of Gaelic and English, but I gathered sufficient sense to realize that he was inquiring, in a soft, level tone that seemed to turn his listeners to stone, as to the identity of the sentinels on duty for the evening.

There was a furtive glancing to and fro, and uneasy movement among the men, who seemed to clump more strongly together in the face of danger. But then the closed ranks parted, and two men stepped out, glanced up—once— then hastily down, and stood shoulder to shoulder, eyes on the ground, outside the protection of their fellows.

It was the McClure brothers, George and Sorley. Close in age, somewhere in their thirties, they stood hang-dog near each other, fingers of the work-toughened hands twitching as though longing to link and clasp together, as some small protection before the coming storm.

There was a brief, wordless pause as Jamie looked over the two delinquent sentinels. Then followed five solid minutes of unpleasantness, all conducted in that same soft, level voice. There wasn't a sound from the grouped men, and the McClures, both burly men, seemed to dwindle and shrink under the weight of it. I wiped my sweating palms on my skirt, glad that I didn't understand it all, and beginning to regret not following Jamie's order to return to the tent.

I regretted it still more in the next moment, when Jamie turned suddenly to Murtagh, who, expecting the command, was ready with a leather strip, some two feet long, knotted at one end to provide a rough grip.

"Strip and stand to me, the both of ye." The McClures moved at once, thick fingers fumbling with shirt fastenings, as though eager to obey, relieved that the preliminaries were over and the reckoning arrived.

I thought perhaps I would be sick, though I gathered that the punishment was light enough, by the standards applied to such things. There was no sound in the clearing, save the slap of the lash and an occasional gasp or groan from the man being flogged.

At the last stroke, Jamie let the thong fall to his side. He was sweating heavily, and the grimed linen of his shirt was pasted to his back. He nodded to the McClures in dismissal, and wiped his wet face on his sleeve as one man bent painfully to retrieve the discarded shirts, his brother, shaky himself, bracing him on the other side.

The men in the clearing seemed to have ceased even breathing, during the punishment. Now there was a tremor through the group, as though a collective breath had been released in a sigh of relief.

Jamie eyed them, shaking his head slightly. The night wind was rising, stirring and lifting the hair on his crown.

"We canna afford carelessness, *mo duinnen*," he said softly. "Not from anyone." He took a deep breath and his mouth twisted wryly. "And that includes me. It was my unshielded fire drew the lad to us." Fresh sweat had sprung out on his brow, and he wiped a hand roughly across his face, drying it on his kilt. He nodded toward Murtagh, standing grimly apart from the other men, and held the leather strap out toward him.

"If ye'll oblige me, sir?"

After a moment's hesitation, Murtagh's gnarled hand reached out and took the strap. An expression that might have been amusement flickered in the little clansman's bright black eyes.

"Wi' pleasure . . . sir."

Jamie turned his back to his men, and began to unfasten his shirt. His eye caught me, standing frozen between the tree trunks, and one eyebrow lifted in ironic question. Did I want to watch? I shook my head frantically, whirled, and blundered away through the trees, belatedly taking his advice.

In fact, I didn't return to the tent. I couldn't bear the thought of its stifling enclosure; my chest felt tight and I needed air.

I found it on the crest of a small rise, just beyond the tent. I stumbled to a stop in a small open space, flung myself full-length on the ground, and put both arms over my head. I didn't want to hear the faintest echo of the drama's final act, down behind me by the fire.

The rough grass beneath me was cold on bare skin, and I hunched to wrap the cloak around me. Cocooned and insulated, I lay quiet, listening to the pounding of my heart, waiting for the turmoil inside me to calm.

Sometime later, I heard men passing by in small groups of four or five, returning to their sleeping spots. Muffled by folds of cloth, I couldn't distinguish their words, but they sounded subdued, perhaps a little awed. Some time passed before I realized that he was there. He didn't speak or make a noise, but I suddenly knew that he was nearby. When I rolled over and sat up, I could see his bulk shadowed on a stone, head resting on forearms, folded across his knees.

Torn between the impulse to stroke his head, and the urge to cave it in with a rock, I did neither.

"Are you all right?" I asked, after a moment's pause, voice neutral as I could make it.

"Aye, I'll do." He unfolded himself slowly, and stretched, moving gingerly, with a deep sigh.

"I'm sorry for your gown," he said, a minute later. I realized that he could see my bare flesh shining dim-white in the darkness, and pulled the edges of my cloak sharply together.

"Oh, for the *gown*?" I said, more than a slight edge to my voice.

He sighed again. "Aye, and for the rest of it, too." He paused, then said, "I thought perhaps ye might be willing to sacrifice your modesty to prevent my havin' to damage the lad, but under the circumstances, I hadna time to ask your permission. If I was wrong, then I'll ask your pardon, lady."

"You mean you would have tortured him further?"

He was irritated, and didn't trouble to hide it. "Torture, forbye! I didna hurt the lad."

I drew the folds of my cloak more tightly around me. "Oh, you don't consider breaking his arm and branding him with a hot knife as hurting him, then?"

"No, I don't." He scooted across the few feet of grass between us, and grasped me by the elbow, pulling me around to face him. "Listen to me. He broke his own silly arm, trying to force his way out of an unbreakable lock. He's brave as any man I've got, but he's no experience at hand-to-hand fighting."

"And the knife?"

Jamie snorted. "Tcha! He's a small sore spot under one ear, that won't pain him much past dinner tomorrow. I expect it hurt a bit, but I meant to scare him, not wound him."

"Oh." I pulled away and turned back to the dark wood, looking for our tent. His voice followed me.

"I could have broken him, Sassenach. It would have been messy, though, and likely permanent. I'd rather not use such means if I dinna have to. Mind ye, Sassenach"—his voice reached me from the shadows, holding a note of warning—"sometime I may have to. I had to know where his fellows were, their arms and the rest of it. I couldna scare him into it; it was trick him or break him."

"He said you couldn't do anything that would make him talk."

Jamie's voice was weary. "Christ, Sassenach, of course I could. Ye can break anyone if you're prepared to hurt them enough. I know that, if anyone does."

"Yes," I said quietly, "I suppose you do."

Neither of us moved for a time, nor spoke. I could hear the murmurs of men bedding down for the night, the occasional stamp of boots on hard earth and the rustle of leaves heaped up as a barrier against the autumn chill. My eyes had adjusted sufficiently to the dark that I could now see the outline of our tent, some thirty feet away in the shelter of a big larch. I could see Jamie, too, his figure black against the lighter darkness of the night.

"All right," I said at last. "All right. Given the choice between what you did, and what you might have done . . . yes, all right."

"Thank you." I couldn't tell whether he was smiling or not, but it sounded like it.

"You were taking the hell of a chance with the rest of it," I said. "If I hadn't given you an excuse for not killing him, what would you have done?"

The large figure stirred and shrugged, and there was a faint chuckle in the shadows.

"I don't know, Sassenach. I reckoned as how you'd think of something. If ye hadn't—well, I suppose I would have had to shoot the lad. Couldna very well disappoint him by just lettin' him go, could I?"

"You bloody Scottish bastard," I said without heat.

He heaved a deep exasperated sigh. "Sassenach, I've been stabbed, bitten, slapped, and whipped since supper—which I didna get to finish. I dinna like to scare children and I dinna like to flog men, and I've had to do both. I've two hundred English camped three miles away, and no idea what to do about them. I'm tired, I'm hungry, and I'm sore. If you've anything like womanly sympathy about ye, I could use a bit!"

He sounded so aggrieved that I laughed in spite of myself. I got up and walked toward him.

"I suppose you could, at that. Come here, and I'll see if I can find a bit for you." He had put his shirt back on loose over his shoulders, not troubling to do it up. I slid my hands under it and over the hot, tender skin of his back. "Didn't cut the skin," I said, feeling gently upward.

"A strap doesn't; it just stings."

I removed the shirt and sat him down to have his back sponged with cold water from the stream.

"Better?" I asked.

"Mmmm." The muscles of his shoulders relaxed, but he flinched slightly as I touched a particularly tender spot.

I turned my attention to the scratch under his ear. "You wouldn't really have shot him, would you?"

"What d'ye take me for, Sassenach?" he said, in mock outrage.

"A Scottish poltroon. Or at best, a conscienceless outlaw. Who knows what a fellow like that would do? Let alone an unprincipled voluptuary."

He laughed with me, and his shoulder shook under my hand. "Turn your head. If you want womanly sympathy, you'll have to keep still while I apply it."

"Mmm." There was a moment of silence. "No," he said at last, "I wouldna have shot him. But I had to save his pride somehow, after making him feel ridiculous over you. He's a brave lad; he deserved to feel he was worth killing."

I shook my head. "I will never understand men," I muttered, smoothing marigold ointment over the scratch.

He reached back for my hands and brought them together under his chin.

"You dinna need to understand me, Sassenach," he said quietly. "So long as ye love me." His head tilted forward and he gently kissed my clasped hands.

"And feed me," he added, releasing them.

"Oh, womanly sympathy, love *and* food?" I said, laughing. "Don't want a lot, do you?"

There were cold bannocks in the saddlebags, cheese, and a bit of cold bacon as well. The tensions and absurdities of the last two hours had been more draining than I realized, and I hungrily joined in the meal.

The sounds of the men surrounding us had now died down, and there was neither sound nor any flicker of an unguarded fire to indicate that we were not a thousand miles from any human soul. Only the wind rattled busily among the leaves, sending the odd twig bouncing down through the branches.

Jamie leaned back against a tree, face dim in the starlight, but body instinct with mischief.

"I gave your champion my word that I'd no molest ye wi' my loathsome advances. I suppose that means unless ye invite me to share your bed, I shall have to go and sleep wi' Murtagh or Kincaid. And Murtagh snores."

"So do you," I said.

I looked at him for a moment, then shrugged, letting half my ruined gown slide off my shoulder. "Well, you've made a good start at ravishing me." I dropped the other shoulder, and the torn cloth fell free to my waist. "You may as well come and finish the job properly."

The warmth of his arms was like heated silk, sliding over my cold skin.

"Aye, well," he murmured into my hair, "war's war, no?"

"I'm very bad at dates," I said to the star-thick sky sometime later. "Has Miguel de Cervantes been born yet?"

Jamie was lying—perforce—on his stomach next to me, head and shoulders protruding from the tent's shelter. One eye slowly opened, and swiveled toward the eastern horizon. Finding no trace of dawn, it traveled slowly back and rested on my face, with an expression of jaundiced resignation.

"You've a sudden urge to discuss Spanish novels?" he said, a little hoarsely.

"Not particularly," I said. "I just wondered whether perhaps you were familiar with the term 'quixotic.' "

He heaved himself onto his elbows, scrubbed at his scalp with both hands to wake himself fully, then turned toward me, blinking but alert.

"Cervantes was born almost two hundred years ago, Sassenach, and, me having had the benefit of a thorough education, aye, I'm familiar with the gentleman. Ye wouldna be implying anything personal by that last remark, would ye?"

"Does your back hurt?"

He hunched his shoulders experimentally. "Not much. A wee bit bruised, I expect."

"Jamie, *why*, for God's sake?" I burst out.

He rested his chin on his folded forearms, the sidelong turn of his head emphasizing the slant of his eyes. The one I could see narrowed still further with his smile.

"Well, Murtagh enjoyed it. He's owed me a hiding since I was nine and put pieces of honeycomb in his boots while he had them off to cool his feet. He couldna catch me at the time, but I learned a good many interesting new words whilst he was chasing me barefoot. He—"

I put a stop to this by punching him as hard as I could on the point of the shoulder. Surprised, he let the arm collapse under him with a sharp "Oof!" and rolled onto his side, back toward me.

I brought my knees up behind him and wrapped an arm around his waist. His back blotted out the stars, wide and smoothly muscled, still gleaming faintly with the moisture of exertion. I kissed him between the shoulder blades, then drew back and blew gently, for the pleasure of feeling his skin shiver under my fingertips and the tiny fine hairs stand up in goose bumps down the furrow of his spine.

"Why?" I said again. I rested my face against his warm, damp back. Shadowed by the darkness, the scars were invisible, but I could feel them, faint tough lines hard under my cheek.

He was quiet for a moment, his ribs rising and falling under my arm with each deep, slow breath.

"Aye, well," he said, then fell silent again, thinking.

"I dinna ken exactly, Sassenach," he said finally. "Could be I thought I owed it to you. Or maybe to myself."

I laid a light palm across the width of one shoulder blade, broad and flat, the edges of the bone clear-drawn beneath the skin.

"Not to me."

"Aye? Is it the act of a gentleman to unclothe his wife in the presence of thirty men?" His tone was suddenly bitter, and my hands stilled, pressing against him. "Is it the act of a gallant man to use violence against a captive enemy, and a child to boot? To consider doing worse?"

"Would it have been better to spare me—or him—and lose half your men in two days' time? You had to know. You couldn't—you *can't* afford to let notions of gentlemanly conduct sway you."

"No," he said softly, "I can't. And so I must ride wi' a man—with the son of my King—whom duty and honor call me to follow—and seek meanwhiles to pervert his cause that I am sworn to uphold. I am forsworn for the lives of those I love—I betray the name of honor that those I honor may survive."

"Honor has killed one bloody hell of a lot of men," I said to the dark groove of his bruised back. "Honor without sense is . . . foolishness. A gallant foolishness, but foolishness nonetheless."

"Aye, it is. And it will change—you've told me. But if I shall be among the first who sacrifice honor for expedience . . . shall I feel nay shame in the doing of it?" He rolled suddenly to face me, eyes troubled in the starlight.

"I willna turn back—I cannot, now—but Sassenach, sometimes I do sorrow for that bit of myself I have left behind."

"It's my fault," I said softly. I touched his face, the thick brows, wide mouth, and the sprouting stubble along the clean, long jaw. "Mine. If I hadn't come . . . and told you what would happen . . ." I felt a true sorrow for his corruption, and shared a sense of loss for the naive, gallant lad he had been. And yet . . . what choice had either of us truly had, being who we were? I had had to tell him, and he had had to act on it. An Old Testament line drifted through my mind: "When I kept silence, my bones waxed old through my roaring all the day long."

As though he had picked up this biblical strain of thought, he smiled faintly.

"Aye, well," he said. "I dinna recall Adam's asking God to take back Eve —and look what she did to *him*." He leaned forward and kissed my forehead as I laughed, then drew the blanket up over my bare shoulders. "Go to sleep, my wee rib. I shall be needin' a helpmeet in the morning."

An odd metallic noise woke me. I poked my head out of the blanket and blinked in the direction of the noise, to find my nose a foot from Jamie's plaid-covered knee.

"Awake, are ye?" Something silvery and chinking suddenly descended in front of my face, and a heavy weight settled around my neck.

"What on earth is this?" I asked, sitting up in astonishment and peering downward. I seemed to be wearing a necklace composed of a large number of three-inch metal objects, each with a divided shank and a hooped top, strung together on a leather bootlace. Some of the objects were rusted at the tops, others brand-new. All showed scratches along the length of the shanks, as though they had been wrenched by force out of some larger object.

"Trophies of war, Sassenach," said Jamie.

I looked up at him, and uttered a small shriek at the sight.

"Oh," he said, putting a hand to his face. "I forgot. I hadna time to wash it off."

"You scared me to death," I said, hand pressed to my palpitating heart. "What *is* it?"

"Charcoal," he said, voice muffled in the cloth he was rubbing over his face. He let it down and grinned at me. The rubbing had removed some of the blackening from nose, chin and forehead, which glowed pinkish-bronze through the remaining smears, but his eyes were still ringed black as a raccoon's, and charcoal lines bracketed his mouth. It was barely dawn, and in the dim light of the tent, his darkened face and hair tended to fade into the drab background of the canvas wall behind him, giving the distinctly unsettling impression that I was speaking to a headless body.

"It was your idea," he said.

"*My* idea? You look like the end man in a minstrel show," I replied. "What the hell have you been doing?"

His teeth gleamed a brilliant white amid the sooty creases of his face.

"Commando raid," he said, with immense satisfaction. "Commando? Is that the right word?"

"Oh, God," I said. "You've been in the English camp? Christ! Not alone, I hope?"

"I couldna leave my men out of the fun, could I? I left three of them to guard you, and the rest of us had a verra profitable night." He gestured at my necklace with pride.

"Cotter pins from the cannon carriages. We couldna take the cannon, or damage them without noise, but they'll no be goin' far, wi' no wheels to them. And the hell of a lot of good sixteen gallopers will do General Cope, stranded out on the moor."

I examined my necklace critically.

"That's well and good, but can't they contrive new cotter pins? It looks like you could make something like this from heavy wire."

He nodded, his air of smugness abating not a whit.

"Oh, aye. They could. But nay bit o' good it will do them, wi' no new wheels to put them to." He lifted the tent flap, and gestured down toward the foot of the hill, where I could now see Murtagh, black as a wizened demon, supervising the activities of several similarly decorated subdemons, who were gaily feeding the last of thirty-two large wooden wheels into a roaring fire. The iron rims of the wheels lay in a stack to one side; Fergus, Kincaid, and one of the other young men had improvised a game with one of them, rolling it to and fro with sticks. Ross sat on a log nearby, sipping at a horn cup and idly twirling another round his burly forearm.

I laughed at the sight.

"Jamie, you *are* clever!"

"I may be clever," he replied, "but *you're* half-naked, and we're leaving now. Have ye something to put on? We left the sentinels tied up in an abandoned sheep-pen, but the rest of them will be up by now, and none so far behind us. We'd best be off."

As though to emphasize his words, the tent suddenly shook above me, as someone jerked free the lines on one side. I uttered an alarmed squeak and dived for the saddlebags as Jamie left to superintend the details of departure.

———◆———

It was midafternoon before we reached the village of Tranent. Perched on the hills above the seaside, the usually tranquil hamlet was reeling under the impact of the Highland army. The main bulk of the army was visible on the hills beyond, overlooking the small plain that stretched toward the shore. But with the usual disorganized comings and goings, there were as many men in Tranent as out of it, with detachments coming and going in more or less military formation, messengers galloping to and fro—some on ponies, some by shanks' mare—and the wives, children, and camp followers, who overflowed the cottages and sat outside, leaning on stone walls and nursing babies in the intermittent sun, calling to passing messengers for word of the most recent action.

We halted at the edge of this seethe of activity, and Jamie sent Murtagh to discover the whereabouts of Lord George Murray, the army's commander in chief, while he made a hasty toilet in one of the cottages.

My own appearance left a good bit to be desired; while not deliberately covered with charcoal, my face undoubtedly sported a few streaks of grime left as tokens of several nights spent sleeping out-of-doors. The goodwife kindly lent me a towel and a comb, and I was seated at her table, doing battle with my ungovernable locks, when the door opened and Lord George himself burst in without ceremony.

His usually impeccable dress was disheveled, with several buttons of his waistcoat undone, his stock slipped loose, and one garter come untied. His wig had been thrust unceremoniously into his pocket, and his own thinning brown curls stood on end, as though he had been tugging at them in frustration.

"Thank God!" he said. "A sane face, at last!" Then he leaned forward, squinting as he peered at Jamie. Most of the charcoal dust had been rinsed from the blazing hair, but gray rivulets ran down his face and dripped on his shirtfront, and his ears, which had been overlooked in the hastiness of his ablutions, were still coal-black.

"What—" began a startled Lord George, but he broke off, shook his head rapidly once or twice as though to dismiss some figment of his imagination, and resumed his conversation as though he had noticed nothing out of the ordinary.

"How does it go, sir?" said Jamie respectfully, also affecting not to notice the ribboned tail of the periwig which hung out of Lord George's pocket, wagging like the tail of a small dog as His Lordship gestured violently.

"How does it go?" he echoed. "Why, I'll tell you, sir! It goes to the east, and then it goes to the west, and then half of it comes downhill to have luncheon, while the other half marches off to devil-knows-where! *That's* how it goes!"

" 'It,' " he said, momentarily relieved by his outburst, "being His Highness's loyal Highland army." Somewhat calmer, he began to tell us of the events transpiring since the army's first arrival in Tranent the day before.

Arriving with the army, Lord George had left the bulk of the men in the village and rushed with a small detachment to take possession of the ridge above the plain. Prince Charles, coming along somewhat later, had been displeased with this action and said so—loudly and publicly. His Highness had then taken half the army and marched off westward, the Duke of Perth—nominally the other commander in chief—tamely in tow, presumably to assess the possibilities of attacking through Preston.

With the army divided, and His Lordship occupied in conferring with villagemen who knew the hell of a lot more about the surrounding terrain than did either His Highness *or* His Lordship, O'Sullivan, one of the Prince's Irish confidants, had taken it upon himself to order a contingent of Lochiel's Cameron clansmen to the Tranent churchyard.

"Cope, of course, brought up a pair of galloper guns and bombarded them," Lord George said grimly. "And I've had the devil of a time with Lochiel this afternoon. He was rather understandably upset at having a number of his men wounded for no evident purpose. He asked that they be withdrawn, which request I naturally acceded to. Whereupon here comes His Highness's frog-spawn, O'Sullivan—pest! Simply because he landed at Eriskay with His Highness, the man thinks he—well, anyway, he comes whining that the presence of the Camerons in the churchyard is essential—*essential,* mind you!—if we are to attack from the west. Told him in no uncertain terms that we attack from the east, if at all. Which prospect is exceedingly doubtful at the moment, insofar as we do not presently know exactly where half of our men are—nor His Highness, come to that," he added, in a tone that made it clear that he considered the whereabouts of Prince Charles a matter of academic interest only.

"And the chiefs! Lochiel's Camerons drew the lot that gives them the honor of fighting on the right hand in the battle—if there is one—but the MacDonalds, having agreed to the arrangement, now energetically deny having done any such thing, and insist that they will not fight at all if they're denied their traditional privilege of fighting on the right."

Having started this recitation calmly enough, Lord George had grown heated again in the telling, and at this point sprang to his feet again, rubbing his scalp energetically with both hands.

"The Camerons have been drilled all day. By now, they've been marched to and fro so much that they can't tell their pricks from their arseholes—saving your presence, mum," he added, with a distracted glance at me, "and Clanranald's men have been having fistfights with Glengarry's." He paused, lower jaw thrust out, face red. "If Glengarry wasn't who he is, I'd . . . ah, well." He dismissed Glengarry with a flip of the hand and resumed his pacing.

"The only saving grace of the matter," he said, "is that the English have been forced to turn themselves about as well, in response to our movements. They've turned Cope's entire force no less than four times, and now he's strung his right flank out nearly to the sea, no doubt wondering what in God's name we'll do next." He bent and peered out the window, as though expecting to see General Cope himself advancing down the main road to inquire.

"Er . . . where exactly *is* your half of the army at present, sir?" Jamie made a move as though to join His Lordship in his random peregrinations about the cottage, but was restrained by my grip on his collar. Armed with a towel and a bowl of warm water, I had occupied myself during His Lordship's exegesis with removing the soot from my husband's ears. They stood out now, glowing pinkly with earnestness.

"On the ridge just south of town."

"We still hold the high ground, then?"

"Yes, it sounds good, doesn't it?" His Lordship smiled bleakly. "However, occupation of the high ground profits us relatively little, in consideration of the fact that the ground just below the ridge is riddled with pools and boggy marsh. God's eyes! There's a six-foot ditch filled with water that runs a hundred feet along the base of that ridge! There's scarce five hundred yards between the armies this moment, and it might as well be five hundred miles, for all we can do." Lord George plunged a hand into his pocket in search of a handkerchief, brought it out, and stood staring blankly at the wig with which he had been about to wipe his face.

I delicately offered him the sooty handkerchief. He closed his eyes, inhaled strongly through both nostrils, then opened them and bowed to me with his usual courtly manner.

"Your servant, mum." He polished his face thoroughly with the filthy rag, handed it politely back to me, and clapped the tousled wig on his head.

"Damn my liver," he said distinctly, "if I let that fool lose this engagement for us." He turned to Jamie with decision.

"How many men have you, Fraser?"

"Thirty, sir."

"Horses?"

"Six, sir. And four ponies for pack animals."

"Pack animals? Ah. Carrying provisions for your men?"

"Yes, sir. And sixty sacks of meal abstracted from an English detachment last night. Oh, and one sixteen-inch mortar, sir."

Jamie imparted this last bit of information with an air of such perfect offhand casualness that I wanted to cram the handkerchief down his throat. Lord George stared at him for a moment, then one corner of his mouth twitched upward in a smile.

"Ah? Well, come with me, Fraser. You can tell me all about it on the way." He wheeled toward the door, and Jamie, with a wide-eyed glance at me, caught up his hat and followed.

At the cottage door, Lord George stopped suddenly, and turned back. He glanced up at Jamie's towering form, shirt collar undone and coat flung hastily over one arm.

"I may be in a hurry, Fraser, but we have still sufficient time to observe the civilities. Go and kiss your wife goodbye, man. Meet me outside."

Turning on his heel, he made a leg to me, bowing deeply, so that the tail of his wig flopped forward.

"Your servant, mum."

I knew enough about armies to realize that nothing apparent was likely to happen for some time, and sure enough, it didn't. Random parties of men marched up and down the single main street of Tranent. Wives, camp followers, and the displaced citizens of Tranent milled aimlessly, uncertain whether to stay or go. Messengers darted sideways through the crowd, carrying notes.

I had met Lord George before, in Paris. He was not a man to stand on ceremony when action would better suit, though I thought it likely that the fraying of his temper at Prince Charles's actions, and a desire to escape the company of O'Sullivan, were more responsible for his coming in person to meet Jamie than any desire either for expeditiousness or confidentiality. When the total strength of the Highland army stood somewhere between fifteen hundred and two thousand, thirty men were neither to be regarded as a gift from the gods, nor sneered at altogether.

I glanced at Fergus, fidgeting to and fro like a hoptoad with St. Vitus's dance, and decided that I might as well send a few messages myself. There is a saying, "In the kingdom of the blind, the one-eyed man is king." I promptly invented its analogy, based on experience: "When no one knows what to do, anyone with a sensible suggestion is going to be listened to."

There was paper and ink in the saddlebags. I sat down, watched with an almost superstitious awe by the goodwife, who had likely never seen a woman write anything before, and composed a note to Jenny Cameron. It was she who had led three hundred Cameron clansmen across the mountains to join Prince Charles, when he had raised his banner at Glenfinnan on the coast. Her brother Hugh, arriving home belatedly and hearing what had happened, had ridden posthaste to Glenfinnan to take the chieftain's place at the head of his men, but Jenny had declined to go home and miss the fun. She had thoroughly enjoyed the brief stop in Edinburgh, where Charles received the plaudits of his loyal subjects, but she had been equally willing to accompany her Prince on his way to battle.

I hadn't a signet, but Jamie's bonnet was in one of the bags, bearing a badge with the Fraser clan crest and motto. I dug it out and pressed it into the splodge of warm candle wax with which I had sealed the note. It looked very official.

"For the Scottish milady with the freckles," I instructed Fergus, and with satisfaction saw him dart out the door and into the melee in the street. I had no idea where Jenny Cameron was at the moment, but the officers were quartered in the manse near the kirk, and that was as good a place to start as any. At least the search would keep Fergus out of mischief.

That errand out of the way, I turned to the cottage wife.

"Now, then," I said. "What have you got in the way of blankets, napkins, and petticoats?"

I soon found that I had been correct in my surmise as to the force of Jenny Cameron's personality. A woman who could raise three hundred men and lead them across the mountains to fight for an Italian-accented fop with a taste for brandywine was bound to have both a low threshold of boredom and a rare talent for bullying people into doing what she wanted.

"Verra sensible," she said, having heard my plan. "Cousin Archie's made some arrangements, I expect, but of course he's wanting to be with the army just now." Her firm chin stuck out a little farther. "That's where the fun is, after all," she said wryly.

"I'm surprised you didn't insist on going along," I said.

She laughed, her small, homely face with its undershot jaw making her look like a good-humored bulldog.

"I would if I could, but I can't," she admitted frankly. "Now that Hugh's come, he keeps trying to make me go home. Told him I was"—she glanced around to be sure we weren't overheard, and lowered her voice conspiratorially—"*damned* if I'd go home and sit. Not while I can be of use here."

Standing on the cottage doorstep, she looked thoughtfully up and down the street.

"I didn't think they'd listen to me," I said. "Being English."

"Aye, you're right," she said, "but they will to me. I don't know how many the wounded will be—pray God not many," and she crossed herself unobtrusively. "But we'd best start with the houses near the manse; it'll be less trouble to carry water from the well." With decision, she stepped off the doorstep and headed down the street, me following close behind.

We were aided not only by the persuasion of Miss Cameron's position and person but by the fact that sitting and waiting is one of the most miserable occupations known to man—not that it usually is known to men; women do it much more often. By the time the sun sank behind Tranent kirk, we had the bare rudiments of a hospital brigade organized.

The leaves were beginning to fall from larch and alder in the nearby wood, lying loose, flat and yellow on the sandy ground. Here and there a leaf had crisped and curled to brown, and took off scudding in the wind like a small boat over rough seas.

One of these spiraled past me, settling gently as its wind current failed. I caught it on my palm and held it for a moment, admiring the perfection of midribs and veins, a lacy skeleton that would remain past the rotting of the blade. There was a sudden puff of wind, and the cup-curled leaf lifted off my hand, to tumble to the ground and go rolling along, down the empty street.

Shading my eyes against the setting sun, I could see the ridge beyond the town where the Highland army was camped. His Highness's half of the army had returned an hour before, sweeping the last stragglers from the village as they marched to join Lord George. At this distance, I could only pick out an occasional tiny figure, black against the graying sky, as here and there a man came over the crest of the ridge. A quarter-mile past the end of the street, I could see the first lighting of the English fires, burning pale in the dying light. The thick smell of burning peat from the cottages joined the sharper scent of the English wood fires, overlying the tang of the nearby sea.

Such preparations as could be made were under way. The wives and families of the Highland soldiers had been welcomed with generous hospitality, and were now mostly housed in the cottages along the main street, sharing their hosts' plain supper of brose and salt herring. My own supper was waiting inside, though I had little appetite.

A small form appeared at my elbow, quiet as the lengthening shadows.

"Will you come and eat, Madame? The goodwife is keeping food for you."

"Oh? Oh, yes, Fergus. Yes, I'll come." I cast a last glance toward the ridge, then turned back to the cottages.

"Are you coming, Fergus?" I asked, seeing him still standing in the street. He was shading his eyes, trying to see the activities on the ridge beyond the town. Firmly ordered by Jamie to stay with me, he was plainly longing to be with the fighting men, preparing for battle on the morrow.

"Uh? Oh, yes, Madame." He turned with a sigh, resigned for the moment to a life of boring peace.

The long days of summer were yielding quickly to darkness, and the lamps were lit well before we had finished our preparations. The night outside was restless with constant movement and the glow of fires on the horizon. Fergus, unable to keep still, flitted in and out of the cottages, carrying messages, collecting rumors and bobbing up out of the shadows periodically like a small, dark ghost, eyes gleaming with excitement.

"Madame," he said, plucking at my sleeve as I ripped linens into strips and threw them into a pile for sterilization. "Madame!"

"What is it this time, Fergus?" I was mildly irritated at the intrusion; I had been in the middle of a lecture to a group of housewives on the importance of washing the hands frequently while treating the wounded.

"A man, Madame. He is wanting to speak with the commander of His Highness's army. He has important information, he says."

"Well, I'm not stopping him, am I?" I tugged at a recalcitrant shirt seam, then used my teeth to wrench loose the end, and yanked. It tore cleanly, with a satisfying ripping sound.

I spit out a thread or two. He was still there, waiting patiently.

"All right," I said, resigned. "What do you—or he—think I can do about it?"

"If you will give me permission, Madame," he said eagerly, "I could guide him to my master. *He* could arrange for the man to speak to the commander."

"He," of course, could do anything, so far as Fergus was concerned; including, no doubt, walking on water, turning water into wine, and inducing Lord George to talk to mysterious strangers who materialized out of the darkness with important information.

I brushed the hair out of my eyes; I had tied it back under a kertch, but curly strands kept escaping.

"Is this man somewhere nearby?"

That was all the encouragement he needed; he disappeared through the open door, returning momentarily with a thin young man whose eager gaze fastened at once on my face.

"Mrs. Fraser?" He bowed awkwardly at my nod, wiping his hands on his breeches as though he didn't know quite what to do with them, but wanted to be ready if something suggested itself.

"I—I'm Richard Anderson, of Whitburgh."

"Oh? Well, good for you," I said politely. "My servant says you have some valuable information for Lord George Murray."

He nodded, bobbing his head like a water ouzel. "Ye see, Mrs. Fraser, I've lived in these parts all my life. I—I know all of that ground where the armies are, know it like the back o' my hand. And there's a way down from the ridge where the Highland troops are camped—a trail that will lead them past the ditch at the bottom."

"I see." I felt a hollowing of the stomach at these words. If the Highlanders were to charge out of the rising sun next morning, they would have to leave the high ground of the ridge during the night watches. And if a charge was to be successful, plainly that ditch must be crossed or bypassed.

While I *thought* I knew what was to come, I had no certainty at all about it. I had been married to an historian—and the usual faint stab came at the thought of Frank—and knew just how unreliable historical sources often were. For that matter, I had no surety that my own presence couldn't or wouldn't change anything.

For the space of a moment, I wondered wildly what might happen if I tried to keep Richard Anderson from speaking to Lord George. Would the outcome of tomorrow's battle be changed? Would the Highland army—including Jamie and his men—be slaughtered as they ran downhill over boggy ground and into a ditch? Would Lord George come up with another plan that would work? Or would Richard Anderson merely go off on his own and find a way of speaking to Lord George himself, regardless of what I did?

It wasn't a risk I cared to take for experiment's sake. I looked down at Fergus, fidgeting with impatience to be gone.

"Do you think you can find your master? It's black as the inside of a coal hole up on that ridge. I wouldn't like either of you to be shot by mistake, traipsing around up there."

"I can find him, Madame," Fergus said confidently. He probably could, I thought. He seemed to have a sort of radar where Jamie was concerned.

"All right, then," I conceded. "But for God's sake, be careful."

"*Oui*, Madame!" In a flash, he was at the door, vibrating with eagerness to be gone.

It was half an hour after they had left that I noticed the knife I had left on the table was gone as well. And only then did I remember, with a sickening lurch of my stomach, that while I had told Fergus to be careful, I had forgotten altogether to tell him to come back.

The sound of the first cannon came in the lightening predawn, a dull, booming noise that seemed to echo through the plank boards on which I slept. My buttocks tightened, the involuntary flattening of a tail I didn't possess, and my fingers clasped those of the woman lying under the blanket next to me. The knowledge that something is going to happen should be some defense, but somehow it never is.

There was a faint moan from one corner of the cottage, and the woman next to me muttered, "Mary, Michael, and Bride preserve us," under her breath. There was a stirring over the floor as the women began to rise. There was little talk, as though all ears were pricked to catch the sounds of battle from the plain below.

I caught sight of one of the Highlanders' wives, a Mrs. MacPherson, as she folded her blanket next to the graying window. Her face was blank with fear, and she closed her eyes with a small shudder as another muffled boom came from below.

I revised my opinion as to the uselessness of knowledge. These women had no knowledge of secret trails, sunrise charges, and surprise routs. All these women knew was that their husbands and sons were now facing the cannon and musket fire of an English army four times their number.

Prediction is a risky business at the best of times, and I knew they would pay me no mind. The best thing I could do for them was to keep them busy. A fleeting image crossed my mind, of the rising sun shining bright off blazing hair, making a perfect target of its owner. A second image followed hard on its heels; a squirrel-toothed boy, armed with a stolen butcher knife and a bright-eyed belief in the glories of war. I closed my own eyes and swallowed hard. Keeping busy was the best thing I could do for myself.

"Ladies!" I said. "We've done a lot, but there's a lot more to do. We shall be needing boiling water. Cauldrons for boiling, cream pans for soaking. Parritch for those who can eat; milk for those who can't. Tallow and garlic for dressings. Wood laths for splints. Bottles and jugs, cups and spoons. Sewing needles and stout thread. Mrs. MacPherson, if you would be so kind . . ."

I knew little of the battle, except which side was supposed to win, and that the casualties of the Jacobite army were to be "light." From the far-off, blurry page of the textbook, I again retrieved that tiny bit of information: ". . . while the Jacobites triumphed, with only thirty casualties."

Casualties. Fatalities, I corrected. Any injury is a casualty, in nursing terms, and there were a good many more than thirty in my cottage as the sun burned its way upward through the sea mist toward noon. Slowly, the victors of the battle were making their way in triumph back toward Tranent, the sound of body helping their wounded comrades.

Oddly enough, His Highness had ordered that the English wounded be retrieved first from the field of battle and carefully tended. "They are my Father's subjects," he said firmly, making the capital "F" thoroughly audible, "and I will have them well cared for." The fact that the Highlanders who had just won the battle for him were also presumably his Father's subjects seemed to have escaped his notice for the moment.

"Given the behavior of the Father and the Son," I muttered to Jenny Cameron on hearing this, "the Highland army had better hope that the Holy Ghost doesn't choose to descend today."

A look of shock at this blasphemous observation crossed the face of Mrs. MacPherson, but Jenny laughed.

The whoops and shrieks of Gaelic celebration overwhelmed the faint groans of the wounded, borne in on makeshift stretchers made of planks or bound-together muskets, or more often, leaning on the arms of friends for support. Some of the casualties staggered in under their own power, beaming and drunk on their own exuberance, the pain of their wounds seeming a minor inconvenience in the face of glorious vindication of their faith. Despite the injuries that brought them here to be tended, the intoxicating knowledge of victory filled the house with a mood of hilarious exhilaration.

"Christ, did ye see 'em scutter like wee mousies wi' a cat on their tails?" said one patient to another, seemingly oblivious of the nasty powder burn that had singed his left arm from knuckles to shoulder.

"And a rare good many of 'em missin' their tails," answered his friend, with a chortle.

Joy was not quite universal; here and there, small parties of subdued Highlanders could be seen making their way across the hills, carrying the still form of a friend, plaid's end covering a face gone blank and empty with heaven's seeing.

It was the first test of my chosen assistants, and they rose to the challenge as well as had the warriors of the field. That is, they balked and complained and made nuisances of themselves, and then, when necessity struck, threw themselves into battle with unparalleled fierceness.

Not that they stopped complaining while they did it.

Mrs. McMurdo returned with yet another full bottle, which she hung in the assigned place on the cottage wall, before stooping to rummage in the tub that held the bottles of honey water. The elderly wife of a Tranent fisherman pressed into army service, she was the waterer on this shift; in charge of going from man to man, urging each to sip as much of the sweetened fluid as could be tolerated—and then making a second round to deal with the results, equipped with two or three empty bottles.

"If ye didna gie them so much to drink, they'd no piss sae much," she complained—not for the first time.

"They need the water," I explained patiently—not for the first time. "It keeps their blood pressure up, and replaces some of the fluids they've lost, and helps avoid shock—well, look, woman, do you see many of them dying?" I demanded, suddenly losing a good deal of my patience in the face of Mrs. McMurdo's continuing dubiousness and complaints; her nearly toothless mouth lent a note of mournfulness to an already dour expression—all is lost, it seemed to say; why trouble further?

"Mphm," she said. Since she took the water and returned to her rounds without further remonstrance, I took this sound for at least temporary assent.

I stepped outside to escape both Mrs. McMurdo and the atmosphere in the cottage. It was thick with smoke, heat, and the fug of unwashed bodies, and I felt a bit dizzy.

The streets were filled with men, drunk, celebrating, laden with plunder from the battlefield. One group of men in the reddish tartan of the MacGillivrays pulled an English cannon, tethered with ropes like a dangerous wild beast. The resemblance was enhanced by the fanciful carvings of crouching wolves that decorated the touch-hole and muzzle. One of General Cope's showpieces, I supposed.

Then I recognized the small black figure riding astride the cannon's muzzle, hair sticking up like a bottle brush. I closed my eyes in momentary thankfulness, then opened them and hastened down the street to drag him off the cannon.

"Wretch!" I said, giving him a shake and then a hug. "What do you mean sneaking off like that? If I weren't so busy, I'd box your ears 'til your head rattled!"

"Madame," he said, blinking stupidly in the afternoon sun. "Madame."

I realized he hadn't heard a word I'd said. "Are you all right?" I asked, more gently.

A look of puzzlement crossed his face, smeared with mud and powder-stains. He nodded, and a sort of dazed smile appeared through the grime.

"I killed an English soldier, Madame."

"Oh?" I was unsure whether he wanted congratulation, or needed comfort. He was ten.

His brow wrinkled, and his face screwed up as though trying very hard to remember something.

"I *think* I killed him. He fell down, and I stuck him with my knife." He looked at me in bewilderment, as though I could supply the answer.

"Come along, Fergus," I said. "We'll find you some food and a place to sleep. Don't think about it anymore."

"*Oui,* Madame." He stumbled obediently along beside me, but within moments, I could see that he was about to fall flat on his face. I picked him up, with some difficulty, and lugged him toward the cottages near the church where I had centered our hospital operation. I had intended to feed him first, but he was sound asleep by the time I reached the spot where O'Sullivan was attempting—with little success—to organize his commissary wagons.

Instead, I left him curled in the box bed in one of the cottages, where a woman was looking after assorted children while their mothers tended wounded men. It seemed the best place for him.

The cottage had filled up with twenty or thirty men by midafternoon, and my two-woman staff was hopping. The house normally held a family of five or six, and the men able to stand were standing on the plaids of those lying down. In the distance across the small flat, I could see officers coming and going to the manse, the minister's residence commandeered by the High Command. I kept an eye on the battered door, which hung constantly ajar, but didn't see Jamie among those arriving to report casualties and receive congratulations.

I batted away the recurrent small gnat of worry, telling myself that I didn't see him among the wounded, either. I had not had time since early on to visit the small tent up the slope, where the dead of the battle were being laid out in orderly rows, as though awaiting a last inspection. But surely he could not be there.

Surely not, I told myself.

The door swung open and Jamie walked in.

I felt my knees give slightly at sight of him, and put out a hand to steady myself on the cottage's wooden chimney. He had been looking for me; his eyes darted around the room before they lighted on me, and a heart-stopping smile lit his face.

He was filthy, grimed with black-powder smoke, splattered with blood, and barefoot, legs and feet caked with mud. But he was whole, and standing. I wasn't inclined to quibble with the details.

Cries of greeting from some of the wounded men on the floor dragged his gaze away from me. He glanced down, smiled at George McClure, grinning up at his commander despite an ear that hung from his head by a sliver of flesh, then looked quickly back at me.

Thank God, his dark-blue eyes said, and *Thank God,* my own echoed back.

There was no time for more; wounded men were still coming in, and every able-bodied nonmilitary person in the village had been pressed into service to care for them. Archie Cameron, Lochiel's doctor brother, bustled back and forth among the cottages, nominally in charge, and actually doing some good here and there.

I had arranged that any Fraser men from Lallybroch should be brought to the cottage where I was conducting my own triage, quickly evaluating the severity of wounds, sending the still-mobile down the street to be dealt with by Jenny Cameron, the dying across to Archie Cameron's headquarters in the church—I did think him competent to dispense laudanum, and the surroundings might provide some consolation.

Serious wounds I dealt with as I could. Broken bones next door, where two surgeons from the Macintosh regiment could apply splints and bandages. Nonfatal chest wounds propped as comfortably as possible against one wall in a half-sitting position to assist breathing; lacking oxygen or facilities for surgical repair, there was little else I could do for them. Serious head wounds were dispatched to the church with the obviously dying; I had nothing to offer them, and they were better off in the hands of God, if not Archie Cameron.

Shattered and missing limbs and abdominal wounds were the worst. There was no possibility of sterility; all I could do was to cleanse my own hands between patients, browbeat my assistants into doing the same—so long as they were under my direct scrutiny, anyway—and try to ensure that the dressings we applied had all been boiled before application. I knew, beyond doubt, that similar precautions were being ignored as a waste of time in the other cottages, despite my lectures. If I couldn't convince the sisters and physicians of L'Hôpital des Anges of the existence of germs, I was unlikely to succeed with a mixed bag of Scottish housewives and army surgeons who doubled as farriers.

I blocked my mind to the thought of the men with treatable injuries who would die from infection. I could give the men of Lallybroch, and a few more, the benefit of clean hands and bandages; I couldn't worry about the rest. One dictum I had learned on the battlefields of France in a far distant war: You cannot save the world, but you might save the man in front of you, if you work fast enough.

Jamie stood a moment in the doorway, assessing the situation, then moved to help with the heavy work, shifting patients, lifting cauldrons of hot water, fetching buckets of clean water from the well in Tranent square. Relieved of fear for him, and caught up in the whirlwind of work and detail, I forgot about him for the most part.

The triage station of any field hospital always bears a strong resemblance to an abattoir, and this was no exception. The floor was pounded dirt, not a bad surface, insofar as it absorbed blood and other liquids. On the other hand, saturated spots did become muddy, making the footing hazardous.

Steam billowed from the boiling cauldron over the fire, adding to the heat of exertion. Everyone streamed with moisture; the workers with the sticky wash of exercise, the wounded men with the stinking sweat of fear and long-spent rage. The dissipating fog of black-powder smoke from the battlefield below drifted through the streets of Tranent and in through the open doors, its eye-stinging haze threatening the purity of the freshly boiled linens, hung dripping from the mackeral-drying rack by the fire.

The flow of the wounded came in waves, washing into the cottage like surf-scour, churning everything into confusion with the arrival of each fresh surge. We thrashed about, fighting the pull of the tide, and were left at last, gasping, to deal with the new flotsam left behind as each wave ebbed.

There are lulls, of course, in the most frantic activity. These began to come more frequently in the afternoon, and toward sundown, as the flow of wounded dropped to a trickle, we began to settle into a routine of caring for the patients who remained with us. It was still busy, but there was at last time to draw breath, to stand in one place for a moment and look around.

I was standing by the open door, breathing in the freshening breeze of the offshore wind, when Jamie came back into the cottage, carrying an armload of firewood. Dumping it by the hearth, he came back to stand by me, one hand resting briefly on my shoulder. Trickles of sweat ran down the edge of his jaw, and I reached up to dab them with a corner of my apron.

"Have you been to the other cottages?" I asked.

He nodded, breath beginning to slow. His face was so blotched with smoke and blood that I couldn't tell for sure, but thought he looked pale.

"Aye. There's still looting going on in the field, and a good many men still missing. All of our own wounded are here, though—none elsewhere." He nodded at the far end of the cottage where the three wounded men from Lallybroch lay or sat companionably near the hearth, trading good-natured insults with the other Scots. The few English wounded in this cottage lay by themselves, near the door. They talked much less, content to contemplate the bleak prospects of captivity.

"None bad?" he asked me, looking at the three.

I shook my head. "George McClure might lose the ear; I can't tell. But no; I think they'll be all right."

"Good." He gave me a tired smile, and wiped his hot face on the end of his plaid. I saw he had wrapped it carelessly around his body instead of draping

it over one shoulder. Probably to keep it out of the way, but it must have been
hot.

Turning to go, he reached for the water bottle hanging from the door peg.

"Not that one!" I said.

"Why not?" he asked, puzzled. He shook the wide-mouthed flask, with a
faint sloshing sound. "It's full."

"I know it is," I said. "That's what I've been using as a urinal."

"Oh." Holding the bottle by two fingers, he reached to replace it, but I
stopped him.

"No, go ahead and take it," I suggested. "You can empty it outside, and
fill this one at the well." I handed him another gray stone bottle, identical with
the first.

"Try not to get them mixed up," I said helpfully.

"Mmphm," he replied, giving me a Scottish look to go along with the
noise, and turned toward the door.

"Hey!" I said, seeing him clearly from the back. "What's that?"

"What?" he said, startled, trying to peer over one shoulder.

"That!" My fingers traced the muddy shape I had spotted above the sagging plaid, printed on the grubby linen of his shirt with the clarity of a stencil.
"It looks like a horseshoe," I said disbelievingly.

"Oh, that," he said, shrugging.

"A *horse* stepped on you?"

"Well, not on purpose," he said, defensive on the horse's behalf. "Horses
dinna like to step on people; I suppose it feels a wee bit squashy underfoot."

"I would suppose it does," I agreed, preventing his attempts to escape by
holding on to one sleeve. "Stand still. How the hell did this happen?"

"It's no matter," he protested. "The ribs don't feel broken, only a trifle
bruised."

"Oh, just a trifle," I agreed sarcastically. I had worked the stained fabric
free in back, and could see the clear, sharp imprint of a curved horseshoe,
embedded in the fair flesh of his back, just above the waist. "Christ, you can see
the horseshoe nails." He winced involuntarily as I ran my finger over the marks.

It had happened during one brief sally by the mounted dragoons, he explained. The Highlanders, mostly unaccustomed to horses other than the small,
shaggy Highland ponies, were convinced that the English cavalry horses had
been trained to attack them with hooves and teeth. Panicked at the horses'
charge, they had dived under the horses' hooves, slashing ferociously at legs
and bellies with swords and scythes and axes.

"And you think they aren't?"

"Of course not, Sassenach," he said impatiently. "He wasna trying to
attack me. The rider wanted to get away, but he was sealed in on either side.
There was noplace to go but over me."

Seeing this realization dawn in the eyes of the horse's rider, a split second before the dragoon applied spurs to his mount's sides, Jamie had flung himself flat on his face, arms over his head.

"Then the next was the breath bursting from my lungs," he explained. "I felt the dunt of it, but it didna hurt. Not then." He reached back and rubbed a hand absently over the mark, grimacing slightly.

"Right," I said, dropping the edge of the shirt. "Have you had a piss since then?"

He stared at me as though I had gone suddenly barmy.

"You've had four-hundredweight of horse step smack on one of your kidneys," I explained, a trifle impatiently. There were wounded men waiting. "I want to know if there's blood in your urine."

"Oh," he said, his expression clearing. "I don't know."

"Well, let's find out, shall we?" I had placed my big medicine box out of the way in one corner; now I rummaged about in it and withdrew one of the small glass urinoscopy cups I had acquired from L'Hôpital des Anges.

"Fill it up and give it back to me." I handed it to him and turned back toward the hearth, where a cauldron full of boiling linens awaited my attention.

I glanced back to find him still regarding the cup with a slightly quizzical expression.

"Need help, lad?" A big English soldier on the floor was peering up from his pallet, grinning at Jamie.

A flash of white teeth showed in the filth of Jamie's face. "Oh, aye," he said. He leaned down, offering the cup to the Englishman. "Here, hold this for me while I aim."

A ripple of mirth passed through the men nearby, distracting them momentarily from their distress.

After a moment's hesitation, the Englishman's big fist closed around the fragile cup. The man had taken a dose of shrapnel in one hip, and his grip was none too steady, but he still smiled, despite the sweat dewing his upper lip.

"Sixpence says you can't make it," he said. He moved the cup, so it stood on the floor three or four feet from Jamie's bare toes. "From where you stand now."

Jamie looked down thoughtfully, rubbing his chin with one hand as he measured the distance. The man whose arm I was dressing had stopped groaning, absorbed in the developing drama.

"Weel, I'll no say it would be easy," Jamie said, letting his Scots broaden on purpose. "But for sixpence? Aye, weel, that's a sum might make it worth the effort, eh?" His eyes, always faintly slanted, turned catlike with his grin.

"Easy money, lad," said the Englishman, breathing heavily but still grinning. "For me."

"Two silver pennies on the lad," called one of the MacDonald clansmen in the chimney corner.

An English soldier, coat turned inside-out to denote his prisoner status, fumbled inside the skirts, searching for the opening of his pocket.

"Ha! A pouch of weed against!" he called, triumphantly holding up a small cloth bag of tobacco.

Shouted wagers and rude remarks began to fly through the air as Jamie squatted down and made a great show of estimating the distance to the cup.

"All right," he said at last, standing up and throwing back his shoulders. "Are ye set, then?"

The Englishman on the floor chuckled. "Oh, *I'm* set, lad."

"Well, then."

An expectant hush fell over the room. Men raised on their elbows to watch, ignoring both discomfort and enmity in their interest.

Jamie glanced around the room, nodded at his Lallybroch men, then slowly raised the hem of his kilt and reached beneath it. He frowned in concentration, groping randomly, then let an expression of doubt flit across his countenance.

"I had it when I went out," he said, and the room erupted in laughter.

Grinning at the success of his joke, he raised his kilt further, grasped his clearly visible weapon and took careful aim. He squinted his eyes, bent his knees slightly, and his fingers tightened their grip.

Nothing happened.

"It's a misfire!" crowed one of the English.

"His powder's wet!" Another hooted.

"No balls to your pistol, lad?" jibed his accomplice on the floor.

Jamie squinted dubiously at his equipment, bringing on a fresh riot of howls and catcalls. Then his face cleared.

"Ha! My chamber's empty, that's all!" He snaked an arm toward the array of bottles on the wall, cocked an eyebrow at me, and when I nodded, took one down and upended it over his open mouth. The water splashed over his chin and onto his shirt, and his Adam's apple bobbed theatrically as he drank.

"Ahhh." He lowered the bottle, swabbed some of the grime from his face with a sleeve, and bowed to his audience.

"Now, then," he began, reaching down. He caught sight of my face, though, and stopped in mid-motion. He couldn't see the open door at his back, nor the man standing in it, but the sudden quiet that fell upon the room must have told him that all bets were off.

His Highness Prince Charles Edward bent his head under the lintel to enter the cottage. Come to visit the wounded, he was dressed for the occasion in plum velvet breeches with stockings to match, immaculate linen, and—to show solidarity with the troops, no doubt—a coat and waistcoat in Cameron tartan, with a subsidiary plaid looped over one shoulder through a cairngorm brooch. His hair was freshly powdered, and the Order of St. Andrew glittered brilliantly upon his breast.

He stood in the doorway, nobly inspiring everyone in sight and noticeably impeding the entrance of those behind him. He looked slowly about him, taking in the twenty-five men crammed cheek by jowl on the floor, the helpers crouching over them, the mess of bloodied dressings tossed into the corner, the scatter of medicines and instruments across the table, and me, standing behind it.

His Highness didn't care overmuch for women with the army in general, but he was thoroughly grounded in the rules of courtesy. I *was* a woman, despite the smears of blood and vomit that streaked my skirt, and the fact that my hair was shooting out from under my kertch in half a dozen random sprays.

"Madame Fraser," he said, bowing graciously to me.

"Your Highness." I bobbed a curtsy back, hoping he didn't intend to stay long.

"Your labors in our behalf are very much appreciate, Madame," he said, his soft Italian accent stronger than usual.

"Er, thank you," I said. "Mind the blood. It's slippery just there."

The delicate mouth tightened a bit as he skirted the puddle I had pointed out. The doorway freed, Sheridan, O'Sullivan, and Lord Balmerino came in, adding to the congestion in the cottage. Now that the demands of courtesy had been attended to, Charles crouched carefully between two pallets.

He laid a gentle hand on the shoulder of one man.

"What is your name, my brave fellow?"

"Gilbert Munro . . . erm, Your Highness," added the man, hastily, awed at the sight of the Prince.

The manicured fingers touched the bandage and splints that swathed what was left of Gilbert Munro's right arm.

"Your sacrifice was great, Gilbert Munro," Charles said simply. "I promise you it will not be forgotten." The hand brushed across a whiskered cheek, and Munro reddened with embarassed pleasure.

I had a man before me with a scalp wound that needed stitching, but was able to watch from the corner of my eye as Charles made the rounds of the cottage. Moving slowly, he went from bed to bed, missing no one, stopping to inquire each man's name and home, to offer thanks and affection, congratulations, and condolence.

The men were stunned into silence, English and Highlander alike, barely managing to answer His Highness in soft murmurs. At last he stood and stretched, with an audible creaking of ligaments. An end of his plaid had trailed in the mud, but he didn't seem to notice.

"I bring you the blessing and the thanks of my Father," he said. "Your deeds of today will always be remembered." The men on the floor were not in the proper mood to cheer, but there were smiles, and a general murmur of appreciation.

Turning to go, Charles caught sight of Jamie, standing out of the way in the corner, so as not to have his bare toes trampled by Sheridan's boots. His Highness's face lighted with pleasure.

"*Mon cher!* I had not seen you today. I feared some malchance had overtaken you." A look of reproach crossed the handsome, ruddy face. "Why did you not come to supper at the manse with the other officers?"

Jamie smiled and bowed respectfully.

"My men are here, Highness."

The Prince's brows shot up at this, and he opened his mouth as though to say something, but Lord Balmerino stepped forward and whispered something in his ear. Charles's expression changed to one of concern.

"But what this is I hear?" he said to Jamie, losing control of his syntax as he did in moments of emotion. "His Lordship tells me that you have yourself suffered a wound."

Jamie looked mildly discomfited. He shot a quick glance my way, to see if I had heard, and seeing that I most certainly had, jerked his eyes back to the Prince.

"It's nothing, Highness. Only a scratch."

"Show me." It was simply spoken, but unmistakably an order, and the stained plaid fell away without protest.

The folds of dark tartan were nearly black on the inner side. His shirt beneath was reddened from armpit to hip, with stiff brown patches where the blood had begun to dry.

Leaving my head injury to mind himself for a moment, I stepped forward and opened the shirt, pulling it gently away from the injured side. Despite the quantity of blood, I knew it must not be a serious wound; he stood like a rock, and the blood no longer flowed.

It was a saber-slash, slanting across the ribs. A lucky angle; straight in and it would have gone deep into the intercostal muscles between the ribs. As it was, an eight-inch flap of skin gaped loose, red beginning to ooze beneath it again with the release of pressure. It would take a goodly number of stitches to repair, but aside from the constant danger of infection, the wound was in no way serious.

Turning to report this to His Highness, I halted, stopped by the odd look on his face. For a split second, I thought it was "rookie's tremors," the shock of a person unaccustomed to the sight of wounds and blood. Many a trainee nurse at the combat station had removed a field dressing, taken one look and bolted, to vomit quietly outside before returning to tend the patient. Battle wounds have a peculiarly nasty look to them.

But it couldn't be that. By no means a natural warrior, still Charles had been blooded, like Jamie, at the age of fourteen, in his first battle at Gaeta. No,

I decided, even as the momentary expression of shock faded from the soft brown eyes. He would not be startled by blood or wounds.

This wasn't a cottar or a herder that stood before him. Not a nameless subject, whose duty was to fight for the Stuart cause. This was a friend. And I thought that perhaps Jamie's wound had suddenly brought it home to him; that blood was shed on *his* order, men wounded for *his* cause—little wonder if the realization struck him, deep as a sword-cut.

He looked at Jamie's side for a long moment, then looked up to meet his eyes. He grasped Jamie by the hand, and bowed his own head.

"Thank you," he said softly.

And just for that one moment, I thought perhaps he might have made a king, after all.

On a small slope behind the church, a tent had been erected at His Highness's order, for the last shelter of those dead in battle. Given preference in treatment, the English soldiers received none here; the men lay in rows, cloths covering their faces, Highlanders distinguished only by their dress, all awaiting burial on the morrow. MacDonald of Keppoch had brought a French priest with him; the man, shoulders sagging with weariness, purple stole worn incongruously over a stained Highland plaid, moved slowly through the tent, pausing to pray at the foot of each recumbent figure.

"Perpetual rest grant unto him, O Lord, and let perpetual light shine upon him." He crossed himself mechanically, and moved on to another corpse.

I had seen the tent earlier, and—heart in mouth—counted the bodies of the Highland dead. Twenty-two. Now, as I entered the tent, I found the toll had risen to twenty-six.

A twenty-seventh lay in the nearby church, on the last mile of his journey. Alexander Kincaid Fraser, dying slowly of the wounds that riddled his belly and chest, of a slow internal seepage that couldn't be halted. I had seen him when they brought him in, bleached white from an afternoon of bleeding slowly to death, alone in the field among the bodies of his foes.

He had tried to smile at me, and I had wetted his cracked lips with water and coated them with tallow. To give him a drink was to kill him at once, as the liquid would rush through his perforated intestines and cause fatal shock. I hesitated, seeing the seriousness of his wounds, and thinking that a quick death might be better . . . but then I had stopped. I realized that he would want to see a priest and make his confession, at least. And so I had dispatched him to the church, where Father Benin tended the dying as I tended the living.

Jamie had made short visits to the church every half-hour or so, but Kincaid held his own for an amazingly long time, clinging to life despite the constant ebbing of its substance. But Jamie had not come back from his latest visit. I knew that the fight was ending now at last, and went to see if I could help.

The space under the windows where Kincaid had lain was empty, save for a large, dark stain. He wasn't in the tent of the dead, either, and neither was Jamie anywhere in sight.

I found them at length some distance up the hill behind the church. Jamie was sitting on a rock, the form of Alexander Kincaid cradled in his arms, curly head resting on his shoulder, the long, hairy legs trailing limp to one side. Both were still as the rock on which they sat. Still as death, though only one was dead.

I touched the white, slack hand, to be sure, and rested my hand on the thick brown hair, feeling still so incongruously alive. A man should not die a virgin, but this one did.

"He's gone, Jamie," I whispered.

He didn't move for a moment, but then nodded, opening his eyes as though reluctant to face the realities of the night.

"I know. He died soon after I brought him out, but I didna want to let him go."

I took the shoulders and we lowered him gently to the ground. It was grassy here, and the night wind stirred the stems around him, brushing them lightly across his face, a welcome to the caress of the earth.

"You didn't want him to die under a roof," I said, understanding. The sky swept over us, cozy with cloud, but endless in its promise of refuge.

He nodded slowly, then knelt by the body and kissed the wide, pale forehead.

"I would have someone do the same for me," he said softly. He drew a fold of the plaid up over the brown curls, and murmured something in Gaelic that I didn't understand.

A medical casualties station is no place for tears; there is much too much to be done. I had not wept all day, despite the things I had seen, but now gave way, if only for a moment. I leaned my face against Jamie's shoulder for strength, and he patted me briefly. When I looked up, wiping the tears from my face, I saw him still staring, dry-eyed, at the quiet figure on the ground. He felt me watching him and looked down at me.

"I wept for him while he was still alive to know it, Sassenach," he said quietly. "Now, how is it in the house?"

I sniffed, wiped my nose, and took his arm as we turned back to the cottage.

"I need your help with one."

"Which is it?"

"Hamish MacBeth."

Jamie's face, strained for so many hours, relaxed a bit under the stains and smudges.

"He's back, then? I'm glad. How bad is he, though?"

I rolled my eyes. "You'll see."

MacBeth was one of Jamie's favorites. A massive man with a curly brown beard and a reticent manner, he had been always there within Jamie's call, ready when something was needed on the journey. Seldom speaking, he had a slow, shy smile that blossomed out of his beard like a night-blooming flower, rare but radiant.

I knew the big man's absence after the battle had been worrying Jamie, even among the other details and stresses. As the day wore on and the stragglers came back one by one, I had been keeping an eye out for MacBeth. But sundown came and the fires sprang up amid the army camp, with no Hamish MacBeth, and I had begun to fear we would find him among the dead, too.

But he had come into the casualties station half an hour before, moving slowly, but under his own power. One leg was stained with blood down to the ankle, and he walked with a ginger, spraddled gait, but he would on no account let a "wumman" lay hands on him to see what was the matter.

The big man was lying on a blanket near a lantern, hands clasped across the swell of his belly, eyes fastened patiently on the raftered ceiling. He swiveled his eyes around as Jamie knelt down beside him, but didn't move otherwise. I lingered tactfully in the background, hidden from view by Jamie's broad back.

"All right, then, MacBeth," said Jamie, laying a hand on the thick wrist in greeting. "How is it, man?"

"I'll do, sir," the giant rumbled. "I'll do. Just that it's a bit . . ." He hesitated.

"Well, then, let's have a look at it." MacBeth made no protest as Jamie flipped back the edge of the kilt. Peeking through a crack between Jamie's arm and body, I could see the cause of MacBeth's hesitations.

A sword or pike had caught him high in the groin and ripped its way downward. The scrotum was torn jaggedly on one side, and one testicle hung halfway out, its smooth pink surface shiny as a peeled egg.

Jamie and the two or three other men who saw the wound turned pale, and I saw one of the aides touch himself reflexively, as though to assure that his own parts were unscathed.

Despite the horrid look of the wound, the testicle itself seemed undamaged, and there was no excessive bleeding. I touched Jamie on the shoulder and shook my head to signify that the wound was not serious, no matter what its effect on the male psyche. Catching my gesture with the tail of his eye, Jamie patted MacBeth on the knee.

"Och, it's none so bad, MacBeth. Nay worry, ye'll be a father yet."

The big man had been looking down apprehensively, but at these words, transferred his gaze to his commander. "Weel, that's no such a consairn to me, sir, me already havin' the six bairns. It's just what my wife'd say, if I . . ." MacBeth blushed crimson as the men surrounding him laughed and hooted.

Casting an eye back at me for confirmation, Jamie suppressed his own grin and said firmly, "That'll be all right, too, MacBeth."

"Thank ye, sir," the man breathed gratefully, with complete trust in his commander's assurance.

"Still," Jamie went on briskly, "it'll need to be stitched up, man. Now, ye've your choice about that."

He reached into the open kit for one of my handmade suture needles. Appalled by the crude objects barber-surgeons customarily used to sew up their customers, I'd made three dozen of my own, by selecting the finest embroidery needles I could get, and heating them in forceps over the flame of an alcohol lamp, bending them gently until I had the proper half-moon curve needed for stitching severed tissues. Likewise, I'd made my own catgut sutures; a messy, disgusting business, but at least I was sure of the sterility of my materials.

The tiny suture needle looked ridiculous, pinched between Jamie's large thumb and index finger. The illusion of medical competence was not furthered by Jamie's cross-eyed attempts to thread the needle.

"Either I'll do it myself," he said, tongue-tip protruding slightly in his concentration, "or—" He broke off as he dropped the needle and fumbled about in the folds of MacBeth's plaid for it. "Or," he resumed, holding it up triumphantly before his patient's apprehensive eyes, "my wife can do it for ye." A slight jerk of the head summoned me into view. I did my best to look as matter-of-fact as possible, taking the needle from Jamie's incompetent grasp and threading it neatly with one thrust.

MacBeth's large brown eyes traveled slowly between Jamie's big paws, which he contrived to make look as clumsy as possible by setting the crooked right hand atop the left, and my own small, swift hands. At last he lay back with a dismal sigh, and mumbled his consent to let a "wumman" lay hands on his private parts.

"Dinna worry yourself, man," Jamie said, patting him companionably on the shoulder. "After all, she's had the handling of my own for some time now, and she's not unmanned me yet." Amid the laughter of the aides and nearby patients, he started to rise, but I stopped him by thrusting a small flask into his hands.

"What's this?" he asked.

"Alcohol and water," I said. "Disinfectant solution. If he's not to have fever or pustulence or something worse, the wound will have to be washed out." MacBeth had plainly walked some way from where the injury had occurred, and there were smears of dirt as well as blood near the wound. Grain alcohol was a harsh disinfectant, even cut 50/50 with distilled sterile water as I used it. Still, it was the single most effective tool I had against infection, and I was adamant about its usage, in spite of complaints from the aides and screams of anguish from the patients who were subjected to it.

Jamie glanced from the alcohol flask to the gaping wound and shuddered slightly. He'd had his own dose when I stitched his side, earlier in the evening.

"Weel, MacBeth, better you than me," he said, and, placing his knee firmly in the man's midriff, sloshed the contents of the flask over the exposed tissues.

A dreadful roar shook the walls, and MacBeth writhed like a cut snake. When the noise at last subsided, his face had gone a mottled greenish color, and he made no objection at all as I began the routine, if painful, job of stitching up the scrotum. Most of the patients, even those horribly wounded, were stoic about the primitive treatment to which we subjected them, and MacBeth was no exception. He lay unmoving in hideous embarrassment, eyes fixed on the lantern flame, and didn't move a muscle as I made my repairs. Only the changing colors of his face, from green to white to red and back again, betrayed his emotions.

At the last, however, he went purple. As I finished the stitching, the limp penis began to stiffen slightly, brushed in passing by my hand. Thoroughly rattled by this justification of his faith in Jamie's word, MacBeth snatched down his kilts the instant I was finished, lurched to his feet, and staggered away into the darkness, leaving me giggling over my kit.

I found a corner where a chest of medical supplies made a seat, and leaned against the wall. A surge of pain shot up my calves; the sudden release of tension, and the nerves' reaction to it. I slipped off my shoes and leaned back against the wall, reveling in the smaller spasms that shot up backbone and neck as the strain of standing was relieved.

Every square inch of skin seems newly sensitive in such a state of fatigue; when the necessity of forcing the body to perform is suddenly suspended, the lingering impetus seems to force the blood to the perimeter of the body, as though the nervous system is reluctant to believe what the muscles have already gratefully accepted; you need not move, just now.

The air in the cottage was warm and noisy with breathing; not the healthy racket of snoring men, but the shallow gasps of men for whom breathing hurts, and the moans of those who have found a temporary oblivion that frees them from the manly obligation of suffering in silence.

The men in this cottage were those badly wounded, but in no immediate danger. I knew, though, that death walks at night in the aisles of a sick ward, searching for those whose defenses are lowered, who may stray unwittingly into its path through loneliness and fear. Some of the wounded had wives who slept next to them, to comfort them in the dark, but none in this cottage.

They had me. If I could do little to heal them or stop their pain, I could at least let them know that they didn't lie alone; that someone stood here, between them and the shadow. Beyond anything I could do, it was my job only to be there.

I rose and made my way slowly once again through the pallets on the floor, stooping at each one, murmuring and touching, straightening a blanket, smoothing tangled hair, rubbing the knots that form in cramped limbs. A sip of water here, a change of dressing there, the reading of an attitude of tense embarrassment that meant a urinal was needed, and the matter-of-fact presentation that allowed the man to ease himself, the stone bottle growing warm and heavy in my hand.

I stepped outdoors to empty one of these, and paused for a moment, gathering the cool, rainy night to myself, letting the soft moisture wipe away the touch of coarse, hairy skin and the smell of sweating men.

"Ye dinna sleep much, Sassenach." The soft Scottish voice came from the direction of the road. The other hospital cottages lay in that direction; the officers' quarters, the other way, in the village manse.

"You dinna sleep much, either," I responded dryly. How long had he gone without sleep? I wondered.

"I slept in the field last night, with the men."

"Oh, yes? Very restful," I said, with an edge that made him laugh. Six hours' sleep in a wet field, followed by a battle in which he'd been stepped on by a horse, wounded by a sword, and done God knows what else. Then he had gathered his men, collected the wounded, tended the hurt, mourned his dead, and served his Prince. And through none of it had I seen him pause for food, drink, or rest.

I didn't bother scolding. It wasn't even worth mentioning that he ought to have been among the patients on the floor. It was his job to be here, as well.

"There are other women, Sassenach," he said gently. "Shall I have Archie Cameron send someone down?"

It was a temptation, but one I pushed away before I could think about it too long, for fear that if I acknowledged my fatigue, I would never move again.

I stretched, hands against the small of my back.

"No," I said. "I'll manage 'til the dawn. Then someone else can take over for a time." Somehow I felt that I must get them through the night; at dawn they would be safe.

He didn't scold, either; just laid a hand on my shoulder and drew me to lean against him for a moment. We shared what strength we had, unspeaking.

"I'll stay with ye, then," he said, drawing away at last. "I canna sleep before light, myself."

"The other men from Lallybroch?"

He moved his head toward the fields near the town where the army was camped.

"Murtagh's in charge."

"Oh, well, then. Nothing to worry about," I said, and saw him smile in the light from the window. There was a bench outside the cottage, where the goodwife would sit on sunny days to clean fish or mend clothes. I drew him down to sit beside me, and he sagged back against the wall of the house with a sigh. His patent exhaustion reminded me of Fergus, and the boy's expression of confused bewilderment after the battle.

I reached to caress the back of Jamie's neck, and he turned his head blindly toward me, resting his brow against my own.

"How was it, Jamie?" I asked softly, fingers rubbing hard and slow over the tight-ridged muscles of his neck and shoulders. "What was it like? Tell me."

There was a short silence, then he sighed, and began to talk, haltingly at first, and then faster, as if wanting to get it out.

"We had no fire, for Lord George thought we must move off the ridge before daylight, and wanted no hint of movement to be seen below. We sat in the dark for a time. Couldna even talk, for the sound would carry to the plain. So we sat.

"Then I felt something grab my thigh in the dark, and near jumped out of my skin." He inserted a finger in his mouth and rubbed gingerly. "Nearly bit my tongue off." I felt the shift of his muscles as he smiled, though his face was hidden.

"Fergus?"

The ghost of a laugh floated through the dark.

"Aye, Fergus. Crawled through the grass on his belly, the little bastard, and I thought he was a snake, at that. He whispered to me about Anderson, and I crawled off after him and took Anderson to see Lord George."

His voice was slow and dreamy, talking under the spell of my touch.

"And then the order came that we'd move, following Anderson's trail. And the whole of the army got to its feet, and set off in the dark."

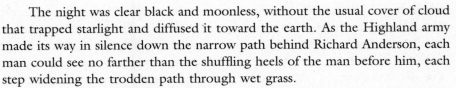

The night was clear black and moonless, without the usual cover of cloud that trapped starlight and diffused it toward the earth. As the Highland army made its way in silence down the narrow path behind Richard Anderson, each man could see no farther than the shuffling heels of the man before him, each step widening the trodden path through wet grass.

The army moved almost without noise. Orders were relayed in murmurs from man to man, not shouted. Broadswords and axes were muffled in the folds of their plaids, powder flasks tucked inside shirts against fast-beating hearts.

Once on sound footing, still in total silence, the Highlanders sat down, made themselves as comfortable as was possible without fire, ate what cold rations there were, and composed themselves to rest, wrapped in their plaids, in sight of the enemy's campfires.

"We could hear them talking," Jamie said. His eyes were closed, hands clasped behind his head, as he leaned against the cottage wall. "Odd, to hear men laughing over a jest, or asking for a pinch of salt or a turn at the wineskin —and know that in a few hours, ye may kill them—or them you. Ye can't help wondering, ye ken; what does the face behind that voice look like? Will you know the fellow if ye meet him in the morning?"

Still, the tremors of anticipated battle were no match for sheer fatigue, and the "Black Frasers"—so called for the traces of charcoal that still adorned their features—and their chief had been awake for more than thirty-six hours by then. He had picked a sheaf of marrow-grass for a pillow, tucked the plaid around his shoulders, and lain down in the waving grass beside his men.

During his time with the French army, years before, one of the sergeants had explained to the younger mercenaries the trick of falling asleep the night before a battle.

"Make yourself comfortable, examine your conscience, and make a good Act of Contrition. Father Hugo says that in time of war, even if there is no priest to shrive you, your sins can be forgiven this way. Since you cannot commit sins while asleep—not even *you*, Simenon!—you will awake in a state of grace, ready to fall on the bastards. And with nothing to look forward to but victory or heaven—how can you be afraid?"

While privately noting a few flaws in this argument, Jamie had found it still good advice; freeing the conscience eased the soul, and the comforting repetition of prayer distracted the mind from fearful imaginings and lulled it toward sleep.

He gazed upward into the black vault of the sky, and willed the tightness of neck and shoulders to relax into the ground's hard embrace. The stars were faint and hazy tonight, no match for the nearby glow of the English fires.

His mind reached out to the men around him, resting briefly on each, one by one. The stain of sin was small weight on his conscience, compared with these. Ross, McMurdo, Kincaid, Kent, McClure . . . he paused to give brief thanks that his wife and the boy Fergus at least were safe. His mind lingered on his wife, wanting to bask in the memory of her reassuring smile, the solid, wonderful warmth of her in his arms, pressed tight against him as he had kissed her goodbye that afternoon. Despite his own weariness and the waiting presence of Lord George outside, he had wanted to tumble her onto the waiting mattress right then and take her quickly, at once, without undressing. Strange how the imminence of fighting made him so ready, always. Even now . . .

But he hadn't yet finished his mental roster, and he felt his eyelids closing already, as tiredness sought to pull him under. He dismissed the faint tightening of his testicles that came at thought of her, and resumed his roll call, a shepherd treacherously lulled to sleep by counting the sheep he was leading to slaughter.

But it wouldn't be a slaughter, he tried to reassure himself. Light casualties for the Jacobite side. Thirty men killed. Out of two thousand, only a slim chance that some of the Lallybroch men would be among that number, surely? If she was right.

He shuddered faintly under the plaid, and fought down the momentary doubt that wrenched his bowels. If. God, if. Still he had trouble believing it, though he had seen her by that cursed rock, face dissolving in terror around the panic-wide gold eyes, the very outlines of her body blurring as he, panicked also, had clutched at her, pulling her back, feeling little more than the frail double bone of her forearm under his hand. Perhaps he should have let her go, back to her own place. No, no perhaps. He knew that he should. But he had pulled her back. Given her the choice, but kept her with him by the sheer force of his wanting her. And so she had stayed. And given *him* the choice—to believe her, or not. To act, or to run. And the choice was made now, and no power on earth could stop the dawn from coming.

His heart beat heavily, pulse echoing in wrists and groin and the pit of his stomach. He sought to calm it, resuming his count, one name to each heartbeat. Willie McNab, Bobby McNab, Geordie McNab . . . thank God, young Rabbie McNab was safe, left at home . . . Will Fraser, Ewan Fraser, Geoffrey McClure . . . McClure . . . had he touched on both George and Sorley? Shifted slightly, smiling faintly, feeling for the soreness left along his ribs. Murtagh. Aye, Murtagh, tough old boot . . . my mind is no troubled on your account, at least. William Murray, Rufus Murray, Geordie, Wallace, Simon . . .

And at last, had closed his eyes, commended all of them to the care of the black sky above, and lost himself in the murmured words that came to him still most naturally in French—*"Mon Dieu, je regrette . . ."*

I made my rounds inside the cottage, changing a blood-soaked dressing on one man's leg. The bleeding should have stopped by now, but it hadn't. Poor nutrition and brittle bones. If the bleeding hadn't stopped before cockcrow, I would have to fetch Archie Cameron or one of the farrier-surgeons to amputate the leg, and cauterize the stump.

I hated the thought of it. Life was sufficiently hard for a man with all his limbs in good working order. Hoping for the best, I coated the new dressing with a light sprinkling of alum and sulfur. If it didn't help, it wouldn't hinder. Likely it *would* hurt, but that couldn't be helped.

"It will burn a bit," I murmured to the man, as I wrapped his leg in the layers of cloth.

"Dinna worry yourself, Mistress," he whispered. He smiled at me, in spite of the sweat that ran down his cheeks, shiny in the light of my candle. "I'll stand it."

"Good." I patted his shoulder, smoothed the hair off his brow, and gave him a drink of water. "I'll check again in an hour, if you can bear it that long."

"I'll stand it," he said again.

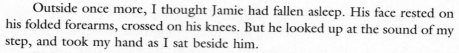

Outside once more, I thought Jamie had fallen asleep. His face rested on his folded forearms, crossed on his knees. But he looked up at the sound of my step, and took my hand as I sat beside him.

"I heard the cannon at dawn," I said, thinking of the man inside, leg broken by a cannonball. "I was afraid for you."

He laughed softly. "So was I, Sassenach. So were we all."

Quiet as wisps of mist, the Highlanders advanced through the sea grass, one foot at a time. There was no sense of darkness lessening, but the feel of the night had changed. The wind had changed, that was it; it blew from the sea over the cold dawning land, and the faint thunder of waves on distant sand could be heard.

Despite his impression of continued dark, the light was coming. He saw the man at his feet just in time; one more step and he would have been headlong across the man's curled body.

Heart pounding from the shock of the near-meeting, he dropped to his haunches to get a better look. A Redcoat, and sleeping, not dead or wounded. He squinted hard into the darkness around them, willing his ears to listen for the breathing of other sleeping men. Nothing but sea sounds, grass and wind sounds, the tiny swish of stealthy feet almost hidden in their muted roar.

He glanced hastily back, licking lips gone dry despite the moist air. There were men close behind him; he dared not hesitate long. The next man might not be so careful where he stepped, and they could risk no outcry.

He set hand to his dirk, but hesitated. War was war, but it went against the grain to slay a sleeping enemy. The man seemed to be alone, some distance from his companions. Not a sentinel; not even the slackest of guards would sleep, knowing the Highlanders to be camped on the ridge above. Perhaps the soldier had gotten up to relieve himself, thoughtfully come some distance from his fellows to do it, then, losing his direction in the dark, lain down to sleep where he was.

The metal of his musket was slick from his sweating palm. He rubbed his hand on his plaid, then stood, grasped the barrel of the musket, and swung the butt in a vicious arc, down and around. The shock of impact jolted him to the shoulder blades; an immobile head is solid. The man's arms had flown out with the force of the impact, but beyond an explosion of breath, he had made no noise, and now lay sprawled on his face, limp as a clout.

Palms tingling, he stooped again and groped beneath the man's jaw, looking for a pulse. He found one, and reassured, stood up. There was a muffled cry of startlement from behind, and he swung around, musket already at his shoulder, to find its barrel poking into the face of one of Keppoch's MacDon-ald clansmen.

"Mon Dieu!" the man whispered, crossing himself, and Jamie clenched his teeth with aggravation. It was Keppoch's bloody French priest, dressed, at O'Sullivan's suggestion, in shirt and plaid like the fighting men.

"The man insisted that it was his duty to bring the sacraments to the wounded and dying on the field," Jamie explained to me, hitching his stained plaid higher on his shoulder. The night was growing colder. "O'Sullivan's idea was that if the English caught him on the battlefield in his cassock, they'd tear him to pieces. As to that, maybe so, maybe no. But he looked a right fool in a plaid," he added censoriously.

Nor had the priest's behavior done anything to ameliorate the impression caused by his attire. Realizing belatedly that his assailant was a Scot, he had sighed in relief, and then opened his mouth. Moving quickly, Jamie had clapped a hand over it before any ill-advised questions could emerge.

"What are ye doing here, Father?" he growled, mouth pressed to the priest's ear. "You're meant to be behind the lines."

A widening of the priest's eyes at this told Jamie the truth—the man of God, lost in the darkness, had thought he *was* behind the lines, and the belated realization that he was, in fact, in the vanguard of the advancing Highlanders, made him buckle slightly at the knees.

Jamie glanced backward; he didn't dare send the priest back through the lines. In the misty dark, he could easily stumble into an advancing Highlander, be mistaken for an enemy, and be killed on the spot. Gripping the smaller man by the back of the neck, he pushed him to his knees.

"Lie flat and stay that way until the firing stops," he hissed into the man's ear. The priest nodded frantically, then suddenly saw the body of the English soldier, lying on the ground a few feet away. He glanced up at Jamie in awed horror, and reached for the bottles of chrism and holy water that he wore at his belt in lieu of a dirk.

Rolling his eyes in exasperation, Jamie made a series of violent motions, meant to indicate that the man was not dead, and thus in no need of the priest's services. These failing to make their point, he bent, seized the priest's hand, and pressed the fingers on the Englishman's neck, as the simplest method of illustrating that the man was not in fact the first victim of the battle. Caught in this ludicrous position, he froze as a voice cut through the mist behind him.

"Halt!" it said. "Who goes there?"

"Have ye got a bit of water, Sassenach?" asked Jamie. "I'm gettin' a bit dry with the talking."

"Bastard!" I said. "You can't stop there! What happened?"

"Water," he said, grinning, "and I'll tell ye."

"All right," I said, handing him a water bottle and watching as he tilted it into his mouth. "What happened then?"

"Nothing," he said, lowering the bottle and wiping his mouth on his sleeve. "What did ye think, I was going to answer him?" He grinned impudently at me and ducked as I aimed a slap at his ear.

"Now, now," he reproved. "No way to treat a man wounded in the service of his King, now is it?"

"Wounded, are you?" I said. "Believe me, Jamie Fraser, a mere saber slash is as nothing compared to what I will do to you if . . ."

"Oh, threats, too, is it? What was that poem ye told me about, 'When pain and anguish wring the brow, a ministering angel' . . . ow!"

"Next time, I twist it right off at the roots," I said, releasing the ear. "Get on with it, I have to go back in a minute."

He rubbed the ear gingerly, but leaned back against the wall and resumed his story.

"Well, we just sat there on our haunches, the padre and I, staring at each other and listening to the sentries six feet away. "What's that?" says the one, and me thinking can I get up in time to take him with my dirk before he shoots me in the back, and what about his friend? For I canna expect help from the priest, unless maybe it's a last prayer over my body."

There was a long, nerve-racking silence, as the two Jacobites squatted in the grass, hands still clasped, afraid to move enough even to let go.

"Ahhh, yer seein' things," came from the other sentry at last, and Jamie felt the shudder of relief run through the priest, as his damp fingers slid free. "Nothin' up there but furze bushes. Never mind, lad," the sentry said reassuringly, and Jamie heard the clap of a hand on a shoulder and the stamp of booted feet, trying to keep warm. "There's the damn lot of 'em, sure, and in this dark, they could be the whole bloody Highland army, for all you can see." Jamie thought he heard the breath of a smothered laugh from one of the "furze bushes," on the hillside within hearing.

He glanced at the crest of the hill, where the stars were beginning to dim. Less than ten minutes to first light, he judged. At which point, Johnnie Cope's troops would swiftly realize that the Highland army was not, as they thought, an hour's march away in the opposite direction, but already face-to-face with their front lines.

There was a noise to the left, in the direction of the sea. It was faint, and indistinct, but the note of alarm was clear to battle-trained ears. Someone, he supposed, had tripped over a furze bush.

"Hey?" The note of alarm was taken up by one of the sentries nearby. "What's happening?"

The priest would have to take care of himself, he thought. Jamie drew the broadsword as he rose, and with one long step, was within reach. The man was no more than a shape in the darkness, but distinct enough. The merciless blade smashed down with all his strength, and split the man's skull where he stood.

"Highlanders!" The shriek broke from the man's companion, and the second sentry sprang out like a rabbit flushed from a copse, bounding away into the fading dark before Jamie could free his weapon from its gory cleft. He put a foot on the fallen man's back and jerked, gritting his teeth against the unpleasant sensation of slack flesh and grating bone.

Alarm was spreading up and down the English lines; he could feel as much as hear it—an agitation of men rudely wakened, groping blindly for weapons, searching in all directions for the unseen threat.

Clanranald's pipers were behind to the right, but no signal as yet came for the charge. Continue the advance, then, heart pounding and left arm tingling from the death blow, belly muscles clenched and eyes straining through the waning dark, the spray of warm blood across his face going cold and sticky in the chill.

"I could hear them first," he said, staring off into the night as though still searching for the English soldiers. He bent forward, hugging his knees. "Then I could see, too. The English, wriggling over the ground like maggots in meat, and the men behind me. George McClure came up with me, and Wallace and Ross on the other side, and we were walkin' still, one pace at a time, but faster and faster, seein' the sassenaches breaking before us."

There was a dull boom off to the right; the firing of a single cannon. A moment later, another, and then, as though this were the signal, a wavering cry rose from the oncoming Highlanders.

"The pipes started then," he said, eyes closed. "I didna remember my musket 'til I heard one fire close behind me; I'd left it in the grass next to the priest. When it's like that, ye dinna see anything but the small bit that's happening round you.

"Ye hear a shout, and of a sudden, you're running. Slow, for a step or two, while ye free your belt, and then your plaid falls free and you're bounding, wi' your feet splashing mud up your legs and the chill of the wet grass on your feet, and your shirttails flying off your bare arse. The wind blows into your shirt and up your belly and out along your arms. . . . Then the noise takes ye and you're screaming, like runnin' down a hill yelling into the wind when you're a bairn, to see can ye lift yourself on the sound."

They rode the waves of their own shrieking onto the plain, and the force of the Highland charge crashed onto the shoals of the English army, smothering them in a boiling surge of blood and terror.

"They ran," he said softly. "One man stood to face me—all during the fight, only one. The others I took from behind." He rubbed a grimy hand over his face, and I could feel a fine tremor start somewhere deep inside him.

"I remember . . . everything," he said, almost whispering. "Every blow. Every face. The man lying on the ground in front of me who wet himself wi' fear. The horses screaming. All the stinks—black powder and blood and the smell of my own sweat. Everything. But it's like I was standin' outside, watching myself. I wasna really there." He opened his eyes and looked sidelong at me. He was bent almost double, head on his knees, the shivering visible now.

"D'ye know?" he asked.

"I know."

While I hadn't fought with sword or knife, I had fought often enough with hands and will; getting through the chaos of death only because there is no other choice. And it did leave behind that odd feeling of detachment; the brain seemed to rise above the body, coldly judging and directing, the viscera obediently subdued until the crisis passed. It was always sometime later that the shaking started.

I hadn't reached that point yet. I slid the cloak from my shoulders and covered him before going back into the cottage.

The dawn came, and relief with it, in the person of two village women and an army surgeon. The man with the wounded leg was pale and shaky, but the bleeding had stopped. Jamie took me by the arm and led me away, down the street of Tranent.

O'Sullivan's constant difficulties with the commissary had been temporarily relieved by the captured wagons, and there was food in plenty. We ate quickly, scarcely tasting the hot porridge, aware of food only as a bodily necessity, like breathing. The feeling of nourishment began to creep through my body, freeing me to think of the next most pressing need—sleep.

Wounded men were quartered in every house and cottage, the sound of body mostly sleeping in the fields outside. While Jamie could have claimed a place in the manse with the other officers, he instead took my arm and turned me aside, heading between the cottages and up a hill, into one of the scattered small groves that lay outside Tranent.

"It's a bit of a walk," he said apologetically, looking down at me, "but I thought perhaps ye'd rather be private."

"I would." While I had been raised under conditions that would strike most people of my time as primitive—often living in tents and mud houses on Uncle Lamb's field expeditions—still, I wasn't used to living crowded cheek by jowl with numbers of other people, as was customary here. People ate, slept, and frequently copulated, crammed into tiny, stifling cottages, lit and warmed by smoky peat fires. The only thing they didn't do together was bathe—largely because they didn't bathe.

Jamie led the way under the drooping limbs of a huge horse chestnut, and into a small clearing, thick with the fallen leaves of ash, alder, and sycamore. The sun was barely up, and it was still cold under the trees, a faint edge of frost rimming some of the yellowed leaves.

He scraped a rough trench in the layer of leaves with one heel, then stood at one end of the hollow, set his hand to the buckle of his belt, and smiled at me.

"It's a bit undignified to get into, but it's verra easy to take off." He jerked the belt loose, and his plaid dropped around his ankles, leaving him clad to mid-thigh in only his shirt. He usually wore the military "little kilt," which buckled about the waist, with the plaid a separate strip of cloth around the shoulders. But now, his own kilt rent and stained from the battle, he had acquired one of the older belted plaids—nothing more than a long strip of cloth, tucked about the waist and held in place with no fastening but a belt.

"How *do* you get into it?" I asked curiously.

"Well, ye lay it out on the ground, like this"—he knelt, spreading the cloth so that it lined the leaf-strewn hollow—"and then ye pleat it every few inches, lie down on it, and roll."

I burst out laughing, and sank to my knees, helping to smooth the thick tartan wool.

"*That,* I want to see," I told him. "Wake me up before you get dressed."

He shook his head good-naturedly, and the sunlight filtering through the leaves glinted off his hair.

"Sassenach, the chances of me wakin' before you do are less than those of a worm in a henyard. I dinna care if another horse steps on me, I'll no be moving 'til tomorrow." He lay down carefully, pushing back the leaves.

"Come lie wi' me." He extended an inviting hand upward. "We'll cover ourselves with your cloak."

The leaves beneath the smooth wool made a surprisingly comfortable mattress, though at this point I would cheerfully have slept on a bed of nails. I relaxed bonelessly against him, reveling in the exquisite delight of simply lying down.

The initial chill faded quickly as our bodies warmed the pocket where we lay. We were far enough from the town that the sounds of its occupation reached us only in wind-borne snatches, and I thought with drowsy satisfaction that it might well *be* tomorrow before anyone looking for Jamie found us.

I had removed my petticoats and torn them up for additional bandages the night before, and there was nothing between us but the thin fabric of skirt and shirt. A hard, solid warmth stirred briefly against my stomach.

"Surely not?" I said, amused despite my tiredness. "Jamie, you must be half-dead."

He laughed tiredly, holding me close with one large, warm hand on the small of my back.

"A lot more than half, Sassenach. I'm knackered, and my cock's the only thing too stupid to know it. I canna lie wi' ye without wanting you, but wanting's all I'm like to do."

I fumbled with the hem of his shirt, then pushed it up and wrapped my hand gently around him. Even warmer than the skin of his belly, his penis was silken under the touch of my stroking thumb, pulsing strongly with each beat of his heart.

He made a small sound of half-painful content, and rolled slowly onto his back, letting his legs sprawl loosely outward, half-covered by my cloak.

The sun had reached our pile of leaves, and my shoulders relaxed under the warming touch of the light. Everything seemed slightly tinged with gold, the mingled result of early autumn and extreme fatigue. I felt languid and vaguely disembodied, watching the small stirrings of his flesh under my fingers. All the terror and the tiredness and the noise of the two days past ebbed slowly away, leaving us alone together.

The haze of fatigue seemed to act as a magnifying glass, exaggerating tiny details and sensations. The tail of his saber wound was visible beneath the rucked-up shirt, crusted black against the fair skin. Two or three small flies buzzed low, investigating, and I waved them away. My ears rang with the silence, the breath of the trees no match for the echoes of the town.

I laid my cheek against him, feeling the hard, smooth curve of his hip bone, close under the skin. His skin was transparent in the crease of his groin, the branching veins blue and delicate as a child's.

His hand rose slowly, floating like the leaves, and rested lightly on my head.

"Claire. I need you," he whispered. "I need ye so."

Without the hampering petticoats, it was easy. I felt as though I were floating myself, rising without volition, drifting my skirts up the length of his body, settling over him like a cloud on a hilltop, sheltering his need.

His eyes were closed, head laid back, the red gold of his hair tumbled coarsely in the leaves. But his hands rose together and settled surely on my waist, resting without weight on the curve of my hips.

My eyes closed as well, and I felt the shapes of his mind, as surely as I felt those of his body under me; exhaustion blocked our every thought and memory; every sensation but the knowledge of each other.

"Not . . . long," he whispered. I nodded, knowing he felt what he did not see, and rose above him, thighs powerful and sure under the stained fabric of my gown.

Once, and twice, and again, and once again, and the tremor rose through him and through me, like the rising of water through the roots of a plant and into its leaves.

The breath left him in a sigh, and I felt his descent into unconsciousness like the dimming of a lamp. I fell beside him, with barely time to draw the heavy folds of the cloak up over us before the darkness filled me, and I lay weighted to the earth by the heavy warmth of his seed in my belly. We slept.

37

Holyrood

The knock on my door surprised me from an inspection of my newly replenished medical boxes. After the stunning victory at Prestonpans, Charles had led his triumphant army back to Edinburgh, to bask in adulation. While he was basking, his generals and chieftains labored, rallying their men and procuring what equipment was to be had, in preparation for whatever was coming next.

Buoyed by early success, Charles talked freely of taking Stirling, then Carlyle, and then, perhaps, of advancing south, even to London itself. I spent my spare time counting suture needles, hoarded willow bark, and stole every spare ounce of alcohol I could find, to be brewed into disinfectant.

"What is it?" I asked, opening the door. The messenger was a young boy, scarcely older than Fergus. He was trying to look grave and deferential, but couldn't suppress his natural curiosity. I saw his eyes dart around the room, resting on the large medicine chest in the corner with fascination. Clearly the rumors concerning me had spread through the palace of Holyrood.

"His Highness has asked for ye, Mistress Fraser," he answered. Bright brown eyes scanned me closely, no doubt looking for signs of supernatural possession. He seemed slightly disappointed at my depressingly normal appearance.

"Oh, has he?" I said. "Well, all right. Where is he, then?"

"In the morning drawing room, Mistress. I'm to take ye. Oh . . ." The thought struck him as he turned, and he swung back before I could close the door. "You're to bring your box of medicines, if ye'd be so kind."

My escort brimmed with self-importance at his mission as he escorted me down the long hallway to the Royal wing of the palace. Plainly someone had been schooling him in the behavior appropriate to a Royal page, but an occasional exuberant skip in his step betrayed his newness to the job.

What on earth did Charles want with me? I wondered. While he tolerated me on Jamie's account, the story of La Dame Blanche had plainly disconcerted him and made him uneasy. More than once, I had surprised him crossing himself surreptitiously in my presence, or making the quick two-fingered "horns" sign against evil. The idea that he would ask me to treat him medically was unlikely in the extreme.

When the heavy cross-timbered door swung open into the small morning drawing room, it seemed still more unlikely. The Prince, plainly in good health, was leaning on the painted harpsichord, picking out a hesitant tune with one finger. His delicate skin was mildly flushed, but with excitement, not fever, and his eyes were clear and attentive when he looked up at me.

"Mistress Fraser! How kind of you to attend me so shortly!" He was dressed this morning with even more lavishness than usual, bewigged and wearing a new cream-colored silk waistcoat, embroidered with flowers. He must be excited about something, I thought; his English went to pot whenever he became agitated.

"My pleasure, Your Highness," I said demurely, dropping a brief curtsy. He was alone, an unusual state of affairs. Could he want my medical services for himself after all?

He made a quick, nervous gesture toward one of the gold damask chairs, urging me to be seated. A second chair was pulled up, facing it, but he walked up and down in front of me, too restless to sit.

"I need your help," he said abruptly.

"Um?" I made a politely inquiring noise. Gonorrhea? I wondered, scanning him covertly. I hadn't heard of any women since Louise de La Tour, but then, it only took once. He worked his lips in and out, as though searching for some alternative to telling me, but finally gave it up.

"I have a *capo*—a chief, you understand?—here. He thinks of joining my Father's cause, but has still some doubt."

"A clan chieftain, you mean?" He nodded, brow furrowed beneath the careful curls of his wig.

"*Oui*, Madame. He is of course in support of my Father's claims . . ."

"Oh, of course," I murmured.

". . . but he is wishing to speak to you, Madame, before he will commit his men to follow me."

He sounded incredulous, hearing his own words, and I realized that the flush on his cheeks came from a combination of bafflement and suppressed fury.

I was more than a little baffled myself. My imagination promptly visualized a clan chieftain with some dread disease, whose adherence to the cause depended on my performing a miraculous cure.

"You're sure he wants to speak to me?" I said. Surely my reputation hadn't gone *that* far.

Charles inclined his head coldly in my direction. "So he says, Madame."

"But I don't *know* any clan chieftains," I said. "Bar Glengarry and Lochiel, of course. Oh, and Clanranald and Keppoch, of course. But they've all committed themselves to you already. And why on earth . . ."

"Well, he is of the opinion you are knowing him," the Prince interrupted, syntax becoming more mangled with his rising temper. He clenched his hands, obviously forcing himself to speak courteously. "It is of importance—*most* importance, Madame, that he should become convinced to join me. I require . . . I *request* . . . you therefore, that you . . . convince him."

I rubbed my nose thoughtfully, looking at him. One more point of decision. One more opportunity to make events move in the path I chose. And once more, the inability to know what best to do.

He was right; it was important to convince this chieftain to commit his resources to the Jacobite cause. With the Camerons, the various MacDonalds, and the others so far committed, the Jacobite army numbered barely two thousand men, and those the most ill-assorted lot of ragtag and draggletail that any general had ever been lumbered with. And yet, that ragged-arsed lot had taken the city of Edinburgh, routed a greatly superior English force at Preston, and showed every disposition to continue going through the countryside like a dose of salts.

We had been unable to stop Charles; perhaps, as Jamie said, the only way to avert calamity was now to do everything possible to help him. The addition of an important clan chieftain to the roster of supporters would greatly influence the odds of others joining. This might be a turning point, where the Jacobite forces could be increased to the level of a true army, actually capable of the proposed invasion of England. And if so, what in bloody hell would happen then?

I sighed. No matter what I decided to do, I couldn't make any decision until I saw this mysterious person. I glanced down to make sure my gown was suitable for interviewing clan chieftains, infected or otherwise, and rose, tucking the medicine box under my arm.

"I'll try, Your Highness," I said.

The clenched hands relaxed, showing the bitten nails, and his frown lessened.

"Ah, good," he said. He turned toward the door of the larger afternoon drawing room. "Come, I shall take you myself."

The guard at the door jumped back in surprise as Charles flung the door open and strode past him without a glance. On the far side of the long, tapestry-hung room was an enormous marble fireplace, lined with white Delft tiles, painted with Dutch country scenes in shades of blue and mulberry. A small sofa was drawn up before the fire, and a big, broad-shouldered man in Highland dress stood beside it.

In a room less imposing, he would have bulked huge, legs like tree trunks in their checkered stockings beneath the kilt. As it was, in this immense room with its high gessoed ceilings, he was merely big—quite in keeping with the heroic figures of mythology that decorated the tapestries at either end of the room.

I stopped dead at sight of the enormous visitor, the shock of recognition still mingled with absolute incredulity. Charles had kept on, and now glanced back with some impatience, beckoning me to join him before the fire. I nodded to the big man. Then I walked slowly around the end of the sofa and gazed down at the man who lay upon it.

He smiled faintly when he saw me, the dove-gray eyes lighting with a spark of amusement.

"Yes," he said, answering my expression. "I hadn't really expected to meet *you* again, either. One might almost believe we are fated." He turned his head and lifted a hand toward his enormous body-servant.

"Angus. Will ye fetch a drop of the brandy for Mistress Claire? I'm afraid the surprise of seeing me may have somewhat discomposed her."

That, I thought, was putting it mildly. I sank into a splay-footed chair and accepted the crystal goblet Angus Mhor held out to me.

Colum MacKenzie's eyes hadn't changed; neither had his voice. Both held the essence of the man who had led clan MacKenzie for thirty years, despite the disease that had crippled him in his teens. Everything else had changed sadly for the worse, though; the black hair streaked heavily with gray, the lines of his face cut deep into skin that had fallen slack over the sharp outlines of bone. Even the broad chest was sunken and the powerful shoulders hunched, flesh fallen away from the fragile skeleton beneath.

He already held a glass half-filled with amber liquid, glowing in the fire-light. He raised himself painfully to a sitting position and lifted the cup in ironic salute.

"You're looking very well . . . niece." From the corner of my eye, I saw Charles's mouth drop open.

"You aren't," I said bluntly.

He glanced dispassionately down at the bowed and twisted legs. In a hundred years' time, they would call this disease after its most famous sufferer —the Toulouse-Lautrec syndrome.

"No," he said. "But then, it's been two years since you saw me last. Mrs. Duncan estimated my survival at less than two years, then."

I took a swallow of the brandy. One of the best. Charles *was* anxious.

"I shouldn't have thought you'd put much stock in a witch's curse," I said.

A smile twitched the fine-cut lips. He had the bold beauty of his brother Dougal, ruined as it was, and when he lifted the veil of detachment from his eyes, the power of the man overshone the wreck of his body.

"Not in curses, no. I had the distinct impression that the lady was dealing in observation, however, not malediction. And I have seldom met a more acute observer than Geillis Duncan—with one exception." He inclined his head gracefully toward me, making his meaning clear.

"Thanks," I said.

Colum glanced up at Charles, who was gaping in bewilderment at these exchanges.

"I thank you for your graciousness in permitting me to use your premises for my meeting with Mrs. Fraser, Your Highness," he said, with a slight bow. The words were sufficiently civil, but the tone made it an obvious dismissal. Charles, who was by no means used to being dismissed, flushed hotly and opened his mouth. Then, recalling himself, he snapped it shut, bowed shortly, and turned on his heel.

"We won't need the guard, either," I called after him. His shoulders hunched and the back of his neck grew red beneath the tail of his wig, but he gestured abruptly, and the guard at the door, with an astonished glance at me, followed him out.

"Hm." Colum cast a brief glance of disapproval at the door, then returned his attention to me.

"I asked to see you because I owe ye an apology," he said, without preamble.

I leaned back in my chair, goblet resting nonchalantly on my stomach.

"Oh, an apology?" I said, with as much sarcasm as could be mustered on short notice. "For trying to have me burnt for witchcraft, I suppose you mean?" I flipped a hand in gracious dismissal. "Pray think nothing of it." I glared at him. *"Apology?!"*

He smiled, not disconcerted in the slightest.

"I suppose it seems a trifle inadequate," he began.

"Inadequate?! For having me arrested and thrown into a thieves' hole for three days without decent food or water? For having me stripped half-naked and whipped before every person in Cranesmuir? For leaving me a hairsbreadth away from a barrel of pitch and a bundle of faggots?" I stopped and took a deep breath. "Now that you mention it," I said, a little more calmly, " 'inadequate' is precisely what I'd call it."

The smile had vanished.

"I beg your pardon for my apparent levity," he said softly. "I had no intent to mock you."

I looked at him, but could see no lingering gleam of amusement in the black-lashed eyes.

"No," I said, with another deep breath. "I don't suppose you did. I suppose you're going to say that you had no intent to have me arrested for witchcraft, either."

The gray eyes sharpened. "You knew that?"

"Geilie said so. While we were in the thieves' hole. She said it was her you meant to dispose of; I was an accident."

"You were." He looked suddenly very tired. "Had ye been in the castle, I could have protected you. What in the name of God led ye to go down to the village?"

"I was told that Geilie Duncan was ill and asking for me," I replied shortly.

"Ah," he said softly. "You were told. By whom, and I may ask?"

"Laoghaire." Even now, I could not repress a brief spurt of rage at the girl's name. Out of thwarted jealousy over my having married Jamie, she had deliberately tried to have me killed. Considerable depths of malice for a sixteen-year-old girl. And even now, mingled with the rage was that tiny spark of grim satisfaction; he's mine, I thought, almost subconsciously. Mine. You'll never take him from me. Never.

"Ah," Colum said again, staring thoughtfully at my flushed countenance. "I thought perhaps that was the way of it. Tell me," he continued, raising one dark brow, "if a mere apology strikes you as inadequate, will ye have vengeance instead?"

"Vengeance?" I must have looked startled at the idea, for he smiled faintly, though without humor.

"Aye. The lass was wed six months ago, to Hugh MacKenzie of Muldaur, one of my tacksmen. He'll do with her as I say, and ye want her punished. What will ye have me do?"

I blinked, taken aback by his offer. He appeared in no hurry for an answer; he sat quietly, sipping the fresh glass of brandy that Angus Mhor poured for him. He wasn't staring at me, but I got up and moved away toward the windows, wanting to be alone for a moment.

The walls here were five feet thick; by leaning forward into the deep window embrasure I could assure myself of privacy. The bright sun illuminated the fine blond hairs on my forearms as I rested them on the sill. It made me think of the thieves' hole, that damp, reeking pit, and the single bar of sunlight that had shone through an opening above, making the dark hole below seem that much more like a grave by contrast.

I had spent my first day there in cold and dirt, full of stunned disbelief; the second in shivering misery and growing fear as I discovered the full extent of Geillis Duncan's treachery and Colum's measures against it. And on the third day, they had taken me to trial. And I had stood, filled with shame and terror, under the clouds of a lowering autumn sky, feeling the jaws of Colum's trap close round me, sprung by a word from the girl Laoghaire.

Laoghaire. Fair-skinned and blue-eyed, with a round, pretty face, but nothing much to distinguish her from the other girls at Leoch. I had thought about her—in the pit with Geillis Duncan, I had had time to think of a lot of things. But furious and terrified as I had been, furious as I remained, I couldn't, either then or now, bring myself to see her as intrinsically evil.

"She was only sixteen, for God's sake!"

"Old enough to marry," said a sardonic voice behind me, and I realized that I had spoken aloud.

"Yes, she wanted Jamie," I said, turning around. Colum was still sitting on the sofa, stumpy legs covered with a rug. Angus Mhor stood silent behind him, heavy-lidded eyes fixed on his master. "Perhaps she thought she loved him."

Men were drilling in the courtyard, amid shouts and clashing of arms. The sun glanced off the metal of swords and muskets, the brass studding of targes— and off the red-gold of Jamie's hair, flying in the breeze as he wiped a hand across his face, flushed and sweating from the exercise, laughing at one of Murtagh's deadpan remarks.

I had perhaps done Laoghaire an injustice, after all, in assuming her feelings to be less than my own. Whether she had acted from immature spite or from a true passion, I could never know. In either case, she had failed. I had survived. And Jamie was mine. As I watched, he rucked up his kilt and casually scratched his bottom, the sunlight catching the reddish-gold fuzz that softened the iron-hard curve of his thigh. I smiled, and went back to my seat near Colum.

"I'll take the apology," I said.

He nodded, gray eyes thoughtful.

"You've a belief in mercy, then, Mistress?"

"More in justice," I said. "Speaking of which, I don't imagine you traveled all the way from Leoch to Edinburgh merely to apologize to me. It must have been a hellish journey."

"Aye, it was." The huge, silent bulk of Angus Mhor shifted an inch or two behind him, and the massive head bent toward his laird in eloquent witness. Colum sensed the movement and raised a hand briefly—it's all right, the gesture said, I'm all right for the present.

"No," Colum went on. "I did not know ye were in Edinburgh, in fact, until His Highness mentioned Jamie Fraser, and I asked." A sudden smile grew on his face. "His Highness isn't over fond of you, Mistress Claire. But I suppose ye knew that?"

I ignored this. "So you really are considering joining Prince Charles?"

Colum, Dougal, and Jamie all had the capacity for hiding what they were thinking when they chose to, but of the three, Colum was undoubtedly best at it. You'd get more from one of the carved heads on the fountain in the front courtyard, if he was feeling uncommunicative.

"I've come to see him" was all he said.

I sat a moment, wondering what, if anything, I could—or should—say in Charles's behalf. Perhaps I would do better to leave it to Jamie. After all, the fact that Colum felt regret over nearly killing me by accident didn't mean he was necessarily inclined to trust me. And while the fact that I was here, part of Charles's entourage, surely argued against my being an English spy, it wasn't impossible that I was.

I was still debating with myself when Colum suddenly put down his glass of brandy and looked straight at me.

"D'ye know how much of this I've had since morning?"

"No." His hands were steady, calloused and roughened from his disease, but well kept. The reddened lids and slightly bloodshot eyes could as easily be from the rigors of travel as from drink. There was no slurring of speech, and no more than a certain deliberateness of movement to indicate that he wasn't sober as a judge. But I had seen Colum drink before, and had a very respectful idea of his capacity.

He waved away Angus Mhor's hand, hovering above the decanter. "Half a bottle. I'll have finished it by tonight."

"Ah." So that was why I had been asked to bring my medicine box. I reached for it, where I had set it on the floor.

"If you're needing that much brandy, there isn't much that will help you besides some form of opium," I said, flicking through my assortment of vials and jars. "I think I have some laudanum here, but I can get you some—"

"That isn't what I want from you." The tone of authority in his voice stopped me, and I looked up. If he could keep his thoughts to himself, he could also let them show when he chose.

"I could get laudanum easily enough," he said. "I imagine there's an apothecarist in the city who sells it—or poppy syrup, or undiluted opium, for that matter."

I let the lid of the small chest fall shut and rested my hands on top of it. So he didn't mean to waste away in a drugged state, leaving the leadership of the clan uncertain. And if it were not a temporary oblivion he sought from me, what else? A permanent one, perhaps. I knew Colum MacKenzie. And the clear, ruthless mind that had planned Geillis Duncan's destruction would not hesitate over his own.

Now it was clear. He had come to see Charles Stuart, to make the final decision whether to commit the MacKenzies of Leoch to the Jacobite cause. Once committed, it would be Dougal who led the clan. And then . . .

"I was under the impression that suicide was considered a mortal sin," I said.

"I imagine it is," he said, undisturbed. "A sin of pride, at least, that I should choose a clean death at the time of my own devising, as best suits my purpose. I don't, however, expect to suffer unduly for my sin, having put no credence in the existence of God since I was nineteen or so."

It was quiet in the room, beyond the crackle of the fire and the muffled shouts of mock battle from below. I could hear his breathing, a slow and steady sigh.

"Why ask me?" I said. "You're right, you could get laudanum where you liked, so long as you have money—and you do. Surely you know that enough of it will kill you. It's an easy death, at that."

"Too easy." He shook his head. "I have had little to depend on in life, save my wits. I would keep them, even to meet death. As for ease . . ." He shifted slightly on the sofa, making no effort to hide his discomfort. "I shall have enough, presently."

He nodded toward my box. "You shared Mrs. Duncan's knowledge of medicines. I thought it possible that you knew what she used to kill her husband. That seemed quick and certain. And appropriate," he added wryly.

"She used witchcraft, according to the verdict of the court." The court that condemned her to death, in accordance with your plan, I thought. "Or do you not believe in witchcraft?" I asked.

He laughed, a pure, carefree sound in the sunlit room. "A man who doesn't believe in God can scarce credit power to Satan, can he?"

I still hesitated, but he was a man who judged others as shrewdly as he did himself. He had asked my pardon before asking my favor, and satisfied himself that I had a sense of justice—or of mercy. And it was, as he said, appropriate. I opened the box and took out the small vial of cyanide that I kept to kill rats.

"I thank ye, Mistress Claire," he said, formal again, though the smile still lingered in his eyes. "Had my nephew not proved your innocence with such flamboyance at Cranesmuir, still I would never believe you a witch. I have no more notion now than I had at our first meeting, as to who you are, or why you are here, but a witch is not one of the possibilities I've ever considered." He paused, one brow raised. "I don't suppose you'd be inclined to tell me who—or what—you are?"

I hesitated for a moment. But a man with belief in neither God nor Devil was not likely to believe the truth of my presence here, either. I squeezed his fingers lightly and released them.

"Better call me a witch," I said. "It's as close as you're likely to get."

On my way out to the courtyard next morning, I met Lord Balmerino on the stairs.

"Oh, Mistress Fraser!" he greeted me jovially. "Just who I was looking for."

I smiled at him; a chubby, cheerful man, he was one of the refreshing features of life in Holyrood.

"If it isn't fever, flux, or French pox," I said, "can it wait for a moment? My husband and his uncle are giving a demonstration of Highland sword-fighting for the benefit of Don Francisco de la Quintana."

"Oh, really? I must say, I should like to see that myself." Balmerino fell into step beside me, head bobbing cheerfully at the level of my shoulder. "I do like a pretty man with a sword," he said. "And anything that will sweeten the Spaniards has my most devout approval."

"Mine, too." Deeming it too dangerous for Fergus to lift His Highness's correspondence inside Holyrood, Jamie was dependent for information on what he learned from Charles himself. This seemed to be quite a lot, though;

Charles considered Jamie one of his intimates—virtually the only Highland chief to be accorded such a mark of favor, small as was his contribution in men and money.

So far as money went, though, Charles had confided that he had high hopes of support from Philip of Spain, whose latest letter to James in Rome had been distinctly encouraging. Don Francisco, while not quite an envoy, was certainly a member of the Spanish Court, and might be relied upon to carry back his report of how matters stood with the Stuart rising. This was Charles's opportunity to see how far his own belief in his destiny would carry him, in convincing Highland chiefs and foreign kings to join him.

"What did you want to see me for?" I asked as we came out onto the walkway that edged the courtyard of Holyrood. A small crowd of spectators was assembling, but neither Don Francisco nor the two combatants were yet in sight.

"Oh!" Reminded, Lord Balmerino groped inside his coat. "Nothing of great importance, my dear lady. I received these from one of my messengers, who obtained them from a kinsman to the South. I thought you might find them amusing."

He handed me a thin sheaf of crudely printed papers. I recognized them as broadsheets, the popular circulars distributed in taverns or that fluttered from doorposts and hedges through towns and villages.

"CHARLES EDWARD STUART, known to all as The Younge Pretender" read one. "Be it Known to all Present that this Depraved and Dangerous Person, having landed Unlawfully upon the shores of Scotland, hath Incited to Riot the Population of that Country, and hath Unleashed upon Innocent Citizens the Fury of an Unjust War." There was quite a lot more of it, all in the same vein, concluding with an exhortation to the Innocent Citizens reading this indictment "to do all in their Power to Deliver ye this Person to the Justice which he so Richly Deserves." The sheet was decorated at the top with what I supposed was meant as a drawing of Charles; it didn't bear much resemblance to the original, but definitely looked Depraved and Dangerous, which I supposed was the general idea.

"That one's quite fairly restrained," said Balmerino, peering over my elbow. "Some of the others show a most impressive range both of imagination and invective, though; look at this one. That's me," he said, pointing at the paper with evident delight.

The broadsheet showed a rawboned Highlander, thickly bewhiskered, with beetling brows and eyes that glared wildly under the shadow of a Scotch bonnet. I looked askance at Lord Balmerino, clad, as was his habit, in breeches and coat in the best of taste; made of fine stuff, but subdued both in cut and color, to flatter his tubby little form. He stared at the broadsheet, meditatively stroking his round, clean-shaven cheeks.

"I don't know," he said. "The whiskers do lend me a most romantic air, do they not? Still, a beard itches most infernally; I'm not sure I could bear it, even for the sake of being picturesque."

I turned to the next page, and nearly dropped the whole sheaf.

"They did a slightly better job in rendering a likeness of your husband," Balmerino observed, "but of course our dear Jamie does actually look somewhat like the popular English conception of a Highland thug—begging your pardon, my dear, I mean no offense. He *is* large, though, isn't he?"

"Yes," I said faintly, perusing the broadsheet's charges.

"Didn't realize your husband was in the habit of roasting and eating small children, did you?" said Balmerino, chortling. "I always thought his size was due to something special in his diet."

The little earl's irreverent attitude did a good deal to steady me. I could almost smile myself at the ridiculous charges and descriptions, though I wondered just how much credence the readers of the broadsheets placed in them. Rather a lot, I was afraid; people so often seemed not only willing but eager to believe the worst—and the worse, the better.

"It's the last one I thought you'd be interested in." Balmerino interrupted my thoughts, flipping over the next-to-last sheet.

"THE STUART WITCH" proclaimed the heading. A long-nosed female with pinpoint pupils stared back at me, over a text which accused Charles Stuart of invoking "ye Pow'rs of Darkness" in support of his unlawful cause. By retaining among his intimate entourage a well-known witch—one holding power of life and death over men, as well as the more usual power of blighting crops, drying up cattle, and causing blindness—Charles gave evidence of the fact that he had sold his own soul to the devil, and thus would "Frye in Hell Forever!" as the tract gleefully concluded.

"I assume it must be you," Balmerino said. "Though I assure you, my dear, the picture hardly does you justice."

"Very entertaining," I said. I gave the sheaf back to his lordship, restraining the urge to wipe my hand on my skirt. I felt a trifle ill, but did my best to smile at Balmerino. He glanced at me shrewdly, then took my elbow with a reassuring squeeze.

"Don't trouble yourself, my dear," he said. "Once His Majesty has regained his crown, all this nonsense will be forgotten in short order. Yesterday's villain is tomorrow's hero in the eyes of the populace; I've seen it time and again."

"Plus ça change, plus c'est la même chose," I murmured. And if His Majesty King James *didn't* regain his crown . . .

"And if our efforts should by misfortune be unsuccessful," Balmerino said, echoing my thoughts, "what the broadsheets say will be the least of our worries."

"En garde." With the formal French opening, Dougal fell into a classic dueler's stance, side-on to his opponent, sword-arm bent with the blade at the ready, back arm raised in a graceful arc, hand dropping from the wrist in open demonstration that no dagger was held in reserve.

Jamie's blade crossed Dougal's, the metal meeting with the whisper of a clash.

"Je suis prest." Jamie caught my eye, and I could see the flicker of humor cross his face. The customary dueler's response was his own clan motto. *Je suis prest.* "I am ready."

For a moment, I thought he might not be, and gasped involuntarily as Dougal's sword shot out in a lunging flash. But Jamie had seen the motion start, and by the time the blade crossed the place where he had been standing, he was no longer there.

Sidestep, a quick beat of the blade, and a counter-lunge that brought the blades screeching together along their lengths. The two swords held fast together at the hilt for only a second, then the swordsmen broke, stepped back, circled and returned to the attack.

With a clash and a beat, a parry and a lunge in *tierce,* Jamie came within an inch of Dougal's hip, swung adroitly aside with a flare of green kilt. A parry and a dodge and a quick upward beat that knocked the pressing blade aside, and Dougal stepped forward, forcing Jamie back a pace.

I could see Don Francisco, standing on the opposite side of the courtyard with Charles, Sheridan, the elderly Tullibardine, and a few others. A small smile curved the Spaniard's lips under a wisp of waxed mustache, but I couldn't tell whether it was admiration for the fighters, or merely a variation on his normally supercilious expression. Colum was nowhere in sight. I wasn't surprised; aside from his normal reluctance to appear in public, he must have been exhausted by the journey to Edinburgh.

Both gifted swordsmen, and both left-handed, uncle and nephew were putting on a skilled display—a show made more impressive by the fact that they were fighting in accordance with the most exacting rules of French dueling, but using neither the rapier-like smallsword that formed part of a gentleman's *costume,* nor the saber of a soldier. Instead, both men wielded Highland broadswords, each a full yard of tempered steel, with a flat blade that could cleave a man from crown to neck. They handled the enormous weapons with a grace and an irony that could not have been managed by smaller men.

I saw Charles murmur in Don Francisco's ear, and the Spaniard nod, never taking his eyes off the flash and clang of the battle in the grass-lined court. Well matched in size and agility, Jamie and his uncle gave every appearance of intending to kill each other. Dougal had been Jamie's teacher in the art of swordsmanship, and they had fought back to back and shoulder to shoulder many times before; each man knew the subtleties of the other's style as well as he knew his own—or at least I hoped so.

Dougal pressed his advantage with a double lunge, forcing Jamie back toward the edge of the courtyard. Jamie stepped quickly to one side, struck Dougal's blade away with one beat, then slashed back the other way, with a speed that sent the blade of his broadsword through the cloth of Dougal's right sleeve. There was a loud ripping noise, and a strip of white linen hung free, fluttering in the breeze.

"Oh, nicely fought, sir!" I turned to see who had spoken, and found Lord Kilmarnock standing at my shoulder. A serious, plain-faced man in his early thirties, he and his young son Johnny were also housed in the guest quarters of Holyrood.

The son was seldom far from his father, and I glanced around in search of him. I hadn't far to look; he was standing on the other side of his father, jaw slightly agape as he watched the swordplay. My eye caught a faint movement from the far side of a pillar: Fergus, black eyes fixed unblinkingly on Johnny. I lowered my brows and glowered at him menacingly.

Johnny, rather overconscious of being Kilmarnock's heir, and still more conscious of his privilege in going to war with his father at the age of twelve, tended to lord it over the other lads. In the manner of lads, most of them either avoided Johnny, or bided their time, waiting for him to step out of his father's protective shadow.

Fergus most definitely fell into the latter group. Taking umbrage at a disparaging remark of Johnny's about "bonnet lairds," which he had—quite accurately—interpreted as an insult to Jamie, Fergus had been forcibly prevented from assaulting Johnny in the rock garden a few days before. Jamie had administered swift justice on a physical level, and then pointed out to Fergus that while loyalty was an admirable virtue, and highly prized by its recipient, stupidity was not.

"That lad is two years older than you, and two stone heavier," he had said, shaking Fergus gently by the shoulder. "D'ye think you'll help me by getting your own head knocked in? There's times to fight wi'out counting the cost, but there's times ye bite your tongue and bide your time. *"Ne pétez plus haut que votre cul,* eh?"

Fergus had nodded, wiping his tear-stained cheeks with the tail of his shirt, but I had my doubts as to whether Jamie's words had made much impression on him. I didn't like the speculative look I saw now in those wide black eyes, and thought that had Johnny been a trifle brighter, he would have been standing between me and his father.

Jamie dropped halfway to one knee, with a murderous jab upward that brought his blade whizzing past Dougal's ear. The MacKenzie jerked back, looking startled for a moment, then grinned with a flash of white teeth, and banged his blade flat on top of Jamie's head, with a resounding *clong*.

I heard the sound of applause from across the square. The fight was degenerating from elegant French duel into Highland brawl, and the spectators were thoroughly enjoying the joke of it.

Lord Kilmarnock, also hearing the sound, looked across the square and grimaced sourly.

"His Highness's advisers are summoned to meet the Spaniard," he observed sarcastically. "O'Sullivan, and that ancient fop Tullibardine. Does he take advice of Lord Elcho? Balmerino, Lochiel, or even my humble self?"

This was plainly a rhetorical question, and I contented myself with a faint murmur of sympathy, keeping my eyes on the fighters. The clash of steel rang off the stones, nearly drowning out Kilmarnock's words. Once having started, though, he seemed unable to contain his bitterness.

"No, indeed!" he said. "O'Sullivan and O'Brien and the rest of the Irish; they risk nothing! If the worst should ever happen, they can plead immunity from prosecution by reason of their nationality. But we—we who are risking property, honor—life itself! We are ignored and treated like common dragoons. I said good morning to His Highness yesterday, and he swept by me, nose in the air, as though I had committed a breach in etiquette by so addressing him!"

Kilmarnock was plainly furious, and with good reason. Ignoring the men whom he had charmed and courted into providing the men and money for his adventure, Charles then had rejected them, turning to the comfort of his old advisers from the Continent—most of whom regarded Scotland as a howling wilderness, and its inhabitants as little more than savages.

There was a whoop of surprise from Dougal, and a wild laugh from Jamie. Dougal's left sleeve hung free from the shoulder, the flesh beneath brown and smooth, unmarred by a scratch or a drop of blood.

"I'll pay ye for that, wee Jamie," Dougal said, grinning. Droplets of sweat ran down his face.

"Will ye, Uncle?" Jamie panted. "With what?" A flash of metal, judged to a nicety, and Dougal's sporran flew jingling across the stones, clipped free from the belt.

I caught a movement from the corner of my eye, and turned my head sharply.

"Fergus!" I said.

Kilmarnock turned in the direction I was looking, and saw Fergus. The boy carried a large stick in one hand, with a casualness so assumed as to be laughable, if it weren't for the implicit threat.

"Don't trouble yourself, my lady Broch Tuarach," said Lord Kilmarnock, after a brief glance. "You may depend upon my son to defend himself honorably, if the occasion demands it." He beamed indulgently at Johnny, then turned back to the swordsmen. I turned back, too, but kept an ear cocked in Johnny's direction. It wasn't that I thought Fergus lacked a sense of honor; I just had the impression that it diverged rather sharply from Lord Kilmarnock's notion of that virtue.

"Gu leoir!" At the cry from Dougal, the fight stopped abruptly. Sweating freely, both swordsmen bowed toward the applause of the Royal party, and stepped forward to accept congratulations and be introduced to Don Francisco.

"Milord!" called a high voice from the pillars. "Please—*le parabola*!"

Jamie turned, half-frowning at the interruption, but then shrugged, smiled, and stepped back into the center of the courtyard. *Le parabola* was the name Fergus had given this particular trick.

With a quick bow to His Highness, Jamie took the broadsword carefully by the tip of the blade, stooped slightly, and with a tremendous heave, sent the blade whirling straight up into the air. Every eye fixed on the basket-hilted sword, the tempered length of it glinting in the sun as it turned end over end over end, with such inertia that it seemed to hang in the air for a moment before plunging earthward.

The essence of the trick, of course, was to hurl the weapon so that it buried itself point-first in the earth as it came down. Jamie's refinement of this was to stand directly under the arc of descent, stepping back at the last moment to avoid being skewered by the falling blade.

The sword chunked home at his feet to the accompaniment of a collective "ah!" from the spectators. It was only as Jamie bent to pull the sword from its grassy sheath that I noticed the ranks of the spectators had been reduced by two.

One, the twelve-year-old Master of Kilmarnock, lay facedown on the grassy verge, the swelling bump on his head already apparent through the lank brown hair. The second was nowhere visible, but I caught a faint whisper from the shadows behind me.

"Ne pétez plus haut que votre cul," it said, with satisfaction. Don't fart above your arsehole.

The weather was unseasonably warm for November, and the omnipresent clouds had broken, letting a fugitive autumn sun shine briefly on the grayness of Edinburgh. I had taken advantage of the transient warmth to be outside, however briefly, and was crawling on my knees through the rock garden behind Holyrood, much to the amusement of several Highlanders hanging about the grounds, enjoying the sunshine in their own manner, with a jug of home-brewed whisky.

"Art huntin' *burras*, Mistress?" called one man.

"Nay, it'll be fairies, surely, not caterpillars," joked another.

"You're more likely to find fairies in that jug than I am under rocks," I called back.

The man held the jug up, closed one eye and squinted theatrically into its depths.

"Aye, well, so long as it isna caterpillars in my jug," he replied, and took a deep swig.

In fact, what I was hunting would make as little—or as much—sense to them as caterpillars, I reflected, shoving one boulder a few inches to the side to expose the orange-brown lichen on its surface. A delicate scraping with the small penknife, and several flakes of the odd symbiont fell into my palm, to be transferred with due care to the cheap tin snuffbox that held my painfully acquired hoard.

Something of the relatively cosmopolitan attitude of Edinburgh had rubbed off on the visiting Highlanders; while in the remote mountain villages, such behavior would have gotten me viewed with suspicion, if not downright hostility, here it seemed no more than a harmless quirk. While the Highlanders treated me with great respect, I was relieved to find that there was no fear mingled with it.

Even my basic Englishness was forgiven, once it was known who my husband was. I supposed I was never going to know more than Jamie had told me about what he had done at the Battle of Prestonpans, but whatever it was, it had mightily impressed the Scots, and "Red Jamie" drew shouts and hails whenever he ventured outside Holyrood.

In fact, a shout from the nearby Highlanders drew my attention at this point, and I looked up to see Red Jamie himself, strolling across the grass, waving absently to the men as he scanned the serried rocks behind the palace.

His face lightened as he saw me, and he came across the grass to where I knelt in the rockery.

"There you are," he said. "Can ye come with me for a bit? And bring your wee basket along, if ye will."

I scrambled to my feet, dusting the dried grass from the knees of my gown, and dropped my scraping knife into the basket.

"All right. Where are we going?"

"Colum's sent word he wishes to speak with us. Both of us."

"Where?" I asked, stretching my steps to keep up with his long stride down the path.

"The kirk in the Canongate."

This was interesting. Whatever Colum wished to see us about, he clearly didn't want the fact that he had spoken with us privately to be known in Holyrood.

Neither did Jamie; hence the basket. Passing arm in arm through the gate, my basket gave an apparent excuse for our venturing up the Royal Mile, whether it were to convey purchases home or distribute medicines to the men and their families quartered in the wynds and closes of Edinburgh.

Edinburgh sloped upward steeply along its one main street. Holyrood sat in dignity at the foot, the creaking Abbey vault alongside conferring a spurious air of gracious security. It loftily ignored the glowering presence of Edinburgh

Castle, perched high on the crest of the rocky hill above. In between the two castles, the Royal Mile rose at a rough angle of forty-five degrees. Puffing red-faced at Jamie's side, I wondered how in hell Colum MacKenzie had ever negotiated the quarter-mile of cobbled slope from the palace to the kirk.

We found Colum in the kirkyard, sitting on a stone bench where the late afternoon sun could warm his back. His blackthorn stick lay on the bench beside him, and his short, bowed legs dangled a few inches above the ground. Shoulders hunched and head bowed in thought, at a distance he looked like a gnome, a natural inhabitant of this man-made rock garden, with its tilted stones and creeping lichens. I eyed a prime specimen on a weathered vault, but supposed we had better not stop.

The grass was soundless under our feet, but Colum raised his head while we were still some distance away. There was nothing wrong with his senses, at least.

The shadow under a nearby lime tree moved slightly at our approach. There was nothing wrong with Angus Mhor's senses, either. Satisfied of our identity, the big servant resumed his silent guardianship, becoming again part of the landscape.

Colum nodded in greeting and motioned to the seat beside him. Near at hand, there was no suggestion of the gnomish, despite his twisted body. Face-to-face, you saw nothing but the man within.

Jamie found me a seat on a nearby stone, before taking up the place indicated next to Colum. The marble was surprisingly cold, even through my thick skirts, and I shifted a bit, the carved skull and crossbones atop the memorial lumpy and uncomfortable under me. I saw the epitaph carved below it and grinned:

> *Here lies Martin Elginbrod,*
> *Have mercie on my soul, Lord God,*
> *As I would do were I Lord God,*
> *And thou wert Martin Elginbrod.*

Jamie raised one brow at me in warning, then turned back to Colum. "You asked to see us, Uncle?"

"I've a question for ye, Jamie Fraser," Colum said, without preamble. "D'ye hold me as your kinsman?"

Jamie was silent for a moment, studying his uncle's face. Then he smiled faintly.

"You've my mother's eyes," he said. "Shall I deny that?"

Colum looked startled for a moment. His eyes were the clear, soft gray of a dove's wing, fringed thick with black lashes. For all their beauty, they could gleam cold as steel, and I wondered, not for the first time, just what Jamie's mother had been like.

"You remember your mother? You were no more than a wee laddie when she died."

Jamie's mouth twisted slightly at this, but he answered calmly.

"Old enough. For that matter, my father's house had a looking glass; I'm told I favor her a bit."

Colum laughed shortly. "More than a bit." He peered closely at Jamie, eyes squinting slightly in the bright sun. "Oh, aye, lad; you're Ellen's son, not a doubt of it. That hair, for the one thing . . ." He gestured vaguely toward Jamie's hair, glinting auburn and amber, roan and cinnabar, a thick, wavy mass with a thousand colors of red and gold. ". . . And that mouth." Colum's own mouth rose at one side, as though in reluctant reminiscence. "Wide as a night-jar's, I used to tease her. Ye could catch bugs like a toad, I'd say to her, had ye no but a sticky tongue."

Taken by surprise, Jamie laughed.

"Willie said that once, to me," he said, and then the full lips clamped shut; he spoke rarely of his dead elder brother, and never, I imagined, had he mentioned Willie to Colum before.

If Colum noticed the slip, he gave no sign of it.

"I wrote to her then," he said, looking abstractedly at one of the tilted stones nearby. "When your brother and the babe died of the pox. That was the first time, since she left Leoch."

"Since she wed my father, ye mean."

Colum nodded slowly, still looking away.

"Aye. She was older than me, ye ken, by two years or so; about the same as between your sister and you." The deep-set gray eyes swiveled back and fixed on Jamie.

"I've never met your sister. Were ye close, the two of you?"

Jamie didn't speak, but nodded slightly, studying his uncle closely, as though looking for the answer to a puzzle in the worn face before him.

Colum nodded, too. "It was that way between Ellen and myself. I was a sickly wee thing, and she nursed me often. I remember the sun shining through her hair, and she telling me tales as I lay in bed. Even later"—the fine-cut lips lifted in a slight smile—"when my legs first gave way; she'd come and go, all about Leoch, and stop each morning and night in my chamber, to tell me who she'd seen and what they'd said. We'd talk, about the tenants and the tacksmen, and how things might be arranged. I was married then, but Letitia had no mind for such matters, and less interest." He flipped a hand, dismissing his wife.

"We talked between us—sometimes with Dougal, sometimes alone—of how the fortunes of the clan might best be maintained; how peace might be kept among the septs, which alliances could be made with other clans, how the lands and the timber should be managed. . . . And then she left," he said abruptly, looking down at the broad hands folded on his knee. "With no asking of leave nor word of farewell. She was gone. And I heard of her from others now and then, but from herself—nothing."

"She didn't answer your letter?" I asked softly, not wanting to intrude. He shook his head, still looking down.

"She was ill; she'd lost a child, as well as having the pox. And perhaps she meant to write later; it's an easy task to put off." He smiled briefly, without humor, and then his face relaxed into somberness. "But by Christmas twelvemonth, she was dead."

He looked directly at Jamie, who met his gaze squarely.

"I was a bit surprised, then, when your father wrote to tell me he was taking you to Dougal, and wished ye then to come to me at Leoch for your schooling."

"It was agreed so, when they wed," Jamie answered. "That I should foster with Dougal, and then come to you for a time." The dry twigs of a larch rattled in a passing wind, and he and Colum both hunched their shoulders against the sudden chill of it, their family resemblance exaggerated by the similarity of the gesture.

Colum saw my smile at their resemblance, and one corner of his mouth turned up in answer.

"Oh, aye," he said to Jamie. "But agreements are worth as much as the men who make them, and nay more. And I didna know your father then."

He opened his mouth to go on, but then seemed to reconsider what he had been about to say. The silence of the kirkyard flowed back into the space their conversation had made, filling in the gap as though no word were ever spoken.

It was Jamie, finally, who broke the silence once more.

"What did ye think of my father?" he asked, and I glimpsed in his tone that curiosity of a child who has lost his parents early, seeking clues to the identity of these people known only from a child's restricted point of view. I understood the impulse; what little I knew of my own parents came almost entirely from Uncle Lamb's brief and unsatisfactory answers to my questions— he was not a man given to character analysis.

Colum, on the other hand, was.

"What was he like, d'ye mean?" He looked his nephew over carefully, then gave a short grunt of amusement.

"Look ye in the mirror, lad," he said, a half-grudging smile lingering on his face. "If it's your mother's face ye see, it's your father looking back at ye through those damned Fraser cat-eyes." He stretched and shifted his position, easing his bones on the lichened stone bench. His lips were pressed tight, by habit, against any exclamation of discomfort, and I could see what had made those deep creases between nose and mouth.

"To answer ye, though," he went on, once more comfortably settled, "I didn't like the man overmuch—nor he me—but I knew him at once for a man of honor." He paused, then said, very softly, "I know you for the same, Jamie MacKenzie Fraser."

Jamie didn't change expression, but there was a faint quiver to his eyelids; only one as familiar with him as I was—or as observant as Colum was—would have noticed.

Colum let out his breath in a long sigh.

"So, lad, that's why I wished to talk with you. I must decide, ye see, whether the MacKenzies of Leoch go for King James or King Geordie." He smiled sourly. "It's a case, I think, of the devil ye know, or the devil ye don't, but it's a choice I must make."

"Dougal—" Jamie began, but his uncle cut him off with a sharp motion of his hand.

"Aye, I know what Dougal thinks—I've had little rest from it, these two years past," he said impatiently. "But I am the MacKenzie of Leoch, and it's mine to decide. Dougal will abide by what I say. I'd know what you'd advise me to do—for the sake of the clan whose blood runs in your veins."

Jamie glanced up, eyes dark blue and impervious, hooded against the afternoon sun that shone in his face.

"I am here, and my men with me," he said. "Surely my choice is plain?"

Colum shifted himself again, head cocked attentively to his nephew, as though to catch any nuances of voice or expression that might give him a clue.

"Is it?" he asked. "Men give their allegiance for any number of reasons, lad, and few of them have much to do with the reasons they speak aloud. I've talked with Lochiel, and Clanranald, and Angus and Alex MacDonald of Scotus. D'ye think they're here only because they feel James Stuart their rightful king? Now I would talk with you—and hear the truth, for the sake of your father's honor."

Seeing Jamie hesitate, Colum went on, still watching his nephew keenly.

"I don't ask for myself; if you've eyes, ye can see that the matter isn't one that will trouble me long. But for Hamish—the lad is your cousin, remember. If there's to be a clan for him to lead, once he's of age—then I must choose rightly, now."

He stopped speaking and sat still, the usual caution now relaxed from his features, the gray eyes open and listening.

Jamie sat as still as Colum, frozen like the marble angel on the tomb behind him. I knew the dilemma that preoccupied him, though no trace of it showed on the stern, chiseled face. It was the same one we had faced before, choosing to come with the men from Lallybroch. Charles's Rising was balanced on a knife edge; the allegiance of a large clan such as the MacKenzies of Leoch might encourage others to join the brash Young Pretender, and lead to his success. But if it ended in failure nonetheless, the MacKenzies of Leoch could well end with it.

At last Jamie turned his head deliberately, and looked at me, blue eyes holding my own. *You have some say in this,* his look said. *What shall I do?*

I could feel Colum's eyes upon me, too, and felt rather than saw the questioning lift of the thick, dark brows above them. But what I saw in my mind's eye was young Hamish, a redheaded ten-year-old who looked enough like Jamie to be his son, rather than his cousin. And what life might be for him, and the rest of his clan, if the MacKenzies of Leoch fell with Charles at Culloden. The men of Lallybroch had Jamie to save them from final slaughter, if it came to that. The men of Leoch would not. And yet the choice could not be mine. I shrugged and bowed my head. Jamie took a deep breath, and made up his mind.

"Go home to Leoch, Uncle," he said. "And keep your men there."

Colum sat motionless for a long minute, looking straight at me. Finally, his mouth curled upward, but the expression was not quite a smile.

"I nearly stopped Ned Gowan, when he went to keep you from burning," he said to me. "I suppose I'm glad I didn't."

"Thanks," I said, my tone matching his.

He sighed, rubbing the back of his neck with a calloused hand, as though it ached under the weight of leadership.

"Well, then. I shall see His Highness in the morning, and tell him my decision." The hand descended, lying inert on the stone bench, halfway between him and his nephew. "I thank ye, Jamie, for your advice." He hesitated, then added, "And may God go with you."

Jamie leaned forward and laid his hand over Colum's. He smiled his mother's wide, sweet smile and said, "And with you, too, *mo caraidh.*"

The Royal Mile was busy, thronged with people taking advantage of the brief hours of warmth. We walked in silence through the crowd, my hand tucked deep into the crook of Jamie's elbow. Finally he shook his head, muttering something to himself in Gaelic.

"You did right," I said to him, answering the thought rather than the words. "I would have done the same. Whatever happens, at least the MacKenzies will be safe."

"Aye, perhaps." He nodded to a greeting from a passing officer, jostling through the crowd that surrounded the World's End. "But what of the rest—the MacDonalds and MacGillivrays, and the others that have come? Will they be destroyed now, where maybe they wouldn't, had I had the nerve to tell Colum to join them?" He shook his head, face clouded. "There's no knowing, is there, Sassenach?"

"No," I said softly, squeezing his arm. "Never enough. Or maybe too much. But we can't do nothing on that account, surely?"

He gave me a half-smile back, and pressed my hand against his side.

"No, Sassenach. I dinna suppose we can. And it's done now, and naught can change it, so it's no good worrying. The MacKenzies will stay out of it."

The sentry at the gate of Holyrood was a MacDonald, one of Glengarry's men. He recognized Jamie and nodded us into the courtyard, barely looking up from his louse-searching. The warm weather made the vermin active, and as they left their cozy nests in crotch and armpit, often they could be surprised while crossing the perilous terrain of shirt or tartan and removed from the body of their host.

Jamie said something to him in Gaelic, smiling. The man laughed, picked something from his shirt, and flicked it at Jamie, who pretended to catch it, eyed the imaginary beastie critically, then, with a wink at me, popped it into his mouth.

"Er, how is your son's head, Lord Kilmarnock?" I inquired politely as we stepped out together onto the floor of Holyrood's Great Gallery. I didn't care greatly, but I thought as the topic couldn't be avoided altogether, it was perhaps better to air it in a place where hostility was unlikely to be openly exhibited.

The Gallery met that criterion, I thought. The long, high-ceiled room with its two vast fireplaces and towering windows had been the scene of frequent balls and parties since Charles's triumphant entry into Edinburgh in September. Now, crowded with the luminaries of Edinburgh's upper class, all anxious to do honor to their Prince—once it appeared that he might actually win—the room positively glittered. Don Francisco, the guest of honor, stood at the far end of the room with Charles, dressed in the depressing Spanish style, with baggy dark pantaloons, shapeless coat, and even a small ruff, which seemed to provoke considerable suppressed amusement among the younger and more fashionable element.

"Oh, well enough, Mistress Fraser," replied Kilmarnock imperturbably. "A dunt on the skull will not discommode a lad of that age for long; though his pride may take a bit more mending," he added, with a sudden humorous twist to his long mouth.

I smiled at him, relieved to see it.

"You're not angry?"

He shook his head, looking down to be sure that his feet were clear of my sweeping skirt.

"I have tried to teach John the things he should know as heir to Kilmarnock. In teaching him humility I seem to have signally failed; perhaps your servant may have had more success."

"I suppose you didn't whack him outside," I said absently.

"Pardon?"

"Nothing," I said flushing. "Look, is that Lochiel? I thought he was ill."

Dancing required most of my breath, and Lord Kilmarnock appeared not to wish for conversation, so I had time to look around. Charles was not dancing; though he was a good dancer, and the young women of Edinburgh vied for his attentions, tonight he was thoroughly engrossed in the entertainment of his guest. I had seen a small cask with a Portuguese brand-mark burned into its side being rolled into the kitchens in the afternoon, and glasses of the ruby liquid kept reappearing by Don Francisco's left hand as though by magic through the evening.

We crossed the path of Jamie, propelling one of the Misses Williams through the figures of the dance. There were three of them, nearly indistinguishable from one another—young, brown-haired, comely, and all "so terribly interested, Mr. Fraser, in this noble Cause." They made me quite tired, but Jamie, ever the soul of patience, danced with them all, one by one, and answered the same silly questions over and over.

"Well, it's a change for them to get out, poor things," he explained kindly. "And their father's a rich merchant, so His Highness would like to encourage the sympathy of the family."

The Miss Williams with him looked enthralled, and I wondered darkly just how encouraging he was being. Then my attention shifted, as Balmerino danced by with Lord George Murray's wife. I saw the Murrays exchange affectionate glances as they passed, he with another of the Misses Williams, and felt mildly ashamed of my noticing who Jamie danced with.

Not surprisingly, Colum wasn't at the ball. I wondered whether he had had a chance to speak to Charles beforehand, but decided probably not; Charles looked much too cheerful and animated to have been the recipient of bad news anytime recently.

At one side of the Gallery, I caught sight of two stocky figures, almost identical in uncomfortable and unaccustomed formal dress. It was John Simpson, Master of the Swordmakers Guild of Glasgow, and his son, also John Simpson. Arrived earlier in the week to present His Highness with one of the magnificent basket-hilted broadswords for which they were famed throughout Scotland, the two artisans had plainly been invited tonight to show Don Francisco the depth of support that the Stuarts enjoyed.

Both men had thick, dark hair and beards, lightly frosted with gray. Simpson senior was salt with a sprinkle of pepper, while Simpson junior gave the impression of a dark hillside with a rim of snow crusted lightly round its frostline, white hairs confined to the temples and upper cheeks. As I watched, the older swordmaker poked his son sharply in the back and nodded with significance toward one of the merchants' daughters, hovering near the edge of the floor under her father's protection.

Simpson junior gave his father a skeptical glance, but then shrugged, stepped out, and offered his arm with a bow to the third Miss Williams.

I watched with amusement and fascination as they whirled out into the steps of the dance, for Jamie, who had met the Simpsons earlier, had told me that Simpson junior was quite deaf.

"From all the hammering at the forge, I should think," he had said, showing me with pride the beautiful sword he had bought from the artisans. "Deaf as a stone; his father does the talkin', but the young one sees everything."

I saw the sharp dark eyes flick rapidly across the floor now, judging to a nicety the distance from one couple to the next. The young swordmaster trod a little heavily, but kept the measure of the dance well enough—at least as well as I did. Closing my eyes, I felt the thrum of the music vibrating through the wooden floor, from the cellos resting on it, and assumed that was what he followed. Then, opening my eyes so as not to crash into anyone, I saw Junior wince at a screeching miscue among the violins. Perhaps he did hear some sounds, then.

The circling of the dancers brought Kilmarnock and myself close to the place where Charles and Don Francisco stood, warming their coattails before the huge, tile-lined fireplace. To my surprise, Charles scowled at me over Don Francisco's shoulder, motioning me away with a surreptitious movement of one hand. Seeing it as we turned, Kilmarnock gave a short laugh.

"So His Highness is afraid to have you introduced to the Spaniard!" he said.

"Really?" I looked back over my shoulder as we whirled away, but Charles had returned to his conversation, waving his hands with expressive Italian gestures as he talked.

"I expect so." Lord Kilmarnock danced skillfully, and I was beginning to relax enough to be able to speak, without worrying incessantly about tripping over my skirts.

"Did you see that silly broadsheet Balmerino was showing everyone?" he asked, and when I nodded, went on, "I imagine His Highness saw it, too. And the Spanish are sufficiently superstitious to be ridiculously sensitive to idiocies of that sort. No person of sense or breeding could take such a thing seriously," he assured me, "but no doubt His Highness thinks it best to be safe. Spanish gold is worth a considerable sacrifice, after all," he added. Apparently including the sacrifice of his own pride; Charles still treated the Scottish earls and the Highland chieftains like beggars at his table, though they had at least been invited to the festivities tonight—no doubt to impress Don Francisco.

"Have you noticed the pictures?" I asked, wanting to change the subject. There were more than a hundred of them lining the walls of the Great Gallery, all portraits, all of kings and queens. And all with a most striking similarity.

"Oh, the nose?" he said, an amused smile replacing the grim expression that had taken possession of his face at sight of Charles and the Spaniard. "Yes, of course. Do you know the story behind it?"

The portraits, it seemed, were all the work of a single painter, one Jacob

DeWitt, who had been commissioned by Charles II, upon that worthy's restoration, to produce portraits of all the King's ancestors, from the time of Robert the Bruce onward.

"To assure everyone of the ancientness of his lineage, and the entire appropriateness of his restoration," Kilmarnock explained, a wry twist to his mouth. "I wonder if King James will undertake a similar project when he regains the throne?"

In any case, he continued, DeWitt had painted furiously, completing one portrait every two weeks in order to comply with the monarch's demand. The difficulty, of course, was that DeWitt had no way of knowing what Charles's ancestors had actually looked like, and had therefore used as sitters anyone he could drag into his studio, merely equipping each portrait with the same prominent nose, by way of ensuring a family resemblance.

"That's King Charles himself," Kilmarnock said, nodding at a full-length portrait, resplendent in red velvet and plumed hat. He cast a critical glance at the younger Charles, whose flushed face gave evidence that he had been hospitably keeping his guest company in his potations.

"A better nose, anyway," the Earl murmured, as though to himself. "His mother was Polish."

It was growing late, and the candles in the silver candelabra were beginning to gutter and go out before the gentlefolk of Edinburgh had had their fill of wine and dancing. Don Francisco, possibly not as accustomed as Charles to unrestrained drinking, was nodding into his ruff.

Jamie, having with an obvious expression of relief restored the last Miss Williams to her father for the journey home, came to join me in the corner where I had found a seat that enabled me to slip off my shoes under cover of my spreading skirts. I hoped I wouldn't have to put them on again in a hurry.

Jamie sat down on a vacant seat beside me, mopping his glowing face with a large white handkerchief. He reached past me to the small table, where a tray with a few leftover cakes was sitting.

"I'm fair starved," he said. "Dancing gives ye a terrible appetite, and the talking's worse." He popped a whole cake into his mouth at once, chewed it briefly, and reached for another.

I saw Prince Charles bend over the slumped form of the guest of honor and shake him by the shoulder, to little effect. The Spanish envoy's head was fallen back and his mouth was slack beneath the drooping mustache. His Highness stood, rather unsteadily, and glanced about for help, but Sheridan and Tullibardine, both elderly gentlemen, had fallen asleep themselves, leaning companionably together like a couple of old village sots in lace and velvet.

"Maybe you'd better give His Highness a hand?" I suggested.

"Mmphm."

Resigned, Jamie swallowed the rest of his cake, but before he could rise, I saw the younger Simpson, who had taken quick note of the situation, nudge his father in the ribs.

Senior advanced and bowed ceremoniously to Prince Charles, then, before the glazed prince could respond, the swordmakers had the Spanish envoy by wrists and ankles. With a heave of forge-toughened muscles, they lifted him from his seat, and bore him away, gently swinging him between them like some specimen of big game. They disappeared through the door at the far end of the hall, followed unsteadily by His Highness.

This rather unceremonious departure signaled the end of the ball.

The other guests began to relax and move about, the ladies disappearing into an anteroom to retrieve shawls and cloaks, the gentlemen standing about in small, impatient knots, exchanging complaints about the time the women were taking to make ready.

As we were housed in Holyrood, we left by the other door, at the north end of the gallery, going through the morning and evening drawing rooms to the main staircase.

The landing and the soaring stairwell were lined with tapestries, their figures dim and silvery in candlelight. And below them stood the giant form of Angus Mhor, his shadow huge on the wall, wavering like one of the tapestry figures as they shimmered in the draft.

"My master is dead," he said.

"His Highness said," Jamie reported, "that perhaps it was as well." He spoke with a tone of sarcastic bitterness.

"Because of Dougal," he added, seeing my shocked bewilderment at this statement. "Dougal has always been more than willing to join His Highness in the field. Now Colum's gone, Dougal is chief. And so the MacKenzies of Leoch will march with the Highland army," he said softly, "to victory—or not."

The lines of grief and weariness were cut deep into his face, and he didn't resist as I moved behind him and laid my hands on the broad swell of his shoulders. He made a small sound of incoherent relief as my fingertips pressed hard into the muscles at the base of his neck, and let his head fall forward, resting on his folded arms. He was seated before the table in our room, and piles of letters and dispatches lay neatly stacked around him. Amid the documents lay a small notebook, rather worn, bound in red morocco leather. Colum's diary, which Jamie had taken from his uncle's rooms in hopes that it would contain a recent entry confirming Colum's decision not to support the Jacobite cause.

"Not that it would likely sway Dougal," he had said, grimly thumbing the close-written pages, "but there's nothing else to try."

In the event, though, there had been nothing in Colum's diary for the last three days, save one brief entry, clearly made upon his return from the church-yard the day before.

Met with young Jamie and his wife. Have made my peace with Ellen at last. And that was, of course, important—to Colum, to Jamie, and possibly to Ellen —but of little use in swaying the convictions of Dougal MacKenzie.

Jamie straightened up after a moment and turned to me. His eyes were dark with worry and resignation.

"What it means is that now we are committed to him, Claire—to Charles, I mean. There's less choice than there ever was. We must try to assure his victory."

My mouth felt dry with too much wine. I licked my lips before answering, to moisten them.

"I suppose so. Damn! Why couldn't Colum have waited a little longer? Just 'til the morning, when he could have seen Charles?"

Jamie smiled lopsidedly.

"I dinna suppose he had so much to say about it, Sassenach. Few men get to choose the hour of their death."

"Colum meant to." I had been of two minds whether to tell Jamie what had passed between me and Colum at our first meeting in Holyrood, but now there was no point in keeping Colum's secrets.

Jamie shook his head in disbelief and sighed, his shoulders slumping under the revelation that Colum had meant to take his own life.

"I wonder then," he murmured, half to himself. "Was it a sign, do ye think, Claire?"

"A sign?"

"Colum's death now, before he could do as he meant to and refuse Charles's plea for help. Is it a sign that Charles is destined to win his fight?"

I remembered my last sight of Colum. Death had come for him as he sat in bed, a glass of brandy untouched near his hand. He had met it as he wished, then, clearheaded and alert; his head had fallen back, but his eyes were wide open, dulled to the sights he had left behind. His mouth was pressed tight, the habitual lines carved deep from nose to chin. The pain that was his constant companion had accompanied him as far as it could.

"God knows," I said at last.

"Aye?" he said, voice once more muffled in his arms. "Aye, well. I hope somebody does."

A Bargain with the Devil

Catarrh settled on Edinburgh like the cloud of cold rain that masked the Castle from sight on its hill. Water ran day and night in the streets, and if the cobbles were temporarily clean of sewage, the relief from stench was more than made up for by the splatter of expectorations that slimed every close and wynd, and the choking cloud of fireplace smoke that filled every room from waist-height to ceiling.

Cold and miserable as the weather was outside, I found myself spending a good deal of time walking the grounds of Holyrood and the Canongate. A faceful of rain seemed preferable to lungfuls of woodsmoke and germ-filled air indoors. The sounds of coughing and sneezing rang through the Palace, though the constraint of His Highness's genteel presence caused most hawking sufferers to spit into filthy handerchiefs or the Delft-lined fireplaces, rather than on the polished Scotch oak floors.

The light failed early at this time of year, and I turned back, halfway up the High Street, in order to reach Holyrood before dark. I had no fear at all of assault in the darkness; even had I not been known by now to all the Jacobite troops occupying the city, the prevailing horror of fresh air kept everyone indoors.

Men still well enough to leave their homes on business completed their errands with dispatch before diving thankfully into the smoke-filled sanctuary of Jenny Ha's tavern, and stayed there, nestled cozily into warm airlessness, where the smell of damp wool, unwashed bodies, whisky, and ale nearly succeeded in overcoming the reek of the stove.

My only fear was of losing my footing in the dark and breaking an ankle on the slippery cobbles. The city was lit only by the feeble lanterns of the town watchmen, and these had a disconcerting habit of ducking from doorway to doorway, appearing and disappearing like fireflies. And sometimes disappearing altogether for half an hour at a time, as the lantern-bearer darted into The World's End at the bottom of the Canongate for a life-saving draught of hot ale.

I eyed the faint glow over the Canongate kirk, estimating how much time remained 'til dark. With luck, I might have time to stop at Mr. Haugh's apothecary's shop. While boasting nothing of the variety to be found in Raymond's Paris emporium, Mr. Haugh did a sound trade in horse chestnuts and slippery-elm bark, and usually was able to provide me with peppermint and barberry, as well. At this time of year, his chief income was derived from the sale of camphor balls, considered a sovereign remedy for colds, catarrh, and consumption. If it was no more effective than modern cold remedies, I reflected, it was no worse, and at least smelled invigoratingly healthy.

Despite the prevalence of red noses and white faces, parties were held at the palace several nights a week, as the noblesse of Edinburgh welcomed their Prince with enthusiasm. Another two hours, and the lanterns of servants accompanying ball-goers would start to flicker in the High Street.

I sighed at the thought of another ball, attended by sneezing gallants, paying compliments in phlegm-thickened voices. Perhaps I'd better add some garlic to the list; worn in a silver pomander-locket about the neck, it was supposed to ward off disease. What it actually did do, I supposed, was to keep disease-ridden companions at a safe distance—equally satisfactory, from my point of view.

The city was occupied by Charles's troops, and the English, while not besieged, were at least sequestered in the Castle above. Still, news—of dubious veracity—tended to leak in both directions. According to Mr. Haugh, the most recent rumor held that the Duke of Cumberland was gathering troops south of Perth, with the intent of marching north almost immediately. I hadn't any idea whether this was true; I doubted it, in fact, recalling no mention of Cumberland's activities much before the spring of 1746, which hadn't arrived. Still, I could hardly ignore the rumor.

The sentry at the gate nodded me in, coughing. The sound was taken up by the guards stationed down the hallways and on the landings. Resisting the impulse to wave my basket of garlic at them like a censer as I passed, I made my way upstairs to the afternoon drawing room, where I was admitted without question.

I found His Highness with Jamie, Aeneas MacDonald, O'Sullivan, His Highness's secretary, and a saturnine man named Francis Townsend, who was lately much in His Highness's good graces. Most of them were red-nosed and sneezing, and splattered phlegm smeared the hearth before the gracious mantel. I cast a sharp look at Jamie, who was slumped wearily in his chair, white-faced and drooping.

Accustomed to my forays into the city, and eager for any intelligence regarding the English movements, the men heard me out with great attention.

"We are indebted greatly to you for your news, Mistress Fraser," said His Highness, with a gracious bow and a smile. "You must tell me if there some way in which I might repay your generous service."

"There is," I said, seizing the opportunity. "I want to take my husband home to bed. Now."

The Prince's eyes bulged slightly, but he recovered himself quickly. Not so restrained, Aeneas MacDonald broke out into a fit of suspiciously strangled coughing. Jamie's white face blazed suddenly crimson. He sneezed, and buried his countenance in a handkerchief, blue eyes shooting sparks at me over its folds.

"Ah . . . your husband," said Charles, rallying gallantly to the challenge. "Um . . ." A soft pink blush began to tint his cheeks.

"He's ill," I said, with some asperity. "Surely you can see that? I want him to go to bed and rest."

"Oh, *rest*," murmured MacDonald, as though to himself.

I searched for some sufficiently courtly words.

"I should be sorry to deprive Your Highness temporarily of my husband's attendance, but if he isn't allowed to take sufficient rest, he isn't likely to go on attending you much longer."

Charles, recovered from his momentary discomposure, seemed now to be finding Jamie's patent discomfiture entertaining.

"To be sure," he said, eyeing Jamie, whose complexion had faded now into a sort of mottled pallor. "We should dislike exceedingly the contemplation of such a prospect as you describe, Madam." He inclined his head in my direction. "It shall be as you wish, Madam. *Cher* James is excused from attendance upon our person until he shall be recovering. By all means, take your husband to your rooms at once, and, er . . . undertake what cure seems . . . ah . . . fitting." The corner of the Prince's mouth twitched suddenly, and pulling a large handkerchief from his pocket, he followed Jamie's example and buried the lower half of his face, coughing delicately.

"Best take care, Highness," MacDonald advised somewhat caustically. "You may catch Mr. Fraser's ailment."

"One could wish to have *half* Mr. Fraser's complaint," murmured Francis Townsend, with no attempt at concealing the sardonic smile that made him look like a fox in a hen coop.

Jamie, now bearing a strong resemblance to a frostbitten tomato, rose abruptly, bowed to the Prince with a brief "I thank ye, Highness," and headed for the door, clutching me by the arm.

"Let go," I snarled as we swept past the guards in the anteroom. "You're breaking my arm."

"Good," he muttered. "As soon as I've got ye in private, I'm going to break your neck." But I caught sight of the curl of his mouth, and knew the gruffness was only a facade.

Once in our apartment, with the door safely shut, he pulled me to him, leaned against the door and laughed, his cheek pressed to the top of my head.

"Thank ye, Sassenach," he said, wheezing slightly.

"You're not angry?" I asked, voice somewhat muffled in his shirtfront. "I didn't mean to embarrass you."

"Nay, I'm no minding it." he said, releasing me. "God, I wouldna ha' cared if ye'd said ye meant to set me on fire in the Great Gallery, so long as I could leave His Highness and come to rest for a bit. I'm tired to death of the man, and every muscle I've got is aching." A sudden spasm of coughing shook his frame, and he leaned against the door once more, this time for support.

"Are you all right?" I stretched up on tiptoe to feel his forehead. I wasn't surprised, but was somewhat alarmed, to feel how hot his skin was beneath my palm.

"You," I said accusingly, "have a fever!"

"Aye well, everyone's got a fever, Sassenach," he said, a bit crossly. "Only some are hotter than others, no?"

"Don't quibble," I said, relieved that he still felt well enough to chop logic. "Take off your clothes. And don't say it," I added crisply, seeing the grin forming as he opened his mouth to reply. "I have no designs whatever on your disease-ridden carcass, beyond getting it into a nightshirt."

"Oh, aye? Ye dinna think I'd benefit from the exercise?" He teased, beginning to unfasten his shirt. "I thought ye said exercise was healthy." His laugh turned suddenly to an attack of hoarse coughing that left him breathless and flushed. He dropped the shirt on the floor, and almost immediately began to shiver with chill.

"Much too healthy for you, my lad." I yanked the thick woolen nightshirt over his head, leaving him to struggle into it as I got him out of kilt, shoes, and stockings. "Christ, your feet are like ice!"

"You could . . . warm them . . . for me." But the words were forced out between chattering teeth, and he made no protest when I steered him toward the bed.

He was shaking too hard to speak by the time I had snatched a hot brick from the fire with tongs, wrapped it in flannel, and thrust it in at his feet.

The chill was hard but brief, and he lay still again by the time I had set a pan of water to steep with a handful of peppermint and black currant.

"What's that?" he asked, suspiciously, sniffing the air as I opened another jar from my basket. "Ye dinna mean me to drink it, I hope? It smells like a duck that's been hung ower-long."

"You're close," I said. "It's goose grease mixed with camphor. I'm going to rub your chest with it."

"No!" He snatched the covers protectively up beneath his chin.

"Yes," I said firmly, advancing with purpose.

In the midst of my labors, I became aware that we had an audience. Fergus stood on the far side of the bed, watching the proceedings with fascination, his nose running freely. I removed my knee from Jamie's abdomen and reached for a handkerchief.

"And what are *you* doing here?" Jamie demanded, trying to yank the front of his nightshirt back into place.

Not noticeably disconcerted by the unfriendly tone of this greeting, Fergus ignored the proffered handkerchief and wiped his nose on his sleeve, meanwhile staring with round-eyed admiration at the broad expanse of muscular, gleaming chest on display.

"The skinny milord sent me to fetch a packet he says you have for him. Do all Scotsmen have such quantities of hair upon their chests, milord?"

"Christ! I forgot all about the dispatches. Wait, I'll take them to Cameron myself." Jamie began to struggle up in bed, a process that brought his nose close to the site of my recent endeavors.

"Phew!" He flapped the nightshirt in an effort to dispel the penetrating aroma, and glared accusingly at me. "How am I to get this reek off me? D'ye expect me to go out in company smellin' like a dead goose, Sassenach?"

"No, I don't," I said. "I expect you to lie quietly in bed and rest, or you'll *be* a dead goose." I uncorked a fairly high-caliber glare of my own.

"I can carry the package, milord," Fergus was assuring him.

"You will do nothing of the kind," I said, noting the boy's flushed cheeks and overbright eyes. I put a hand to his forehead.

"Don't tell me," said Jamie sarcastically. "He's got a fever?"

"Yes, he has."

"Ha," he said to Fergus with gloomy satisfaction. "Now you're for it. See how *you* like bein' basted."

A short period of intense effort saw Fergus tucked up in his pallet by the fire, goose grease and medicinal hot tea administered lavishly all round, and a clean handkerchief deposited beneath the chin of each sufferer.

"There," I said, fastidiously rinsing my hands in the basin. "Now, *I* will take this precious packet of dispatches across to Mr. Cameron. *You* will both rest, drink hot tea, rest, blow your nose, and rest, in that order. Got it, troops?"

The tip of a long, reddened nose was barely visible above the bedclothes. It oscillated slowly back and forth as Jamie shook his head.

"Drunk wi' power," he remarked disapprovingly to the ceiling. "Verra unwomanly attitude, that."

I dropped a kiss on his hot forehead and swung my cloak down from its hook.

"How little you know of women, my love," I said.

Ewan Cameron was in charge of what passed for intelligence operations at Holyrood. His quarters were at the end of the west wing, tucked away near the kitchens. On purpose, I suspected, having witnessed the man's appetite in action. Possibly a tapeworm, I thought, viewing the officer's cadaverous countenance as he opened the packet and scanned the dispatches.

"All in order?" I asked after a moment. I had to repress the automatic urge to add "sir."

Startled from his train of thought, he jerked his head up from the dispatches and blinked at me.

"Um? Oh!" Recalled to himself, he smiled and hastened to make apologies.

"I'm sorry, Mistress Fraser. How impolite of me to forget myself and leave you standing there. Yes, everything appears to be in order—most interesting," he murmured to himself. Then, snapping back to an awareness of me, "Would you be so kind as to tell your husband that I wish to discuss these with him as soon as possible? I understand that he is unwell," he added delicately, carefully avoiding my eye. Apparently it hadn't taken Aeneas MacDonald long to relay an account of my interview with the Prince.

"He is," I said unhelpfully. The last thing I wanted was Jamie leaving his bed and sitting up poring over intelligence dispatches all night with Cameron and Lochiel. That would be nearly as bad as staying up dancing all night with the ladies of Edinburgh. Well, possibly not *quite* as bad, I amended to myself, recalling the three Misses Williams.

"I'm sure he will attend upon you as soon as he's able," I said, pulling the edges of the cloak together. "I'll tell him." And I would—tomorrow. Or possibly the next day. Wherever the English forces presently were, I was positive they weren't within a hundred miles of Edinburgh.

A quick peek into the bedroom upon my return showed two lumps, immobile beneath the bedclothes, and the sounds of breathing—slow and regular, if a trifle congested—filled the room. Reassured, I removed my cloak and sat down in the sitting room with a preventative cup of hot tea, to which I had added a fair dollop of medicinal brandy.

Sipping slowly, I felt the liquid heat flow down the center of my chest, spread comfortably through my abdomen, and begin working its steady way down toward my toes, quick-frozen after a dash across the courtyard, undertaken in preference to the circuitous inside passage with its endless stairs and turnings.

I held the cup below my chin, inhaling the pleasant, bitter smell, feeling the heated fumes of the brandy clarify my sinuses. Sniffing, it occurred to me to wonder exactly *why*, in a city and a building plagued with colds and influenza, my own sinuses remained unclogged.

In fact, aside from the childbed fever, I had not been ill once since my passage through the stone circle. That *was* odd, I thought; given the standards of hygiene and sanitation, and the crowded conditions in which we frequently lived, I ought surely to have come down at least with a case of sniffles by this time. But I remained as disgustingly healthy as always.

Plainly I was not immune to all diseases, or I would not have had the fever. But the common communicable ones? Some were explainable on the basis of vaccination, of course. I couldn't, for example, catch smallpox, typhus, cholera, or yellow fever. Not that yellow fever was likely, but still. I set down the cup and felt my left arm, through the cloth of the sleeve. The vaccination scar had faded with time, but was still prominent enough to be detectable; a roughly circular patch of pitted skin, perhaps a half-inch in diameter.

I shuddered briefly, reminded again of Geillis Duncan, then pushed the thought away, diving back into a contemplation of my state of health in order to avoid thinking either of the woman who had gone to a death by fire, or of Colum MacKenzie, the man who had sent her there.

The cup was nearly empty, and I rose to refill it, thinking. An acquired immunity, perhaps? I had learned in nurses' training that colds are caused by innumerable viruses, each distinct and ever-evolving. Once exposed to a particular virus, the instructor had explained, you became immune to it. You continued to catch cold as you encountered new and different viruses, but the chances of meeting something you hadn't been exposed to before became smaller as you got older. So, he had said, while children caught an average of six colds per year, people in middle age caught only two, and elderly folk might go for years between colds, only because they had already met most of the common viruses and become immune.

Now there was a possibility, I thought. What if some types of immunity became hereditary, as viruses and people co-evolved? Antibodies to many diseases could be passed from mother to child, I knew that. Via the placenta or the breast milk, so that the child was immune—temporarily—to any disease to which the mother had been exposed. Perhaps I never caught cold because I harbored ancestral antibodies to eighteenth-century viruses—benefiting from the colds caught by all my ancestors for the past two hundred years?

I was pondering this entertaining idea, so caught up in it that I hadn't bothered to sit down, but was sipping my tea standing in the middle of the room, when a soft knock sounded on the door.

I sighed impatiently, annoyed at being distracted. I didn't bother to set the cup down, but came to the door prepared to receive—and repel—the expected inquiries about Jamie's health. Likely Cameron had come across an unclear passage in a dispatch, or His Highness had thought better of his generosity in dismissing Jamie from attendance at the ball. Well, they would get him out of bed tonight only over my dead and trampled body.

I yanked open the door, and the words of greeting died in my throat. Jack Randall stood in the shadows of the doorway.

The wetness of the spilled tea soaking through my skirt brought me to my senses, but he had already stepped inside. He looked me up and down with his usual air of disdainful appraisal, then glanced at the closed bedroom door.

"You are alone?"

"Yes!"

The hazel glance flickered back and forth between me and the door, assessing my truthfulness. His face was lined from ill health, pale from poor nutrition and a winter spent indoors, but showed no diminution of alertness. The quick, ruthless brain had retreated a bit further back, behind the curtain of those ice-glazed eyes, but it was still there; no doubt of that.

Making his decision, he grasped me by the arm, scooping up my discarded cloak with his other hand.

"Come with me."

I would have allowed him to chop me in pieces before I made a sound that would cause the bedroom door to open.

We were halfway down the corridor outside before I felt it safe to speak. There were no guards stationed within the confines of the staff quarters, but the grounds were heavily patrolled. He couldn't hope to get me through the rockery or the side gates without detection, let alone through the main palace entrance. Therefore, whatever he wanted with me, it must be a business that could be conducted within the precincts of Holyrood.

Murder, perhaps, in revenge for the injury Jamie had done him? Stomach lurching at the thought, I inspected him as closely as I could as we walked swiftly through the pools of light cast from the candleholders on the wall. Not intended for decoration or for graciousness, the candles in this part of the palace were small and widely spaced and the flames feeble, meant only to provide sufficient light to assist visitors returning to their chambers.

He wasn't in uniform, and appeared completely unarmed. He was dressed in nondescript homespun, with a thick coat over plain brown breeks and hose. Nothing but the straightness of his carriage and the arrogant tilt of his unwigged head gave evidence of his identity—he could easily have slipped inside the grounds with one of the parties arriving for the ball, posing as a servant.

No, I decided, glancing warily at him as we passed from dimness to light, he *wasn't* armed, though his hand clamped around my arm was hard as iron. Still, if it was strangling he had in mind, he wouldn't find me an easy victim; I was nearly as tall as he was, and a good deal better nourished.

As though he sensed my thought, he paused near the end of the corridor and turned me to face him, hands tight above my elbows.

"I mean you no harm," he said, low-voiced but firm.

"Tell me another one," I said, estimating the chances of anyone hearing me if I screamed here. I knew there would be a guard at the foot of the stair, but that was on the other side of two doors, a short landing, and a long staircase.

On the other hand, it was stalemate. If he couldn't take me farther, neither could I summon aid where I was. This end of the corridor was sparsely populated, and such residents as there were would undoubtedly be in the other wing now, either attending the ball or serving at it.

He spoke impatiently.

"Don't be idiotic. If I wished to kill you, I could do it here. It would be a great deal safer than taking you outside. For that matter," he added, "if I meant you harm, inside or out, why should I have brought your cloak?" He lifted the garment from his arm in illustration.

"How the hell should I know?" I said, though it seemed a definite point. "Why *did* you bring it?"

"Because I wish you to go outside with me. I have a proposal to make to you, and I will brook no chance of being overheard." He glanced toward the door at the end of the corridor. Like all the others in Holyrood, it was constructed in the cross-and-Book style, the upper four panels arranged to form a cross, the lower two panels standing tall, forming the likeness of an open Bible. Holyrood had once been an abbey.

"Will you come into the church? We can speak there without fear of interruption." This was true; the church adjoining the palace, part of the original Abbey, was abandoned, rendered unsafe by lack of maintenance over the years. I hesitated, wondering what to do.

"Think, woman!" He gave me a slight shake, then released me and stood back. The candlelight silhouetted him, so that his features were no more than a dark blur facing me. "Why should I take the risk of entering the palace?"

This was a good question. Once he had left the shelter of the Castle in disguise, the streets of Edinburgh were open to him. He could have lurked about the alleys and wynds until he caught sight of me on my daily expeditions, and waylaid me there. The only possible reason not to do so was the one he gave; he needed to speak to me without risk of being overseen or overheard.

He saw conclusion dawn in my face, and his shoulders relaxed slightly. He spread the cloak, holding it for me.

"You have my word that you will return from our conversation unmolested, Madam."

I tried to read his expression, but nothing showed on the thin, chiseled features. The eyes were steady, and told me no more than would my own, seen in a looking glass.

I reached for the cloak.

"All right," I said.

We went out into the dimness of the rock garden, passing the sentry with no more than a nod. He recognized me, and it was not unusual for me to go out at night, to attend to an urgent case of sickness in the city. The guard glanced sharply at Jack Randall—it was usually Murtagh who accompanied me, if Jamie could not—but dressed as he was, there was no hint of the Captain's real identity. He returned the guard's glance with indifference, and the door of the palace closed behind us, leaving us in the chill dark outside.

It had been raining earlier, but the storm was breaking up. Thick clouds shredded and flew overhead, driven by a wind that whipped aside my cloak and plastered my skirt to my legs.

"This way." I clutched the heavy velvet close around me, bent my head against the wind, and followed Jack Randall's lean figure through the path of the rockery.

We emerged at the lower end, and after a pause for a quick look around, crossed rapidly across the grass to the portal of the church.

The door had warped and hung ajar; it had been disused for several years because of structural faults that made the building dangerous, and no one had troubled to repair it. I kicked my way through a barrier of dead leaves and rubbish, ducking from the flickering moonlight of the palace's back garden into the absolute darkness of the church.

Or not quite absolute; as my eyes grew accustomed to the dark, I could see the tall lines of the pillars that marched down each side of the nave, and the delicate stonework of the enormous window at the far end, glass mostly gone.

A movement in the shadows showed me where Randall had gone; I turned between the pillars and found him in a space where a recess once used as a baptismal font had left a stone ledge along the wall. To either side were pale blotches on the walls; the memorial tablets of those buried in the church. Others lay flat, embedded in the floor on either side of the central aisle, the names blurred by the traffic of feet.

"All right," I said. "We can't be overheard now. What do you want of me?"

"Your skill as a physician, and your complete discretion. In exchange for such information as I possess regarding the movements and plans of the Elector's troops," he answered promptly.

That rather took my breath away. Whatever I had been expecting, it wasn't this. He couldn't possibly mean . . .

"You're looking for medical treatment?" I asked, making no effort to disguise the mingled horror and amazement in my voice. "From me? I understood that you . . . er, I mean . . ." With a major effort of will, I stopped myself floundering and said firmly, "Surely you have already received whatever medical treatment is possible? You appear to be in reasonably good condition." Externally, at least. I bit my lip, suppressing an urge toward hysteria.

"I am informed that I am fortunate to be alive, Madam," he answered coldly. "The point is debatable." He set the lantern in a niche in the wall, where the scooped basin of a piscina lay dry and empty in its recess.

"I assume your inquiry to be motivated by medical curiosity rather than concern for my welfare," he went on. The lanternlight, shed at waist height, illuminated him from the ribs downward, leaving head and shoulders hidden. He laid a hand on the waistband of his breeches, turning slightly toward me.

"Do you wish to inspect the injury, in order to judge the effectiveness of treatment?" The shadows hid his face, but the splinters of ice in his voice were tipped with poison.

"Perhaps later," I said, as cool as he. "If not yourself, for whom do you seek my skill?"

He hesitated, but it was far too late for reticence.

"For my brother."

"Your brother?" I couldn't keep the shock from my voice. "Alexander?"

"Since my elder brother William is, so far as I know, virtuously engaged in stewardship of the family estates in Sussex, and in need of no assistance," he said dryly. "Yes, my brother Alex."

I spread my hands on the cold stone of a sarcophagus to steady myself.

"Tell me about it," I said.

It was a simple enough story, and a sad one. Had it been anyone other than Jonathan Randall who told it, I might have found myself prey to sympathy.

Deprived of his employment with the Duke of Sandringham because of the scandal over Mary Hawkins, and too frail of health to secure another appointment, Alexander Randall had been forced to seek aid from his brothers.

"William sent him two pounds and a letter of earnest exhortations." Jack Randall leaned back against the wall, crossing his ankles. "William is a very earnest sort, I'm afraid. But he wasn't prepared to have Alex come home to Sussex. William's wife is a bit . . . extreme, shall we say? in her religious opinions." There was a wisp of amusement in his voice that suddenly made me like him for a moment. In different circumstances, might he have been like the great-grandson he resembled?

The sudden thought of Frank so unsettled me that I missed his next remark.

"I'm sorry. What did you say?" I clutched my left hand with my right, fingers pinching tight on my gold wedding ring. Frank was gone. I must stop thinking of him.

"I said that I had procured rooms for Alex near the Castle, so that I might look in on him myself, as my funds did not stretch far enough to allow of employing a proper servant for him."

But the occupation of Edinburgh had of course made such attendance difficult, and Alex Randall had been left more or less to his own devices for the past month, aside from the intermittent offices of a woman who came in to clean now and then. In ill health to start with, his condition had been worsened by cold weather, poor diet, and squalid conditions until, seriously alarmed, Jack Randall had been moved to seek my help. And to offer for that help, the betrayal of his King.

"Why would you come to me?" I asked at last, turning from the plaque.

He looked faintly surprised.

"Because of who you are." His lips curved in a slight, self-mocking smile.

"If one seeks to sell one's soul, is it not proper to go to the powers of darkness?"

"You really think that I'm a power of darkness, do you?" Plainly he did; he was more than capable of mockery, but there had been none in his original proposal.

"Aside from the stories about you in Paris, you told me so yourself," he pointed out. "When I let you go from Wentworth." He turned in the dark, shifting himself on the stone ledge.

"That was a serious mistake," he said softly. "You should never have left that place alive, dangerous creature. And yet I had no choice; your life was the price he set. And I would have paid still higher stakes than that, for what he gave me."

I made a slight hissing noise, which I muffled at once, but too late to stop him hearing me. He half-sat on the ledge, one hip resting on the stone, one leg stretched down to balance him. The moon broke through the scudding clouds outside, backlighting him through the broken window. In the dimness, head half-turned and the lines of cruelty around his mouth erased by darkness, I could mistake him again, as I had once before, for a man I had loved. For Frank.

Yet I had betrayed that man; because of my choice, that man would never be. *For the sins of the fathers shall be visited on the children . . . and thou shalt destroy him, root and branch, so that his name shall no more be known among the tribes of Israel.*

"Did he tell you?" the light, pleasant voice asked from the shadows. "Did he ever tell you all the things that passed between us, him and me, in that small room at Wentworth?" Through my shock and rage, I noticed that he obeyed Jamie's injunction; not once did he use his name. "He." "Him." Never "Jamie." That was mine.

My teeth were clenched tight, but I forced the words through them.

"He told me. Everything."

He made a small sound, half a sigh.

"Whether the idea pleases you or not, my dear, we are linked, you and I. I cannot say it pleases me, but I admit the truth of it. You know, as I do, the touch of his skin—so warm, is he not? Almost as though he burned from within. You know the smell of his sweat and the roughness of the hairs on his thighs. You know the sound that he makes at the last, when he has lost himself. So do I."

"Be quiet," I said. *"Be still!"* He ignored me, leaning back, speaking thoughtfully, as though to himself. I recognized, with a fresh burst of rage, the impulse that led him to this—not the intention, as I had thought, to upset me, but an overwhelming urge to talk of a beloved; to rehearse aloud and live again vanished details. For after all, to whom might he speak of Jamie in this way, but to me?

"I am leaving!" I said loudly, and whirled on my heel.

"Will you leave?" said the calm voice behind me. "I can deliver General Hawley into your hands. Or you can let him take the Scottish army. Your choice, Madam."

I had the strong urge to reply that General Hawley wasn't worth it. But I thought of the Scottish chieftains now quartered in Holyroodhouse—Kilmarnock and Balmerino and Lochiel, only a few feet away on the other side of the abbey wall. Of Jamie himself. Of the thousands of clansmen they led. Was the chance of victory worth the sacrifice of my feelings? And was this the turning point, again a place of choice? If I didn't listen, if I didn't accept the bargain Randall proposed, what then?

I turned, slowly. "Talk, then," I said. "If you must." He seemed unmoved by my anger, and unworried by the possibility that I would refuse him. The voice in the dark church was even, controlled as a lecturer's.

"I wonder, you know," he said. "Whether you have had from him as much as I?" He tilted his head to one side, sharp features coming into focus as he moved out of the shadow. The fugitive light caught him momentarily from the side, lighting the pale hazel of his eyes and making them shine, like those of a beast glimpsed hiding in the bushes.

The note of triumph in his voice was faint, but unmistakable.

"I," he said softly, "I have had him as you could never have him. You are a woman; you cannot understand, even witch as you are. I have held the soul of his manhood, have taken from him what he has taken from me. I know him, as he now knows me. We are bound, he and I, by blood."

I give ye my Body, that we Two may be One . . .

"You choose a very odd way of seeking my help," I said, my voice shaking. My hands were clenched in the folds of my skirt, the fabric cold and bunched between my fingers.

"Do I? I think it best you understand, Madam. I do not beseech your pity, do not call upon your power as a man might seek mercy from a woman, depending upon what people call womanly sympathy. For that cause, you might come to my brother on his own account." A lock of dark hair fell loose across his forehead; he brushed it back with one hand.

"I prefer that it be a straight bargain made between us, Madam; of service rendered and price paid—for realize, Madam, that my feelings toward you are much as yours toward me must be."

That was a shock; while I struggled to find an answer, he went on.

"We are linked, you and I, through the body of one man—through *him*. I would have no such link formed through the body of my brother; I seek your help to heal his body, but I take no risk that his soul shall fall prey to you. Tell me, then; is the price I offer acceptable to you?"

I turned away from him and walked down the center of the echoing nave. I was shaking so hard that my steps felt uncertain, and the shock of the hard stone beneath my soles jolted me. The tracery of the great window over the disused altar stood black against the white of racing clouds, and dim shafts of moonlight lit my path.

At the end of the nave, as far as I could get from him, I stopped and pressed my hands against the wall for support. It was too dark even to see the letters of the marble tablet under my hands, but I could feel the cool, sharp lines of the carving. The curve of a small skull, resting on crossed thigh bones, a pious version of the jolly Roger. I let my head fall forward, forehead to forehead with the invisible skull, smooth as bone against my skin.

I waited, eyes closed, for my gorge to subside, and the heated pulse that throbbed in my temples to cool.

It makes no difference, I told myself. No matter what he is. No matter what he says.

We are linked, you and I, through the body of one man . . . Yes, but not through Jamie. *Not through him!* I insisted, to him, to myself. Yes, you took him, you bastard! But I took him back, I freed him from you. *You have no part of him!* But the sweat that trickled down my ribs and the sound of my own sobbing breath belied my conviction.

Was this the price I must pay for the loss of Frank? A thousand lives that might be saved, perhaps, in compensation for that one loss?

The dark mass of the altar loomed to my right, and I wished with all my heart that there might be some presence there, whatever its nature; something to turn to for an answer. But there was no one here in Holyrood; no one but me. The spirits of the dead kept their own counsel, silent in the stones of wall and floor.

I tried to put Jack Randall out of my mind. If it weren't him, if it were any other man who asked, would I go? There was Alex Randall to be considered, all other things aside. "For that cause, you might come to my brother on his own account," the Captain had said. And of course I would. Whatever I might offer him in the way of healing, could I withhold it because of the man who asked it?

It was a long time before I straightened, pushing myself wearily erect, my hands damp and slick on the curve of the skull. I felt drained and weak, my neck aching and my head heavy, as though the sickness in the city had laid its hand on me after all.

He was still there, patient in the cold dark.

"Yes," I said abruptly, as soon as I came within speaking distance. "All right. I'll come tomorrow, in the forenoon. Where?"

"Ladywalk Wynd," he said. "You know it?"

"Yes." Edinburgh was a small city—no more than the single High Street, with the tiny, ill-lit wynds and closes opening off it. Ladywalk Wynd was one of the poorer ones.

"I will meet you there," he said. "I shall have the information for you."

He slid to his feet and took a step forward, then stood, waiting for me to move. I saw that he didn't want to pass close by me, in order to reach the door.

"Afraid of me, are you?" I said, with a humorless laugh. "Think I'll turn you into a toadstool?"

"No," he said, surveying me calmly. "I do not fear you, Madam. You cannot have it both ways, you know. You sought to terrify me at Wentworth, by giving me the day of my death. But having told me that, you cannot now threaten me, for if I shall die in April of next year, you cannot harm me now, can you?"

Had I had a knife with me, I might have shown him otherwise, in a soul-satisfying moment of impulse. But the doom of prophecy lay on me, and the weight of a thousand Scottish lives. He was safe from me.

"I keep my distance, Madam," he said, "merely because I would prefer to take no chance of touching you."

I laughed once more, this time genuinely.

"And that, Captain," I said, "is an impulse with which I am entirely in sympathy." I turned and left the church, leaving him to follow as he would.

I had no need to ask or to wonder whether he would keep his word. He had freed me once from Wentworth, because he had given his word to do so. His word, once given, was his bond. Jack Randall was a gentleman.

What did you feel, when I gave my body to Jack Randall? Jamie had asked me.

Rage, I had said. *Sickness. Horror.*

I leaned against the door of the sitting room, feeling them all again. The fire had died out and the room was cold. The smell of camphorated goose grease tingled in my nostrils. It was quiet, save for the heavy rasp of breathing from the bed, and the faint sound of the wind, passing by the six-foot walls.

I knelt at the hearth and began to rebuild the fire. It had gone out completely, and I pushed back the half-burnt log and brushed the ashes away before breaking the kindling into a small heap in the center of the hearthstone. We had wood fires in Holyrood, not peat. Unfortunate, I thought; a peat fire wouldn't have gone out so easily.

My hands shook a little, and I dropped the flint box twice before I succeeded in striking a spark. The cold, I said to myself. It was very cold in here.

Did he tell you all the things that passed between us? said Jack Randall's mocking voice.

"All I need to know," I muttered to myself, touching a paper spill to the tiny flame and carrying it from point to point, setting the tinder aglow in half a dozen spots. One at a time, I added small sticks, poking each one into the flame and holding it there until the fire caught. When the pile of kindling was burning merrily, I reached back and caught the end of the big log, lifting it carefully into the heart of the fire. It was pinewood; green, but with a little sap, bubbling from a split in the wood in a tiny golden bead.

Crystallized and frozen with age, it would make a drop of amber, hard and permanent as gemstone. Now, it glowed for a moment with the sudden heat, popped and exploded in a tiny shower of sparks, gone in an instant.

"All I need to know," I whispered. Fergus's pallet was empty; waking and finding himself cold, he had crawled off in search of a warm haven.

He was curled up in Jamie's bed, the dark head and the red one resting side by side on the pillow, mouths slightly open as they snored peacefully together. I couldn't help smiling at the sight, but I didn't mean to sleep on the floor myself.

"Out you go," I murmured to Fergus, manhandling him to the edge of the bed, and rolling him into my arms. He was light-boned and thin for a ten-year-old, but still awfully heavy. I got him to his pallet without difficulty and plunked him in, still unconscious, then came back to Jamie's bed.

I undressed slowly, standing by the bed, looking down at him. He had turned onto his side and curled himself up against the cold. His lashes lay long and curving against his cheek; they were a deep auburn, nearly black at the tips, but a pale blond near the roots. It gave him an oddly innocent air, despite the long, straight nose and the firm lines of mouth and chin.

Clad in my chemise, I slid into bed behind him, snuggling against the wide, warm back in its woolen nightshirt. He stirred a little, coughing, and I put a hand on the curve of his hip to soothe him. He shifted, curling further and thrusting himself back against me with a small exhalation of awareness. I put my arm around his waist, my hand brushing the soft mass of his testicles. I could rouse him, I knew, sleepy as he was; it took very little to bring him standing, no more than a few firm strokes of my fingers.

I didn't want to disturb his rest, though, and contented myself with gently patting his belly. He reached back a large hand and clumsily patted my thigh in return.

"I love you," he muttered, half-awake.

"I know," I said, and fell asleep at once, holding him.

Family Ties

It was not quite a slum, but the next thing to it. I stepped gingerly aside to avoid a substantial puddle of filth, left by the emptying of chamber pots from the windows overhead, awaiting removal by the next hard rain.

Randall caught my elbow to save my slipping on the slimy cobblestones. I stiffened at the touch, and he withdrew his hand at once.

He saw my glance at the crumbling doorpost, and said defensively, "I couldn't afford to move him to better quarters. It isn't so bad inside."

It wasn't—quite. Some effort had been made at furnishing the room comfortably, at least. There was a large bowl and ewer, a sturdy table with a loaf, a cheese, and a bottle of wine upon it, and the bed was equipped with a feather mattress, and several thick quilts.

The man who lay on the mattress had thrown off the quilts, overheated by the effort of coughing, I assumed. He was quite red in the face, and the force of his coughing shook the bed frame, sturdy as it was.

I crossed to the window and threw it up, disregarding Randall's exclamation of protest. Cold air swept into the stifling room, and the stench of unwashed flesh, unclean linen, and overflowing chamber pot lightened a bit.

The coughing gradually eased, and Alexander Randall's flushed countenance faded to a pasty white. His lips were slightly blue, and his chest labored as he fought to recover his breath.

I glanced around the room, but didn't see anything suitable to my purpose. I opened my medical kit and drew out a stiff sheet of parchment. It was a trifle frayed at the edges, but would still serve. I sat down on the edge of the bed, smiling as reassuringly at Alexander as I could manage.

"It was . . . kind of you . . . to come," he said, struggling not to cough between words.

"You'll be better in a moment," I said. "Don't talk, and don't fight the cough. I'll need to hear it."

His shirt was unfastened already; I spread it apart to expose a shockingly sunken chest. It was nearly fleshless; the ribs were clearly visible from abdomen to clavicle. He had always been thin, but the last year's illness had left him emaciated.

I rolled the parchment into a tube and placed one end against his chest, my ear against the other. It was a crude stethoscope, but amazingly effective.

I listened at various spots, instructing him to breathe deeply. I didn't need to tell him to cough, poor boy.

"Roll onto your stomach for a moment." I pulled up the shirt and listened, then tapped gently on his back, testing the resonance over both lungs. The bare flesh was clammy with sweat under my fingers.

"All right. Onto your back again. Just lie still, now, and relax. This won't hurt at all." I kept up the soothing talk as I checked the whites of his eyes, the swollen lymph glands in his neck, the coated tongue and inflamed tonsils.

"You've a touch of catarrh," I said, patting his shoulder. "I'll brew you something that will ease the cough. Meanwhile . . ." I pointed a toe distastefully at the lidded china receptacle under the bed, and glanced at the man who stood waiting by the door, back braced and rigid as though on parade.

"Get rid of that," I ordered. Randall glared at me, but came forward and stooped to obey.

"Not out the window!" I said sharply, as he made a move toward it. "Take it downstairs." He about-faced and left without looking at me.

Alexander drew a shallow breath as the door closed behind his brother. He smiled up at me, hazel eyes glowing in his pale face. The skin was nearly transparent, stretched tight over the bones of his face.

"You'd better hurry, before Johnny comes back. What is it?"

His dark hair was disordered by the coughing; trying to restrain the feelings it roused in me, I smoothed it for him. I didn't want to tell him, but he clearly knew already.

"You have got catarrh. You also have tuberculosis—consumption."

"And?"

"And congestive heart failure," I said, meeting his eyes straight on.

"Ah. I thought . . . something of the kind. It flutters in my chest sometimes . . . like a very small bird." He laid a hand lightly over his heart.

I couldn't bear the look of his chest, heaving under its impossible burden, and I gently closed his shirt and fastened the tie at the neck. One long, white hand grasped mine.

"How long?" he said. His tone was light, almost unconcerned, displaying no more than a mild curiosity.

"I don't know," I said. "That's the truth. I don't know."

"But not long," he said, with certainty.

"No. Not long. Months perhaps, but almost surely less than a year."

"Can you . . . stop the coughing?"

I reached for my kit. "Yes. I can help it, at least. And the heart palpitations; I can make you a digitalin extract that will help." I found the small packet of dried foxglove leaves; it would take a little time to brew them.

"Your brother," I said, not looking at him. "Do you want me—"

"No," he said, definitely. One corner of his mouth curved up, and he looked so like Frank that I wanted momentarily to weep for him.

"No," he said. "He'll know already, I think. We've always . . . known things about each other."

"Have you, then?" I asked, looking directly at him. He didn't turn away from my eyes, but smiled faintly.

"Yes," he said softly. "I know about him. It doesn't matter."

Oh, doesn't it? I thought. Not to you, perhaps. Not trusting either my face or my voice, I turned away and busied myself in lighting the small alcohol lamp I carried.

"He *is* my brother," the soft voice said behind me. I took a deep breath and steadied my hands to measure out the leaves.

"Yes," I said, "at least he's that."

Since news had spread of Cope's amazing defeat at Prestonpans, offers of support, of men and money, poured in from the north. In some cases, these offers even materialized: Lord Ogilvy, the eldest son of the Earl of Airlie, brought six hundred of his father's tenants, while Stewart of Appin appeared at the head of four hundred men from the shires of Aberdeen and Banff. Lord Pitsligo was single-handedly responsible for most of the Highland cavalry, bringing in a large number of gentlemen and their servants from the northeastern counties, all well mounted and well armed—at least by comparison with some of the miscellaneous clansmen, who came armed with claymores saved by their grandsires from the Rising of the '15, rusty axes, and pitchforks lately removed from the more homely tasks of cleaning cow-byres.

They were a motley crew, but none the less dangerous for that, I reflected, making my way through a knot of men gathered round an itinerant knife-grinder, who was sharpening dirks, razors, and scythes with perfect indifference. An English soldier facing them might be risking tetanus rather than instant death, but the results were likely to be the same.

While Lord Lewis Gordon, the Duke of Gordon's younger brother, had come to do homage to Charles in Holyrood, holding out the glittering prospect of raising the whole of clan Gordon, it was a long way from hand-kissing to the actual provisioning of men.

And the Scottish Lowlands, while perfectly willing to cheer loudly at news of Charles's victory, were singularly unwilling to send men to support him; nearly the whole of the Stuart army was composed of Highlanders, and likely to remain so. The Lowlands hadn't been a total washout, though; Lord George Murray had told me that levies of food, goods, and money on the southern burghs had resulted in a very useful sum being contributed to the army's treasury, which might tide them over for a time.

"We've gotten fifty-five hundred pounds from Glasgow, alone. Though it's but a pittance, compared to the promised moneys from France and Spain," His Lordship had confided to Jamie. "But I'm not inclined to turn up my nose at it, particularly as His Highness has had nothing from France but soothing words, and no gold."

Jamie, who knew just how unlikely the French gold was to materialize, had merely nodded.

"Have ye found out anything more today, *mo duinne?*" he asked me as I came in. He had a half-written dispatch in front of him, and stuck his quill into the inkpot to wet it again. I pulled the damp hood off my hair with a crackle of static electricity, nodding.

"There's a rumor that General Hawley is forming cavalry units in the south. He has orders for the formation of eight regiments."

Jamie grunted. Given the Highlanders' aversion to cavalry, this wasn't good news. Absentmindedly, he rubbed his back, where the hoofprint-shaped bruise from Prestonpans had all but faded.

"I'll put it down for Colonel Cameron, then," he said. "How good a rumor do ye think it is, Sassenach?" Almost automatically, he glanced over his shoulder, to be sure we were alone. He called me "Sassenach" now only in privacy, using the formality of "Claire" in public.

"You can take it to the bank," I said. "I mean, it's good."

It wasn't a rumor at all; it was the latest bit of intelligence from Jack Randall, the latest installment payment on the debt he insisted on assuming for my care of his brother.

Jamie knew, of course, that I visited Alex Randall, as well as the sick of the Jacobite army. What he didn't know, and what I could never tell him, was that once a week—sometimes more often—I would meet Jack Randall, to hear what news seeped into Edinburgh Castle from the South.

Sometimes he came to Alex's room when I was there; other times, I would be coming home in the winter twilight, watching my footing on the slippery cobbles of the Royal Mile, when suddenly a stick-straight form in brown home-spun would beckon from the mouth of a close, or a quiet voice come out of the mist behind my shoulder. It was unnerving; like being haunted by Frank's ghost.

It would have been simpler in many ways for him to leave a letter for me at Alex's lodging, but he would have nothing put in writing, and I could see his point. If such a letter was ever found, even unsigned, it could implicate not only him but Alex as well. As it was, Edinburgh teemed with strangers; volunteers to King James's standard, curious visitors from south and north, foreign envoys from France and Spain, spies and informers in plenty. The only people not abroad on the streets were the officers and men of the English garrison, who remained mewed up in the Castle. So long as no one heard him speak to me, no one would recognize him for what he was, nor think anything odd of our encounters, even were we seen—and we seldom were, such were his precautions.

For my part, I was just as pleased; I would have had to destroy anything put in writing. While I doubted that Jamie would recognize Randall's hand, I couldn't explain a regular source of information without outright lying. Far better to make it appear that the information he gave me was merely part of the gleanings of my daily rounds.

The drawback, of course, was that by treating Randall's contributions in the same light as the other rumors I collected, they might be discounted or ignored. Still, while I believed that Jack Randall was supplying information in good faith—assuming one could entertain such a concept in conjunction with the man—it didn't necessarily follow that it was always correct. As well to have it regarded skeptically.

I relayed the news of Hawley's new regiments with the usual faint twinge of guilt at my quasi deception. However, I had concluded that while honesty between husband and wife was essential, there was such a thing as carrying it too bloody far. And I saw no reason why the supplying of useful information to the Jacobites should cause Jamie further pain.

"The Duke of Cumberland is still waiting for his troops to return from Flanders," I added. "And the siege of Stirling Castle is getting nowhere."

Jamie grunted, scribbling busily. "That much I knew; Lord George had a dispatch from Francis Townsend two days ago; he holds the town, but the ditches His Highness insisted on are wasting men and time. There's no need for them; they'd do better just to batter the Castle from a distance with cannon fire, and then storm it."

"So why are they digging ditches?"

Jamie waved a hand distractedly, still concentrating on his writing. His ears were pink with frustration.

"Because the Italian army dug ditches when they took Verano Castle, which is the only siege His Highness has seen, so plainly that's how it must be done, aye?"

"Och, aye," I said.

It worked; he looked up at me and laughed, his eyes slanting half-shut with it.

"That's a verra fair try, Sassenach," he said. "What else can ye say?"

"Settle for the Lord's Prayer in Gaelic, would you?" I asked.

"No," he said, scattering sand across his dispatch. He got up, kissed me briefly, and reached for his coat. "But I'll settle for some supper. Come along, Sassenach. We'll find a nice, cozy tavern and I'll teach you a lot of things ye mustn't say in public. They're all fresh in my mind."

Stirling Castle fell at last. The cost had been high, the likelihood of holding it low, and the benefit in keeping it dubious. Still, the effect on Charles was euphoric—and disastrous.

"I have succeeded at last in convincing Murray—such a stubborn fool as he is!" Charles interjected, frowning. Then he remembered his victory, and beamed around the room once more. "I have prevailed, I say, though. We march into England on this day a week, to reclaim *all* of my Father's lands!"

The Scottish chieftains gathered in the morning drawing room glanced at each other, and there was considerable coughing and shifting of weight. The overall mood didn't seem to be one of wild enthusiasm at the news.

"Er, Your Highness," Lord Kilmarnock began, carefully. "Would it not be wiser to consider . . . ?"

They tried. They all tried. Scotland, they pointed out, already belonged to Charles, lock, stock, and barrel. Men were still pouring in from the north, while from the south there seemed little promise of support. And the Scottish lords were all too aware that the Highlanders, while fierce fighters and loyal followers, were also farmers. Fields needed to be tilled for the spring planting; cattle needed to be provisioned for overwintering. Many of the men would resist going deeply into the South in the winter months.

"And these men—they are not my subjects? They go not where I command them? Nonsense," Charles said firmly. And that was that. Almost.

"James, my friend! Wait, I speak with you a moment in private, if you please." His Highness turned from a few sharp words with Lord Pitsligo, his long, stubborn chin softening a bit as he waved a hand at Jamie.

I didn't think I was included in this invitation. I hadn't any intention of leaving, though, and settled more firmly into one of the gold damask chairs as the Jacobite lords and chieftains filed out, muttering to each other.

"Ha!" Charles snapped his fingers contemptuously in the direction of the closing door. "Old women, all of them! They will see. So will my cousin Louis, so will Philip—do I need their help? I show them all." I saw the pale, manicured fingers touch briefly at a spot just over his breast. A faint rectangular outline showed through the silk of his coat. He was carrying Louise's miniature; I had seen it.

"I wish Your Highness every good fortune in the endeavor," Jamie murmured, "but . . ."

"Ah, I thank you, *cher* James! *You* at least believe in me!" Charles threw an arm about Jamie's shoulders, massaging his deltoids affectionately.

"I am desolated that you will not accompany me, that you will not be at my side to receive the applause of my subjects as we march into England," Charles said, squeezing vigorously.

"I won't?" Jamie looked stunned.

"Alas, *mon cher ami,* duty demands of you a great sacrifice. I know how much your great heart yearns for the glories of battle, but I require you for another task."

"You do?" said Jamie.

"What?" I said bluntly.

Charles cast a glance of well-mannered dislike in my direction, then turned back to Jamie and resumed the bonhomie.

"It is a task of the greatest import, my James, and one that only you can do. It is true that men flock to my Father's standard; more come every day. Still, we must not haste to feel secure, no? By such luck, your kinsmen the MacKenzies have come to my aid. But you have to your family another side, eh?"

"No," Jamie said, a look of horror dawning on his face.

"But yes," said Charles, with a final squeeze. He swung around to face Jamie, beaming. "You will go to the north, to the land of your fathers, and return to me at the head of the men of clan Fraser!"

40

The Fox's Lair

"Oo you know your grandfather well?" I asked, waving away an unseasonable deerfly that seemed unable to make up its mind whether I or the horse would make a better meal.

Jamie shook his head.

"No. I've heard he acts like a terrible auld monster, but ye shouldna be scairt of him." He smiled at me as I swatted at the deerfly with the end of my shawl. "I'll be with you."

"Oh, crusty old gentlemen don't bother me," I assured him. "I've seen a good many of those in my time. Soft as butter underneath, the most of them. I imagine your grandfather's much the same."

"Mm, no," he replied thoughtfully. "He really *is* a terrible auld monster. It's only, if ye act scairt of him, it makes him worse. Like a beast scenting blood, ye ken?"

I cast a look ahead, where the far-off hills that hid Beaufort Castle suddenly loomed in a rather sinister manner. Taking advantage of my momentary lack of attention, the deerfly made a strafing run past my left ear. I squeaked and ducked to the side, and the horse, taken aback by this sudden movement, shied in a startled manner.

"Hey! *Cuir stad*!" Jamie dove sideways to grab my reins, dropping his own. Better schooled than my own mount, his horse snorted, but accommodated this maneuver, merely flicking its ears in a complacently superior way.

Jamie dug his knees into his horse's sides, pulling mine to a stop alongside.

"Now then," he said, narrowed eyes following the zigzag flight of the humming deerfly. "Let him light, Sassenach, and I'll get him." He waited, hands raised at the ready, squinting slightly in the sunlight.

I sat like a mildly nervous statue, half-hypnotized by the menacing buzz. The heavy winged body, deceptively slow, hummed lazily back and forth between the horse's ears and my own. The horse's ears twitched violently, an impulse with which I was in complete sympathy.

"If that thing lands in my ear, Jamie, I'm going to—" I began.

"Shh!" he ordered, leaning forward in anticipation, left hand cupped like a panther about to strike. "Another second, and I'll have him."

Just then I saw the dark blob alight on his shoulder. Another deerfly, seeking a basking place. I opened my mouth again.

"Jamie . . ."

"Hush!" He clapped his hands together triumphantly on my tormentor, a split second before the deerfly on his collar sank its fangs into his neck.

Scottish clansmen fought according to their ancient traditions. Disdaining strategy, tactics, and subtlety, their method of attack was simplicity itself. Spotting the enemy within range, they dropped their plaids, drew their swords, and charged the foe, shrieking at the tops of their lungs. Gaelic shrieking being what it is, this method was more often successful than not. A good many enemies, seeing a mass of hairy, bare-limbed banshees bearing down on them, simply lost all nerve and fled.

Well schooled as it might ordinarily be, nothing had prepared Jamie's horse for a grade-A, number one Gaelic shriek, uttered at top volume from a spot two feet behind its head. Losing all nerve, it laid back its ears and fled as though the devil itself were after it.

My mount and I sat transfixed in the road, watching an outstanding exhibition of Scottish horsemanship as Jamie, both stirrups lost and the reins free, flung half out of his saddle by his horse's abrupt departure, heaved himself desperately forward, grappling for the mane. His plaid fluttered madly about him, stirred by the wind of his passing, and the horse, thoroughly panicked by this time, took the thrashing mass of color as an excuse to run even faster.

One hand tangled in the long mane, Jamie was grimly hauling himself upright, long legs clasping the horse's sides, ignoring the stirrup irons that danced beneath the beast's belly. Scraps of what even my limited Gaelic recognized as extremely bad language floated back on the gentle wind.

A slow, clopping sound made me look behind, to where Murtagh, leading the pack horse, was coming over the small rise we had just descended. He made his careful way down the road to where I waited. He pulled his animal to a leisurely stop, shaded his eyes, and looked ahead, to the spot where Jamie and his panicked mount were just vanishing over the next hilltop.

"A deerfly," I said, in explanation.

"Late for them. Still, I didna think he'd be in such a hurry to meet his grandsire as to leave ye behind," Murtagh remarked, with his customary dryness. "Not that I'd say a wife more or less will make much difference in his reception."

He picked up his reins and booted his pony into reluctant motion, the packhorse amiably coming along for the journey. My own mount, cheered by the company and reassured by a temporary absence of flies, stepped out quite gaily alongside.

"Not even an English wife?" I asked curiously. From the little I knew, I didn't think Lord Lovat's relations with anything English were much to cheer about.

"English, French, Dutch, or German. It isna like to make much difference; it'll be the lad's liver the Old Fox will be eatin' for breakfast, not yours."

"What do you mean by that?" I stared at the dour little clansman, looking much like one of his own bundles, under the loose wrapping of plaid and shirt. Somehow every garment that Murtagh put on, no matter how new or how well tailored, immediately assumed the appearance of something narrowly salvaged from a rubbish heap.

"What kind of terms is Jamie on with Lord Lovat?"

I caught a sidelong glance from a small, shrewd black eye, and then his head turned toward Beaufort Castle. He shrugged, in resignation or anticipation.

"No terms at all, 'til now. The lad's never spoken to his grandsire in his life."

"But how do you know so much about him if you've never met him?"

At least I was beginning to understand Jamie's earlier reluctance to approach his grandfather for help. Reunited with Jamie and his horse, the latter looking rather chastened, and the former irritable to a degree, Murtagh had gazed speculatively at him, and offered to ride ahead to Beaufort with the pack animal, leaving Jamie and me to enjoy lunch at the side of the road.

Over a restorative ale and oatcake, he had at length told me that his grandfather, Lord Lovat, had not approved of his son's choice of bride, and had not seen fit either to bless the union or to communicate with his son—or his son's children—anytime since the marriage of Brian Fraser and Ellen Mac-Kenzie, more than thirty years before.

"I've heard a good bit about him, one way and another, though." Jamie replied, chewing a bite of cheese. "He's the sort of man that makes an impression on folk, ye ken."

"So I gather." The elderly Tullibardine, one of the Parisian Jacobites, had regaled me with a number of uncensored opinions regarding the leader of clan Fraser, and I thought that perhaps Brian Fraser had not been desolated at his father's inattention. I said as much, and Jamie nodded.

"Oh, aye. I canna recall my father having much good to say of the old man, though he wouldna be disrespectful of him. He just didna speak of him often." He rubbed at the side of his neck, where a red welt from the deerfly bite was beginning to show. The weather was freakishly warm, and he had unfolded his plaid for me to sit on. The deputation to the head of clan Fraser had been thought worth some investment in dignity, and Jamie wore a new kilt, of the buckled military cut, with the plaid a separate strip of cloth. Less enveloping for shelter from the weather than the older, belted plaid, it was a good deal more efficient to put on in a hurry.

"I wondered a bit," he said thoughtfully, "whether my father was the sort of father he was because of the way old Simon treated *him*. I didna realize it at the time, of course, but it's no so common for a man to show his feelings for his sons."

"You've thought about it a lot." I offered him another flask of ale, and he took it with a smile that lingered on me, more warming than the feeble autumn sun.

"Aye, I did. I was wondering, ye see, what sort of father I'd be to my own bairns, and looking back a bit to see, my own father being the best example I had. Yet I knew, from the bits that he said, or that Murtagh told me, that his own father was nothing like him, so I thought as how he must have made up his mind to do it all differently, once he had the chance."

I sighed a bit, setting down my bit of cheese.

"Jamie," I said. "Do you really think we'll ever—"

"I do," he said, with certainty, not letting me finish. He leaned over and kissed my forehead. "I know it, Sassenach, and so do you. You were meant to be a mother, and I surely dinna intend to let anyone else father your children."

"Well, *that's* good," I said. "Neither do I."

He laughed and tilted my chin up to kiss my lips. I kissed him back, then reached up to brush away a breadcrumb that clung to the stubble around his mouth.

"Ought you to shave, do you think?" I asked. "In honor of seeing your grandfather for the first time?"

"Oh, I've seen him the once before," he said casually. "And he's seen me, for that matter. As for what he thinks of my looks now, he can take me as I am, and be damned to him."

"But Murtagh said you'd never met him!"

"Mphm." He brushed the rest of the crumbs from his shirtfront, frowning slightly as if deciding how much to tell me. Finally he shrugged and lay back in the shade of a gorse bush, hands clasped behind his head as he stared at the sky.

"Well, we never have *met,* as ye'd say. Or not exactly. 'Twas like this . . ."

At the age of seventeen, young Jamie Fraser set sail for France, to finish his education at the University of Paris, and to learn further such things as are not taught in books.

"I sailed from the harbor at Beauly," he said, nodding over the next hill, where a narrow slice of gray on the far horizon marked the edge of the Moray Firth. "There were other ports I could have gone by—Inverness would have been most like—but my father booked my passage, and from Beauly it was. He rode with me, to see me off into the world, ye might say."

Brian Fraser had seldom left Lallybroch in the years since his marriage, and took pleasure as they rode in pointing out various spots to his son, where he had hunted or traveled as boy and young man.

"But he grew much quieter as we drew near Beaufort. He hadna spoken of my grandsire on this trip, and I knew better than mention him myself. But I kent he had reason for sending me from Beauly."

A number of small sparrows edged their way cautiously nearer, popping in and out of the low shrubs, ready to dart back to safety at the slightest hint of danger. Seeing them, Jamie reached for a remnant of bread, and tossed it with considerable accuracy into the middle of the flock, which exploded like shrapnel, all fleeing the sudden intrusion.

"They'll be back," he said, motioning toward the scattered birds. He put an arm across his face as though to shield it from the sun, and went on with his story.

"There was a sound of horses along the road from the castle, and when we turned to see, there was a small party coming down, six horsemen with a wagon, and one of them held Lovat's banner, so I knew my grandfather was with them. I looked quick at my father, to see did he mean to do anything, but he just smiled and squeezed my shoulder quick and said, 'Let's go aboard, then, lad.'

"I could feel my grandsire's eyes on me as I walked down the shore, wi' my hair and my height fair shriekin' 'MacKenzie,' and I was glad I had my best clothes on and didna look a beggar. I didna look round, but I stood as tall as I could, and was proud that I had half a head's height above the tallest man there. My father walked by my side, quiet like he was, and he didna look aside, either, but I could feel him there, proud that he'd sired me."

He smiled at me, lopsided.

"That was the last time I was sure I'd done well by him, Sassenach. I wasna so sure, times after, but I was glad of that one day."

He locked his arms around his knees, staring ahead as though reliving the scene on the quay.

"We stepped aboard the ship, and met the master, then we stood by the rail, talking a bit about nothing, both of us careful not to look at the men from Beaufort who were loading the bundles, or glance to the shore where the horsemen stood. Then the master gave the order to cast off. I kissed my father, and he jumped over the rail, down to the dock, and walked to his horse. He didna look back until he was mounted, and by then the ship had started out into the harbor.

"I waved, and he waved back, then he turned, leading my horse, and started on the road back to Lallybroch. And the party from Beaufort turned then, too, and started back. I could see my grandsire at the head of the party, sitting straight in his saddle. And they rode, my father and grandfather, twenty yards apart, up the hill and over it, out of my sight, and neither one turned to the other, or acted as though the other one was there at all."

He turned his head down the road, as though looking for signs of life from the direction of Beaufort.

"I met his eyes," he said softly. "The once. I waited until Father reached his horse, and then I turned and looked at Lord Lovat, bold as I could. I wanted him to know we'd ask nothing of him, but that I wasna scairt of him." He smiled at me, one-sided. "I was, though."

I put a hand over his, stroking the grooves of his knuckles.

"Was he looking back at you?"

He snorted briefly.

"Aye, he was. Reckon he didna take his eyes off me from the time I came down the hill 'til my ship sailed away; I could feel them borin' into my back like an auger. And when I looked at him, there he was, wi' his eyes black under his brows, starin' into mine."

He fell silent, still looking at the castle, 'til I gently prodded him.

"How did he look, then?"

He pulled his eyes from the dark cloud mass on the far horizon to look down at me, the customary expression of good humor missing from the curve of his mouth, the depths of his eyes.

"Cold as stone, Sassenach," he replied. "Cold as the stone."

We were lucky in the weather; it had been warm all the way from Edinburgh.

"It's no going to last," Jamie predicted, squinting toward the sea ahead. "See the bank of cloud out there? It will be inland by tonight." He sniffed the air, and pulled his plaid across his shoulders. "Smell the air? Ye can feel weather coming."

Not so experienced at olfactory meteorology, I still thought that perhaps I *could* smell it; a dampness in the air, sharpening the usual smells of dried heather and pine resin, with a faint, moist scent of kelp from the distant shore mixed in.

"I wonder if the men have got back to Lallybroch yet," I said.

"I doubt it." Jamie shook his head. "They've less distance to go than we've had, but they're all afoot, and it will ha' been slow getting them all away." He rose in his stirrups, shading his eyes to peer toward the distant cloud bank. "I hope it's just rain; that willna trouble them overmuch. And it might not be a big storm, in any case. Perhaps it willna reach so far south."

I pulled my arisaid, a warm tartan shawl, tighter around my own shoulders, in response to the rising breeze. I had thought this few days' stretch of warm weather a good omen; I hoped it hadn't been deceptive.

Jamie had spent an entire night sitting by the window in Holyrood, after receipt of Charles's order. And in the morning, he had gone first to Charles, to tell His Highness that he and I would ride alone to Beauly, accompanied only by Murtagh, to convey His Highness's respects to Lord Lovat, and his request that Lovat honor his promise of men and aid.

Next, Jamie had summoned Ross the smith to our chamber, and given him his orders, in a voice so low that I could not make out the words from my place near the fire. I had seen the burly smith's shoulders rise, though, and set firm, as he absorbed their import.

The Highland army traveled with little discipline, in a ragtag mob that could scarcely be dignified as a "column." In the course of one day's movement, the men of Lallybroch were to drop away, one by one. Stepping aside into the shrubbery as though to rest a moment or relieve themselves, they were not to return to the main body, but to steal quietly away, and make their way, one by one, to a rendezvous with the other men from Lallybroch. And once regathered under the command of Ross the smith, they were to go home.

"I doubt they'll be missed for some time, if at all," Jamie had said, discussing the plan with me beforehand. "Desertion is rife, all through the army. Ewan Cameron told me they'd lost twenty men from his regiment within the last week. It's winter, and men want to be settling their homes and making things ready for the spring planting. In any case, it's sure there's no one to spare to go after them, even should their leavin' be noticed."

"Have you given up, then, Jamie?" I had asked, laying a hand on his arm. He had rubbed a hand tiredly over his face before answering.

"I dinna ken, Sassenach. It may be too late; it may not. I canna tell. It was foolish to go south so near to the winter; and more foolish still to waste time in beseiging Stirling. But Charles hasna been defeated, and the chiefs—some of them—are coming in answer to his summons. The MacKenzies, now, and others because of them. He's twice as many men now as we had at Preston. What will that mean?" He flung up his hands, frustrated.

"I dinna ken. There's no opposition; the English are terrified. Well, ye know; you've seen the broadsheets." He smiled without humor. "We spit small children and roast them ower the fire, and dishonor the wives and daughters of honest men." He gave a snort of wry disgust. While such crimes as theft and insubordination were common among the Highland army, rape was virtually unknown.

He sighed, a brief, angry sound. "Cameron's heard a rumor that King Geordie's makin' ready to flee from London, in fear that the Prince's army will take the city soon." He had—a rumor that had reached Cameron through me, from Jack Randall. "And there's Kilmarnock, and Cameron. Lochiel, and Balmerino, and Dougal, with his MacKenzies. Bonny fighters all. And should Lovat send the men he's promised—God, maybe it would be enough. Christ, should we march into London—" He hunched his shoulders, then stretched suddenly, shrugging as though to fight his way out of a strangling shirt.

"But I canna risk it," he said simply. "I canna go to Beauly, and leave my own men here, to be taken God knows where. If I were there to head them— that would be something else. But damned if I'll leave them for Charles or Dougal to throw at the English, and me a hundred miles away at Beauly."

So it was arranged. The Lallybroch men—including Fergus, who had protested vociferously, but been overruled—would desert, and depart inconspicuously for home. Once our business at Beauly was completed, and we had returned to join Charles—well, then it would be time enough to see how matters went.

"That's why I'm takin' Murtagh with us," Jamie had explained. "If it looks all right, then I shall send him to Lallybroch to fetch them back." A brief smile lightened his somber face. "He doesna look much on a horse, but he's a braw rider, is Murtagh. Fast as chain lightning."

He didn't look it at the moment, I reflected, but then, there was no emergency at hand. In fact, he was moving even slower than usual; as we topped one hill, I could see him at the bottom, pulling his horse to a halt. By the time we had reached him, he was off, glaring at the packhorse's saddle.

"What's amiss, then?" Jamie made to get down from his own saddle, but Murtagh waved him irritably off.

"Nay, nay, naught to trouble ye. A binding's snapped, is all. Get ye on."

With no more than a nod of acknowledgment, Jamie reined away, and I followed him.

"Not very canty today, is he?" I remarked, with a flip of the hand back in Murtagh's direction. In fact, the small clansman had grown more testy and irritable with each step in the direction of Beauly. "I take it he's not enchanted with the prospect of visting Lord Lovat?"

Jamie smiled, with a brief backward glance at the small, dark figure, bent in absorption over the rope he was splicing.

"Nay, Murtagh's no friend of Old Simon. He loved my father dearly"— his mouth quirked to one side—"and my mother, as well. He didna care for Lovat's treatment of them. Or for Lovat's methods of getting wives. Murtagh's got an Irish grandmother, but he's related to Primrose Campbell through his mother's side," he explained, as though this made everything crystal clear.

"Who's Primrose Campbell?" I asked, bewildered.

"Oh." Jamie scratched his nose, considering. The wind off the sea was rising steadily, and his hair was being whipped from its lacing, ruddy wisps flickering past his face.

"Primrose Cambell was Lovat's third wife—still is, I suppose," he added, "though she's left him some years since and gone back to her father's house."

"Popular with women, is he?" I murmured.

Jamie snorted. "I suppose ye can call it that. He took his first wife by a forced marriage. Snatched the Dowager Lady Lovat from her bed in the middle o' the night, married her then and there, and went straight back to bed with her. Still," he added fairly, "she did later decide she loved him, so maybe he wasna so bad."

"Must have been rather special in bed, at least," I said flippantly. "Runs in the family, I expect."

He cast me a mildly shocked look, which dissolved into a sheepish grin.

"Aye, well," he said. "If he was or no, it didna help him much. The Dowager's maids spoke up against him, and Simon was outlawed and had to flee to France."

Forced marriages and outlawry, hm? I refrained from further remark on family resemblances, but privately trusted that Jamie wouldn't follow in his grandfather's footsteps with regard to subsequent wives. One had apparently been insufficient for Simon.

"He went to visit King James in Rome and swear his fealty to the Stuarts," Jamie went on, "and then turned round and went straight to William of Orange, King of England, who was visiting in France. He got James to promise him his title and estates, should a restoration come about, and then—God knows how—got a full pardon from William, and was able to come home to Scotland."

Now it was my turn for raised eyebrows. Apparently it wasn't just attractiveness to the opposite sex, then.

Simon had continued his adventures by returning later to France, this time to spy on the Jacobites. Being found out, he was thrown into prison, but escaped, returned to Scotland, masterminded the assembling of the clans under the guise of a hunting-party on the Braes of Mar in 1715—and then managed to get full credit with the English Crown for putting down the resultant Rising.

"Proper old twister, isn't he?" I said, completely intrigued. "Though I suppose he can't have been so old then; only in his forties." Having heard that Lord Lovat was now in his middle seventies, I had been expecting something fairly doddering and decrepit, but was rapidly revising my expectations, in view of these stories.

"My grandsire," Jamie observed evenly, "has by all reports got a character that would enable him to hide conveniently behind a spiral staircase. Anyway," he went on, dismissing his grandfather's character with a wave of his hand, "then he married Margaret Grant, the Grant o' Grant's daughter. It was after she died that he married Primrose Campbell. She was maybe eighteen at the time."

"Was Old Simon enough of a catch for her family to force her into it?" I asked sympathetically.

"By no means, Sassenach." He paused to brush the hair out of his face, tucking the stray locks back behind his ears. "He kent well enough that she wouldna have him, no matter if he was rich as Croesus—which he wasn't—so he had her sent a letter, saying her mother was fallen sick in Edinburgh, and giving the house there she was to go to."

Hastening to Edinburgh, the young and beautiful Miss Campbell had found not her mother, but the old and ingenious Simon Fraser, who had informed her that she was in a notorious house of pleasure, and that her only hope of preserving her good name was to marry him immediately.

"She must have been a right gump, to fall for that one," I remarked cynically.

"Well, she was verra young," Jamie said defensively, "and it wasna an idle threat, either; had she refused him, Old Simon would ha' ruined her reputation without a second thought. In any event, she married him—and regretted it."

"Hmph." I was busy doing sums in my head. The encounter with Primrose Campbell had been only a few years ago, he'd said. Then . . . "Was it the Dowager Lady Lovat or Margaret Grant who was your grandmother?" I asked curiously.

The high cheekbones were chapped by sun and wind; now they flushed a sudden, painful red.

"Neither one," he said. He didn't look at me, but kept his gaze fixed straight ahead, in the direction of Beaufort Castle. His lips were pressed tightly together.

"My father was a bastard," he said at last. He sat straight as a sword in the saddle, and his knuckles were white, fist clenched on the reins. "Acknowledged, but a bastard. By one of the Castle Downie maids."

"Oh," I said. There didn't seem a lot to add.

He swallowed hard; I could see the ripple in his throat.

"I should ha' told ye before," he said stiffly. "I'm sorry."

I reached out to touch his arm; it was hard as iron.

"It doesn't matter, Jamie," I said, knowing even as I spoke that nothing I said could make a difference. "I don't mind in the slightest."

"Aye?" he said at last, still staring straight ahead. "Well . . . I do."

The steadily freshening wind off Moray Firth rustled its way through a hillside of dark pines. The country here was an odd combination of mountain slope and seashore. Thick growth of alders, larch, and birch blanketed the ground on both sides of the narrow track we followed, but as we approached the dark bulk of Beaufort Castle, over everything floated the effluvium of mud flats and kelp.

We were in fact expected; the kilted, ax-armed sentries at the gate made no challenge as we rode through. They looked at us curiously enough, but seemingly without enmity. Jamie sat straight as a king in his saddle. He nodded once to the man on his side, and received a similar nod in return. I had the distinct feeling that we entered the castle flying a white flag of truce; how long that state would last was anyone's guess.

We rode unchallenged into the courtyard of Beaufort Castle, a small edifice as castles went, but sufficiently imposing, for all that, built of the native stone. Not so heavily fortified as some of the castles I had seen to the south, it looked still capable of withstanding a certain amount of abrasion. Wide-mouthed gun-holes gaped at intervals along the base of the outer walls, and the keep still boasted a stable opening onto the courtyard.

Several of the small Highland ponies were housed in this, heads poking over the wooden half-door to whicker in welcome to our own mounts. Near the wall lay a number of packs, recently unloaded from the ponies in the stable.

"Lovat's summoned a few men to meet us," Jamie observed grimly, noting the packs. "Relatives, I expect." He shrugged. "At least they'll be friendly enough to start with."

"How do you know?"

He slid to the ground and reached up to help me down.

"They've left the broadswords wi' the luggage."

Jamie handed over the reins to an ostler who came out of the stables to meet us, dusting his hands on his breeks.

"Er, now what?" I murmured to Jamie under my breath. There was no sign of chatelaine or majordomo; nothing like the cheery, authoritative figure of Mrs. FitzGibbons that had welcomed us to Castle Leoch two years before.

The few ostlers and stable-lads about glanced at us now and then, but continued about their tasks, as did the servants who crossed the courtyard, lugging baskets of laundry, bundles of peat, and all the other cumbrous paraphernalia that living in a stone castle demanded. I looked approvingly after a burly manservant sweating under the burden of two five-gallon copper cans of water. Whatever its shortcomings in the hospitality department, Beaufort Castle at least boasted a bathtub somewhere.

Jamie stood in the center of the courtyard, arms crossed, surveying the place like a prospective buyer of real estate who harbors black doubts about the drains.

"Now we wait, Sassenach," he said. "The sentries will ha' sent word that we're here. Either someone will come down to us . . . or they won't."

"Um," I said. "Well, I hope they make up their minds about it soon; I'm hungry, and I could do with a wash."

"Aye, ye could," Jamie agreed, with a brief smile as he looked me over. "You've a smut on your nose, and there's teasel-heads caught in your hair. No, leave them," he added, as my hand went to my head in dismay. "It looks bonny, did ye do it on purpose or no."

Definitely no, but I left them. Still, I sidled over to a nearby watering trough, to inspect my appearance and remedy it so far as was possible using nothing but cold water.

It was something of a delicate situation, so far as old Simon Fraser was concerned, I thought, bending over the trough and trying to make out which blotches on my reflected complexion were actual smudges and which caused by floating bits of hay.

On the one hand, Jamie was a formal emissary from the Stuarts. Whether Lovat's promises of support for the cause were honest, or mere lip service, chances were that he would feel obliged to welcome the Prince's representative, if only for the sake of courtesy.

On the other hand, said representative was an illegitimately descended grandson who, if not precisely disowned in his own person, certainly wasn't a bosom member of the family, either. And I knew enough by now of Highland feuds to know that ill feeling of this sort was unlikely to be diminished by the passage of time.

I ran a wet hand across my closed eyes and back across my temples, smoothing down stray wisps of hair. On the whole, I didn't think Lord Lovat would leave us standing in the courtyard. He might, however, leave us there long enough to realize fully the dubious nature of our reception.

After that—well, who knew? We would most likely be received by Lady Frances, one of Jamie's aunts, a widow who—from all we had heard from Tullibardine—managed domestic affairs for her father. Or, if he chose to receive us as a diplomatic ambassage rather than as family connections, I supposed that Lord Lovat himself might appear to receive us, supported by the formal panoply of secretary, guards, and servants.

This last possibility seemed most likely, in view of the time it was taking; after all, you wouldn't keep a full-dress entourage standing about—it would take some time to assemble the necessary personnel. Envisioning the sudden appearance of a fully equipped earl, I had second thoughts about leaving teaselheads tangled in my hair, and leaned over the trough again.

At this point, I was interrupted by the sound of footsteps in the passageway behind the mangers. A squat-bodied elderly man in open shirt and unbuckled breeks stepped out into the courtyard, shoving aside a plump chestnut mare with a sharp elbow and an irritable "Tcha!" Despite his age, he had a back like a ramrod, and shoulders nearly as broad as Jamie's.

Pausing by the horse trough, he glanced around the courtyard as though looking for someone. His eye passed over me without registering, then suddenly snapped back, clearly startled. He stepped forward and thrust his face pugnaciously forward, an unshaven gray beard bristling like a porcupine's quills.

"Who the hell are you?" he demanded.

"Claire Fraser, er, I mean, Lady Broch Tuarach," I said, belatedly remembering my dignity. I gathered my self-possession, and wiped a drop of water off my chin. "Who the hell are *you*?" I demanded.

A firm hand gripped my elbow from behind, and a resigned voice from somewhere above my head said, "That, Sassenach, is my grandsire. My lord, may I present my wife?"

"Ah?" said Lord Lovat, giving me the benefit of a cold blue eye. "I'd heard you'd married an Englishwoman." His tone made it clear that this act confirmed all his worst suspicions about the grandson he'd never met.

He raised a thick gray brow in my direction, and shifted the gimlet stare to Jamie. "No more sense than your father, it seems."

I could see Jamie's hands twitch slightly, resisting the urge to clench into fists.

"At the least, I had nay need to take a wife by rape or trickery," he observed evenly.

His grandfather grunted, unfazed by the insult. I thought I saw the corner of his wrinkled mouth twitch, but wasn't sure.

"Aye, and ye've gained little enough by the bargain ye struck," he observed. "Though at that, this one's less expensive than that MacKenzie harlot Brian fell prey to. If this sassenach wench brings ye naught, at least she looks as though she costs ye little." The slanted blue eyes, so much like Jamie's own, ran over my travel-stained gown, taking in the unstitched hem, the burst seam, and the splashes of mud on the skirt.

I could feel a fine vibration run through Jamie, and wasn't sure whether it was anger or laughter.

"Thanks," I said, with a friendly smile at his lordship. "I don't eat much, either. But I could use a bit of a wash. Just water; don't bother about the soap, if it comes too dear."

This time I was sure about the twitch.

"Aye, I see," his lordship said. "I shall send a maid to see ye to your rooms, then. *And* provide ye with soap. We shall see ye in the library before supper . . . grandson," he added to Jamie, and turning on his heel, disappeared back under the archway.

"Who's *we?*" I asked.

"Young Simon, I suppose," Jamie answered. "His lordship's heir. A stray cousin or two, maybe. And some of the tacksmen, I should imagine, judging from the horses in the courtyard. If Lovat's going to consider sending troops to join the Stuarts, his tacksmen and tenants may have a bit to say about it."

"Ever seen a small worm in a barnyard, in the middle of a flock of chickens?" he murmured as we walked down the hall an hour later behind a servant. "That's me—or us, I should say. Stick close to me, now."

The various connections of clan Fraser were indeed assembled; when we were shown into the Beaufort Castle library, it was to find more than twenty men seated around the room.

Jamie was formally introduced, and gave a formal statement on behalf of the Stuarts, giving the respects of Prince Charles and King James to Lord Lovat and appealing for Lovat's help, to which the old man replied briefly, eloquently and noncommittally. Etiquette attended to, I was then brought forward and introduced, and the general atmosphere became more relaxed.

I was surrounded by a number of Highland gentlemen, who took turns exchanging words of welcome with me as Jamie chatted with someone named Graham, who seemed to be Lord Lovat's cousin. The tacksmen eyed me with a certain amount of reserve, but were all courteous enough—with one exception.

Young Simon, much like his father in squatty outline, but nearly fifty years younger, came forward and bowed over my hand. Straightening up, he looked me over with an attention that seemed just barely this side of rudeness.

"Jamie's wife, hm?" he asked. He had the slanted eyes of his father and half-nephew, but his were brown, muddy as bogwater. "I suppose that means I may call ye 'niece,' does it not?" He was just about Jamie's age, clearly a few years younger than I.

"Ha-ha," I said politely, as he chortled at his own wit. I tried to retrieve my hand, but he wasn't letting go. Instead, he smiled jovially, giving me the once-over again.

"I'd heard of ye, you know," he said. "You've a bit of fame through the Highlands, Mistress."

"Oh, really? How nice." I tugged inconspicuously; in response, his hand tightened around mine in a grip that was nearly painful.

"Oh, aye. I've heard you're verra popular with the men of your husband's command," he said, smiling so hard his eyes narrowed to dark-brown slits. "They call ye *neo-geimnidh meala*, I hear. That means 'Mistress Honeylips,' " he translated, seeing my look of bewilderment at the unfamiliar Gaelic.

"Why, thank you . . ." I began, but got no more than the first words out before Jamie's fist crashed into Simon Junior's jaw and sent his half-uncle reeling into a piecrust table, scattering sweetmeats and serving spoons across the polished slates with a terrific clatter.

He dressed like a gentleman, but he had a brawler's instincts. Young Simon rolled up onto his knees, fists clenched, and froze there. Jamie stood over him, fists doubled but loose, his stillness more menacing than open threat.

"No," he said evenly, "she doesna have much Gaelic. And now that ye've proved it to everyone's satisfaction, ye'll kindly apologize to my wife, before I kick your teeth down your throat." Young Simon glowered up at Jamie, then glanced aside at his father, who nodded imperceptibly, looking impatient at this interruption. The younger Fraser's shaggy black hair had come loose from its lacing, and hung like tree moss about his face. He eyed Jamie warily, but with a strange tinge of what looked like amusement as well, mingled with respect. He wiped the back of his hand across his mouth and bowed gravely to me, still on his knees.

"Your pardon, Mistress Fraser, and my apologies for any offense ye may have suffered."

I could do no more than nod graciously in return, before Jamie was steering me out into the corridor. We had almost reached the door at the end before I spoke, glancing back to see that we were not overheard.

"*What* on earth does *neo-geimnidh meala* mean?" I said, jerking on his sleeve to slow him. He glanced down, as though I had just been recalled to his wandering attention.

"Ah? Oh, it means honeylips, all right. More or less."

"But—"

"It's no your mouth he was referring to, Sassenach," Jamie said dryly.

"Why, that—" I made as if to turn back to the study, but Jamie tightened his grip on my arm.

"Cluck, cluck, cluck," he murmured in my ear. "Dinna worry, Sassenach. They're only tryin' me. It will be all right."

I was left in the care of Lady Frances, Young Simon's sister, while Jamie returned to the library, shoulders squared for battle. I hoped he wouldn't hit any more of his relatives; while the Frasers were, on the whole, not as sizable as the MacKenzies, they had a sort of tough watchfulness that boded ill for anyone trying something on in their immediate vicinity.

Lady Frances was young, perhaps twenty-two, and inclined to view me with a sort of terrorized fascination, as though I might spring upon her if not incessantly placated with tea and sweetmeats. I exerted myself to be as pleasant and unthreatening as possible, and after a time, she relaxed sufficiently to confess that she had never met an Englishwoman before. "Englishwoman," I gathered, was an exotic and dangerous species.

I was careful to make no sudden moves, and after a bit, she grew comfortable enough to introduce me shyly to her son, a sturdy little chap of three or so, maintained in a state of unnatural cleanliness by the constant watchfulness of a stern-faced maidservant.

I was telling Frances and her younger sister Aline about Jenny and her family, whom they had never met, when there was a sudden crash and a cry in the hallway outside. I sprang to my feet, and reached the sitting-room door in time to see a huddled bundle of cloth struggling to rise to its feet in the stone corridor. The heavy door to the library stood open, and the squat figure of Simon Fraser the elder stood framed in it, malevolent as a toad.

"Ye'll get worse than that, my lass, and ye make no better job of it," he said. His tone was not particularly menacing; only a statement of fact. The bundled figure raised its head, and I saw an odd, angularly pretty face, dark eyes wide over the red blotch deepening on her cheekbone. She saw me, but made no acknowledgment of my presence, only getting to her feet and hurrying away without a word. She was very tall and extremely thin, and moved with the strange, half-clumsy grace of a crane, her shadow following her down the stones.

I stood staring at Old Simon, silhouetted against the firelight from the library behind him. He felt my eyes upon him, and turned his head to look at me. The old blue eyes rested on me, cold as sapphires.

"Good evening, my dear," he said, and closed the door.

I stood looking blankly at the dark wooden door.

"What was *that* all about?" I asked Frances, who had come up behind me.

"Nothing," she said, licking her lips nervously. "Come away, Cousin." I let her pull me away, but resolved to ask Jamie later what had happened in the library.

We had reached the chamber allotted us for the night, and Jamie graciously dismissed our small guide with a pat on the head.

I sank down on the bed, gazing around helplessly.

"*Now* what do we do?" I asked. Dinner had passed with little to remark, but I had felt the weight of Lovat's eyes on me from time to time.

Jamie shrugged, pulling his shirt over his head.

"Damned if I know, Sassenach," he said. "They asked me the state of the Highland army, the condition of the troops, what I knew of His Highness's plans. I told them. And then they asked it all again. My grandfather's no inclined to think anyone could be giving him a straight answer," he added dryly. "He thinks everyone must be as twisted as himself, wi' a dozen different motives; one for every occasion."

He shook his head and tossed the shirt onto the bed next to me.

"He canna tell whether I might be lying about the state of the Highland army or no. For if I wanted him to join the Stuarts, then I might say as how things were better than they are, where if I didna care personally, one way or the other, then I might tell the truth. And he doesna mean to commit himself one way or the other until he thinks he knows where I stand."

"And just how does he mean to tell whether you *are* telling the truth?" I asked skeptically.

"He has a seer," he replied casually, as though this were one of the normal furnishings of a Highland castle. For all I knew, it was.

"Really?" I sat up on the bed, intrigued. "Is that the odd-looking woman he threw out into the hall?"

"Aye. Her name's Maisri, and she's had the Sight since she was born. But she couldna tell him anything—or wouldn't," he added. "It was clear enough she knows *something,* but she'd do naught but shake her head and say she couldn't see. That's when my grandsire lost patience and struck her."

"Bloody old crumb!" I said, indignant.

"Well, he's no the flower o' gallantry," Jamie agreed.

He poured out a basin of water and began to splash handfuls over his face. He looked up, startled and streaming, at my gasp.

"Hah?"

"Your stomach . . ." I said, pointing. The skin between breastbone and kilt was mottled with a large fresh bruise, spreading like a large, unsightly blossom on his fair skin.

Jamie glanced down, said "Oh, that," dismissively, and returned to his washing.

"Yes, *that*," I said, coming to take a closer look. "What happened?"

"It's no matter," he said, speech coming thickly through a towel. "I spoke a bit hasty this afternoon, and my grandsire had Young Simon give me a small lesson in respect."

"So he had a couple of minor Frasers hold you while he punched you in the belly?" I said, feeling slightly ill.

Tossing the towel aside, Jamie reached for his nightshirt.

"Verra flattering of you to suppose it took two to hold me," he said, grinning as his head popped through the opening. "Actually, there were three; one was behind, chokin' me."

"Jamie!"

He laughed, shaking his head ruefully as he pulled back the quilt on the bed.

"I don't know what it is about ye, Sassenach, that always makes me want to show off for ye. Get myself killed one of these days, tryin' to impress ye, I expect." He sighed, gingerly smoothing the woolen shirt over his stomach. "It's only play-acting, Sassenach; ye shouldna worry."

"Play-acting! Good God, Jamie!"

"Have ye no seen a strange dog join a pack, Sassenach? The others sniff at him, and nip at his legs, and growl, to see will he cower or growl back at them. And sometimes it comes to biting, and sometimes not, but at the end of it, every dog in the pack knows his place, and who's leader. Old Simon wants to be sure I ken who leads this pack; that's all."

"Oh? And do you?" I lay down, waiting for him to come to bed. He picked up the candle and grinned down at me, the flickering light picking up a blue gleam in his eyes.

"Woof," he said, and blew out the candle.

I saw very little of Jamie for the next two weeks, save at night. During the day, he was always with his grandfather, hunting or riding—for Lovat was a vigorous man, despite his age—or drinking in the study, as the Old Fox slowly drew his conclusions and laid his plans.

I spent most of my time with Frances and the other women. Out of the shadow of her redoubtable old father, Frances gained enough courage to speak her own mind, and proved an intelligent and interesting companion. She had the responsibility for the smooth running of the castle and its staff, but when her father appeared on the scene, she dwindled into insignificance, seldom raising her eyes or speaking above a whisper. I wasn't sure I blamed her.

Two weeks after our arrival, Jamie came to fetch me from the drawing room where I sat with Frances and Aline, saying that Lord Lovat wished to see me.

Old Simon waved a casual hand at the decanters set on the table by the wall, then sat down in a wide-seated chair of carved walnut, with crushed padding in well-worn blue velvet. The chair fitted his short, stocky form as though it had been built around him; I wondered whether it had in fact been built to order, or whether, from long use, he had grown into the shape of the chair.

I sat down quietly in a corner with my glass of port, and kept quiet while Simon questioned Jamie once again about Charles Stuart's situation and prospects.

For the twentieth time in a week, Jamie patiently rehearsed the number of troops available, the structure of command—insofar as one existed—the armament on hand and its condition—mostly poor—the prospects of Charles being joined by Lord Lewis Gordon or the Farquharsons, what Glengarry had said following Prestonpans, what Cameron knew or deduced of the movement of English troops, why Charles had decided to march south, and so on and so forth. I found myself nodding over the cup in my hand, and jerked myself into wakefulness, just in time to keep the ruby liquid from tipping onto my skirt.

". . . and Lord George Murray and Kilmarnock both think His Highness would be best advised to pull back into the Highlands for the winter," Jamie concluded, yawning widely. Cramped on the narrow-backed chair he had been given, he rose and stretched, his shadow flickering on the pale hangings that covered the stone walls.

"And what d'ye think, yourself?" Old Simon's eyes glittered under half-fallen lids as he leaned back in his chair. The fire burned high and bright on the hearth; Frances had smoored the fire in the main hall, covering it with peats, but this one had been rekindled at Lovat's order, and with wood, not peat. The smell of pine resin from the burning wood was sharp, mingled with the thicker smell of smoke.

The light cast Jamie's shadow high on the wall as he turned restlessly, not wanting to sit down again. It was close and dark in the small study, with the window draped against the night—very different from the open, sunny kirkyard in which Colum had asked him the same question. And the situation now had shifted; no longer the popular darling to whom clan chieftains deferred, Charles now was sending to the chiefs, grimly calling in his obligations. But the shape of the problem was the same—a dark, amorphous shape, hanging like a shadow over us.

"I've told ye what I think—a dozen times or more." Jamie spoke abruptly. He moved his shoulders impatiently, shrugging as though the fit of his coat was too tight.

"Oh, aye. You've told me. But this time I think we shall have the truth."

The old man settled more comfortably into his padded chair, hands linked across his belly.

"Will ye, then?" Jamie uttered a short laugh, and turned to face his grandfather. He leaned back against the table, hands braced behind him. Despite the differences in posture and figure, there was a tension between the two men that brought out a fugitive resemblance between them. The one tall and the other squat, but both of them strong, stubborn, and determined to win this encounter.

"Am I not your kinsman? And your chief? I command your loyalty, do I not?"

So that was the point. Colum, so accustomed to physical weakness, had known the secret of turning another man's weakness to his own purposes. Simon Fraser, strong and vigorous even in old age, was accustomed to getting his own way by more direct means. I could see from the sour smile on Jamie's face that he, too, was contrasting Colum's appeal with his grandfather's demand.

"Can ye? I dinna recall that I've sworn ye an oath."

Several long stiff hairs grew out of Simon's eyebrows, in the way of old men. These quivered in the firelight, though I couldn't tell whether with indignation or amusement.

"Oath, is it? And is it not Fraser blood in your veins?"

Jamie's mouth twisted wryly as he answered. "They do say that it's a wise child as kens his own father, no? My mother was a MacKenzie; I know that much."

Simon's face grew dark with blood, and his brows drew together. Then his mouth fell open, and he shouted with laughter. He laughed until he was forced to pull himself up in the chair and bend forward, sputtering and choking. At last, beating one hand on the arm of the chair in helpless mirth, he reached into his mouth with the other and pulled out his false teeth.

"Dod," he sputtered, gasping and wheezing. Face streaming with tears and saliva, he groped blindly for the small table by his chair, and dropped the teeth onto the cake plate. The gnarled fingers closed on a linen napkin, and he pressed it to his face, still emitting strangled grunts of laughter as he conducted his mopping up.

"Chrith, laddie," he said at last, lisping heavily. "Path me the whithky."

Eyebrows raised, Jamie took the decanter from the table behind him and passed it to his grandfather, who removed the stopper and gulped a substantial amount of the contents without bothering about the formality of a glass.

"You think you're not a Frather?" he said, lowering the decanter and exhaling gustily. "Ha!" He leaned back once more, belly rising and falling rapidly as he caught his breath. He pointed a long, skinny finger at Jamie.

"Your own father thtood right where you're thstanding, laddie, and told me jutht what you did, the day he left Beaufort Cathtle once and for all." The old man was growing calmer now; he coughed several times and wiped his face again.

"Did ye know that I'd tried to thtop your parents' marriage by claiming that Ellen MacKenzie's child wathn't Brian's?"

"Aye, I knew." Jamie was leaning back on the table again, surveying his grandfather through narrowed eyes.

Lord Lovat snorted. "I'll not thay there's been always goodwill atween me and mine, but I know my thons. *And* my grandthons," he added pointedly. "De'il take me and I think any one of 'em could be a cuckold, nay more than I could."

Jamie didn't turn a hair, but I couldn't stop myself from glancing away from the old man. I found myself staring at his discarded teeth, the stained beechwood gleaming wetly amid the cake crumbs. Luckily Lord Lovat hadn't noticed my slight motion.

He went on, serious once more. "Now, then. Dougal MacKenzie of Leoch hath declared for Charles. D'ye call him your chief? Is that what ye're telling me—that ye've given him an oath?"

"No. I havena sworn to anyone."

"Not even Charles?" The old man was fast, pouncing on this like a cat on a mouse. I could almost see his tail twitch as he watched Jamie, slanted eyes deep-set and gleaming under crepey lids.

Jamie's eyes were fixed on the leaping flames, his shadow motionless on the wall behind him.

"He hasna asked me." This was true. Charles had had no need to request an oath from Jamie—having precluded the necessity by signing Jamie's name to his Bond of Association. Still, I knew that he had not, in fact, given his word to Charles was important to Jamie. If he must betray the man, let it not be as an acknowledged chief. The idea that the entire world thought such an oath existed was a matter of much less concern.

Simon grunted again. Without his false teeth, his nose and chin came close together, making the lower half of his face oddly foreshortened.

"Then nothing hampers you to thwear to me, as chief of your clan," he said quietly. The twitching tail was less visible, but still there. I could almost hear the thoughts in his head, gliding round on padded feet. With Jamie's loyalty sworn to him, rather than Charles, Lovat's power would be increased. As would his wealth, with a share of the income from Lallybroch that he might claim as his chieftain's due. The prospect of a dukedom drew slightly nearer, gleaming through the mist.

"Nothing save my own will," Jamie agreed pleasantly. "But that's some small obstacle, no?" His own eyes creased at the corners as they narrowed further.

"Mmphm." Lovat's eyes were almost closed, and he shook his head slowly from side to side. "Oh, aye, lad, you're your father's thon. Thtubborn as a block, and twith ath thtupid. I thould have known that Brian would thire nothing but fools from that harlot."

Jamie reached forward and plucked the beechwood teeth from the plate. "Ye'd better put these back, ye auld gomerel," he said rudely. "I canna understand a word ye say."

His grandfather's mouth widened in a humorless smile that showed the yellowed stump of a lone broken tooth in the lower jaw.

"No?" he said. "Will ye underthand a bargain?" He shot a quick look at me, seeing nothing more than another counter to be put into play. "Your oath for your wife's honor, how's that?"

Jamie laughed out loud, still holding the teeth in one hand.

"Oh, aye? D'ye mean to force her before my eyes, then, Grandsire?" He lounged back contemptuously, hand on the table. "Go ahead, and when she's done wi' ye, I'll send Aunt Frances up to sweep up the pieces."

His grandfather looked him over calmly. "Not I, lad." One side of the toothless mouth rose in a lopsided smile as he turned his head to look at me. "Though I've taken my pleasure with worthe." The cold malice in the dark eyes made me want to pull my cloak over my breasts in protection; unfortunately, I wasn't wearing one.

"How many men are there in Beaufort, Jamie? How many, who'd be of a mind to put your thathenach wench to the only uth thee's good for? You cannot guard her night and day."

Jamie straightened slowly, the great shadow echoing his movements on the wall. He stared down at his grandfather with no expression on his face.

"Oh, I think I needna worry, Grandsire," he said softly. "For my wife's a rare woman. A wisewoman, ye ken. A white lady, like Dame Aliset."

I had never heard of Dame Aliset, but Lord Lovat plainly had; his head jerked round to stare at me, eyes sprung wide with shocked alarm. His mouth drooped open, but before he could speak, Jamie had gone on, an undercurrent of malice clearly audible in his smooth speech.

"The man that takes her in unholy embrace will have his privates blasted like a frostbitten apple," he said, with relish, "and his soul will burn forever in hell." He bared his teeth at his grandfather, and drew back his hand. "Like this." The beechwood teeth landed in the midst of the fire with a plop, and at once began to sizzle.

41

The Seer's Curse

ost of the Lowland Scots had gone over to Presbyterianism in the two centuries before. Some of the Highland clans had gone with them, but others, like the Frasers and Mac-Kenzies, had kept their Catholic faith. Especially the Frasers, with their strong family ties to Catholic France.

There was a small chapel in Beaufort Castle, to serve the devotional uses of the Earl and his family, but Beauly Priory, ruined as it was, remained the burying place of the Lovats, and the floor of the open-roofed chancel was paved thick with the flat tombstones of those who lay under them.

It was a peaceful place, and I walked there sometimes, in spite of the cold, blustery weather. I had no idea whether Old Simon had meant his threat against me, or whether Jamie's comparing me to Dame Aliset—who turned out to be a legendary "white woman" or healer, the Scottish equivalent of La Dame Blanche—was sufficient to put a stop to that threat. But I thought that no one was likely to accost me among the tombs of extinct Frasers.

One afternoon, a few days after the scene in the study, I walked through a gap in the ruined Priory wall and found that for once, I didn't have it to myself. The tall woman I had seen outside Lovat's study was there, leaning against one of the red-stone tombs, arms folded about her for warmth, long legs thrust out like a stork.

I made to turn aside, but she saw me, and motioned me to join her.

"You'll be my lady Broch Tuarach?" she said, though there was no more than a hint of question in her soft Highland voice.

"I am. And you're . . . Maisri?"

A small smile lit her face. She had a most intriguing face, slightly asymmetrical, like a Modigliani painting, and long black hair that flowed loose around her shoulders, streaked with white, though she was plainly still young. A seer, hm? I thought she looked the part.

"Aye, I have the Sight," she said, the smile widening a bit on her lopsided mouth.

"Do mind-reading, too, do you?" I asked.

She laughed, the sound vanishing on the wind that moaned through the ruined walls.

"No, lady. But I do read faces, and . . ."

"And mine's an open book. I know," I said, resigned.

We stood side by side for a time then, watching tiny spatters of fine sleet dashing against the sandstone and the thick brown grass that overgrew the kirkyard.

"They do say as you're a white lady," Maisri observed suddenly. I could feel her watching me intently, but with none of the nervousness that seemed common to such an observation.

"They do say that," I agreed.

"Ah." She didn't speak again, just stared down at her feet, long and elegant, stockinged in wool and clad in leather sandals. My own toes, rather more sheltered, were growing numb, and I thought hers must be frozen solid, if she'd been here any time.

"What are you doing up here?" I asked. The Priory was a beautiful, peaceful place in good weather, but not much of a roost in the cold winter sleet.

"I come here to think," she said. She gave me a slight smile, but was plainly preoccupied. Whatever she was thinking, her thoughts weren't overly pleasant.

"To think about what?" I asked, hoisting myself up to sit on the tomb beside her. The worn figure of a knight lay on the lid, his claymore clasped to his bosom, the hilt forming a cross over his heart.

"I want to know why!" she burst out. Her thin face was suddenly alight with indignation.

"Why what?"

"Why! Why can I see what will happen, when there's no mortal thing I can be doin' to change it or stop it? What's the good of a gift like that? It's no a gift, come to that—it's a damn curse, though I havena done anything to be cursed like this!"

She turned and glared balefully at Thomas Fraser, serene under his helm, with the hilt of his sword clasped under crossed hands.

"Aye, and maybe it's *your* curse, ye auld gomerel! You and the rest o' your damned family. Did ye ever think that?" she asked suddenly, turning to me. Her brows arched high over brown eyes that sparked with furious intelligence.

"Did ye ever think perhaps that it's no your own fate at all that makes you what ye are? That maybe ye have the Sight or the power only because it's necessary to someone else, and it's nothing to do wi' you at all—except that it's you has it, and has to suffer the having of it. Have you?"

"I don't know," I said slowly. "Or yes, since you say it, I have wondered. Why me? You ask that all the time, of course. But I've never come up with a satisfactory answer. You think perhaps you have the Sight because it's a curse on the Frasers—to know their deaths ahead of time? That's a hell of an idea."

"A hell is right," she agreed bitterly. She leaned back against the sarcophagus of red stone, staring out at the sleet that sprayed across the top of the broken wall.

"What d'ye think?" she asked suddenly. "Do I tell him?"

I was startled.

"Who? Lord Lovat?"

"Aye, his lordship. He asks what I see, and beats me when I tell him there's naught to see. He knows, ye ken; he sees it in my face when I've had the Sight. But that's the only power I've got; the power not to say." The long white fingers snaked out from her cloak, playing nervously with the folds of soaked cloth.

"There's always the chance of it, isn't there?" she said. Her head was bent so that the hood of her cloak shielded her face from my gaze. "There's a chance that my telling would make a difference. It has, now and then, ye know. I told Lachlan Gibbons when I saw his son-in-law wrapped in seaweed, and the eels stirring beneath his shirt. Lachlan listened; he went out straightaway and stove a hole in his son-in-law's boat." She laughed, remembering. "Lord, there was the kebbie-lebbie to do! But when the great storm came the next week, three men were drowned, and Lachlan's son-in-law was safe at hame, still mending his boat. And when I saw him next, his shirt hung dry on him, and the seaweed was gone from his hair."

"So it can happen," I said softly. "Sometimes."

"Sometimes," she said, nodding, still staring at the ground. Lady Sarah Fraser lay at her feet, the lady's stone surmounted with a skull atop crossed bones. *Hodie mihi cras tibi,* said the inscription. *Sic transit gloria mundi.* My turn today, yours tomorrow. And thus passes away the glory of the world.

"Sometimes not. When I see a man wrapped in his winding sheet, the illness follows—and there's naught to be done about that."

"Perhaps," I said. I looked at my own hands, spread on the stone beside me. Without medicine, without instruments, without knowledge—yes, then illness was fate, and naught to be done. But if a healer was near, and had the things to heal with . . . was it possible that Maisri saw the shadow of a coming illness, as a real—if usually invisible—symptom, much like a fever or a rash? And then only the lack of medical facilities made the reading of such symptoms a sentence of death? I would never know.

"We aren't ever going to know," I said, turning to her. "We can't say. We know things that other people don't know, and we can't say why or how. But we have got it—and you're right, it's a curse. But if you have knowledge, and it *may* prevent harm . . . do you think it could *cause* harm?"

She shook her head.

"I canna say. If you knew ye were to die soon, are there things you'd do? And would they be good things only that ye'd do, or would ye take the last chance ye might have to do harm to your enemies—harm that might otherwise be left alone?"

"Damned if I know." We were quiet for a time, watching the sleet turn to snow, and the blowing flakes whirl up in gusts through the ruined tracery of the Priory wall.

"Sometimes I know there's something there, like," Maisri said suddenly, "but I can block it out of my mind, not look. 'Twas like that with his lordship; I knew there was something, but I'd managed not to see it. But then he bade me look, and say the divining spell to make the vision come clear. And I did." The hood of her cloak slipped back as she tilted her head, looking up at the wall of the Priory as it soared above us, ochre and white and red, with the mortar crumbling between its stones. White-streaked black hair spilled down her back, free in the wind.

"He was standing there before the fire, but it was daylight, and clear to see. A man stood behind him, still as a tree, and his face covered in black. And across his lordship's face there fell the shadow of an ax."

She spoke matter-of-factly, but the shiver ran up my spine nonetheless. She sighed at last, and turned to me.

"Weel, I will tell him, then, and let him do what he will. Doom him or save him, that I canna do. It's his choice—and the Lord Jesus help him."

She turned to go, and I slid off the tomb, landing on the Lady Sarah's slab.

"Maisri," I said. She turned back to look at me, eyes black as the shadows among the tombs.

"Aye?"

"What do you see, Maisri?" I asked, and stood waiting, facing her, hands dropped to my sides.

She stared at me hard, above and below, behind and beside. At last she smiled faintly, nodding.

"I see naught but you, lady," she said softly. "There's only you."

She turned and disappeared down the path between the trees, leaving me among the blowing flakes of snow.

Doom, or save. That I cannot do. For I have no power beyond that of knowledge, no ability to bend others to my will, no way to stop them doing what *they* will. There is only me.

I shook the snow from the folds of my cloak, and turned to follow Maisri down the path, sharing her bitter knowledge that there was only me. And I was not enough.

Old Simon's manner was much as usual over the course of the next two or three weeks, but I imagined that Maisri had kept her intention of telling him about her visions. While he had seemed on the verge of summoning the tacksmen and tenants to march, suddenly he backed off, saying that there was no hurry, after all. This shilly-shallying infuriated Young Simon, who was champing at the bit to go to war and cover himself with glory.

"It's not a matter of urgency," Old Simon said, for the dozenth time. He lifted an oatcake, sniffed at it, and set it down again. "Perhaps we'll do best to wait for the spring planting, after all."

"They could be in London before spring!" Young Simon glowered across the dinner table at his father and reached for the butter. "If ye will not go yourself, then let me take the men to join His Highness!"

Lord Lovat grunted. "You've the Devil's own impatience," he said, "but not half his judgment. Will ye never learn to wait?"

"The time for waiting's long since past!" Simon burst out. "The Camerons, the MacDonalds, the MacGillivrays—they've all been there since the first. Are we to come meachin' along at the finish, to find ourselves beggars, and taking second place to Clanranald and Glengarry? Fat chance you'll have of a dukedom then!"

Lovat had a wide, expressive mouth; even in old age, it retained some trace of humor and sensuality. Neither was visible at the moment. He pressed his lips tight together, surveying his heir without enthusiasm.

"Marry in haste, repent at leisure," he said. "And it's more true when choosing a laird than a lass. A woman can be got rid of."

Young Simon snorted and looked at Jamie for support. Over the last two months, his initial suspicious hostility had faded into a reluctant respect for his bastard relative's obvious expertise in the art of war.

"Jamie says . . ." he began.

"I ken well enough what he says," Old Simon interrupted. "He's said it often enough. I shall make up my own mind in my own time. But bear it in mind, lad—when it comes to declaring yourself in a war, there's little to be lost by waiting."

"Waiting to see who wins," Jamie murmured, studiously wiping his plate with a bit of bread. The old man looked up sharply, but evidently decided to ignore this contribution.

"Ye gave your word to the Stuarts," Young Simon continued stubbornly, paying no heed to his father's displeasure. "Ye dinna mean to break it, surely? What will people say of your honor?"

"The same things they said in '15," his father calmly replied. "Most of those who 'said things' then are dead, bankrupt, or paupers in France. But I am still here."

"But . . ." Young Simon was red in the face, the usual result of this sort of conversation with his father.

"That will do," the old Earl interrupted sharply. He shook his head as he glared at his son, lips tight with disapproval. "Christ. Sometimes I could wish that Brian hadna died. He may have been a fool, too, but at least he knew when to stop talking."

Both Young Simon and Jamie flushed with anger, but after a wary glance at each other, turned their attentions to their food.

"And what are you looking at?" Lord Lovat growled, catching my eye on him as he turned away from his son.

"You," I said bluntly. "You don't look at all well." He didn't, even for a man in his seventies. No more than middle-height, slumped and broadened by age, he was normally still a solid-looking man, giving the impression that his barrel chest and rounded paunch were firm and healthy under his linen. Lately he had begun to look flabby, though, as if he had shrunk a bit within his skin. The wrinkled bags beneath his eyes were darkened, and his skin had a sickly pallor to it.

"Mphm," he grunted. "And why not? I get nay rest when I sleep, nor comfort when I'm awake. No wonder if I dinna look like a bridegroom."

"Oh, but ye do, Father," said Young Simon maliciously, seeing a chance to get a bit of his own back. "One at the end of his honeymoon, wi' all the juice sapped out of him."

"Simon!" said Lady Frances. Still, there was a ripple of laughter around the table at this, and even Lord Lovat's mouth twitched slightly.

"Aye?" he said. "Well, I'd sooner suffer soreness from that cause, I'll tell ye, lad." He shifted uncomfortably in his seat, and pushed away the platter of boiled turnips being offered. He reached for his wineglass, raised it to his nose for a sniff, then morosely put it down again.

"It's ill-mannered to stare," he remarked coldly to me. "Or perhaps the English have different standards of politeness?"

I flushed slightly, but didn't drop my eyes. "I was just wondering—you don't have an appetite, and you don't drink. What other symptoms have you?"

"Going to prove yourself some worth, eh?" Lovat leaned back in his chair, folding his hands across his broad stomach like an elderly frog. "A healer, my grandson says. A white lady, aye?" He flicked a basilisk glance at Jamie, who simply went on eating, ignoring his grandfather. Lovat grunted, and tilted his head ironically in my direction.

"Well, I dinna drink, lady, for I canna piss, and I've little wish to blow up like a pig's bladder. And I dinna rest, for I rise a dozen times a night to make use of my pot, and damn little use it gets. So what have ye to say to that, Dame Aliset?"

"Father," murmured Lady Frances, "really, I don't think you should . . ."

"Could be an infection of the bladder, but it sounds like prostatitis to me," I replied. I picked up my wineglass and took a mouthful, savoring it before letting it slide down my throat. I smiled demurely at his lordship across my glass as I set it down.

"Oh, it does?" he said, eyebrows raised high. "And what's that, pray?"

I pushed back my sleeves and raised my hands, flexing my fingers like a magician about to perform some act of prestidigitation. I held up my left forefinger.

"The prostate gland in males," I said instructively, "encircles the tube of the urethra—which is the passage that leads from the bladder to the outside." I clasped two fingers of my right hand in a circle around my left forefinger, in illustration. "When the prostate becomes inflamed or enlarged—and that's called prostatitis, when it does—it clamps down on the urethra"—I narrowed the circle of my fingers—"cutting off the flow of urine. Very common in older men. Do you see?"

Lady Frances, failing to make any impression on her father with her opinions of proper dinner conversation, was whispering agitatedly to her younger sister, both of them watching me with deeper suspicion than usual.

Lord Lovat watched my little demonstration in fascination.

"Aye, I see," he said. The slanted cat-eyes narrowed, looking speculatively at my fingers. "What's to do about it, then, if ye've so much learning on the subject?"

I thought, frowning as I searched my memory. I had never actually seen— much less treated—a case of prostatitis, as it wasn't a condition that much afflicted young soldiers. Still, I had read medical texts where it was described; I remembered the treatment, because it had caused such hilarity among the student nurses, who had pored in fascinated horror over the rather graphic illustrations in the text.

"Well," I said, "barring surgery, there are really only two things you can do. You can insert a metal rod through the penis and up into the bladder, to force the urethra open"—I jabbed my forefinger through the constricting circle —"or you can massage the prostate itself, to reduce the swelling. Through the rectum," I added helpfully.

I heard a faint choking noise next to me, and glanced up at Jamie. His eyes were still fixed on his plate, but the tide of crimson was creeping upward from his collar, and the tips of his ears blazed red. He quivered slightly. I looked around the table, to find a phalanx of fascinated gazes fixed on me. The Lady Frances, Aline, and the other women were staring at me with varying expressions, ranging from curiosity to disgust, while the men all wore variations of revolted horror.

The exception to the general reaction was Lord Lovat himself, who was rubbing his chin thoughtfully, eyes half-closed.

"Mmphm," he said. "Hell of a choice, there. A stick up the cock, or a finger up the backside, eh?"

"More like two or three," I said. "Repeatedly." I gave him a small, decorous smile.

"Ah." A similar small smile decorated Lord Lovat's mouth, and he slowly lifted his gaze, fixing deep blue eyes on mine with an expression of mockery tinged with challenge.

"That sounds . . . diverting," he observed mildly. The slanted eyes slid down over my hands, assessing.

"You've lovely hands, my dear," he said. "Prettily kept, and such long white slender fingers, aye?"

Jamie brought both his own hands down on the table with a crash and stood up. He leaned across the table, bringing his face within a foot of his grandfather's.

"And you're needing such attentions, Grandsire," he said. "I'll see to it myself." He spread out his hands on the tabletop, broad and massive, each long finger the rough diameter of a pistol barrel. "It's no pleasure to me to be stickin' my fingers up your hairy auld arse," he informed his grandfather, "but I expect it's my filial duty to save ye from exploding in a shower of piss, no?"

Frances emitted a faint squeak.

Lord Lovat eyed his grandson with considerable disfavor, then rose slowly from his seat.

"Don't trouble yourself," he said shortly. "I'll ha' one of the maidservants do it." He waved a hand at the company, giving notice that we might continue the meal, and left the hall, pausing to look speculatively at a young serving girl coming in with a platter of sliced pheasant. Eyes wide, she turned sideways to edge past him.

There was a dead silence over the dinner table following his lordship's exit. Young Simon looked at me and opened his mouth. Then he glanced at Jamie, and closed it again. He cleared his throat.

"I'll have the salt, if ye please," he said.

". . . and in consequence of the regrettable infirmity that prevents me from personal attendance upon Your Highness, I send by the hand of my son and heir a token of the loyalty—nay, make that 'regard'—a token of the regard in which I have long cherished His Majesty and Your Highness." Lord Lovat paused, frowning at the ceiling.

"What shall we send, Gideon?" he asked the secretary. "Rich-looking, but not so much I can't say it was only a trifling present of no importance."

Gideon sighed and wiped his face with a handkerchief. A stout, middle-aged man with thinning hair and round red cheeks, he plainly found the heat of the bedroom fire oppressive.

"The ring your lordship had from the Earl of Mar?" he suggested, without hope. A drop of sweat fell from his double chin onto the letter he was taking down, and he surreptitiously blotted it with his sleeve.

"Not expensive enough," his lordship judged, "and too many political associations." The mottled fingers tapped pensively on the coverlet as he thought.

Old Simon had done it up brown, I thought. He was wearing his best nightshirt, and was propped up in bed with an impressive panoply of medicines arrayed on the table, attended by his personal physician, Dr. Menzies, a small man with a squint who kept eyeing me with considerable doubt. I supposed the old man simply distrusted Young Simon's powers of imagination, and had staged this elaborate tableau so that his heir might faithfully report Lord Lovat's state of decrepitude when he presented himself to Charles Stuart.

"Ha," said his lordship with satisfaction. "We'll send the gold and sterling picnic set. That's rich enough, but too frivolous to be interpreted as political support. Besides," he added practically, "the spoon's dented. All right then," he said to the secretary, "let's go on with 'As Your Highness is aware . . .'"

I exchanged a glance with Jamie, who hid a smile in response.

"I think you've given him what he needs, Sassenach," he had told me as we undressed after our fateful dinner the week before.

"And what's that?" I asked, "an excuse to molest the maidservants?"

"I doubt he bothers greatly wi' excuses of that sort," Jamie said dryly. "Nay, you've given him a way to walk both sides—as usual. If he's got an impressive-sounding disease that keeps him to his bed, then he canna be blamed for not appearing himself wi' the men he promised. At the same time, if he sends his heir to fight, the Stuarts will credit Lovat with keeping his promise, and if it goes wrong, the Old Fox will claim to the English that he didna intend to give any aid to the Stuarts, but Young Simon went on his own account."

"Spell 'prostatitis' for Gideon, would ye, lass?" Lord Lovat called to me, breaking into my thoughts. "And mind ye write it out carefully, clot," he said to his secretary, "I dinna want His Highness to misread it."

"P-r-o-s-t-a-t-i-t-i-s," I spelled slowly, for Gideon's benefit. "And how is it this morning, anyway?" I asked, coming to stand by his lordship's bedside.

"Greatly improved, I thank ye," the old man said, grinning up at me with a fine display of false teeth. "Want to see me piss?"

"Not just now, thanks," I said politely.

It was a clear, icy day in mid-December when we left Beauly to join Charles Stuart and the Highland army. Against all advice, Charles had pressed on into England, defying weather and common sense, as well as his generals. But at last, in Derby, the generals had prevailed, the Highland chiefs refusing to go farther, and the Highland army was returning northward. An urgent letter from Charles to Jamie had urged us to head south "without delay," to rendezvous with His Highness upon his return to Edinburgh. Young Simon, looking every inch the clan chieftain in his crimson tartan, rode at the head of a column of men. Those men with mounts followed him, while the larger number on foot walked behind.

Being mounted, we rode with Simon at the head of the column, until such time as we would reach Comar. There we would part company, Simon and the Fraser troops to go to Edinburgh, Jamie ostensibly escorting me to Lallybroch before returning to Edinburgh himself. He had, of course, no intention of so returning, but that was none of Simon's business.

At midmorning, I emerged from a small wooded clump by the side of the track, to find Jamie waiting impatiently. Hot ale had been served to the departing men, to hearten them for the journey. And while I had myself found that hot ale made a surprisingly good breakfast, I had also found it had a marked effect on the kidneys.

Jamie snorted. "Women," he said. "How can ye all take such the devil of a time to do such a simple thing as piss? Ye make as much fuss over it as my grandsire."

"Well, you can come along next time and watch," I suggested acerbically. "Perhaps you'll have some helpful suggestions."

He merely snorted again, and turned back to watch the column of men filing past, but he was smiling nonetheless. The clear, bright day raised everyone's spirits, but Jamie was in a particularly good mood this morning. And no wonder; we were going home. I knew he didn't deceive himself that all would be well; this war would have its price. But if we had failed to stop Charles, it might still be that we could save the small corner of Scotland that lay closest to us—Lallybroch. That much might be still within our power.

I glanced at the trailing column of clansmen.

"Two hundred men make a fair show."

"A hundred and seventy," Jamie corrected absently, reaching for his horse's reins.

"Are you sure?" I asked curiously. "Lord Lovat said he was sending two hundred. I heard him dictating the letter saying so."

"Well, he didn't." Jamie swung into the saddle, then stood up in his stirrups, pointing down the slope ahead, to the distant spot where the Fraser banner with its stag's-head crest fluttered at the head of the column.

"I counted them while I waited for you," he explained. "Thirty cavalry up there wi' Simon, then fifty wi' broadswords and targes—those will be the men from the local Watch—and then the cottars, wi' everything from scythes to hammers at their belts, and there's ninety of those."

"I suppose your grandfather's betting on Prince Charles not counting them personally," I observed cynically. "Trying to get credit for more than he's sent."

"Aye, but the names will be entered on the army rolls when they reach Edinburgh," Jamie said, frowning. "I'd best see."

I followed more sedately. I judged my mount to be approximately twenty years old, and capable of no more than a staid amble. Jamie's mount was a trifle friskier, though still no match for Donas. The huge stallion had been left in Edinburgh, as Prince Charles wished to ride him on public occasions. Jamie had acceded to this request, as he harbored suspicions that Old Simon might well be capable of appropriating the big horse, should Donas come within reach of his rapacious grasp.

Judging from the tableau unfolding before me, Jamie's estimate of his grandfather's character had not been in error. Jamie had first ridden up alongside Young Simon's clerk, and what looked from my vantage point like a heated argument ended when Jamie leaned from his saddle, grabbed the clerk's reins, and dragged the indignant man's horse out of line, onto the verge of the muddy track.

The two men dismounted and stood face-to-face, obviously going at it hammer and tongs. Young Simon, seeing the altercation, reined aside himself, motioning the rest of the column to proceed. A good deal of to and fro then ensued; we were close enough to see Simon's face, flushed red with annoyance, the worried grimace on the clerk's countenance, and a series of rather violent gestures on Jamie's part.

I watched this pantomime in fascination, as the clerk, with a shrug of resignation, unfastened his saddlebag, scrabbled in the depths, and came up with several sheets of parchment. Jamie snatched these and skimmed rapidly through them, forefinger tracing the lines of writing. He seized one sheet, letting the rest drop to the ground, and shook it in Simon Fraser's face. The Young Fox looked taken aback. He took the sheet, peered at it, then looked up in bewilderment. Jamie grabbed back the sheet, and with a sudden effort, ripped the tough parchment down, then across, and stuffed the pieces into his sporran.

I had halted my pony, who took advantage of the recess to nose about among the meager shreds of plant life still to be found. The back of Young Simon's neck was bright red as he turned back to his horse, and I decided to keep out of the way. Jamie, remounted, came trotting back along the verge to join me, red hair flying like a banner in the wind, eyes gleaming with anger over tight-set lips.

"The filthy auld arse-wipe," he said without ceremony.

"What's he done?" I inquired.

"Listed the names of my men on his own rolls," Jamie said. "Claimed them as part of his Fraser regiment. Mozie auld pout-worm!" He glanced back up the track with longing. "Pity we've come such a way; it's too far to go back and proddle the auld mumper."

I resisted the temptation to egg Jamie on to call his grandfather more names, and asked instead, "Why would he do that? Just to make it look as though he were making more of a contribution to the Stuarts?"

Jamie nodded, the tide of fury receding slightly from his cheeks.

"Aye, that. Make himself look better, at no cost. But not only that. The wretched auld nettercap wants my land back—he has, ever since he was forced to give it up when my parents wed. Now he thinks if it all comes right and he's made Duke of Inverness, he can claim Lallybroch has been his all along, and me just his tenant—the proof being that he's raised men from the estate to answer the Stuarts' call to the clans."

"Could he actually get away with something like that?" I asked doubtfully.

Jamie drew in a deep breath and released it, the cloud of vapor rising like dragon smoke from his nostrils. He smiled grimly and patted the sporran at his waist.

"Not now he can't," he said.

It was a two-day trip from Beauly to Lallybroch in good weather, given sound horses and dry ground, pausing for nothing more than the necessities of eating, sleeping, and personal hygiene. As it was, one of the horses went lame six miles out of Beauly, it snowed and sleeted and blew by turns, the boggy ground froze in patches of slippery ice, and what with one thing and another, it was nearly a week before we made our way down the last slope that led to the farmhouse at Lallybroch—cold, tired, hungry, and far from hygienic.

We were alone, just the two of us. Murtagh had been sent to Edinburgh with Young Simon and the Beaufort men-at-arms, to judge how matters stood with the Highland army.

The house stood solid among its outbuildings, white as the snow-streaked fields that surrounded it. I remembered vividly the emotions I had felt when I first saw the place. Granted, I had seen it first in the glow of a fine autumn day, not through sheets of blowing, icy snow, but even then it had seemed a welcoming refuge. The house's impression of strength and serenity was heightened now by the warm lamplight spilling through the lower windows, soft yellow in the deepening gray of early evening.

The feeling of welcome grew even stronger when I followed Jamie through the front door, to be met by the mouth-watering smell of roasting meat and fresh bread.

"Supper," Jamie said, closing his eyes in bliss as he inhaled the fragrant aromas. "God, I could eat a horse." Melting ice dripped from the hem of his cloak, making wet spots on the wooden floor.

"I thought we were going to *have* to eat one of them," I remarked, untying the strings of my cloak and brushing melting snow from my hair. "That poor creature you traded in Kirkinmill could barely hobble."

The sound of our voices carried through the hall, and a door opened overhead, followed by the sound of small running feet and a cry of joy as the younger Jamie spotted his namesake below.

The racket of their reunion attracted the attention of the rest of the household, and before we knew it, we were enveloped in greetings and embraces as Jenny and the baby, little Maggie, Ian, Mrs. Crook, and assorted maidservants all rushed into the hall.

"It's so good to see ye, my dearie!" Jenny said for the third time, standing on tiptoe to kiss Jamie. "Such news as we've heard of the army, we feared it would be months before ye came home."

"Aye," Ian said, "have ye brought any of the men back with ye, or is this only a visit?"

"Brought them back?" Arrested in the act of greeting his elder niece, Jamie stared at his brother-in-law, momentarily forgetting the little girl in his arms. Brought to a realization of her presence by her yanking his hair, he kissed her absently and handed her to me.

"What d'ye mean, Ian?" he demanded. "The men should all ha' returned a month ago. Did some of them not come home?"

I held small Maggie tight, a dreadful feeling of foreboding coming over me as I watched the smile fade from Ian's face.

"None of them came back, Jamie," he said slowly, his long, good-humored face suddenly mirroring the grim expression he saw on Jamie's. "We havena seen hide nor hair of any of them, since they marched awa' with you."

There was a shout from the dooryard outside, where Rabbie MacNab was putting away the horses. Jamie whirled, turned to the door and pushed it open, leaning out into the storm.

Over his shoulder, I could see a rider coming through the blowing snow. Visibility was too poor to make out his face, but that small, wiry figure, clinging monkeylike to the saddle, was unmistakable. "Fast as chain lightning," Jamie had said, and clearly he was right; to make the trip from Beauly to Edinburgh, and then to Lallybroch in a week was a true feat of endurance. The coming rider was Murtagh, and it didn't take Maisri's gift of prophecy to tell us that the news he bore was ill.

42

Reunions

White with rage, Jamie flung back the door of Holyrood's morning drawing room with a crash. Ewan Cameron leaped to his feet, upsetting the inkpot he had been using. Simon Fraser, Master of Lovat, was seated across the table, but merely raised thick black brows at his half-nephew's entrance.

"Damn!" Ewan said, scrabbling in his sleeve for a handkerchief to mop the spreading puddle with. "What's the matter wi' ye, Fraser? Oh, good morning to ye, Mistress Fraser," he added, seeing me behind Jamie.

"Where's His Highness?" Jamie demanded without preamble.

"Stirling Castle," Cameron replied, failing to find the handkerchief he was searching for. "Got a cloth, Fraser?"

"If I did, I'd choke ye with it," Jamie said. He had relaxed slightly, upon finding that Charles Stuart was not in residence, but the corners of his lips were still tight. "Why have ye let my men be kept in the Tolbooth? I've just seen them, kept in a place I wouldna let pigs live! Surely to God you could have done something!"

Cameron flushed at this, but his clear brown eyes met Jamie's steadily.

"I tried," he said. "I told his Highness that I was sure it was a mistake— aye, and the thirty of them ten miles from the army when they were found, some mistake!—and besides, even if they'd really meant to desert, he didna have such a strength of men that he could afford to do without them. That's all that kept him from ordering the lot of them to be hanged on the spot, ye ken," he said, beginning to grow angry as the shock of Jamie's entrance wore off. "God, man, it's treason to desert in time of war!"

"Aye?" Jamie said skeptically. He nodded briefly to Young Simon, and pushed a chair in my direction before sitting down himself. "And have you sent orders to hang the twenty of your men who've gone home, Ewan? Or is it more like forty, now?"

Cameron flushed more deeply and dropped his eyes, concentrating on mopping up the ink with the cloth Simon Fraser handed him.

"They weren't caught," he muttered at last. He glanced up at Jamie, his thin face earnest. "Go to His Highness at Stirling," he advised. "He was furious about the desertion, but after all, it was his orders sent ye to Beauly and left your men untended, aye? And he's always thought well of ye, Jamie, and called ye friend. It might be he'll pardon your men, and ye beg him for their lives."

Picking up the ink-soaked cloth, he looked dubiously at it, then, with a muttered excuse, left to dispose of it outside, obviously eager to get away from Jamie.

Jamie sat sprawled in his chair, breathing through clenched teeth with a small hissing noise, eyes fixed on the small embroidered hanging on the wall that showed the Stuart coat of arms. The two stiff fingers of his right hand tapped slowly on the table. He had been in much the same state ever since Murtagh's arrival at Lallybroch with the news that the thirty men of Jamie's command had been apprehended in the act of desertion and imprisoned in Edinburgh's notorious Tolbooth Prison, under sentence of death.

I didn't myself think that Charles intended to execute the men. As Ewan Cameron pointed out, the Highland army had need of every able-bodied man it could muster. The push into England that Charles had argued for had been costly, and the influx of support he had foreseen from the English countryside had not materialized. Not only that; to execute Jamie's men in his absence would have been an act of political idiocy and personal betrayal too great even for Charles Stuart to contemplate.

No, I imagined that Cameron was right, and the men would be pardoned eventually. Jamie undoubtedly realized it, too, but the realization was poor consolation to him, faced with the matching realization that rather than seeing his men safely removed from the risks of a deteriorating campaign, his orders had landed them in one of the worst prisons in all of Scotland, branded as cowards and sentenced to a shameful death by hanging.

This, coupled with the imminent prospect of leaving the men in their dark, filthy imprisonment, to go to Stirling and face the humiliation of pleading with Charles, was more than sufficient to explain the look on Jamie's face—that of a man who has just breakfasted on broken glass.

Young Simon also was silent, frowning, wide forehead creasing with thought.

"I'll come with ye to His Highness," he said abruptly.

"You will?" Jamie glanced at his half-uncle in surprise, then his eyes narrowed at Simon. "Why?"

Simon gave a half-grin. "Blood's blood, after all. Or do ye think I'd try to claim your men, like Father did?"

"Would you?"

"I might," Simon said frankly, "if I thought there was a chance of it doing me some good. More likely to cause trouble, though, is what I think. I've no wish to fight wi' the MacKenzies—or you, nevvie," he added, the grin widening. "Rich as Lallybroch might be, it's a good long way from Beauly, and likely to be the devil of a fight to get hold of it, either by force or by the courts. I told Father so, but he hears what he wants to."

The young man shook his head and settled his swordbelt around his hips.

"There's like to be better pickings with the army; certainly there will be with a restored king. And—" he concluded, "if that army's going to fight again like they did at Preston, they'll need every man they can get. I'll go with ye," he repeated firmly.

Jamie nodded, a slow smile dawning on his face. "I thank ye, then, Simon. It will be of help."

Simon nodded. "Aye, well. It wouldna hurt matters any for ye to ask Dougal MacKenzie to come speak for ye, either. He's in Edinburgh just now."

"Dougal MacKenzie?" Jamie's brows rose quizzically. "Aye, I suppose it would do no harm, but . . . ."

"Do no harm? Man, did ye no hear? The MacKenzie's Prince Charles's fair-haired boy the noo." Simon lounged back in his seat, looking mockingly at his half-nephew.

"What for?" I asked. "What on earth has he done?" Dougal had brought two hundred and fifty men-at-arms to fight for the Stuart cause, but there were a number of chieftains who had made greater contributions.

"Ten thousand pounds," Simon said, savoring the words as he rolled them around on his tongue. "Ten thousand pounds in fine sterling, Dougal Mac-Kenzie's brought to lay at the feet of his sovereign. And it willna come amiss, either," he said matter-of-factly, dropping his lounging pose. "Cameron was just telling me that Charles had gone through the last of the Spanish money, and damn little coming in from the English supporters he'd counted on. Dougal's ten thousand will keep the army in weapons and food for a few more weeks, at least, and with luck, by then he'll ha' got more from France." At last, realizing that his reckless cousin was providing him with an excellent distraction for the English, Louis was reluctantly agreeing to cough up a bit of money. It was a long time coming, though.

I stared at Jamie, his face reflecting my own bewilderment. Where on earth would Dougal MacKenzie have gotten ten thousand pounds? Suddenly I remembered where I had heard that sum mentioned once before—in the thieves' hole at Cranesmuir, where I had spent three endless days and nights, awaiting trial on charges of witchcraft.

"Geillis Duncan!" I exclaimed. I felt cold at the memory of that conversation, carried out in the pitch-blackness of a miry pit, my companion no more than a voice in the dark. The drawing-room fire was warm, but I pulled my cloak tighter around me.

"I diverted near on to ten thousand pounds," Geillis had said, boasting of the thefts accomplished by judicious forgery of her late husband's name. Arthur Duncan, whom she had killed by poison, had been the procurator fiscal for the district. "Ten thousand pounds for the Jacobite cause. When it comes to rebellion, I shall know that I helped."

"She stole it," I said, feeling a tremor run up my arms at the thought of

Geillis Duncan, convicted of witchcraft, gone to a fiery death beneath the branches of a rowan tree. Geillis Duncan, who had escaped death just long enough to give birth to the child she bore to her lover—Dougal MacKenzie. "She stole it and she gave it to Dougal; or he took it from her, no telling which, now." Agitated, I stood up and paced back and forth before the fire.

"That bastard!" I said. "That's what he was doing in Paris two years ago!"

"What?" Jamie was frowning at me, Simon staring openmouthed.

"Visiting Charles Stuart. He came to see whether Charles were really planning a rebellion. Maybe he promised the money then, maybe that's what encouraged Charles to risk coming to Scotland—the promise of Geillis Duncan's money. But Dougal couldn't give Charles the money openly while Colum was alive—Colum would have asked questions; he was much too honest a man to have used stolen money, no matter who stole it in the first place."

"I see." Jamie nodded, eyes hooded in thought. "But now Colum is dead," he said quietly. "And Dougal MacKenzie is the Prince's favorite."

"Which is all to the good for you, as I've been saying," Simon put in, impatient with talk of people he didn't know and matters he only half-understood. "Go find him; likely he'll be in the World's End at this time o' day."

"Do you think he'll speak to the Prince for you?" I asked Jamie, worried. Dougal had been Jamie's foster father for a time, but the relationship had assuredly had its ups and downs. Dougal might not want to risk his newfound popularity with the Prince by speaking out for a bunch of cowards and deserters.

The Young Fox might lack his father's years, but he had a good bit of his sire's acumen. The heavy black brows quirked upward.

"MacKenzie still wants Lallybroch, no? And if he thinks Father and I might have an eye on reclaiming your land, he'll be more eager to help you get your men back, aye? Cost him a lot more to fight us for it than to deal wi' you, once the war's over." He nodded, happily chewing his upper lip as he contemplated the ramifications of the situation.

"I'll go wave a copy of Father's list under his nose before ye speak to him. You come in and tell him you'll see me in hell before ye let me claim your men, and then we'll all go to Stirling together." He grinned at Jamie complicitously.

"I always thought there was some reason why 'Scot' rhymed with 'plot,' " I remarked.

"What?" Both men looked up, startled.

"Never mind," I said, shaking my head. "Blood will tell."

———◄——————►———

I stayed in Edinburgh while Jamie and his rival uncles rode to Stirling to straighten out matters with the Prince. Under the circumstances, I couldn't stay at Holyroodhouse, but found lodgings in one of the wynds above the Canongate. It was a small, cold, cramped room, but I wasn't in it much.

The Tolbooth prisoners couldn't come out, but there was nothing barring visitors who wanted to get in. Fergus and I visited the prison daily, and a small amount of discriminating bribery allowed me to pass food and medicine to the men from Lallybroch. Theoretically, I wasn't allowed to talk privately to the prisoners, but here again, the system had a certain amount of slip to it, when suitably greased, and I managed to talk alone with Ross the smith on two or three occasions.

"'Twas my fault, lady," he said at once, the first time I saw him. "I should ha' had the sense to make the men go in small groups of three and four, not altogether like we did. I was afraid of losing some, though; the most of them had never been more than five mile from home before."

"You needn't blame yourself," I assured him. "From what I heard, it was only ill luck that you were caught. Don't worry; Jamie has gone to see the Prince at Stirling; he'll have you out of here in no time."

He nodded, tiredly brushing back a lock of hair. He was filthy and unkempt, and a good bit diminished from the burly, robust craftsman he had been a few months before. Still, he smiled at me, and thanked me for the food.

"It willna come amiss," he said frankly. "It's little we get but slops. D'ye think . . ." He hesitated. "D'ye think ye might manage a few blankets, my lady? I wouldna ask, only four of the men have the ague, and . . ."

"I'll manage," I said.

I left the prison, wondering exactly *how* I would manage. While the main army had gone south to invade England, Edinburgh was still an occupied city. With soldiers, lords, and hangers-on drifting constantly in and out, goods of all sorts were high-priced and in short supply. Blankets and warm clothes could be found, but they would cost a lot, and I had precisely ten shillings left in my purse.

There was a banker in Edinburgh, a Mr. Waterford, who had in the past handled some of Lallybroch's business and investments, but Jamie had removed all his funds from the bank some months before, fearing that bank-held assets might be seized by the Crown. The money had been converted to gold, some of it sent to Jared in France for safekeeping, the rest of it hidden in the farmhouse. All of it equally inaccessible to me at the moment.

I paused on the street to think, passersby jostling past me on the cobbles. If I didn't have money, I had still a few things of value. The crystal Raymond had given me in Paris—while the crystal itself was of no particular value, its gold mounting and chain were. My wedding rings—no, I didn't want to part with those, even temporarily. But the pearls . . . I felt inside my pocket, checking to see that the pearl necklace Jamie had given me on our wedding day was still safely sewn into the seam of my skirt.

It was; the small, irregular beads of the freshwater pearls were hard and smooth under my fingers. Not as expensive as oriental pearls, but it was still a fine necklace, with gold pierced-work roundels between the pearls. It had be-

longed to Jamie's mother, Ellen. I thought she would have liked to see it used
to comfort his men.

"Five pounds," I said firmly. "It's worth ten, and I could get six for it, if I
cared to walk all the way up the hill to another shop." I had no idea whether
this was true or not, but I reached out as though to pick up the necklace from
the counter anyway, pretending that I was about to leave the pawnbroker's
shop. The pawnbroker, Mr. Samuels, placed a quick hand over the necklace, his
eagerness letting me know that I should have asked six pounds to start with.

"Three pound ten, then," he said. "It's beggaring me own family to do it,
but for a fine lady like yourself . . ."

The small bell over the shop door chimed behind me as the door opened,
and there was the sound of hesitant footsteps on the worn boards of the pawn-
shop floor.

"Excuse me," began a girl's voice, and I whirled around, pearl necklace
forgotten, to see the shadow of the pawnbroker's balls falling across the face of
Mary Hawkins. She had grown in the last year, and filled out as well. There was
a new maturity and dignity in her manner, but she was still very young. She
blinked once, and then fell on me with a shriek of joy, her fur collar tickling my
nose as she hugged me tight.

"What are you doing here?" I asked, disentangling myself at last.

"Father's sister lives here," she replied. "I'm st-staying with her. Or do
you mean why am I here?" She waved a hand at the dingy confines of Mr.
Samuels's emporium.

"Well, that too," I said. "But that can wait a bit." I turned to the pawnbroker. "Four pound six, or I'll walk up the hill," I told him. "Make up your
mind, I'm in a hurry."

Grumbling to himself, Mr. Samuels reached beneath his counter for the
cash box, as I turned back to Mary.

"I have to buy some blankets. Can you come with me?"

She glanced outside, to where a small man in a footman's livery stood by
the door, clearly waiting for her. "Yes, if you'll come with me afterward. Oh,
Claire, I'm *so* glad to see you!"

"He sent a message to me," Mary confided, as we walked down the hill.
"Alex. A friend brought me his letter." Her face glowed as she spoke his name,
but there was a small frown between her brows as well.

"When I found he was in Edinburgh, I m-made Father send me to visit
Aunt Mildred. He didn't mind," she added bitterly. "It m-made him ill to look
at me, after what happened in Paris. He was happy to get me out of his house."

"So you've seen Alex?" I asked. I wondered how the young curate had
fared, since I had last seen him. I also wondered how he had found the courage
to write to Mary.

"Yes. He didn't ask me to come," she added quickly. "I c-came by my-self." Her chin lifted in defiance, but there was a small quiver as she said, "He. . . . he wouldn't have written to me, but he thought he was d-dying, and he wanted me to know . . . to know . . ." I put an arm about her shoulders and turned quickly into one of the closes, standing with her out of the flow of jostling street traffic.

"It's all right," I said to her, patting her helplessly, knowing that nothing I could do would make it right. "You came, and you've seen him, that's the important thing."

She nodded, speechless, and blew her nose. "Yes," she said thickly, at last. "We've had . . . two months. I k-keep telling myself that that's more than most people ever have, two months of happiness . . . but we lost so much time that we might have h-had, and . . . it's not enough. Claire, it isn't enough!"

"No," I said quietly. "A lifetime isn't enough, for that kind of love." With a sudden pang, I wondered where Jamie was, and how he was faring.

Mary, more composed now, clutched me by the sleeve. "Claire, can you come with me to see him? I know there's n-not much you can do . . ." Her voice faltered, and she steadied it with a visible effort. "But maybe you could . . . help." She caught my look at the footman, who stood stolidly outside the wynd, oblivious to the passing traffic. "I pay him," she said simply. "My aunt thinks I go w-walking every afternoon. Will you come?"

"Yes, of course." I glanced between the towering buildings, judging the level of the sun over the hills outside the city. It would be dark in an hour; I wanted the blankets delivered to the prison before night made the damp stone walls of the Tolbooth still colder. Making a sudden decision, I turned to Fergus, who had been standing patiently next to me, watching Mary with interest. Returned to Edinburgh with the rest of the Lallybroch men, he had escaped imprisonment by virtue of his French citizenship, and had survived hardily by reverting to his customary trade. I had found him faithfully hanging about near the Tolbooth, where he brought bits of food for his imprisoned companions.

"Take this money," I said, handing him my purse, "and find Murtagh. Tell him to get as many blankets as that will buy, and see they're taken to the gaolkeeper at the Tolbooth. He's been bribed already, but keep back a few shillings, just in case."

"But Madame," he protested, "I promised milord I would not let you go alone . . ."

"Milord isn't here," I said firmly, "and I am. Go, Fergus."

He glanced from me to Mary, evidently decided she was less a threat to me than my temper was to him, and departed, shrugging his shoulders and mutter-ing in French about the stubbornness of women.

The little room at the top of the building had changed considerably since my last visit. It was clean, for one thing, with polish gleaming on every horizontal surface. There was food in the hutch, a down quilt on the bed, and numerous small comforts provided for the patient. Mary had confided on the way that she had been quietly pawning her mother's jewelry, to ensure that Alex Randall was as comfortable as money could make him.

There were limits to what money could manage, but Alex's face glowed like a candle flame when Mary came through the door, temporarily obscuring the ravages of illness.

"I've brought Claire, dearest." Mary dropped her cloak unheeded onto a chair and knelt beside him, taking his thin, blue-veined hands in her own.

"Mrs. Fraser." His voice was light and breathless, though he smiled at me. "It's good to see a friendly face again."

"Yes, it is." I smiled at him, noting half-consciously the rapid, fluttering pulse visible in his throat, and the transparency of his skin. The hazel eyes were soft and warm, holding most of the life left in his frail body.

Lacking medicine, there was nothing I could do for him, but I examined him carefully, and saw him tucked up comfortably afterward, his lips slightly blue from the minor exertion of the examination.

I covered the anxiety I felt at his condition, and promised to come next day with some medicine to help him sleep more easily. He hardly noticed my assurances; all his attention was for Mary, sitting anxiously by him, holding his hand. I saw her glance at the window, where light was fading rapidly, and realized her concern; she would have to return to her aunt's house before nightfall.

"I'll take my leave, then," I told Alex, removing myself as tactfully as I could, to leave them a few precious moments alone together.

He glanced from me to Mary, then smiled back at me in gratitude.

"God bless you, Mrs. Fraser," he said.

"I'll see you tomorrow," I said, and left, hoping that I would.

◆───◆

I was busy over the next few days. The men's arms had been confiscated, of course, when they were arrested, and I did my best to recover what I could, bullying and threatening, bribing and charming where necessary. I pawned two brooches that Jared had given me as a farewell present, and bought enough food to ensure that the men of Lallybroch ate as well as the army in general— poorly as that might be.

I talked my way into the cells of the prison, and spent some time in treating the prisoners' ailments, ranging from scurvy and the more generalized malnutrition common in winter, to chafing sores, chilblains, arthritis, and a variety of respiratory ailments.

I made the rounds of those chieftains and lords still in Edinburgh—not many—who might be helpful to Jamie, if his visit to Stirling should fail. I didn't think it would, but it seemed wise to take precautions.

And among the other activities of my days, I made time to see Alex Randall once a day. I took pains to come in the mornings, so as not to use up his time with Mary. Alex slept little, and that little, ill; consequently, he tended to be tired and drooping in the morning, not wanting to talk, but always smiling in welcome when I arrived. I would give him a light mixture of mint and lavender, with a few drops of poppy syrup stirred in; this would generally allow him a few hours of sleep, so that he could be alert when Mary arrived in the afternoon.

Aside from me and Mary, I had seen no other visitors at the top of the building. I was therefore surprised, coming up the stairs to his room one morning, to hear voices behind the closed door.

I knocked once, briefly, as was our agreed custom, and let myself in. Jonathan Randall was sitting by his brother's bed, clad in his captain's uniform of red and fawn. He rose at my entrance and bowed correctly, face cold.

"Madam," he said.

"Captain," I said. We then stood awkwardly in the middle of the room, staring at each other, each unwilling to go further.

"Johnny," said Alex's hoarse voice from the bed. It had a note of coaxing, as well as one of command, and his brother shrugged irritably when he heard it.

"My brother has summoned me to give you a bit of news," he said, tight-lipped. He wore no wig this morning, and with his dark hair tied back, his resemblance to his brother was startling. Pale and frail as Alex was, he looked like Jonathan's ghost.

"You and Mr. Fraser have been kind to my Mary," Alex said, rolling onto his side to look at me. "And to me as well. I . . . knew of my brother's bargain with you"—the faintest of pinks rose in his cheeks—"but I know, too, what you and your husband did for Mary . . . in Paris." He licked his lips, cracked and dry from the constant heat in the room. "I think you should hear the news Johnny brought from the Castle yesterday."

Jack Randall eyed me with dislike, but he was good as his word.

"Hawley has succeeded Cope, as I told you earlier that he would," he said. "Hawley has little gift for leadership, bar a certain blind confidence in the men under his command. Whether that will stand him in better stead than did Cope's cannon—" He shrugged impatiently.

"Be that as it may, General Hawley has been directed to march north to recover Stirling Castle."

"Has he?" I said. "Do you know how many troops he has?"

Randall nodded shortly. "He has eight thousand troops at the moment, thirteen hundred of them cavalry. He is also in daily expectation of the arrival of six thousand Hessians." He frowned, thinking. "I have heard that the chief of clan Campbell is sending a thousand men to join with Hawley's forces as well, but I cannot say whether that information is reliable; there seems no way of predicting what Scots will do."

"I see." This was serious; the Highland army at this point had between six and seven thousand men. Against Hawley, minus his expected reinforcements, they might manage. To wait until his Hessians and Campbells arrived was clearly madness, to say nothing of the fact that the Highlanders' fighting skills were much better suited to attack than defense. This news had best reach Lord George Murray at once.

Jack Randall's voice called me back from my ruminations.

"Good day to you, Madam," he said, formal as ever, and there was no trace of humanity on the hard, handsome features as he bowed to me and took his leave.

"Thank you," I said to Alex Randall, waiting for Jonathan to descend the long, twisting stair before leaving myself. "I appreciate it very much."

He nodded. The shadows under his eyes were pronounced; another bad night.

"You're welcome," he said simply. "I suppose you'll be leaving some of the medicine for me? I imagine it may be some time before I see you again."

I halted, struck by his assumption that I would go myself to Stirling. That was what every fiber of my being urged me to do, but there was the matter of the men in the Tolbooth to be considered.

"I don't know," I said. "But yes; I'll leave the medicine."

I walked slowly back to my lodgings, my mind still spinning. Obviously, I must get word to Jamie immediately. Murtagh would have to go, I supposed. Jamie would believe me, of course, if I wrote him a note. But could he convince Lord George, the Duke of Perth, or the other army commanders?

I couldn't tell him where I had come by this knowledge; would the commanders be willing to believe a woman's unsupported, written word? Even the word of a woman popularly supposed to have supernatural powers? I thought of Maisri suddenly, and shivered. *It's a curse,* she had said. Yes, but what choice was there? *I have no power but the power not to say what I know.* I had that power, too, but dared not risk using it.

To my surprise, the door to my small room was open, and there were clashing, banging noises coming from inside it. I had been storing the recovered arms under my bed, and stacking swords and assorted blades by the hearth once the space under the bed was filled, until there was virtually no floor space left, save the small square of floorboards where Fergus laid his blankets.

I stood on the stair, amazed at the scene visible through the open door above. Murtagh, standing on the bed, was overseeing the handing-out of weaponry to the men who crowded the room to overflowing—the men of Lallybroch.

"Madame!" I turned at the cry, to find Fergus at my elbow, beaming up at me, a square-toothed grin on his sallow face.

"Madame! Is it not wonderful? Milord has received pardon for his men—a messenger came from Stirling this morning, with the order to release them, and we are ordered at once to join milord at Stirling!"

I hugged him, grinning a bit myself. "That *is* wonderful, Fergus." A few of the men had noticed me, and were beginning to turn to me, smiling and plucking at each other's sleeves. An air of exhilaration and excitement filled the small room. Murtagh, perched on the bedstead like the Gnome King on a toadstool, saw me then, and smiled—an expression which rendered him virtually unrecognizable, so much did it transform his face.

"Will Mr. Murtagh take the men to Stirling?" Fergus asked. He had received a whinger, or short sword, as his share of the weaponry, and was practicing drawing and sheathing it as he spoke.

I met Murtagh's eye and shook my head. After all, I thought, if Jenny Cameron could lead her brother's men to Glenfinnan, I could take my husband's troops to Stirling. And just let Lord George and His Highness try to disregard my news, delivered in person.

"No," I said. "I will."

43

Falkirk

I could feel the men close by, all around me in the dark. There was a piper walking next to me; I could hear the creak of the bag under his arm and see the outline of the drones, poking out behind. They moved as he walked, so that he seemed to be carrying a small, feebly struggling animal.

I knew him, a man named Labhriunn MacIan. The pipers of the clans took it in turns to call the dawn at Stirling, walking to and fro in the encampment with the piper's measured stride, so that the wail of the drones bounced from the flimsy tents, calling all within to the battle of the new day.

Again in the evening a single piper would come out, strolling slow across the yard, and the camp would stop to listen, voices stilling and the glow of the sunset fading from the tents' canvas. The high, whining notes of the pibroch called down the shadows from the moor, and when the piper was done, the night had come.

Evening or morning, Labhriunn MacIan played with his eyes closed, stepping sure and slow across the yard and back, elbow tight on the bag and his fingers lively on the chanters' holes. Despite the cold, I sat sometimes to watch in the evenings, letting the sound drive its spikes through my heart. MacIan paced to and fro, ignoring everything around him, making his turns on the ball of his foot, pouring his being out through his chanter.

There are the small Irish pipes, used indoors for making music, and the Great Northern pipes, used outdoors for reveille, and for calling of clans to order, and the spurring of men to battle. It was the Northern pipes that MacIan played, walking to and fro with his eyes shut tight.

Rising from my seat as he finished one evening, I waited while he pressed the last of the air from his bag with a dying wail, and fell in alongside him as he came in through Stirling's gate with a nod to the guard.

"Good e'en to ye, Mistress," he said. His voice was soft, and his eyes, now open, softer still with the unbroken spell of his playing still on him.

"Good evening to you, MacIan," I said. "I wondered, MacIan, why do you play with your eyes tight shut?"

He smiled and scratched his head, but answered readily enough.

"I suppose it is because my grandsire taught me, Mistress, and he was blind. I see him always when I play, pacing the shore with his beard flying in the wind and his blind eyes closed against the sting of the sand, hearing the sound of the pipes come down to him off the rocks of the cliffside and knowing from that where he was in his walk."

"So you see him, and you play, too, to the cliffs and the sea? From where do you come, MacIan?" I asked. His speech was low and sibilant, even more than that of most Highlanders.

"It is from the Shetlands, Mistress," he replied, making the last word almost "Zetlands." "A long way from here." He smiled again, and bowed to me as we came to the guest quarters, where I would turn. "But then, I am thinking that you have come farther still, Mistress."

"That's true," I said. "Good night, MacIan."

Later that week, I wondered whether his skill at playing unseeing would help him, here in the dark. A large body of men moving makes a good bit of noise, no matter how quietly they go, but I thought any echoes they created would be drowned in the howl of the rising wind. The night was moonless, but the sky was light with clouds, and an icy sleet was falling, stinging my cheeks.

The men of the Highland army covered the ground in small groups of ten or twenty, moving in uneven bumps and patches, as though the earth thrust up small hillocks here and there, or as though the groves of larch and alder were walking through the dark. My news had not come unsupported; Ewan Cameron's spies had reported Hawley's moves as well, and the Scottish army was now on its way to meet him, somewhere south of Stirling Castle.

Jamie had given up urging me to go back. I had promised to stay out of the way, but if there was a battle to be fought, then the army's physicians must be at hand afterward. I could tell when his attention shifted to his men, and the prospects ahead, by the sudden cock of his head. On Donas, he sat high enough to be visible as a shadow, even in the dark, and when he threw up an arm, two smaller shadows detached themselves from the moving mass and came up beside his stirrup. There was a moment's whispered conversation; then he straightened in his saddle and turned to me.

"The scouts say we've been seen; English guards have gone flying for Callendar House, to warn General Hawley. We shallna wait longer; I'm taking my men and circling beyond Dougal's troops to the far side of Falkirk Hill. We'll come down from behind as the MacKenzies come in from the west. There's a wee kirk up the hill to your left, maybe a quarter-mile. That's your place, Sassenach. Ride there now, and stay." He groped for my arm in the darkness, found it, and squeezed.

"I shall come for ye when I can, or send Murtagh if I can't. If things should go wrong, go into the kirk and claim sanctuary there. It's the best I can think of."

"Don't worry about me," I said. My lips were cold, and I hoped my voice didn't sound as shaky as I felt. I bit back the "Be careful" that would have been my next words, and contented myself with touching him quickly, the cold surface of his cheek hard as metal under my hand, and the brush of a lock of hair, cold and smooth as a deer's pelt.

I reined to the left, picking my way slowly as the oncoming men flowed around me. The gelding was excited by the stir; he tossed his head, snorting, and fidgeted under me. I pulled him up sharply, as Jamie had taught me, and kept a close rein as the ground sloped suddenly up beneath the horse's hooves. I glanced back once, but Jamie had disappeared into the night, and I needed all my attention to find the church in the dark.

It was a tiny building, stone with a thatched roof, crouched in a small depression of the hill, like a cowering animal. I felt a strong feeling of kinship with it. The English watchfires were visible from here, glimmering through the sleet, and I could hear shouting in the distance—Scots or English, I couldn't tell.

Then the pipes began, a thin, eerie scream in the storm. There were discordant shrieks, rising unearthly from several different places on the hill. Having seen it before at close hand, I could imagine the pipers blowing up their bags, chests inflating with quick gasps and blue lips clamped tight on the chanters' stems, cold-stiff fingers fumbling to guide the blowing into coherence.

I could almost feel the stubborn resistance of the leathern bag, kept warm and flexible under a plaid, but reluctant to be coaxed into fullness, then suddenly springing to life, part of the piper's body, like a third lung, breathing for him when the wind stole his breath, as though the shouting of the clansmen near him filled it.

The shouting was louder, now, and reached me in waves as the wind turned, carrying eddying blasts of sleet. There was no porch to give shelter, or any trees on the hillside to break the wind. My horse turned and put his head down, facing into the wind, and his mane whipped hard against my face, rough with ice.

The church offered sanctuary from the elements, as well as from the English. I pushed the door open and, tugging on the bridle, led the horse inside after me.

It was dark inside, with the single oiled-skin window no more than a dim patch in the blackness over the altar. It seemed warm, by contrast with the weather outside, but the smell of stale sweat made it suffocating. There were no seats for the horse to knock over; nothing save a small shrine set into one wall, and the altar itself. Oppressed by the strong smell of people, the horse stood still, snorting and blowing, but not fidgeting overmuch. Keeping a wary eye on him, I went back to the door and thrust my head out.

No one could tell what was happening on Falkirk Hill. The sparks of gunfire twinkled randomly in the dark. I could hear, faint and intermittent, the ring of metal and the thump of an occasional explosion. Now and then came the scream of a wounded man, high as a bagpipe's screech, different from the

Gaelic cries of the warriors. And then the wind would turn, and I would hear nothing, or would imagine I heard voices that were nothing but the shrieking wind.

I had not seen the fight at Prestonpans; subconsciously accustomed to the ponderous movements of huge armies bound to tanks and mortars, I had not realized just how quickly things could happen in a small pitched battle of hand-to-hand fighting and small, light arms.

The first warning I had was a shout from near at hand. *"Tulach Ard!"* Deafened by wind, I hadn't heard them as they came up the hill. *"Tulach Ard!"* It was the battle cry of clan MacKenzie; some of Dougal's troops, forced backward in the direction of my sanctuary. I ducked back inside, but kept the door ajar, so that I could peer out.

They were coming up the hill, a small group of men in flight. Highlanders, both from the sound and the sight of them, plaids and beards and hair flying around them, so they looked like black clouds against the grassy slope, scudding uphill before the wind.

I jumped back into the church as the first of them burst through the door. Dark as it was, I couldn't see his face, but I recognized his voice when he crashed headfirst into my horse.

"Jesus!"

"Willie!" I shouted. "Willie Coulter!"

"Sweet bleeding Jesus! Who's that!"

I hadn't time to answer before the door crashed against the wall, and two more black forms shot into the tiny church. Incensed by this noisy intrusion, my horse reared and whinnied, pawing the air. This gave rise to cries of alarm from the intruders, who clearly had thought the building unoccupied, and were disconcerted to find otherwise.

The entrance of several more men only increased the confusion, and I gave up any idea of trying to subdue the horse. Forced to the rear of the church, I squeezed myself into the small space between altar and wall and waited for things to sort themselves out.

They began to show signs of doing so when one of the confused voices in the darkness rose above the others.

"Be QUIET!" it shouted, in a tone that brooked no opposition. Everyone but the horse obeyed, and as the racket died down, even the horse subsided, backing into a corner and making snorting noises, mixed with querulous squeals of disgust.

"It is MacKenzie of Leoch," said the imperious voice. "Who else bides here?"

"It is Geordie, Dougal, and my brother with me," said a voice nearby, in tones of profound relief. "We've brought Rupert with us, too; he's wounded. Christ, I thought it was the de'il himself in here!"

"Gordon McLeod of Ardsmuir," said another voice I didn't recognize.

"And Ewan Cameron of Kinnoch," said another. "Whose is the horse?"

"Mine," I said, sidling cautiously out from behind the altar. The sound of my voice caused another outbreak, but Dougal put a stop to it once more, raising his own voice above the racket.

"QUIET, damn the lot of ye! Is that you, Claire Fraser?"

"Well, it isn't the Queen," I said testily. "Willie Coulter's in here, too, or he was a minute ago. Hasn't anyone got a flint box?"

"No light!" said Dougal. "Little chance that the English will overlook this place if they follow us, but little sense in drawing their attention to it if they don't."

"All right," I said, biting my lip. "Rupert, can you talk? Say something so I can tell where you are." I didn't know how much I could do for him in the dark; as it was, I couldn't even reach my medicine box. Still, I couldn't leave him to bleed to death on the floor.

There was a nasty-sounding cough from the side of the church opposite me, and a hoarse voice said, "Here, lass," and coughed again.

I felt my way across the floor, cursing under my breath. I could tell merely from the bubbling sound of that cough that it was bad; the sort of bad that my medicine box wasn't likely to help. I crouched and duck-walked the last few feet, waving my arms in a wide swathe to feel what might be in my way.

One hand struck a warm body, and a big hand fastened on to me. It had to be Rupert; I could hear him breathing, a stertorous sound with a faint gurgle behind it.

"I'm here," I said, patting him blindly in what I hoped was a reassuring spot. I supposed it was, because he gave a sort of gasping chuckle and arched his hips, pressing my hand down hard against him.

"Do that again, lass, and I'll forget all about the musket ball," he said.

I grabbed my hand back.

"Perhaps a bit later," I said dryly. I moved my hand upward, skimming over his body in search of his head. The thick bristle of beard told me I'd reached my goal, and I felt carefully under the dense growth for the pulse in his throat. Fast and light, but still fairly regular. His forehead was slick with sweat, though his skin felt clammy to the touch. The tip of his nose was cold when I brushed it, chilled from the air outside.

"Pity I'm no a dog," he said, a thread of laughter coming between the gasps for air. "Cold nose . . . would be a good sign."

"Be a better sign if you'd quit talking," I said. "Where did the ball take you? No, don't tell me, take my hand and put it on the wound . . . and if you put it anywhere else, Rupert MacKenzie, you can die here like a dog, and good riddance to you."

I could feel the wide chest vibrate with suppressed laughter under my hand. He drew my hand slowly under his plaid, and I pushed back the obstructing fabric with my other hand.

"All right, I've got it," I whispered. I could feel the small tear in his shirt, damp with blood around the edges, and I put both hands to it and ripped it open. I brushed my fingers very lightly down his side, feeling the ripple of gooseflesh under them, and then the small hole of the entrance wound. It seemed a remarkably small hole, compared to the bulk of Rupert, who was a burly man.

"Did it come out anywhere?" I whispered. The inside of the church was quiet, except for the horse, who was moving restlessly in his own corner. With the door closed, the sounds of battle outside were still audible, but diffuse; it was impossible to tell how close they were.

"No," he said, and coughed again. I could feel his hand move toward his mouth, and I followed it with a fold of his plaid. My eyes were as accustomed to the darkness as they were likely to get, but he was still no more than a hunched black shape on the floor before me. For some things, though, touch was enough. There was little bleeding at the site of the wound, but the cloth I held to his mouth flooded my hand with sudden damp warmth.

The ball had taken him through one lung at least, possibly both, and his chest was filling with blood. He could last a few hours in this condition, perhaps a day if one lung remained functional. If the pericardium had been nicked, he would go faster. But only surgery would save him, and that of a kind I couldn't do.

I could feel a warm presence behind me, and heard normal breathing as someone groped toward me. I reached back and felt my hand gripped tight. Dougal MacKenzie.

He made his way up beside me, and laid a hand on Rupert's supine body. "How is it, man?" he asked softly. "Can ye walk?" My other hand still on Rupert, I could feel his head shake in answer to Dougal's question. The men in the church behind us had begun to talk among themselves in whispers.

Dougal's hand pressed down on my shoulder.

"What d'ye need to help him? Your wee box? Is it on the horse?" He had risen before I could tell him that there was nothing in the box to help Rupert.

A sudden loud crack from the altar stopped the whispers, and there was a quick movement all around, as men snatched up the weapons they had laid down. Another crack, and a ripping noise, and the oiled-skin covering of the window gave way to a rush of cold, clean air and a few swirling snowflakes.

"Sassenach! Claire! Are ye there?" The low voice from the window brought me to my feet in momentary forgetfulness of Rupert.

"Jamie!" All around me was a collective exhalation, and the clank of falling swords and targes. The new faint light from outdoors was blotted out for a moment by the bulk of Jamie's head and shoulders. He dropped down lightly from the altar, silhouetted against the open window.

"Who's here?" he said softly, looking around. "Dougal, is that you?"

"Aye, it's me, lad. Your wife and a few more. Did ye see the sassenach bastards anywhere near outside?"

Jamie uttered a short laugh.

"Why d'ye think I came in through the window? There's maybe twenty of them at the foot of the hill."

Dougal made a displeased noise deep in his throat. "The bastards that cut us off from the main troop, I'll be bound."

"Just so. *Ho, mo cridh! Ciamar a tha thu?*" Recognizing a familiar voice in the midst of madness, my horse had thrust its nose up with a loud whinny of greeting.

"Hush, ye wee fool!" Dougal said to it violently. "D'ye want the English to hear?"

"I dinna suppose the English would hang *him*," Jamie observed mildly. "As for them telling you're here, they won't need ears, if they've eyes in their heads; the slope's half mud outside, and the prints of all your feet show clear."

"Mmphm." Dougal cast an eye toward the window, but Jamie was already shaking his head.

"No good, Dougal. The main body's to the south, and Lord George Murray's gone to meet them, but there's the few English from the party we met still left on this side. A group of them chased me over the hill; I dodged to the side and crawled up to the church on my belly through the grass, but I'll guess they're still combing the hillside above." He reached out a hand in my direction, and I took it. It was cold and damp from crawling through grass, but I was glad just to touch him, to have him there.

"Crawled in, eh? And how were ye planning to get out again?" Dougal asked.

I could feel Jamie shrug. He tilted his head in the direction of my horse.

"I'd thought I might burst out and ride them down; they'll not know about the horse. That would cause enough kerfuffle maybe for Claire to slip free."

Dougal snorted. "Aye, and they'd pick ye off your horse like a ripe apple."

"It hardly matters," Jamie said dryly. "I canna see the lot of ye to be slipping out quietly with no one noticing, no matter how much fuss I made over it."

As though in confirmation of this, Rupert gave a loud groan by the wall. Dougal and I dropped onto our knees beside him at once, followed more slowly by Jamie.

He wasn't dead, but wasn't doing well, either. His hands were chilly, and his breathing had a wheezing, whining note to it.

"Dougal," he whispered.

"I'm here, Rupert. Be still, man, you'll be all right soon." The MacKenzie chieftain quickly pulled off his own plaid and folded it into a pillow, which he thrust beneath Rupert's head and shoulders. Raised a bit, his breathing seemed easier, but a touch below his beard showed me wet blotches on his shirt. He still had some strength; he reached out a hand and grasped Dougal's arm.

"If . . . they'll find us anyway . . . give me a light," he said, gasping. "I'd see your face once more, Dougal."

Close as I was to Dougal, I felt the shock run through him at these words and their implication. His head turned sharply toward me, but of course he couldn't see my face. He muttered an order over his shoulder, and after a bit of shuffling and murmuring, someone cut loose a handful of the thatch, which was twisted into a torch and lit with a spark from a flint. It burned fast, but gave enough light for me to examine Rupert while the men worked at chiseling loose a long splinter of wood from the poles of the roof, to serve as a less temporary torch.

He was white as a fish belly, hair matted with sweat, and a faint smear of blood still showed on the flesh of his full lower lip. Dark spots showed on the glossy black beard, but he smiled faintly at me as I bent over him to check his pulse again. Lighter, and very fast, missing beats now and then. I smoothed the hair back from his face, and he touched my hand in thanks.

I felt Dougal's hand on my elbow, and sat back on my heels, turning to face him. I had faced him once like this before, over the body of a man mortally wounded by a boar. He had asked me then, "Can he live?" and I saw the memory of that day cross his face. The same question stood in his eyes again, but this time in eyes glazed with fear of my answer. Rupert was his closest friend, the kinsman who rode and who fought on his right-hand side, as Ian did for Jamie.

This time I didn't answer; Rupert did it for me.

"Dougal," he said, and smiled as his friend bent anxiously over him. He closed his eyes for a moment and breathed as deeply as he could, gathering strength for the moment.

"Dougal," he said again, opening his eyes. "Ye'll no grieve for me, man."

Dougal's face twitched in the torchlight. I could see the denial of death come to his lips, but he bit it back and forced it aside.

"I'm your chief, man," he said, with a quivering half-smile. "Ye'll not order me; I shall grieve ye and I like." He clasped Rupert's hand, where it lay across his chest, and held it tightly.

There was a faint, wheezing chuckle from Rupert, and another coughing spell.

"Weel, grieve for me and ye will, Dougal," he said, when he'd finished. "And I'm glad for it. But ye canna grieve 'til I be deid, can ye? I would die by your hand, *mo caraidh,* not in the hands of the strangers."

Dougal jerked, and Jamie and I exchanged appalled glances behind his back.

"Rupert . . ." Dougal began helplessly, but Rupert interrupted him, clasping his hand and shaking it gently.

"You *are* my chief, man, and it's your duty," he whispered. "Come now. Do it now. This dying hurts me, Dougal, and I would have it over." His eyes moved restlessly, lighting on me.

"Will ye hold my hand while I go, lass?" he asked. "I'd like it so."

There seemed nothing else to do. Moving slowly, feeling that this was all a dream, I took the broad, black-haired hand in both of mine, pressing it as though I might force my own warmth into the cooling flesh.

With a grunt, Rupert heaved himself slightly to one side and glanced up at Jamie, who sat by his head.

"She should ha' married me, lad, when she had the choice," he wheezed. "You're a poor weed, but do your best." One eye squeezed shut in a massive wink. "Gi'e her a good one for me, lad."

The black eyes swiveled back to me, and a final grin spread across his face.

"Goodbye, bonnie lassie," he said softly.

Dougal's dirk took him under the breastbone, hard and straight. The burly body convulsed, turning to the side with an coughing explosion of air and blood, but the brief sound of agony came from Dougal.

The MacKenzie chieftain stayed frozen for a moment, eyes shut, hands clenched on the hilt of the dirk. Then Jamie rose, took him by the shoulders, and turned him away, murmuring something in Gaelic. Jamie glanced at me, and I nodded and held out my arms. He turned Dougal gently toward me, and I gathered him to me as we both crouched on the floor, holding him while he wept.

Jamie's own face was streaked with tears, and I could hear the brief sighs and sobbing breaths of the other men. I supposed it was better they wept for Rupert than for themselves. If the English did come for us here, all of us stood to be hanged for treason. It was easier to mourn for Rupert, who was safely gone, sped on his way by the hand of a friend.

⟿

They did not come anytime in the long winter night. We huddled together against one wall, under plaids and cloaks, waiting. I dozed fitfully, leaning against Jamie's shoulder, with Dougal hunched and silent on my other side. I thought that neither of them slept, but kept watch through the night over Rupert's corpse, quiet under his own draped plaid across the church, on the other side of the abyss that separates the dead from the living.

We spoke little, but I knew what they were thinking. They were wondering, as I was, whether the English troops had left, regrouping with the main army at Callendar House below, or whether they still watched outside, waiting for the dawn before making a move, lest anyone in the tiny church escape under cover of darkness.

The matter was settled with the coming of first light.

"Ho, the church! Come out and give yourselves up!" The call came from the slope below, in a strong English voice.

There was a stir among the men in the church, and the horse, who had been dozing in his corner, snapped his head up with a startled snort at the movement nearby. Jamie and Dougal exchanged a glance, then, as though they had planned it together, rose and stood, shoulder to shoulder, before the closed door. A jerk of Jamie's head sent me to the rear of the church, back to my shelter behind the altar.

Another shout from the outside was met with silence. Jamie drew the snaphance pistol from his belt and checked the loading of it, casually, as though there were all the time in the world. He sank to one knee and braced the pistol, pointing it at the door at the level of a man's head.

Geordie and Willie guarded the window to the rear, swords and pistols to the ready. But it was likely from the front that an attack would come; the hill behind the church sloped steeply up, with barely room between the slope and the wall of the church for one man to squeeze past.

I heard the squelching of footsteps, approaching the door through the mud, and the faint clanking of sidearms. The sounds stopped at a distance, and a voice came again, closer and louder.

"In the name of His Majesty King George, come out and surrender! We know you are there!"

Jamie fired. The report inside the tiny church was deafening. It must have been sufficiently impressive from outside as well; I could hear the hasty sounds of slipping retreat, accompanied by muffled curses. There was a small hole in the door, made by the pistol ball; Dougal sidled up to it and peered out.

"Damn," he said under his breath. "There's a lot of them."

Jamie cast a glance at me, then set his lips and turned his attention to reloading his pistol. Clearly, the Scots had no intention of surrendering. Just as clearly, the English had no desire to storm the church, given the easily defended entrances. They couldn't mean to starve us out? Surely the Highland army would be sending out men to search for the wounded of the battle from the night before. If they arrived before the English had opportunity to bring a cannon to bear on the church, we might be saved.

Unfortunately, there was a thinker outside. The sound of footsteps came once more, and then a measured English voice, full of authority.

"You have one minute to come out and give yourselves up," it said, "or we fire the thatch."

I glanced upward in complete horror. The walls of the church were stone, but the thatch would burn in short order, even soaked with rain and sleet, and once well caught, would send flames and smoking embers raining down to engulf us. I remembered the awful speed with which the torch of twisted reed had burned the night before; the charred remnant lay on the floor near Rupert's shrouded corpse, a grisly token in the gray dawn light.

"No!" I screamed. "Bloody bastards! This is a church! Have you never heard of sanctuary?"

"Who is that?" came the sharp voice from outside. "Is that an English-woman in there?!"

"Yes!" shouted Dougal, springing to the door. He cracked it ajar and bellowed out at the English soldiers on the hillside below. "Yes! We hold an English lady captive! Fire the thatch, and she dies with us!"

There was an outbreak of voices at the bottom of the hill, and a sudden shifting among the men in the church. Jamie whirled on Dougal with a scowl, saying, "What . . . !"

"It's the only chance!" Dougal hissed back. "Let them take her, in return for our freedom. They'll not harm her if they think she's our hostage, and we'll get her back later, once we're free!"

I came out of my hiding space and went to Jamie, gripping his sleeve.

"Do it!" I said urgently. "Dougal is right, it's the only chance!"

He looked down at me helplessly, rage and fear mingled on his face. And under it all, a trace of humor at the underlying irony of the situation.

"I am a sassenach, after all," I said, seeing it.

He touched my face briefly with a rueful smile.

"Aye, *mo duinne*. But you're *my* sassenach." He turned to Dougal, squaring his shoulders. He drew in a deep breath, and nodded.

"All right. Tell them we took her"—he thought quickly, rubbing one hand through his hair—"from Falkirk road, late yesterday."

Dougal nodded, and without waiting for more, slipped out of the church door, a white handkerchief held high overhead in signal of truce.

Jamie turned to me, frowning, glancing at the church door, where the sounds of English voices were still audible, though we couldn't make out words as they talked.

"I don't know what you're to tell them, Claire; perhaps ye'd better pretend to be so shocked that ye canna speak of it. It's maybe better than telling a tale; for if they should realize who you are—" He stopped suddenly and rubbed his hand hard over his face.

If they realized who I was, it would be London, and the Tower—followed quite possibly by swift execution. But while the broadsheets had made much of "the Stuart Witch," no one, so far as I knew, had realized or published the fact that the witch was English.

"Don't worry," I said, realizing just what a silly remark this was, but unable to come up with anything better. I laid a hand on his sleeve, feeling the swift pulse that beat in his wrist. "You'll get me back before they have a chance to realize anything. Do you think they'll take me to Callendar House?"

He nodded, back in control. "Aye, I think so. If ye can, try to be alone near a window, just after nightfall. I'll come for ye then."

There was time for no more. Dougal slipped back through the door, closing it carefully behind him.

"Done," he said, looking from me to Jamie. "We give them the woman, and we'll be allowed to leave unmolested. No pursuit. We keep the horse. We'll need it, for Rupert, ye see," he said to me, half-apologetically.

"It's all right," I told him. I looked at the door, with its small dark spot where the bullet had passed, the same size as the hole in Rupert's side. My mouth was dry and I swallowed hard. I was a cuckoo's egg, about to be laid in the wrong nest. The three of us hesitated before the door, all reluctant to take the final step.

"I'd b-better go," I said, trying hard to control my shaking voice and limbs. "They'll wonder what's keeping us."

Jamie closed his eyes for a moment, nodded, then stepped toward me.

"I think you'd better swoon, Sassenach," he said. "It will be easier that way, maybe." He stooped, picked me up in his arms, and carried me through the door that Dougal held open.

His heart pounded beneath my ear, and I could feel the trembling in his arms as he carried me. After the stuffiness of the church, with its smells of sweat, blood, black powder and horse manure, the cold fresh air of early morning took my breath away, and I huddled against him, shivering. His hands tightened under my knees and shoulders, hard as a promise; he would never let me go.

"God," he said once, under his breath, and then we had reached them. Sharp questions, mumbled answers, the reluctant loosening of his grip as he laid me on the ground, and then the swish of his feet, going away through wet grass. I was alone, in the hands of the strangers.

44

In Which Quite a Lot of Things Gang Agley

I hunched closer to the fire, holding out my hands to thaw. They were grimy from holding the reins all day, and I wondered briefly whether it was worthwhile walking the distance to the stream to wash them. Maintaining modern standards of hygiene in the absence of all forms of plumbing sometimes seemed a good deal more trouble than it was worth. No bloody wonder if people got ill and died frequently, I thought sourly. They died of simple filth and ignorance more than anything.

The thought of dying in filth was sufficient to get me to my feet, tired as I was. The tiny streamlet that passed by the campsite was boggy near the edges, and my shoes sank deep into the marshy growth. Having traded dirty hands for wet feet, I slogged back to the fire, to find Corporal Rowbotham waiting for me with a bowl of what he said was stew.

"The Captain's compliments, Mum," he said, actually tugging his forelock as he handed me the bowl, "and he says to tell yer as we'll be in Tavistock tomorrow. There's an inn there." He hesitated, his round, homely, middle-aged face concerned, then added, "The Captain's apologies for the lack of accommodation, Mum, but we've fixed a tent for yer for tonight. 'S not much, but mebbe'll keep the rain off yer."

"Thank the Captain for me, Corporal," I said, as graciously as I could manage. "And thank *you*, too," I added, with more warmth. I was entirely aware that Captain Mainwaring considered me a burdensome nuisance, and would have taken no thought at all for my night's shelter. The tent—a spare length of canvas draped carefully over a tree limb and pegged at both sides— was undoubtedly the sole idea of Corporal Rowbotham.

The Corporal went away and I sat by myself, slowly eating scorched potatoes and stringy beef. I'd found a late patch of charlock near the stream, leaves wilting and brown around the edges, and had brought back a handful in my pocket, along with a few juniper berries picked during a stop earlier in the day. The mustard leaves were old and very bitter, but I managed to get them down by wodging them between bites of potato. I finished the meal with the juniper berries, biting each one briefly to avoid choking and then swallowing the tough, flattened berry, seed and all. The oily burst of flavor sent fumes up the back of my throat that made my eyes water, but they did cleanse my tongue of the taste of grease and scorch, and would, with the charlock leaves, maybe be sufficient to ward off scurvy.

I had had a large store of dried fiddleheads, rose hips, dried apples and dill seeds in the larger of my two medicine chests, carefully collected as a defense against nutritional deficiency during the long winter months. I hoped Jamie was eating them.

I put my head down on my knees; I didn't think anyone was looking at me, but I didn't want my face to show when I thought of Jamie.

I had stayed in my pretended swoon on Falkirk Hill as long as I could, but was roused before too long by a British dragoon trying to force brandy from a pocket flask down my throat. Unsure quite what to do with me, my "rescuers" had taken me to Callendar House and turned me over to General Hawley's staff.

So far, all had gone according to plan. Within the hour, though, things had gone rather seriously awry. From sitting in an anteroom and listening to everything that was said around me, I soon learned that what I had thought was a major battle during the night had in fact been no more than a small skirmish between the MacKenzies and a detachment of English troops on their way to join the main body of the army. Said army was even now assembling itself to meet the expected Highland charge on Falkirk Hill; the battle I thought I had lived through had not, in fact, happened yet!

General Hawley himself was overseeing this process, and as no one seemed to have any idea what ought to be done with me, I was consigned to the custody of a young private, along with a letter describing the circumstances of my rescue, and dispatched to a Colonel Campbell's temporary headquarters at Kerse. The young private, a stocky specimen named Dobbs, was distressingly zealous in his urge to perform his duty, and despite several tries along the way, I had been unable to get away from him.

We had arrived in Kerse, only to find that Colonel Campbell was not there, but had been summoned to Livingston.

"Look," I had suggested to my escorting gaoler, "plainly Colonel Campbell is not going to have time or inclination to talk to me, and there's nothing I could tell him in any case. Why don't I just find lodging in the town here, until I can make some arrangement for continuing my journey to Edinburgh?" For lacking any better idea, I had given the English basically the same story I had given to Colum MacKenzie, two years earlier; that I was a widowed lady from Oxford, traveling to visit a relative in Scotland, when I had been set upon and abducted by Highland brigands.

Private Dobbs shook his head, flushing stubbornly. He couldn't be more than twenty, and he wasn't very bright, but once he got an idea in his head, he hung on to it.

"I can't let you do that, Mrs. Beauchamp," he said—for I had used my own maiden name as an alias—"Captain Bledsoe'll have my liver for it, an' I don't bring you safe to the Colonel."

So to Livingston we had gone, mounted on two of the sorriest-looking nags I had ever seen. I was finally relieved of the attentions of my escort, but with no improvement in my circumstances. Instead, I found myself immured in an upper room in a house in Livingston, telling the story once again, to one Colonel Gordon MacLeish Campbell, a Lowland Scot in command of one of the Elector's regiments.

"Aye, I see," he said, in the sort of tone that suggested that he didn't see at all. He was a small, foxy-faced man, with balding reddish hair brushed back from his temples. He narrowed his eyes still further, glancing down at the crumpled letter on his blotter.

"This says," he said, placing a pair of half-spectacles on his nose in order to peer more closely at the sheet of paper, "that one of your captors, Mistress, was a Fraser clansman, very large, and with red hair. Is this information correct?"

"Yes," I said, wondering what he was getting at.

He tilted his head so the spectacles slid down his nose, the better to fix me with a piercing stare over the tops.

"The men who rescued you near Falkirk gave it as their impression that one of your captors was none other than the notorious Highland chief known as 'Red Jamie.' Now, I am aware, Mrs. Beauchamp, that you were . . . distressed, shall we say?"—his lips pulled back from the word, but it wasn't a smile —"during the period of your captivity, and perhaps in no fit frame of mind to make close observations, but did you notice at any time whether the other men present referred to this man by name?"

"They did. They called him Jamie." I couldn't imagine any harm that could be done by telling him this; the broadsheets I had seen made it abundantly clear that Jamie was a supporter of the Stuart cause. The placing of Jamie at the battle of Falkirk was possibly of interest to the English, but could hardly incriminate him further.

"They canna very well hang me more than once," he'd said. Once would be more than enough. I glanced at the window. Night had fallen half an hour ago, and lanterns glowed in the street below, carried by soldiers passing to and fro. Jamie would be at Callendar House, searching for the window where I should be waiting.

I had the absurd certainty, all of a sudden, that he had followed me, had known somehow where I was going, and would be waiting in the street below, for me to show myself.

I rose abruptly and went to the window. The street below was empty, save for a seller of pickled herrings, seated on a stool with his lantern at his feet, waiting for the possibility of customers. It wasn't Jamie, of course. There was no way for him to find me. No one in the Stuart camp knew where I was; I was entirely alone. I pressed my hands hard against the glass in sudden panic, not caring that I might shatter it.

"Mistress Beauchamp! Are ye well?" The Colonel's voice behind me was sharp with alarm.

I clamped my lips tight together to stop them shaking and took several deep breaths, clouding the glass so the street below vanished in mist. Outwardly calm, I turned back to face the Colonel.

"I'm quite well," I said. "If you've finished asking questions, I'd like to go now."

"Would ye? Mmm." He looked me over with something like doubt, then shook his head decidedly.

"Ye'll stay the night here," he declared. "In the morning, I shall be sendin' ye southward."

I felt a spasm of shock clench my insides. "South! What the hell for?" I blurted.

His fox-fur eyebrows rose in astonishment and his mouth fell open. Then he shook himself slightly, and clamped it shut, opening it only a slit to deliver himself of his next words.

"I have orders to send on any information pertaining to the Highland criminal known as Red Jamie Fraser," he said. "Or any person associated with him."

"I'm not associated with him!" I said. Unless you wanted to count marriage, of course.

Colonel Campbell was oblivious. He turned to his desk and shuffled through a stack of dispatches.

"Aye, here it is. Captain Mainwaring will be the officer who escorts you. He will come to fetch ye here at dawn." He rang a small silver bell shaped like a goblin, and the door opened to reveal the inquiring face of his private orderly. "Garvie, ye'll see the lady to her quarters. Lock the door." He turned to me and bowed perfunctorily. "I think we shall not meet again, Mrs. Beauchamp; I wish ye good rest and God-speed." And that was that.

I didn't know quite how fast God-speed was, but it was likely faster than Captain Mainwaring's detachment had ridden. The Captain was in charge of a supply train of wagons, bound for Lanark. After delivery of these and their drivers, he was then to proceed south with the rest of his detachment, delivering nonvital dispatches as he went. I was apparently in the category of nonurgent intelligence, for we had been more than a week on the road, and no sign of reaching whatever place I was bound for.

"South." Did that mean London? I wondered, for the thousandth time. Captain Mainwaring had not told me my final destination, but I could think of no other possibility.

Lifting my head, I caught one of the dragoons across the fire staring at me. I stared flatly back at him, until he flushed and dropped his eyes to the bowl in his hands. I was accustomed to such looks, though most were less bold about it.

It had started from the beginning, with a certain reserved embarrassment on the part of the young idiot who had taken me to Livingston. It had taken some little time for me to realize that what caused the attitude of distant reserve on the part of the English officers was not suspicion, but a mixture of contempt and horror, mingled with a trace of pity and a sense of official responsibility that kept their true feelings from showing openly.

I had not merely been rescued from a band of the rapacious, marauding Scots. I had been delivered from a captivity during which I had spent an entire night in a single room with a number of men who were, to the certain knowledge of all right-thinking Englishmen, "Little more than Savage Beasts, guilty of Rapine, Robbery, and countless other such Hideous Crimes." Not thinkable, therefore, that a young Englishwoman had passed a night in the company of such beasts and emerged unscathed.

I reflected grimly that Jamie's carrying me out in an apparent swoon might have eased matters originally, but had undoubtedly contributed to the overall impression that he—and the other assorted Scots—had been having their forcible way with me. And thanks to the detailed letter written by the captain of my original band of rescuers, everyone to whom I had later been passed on—and everyone to whom they talked, I imagined—knew about it. Schooled in Paris, I understood the mechanics of gossip very well.

Corporal Rowbotham had certainly heard the stories, but continued to treat me kindly, with none of the smirking speculation I occasionally surprised on the faces of the other soldiers. If I had been inclined to offer up bedtime prayers, I would have included his name therein.

I rose, dusted off my cloak, and went to my tent. Seeing me go, Corporal Rowbotham also rose, and circling the fire discreetly, sat down by his comrades again, his back in direct line with the entrance to my tent. When the soldiers retired to their beds, I knew he would seek a spot at a respectful distance, but still within call of my resting place. He had done this for the past three nights, whether we slept in inn or field.

Three nights earlier I had tried yet another escape. Captain Mainwaring was well aware that I traveled with him under compulsion, and while he didn't like being burdened with me, he was too conscientious a soldier to shirk the responsibility. I had two guards, who watched me closely, riding on each side by day.

At night, the guard was relaxed, the Captain evidently thinking it unlikely that I would strike out on foot over deserted moors in the dead of winter. The Captain was correct. I had no interest in committing suicide.

On the night in question, however, we had passed through a small village about two hours before we stopped for the night. Even on foot, I was sure I could backtrack and reach the village before dawn. The village boasted a small distillery, from which wagons bearing loads of barrels departed for several towns in the surrounding region. I had seen the distiller's yard, piled high with barrels, and thought I had a decent chance of hiding there, and leaving with the first wagon.

So after the camp was quiet, and the soldiers lumped and snoring in their blankets round the fire, I had crept out of my own blanket, carefully laid near the edge of a willow grove, and made my way through the trailing fronds, with no more sound than the rustle of the wind.

Leaving the grove, I had thought it was the rustle of the wind behind me, too, until a hand clamped down on my shoulder.

"Don't scream. Y' don't want the Capting to know yer out wi'out leave." I didn't scream, only because all the breath had been startled out of me. The soldier, a tallish man called "Jessie" by his mates, because of the trouble he took in combing out his yellow curls, smiled at me, and I smiled a little uncertainly back at him.

His eyes dropped to my bosom. He sighed, raised his eyes to mine, and took a step toward me. I took three steps back, fast.

"It doesn't matter, really, does it, sweet'art?" he said, still smiling lazily. "Not after what's 'appened already. What's once more, eh? And I'm an Englishman, too," he coaxed. "Not a filthy Scot."

"Leave the poor woman alone, Jess," Corporal Rowbotham said, emerging silently from the screen of willows behind him. "She's had enough trouble, poor lady." He spoke softly enough, but Jessie glared at him, then, thinking better of whatever he'd had in mind, turned without another word and disappeared under the willow leaves.

The Corporal had waited, unspeaking, for me to gather up my fallen cloak, and then had followed me back to the camp. He had gone to pick up his own blanket, motioned to me to lie down, and placed himself six feet away, sitting up with his blanket about his shoulders Indian-style. Whenever I woke during the night, I had seen him still sitting there, staring shortsightedly into the fire.

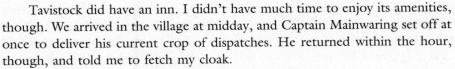

Tavistock did have an inn. I didn't have much time to enjoy its amenities, though. We arrived in the village at midday, and Captain Mainwaring set off at once to deliver his current crop of dispatches. He returned within the hour, though, and told me to fetch my cloak.

"Why?" I said, bewildered. "Where are we going?"

He glanced at me indifferently and said "To Bellhurst Manor."

"Right," I said. It sounded a trifle more impressive than my current surroundings, which featured several soldiers playing at chuck-a-luck on the floor, a flea-ridden mongrel asleep by the fire, and a strong smell of hops.

The manor house, without regard to the natural beauty of its site, stubbornly turned its back on the open meadows and huddled inland instead, facing the stark cliffside.

The drive was straight, short, and unadorned, unlike the lovely curving approaches to French manors. But the entrance was equipped with two utilitarian stone pillars, each bearing the heraldic device of the owner. I stared at it as my horse clopped past, trying to place it. A cat—perhaps a leopard?—couchant, with a lily in its paw. It was familiar, I knew. But whose?

There was a stir in the long grass near the gate, and I caught a quick glimpse of pale blue eyes as a hunched bundle of rags scuttled into the shadows, away from the churn of the horses' hooves. Something about the ragged beggar seemed faintly familiar, too. Perhaps I was merely hallucinating; grasping at anything that didn't remind me of English soldiers.

The escort waited in the dooryard, not bothering to dismount, while I mounted the steps with Captain Mainwaring, and waited while he hammered at the door, rather wondering what might be on the other side of it.

"Mrs. Beauchamp?" The butler, if that's what he was, looked rather as though he suspected the worst. No doubt he was right.

"Yes," I said. "Er, whose house is this?"

But even as I asked, I raised my eyes and looked into the gloom of the inner hall. A face stared back at me, doe-eyes wide and startled.

Mary Hawkins.

As the girl opened her mouth, I opened mine as well. And screamed as loudly as I could. The butler, taken unprepared, took a step back, tripped on a settee, and fell over sideways like a bowls pin. I could hear the startled noises of the soldiers outside, coming up the steps.

I picked up my skirts, shrieked "A mouse! A mouse!" and fled toward the parlor, yelling like a banshee.

Infected by my apparent hysteria, Mary shrieked as well, and clutched me about the middle as I cannoned into her. I bore her back into the recesses of the parlor with me, and grabbed her by the shoulders.

"Don't tell anyone who I am," I breathed into her ear. "No one! My life depends on it!" I had thought I was being melodramatic, but it occurred to me, as I spoke the words, that I could very well be telling the exact truth. Being married to Red Jamie Fraser was likely a dicey proposition.

Mary had time only to nod in a dazed sort of way, when the door at the far side of the room opened, and a man came in.

"Whatever is all this wretched noise, Mary?" he demanded. A plump, contented-looking man, he had also the firm chin and tightly satisfied lips of the man who is contented because he generally gets his own way.

"N-nothing, Papa," said Mary, stuttering in her nervousness. "Only a m-m-mouse."

The baronet squeezed his eyes shut and inhaled deeply, seeking patience. Having found a simulacrum of that state, he opened them and gazed at his offspring.

"Say it again, child," he ordered. "But straight. I'll not have you mumbling and blithering. Take a deep breath, steady yourself. Now. Again."

Mary obeyed, inhaling 'til the laces of her bodice strained across the budding chest. Her fingers wound themselves in the silk brocade of her skirt, seeking support.

"It w-was a mouse, Papa. Mrs. Fr . . . er, this lady was frightened by a mouse."

Dismissing this attempt as barely satisfactory, the baronet stepped forward, examining me with interest.

"Oh? And who might you be, Madam?"

Captain Mainwaring, arriving belatedly after the search for the mythical mouse, popped up at my elbow and introduced me, handing over the note of introduction from Colonel MacLeish.

"Hum. So, it seems His Grace is to be your host, Madam, at least temporarily." He handed the note to the waiting butler, and took the hat the latter had taken from the nearby rack.

"I regret that our acquaintance should be so short, Mrs. Beauchamp. I was just leaving myself." He glanced over his shoulder, to a short stairway that branched off the hall. The butler, dignity restored, was already mounting it, grubby note reposing on a salver held before him. "I see Walmisley has gone to tell His Grace of your arrival. I must go, or I shall miss the post-coach. *Adieu,* Mrs. Beauchamp."

He turned to Mary, hanging back against the paneled wainscoting.

"Goodbye, daughter. Do try to . . . well." The corners of his mouth turned up in what was meant to be a fatherly smile. "Goodbye, Mary."

"Goodbye, Papa," she murmured, eyes on the ground. I glanced from one to the other. What on earth was Mary Hawkins, of all people, doing here? Plainly she was staying at the house; I supposed the owner must be some connection of her family's.

"Mrs. Beauchamp?" A small, tubby footman was bowing at my elbow. "His Grace will see you now, Madam."

Mary's hands clutched at my sleeve as I turned to follow the footman.

"B-b-b-but . . ." she began. In my keyed-up state, I didn't think I could manage sufficient patience to hear her out. I smiled vaguely and patted her hand.

"Yes, yes," I said. "Don't worry, it will be all right."

"B-but it's my . . ."

The footman bowed and pushed open a door at the end of the corridor.

Light within fell on the richness of brocade and polished wood. The chair I could see to one side had a family crest embroidered on its back; a clearer version of the worn stone shield I had seen outside.

A leopard couchant, holding in its paw a bunch of lilies—or were they crocuses? Alarm bells rang in my mind as the chair's occupant rose, his shadow falling across the polished doorsill as he turned. Mary's final anguished word made it out, neck and neck with the footman's announcement.

"My *g-g-godfather!*" she said.

"His Grace, the Duke of Sandringham," said the footman.

"Mrs. . . . Beauchamp?" said the Duke, his mouth dropping open in astonishment.

"Well," I said weakly. "Something like that."

<hr />

The door of the drawing room closed behind me, leaving me alone with His Grace. My last sight of Mary had been of her standing out in the hall, eyes like saucers, mouth opening and shutting silently like a goldfish.

There were huge Chinese jars flanking the windows, and inlaid tables under them. A bronze Venus posed coquettishly on the mantelpiece, companioned by a pair of gold-rimmed porcelain bowls and silver-gilt candelabra, blazing with beeswax candles. A close-napped carpet that I recognized as a very good Kermanshah covered most of the floor and a spinet crouched in one corner; what little space was left bare was occupied by marquetried furniture and the odd bit of statuary.

"Nice place you have here," I remarked graciously to the Duke, who had been standing before the fire, hands folded beneath his coattail as he watched me, an expression of wary amusement on the broad, florid face.

"Thank you," he said, in the piping tenor that came so oddly from that barrel-chested frame. "Your presence adorns it, my dear." Amusement won out over wariness, and he smiled, a bluff, disarming grin.

"Why Beauchamp?" he asked. "That isn't by chance your real name, is it?"

"My maiden name," I answered, rattled into the truth. His thick blond eyebrows shot up.

"*Are* you French?"

"No. English. I couldn't use Fraser, though, could I?"

"I see." Brows still raised, he nodded at a small brocaded love seat, inviting me to be seated. It was richly carved and beautifully proportioned, a museum piece, like everything else in the room. I swept my sodden skirts to one side as gracefully as I could, ignoring their liberal stains of mud and horsehair, and delicately lowered myself onto the primrose satin.

The Duke paced slowly back and forth before the fire, watching me, still with a slight smile on his features. I fought the growing warmth and comfort that spread through my aching legs, threatening to drag me into the abyss of fatigue that gaped open at my feet. This was no time to let down my guard.

"Which are you?" the Duke inquired suddenly. "An English hostage, a fervent Jacobite, or a French agent?"

I rubbed two fingers over the ache between my eyes. The correct answer was "none of the above," but I didn't think it would get me very far.

"The hospitality of this house seems a trifle lacking by comparison with its appointments," I said, as haughtily as I could manage under the circumstances, which wasn't all that much. Still, Louise's example of great-ladydom had not been entirely in vain.

The Duke laughed, a high, chittering sort of laugh, like a bat that has just heard a good one.

"Your pardon, Madam. You're quite right; I should have thought to offer you refreshment before presuming to question you. *Most* thoughtless of me."

He murmured something to the footman who appeared in answer to his ring, then waited calmly before the fire for the tray to arrive. I sat in silence, glancing around the room, occasionally stealing a look at my host. Neither of us was interested in making small talk. Despite his outward geniality, this was an armed truce, and both of us knew it.

What I wanted to know was why. No stranger to people wondering who in hell I was, I rather wondered myself where the Duke came into it. Or where he thought *I* did. He had met me twice before, as Mrs. Fraser, wife of the laird of Lallybroch. Now I had turned up on his doorstep, posing as an English hostage named Beauchamp lately rescued from a gang of Scottish Jacobites. That was enough to make anyone wonder. But his attitude toward me went a long way past simple curiosity.

The tea arrived, complete with scones and cake. The Duke picked up his own cup, motioned to mine with a lift of one brow, and we took tea, still both in silence. Somewhere on the other side of the house, I could hear a muffled banging, as of someone hammering. The soft chime of the Duke's cup against its saucer was the signal for the resumption of hostilities.

"Now, then," he said, with as much firmness as a man who sounded like Mickey Mouse could manage. "Let me begin, Mrs. Fraser—I may call you so? Thank you. Let me begin by saying that I know a great deal about you already. I intend to know more. You will do well to answer me fully and without hesitations. I must say, Mrs. Fraser, that you are amazingly difficult to kill"—he bowed slightly in my direction, that smile still on his lips—"but I feel sure that it could be accomplished, given sufficient determination."

I stared at him, unmoving; not out of any native sang-froid, but from simple dumbfoundedness. Adopting another of Louise's mannerisms, I raised both eyebrows inquiringly, sipped tea, then patted my lips delicately with the monogrammed serviette provided.

"I am afraid you will think me dense, Your Grace," I said politely, "but I haven't the faintest idea what you're talking about."

"Haven't you, my dear?"

The small, jolly blue eyes didn't blink. He reached for the silver-gilt bell on the tray and rang it once.

The man must have been waiting in the next room for the summons, for the door opened immediately. A tall, lean man in the dark habiliments and good linen of an upper servant advanced to the Duke's side and bowed deeply.

"Your Grace?" He spoke English, but the French accent was unmistakable. The face was French, too; long-nosed and white, with thin, tight lips and a pair of ears that stood out from his head like small wings on either side, their tips fiercely red. His lean face grew still paler as he looked up and spotted me, and he took an involuntary step backward.

Sandringham watched this with a frown of irritation, then switched his gaze to me.

"You don't recognize him?" he asked.

I was beginning to shake my head, when the man's right hand twitched suddenly against the cloth of his breeches. As unobtrusively as possible, he was making the sign of the horns, middle fingers folded down, index and little finger pointed at me. I knew, then, and in the next instant had seen the confirmation of my knowledge—the small beauty mark above the fork of his thumb.

I hadn't the slightest doubt; it was the man in the spotted shirt who had attacked me and Mary in Paris. And all too obviously in the Duke's employ.

"You bloody *bastard*!" I said. I leaped to my feet, overturning the tea table, and snatched up the nearest object to hand, a carved alabaster tobacco jar. I hurled it at the man's head, and he turned and fled precipitately, the heavy jar missing him by inches to smash against the door frame.

The door slammed to as I started after him, and I stopped in my tracks, breathing heavily. I glared at Sandringham, hands braced on my hips.

"Who is he?" I demanded.

"My valet," said the Duke calmly. "Albert Danton, by name. A good fellow with neckcloths and stockings, but a trifle excitable, as so many of these Frenchmen are. Incredibly superstitious, too." He frowned disapprovingly at the closed door. "Bloody papists, with all these saints and smells and such. Believe anything at all."

My breathing was slowing, though my heart still banged against the whalebones of my bodice. I had trouble drawing a deep breath.

"You filthy, disgusting, outrageous. . . . *pervert*!"

The Duke seemed bored by this, and nodded negligently.

"Yes, yes, my dear. All that, I'm sure, and more. A trifle unlucky, too, at least on that occasion."

"Unlucky? Is that what you'd call it?" Unsteadily, I moved to the love seat, and sat down. My hands were shaking with nerves, and I clasped them together, hidden in the folds of my skirt.

"On several counts, my dear lady. Just look at it." He spread out both hands in graceful entreaty. "I send Danton to dispose of you. He and his companions decide to entertain themselves a bit first; that's all well and good, but in the process, they get a good look at you, leap unaccountably to the conclusion that you're a witch of some kind, lose their heads entirely and run off. But not before debauching my goddaughter, who is present by accident, thus ruining all chance of the excellent marriage I had painstakingly arranged for her. Consider the irony of it!"

The shocks were coming thick and fast, and I hardly knew which to respond to first. There seemed one particularly striking statement in this speech, though.

"What do you mean 'dispose of me'?" I demanded. "Do you mean to say you actually tried to have me *killed*?" The room seemed to be swaying a bit, and I took a deep gulp of tea as being the nearest thing to a restorative available. It wasn't terribly effective.

"Well, yes," Sandringham said pleasantly. "That was the point I was endeavoring to make. Tell me, my dear, would you care for a cup of sherry?"

I eyed him narrowly for a moment. Having just stated that he'd tried to have me killed, he now expected me to accept a cup of sherry from his hands?

"Brandy," I said. "Lots of it."

He giggled in that high-pitched way again, and made his way to the sideboard, remarking over his shoulder, "Captain Randall said you were a most diverting woman. Quite an encomium from the Captain, you know. He hasn't much use for women ordinarily, though they swarm over him. His looks, I suppose; it can't be his manner."

"So Jack Randall *does* work for you," I said, taking the glass he handed me. I had watched him pour out two glasses, and was sure that both contained nothing but brandy. I took a large and sorely needed swallow.

The Duke matched me, blinking his eyes at the effect of the pungent liquid.

"Of course," he said. "Often the best tool is the most dangerous. One doesn't hesitate to use it on that account; one merely makes sure to take adequate precautions."

"Dangerous, eh? Just how much do you know about Jonathan Randall?" I asked curiously.

The Duke tittered. "Oh, virtually everything, I should think, my dear. Most likely a great deal more than you do, in fact. It doesn't do to employ a man like that without having a means at hand to control him, you know. And money is a good bridle, but a weak rein."

"Unlike blackmail?" I said dryly.

He sat back, hands clasped across his bulging stomach, and regarded me with bland interest.

"Ah. You are thinking that blackmail might work both ways, I suppose?" He shook his head, dislodging a few grains of snuff that floated down onto the silk waistcoat.

"No, my dear. For one thing, there is something of a difference in our stations. While rumor of that sort might affect my reception in some circles of society, that is not a matter of grave concern to me. While for the good Captain —well, the army takes a very dim view of such unnatural predilections. The penalty is often death, in fact. No, not much comparison, really." He cocked his head to one side, so far as the multiple chins allowed.

"But it is neither the promise of wealth nor the threat of exposure that binds John Randall to me," he said. The small, watery blue eyes gleamed in their orbits. "He serves me because I can give him what he desires."

I eyed the corpulent frame with unconcealed disgust, making His Grace shake with laughter.

"No, not that," he said. "The Captain's tastes are somewhat more refined than that. Unlike my own."

"What, then?"

"Punishment," he said softly. "But you know that, don't you? Or at least your husband does."

I felt unclean simply from being near him, and rose to get away. The shards of the alabaster tobacco jar lay on the floor, and I kicked one inadvertently, so that it pinged off the wall, ricocheting and spinning off under the love seat, reminding me of the recent Danton.

I wasn't at all sure that I wanted to discuss the subject of my aborted murder with him, but it seemed at the moment preferable to some alternatives.

"What did you want to kill me for?" I asked abruptly, turning to face him. I glanced quickly over the collection of objects on a piecrust table, looking for a suitable weapon of defense, just in case he still felt the urge.

He didn't seem to. Instead, he bent laboriously over and picked up the teapot—miraculously unbroken—and set it upright on the restored tea table.

"It seemed expedient at the time," he said calmly. "I had learned that you and your husband were attempting to thwart a particular affair in which I had interested myself. I considered removing your husband instead, but it seemed too dangerous, what with his close relation to two of the greatest families in Scotland."

"Considered removing him?" A light dawned—one of many that were going off in my skull like fireworks. "Was it you who sent the seamen who attacked Jamie in Paris?"

The Duke nodded in an offhand manner.

"That seemed the simplest method, if a bit crude. But then, Dougal Mac-

Kenzie turned up in Paris, and I wondered whether in fact your husband was in fact working *for* the Stuarts. I became unsure where his interests lay."

What I was wondering was just where the *Duke*'s interests lay. This odd speech made it sound very much as though he was a secret Jacobite—and if so, he'd done a really masterly job of keeping his secrets.

"And then," he went on, delicately placing the teapot's lid back in place, "there was your growing friendship with Louis of France. Even had your husband failed with the bankers, Louis could have supplied Charles Stuart with what he needed—provided you kept your pretty nose out of the affair."

He frowned closely at the scone he was holding, flicked a couple of threads off it, then decided against eating it and tossed it onto the table.

"Once it became clear what was really happening, I tried to lure your husband back to Scotland, with the offer of a pardon; very expensive, that was," he said reflectively. "And all for nothing, too!

"But then I recalled your husband's apparent devotion to you—quite touching," he said, with a benevolent smile that I particularly disliked. "I supposed that your tragic demise might well distract him from the endeavor in which he was engaged without provoking the sort of interest his own murder would have involved."

Suddenly thinking of something, I turned to look at the harpsichord in the corner of the room. Several sheets of music adorned its rack, written in a fine, clear hand. *Fifty thousand pounds, upon the occasion of Your Highness's setting foot in Scotland.* Signed S. "S," of course, for Sandringham. The Duke laughed, in apparent delight.

"That was really very clever of you, my dear. It must have been you; I'd heard of your husband's unfortunate inability with music."

"Actually, it wasn't," I replied, turning back from the piano. The table at my side lacked anything useful in the way of letter openers or blunt objects, but I hastily picked up a vase, and buried my face in the mass of hothouse flowers it held. I closed my eyes, feeling the brush of cool petals against my suddenly heated cheeks. I didn't dare to look up, for fear my telltale face would give me away.

For behind the Duke's shoulder, I had seen a round, leathery object, shaped like a pumpkin, framed by the green velvet draperies like one of the Duke's exotic art objects. I opened my eyes, peering cautiously through the petals, and the wide, snaggle-toothed mouth split in a grin like a jack-o'-lantern's.

I was torn between terror and relief. I had been right, then, about the beggar near the gate. It was Hugh Munro, an old companion from Jamie's days as a Highland outlaw. A one-time schoolmaster, he had been captured by the Turks at sea, disfigured by torture, and driven to beggary and poaching—professions he augmented by successful spying. I had heard he was an agent of the Highland army, but hadn't realized his activities had brought him so far south.

How long had he been there, perched like a bird on the ivy outside the second-story window? I didn't dare try to communicate with him; it was all I could do to keep my eyes fixed on a point just above the Duke's shoulder, gazing with apparent indifference into space.

The Duke was regarding me with interest. "Really? Not Gerstmann, surely? I shouldn't have thought he had a sufficiently devious mind."

"And you think I do? I'm flattered." I kept my nose in the flowers, speaking distractedly into a peony.

The figure outside released his grip on the ivy long enough to bring one hand up into view. Deprived of his tongue by his Saracen captors, Hugh Munro's hands spoke for him. Staring intently at me, he pointed deliberately, first at me, then at himself, then off to one side. The broad hand tilted and the first two fingers became a pair of running legs, racing away to the east. A final wink, a clenched fist in salute, and he was gone.

I relaxed, trembling slightly with reaction, and took a deep, restorative breath. I sneezed, and put the flowers down.

"So you're a Jacobite, are you?" I asked.

"Not necessarily," the Duke answered genially. "The question is, my dear —are you?" Completely unselfconscious, he took off his wig and scratched his fair, balding head before putting it back on.

"You tried to stop the effort to restore King James to his throne when you were in Paris. Failing at that, you and your husband appear now to be His Highness's most loyal supporters. Why?" The small blue eyes showed nothing more than a mild interest, but it wasn't a mild interest that had tried to have me killed.

Ever since finding out who my host was, I had been trying as hard as I could to remember what it was that Frank and the Reverend Mr. Wakefield had once said about him. *Was* he a Jacobite? So far as I could recall, the verdict of history—in the persons of Frank and the Reverend—was uncertain. So was I.

"I don't believe I'm going to tell you," I said slowly.

One blond brow arched high, the Duke took a small enameled box from his pocket and abstracted a pinch of the contents.

"Are you sure that's wise, my dear? Danton is still within call, you know."

"Danton wouldn't touch me with a ten-foot pole," I said bluntly. "Neither would you, for that matter. Not," I added hastily, seeing his mouth open, "on that account. But if you want so badly to know which side I'm on, you aren't going to kill me before finding out, now, are you?"

The Duke choked on his pinch of snuff and coughed heavily, thumping himself on the chest of his embroidered waistcoat. I drew myself up and stared coldly down my nose at him as he sneezed and spluttered.

"You're trying to frighten me into telling you things, but it won't work," I said, with a lot more confidence than I felt.

Sandringham dabbed gently at his streaming eyes with a handkerchief. At last he drew a deep breath, and blew it out between plump, pursed lips as he stared at me.

"Very well, then," he said, quite calmly. "I imagine my workmen have finished their alterations to your quarters by now. I shall summon a maid to take you to your room."

I must have gawped foolishly at him, for he smiled derisively as he hoisted himself out of his chair.

"To a point, you know, it doesn't matter," he said. "Whatever else you may be or whatever information you may possess, you have one invaluable attribute as a houseguest."

"And what's that?" I demanded. He paused, hand on the bell, and smiled.

"You're Red Jamie's wife," he said softly. "And he *is* fond of you, my dear, is he not?"

As prisons go, I had seen worse. The room measured perhaps thirty feet in each dimension, and was furnished with a lavishness exceeded only by the sitting room downstairs. The canopied bed stood on a small dais, with baldachins of ostrich feathers sprouting from the corners of its damask drapes, and a pair of matching brocaded chairs squatted comfortably before a huge fireplace.

The maidservant who had accompanied me in set down the basin and ewer she carried, and hurried to light the ready-laid fire. The footman laid his covered supper-tray on the table by the door, then stood stolidly in the doorway, dishing any thoughts I might have had of trying a quick dash down the hall. Not that it would do me much good to try, I thought gloomily; I'd be hopelessly lost in the house after the first turn of the corridor; the bloody place was as big as Buckingham Palace.

"I'm sure His Grace hopes as you'll be comfortable, ma'am," said the servant, curtsying prettily on her way out.

"Oh, I'll bet he does," I said, ungraciously.

The door closed behind her with a depressingly solid thud, and the grating sound of the big key turning seemed to scrape away the last bit of insulation covering my raw nerves.

Shivering in the chill of the vast room, I clutched my elbows and walked to the fire, where I subsided into one of the chairs. My impulse was to take advantage of the solitude to have a nice private little fit of hysterics. On the other hand, I was afraid that if I allowed my tight-reined emotions any play at all, I would never get them in check again. I closed my eyes tight and watched the red flicker of the firelight on my inner eyelids, willing myself to calmness.

After all, I was in no danger for the moment, and Hugh Munro was on his way to Jamie. Even if Jamie had lost my trail over the course of the week's travel, Hugh would find him and lead him right. Hugh knew every cottar and tinker, every farmhouse and manor within four parishes. A message from the speechless man would travel through the network of news and gossip as quickly as the wind-driven clouds passed over the mountains. If he had made it down from his lofty perch in the ivy and safely off the Duke's grounds without being apprehended, that was.

"Don't be ridiculous," I said aloud, "the man's a professional poacher. Of course he made it." The echo of my words against the ornate white-plaster ceiling was somehow comforting.

"And if so," I continued firmly, still talking to hear myself, "then Jamie will come."

Right, I thought suddenly. And Sandringham's men will be waiting for him, when he does. *You're Red Jamie's wife,* the Duke had said. My one invaluable attribute. I was bait.

"I'm a salmon egg!" I exclaimed, sitting up straight in my chair. The sheer indignity of the image summoned up a small but welcome spurt of rage that pushed the fear back a little way. I tried to fan the flames of anger by getting up and striding back and forth, thinking of new names to call the Duke next time we met. I'd gotten as far in my compositions as "skulking pederast," when a muffled shouting from outside distracted my attention.

Pushing back the heavy velvet drapes from the window, I found that the Duke had been as good as his word. Stout wooden bars crisscrossed the window frame, latticed so closely together that I could scarcely thrust an arm between them. I could see, though.

Dusk had fallen, and the shadows under the park trees were black as ink. The shouting was coming from there, matched by answering cries from the stables, where two or three figures suddenly appeared, bearing lit torches.

The small, dark figures ran toward the wood, the fire of their pine torches streaming backward, flaring orange in the cold, damp wind. As they reached the edge of the park, a knot of vaguely human shapes became visible, tumbling onto the grass before the house. The ground was wet, and the force of their struggle left deep gashes of black in the winter-dead lawn.

I stood on tiptoe, gripping the bars and pressing my head against the wood in an effort to see more. The light of the day had failed utterly, and by the torchlight, I could distinguish no more than the occasional flailing limb in the riot below.

It couldn't be Jamie, I told myself, trying to swallow the lump in my throat that was my heart. Not so soon, not now. And not alone, surely he wouldn't have come alone? For I could see by now that the fight centered on one man, now on his knees, no more than a hunched black shape under the fists and sticks of the Duke's gamekeepers and stable-lads.

Then the hunched figure sprawled flat, and the shouting died, though a few more blows were given for good measure before the small gang of servants stood back. A few words of conversation were exchanged, inaudible from my vantage point, and two of the men stooped and seized the figure beneath the arms. As they passed beneath my third-floor window on their way toward the back of the house, the torchlight illuminated a pair of dragging, sandal-shod feet, and the tatters of a grimy smock. Not Jamie.

One of the stable-lads scampered alongside, triumphantly carrying a thick leather wallet on a strap. I was too far above to hear the clink of the tiny metal ornaments on the strap, but they glittered in the torchlight, and all the strength went from my arms in a rush of horror and despair.

They were coins and buttons, the small metal objects. And gaberlunzies. The tiny lead seals that gave a beggar license to plead his poverty through a given parish. Hugh Munro had four of them, a mark of favor for his trials at the hands of the Turk. Not Jamie, but Hugh.

I was shaking so badly that my legs would hardly carry me, but I ran to the door and pounded on it with all my strength.

"Let me out!" I shrieked. "I have to see the Duke! Let me out, I say!"

There was no response to my continued yelling and pounding, and I dashed back to the window. The scene below was eminently peaceful now; a boy stood holding a torch for one of the gardeners, who was kneeling at the edge of the lawn, tenderly replacing the divots of turf dug up by the fight.

"Hoy!" I roared. Covered as they were by bars, I couldn't crank the casements outward. I ran across the room to fetch one of the heavy silver candlesticks, dashed back, and smashed a pane of glass, heedless of the flying fragments.

"Help! Ahoy, down there! Tell the Duke I want to see him! Now! Help!" I thought one of the figures turned its head toward me, but neither made any motion toward the house, going on with their work as though no more than a night bird's cry disturbed the darkness around them.

Back to the door I ran, hammering and shouting, and back to the window, and back to the door again. I shouted, pleaded, and threatened until my throat was raw and hoarse, and beat upon the unyielding door until my fists were red and bruised, but no one came. I might have been alone in the great house, for all I could hear. The silence in the hallway was as deep as that of the night outside; as silent as the grave. All check on my fear was gone, and I sank at last to my knees before the door, sobbing without restraint.

I woke, chilled and stiff, with a throbbing headache, to feel something wide and solid shoving me across the floor. I came awake with a jerk as the opening edge of the heavy door pinched my thigh against the floor.

"Ow!" I rolled clumsily, then scrabbled to my hands and knees, hair hanging in my face.

"Claire! Oh, do be quiet, p-please! Darling, are you hurt?" With a rustle of starched lawn, Mary dropped to her knees beside me. Behind her, the door swung shut and I heard the click of the lock above.

"Yes—I mean, no. I'm all right," I said dazedly. "But Hugh . . ." I clamped my lips shut and shook my head, trying to clear it. "What in bloody hell are you doing here, Mary?"

"I b-bribed the housekeeper to let me in," she whispered. "Must you talk so loudly?"

"It doesn't matter much," I said, in a normal tone of voice. "That door's so thick, nothing short of a football match could be heard through it."

"A what?"

"Never mind." My mind was beginning to clear, though my eyes were sticky and swollen and my head still throbbed like a drum. I pushed myself to my feet and staggered to the basin, where I splashed cold water over my face.

"You bribed the housekeeper?" I said, wiping my face with a towel. "But we're still locked in, aren't we? I heard the key turn."

Mary was pale in the dimness of the room. The candle had guttered out while I slept on the floor, and there was no light but the deep red glow of the fireplace embers. She bit her lip.

"It was the b-best I could do. Mrs. Gibson was too afraid of the Duke to give me a key. All she would do was agree to lock me in with you, and let me out in the morning. I thought you m-might like company," she added timidly.

"Oh," I said. "Well . . . thank you. It was a kind thought." I took a new candle from the drawer and went to the fireplace to light it. The candlestick was clotted with wax from the burned-out candle; I tipped a small puddle of melted wax onto the tabletop and set the fresh candle in it, heedless of damage to the Duke's intaglio.

"Claire," Mary said. "Are you . . . are you in trouble?"

I bit my lip to prevent a hasty reply. After all, she was only seventeen, and her ignorance of politics was probably even more profound than her lack of knowledge of men had been.

"Er, yes," I said. "Rather a lot, I'm afraid." My brain was starting to work again. Even if Mary was not equipped to be of much practical help in escaping, she might at least be able to provide me with information about her godfather and the doings of his household.

"Did you hear the racket out by the wood earlier?" I asked. She shook her head. She was beginning to shiver; in such a large room, the heat of the fire died away long before it reached the bed dais.

"No, but I heard one of the cookmaids saying the keepers had caught a poacher in the park. It's awfully cold. Can't we get into b-bed?"

She was already crawling across the coverlet, burrowing beneath the bolster for the edge of the sheet. Her bottom was round and neat, childlike under the white nightdress.

"That wasn't a poacher," I said. "Or rather it was, but it was also a friend. He was on his way to find Jamie, to tell him I was here. Do you know what happened after the keepers took him?"

Mary swung around, face a pale blur within the shadows of the bed hangings. Even in this light, I could see that the dark eyes had grown huge.

"Oh, Claire! I'm so sorry!"

"Well, so am I," I said impatiently. "Do you know where the poacher is, though?" If Hugh had been imprisoned somewhere accessible, like the stables, there was a bare chance that Mary might be able to release him somehow in the morning.

The trembling of her lips, making her normal stutter seem comprehensible by comparison, should have warned me. But the words, once she got them out, struck through my heart, sharp and sudden as a thrown dirk.

"Th-they h-h-hanged him," she said. "At the p-park g-gate."

It was some time before I was able to pay attention to my surroundings. The flood of shock, grief, fear, and shattered hope washed over me, swamping me utterly. I was dimly conscious of Mary's small hand timidly patting my shoulder, and her voice offering handkerchiefs and drinks of water, but remained curled in a ball, not speaking, but shaking, and waiting for the relaxation of the wrenching despair that clenched my stomach like a fist. Finally I exhausted the panic, if not myself, and opened my eyes blearily.

"I'll be all right," I said at last, sitting up and wiping my nose inelegantly on my sleeve. I took the proffered towel and blotted my eyes with it. Mary hovered over me, looking concerned, and I reached out and squeezed her hand reassuringly.

"Really," I said. "I'm all right now. And I'm very glad you're here." A thought struck me, and I dropped the towel, looking curiously at her.

"Come to think of it, why *are* you here?" I asked. "In this house, I mean."

She looked down, blushing, and picked at the coverlet.

"The D-Duke is my godfather, you know."

"Yes, so I gathered," I said. "Somehow I doubt that he merely wanted the pleasure of your company, though."

She smiled a little at the remark. "N-no. But he—the Duke, I mean—he thinks he's found another h-h-husband for me." The effort to get out "husband" left her red-faced. "Papa brought me here to meet him."

I gathered from her demeanor that this wasn't news requiring immediate congratulations. "Do you know the man?"

Only by name, it turned out. A Mr. Isaacson, an importer, of London. Too busy to travel all the way to Edinburgh to meet his intended, he had agreed to come to Bellhurst, where the marriage would take place, all parties being agreeable.

I picked up the silver-backed hairbrush from the bed table and abstractedly began to tidy my hair. So, having failed to secure an alliance with the French nobility, the Duke was intending to sell his goddaughter to a wealthy Jew.

"I have a new trousseau," Mary said, trying to smile. "Forty-three embroidered petticoats—two with g-gold thread." She broke off, her lips pressed tight together, staring down sightlessly at her bare left hand. I put my own hand over it.

"Well." I tried to be encouraging. "Perhaps he'll be a kind man."

"That's what I'm af-fraid of." Avoiding my questioning look, she glanced down, twisting her hands together in her lap.

"They didn't tell Mr. Isaacson—about P-Paris. And they say I mustn't, either." Her face crumpled miserably. "They brought a horrible old woman to tell me how I must act on my w-w-wedding night, to—to pretend it's the first time, but I . . . oh, Claire, how can I do it?" she wailed. "And Alex—I didn't tell him; I couldn't! I was such a coward, I d-didn't even say goodbye!"

She threw herself into my arms, and I patted her back, losing a little of my own grief in the effort to comfort her. At length, she grew calmer, and sat up, hiccuping, to take a little water.

"Are you going to go through with it?" I asked. She looked up at me, her lashes spiked and wet.

"I haven't any choice," she said simply.

"But—" I started, and then stopped, helpless.

She was quite right. Young and female, with no resources, and no man who could come to her rescue, there was simply nothing to do but to accede to her father's and godfather's wishes, and marry the unknown Mr. Isaacson of London.

Heavyhearted, neither of us had any appetite for the food on the tray. We crawled under the covers to keep warm, and Mary, worn out with emotion, was sound asleep within minutes. No less exhausted, I found myself unable to sleep, grieving for Hugh, worried for Jamie, and curious about the Duke.

The sheets were chilly, and my feet seemed like chunks of ice. Avoiding the more distressful things on my mind, I turned my thoughts to Sandringham. What was his place in this affair?

To all appearances, the man was a Jacobite. He had, by his own admission, been willing to do murder—or pay for it, at least—in order to ensure that Charles got the backing he needed to launch his expedition to Scotland. And the evidence of the musical cipher made it all but certain that it was the Duke who had finally induced Charles to set sail in August, with his promise of help.

There were certainly men who took pains to conceal their Jacobite sympathies; given the penalties for treason, it was hardly peculiar. And the Duke had a good deal more to lose than some, should he back a failing cause.

Still, Sandringham hardly struck me as an enthusiastic supporter of the Stuart monarchy. Given his remarks about Danton, clearly he wouldn't be in sympathy with a Catholic ruler. And why wait so long to provide support, when Charles was in desperate need of money now—and had been, in fact, ever since his arrival in Scotland?

I could think of two conceivable reasons for the Duke's behavior, neither particularly creditable to the gentleman, but both well within the bounds of his character.

He could in fact be a Jacobite, willing to countenance an unpalatable Catholic king in return for the future benefits he might anticipate as chief backer of the restored Stuart monarchy. I could see that; "principle" wasn't in the man's vocabulary, whereas "self-interest" clearly was a term he knew well. He might wish to wait until Charles reached England, in order that the money not be wasted before the Highland army's final, crucial push to London. Anyone familiar with Charles Stuart could see the common sense in not entrusting him with too much money at once.

Or, for that matter, he might have wished to ensure that the Stuarts did in fact have some substantial backing for their cause before becoming financially involved himself; after all, contributing to a rebellion is not the same thing as supporting an entire army single-handed.

Contrariwise, I could see a much more sinister reason for the conditions of the Duke's offer. Making support conditional on the Jacobite army reaching English soil ensured that Charles would struggle on against the increasing opposition of his own leaders, dragging his reluctant, straggling army farther and farther south, away from the sheltering mountains in which they might find refuge.

If the Duke could expect benefits from the Stuarts for help in restoring them, what might he expect from the Hanovers, in return for luring Charles Stuart within their reach—and betraying him and his followers into the hands of the English army?

History had not been able to say what the Duke's true leanings had been. That struck me as odd; surely he would have to reveal his true intent sooner or later. Of course, I mused, the Old Fox, Lord Lovat, had managed to play off both sides of the Jacobite Rising last time, simultaneously ingratiating himself with the Hanovers and retaining the favor of the Stuarts. And Jamie had done it himself, for a time. Maybe it wasn't all that difficult to hide one's loyalties, in the constantly shifting morass of Royal politics.

The chill was creeping up my feet, and I moved my legs restlessly, my skin seeming numb as I rubbed my calves together. Legs obviously generated much less friction than dry sticks; no perceptible warmth resulted from this activity.

Lying sleepless, restless and clammy, I suddenly became aware of a tiny, rhythmic popping noise next to me. I turned my head, listening, then raised up on one elbow and peered incredulously at my companion. She was curled on her side, delicate skin flushed with sleep, so that she looked like a hothouse flower in full bloom, thumb tucked securely in the soft pink recesses of her mouth. Her lower lip moved as I watched, in the faintest of sucking motions.

I wasn't sure whether to laugh or cry. In the end, I did neither; merely pulled the thumb gently free and laid the limp hand curled upon her bosom. I blew out the candle and cuddled close to Mary.

Whether it was the innocence of that small gesture, with the far-off memories of trust and safety it provoked, the simple comfort of a warm body nearby, or only the exhaustion of fear and grief, my feet thawed, I relaxed at last, and fell asleep.

Wrapped in a warm cocoon of quilts, I slept deep and dreamlessly. It was all the greater a shock, then, when I was jerked abruptly from the soft, quiet dark of oblivion. It was still dark—black as a coachman's hat, in fact, as the fire had gone out—but the surroundings were neither soft nor quiet. Something heavy had landed suddenly on the bed, striking my arm in the process, and was apparently in the process of murdering Mary.

The bed heaved and the mattress tilted sharply under me, the bedframe shuddering with the force of the struggle taking place next to me. Agonized grunts and whispered threats came from close at hand, and a flailing hand—Mary's, I thought—struck me in the eye.

I rolled hastily out of bed, tripping on the step of the dais and falling flat on the floor. The sounds of struggle above me intensified, with a horrible, high-pitched squealing noise that I took to be Mary's best effort at a scream while being strangled.

There was a sudden startled exclamation, in a deep male voice, then a further convulsion of bedclothes, and the squealing stopped abruptly. Moving hastily, I found the flint box on the table and struck a light for the candle. Its wavering flame strengthened and rose, revealing what I had suspected from the sound of that vigorous Gaelic expletive—Mary, invisible save for a pair of wildly scrabbling hands, face smothered under a pillow and body flattened by the prostrate form of my large and agitated husband, who despite his advantage of size, appeared to have his hands well and truly full.

Intent on subduing Mary, he hadn't glanced up at the newly lit candle, but went on trying to capture her hands, while simultaneously holding the pillow over her face. Suppressing the urge to laugh hysterically at the spectacle, I instead set down the candle, leaned over the bed, and tapped him on the shoulder.

"Jamie?" I said.

"Jesus!" He leaped like a salmon, springing off the bed and coming to rest on the floor in a crouch, dirk half-drawn. He saw me then, and sagged in relief, closing his eyes for an instant.

"Jesus God, Sassenach! Never do that again, d'ye hear? Be quiet," he said briefly to Mary, who had escaped from the pillow and was now sitting bolt upright in bed, bug-eyed and spluttering. "I didna mean ye harm; I thought ye were my wife." He strode purposefully round the bed, took me by both shoulders and kissed me hard, as though to reassure himself that he'd got the right woman now. He had, and I kissed him back with considerable fervor, reveling in the scrape of his unshaven beard and the warm, pungent scent of him; damp linen and wool, with a strong hint of male sweat.

"Get dressed," he said, letting go. "The damn house is crawling wi' servants. It's like an ant's nest below."

"How did you get in here?" I asked, looking around for my discarded gown.

"Through the door, of course," he said impatiently. "Here." He seized my gown from the back of a chair and tossed it at me. Sure enough, the massive door stood open, a great ring of keys protruding from the lock.

"But how . . ." I began.

"Later," he said brusquely. He spotted Mary, out of bed and struggling into her nightrobe. "Best get back in bed, lassie," he advised. "The floor's cold."

"I'm coming with you." The words were muffled by the folds of cloth, but her determination was evident as her head popped through the neck of the robe and emerged, tousled-haired and defiant.

"The hell you are," Jamie said. He glared at her, and I noticed the fresh, raw scratches down his cheek. Seeing the quiver of her lips, though, he mastered his temper with an effort, and spoke reassuringly. "Dinna mind, lassie. You'll have no trouble over it. I'll lock the door behind us, and ye can tell everyone in the morning what's happened. No one shall hold ye to blame."

Ignoring this, Mary thrust her feet hastily into her slippers and ran toward the door.

"Hey! Where d'ye think you're going?" Startled, Jamie swung around after her, but not soon enough to stop her reaching the door. She stood in the hallway just outside, poised like a deer.

"I'm going with you!" she said fiercely. "If you don't take me, I shall run down the corridor, screaming as loudly as I can. So there!"

Jamie stared at her, his hair gleaming copper in the candlelight and the blood rising in his face, obviously torn between the necessity for silence and the urge to kill her with his bare hands and damn the noise. Mary glared back, one hand holding up her skirts, ready to run. Now dressed and shod, I poked him in the ribs, breaking his concentration.

"Take her," I said briefly. "Let's go."

He gave me a look that was twin to the one he'd been giving Mary, but hesitated no more than a moment. With a short nod, he took my arm and the three of us hurried out into the chill darkness of the corridor.

The house was at once deathly still and full of noises; boards squeaked loud beneath our feet and our garments rustled like leaves in a gale. The walls seemed to breathe with the settlings of wood, and small, half-heard sounds beyond the corridor suggested the secretive burrowings of animals underground. And over all was the deep and frightening silence of a great, dark house, sunk in a sleep that must not be broken.

Mary's hand was tight on my arm, as we crept down the hall behind Jamie. He moved like a shadow, hugging the wall, but quickly, for all his silence.

As we passed one door, I heard the sound of soft footsteps on the other side. Jamie heard them, too, and flattened himself against the wall, motioning Mary and me ahead of him. The plaster of the wall was cold against the palms of my hands, as I tried to press backward into it.

The door opened cautiously, and a head in a puffy white mobcap poked out, peering down the hall in the direction away from us.

"Hullo?" it said in a whisper. "Is that you, Albert?" A tickle of cold sweat ran down my spine. A housemaid, apparently expecting a visitation from the Duke's valet, who seemed to be keeping up the reputation of Frenchmen.

I didn't think she was going to consider an armed Highlander an adequate substitute for her absent lover. I could feel Jamie tense beside me, trying to overcome his scruples against striking a woman. Another instant, and she would turn, see him, and scream the house down.

I stepped out from the wall.

"Er, no," I said apologetically, "I'm afraid it's only me."

The maidservant started convulsively, and I took a swift step past, so that she was facing me, with Jamie still behind her.

"Sorry to alarm you," I said, smiling cheerily. "I couldn't sleep, you see. Thought I'd try a spot of hot milk. Tell me, am I headed right for the kitchens?"

"Eh?" The maid, a plump miss in her early twenties, gaped unbecomingly, exposing evidence of a distressing lack of concern for dental hygiene. Luckily, it wasn't the same maid who had seen me to my room; she might not realize that I was a prisoner, not a guest.

"I'm a guest in the house," I said, driving the point home. Continuing on the principle that the best defense is a good offense, I stared accusingly at her.

"Albert, eh? Does His Grace know that you are in the habit of entertaining men in your room at night?" I demanded. This seemed to hit a nerve, for the woman paled and dropped to her knees, clutching at my skirt. The prospect of exposure was so alarming that she didn't pause to ask exactly why a guest should be wandering about the halls in the wee hours of the morning, wearing not only gown and shoes, but a traveling cloak as well.

"Oh, mum! Please, you won't say nothing to His Grace, will you? I can see you've a kind face, mum, surely you'd not want to see me dismissed from my place? Have pity on me, my lady, I've six brothers and sisters still at home, and I . . ."

"Now, now," I soothed, patting her on the shoulder. "Don't worry about it. I won't tell the Duke. You just go back to your bed, and . . ." Talking in the sort of voice one uses with children and mental patients, I eased her, still volubly protesting her innocence, back into the small closet of a room.

I shut the door on her and leaned against it for support. Jamie's face loomed up from the shadows before me, grinning. He said nothing, but patted me on the head in congratulation, before taking my arm and urging me down the hall once more.

Mary was waiting under the window on the landing, her nightrobe glowing white in the moonlight that beamed momentarily through scudding clouds outside. A storm was gathering, from the looks of it, and I wondered whether this would help or hinder our escape.

Mary clutched at Jamie's plaid as he stepped onto the landing.

"Shh!" she whispered. "Someone's coming!"

Someone was; I could hear the faint thud of footsteps coming from below, and the pale wash of a candle lit the stairwell. Mary and I looked wildly about, but there was absolutely no place to hide. This was a back stair, meant for the servants' use, and the landings were simple squares of flooring, totally unrelieved by furniture or convenient hangings.

Jamie sighed in resignation. Then, motioning me and Mary back into the hallway from which we had come, he drew his dirk and waited, poised in the shadowed corner of the landing.

Mary's fingers clutched and twined with mine, squeezing tight in an agony of apprehension. Jamie had a pistol hanging from his belt, but plainly couldn't use it within the house—and a servant would realize that, making it useless for threat. It would have to be the knife, and my stomach quivered with pity for the hapless servant who was just about to come face-to-face with fifteen stone of keyed-up Scot and the threat of black steel.

I was taking stock of my apparel, and thinking that I could spare one of my petticoats to be used for bindings, when the bowed head of the candle-bearer came in sight. The dark hair was parted down the middle and slicked with a stinkingly sweet pomade that at once brought back the memory of a dark Paris street and the curve of thin, cruel lips beneath a mask.

My gasp of recognition made Danton look up sharply, one step below the landing. The next instant, he was grasped by the neck and flung against the wall of the landing with a force that sent the candlestick flying through the air.

Mary had seen him too.

"That's him!" she exclaimed, in her shock forgetting either to whisper or to stutter. "The man in Paris!"

Jamie had the feebly struggling valet squashed against the wall, held by one muscled forearm pressed across his chest. The man's face, fading in and out as the light ebbed and flooded with the passing clouds, was ghastly pale. It grew paler in the next moment, as Jamie laid the edge of his blade against Danton's throat.

I stepped onto the landing, not sure either what Jamie would do, or what I wanted him to do. Danton let out a strangled moan when he saw me, and made an abortive attempt to cross himself.

"La Dame Blanche!" he whispered, eyes starting in horror.

Jamie moved with sudden violence, grasping the man's hair and jerking his head back so hard that it thumped against the paneling.

"Had I time, *mo garhe,* ye would die slow," he whispered, and his voice lacked nothing in conviction, quiet as it was. "Count it God's mercy I have not." He yanked Danton's head back even further, so I could see the bobbing of his Adam's apple as he swallowed convulsively, his eyes fixed on me in fear.

"You call her 'Dame Blanche,' " Jamie said, between his teeth. "I call her wife! Let her face be the last that ye see, then!"

The knife ripped across the man's throat with a violence that made Jamie grunt with the effort, and a dark sheet of blood sprayed over his shirt. The stench of sudden death filled the landing, with a wheezing, gurgling sound from the crumpled heap on the floor that seemed to go on for a very long time.

The sounds behind me brought me finally to my senses: Mary, being violently sick in the hallway. My first coherent thought was that the servants were going to have the hell of a mess to clean up in the morning. My second was for Jamie, seen in a flash of the fleeting moon. His face was spattered and his hair matted with droplets of blood, and he was breathing heavily. He looked as though he might be going to be sick, too.

I turned toward Mary, and saw, far beyond her down the hall, the crack of light behind an opening door. Someone was coming to investigate the noise. I grabbed the hem of her nightrobe, wiped it roughly across her mouth, and seized her by the arm, tugging her toward the landing.

"Come on!" I said. "Let's get out of here!" Starting from his dazed contemplation of Danton's corpse, Jamie shook himself suddenly, and returning to his senses, turned to the stair.

He seemed to know where we were going, leading us through the darkened corridors without hesitation. Mary stumbled along beside me, puffing, her breath loud as an engine in my ear.

At the scullery door, Jamie came to a sudden halt, and gave a low whistle. This was returned immediately, and the door swung open on a darkness inhabited by indistinct forms. One of these detached itself from the murk and hastened forward. A few muttered words were exchanged, and the man—whichever it was—reached for Mary and pulled her into the shadows. A cold draft told me there was an open door somewhere ahead.

Jamie's hand on my shoulder steered me through the obstacles of the darkened scullery and some smaller chamber that seemed to be a lumber room of some sort; I barked my shin against something, but bit back the exclamation of pain.

Out in the free night at last, the wind seized my cloak and whirled it out in a exuberant balloon. After the nerve-stretching trek through the darkened house, I felt as though I might take wing, and sail for the sky.

The men around me seemed to share the mood of relief; there was a small outbreak of whispered remarks and muffled laughter, quickly shushed by Jamie. One at a time, the men flitted across the open space before the house, no more than shadows under the dancing moon. At my side, Jamie watched as they disappeared into the woods of the park.

"Where's Murtagh?" he muttered, as though to himself, frowning after the last of his men. "Gone to look for Hugh, I suppose," he said, in answer to his own question. "D'ye ken where he might be, Sassenach?"

I swallowed, feeling the wind bite cold beneath my cloak, memory killing the sudden exhilaration of freedom.

"Yes," I said, and told him the bad news, as briefly as I could. His expression darkened under its mask of blood, and by the time I had finished, his face was hard as stone.

"D'ye mean just to stand there all night," inquired a voice behind us, "or ought we to sound an alarm, so they'll know where to look first?"

Jamie's expression lightened slightly as Murtagh appeared from the shadows beside us, quiet as a wraith. He had a cloth-wrapped bundle under one arm; a joint from the kitchens, I thought, seeing the blotch of dark blood on the cloth. This impression was borne out by the large ham he had tucked beneath the other arm, and the strings of sausages about his neck.

Jamie wrinkled his nose, with a faint smile.

"Ye smell like a butcher, man. Can ye no go anywhere without thinkin' of your stomach?"

Murtagh cocked his head to one side, taking in Jamie's blood-spattered appearance.

"Better to look like the butcher than his wares, lad," he said. "Shall we go?"

The trip through the park was dark and frightening. The trees were tall and widely spaced here, but there were saplings left to grow between them that changed abruptly into the menacing shapes of gamekeepers in the uncertain light. The clouds were gathering thicker, at least, and the full moon made fewer appearances, which was something to be grateful for. As we reached the far side of the park, it began to rain.

Three men had been left with the horses. Mary was already mounted before one of Jamie's men. Plainly embarrassed by the necessity of riding astride, she kept tucking the folds of her nightrobe under her thighs, in a vain attempt to hide the fact that she had legs.

More experienced, but still cursing the heavy folds of my skirt, I plucked them up and set a foot in Jamie's offered hand, swinging aboard with a practiced thump. The horse snorted at the impact and set his ears back.

"Sorry, cully," I said without sympathy. "If you think that's bad, just wait 'til *he* gets back on."

Glancing around for the "he" in question, I found him under one of the trees, hand on the shoulder of a strange boy of about fourteen.

"Who's that?" I asked, leaning over to attract the attention of Geordie Paul Fraser, who was busy tightening his girth next to me.

"Eh? Oh, him." He glanced at the boy, then back at his reluctant girth, frowning. "His name's Ewan Gibson. Hugh Munro's eldest stepson. He was wi' his da, seemingly, when the Duke's keepers came on 'em. The lad got awa', and we found him near the edge o' the moor. He brought us here." With a final unnecessary tug, he glared at the girth as though daring it to say something, then looked up at me.

"D'ye ken where the lad's da is?" he asked abruptly.

I nodded, and the answer must have been plain in my face, for he turned to look at the boy. Jamie was holding the boy, hugged hard against his chest, and patting his back. As we watched, he held the boy away from him, both hands on his shoulders, and said something, looking down intently into his face. I couldn't hear what it was, but after a moment, the boy straightened himself and nodded. Jamie nodded as well, and with a final clap on the shoulder, turned the lad toward one of the horses, where George McClure was already reaching down a hand to him. Jamie strode toward us, head down, and the end of his plaid fluttering free behind him, despite the cold wind and the spattering rain.

Geordie spat on the ground. "Poor bugger," he said, without specifying whom he meant, and swung into his own saddle.

Near the southeast corner of the park we halted, the horses stamping and twitching, while two of the men disappeared back into the trees. It cannot have been more than twenty minutes, but it seemed twice as long before they came back.

The men rode double now, and the second horse bore a long, hunched shape bound across its saddle, wrapped in a Fraser plaid. The horses didn't like it; mine jerked its head, nostrils flaring, as the horse bearing Hugh's corpse came alongside. Jamie yanked the rein and said something angrily in Gaelic, though, and the beast desisted.

I could feel Jamie rise in the stirrups behind me, looking backward as though counting the remaining members of his band. Then his arm came around my waist, and we set off, on our way north.

We rode all night, with only brief stops for rest. During one of these, sheltering under a horse-chestnut tree, Jamie reached to embrace me, then suddenly stopped.

"What is it?" I said, smiling. "Afraid to kiss your wife in front of your men?"

"No," he said, proving it, then stepped back, smiling. "No, I was afraid for a moment ye were going to scream and claw my face." He dabbed gingerly at the marks Mary had left on his cheek.

"Poor thing," I said, laughing. "Not the welcome you expected, was it?"

"Well, by that time, actually it was," he said, grinning. He had taken two sausages from one of Murtagh's strings, and now handed me one. I couldn't remember when I had last eaten, but it must have been quite some time, for not even my fears of botulism kept the fatty, spiced meat from being delicious.

"What do you mean by that? You thought I wouldn't recognize you after only a week?"

He shook his head, still smiling, and swallowed the bite of sausage.

"Nay. It's only, when I got in the house to start, I kent where ye were, more or less, because of the bars on your windows." He arched one brow. "From the looks of them, ye must have made one hell of an impression on His Grace."

"I did," I said shortly, not wanting to think about the Duke. "Go on."

"Well," he said, taking another bite and shifting it expertly to his cheek while he talked, "I kent the room, but I needed the key, didn't I?"

"Oh, yes," I said. "You were going to tell me about that."

He chewed briefly and swallowed.

"I got it from the housekeeper, but not without trouble." He rubbed himself tenderly, a few inches below the belt. "From appearances, I'd say the woman's been waked in her bed a few times before—and didna care for the experience."

"Oh, yes," I said, entertained by the mental picture this provoked. "Well, I daresay you came as rare and refreshing fruit to her."

"I doubt it extremely, Sassenach. She screeched like a banshee and kneed me in the stones, then came altogether too near to braining me wi' a candlestick whilst I was doubled up groaning."

"What did you do?"

"Thumped her a good one—I wasna feeling verra chivalrous just at the moment—and tied her up wi' the strings to her nightcap. Then I put a towel in her mouth to put a stop to the things she was callin' me, and searched her room 'til I found the keys."

"Good work," I said, something occurring to me, "but how did you know where the housekeeper slept?"

"I didn't," he said calmly. "The laundress told me—after I told her who I was, and threatened to gut her and roast her on a spit if she didna tell me what I wanted to know." He gave me a wry smile. "Like I told ye, Sassenach, sometimes it's an advantage to be thought a barbarian. I reckon they've all heard of Red Jamie Fraser by now."

"Well, if they hadn't, they will," I said. I looked him over, as well as I could in the dim light. "What, didn't the laundress get a lick in?"

"She pulled my hair," he said reflectively. "Took a clump of it out by the roots. I'll tell ye, Sassenach; if ever I feel the need to change my manner of employment, I dinna think I'll take up attacking women—it's a bloody hard way to make a living."

It was beginning to sleet heavily near dawn, but we rode for some time before Ewan Gibson dragged his pony uncertainly to a stop, rose up clumsily in the stirrups to look around, then motioned up the hillside that rose to the left.

Dark as it was, it was impossible to ride the horses uphill. We had to descend to the ground and lead them, foot by muddy, slogging foot, along the nearly invisible track that zigzagged through heather and granite. Dawn was beginning to lighten the sky as we paused for breath at the crest of the hill. The horizon was hidden, thick with clouds, but a dull gray of no apparent source began to replace the darker gray of the night. Now I could at least see the cold streamlets that I sank in, ankle-deep, and avoid the worst of the foot-twisting snags of rock and bramble that we encountered on the way down the hill.

At the bottom was a small corrie, with six houses—though "house" was an overdignified word for the rude structures crouched beneath the larch trees there. The thatched roofs came down within a few feet of the ground, leaving only a bit of the stone walls showing.

Outside one bothy, we came to a halt. Ewan looked at Jamie, hesitating as though lost for direction, then at his nod, ducked and disappeared beneath the low rooftree of the hut. I drew closer to Jamie, putting my hand on his arm.

"This is Hugh Munro's house," he said to me, low-voiced. "I've brought him home to his wife. The lad's gone in to tell her."

I glanced from the dark, low doorway of the hut to the limp, plaid-draped bundle that two of the men were now unstrapping from the horse. I felt a small tremor run through Jamie's arm. He closed his eyes for a moment, and I saw his lips move; then he stepped forward and held out his arms for the burden. I drew a deep breath, brushed my hair back from my face, and followed him, stooping below the lintel of the door.

It wasn't as bad as I had feared it might be, though bad enough. The woman, Hugh's widow, was quiet, accepting Jamie's soft Gaelic speech of condolence with bowed head, the tears slipping down her face like rain. She reached tentatively for the covering plaid, as though meaning to draw it down, but then her nerve failed, and she stood, one hand resting awkwardly on the curve of the shroud, while the other drew a small child close against her thigh.

There were several children huddled near the fire—Hugh's stepchildren—and a swaddled mass in the rough cradle nearest the hearth. I felt some small comfort, looking at the baby; at least this much of Hugh was left. Then the comfort was overwhelmed with a cold fear as I looked at the children, grimy faces blending with the shadows. Hugh had been their main support. Ewan was brave and willing, but he was no more than fourteen, and the next eldest child was a girl of twelve or so. How would they manage?

The woman's face was worn and lined, nearly toothless. I realized with a shock that she could be only a few years older than I was. She nodded toward the single bed, and Jamie laid the body gently on it. He spoke to her again in Gaelic; she shook her head hopelessly, still staring down at the long shape upon her bed.

Jamie knelt down by the bed, bowed his head, and placed one hand on the corpse. His words were soft, but clearly spoken, and even my limited Gaelic could follow them.

"I swear to thee, friend, and may God Almighty bear me witness. For the sake of your love to me, never shall those that are yours go wanting, while I have aught to give." He knelt unmoving for a long moment, and there was no sound in the cottage but the crackle of the peat on the hearth and the soft patter of rain on the thatch. The wet had darkened Jamie's bowed head; droplets of moisture shone jewel-like in the folds of his plaid. Then his hand tightened once in final farewell, and he rose.

Jamie bowed to Mrs. Munro and turned to take my arm. Before we could leave, though, the cowhide that hung across the low doorway was thrust aside, and I stood back to make way for Mary Hawkins, followed by Murtagh.

Mary looked both bedraggled and bewildered, a damp plaid clasped around her shoulders and her muddy bedroom slippers protruding under the sodden hem of her nightrobe. Spotting me, she pressed close to me as though grateful for my presence.

"I didn't w-want to come in," she whispered to me, glancing shyly at Hugh Munro's widow, "but Mr. Murtagh insisted."

Jamie's brows were raised in inquiry, as Murtagh nodded respectfully to Mrs. Munro and said something to her in Gaelic. The little clansman looked just as he always did, dour and competent, but I thought there was an extra hint of dignity in his demeanor. He carried one of the saddlebags before him, bulging heavily with something. Perhaps a parting gift for Mrs. Munro, I thought.

Murtagh laid the bag on the floor at my feet, then straightened up and looked from me to Mary, to Hugh Munro's widow, and at last to Jamie, who looked as puzzled as I felt. Having thus assured himself of his audience, Murtagh bowed formally to me, a lock of wet dark hair falling free over his brow.

"I bring ye your vengeance, lady," he said, as quietly as I'd ever heard him speak. He straightened and inclined his head in turn to Mary and Mrs. Munro. "And justice for the wrong done to ye."

Mary sneezed, and wiped her nose hastily with a fold of her plaid. She stared at Murtagh, eyes wide and baffled. I gazed down at the bulging saddle-bag, feeling a sudden deep chill that owed nothing to the weather outside. But it was Hugh Munro's widow who sank to her knees, and with steady hands opened the bag and drew out the head of the Duke of Sandringham.

45

Damn All Randalls

It was a torturous trip northward into Scotland. We had to dodge and hide, always afraid of being recognized as Highlanders, unable to buy or beg food, needing to steal small bits from unattended sheds or pluck the few edible roots I could find in the fields.

Slowly, slowly, we made our way north. There was no telling where the Scottish army was by now, except that it lay to the north. With no way of telling where the army was, we decided to make for Edinburgh; there at least there would be news of the campaign. We had been out of touch for several weeks; I knew the relief of Stirling Castle by the English had failed, Jamie knew the Battle of Falkirk had succeeded, ending in victory for the Scots. But what had come after?

When we rode at last into the cobbled gray street of the Royal Mile, Jamie went at once to the army's headquarters, leaving me to go with Mary to Alex Randall's quarters. We hurried up the street together, barely speaking, both too afraid of what we might find.

He was there, and I saw Mary's knees give way as she entered the room and collapsed by his bed. Startled from a doze, he opened his eyes and blinked once, then Alex Randall's face blazed as though he had received a heavenly visitation.

"Oh, God!" he kept muttering brokenly into her hair. "Oh, God. I thought . . . oh, Lord, I had prayed . . . one more sight of you. Just one. Oh, Lord!"

Simply averting my gaze seemed insufficient; I went out onto the landing, and sat on the stairs for half an hour, resting my weary head on my knees.

When it seemed decent to return, I went back into the small room, grown grimy and cheerless again in the weeks of Mary's absence. I examined him, my hands gentle on the wasted flesh. I was surprised that he had lasted so long; it couldn't be much longer.

He saw the truth in my face, and nodded, unsurprised.

"I waited," he said softly, lying back in exhaustion on his pillows. "I hoped . . . she would come once more. I had no reason . . . but I prayed. And now it is answered. I shall die in peace now."

"Alex!" Mary's cry of anguish burst out of her as though his words had struck her a physical blow, but he smiled and pressed her hand.

"We have known it for a long time, my love," he whispered to her. "Don't despair. I will be with you always, watching you, loving you. Don't cry, my dearest." She brushed obediently at her pink-washed cheeks, but could do nothing to stem the tears that came streaming down them. Despite her obvious despair, she had never looked so blooming.

"Mrs. Fraser," Alex said, clearly mustering his strength to ask one more favor. "I must ask . . . tomorrow . . . will you come again, and bring your husband? It is important."

I hesitated for a moment. Whatever Jamie found out, he was going to want to leave Edinburgh immediately, to join the army and find the rest of his men. But surely one more day could make no difference to the outcome of the war—and I could not deny the appeal in the two pairs of eyes that looked at me so hopefully.

"We'll come," I said.

"I am a fool," Jamie grumbled, climbing the steep, cobbled streets to the wynd where Alex Randall had his lodgings. "We should have left yesterday, at once, as soon as we got back your pearls from the pawnbroker! D'ye no ken how far it is to Inverness? And we wi' little more than nags to get us there?"

"I know," I said impatiently. "But I promised. And if you'd seen him . . . well, you will see him in a moment, and then you'll understand."

"Mphm." But he held the street door for me and followed me up the winding stair of the decrepit building without further complaint.

Mary was half-sitting, half-lying on the bed. Still dressed in her tattered traveling clothes, she was holding Alex, cradling him fiercely against her bosom. She must have stayed with him so all night.

Seeing me, he gently freed himself from her grasp, patting her hands as he laid them aside. He propped himself on one elbow, face paler than the linen sheets on which he lay.

"Mrs. Fraser," he said. He smiled faintly, despite the sheen of unhealthy sweat and the gray pallor that betokened a bad attack.

"It was good of you to come," he said, gasping a little. He glanced beyond me. "Your husband . . . he is with you?"

As though in answer, Jamie stepped into the room behind me. Mary, stirred from her misery by the noise of our entry, glanced from me to Jamie, then rose to her feet, laying a hand timidly on his arm.

"I . . . we . . . n-need you, Lord Tuarach." I thought it was the stammer, more than the use of his title, that touched him. Though he was still grim-faced, some of the tension went out of him. He inclined his head courteously toward her.

"I asked your wife to bring you, my lord. I am dying, as you see." Alex Randall had pushed himself upright, sitting on the edge of the bed. His slender shins gleamed white as bone beneath the frayed hem of his nightshirt. The toes, long, slim, and bloodless, were shadowed with the bluing of poor circulation.

I had seen death often enough before, in all its forms, but this was always the worst—and the best; a man who met death with knowledge and courage, while the healer's futile arts fell aside. Futile or not, I rummaged through the contents of my case for the digitalin I had made for him. I had several infusions, in varying strengths, a spectrum of brown liquids in glass vials. I chose the darkest vial without hesitation; I could hear his breath bubbling through the water in his lungs.

It wasn't digitalin, but his purpose that sustained him now, lighting him with a glow as though a candle burned behind the waxy skin of his face. I had seen that a few times before, too; the man—or woman—whose will was strong enough to override for a time the imperatives of the body.

I thought that was perhaps how some ghosts were made; where a will and a purpose had survived, heedless of the frail flesh that fell by the wayside, unable to sustain life long enough. I didn't much want to be haunted by Alex Randall; that, among other reasons, was why I had made Jamie come with me today.

Jamie himself appeared to be coming to similar conclusions.

"Aye," he said softly. "I do see. Do ye ask aught of me?"

Alex nodded, closing his eyes briefly. He lifted the vial I handed him and drank, shuddering briefly at the bitter taste. He opened his eyes and smiled at Jamie.

"The indulgence of your presence only. I promise I shall not detain you long. We are waiting for one more person."

While we waited, I did what I could for Alex Randall, which under the circumstances was not much. The foxglove infusion again, and a bit of camphor to help ease his breathing. He seemed a little better after the administration of such medicine as I had, but placing my homemade stethoscope against the sunken chest, I could hear the labored thud of his heart, interrupted by such frequent flutters and palpitations that I expected it to stop at any moment.

Mary held his hand throughout, and he kept his eyes fixed on her, as though memorizing every line of her face. It seemed almost an intrusion to be in the same room with them.

The door opened, and Jack Randall stood on the threshold. He looked uncomprehendingly at me and Mary for a moment, then his gaze lighted on Jamie and he turned to stone. Jamie met his eyes squarely, then turned, nodding toward the bed.

Seeing that haggard face, Jack Randall crossed the room rapidly and fell on his knees beside the bed.

"Alex!" he said. "My God, Alex . . ."

"It's all right," his brother said. He held Jack's face between frail hands and smiled at him, trying to reassure him. "It's all right, Johnny," he said.

I put a hand under Mary's elbow, gently urging her off the bed. Whatever Jack Randall might be, he deserved a few last words in privacy with his brother. Stunned with despair, she didn't resist, but came with me to the far side of the room, where I perched her on a stool. I poured a little water from the ewer and wet my handkerchief. I tried to give it to her to swab her eyes, but she simply sat, clutching it lifelessly. Sighing, I took it and wiped her face, smoothing her hair as much as I could.

There was a small, choked sound from behind that made me glance toward the bed. Jack, still on his knees, had his face buried in his brother's lap, while Alex stroked his head, holding one of his hands.

"John," he said. "You'll know that I do not ask this lightly. But for the sake of your love for me . . ." He broke off to cough, the effort flushing his cheeks with hectic color.

I felt Jamie's body stiffen still further, if such a thing were possible. Jonathan Randall stiffened, too, as though he felt the force of Jamie's eyes upon him, but didn't look up.

"Alex," he said quietly. He laid a hand on his younger brother's shoulder, as though to quiet the cough. "Don't trouble your mind, Alex. You know you needn't ask; I'll do whatever you wish. Is it the—the girl?" He glanced in Mary's direction, but couldn't quite bring himself to look at her.

Alex nodded, still coughing.

"It's all right," John said. He put both hands on Alex's shoulders, trying to ease him back on the pillow. "I won't let her want for anything. Put your mind at rest."

Jamie looked down at me, eyes wide. I shook my head slowly, feeling the hair prickle from my neck to the base of my spine. Everything made sense now; the bloom on Mary's cheeks, despite her distress, and her apparent willingness to wed the wealthy Jew of London.

"It isn't money," I said. "She's with child. He wants . . ." I stopped, clearing my throat, "I think he wants you to marry her."

Alex nodded, eyes still closed. He breathed heavily for a moment, then opened them, bright pools of hazel, fixed on his brother's stunned and incomprehending face.

"Yes," he said. "John . . . Johnny, I need you to take care of her for me. I want . . . my child to have the Randall name. You can . . . give them some position in the world—so much more than I could." He reached out a hand, groping, and Mary seized it, clutching it to her bosom as though it were a life preserver. He smiled tenderly at her, and stretched up a hand to touch the shiny, dark ringlets that fell by her cheek, hiding her face.

"Mary. I wish . . . well, you know what I wish, my dear; so many things. And so many things I am sorry for. But I cannot regret the love between us. Having known such joy, I would die content, save for my fear that you might be exposed to shame and disgrace."

"I don't care!" Mary burst out fiercely. "I don't care who knows!"

"But I care for you," Alex said, softly. He stretched out a hand to his brother, who took it after a moment's hesitation. Then he brought them together, laying Mary's hand in Randall's. Mary's lay inert, and Jack Randall's stiff, like a dead fish on a wooden slab, but Alex pressed his hands tightly around the two, pressing them together.

"I give you to each other, my dear ones," he said softly. He looked from one face to the other, each reflecting the horror of the suggestion, submerged in the overwhelming grief of impending loss.

"But . . ." For the first time in our acquaintance, I saw Jonathan Randall completely at a loss for words.

"Good." It was almost a whisper. Alex opened his eyes and let out the breath he had been holding, smiling at his brother. "There is not much time. I shall marry you myself. Now. That is why I asked Mrs. Fraser to bring her husband—if you will be witness with your wife, sir?" He looked up at Jamie, who, after a moment's stunned immobility, nodded his head like an automation.

I do not believe I have ever seen three people look so entirely wretched.

Alex was so weak that his brother, with a face like stone, had to help him, tying his minister's high white stock about the pallid throat. Jonathan himself looked little better. Gaunt from illness, the lines in his face were carved so deep that he looked years older than his age, and his eyes peered out from deep sockets like caves of bone. Impeccably attired as always, he looked like a badly made tailor's dummy, features carelessly hacked from a block of wood.

As for Mary, she sat miserably on the bed, weeping helplessly into the folds of her cloak, hair disheveled and static with electricity. I did what I could for her, straightening her gown and combing out her hair. She sat drearily sniffling, her eyes fixed on Alex.

Bracing himself with a hand on the bureau, Alex groped in the drawer, coming at last with his large *Book of Common Prayer*. It was too heavy for him to hold open before him in the normal fashion. He couldn't stand, but sat heavily on the bed, holding the book open on his knees. He closed his eyes, breathing heavily, and a drop of sweat fell from his face, making a blot on the page.

"Dearly beloved," Alex began, and I hoped for his own sake, as well as everyone else's, that he was using the short form of the ceremony.

Mary had stopped crying, but her nose was red and shiny in her white face, and a small snail track showed on her upper lip. Jonathan saw it, and expressionless, pulled a large square of linen from his sleeve and offered it to her silently.

She took it with a faint nod, not looking at him, and carelessly mopped her face.

"I will," she said, when the time came, as though not caring at all what she said now.

Jack Randall made his promises in a firm voice, but one remote from the scene. It gave me an odd feeling to see a marriage contracted between two people who were quite unaware of each other; the complete attention of both was focused on the man who sat before them, eyes fixed on the pages of his book.

It was done. Congratulations to the bridal pair hardly seemed in order, and there was an awkward silence. Jamie glanced at me questioningly and I shrugged. I had fainted immediately after marrying him, and Mary looked rather as though she meant to follow my example.

The act complete, Alex sat quite still for a moment. He smiled slightly, and looked deliberately round the room, his eyes resting for a moment on each face in turn. Jonathan, Jamie, Mary, and me. I saw the glow in those soft hazel depths as his glance met mine. The candle's stub grew low, but the last of the wick blazed up, for a moment bright and strong.

His gaze lingered on Mary's face, then he closed his eyes briefly, as though he could not stand to look upon her, and I could hear the slow, labored rasp of his breathing. The glow of his skin was blanching and fading, the candle guttering.

Without opening his eyes, he reached up a hand, groping blindly. Jonathan grasped it, caught him behind the shoulders and eased him slowly back, onto the pillows. The long hands, smooth as a boy's, twitched uneasily, whiter than the shirt they lay against.

"Mary." The blue lips moved in a whisper, and she trapped the nervous hands between her own, holding them still against her bosom.

"I'm here, Alex. Oh, Alex, I'm here!" She bent close to him, murmuring in his ear. The movement forced Jonathan Randall back a bit, so that he stepped away from the bed. He stood, staring expressionlessly down.

The heavy, domed lids lifted once more, only halfway this time, seeking a face and finding it.

"Johnny. So . . . good to me. Always, Johnny."

Mary bent over him, the shadow of her fallen hair hiding his face. Jonathan Randall stood, still as one of the stones in a henge, watching his brother and his wife. There was no sound in the room but the whisper of the fire and the soft sobbing of Mary Randall.

I felt a touch on my shoulder, and looked up at Jamie. He nodded in Mary's direction.

"Stay with her," he said quietly. "It wilna be long, will it?"

"No."

He nodded. Then he took a deep breath, let it out slowly, and crossed the room to Jonathan Randall. He took the frozen figure by one arm and turned him gently toward the door.

"Come, man," he said quietly. "I'll see ye safe to your quarters."

The crooked door creaked to as he left, assisting Jack Randall to the place where he would spend his wedding night, alone.

I closed the door of our inn room behind me and leaned against it, exhausted. It was first dark outside, and the watchmen's cries echoed down the street.

Jamie was by the window, watching for me. He came to me at once, pulling me tight against him before I had even got my cloak off. I sagged against him, grateful for his warmth and solid strength. He scooped me up with an arm beneath my knees and carried me to the window seat.

"Have a bit of a drink, Sassenach," he urged. "Ye look all in, and no wonder." He took the flask from the table and mixed something that appeared to be brandy and water without the water.

I shoved a hand tiredly through my hair. It had been just after breakfast when we went to the room in Ladywalk Wynd; now it was past six o'clock. It seemed as though I had been gone for days.

"It wasn't long, poor chap. It was as though he was only waiting to see her safely taken care of. I sent word to her aunt's house; the aunt and two cousins came to fetch her. They'll take care of . . . him." I sipped gratefully at the brandy. It burned my throat and the fumes rose inside my head like fog on the moors, but I didn't care.

"Well," I said, attempting a smile, "at least we know Frank is safe, after all."

Jamie glowered down at me, ruddy brows nearly touching each other.

"Damn Frank!" he said ferociously. "Damn all Randalls! Damn Jack Randall, and damn Mary Hawkins Randall, and damn Alex Randall—er, God rest his soul, I mean," he amended hastily, crossing himself.

"I thought you didn't begrudge—" I started. He glared at me.

"I lied."

He grabbed me by the shoulders and shook me slightly, holding me at arm's length.

"And damn you, too, Claire Randall Fraser, while I'm at it!" he said. "Damn right I begrudge! I grudge every memory of yours that doesna hold me, and every tear ye've shed for another, and every second you've spent in another man's bed! Damn you!" He knocked the brandy glass from my hand—accidentally, I think—pulled me to him and kissed me hard.

He drew back enough to shake me again.

"You're mine, damn ye, Claire Fraser! Mine, and I wilna share ye, with a man or a memory, or anything whatever, so long as we both shall live. You'll no mention the man's name to me again. D'ye hear?" He kissed me fiercely to emphasize the point. "Did ye hear me?" he asked, breaking off.

"Yes," I said, with some difficulty. "If you'd . . . stop . . . shaking me, I might . . . answer you."

Rather sheepishly, he released his grip on my shoulders.

"I'm sorry, Sassenach. It's only . . . God, why did ye . . . well, aye, I see why . . . but did you have to—" I interrupted this incoherent sputtering by putting my hand behind his head and drawing him down to me.

"Yes," I said firmly, releasing him. "I had to. But it's over now." I loosened the ties of my cloak and let it fall back off my shoulders to the floor. He bent to pick it up, but I stopped him.

"Jamie," I said. "I'm tired. Will you take me to bed?"

He drew a deep breath and let it out slowly, staring down at me, eyes sunk deep with tiredness and strain.

"Aye," he said softly, at last. "Aye, I will."

He was silent, and rough at the start, the edges of his anger sharpening his love.

"Ooh!" I said, at one point.

"Christ, I'm sorry, *mo duinne*. I couldna . . ."

"It's all right." I stopped his apologies with my mouth and held him tightly, feeling the wrath ebb away as the tenderness grew between us. He didn't break away from the kiss, but held himself motionless, gently exploring my lips, the tip of his tongue caressing, barely stroking.

I touched his tongue with my own, and held his face between my hands. He hadn't shaved since morning, and the faint red stubble rasped pleasantly beneath my fingertips.

He lowered himself and rolled slightly to one side, so as not to crush me with his weight, and we went on, touching all along our lengths, joined in closeness, speaking in silent tongues.

Alive, and one. We are one, and while we love, death will never touch us. "The grave's a fine and private place / But none, I think, do there embrace." Alex Randall lay cold in his bed, and Mary Randall alone in hers. But we were here together, and no one and nothing mattered beyond that fact.

He grasped my hips, large hands warm on my skin, and pulled me toward him, and the shudder that went through me went through him, as though we shared one flesh.

I woke in the night, still in his arms, and knew he was not asleep.

"Go back to sleep, *mo duinne*." His voice was soft, low and soothing, but with a catch that made me reach up to feel the wetness on his cheeks.

"What is it, love?" I whispered. "Jamie, I do love you."

"I know it," he said quietly. "I do know it, my own. Let me tell ye in your sleep how much I love you. For there's no so much I can be saying to ye while ye wake, but the same poor words, again and again. While ye sleep in my arms,

I can say things to ye that would be daft and silly waking, and your dreams will know the truth of them. Go back to sleep, *mo duinne*."

I turned my head, enough that my lips brushed the base of his throat, where his pulse beat slow beneath the small three-cornered scar. Then I laid my head upon his chest and gave my dreams up to his keeping.

46

Timor Mortis Conturbat Me

There were men and their traces all around, as we made our way north, following the retreat of the Highland army. We passed small groups of men on foot, walking doggedly, heads down against the windy rain. Others lay in the ditches and under the hedgerows, too exhausted to go on. Equipment and weapons had been abandoned along the way; here a wagon lay overturned, its sacks of flour split and ruined in the wet, there a brace of small culverin stood beneath a tree, twin barrels gleaming darkly in the shadows.

The weather had been bad all the way, delaying us. It was April 13, and I rode and walked with a constant, gnawing feeling of dread beneath my heart. Lord George and the clan chieftains, the Prince and his chief advisers—all were at Culloden House, or so we had been told by one of the MacDonalds that we met along the way. He knew little more than that, and we did not detain him; the man stumbled away into the mist, moving like a zombie. Rations had been short when I was captured by the English a month gone; matters had plainly gone from bad to worse. The men we saw moved slowly, many of them staggering with exhaustion and starvation. But they moved stubbornly north, all the same, following their Prince's orders. Moving toward the place the Scots called Drumossie Moor. Toward Culloden.

At one point, the road became too bad for the faltering ponies. They would have to be led around the outer edge of a small wood, through the wet spring heather, to where the road became passable, a half-mile beyond.

"It will be swifter to walk through the wood," Jamie told me, taking the reins from my numbed hand. He nodded toward the small grove of pine and oak, where the sweet, cool smell of wet leaves rose from the soaked ground. "D'ye go that way, Sassenach; we'll meet wi' ye on the other side."

I was too tired to argue. Putting one foot in front of the other was a distinct effort, and the effort would undoubtedly be less on the smooth layer of leaves and fallen pine needles in the wood than through the boggy, treacherous heather.

It was quiet in the wood, the whine of the wind softened by the pine boughs overhead. What rain came through the branches pattered lightly on the layers of leathery fallen oak leaves, rustling and crackled, even when wet.

He lay only a few feet from the far edge of the wood, next to a big gray boulder. The pale green lichens of the rock were the same color as his tartan, and its browns blended with the fallen leaves that had drifted half across him. He seemed so much a part of the wood that I might have stumbled over him, had I not been stopped by the patch of brilliant blue.

Soft as velvet, the strange fungus spread its cloak over the naked, cold white limbs. It followed the curve of bone and sinew, sending up small trembling fronds, like the grasses and trees of a forest, invading barren land.

It was an electric, vivid blue, stark and alien. I had never seen it, but had heard of it, from an old soldier I had nursed, who had fought in the trenches of the first world war.

"We called it corpse-candle," he had told me. "Blue, bright blue. You never see it anywhere but on a battlefield—on dead men." He had looked up at me, old eyes puzzled beneath the white bandage.

"I always wondered where it lives, between wars."

In the air, perhaps, its invisible spores waiting to seize an opportunity, I thought. The color was brilliant, incongruous, bright as the woad with which this man's ancestors had painted themselves before going forth to war.

A breeze passed through the wood, ruffling the man's hair. It stirred and rose, silky and lifelike. There was a crunch of leaves behind me, and I started convulsively from the trance in which I had stood, staring at the corpse.

Jamie stood beside me, looking down. He said nothing; only took me by the elbow and led me from the wood, leaving the dead man behind, clothed in the saprophytic hues of war and sacrifice.

➤

It was mid-morning of April 15 by the time we came to Culloden House, having pushed ourselves and our ponies unmercifully to reach it. We approached it from the south, coming first through a cluster of outbuildings. There was a stir—almost a frenzy—of men on the road, but the stableyard was curiously deserted.

Jamie dismounted and handed his reins to Murtagh.

"D'ye wait here a moment," he said. "Something doesna seem quite right here."

Murtagh glanced at the door of the stables, standing slightly ajar, and nodded. Fergus, mounted behind the clansman, would have followed Jamie, but Murtagh prevented him with a curt word.

Stiff from the ride, I slid off my own horse and followed Jamie, slipping in the mud of the stableyard. There *was* something odd about the stableyard. Only as I followed him through the door of the stable building did I realize what it was—it was too quiet.

Everything inside was still; the building was cold and dim, without the usual warmth and stir of a stable. Still, the place was not entirely devoid of life; a dark figure stirred in the gloom, too big to be a rat or a fox.

"Who is that?" Jamie said, stepping forward to put me behind him automatically. "Alec? Is it you?"

The figure in the hay raised its head slowly, and the plaid fell back. The Master of Horse of Castle Leoch had but one eye; the other, lost in an accident many years before, was patched with black cloth. Normally, one eye sufficed him; brisk and snapping blue, it was enough to command the obedience of stable-lads and horses, grooms and riders alike.

Now Alec McMahon MacKenzie's eye was dull as dusty slate. The broad, once vigorous body was curled in upon itself, and the cheeks of his face were sunk with the apathy of starvation.

Knowing the old man suffered from arthritis in damp weather, Jamie squatted beside him to prevent him rising.

"What has been happening?" he asked. "We are newly come; what is happening here?"

It seemed to take Old Alec a long time to absorb the question, assimilate it, and form his reply into words; perhaps it was only the stillness of the empty, shadowed stable that made his words ring hollow when they finally came.

"It has all gone to pot," he said. "They marched to Nairn two nights ago, and came fleeing back yesterday. His Highness has said they will take a stand on Culloden; Lord George is there now, with what troops he has gathered."

I couldn't repress a small moan at the name of Culloden. It was here, then. Despite everything, it had come to pass, and we were here.

A shiver passed through Jamie, as well; I saw the red hairs standing erect on his forearms, but his voice betrayed nothing of the anxiety he must feel.

"The troops—they are ill-provisioned to fight. Does Lord George not realize they must have rest, and food?"

The creaking sound from Old Alec might have been the shade of a laugh.

"What His Lordship knows makes little difference, lad. His Highness has taken command of the army. And His Highness says we shall stand against the English on Drumossie. As for food—" His old-man's eyebrows were thick and bushy, gone altogether white in the last year, with coarse hairs sprouting from them. One brow raised now, heavily, as though even this small change of expression was an exhaustion. One gnarled hand stirred in his lap, gesturing toward the empty stalls.

"They ate the horses last month," he said, simply. "There's been little else, since."

Jamie stood abruptly, and leaned against the wall, head bowed in shock. I couldn't see his face, but his body was stiff as the boards of the stable.

"Aye," he said at last. "Aye. My men—did they have their fair share of the meat? Donas . . . he was . . . a good-sized horse." He spoke quietly, but I saw from the sudden sharpness of Alec's one-eyed glance that he heard as well as I did the effort that kept Jamie's voice from breaking.

The old man rose slowly from the hay, crippled body moving with painful deliberation. He set one gnarled hand on Jamie's shoulder; the arthritic fingers could not close, but the hand rested there, a comforting blunt weight.

"They didna take Donas," he said quietly. "They kept him—for Prince *Tcharlach* to ride, on his triumphal return to Edinburgh. O'Sullivan said it wouldna be . . . fitting . . . for His Highness to walk."

Jamie covered his face in his hands and stood shaking against the boards of the empty stall.

"I am a fool," he said at last, gasping to recover his breath. "Oh, God, I am a fool." He dropped his hands, showing his face, tears streaking through the grime of travel. He dashed the back of his hand across his cheek, but the moisture continued to overflow from his eyes, as though it were a process quite out of his control.

"The cause is lost, my men are being taken to slaughter, there are dead men rotting in the wood . . . and I am weeping for a horse! Oh, God," he whispered, shaking his head. "I am a fool."

Old Alec heaved a sigh, and his hand slid heavily down Jamie's arm.

"It's as well that ye still can, lad," he said. "I'm past it, myself."

The old man folded one leg awkwardly at the knee and eased himself down once more. Jamie stood for a moment, looking down at Old Alec. The tears still streamed unchecked down his face, but it was like rain washing over a sheet of polished granite. Then he took my elbow, and turned away without a word.

I looked back at Alec when we reached the stable door. He sat quite still, a dark, hunched shape shawled in his plaid, the one blue eye unseeing as the other.

Men sprawled through the house, worn to exhaustion, seeking oblivion from gnawing hunger and the knowledge of certain and imminent disaster. There were no women here; those chiefs whose womenfolk had accompanied them had sent the ladies safely away—the coming doom cast a long shadow.

Jamie left me with a murmured word outside the door that led to the Prince's temporary quarters. My presence would help nothing. I walked softly through the house, murmurous with the heavy breathing of sleeping men, the air thick with the dullness of despair.

At the top of the house, I found a small lumber-room. Crowded with junk and discarded furniture, it was otherwise unoccupied. I crept into this warren of oddities, feeling much like a small rodent, seeking refuge from a world in which huge and mysterious forces were let loose to destruction.

There was one small window, filled with the misty gray morning. I rubbed dirt away from one pane with the corner of my cloak, but there was nothing to be seen but the encompassing mist. I leaned my forehead against the cold glass. Somewhere out there was Culloden Field, but I saw nothing but the dim silhouette of my own reflection.

News of the gruesome and mysterious death of the Duke of Sandringham had reached Prince Charles, I knew; we had heard of it from almost everyone we spoke to as we passed to the north and it became safe for us to show ourselves again. What exactly had we done? I wondered. Had we doomed the Jacobite cause for good and all in that one night's adventure, or had we inadvertently saved Charles Stuart from an English trap? I drew a squeaking finger in a line down the misty glass, chalking up one more thing I would never find out.

It seemed a very long time before I heard a step on the uncarpeted boards of the stair outside my refuge. I came to the door to find Jamie coming onto the landing. One look at his face was enough.

"Alec was right," he said, without preliminaries. The bones of his face were stark beneath the skin, made prominent by hunger, sharpened by anger. "The troops are moving to Culloden—as they can. They havena slept or eaten in two days, there is no ordnance for the cannon—but they are going." The anger erupted suddenly and he slammed his fist down on a rickety table. A cascade of small brass dishes from the pile of household rubble woke the echoes of the attic with an ungodly clatter.

With an impatient gesture, he snatched the dirk from his belt and jabbed it violently into the table, where it stood, quivering with the force of the blow.

"The country folk say that if ye see blood on your dirk, it means death." He drew in his breath with a hiss, fist clenched on the table. "Well, I have seen it! So have they all. They know—Kilmarnock, Lochiel, and the rest. And no bit of good does the seeing of it do!"

He bent his head, hands braced on the table, staring at the dirk. He seemed much too large for the confines of the room, an angry smoldering presence that might break suddenly into flame. Instead, he flung up his hands, and threw himself onto a decrepit settle, where he sat, head buried in his hands.

"Jamie," I said, and swallowed. I could barely speak the next words, but they had to be said. I had known what news he would bring, and I had thought of what might still be done. "Jamie. There's only one thing left—only the one possibility."

His head was bent, forehead resting on his knuckles. He shook his head, not looking at me.

"There is no way," he said. "He's bent on it. Murray has tried to turn him, so has Lochiel. Balmerino. Me. But the men are standing on the plain this hour. Cumberland has set out for Drumossie. There is no way."

The healing arts are powerful ones, and any physician versed in the use of substances that heal knows also the power of those that harm. I had given Colum the cyanide he had not had time to use, and taken back the deadly vial from the table by the bed where his body lay. It was in my box now, the crudely distilled crystals a dull brownish-white, deceptively harmless in appearance.

My mouth was so dry that I couldn't speak at once. There was a little wine left in my flask; I drank it, the acid taste like bile on my tongue.

"There is one way," I said. "Only one."

Jamie's head stayed sunk in his hands. It had been a long ride, and the shock of Alec's news had added depression to his tiredness. We had detoured to find his men, or most of them, a miserable, ragged crew, indistinguishable from the skeletal Frasers of Lovat who surrounded them. The interview with Charles was far beyond the last straw.

"Aye?" he said.

I hesitated, but had to speak. The possibility had to be mentioned; whether he—or I—could bring ourselves to it or not.

"It's Charles Stuart," I said, at last. "It's him—everything. The battle, the war—everything depends on him, do you see?"

"Aye?" Jamie was looking up at me now, bloodshot eyes quizzical.

"If he were dead. . . ." I whispered at last.

Jamie's eyes closed, and the last vestiges of blood drained from his face.

"If he were to die . . . now. Today. Or tonight. Jamie, without Charles, there's nothing to fight for. No one to order the men to Culloden. There wouldn't be a battle."

The long muscles of his throat rippled briefly as he swallowed. He opened his eyes and stared at me, appalled.

"Christ," he whispered. "Christ, ye canna mean it."

My hand closed on the smoky, gold-mounted crystal around my neck.

They had called me to attend the Prince, before Falkirk. O'Sullivan, Tullibardine, and the others. His Highness was ill—an indisposition, they said. I had seen Charles, made him bare his breast and arms, examined his mouth and the whites of his eyes.

It was scurvy, and several of the other diseases of malnutrition. I said as much.

"Nonsense!" said Sheridan, outraged. "His Highness cannot suffer from the yeuk, like a common peasant!"

"He's been eating like one," I retorted. "Or rather worse than one." The "peasants" were forced to eat onions and cabbage, having nothing else. Scorning such poor fare, His Highness and his advisers ate meat—and little else. Looking around the circle of scared, resentful faces, I saw few that didn't show symptoms of the lack of fresh food. Loose and missing teeth, soft, bleeding gums, the pus-filled, itching follicles of "the yeuk" that so lavishly decorated His Highness's white skin.

I was loath to surrender any of my precious supply of rose hips and dried berries, but had offered, reluctantly, to make the Prince a tea of them. The offer had been rejected, with a minimum of courtesy, and I understood that Archie Cameron had been summoned, with his bowl of leeches and his lancet, to see whether a letting of the Royal blood would relieve the Royal itch.

"I could do it," I said. My heart was beating heavily in my chest, making it hard to breathe. "I could mix him a draught. I think I could persuade him to take it."

"And if he should die upon drinking your medicine? Christ, Claire! They would kill ye on the spot!"

I folded my hands beneath my arms, trying to warm them.

"D-does that matter?" I asked, desperately trying to steady my voice. The truth was that it did. Just at the moment, my own life weighed a good deal more in the balance than did the hundreds I might save. I clenched my fists, shaking with terror, a mouse in the jaws of the trap.

Jamie was at my side in an instant. My legs didn't work very well; he half-carried me to the broken settle and sat down with me, his arms wrapped tight around me.

"You've the courage of a lion, *mo duinne*," he murmured in my ear. "Of a bear, a wolf! But you know I willna let ye do it."

The shivering eased slightly, though I still felt cold, and sick with the horror of what I was saying.

"There might be another way," I said. "There's little food, but what there is goes to the Prince. I think it might not be difficult to add something to his dish without being noticed; things are so disorganized." This was true; all over the house, officers lay sleeping on tables and floors, still clad in their boots, too tired to lay aside their arms. The house was in chaos, with constant comings and goings. It would be a simple matter to distract a servant long enough to add a deadly powder to the evening dish.

The immediate terror had receded slightly, but the awfulness of my suggestion lingered like poison, chilling my own blood. Jamie's arm tightened briefly around my shoulders, then fell away as he contemplated the situation.

The death of Charles Stuart would not end the matter of the Rising; things had gone much too far for that. Lord George Murray, Balmerino, Kilmarnock, Lochiel, Clanranald—all of us were traitors, lives and property forfeit to the Crown. The Highland army was in tatters; without the figurehead of Charles to rally to, it would dissipate like smoke. The English, terrorized and humiliated at Preston and Falkirk, would not hesitate to pursue the fugitives, seeking to retrieve their lost honor and wash out the insult in blood.

There was little chance that Henry of York, Charles's pious younger brother, already bound by churchly vows, would take his brother's place to continue the fight for restoration. There was nothing ahead but catastrophe and wreck, and no possible way to avert it. All that might be salvaged now was the lives of the men who would die on the moor tomorrow.

It was Charles who had chosen to fight at Culloden, Charles whose stubborn, shortsighted autocracy had defied the advice of his own generals and gone to invade England. And whether Sandringham had meant his offer for good or ill, it had died with him. There was no support from the South; such

English Jacobites as there were did not rally as expected to the banner of their king. Forced against his will to retreat, Charles had chosen this last stubborn stand, to place ill-armed, exhausted, starving men in a battle line on a rain-soaked moor, to face the wrath of Cumberland's cannon fire. If Charles Stuart were dead, the battle of Culloden might not take place. One life, against two thousand. One life—but that life a Royal one, and taken not in battle, but in cold blood.

The small room where we sat had a hearth, but a fire had not been lit—there was no fuel. Jamie sat gazing at it as though seeking an answer in invisible flames. Murder. Not only murder, but regicide. Not only murder, but the killing of a sometime friend.

And yet—the clansmen of the Highlands shivered already on the open moor, shifting in their serried ranks as the plan of battle was adjusted, re-arranged, reordered, as more men drifted to join them. Among them were the MacKenzies of Leoch, the Frasers of Beauly, four hundred men of Jamie's blood. And the thirty men of Lallybroch, his own.

His face was blank, immobile as he thought, but the hands laced together on his knee knotted tight with the struggle. The crippled fingers and the straight strove together, twisting. I sat beside him, scarcely daring to breathe, awaiting his decision.

At last the breath went from him in an almost inaudible sigh, and he turned to me, a look of unutterable sadness in his eyes.

"I cannot," he whispered. His hand touched my face briefly, cupping my cheek. "Would God that I could, Sassenach. I cannot do it."

The wave of relief that washed through me robbed me of speech, but he saw what I felt, and grasped my hands between his own.

"Oh, God, Jamie, I'm glad of it!" I whispered.

He bowed his head over my hands. I turned my head to lay my cheek against his hair, and froze.

In the doorway, watching me with a look of absolute revulsion, was Dougal MacKenzie.

The last months had aged him; Rupert's death, the sleepless nights of fruitless argument, the strains of the hard campaign, and now the bitterness of imminent defeat. There were gray hairs in the russet beard, a gray look to his skin, and deep lines in his face that had not been there in November. With a shock, I realized that he looked like his brother, Colum. He had wanted to lead, Dougal MacKenzie. Now he had inherited the chieftainship, and was paying its price.

"Filthy . . . traitorous . . . whoring. . . . *witch*!"

Jamie jerked as though he had been shot, face gone white as the sleet outside. I sprang to my feet, overturning the bench with a clatter that echoed through the room.

Dougal MacKenzie advanced on me slowly, putting aside the folds of his cloak, so that the hilt of his sword was freed to his hand. I hadn't heard the door behind me open; it must have stood ajar. How long had he been on the other side, listening?

"You," he said softly. "I should have known it; from the first I saw ye, I should have known." His eyes were fixed on me, something between horror and fury in the cloudy green depths.

There was a sudden stir in the air beside me; Jamie was there, a hand on my arm, urging me back behind him.

"Dougal," he said. "It isna what ye think, man. It's—"

"No?" Dougal cut in. His gaze left me for a second, and I shrank behind Jamie, grateful for the respite.

"Not what I think?" he said, still speaking softly. "I hear the woman urging ye to foul murder—to the murder of your Prince! Not only vile murder, but treason as well! And ye tell me I havena heard it?" He shook his head, the tangled russet curls lank and greasy on his shoulders. Like the rest of us, he was starving; the bones jutted in his face, but his eyes burned from their shadowy orbits.

"I dinna blame ye, lad," he said. His voice was suddenly weary, and I remembered that he was a man in his fifties. "It isna your fault, Jamie. She's bewitched ye—anyone can see that." His mouth twisted as he looked again at me.

"Aye, I ken weel enough how it's been for ye. She's worked the same sorcery on me, betimes." His eyes raked over me, burning. "A murdering, lying slut, would take a man by the cock and lead him to his doom, wi' her claws sunk deep in his balls. That's the spell that they lay on ye, lad—she and the other witch. Take ye to their beds and steal the soul from you as ye lie sleeping wi' your head on their breasts. They take your soul, and eat your manhood, Jamie."

His tongue darted out and wetted his lips. He was still staring at me, and his hand tightened on the hilt of his sword.

"Stand aside, laddie. I'll free ye of the *sassenach* whore."

Jamie stepped in front of me, momentarily blocking Dougal from my view.

"You're tired, Dougal," he said, speaking calmly, soothingly. "Tired, and hearin' things, man. D'ye go down now. I shall—"

He had no chance to finish. Dougal wasn't listening to him; the deep-set green eyes were fixed on my face, and the MacKenzie chief had drawn the dirk from its sheath at his waist.

"I shall cut your throat," he said to me softly. "I should ha' done it when first I saw ye. It would have saved us all a great grief."

I wasn't sure that he wasn't right, but that didn't mean I intended to let him remedy the matter. I took three quick steps back, and fetched up hard against the table.

"Get back, man!" Jamie thrust himself before me, holding up a shielding forearm as Dougal advanced on me.

The MacKenzie chieftain shook his head, bull-like, red-rimmed eyes fixed on me.

"She's mine," he said hoarsely. "Witch. Traitoress. Step aside, lad. I wouldna harm ye, but by God, if ye shield that woman, I shall kill you, too, foster son or no."

He lunged past Jamie, grabbing my arm. Exhausted, starved, and aging as he was, he was still a formidable man, and his fingers bit deep into my flesh.

I yelped with pain, and kicked frantically at him as he jerked me toward him. He snatched at my hair and caught it, forcing my head hard back. His breath was hot and sour on my face. I shrieked and struck at him, digging my nails into his cheek in an effort to get free.

The air exploded from his lungs as Jamie's fist struck him in the ribs, and his grip on my hair tore loose as Jamie's other fist came down in a numbing blow on the point of his shoulder. Suddenly freed, I fell back against the table, whimpering with shock and pain.

Dougal whirled to face Jamie then, dropping into a fighter's crouch, the dirk held blade upward.

"Let it be, then," he said, breathing heavily. He swayed slightly from side to side, shifting his weight as he sought the advantage. "Blood will tell. Ye damned Fraser spawn. Treachery runs in your blood. Come here to me, fox cub. I'll kill ye quick, for your mother's sake."

There was little room for maneuver in the small attic. No room to draw a sword; with his dirk stuck fast in the tabletop, Jamie was effectively unarmed. He matched Dougal's stance, eyes watchful, fixed on the point of the menacing dirk.

"Put it down, Dougal," he said. "If ye bear my mother in mind, then listen to me, for her sake!"

The MacKenzie made no answer, but jabbed suddenly, a ripping blow aimed upward.

Jamie dodged aside, dodged again the wide-armed sweep that came from the other side. Jamie had the agility of youth on his side—but Dougal held the knife.

Dougal closed with a rush, and the dirk slid up Jamie's side, ripping his shirt, scoring a dark line in his flesh. With a hiss of pain, he jerked back, grabbing for Dougal's wrist, catching it as the blade struck down.

The dull gleam of the blade flashed once, disappeared between the struggling bodies. They strove together, locked like lovers, the air filled with the smell of male sweat and fury. The blade rose again, two hands grappling on its rounded hilt. A shift, and a jerk, a sudden grunt of effort, one of pain. Dougal stepped back, staggering, face congested and pouring sweat, the hilt of the dagger socketed at the base of his throat.

Jamie half-fell, gasping, and leaned against the table. His eyes were dark with shock, and his hair sweat-soaked, the rent edges of his shirt tinged with blood from the scratch.

There was a terrible sound from Dougal, a sound of shock and stifled breath. Jamie caught him as he tottered and fell, Dougal's weight bringing him to his knees. Dougal's head lay on Jamie's shoulder, Jamie's arms locked around his foster father.

I dropped to my knees beside them, reaching to help, trying to get hold of Dougal. It was too late. The big body went limp, then spasmed, sliding out of Jamie's grasp. Dougal lay crumpled on the floor, muscles jerking with involuntary contractions, struggling like a fish out of water.

His head was pillowed on Jamie's thigh. One heave brought his face into view. It was contorted, and dark red, eyes gone to slits. His mouth moved continuously, saying something, talking with great force—but without sound, save the bubbling rasp from his ruined throat.

Jamie's face was ashen; apparently he could tell what Dougal was saying. He struggled violently, trying to hold the thrashing body still. There was a final spasm, then a dreadful rattling sound, and Dougal MacKenzie lay still, Jamie's hands clenched tight upon his shoulders, as though to prevent his rising again.

"Blessed Michael defend us!" The hoarse whisper came from the doorway. It was Willie Coulter MacKenzie, one of Dougal's men. He stared in stupefied horror at the body of his chief. A small puddle of urine was forming under it, creeping out from under the sprawled plaid. The man crossed himself, still staring.

"Willie." Jamie rose, passing a trembling hand across his face. "Willie." The man seemed struck dumb. He looked at Jamie in complete bewilderment, mouth open.

"I need one hour, man." Jamie had a hand on Willie Coulter's shoulder, easing him into the room. "An hour to see my wife safe. Then I shall come back to answer for this. I give ye my word, on my honor. But I must have an hour free. One hour. Will ye give me one hour, man, before ye speak?"

Willie licked dry lips, looking back and forth between the body of his chief and his chieftain's nephew, clearly frightened out of his wits. At last he nodded, plainly having no idea what to do, choosing to follow this request because no reasonable alternative presented itself.

"Good." Jamie swallowed heavily, and wiped his face on his plaid. He patted Willie on the shoulder. "Stay here, man. Pray for his soul"—he nodded toward the still form on the floor, not looking at it—"and for mine." He leaned past Willie to pry his dirk from the table, then pushed me before him, out the door and down the stairs.

Halfway down, he stopped, leaning against the wall with his eyes closed. He drew deep, ragged breaths, as though he were about to faint, and I put my hands on his chest, alarmed. His heart was beating like a drum, and he was trembling, but after a moment, he drew himself upright, nodded at me, and took my arm.

"I need Murtagh," he said.

We found the clansman just outside, cowled in his plaid against the sleety rain, sitting in a dry spot beneath the eaves of the house. Fergus was curled up next to him, dozing, tired from the long ride.

Murtagh took one look at Jamie's face, and rose to his feet, dark and dour, ready for anything.

"I've killed Dougal MacKenzie," Jamie said bluntly, without preliminary.

Murtagh's face went quite blank for a moment, then his normal expression of wary grimness reasserted itself.

"Aye," he said. "What's to do, then?"

Jamie groped in his sporran and brought out a folded paper. His hands shook as he tried to unfold it, and I took it from him, spreading it out under the shelter of the eaves.

"Deed of Sasine" it said, at the top of the sheet. It was a short document, laid out in a few black lines, conveying title of the estate known as Broch Tuarach to one James Jacob Fraser Murray, said property to be held in trust and administered by the said James Murray's parents, Janet Fraser Murray and Ian Gordon Murray, until the said James Murray's majority. Jamie's signature was at the bottom, and there were two blank spaces provided below, each with the word "Witness" written alongside. It was dated 1 July, 1745—a month before Charles Stuart had launched his rebellion on the shores of Scotland, and made Jamie Fraser a traitor to the Crown.

"I need ye to sign this, you and Claire," Jamie said, taking the note from me and handing it to Murtagh. "But it means forswearing yourself; I have nay right to ask it."

Murtagh's small black eyes scanned the deed quickly. "No," he said dryly. "No right—nor any need, either." He nudged Fergus with a foot, and the boy sat bolt upright, blinking.

"Nip into the house and fetch your chief ink and a quill, lad," Murtagh said. "And quick about it—go!"

Fergus shook his head once to clear it, glanced at Jamie for a confirming nod—and went.

Water was dripping from the eaves down the back of my neck. I shivered and drew the woolen arisaid closer around my shoulders. I wondered when Jamie had written the document. The false date made it seem the property had been transferred before Jamie became a traitor, with his goods and lands subject to seizure—if it was not questioned, the property would pass safely to small Jamie. Jenny's family at least would be safe, still in possession of land and farmhouse.

Jamie had seen the possible need for this; yet he had not executed the document before we left Lallybroch; he had hoped somehow to return, and claim his own place once again. Now that was impossible, but the estate might still be saved from seizure. There was no one to say when the document had really been signed—save the witnesses, me and Murtagh.

Fergus returned, panting, with a small glass inkpot and a ragged quill. We signed one at a time, leaning against the side of the house, careful to shake the quill first to keep the ink from dripping down. Murtagh went first; his middle name, I saw, was FitzGibbons.

"Will ye have me take it to your sister?" Murtagh asked as I shook the paper carefully to dry it.

Jamie shook his head. The rain made damp, coin-sized splotches on his plaid, and glittered on his lashes like tears.

"No. Fergus will take it."

"Me?" The boy's eyes went round with astonishment.

"You, man." Jamie took the paper from me, folded it, then knelt and tucked it inside Fergus's shirt.

"This must reach my sister—Madame Murray—without fail. It is worth more than my life, man—or yours."

Practically breathless with the enormity of the responsibility entrusted to him, Fergus stood up straight, hands clasped over his middle.

"I will not fail you, milord!"

A faint smile crossed Jamie's lips, and he rested a hand briefly on the smooth cap of Fergus's hair.

"I know that, man, and I am grateful," he said. He twisted the ring off his left hand; the cabochon ruby that had belonged to his father. "Here," he said, handing it to Fergus. "Go to the stables, and show this to the old man ye'll see there. Tell him I said you are to take Donas. Take the horse, and ride for Lallybroch. Stop for nothing, except as you must, to sleep, and when ye do sleep, hide yourself well."

Fergus was speechless with alarmed excitement, but Murtagh frowned dubiously at him.

"D'ye think the bairn can manage yon wicked beast?" he said.

"Aye, he can," Jamie said firmly. Overcome, Fergus stuttered, then sank to his knees and kissed Jamie's hand fervently. Springing to his feet, he darted away in the direction of the stables, his slight figure disappearing in the mist.

Jamie licked dry lips, and closed his eyes briefly, then turned to Murtagh with decision.

"And you—*mo caraidh*—I need ye to gather the men."

Murtagh's sketchy brows shot up, but he merely nodded.

"Aye," he said. "And when I have?"

Jamie glanced at me, then back at his godfather. "They'll be on the moor now, I think, with Young Simon. Just gather them together, in one place. I shall see my wife safe, and then—" He hesitated, then shrugged. "I will find you. Wait my coming."

Murtagh nodded once more, and turned to go. Then he paused, and turned back to face Jamie. The thin mouth twitched briefly, and he said, "I would ask the one thing of ye, lad—let it be the English. Not your ain folk."

Jamie flinched slightly, but after a moment, he nodded. Then, without speaking, he held out his arms to the older man. They embraced quickly, fiercely, and Murtagh, too, was gone, in a swirl of ragged tartan.

I was the last bit of business on the agenda.

"Come on, Sassenach," he said, seizing me by the arm. "We must go."

No one stopped us; there was so much coming and going by the roads that we were scarcely noticed while we were near the moor. Farther away, when we left the main road, there was no one to see.

Jamie was completely silent, concentrating single-mindedly on the job at hand. I said nothing to him, too occupied with my own shock and dread to wish for conversation.

"I shall see my wife safe." I hadn't known what he meant by that, but it became obvious within two hours, when he turned the head of his horse farther south, and the steep green hill called Craigh na Dun came in view.

"No!" I said, when I saw it, and realized where we were headed. "Jamie, no! I won't go!"

He didn't answer me, only spurred his horse and galloped ahead, leaving me no option but to follow.

My feelings were in turmoil; beyond the doom of the coming battle and the horror of Dougal's death, now there was the prospect of the stones. That accursed circle, through which I had come here. Plainly Jamie meant to send me back, back to my own time—if such a thing was possible.

He could mean all he liked, I thought, clenching my jaw as I followed him down the narrow trail through the heather. There was no power on earth that could make me leave him now.

We stood together on the hillside, in the small dooryard of the ruined cottage that stood below the crest of the hill. No one had lived there for years; the local folk said the hill was haunted—a fairy's dun.

Jamie had half-urged, half-dragged me up the slope, paying no attention to my protests. At the cottage he had stopped, though, and sunk to the ground, chest heaving as he gasped for breath.

"It's all right," he said at last. "We have a bit of time now; no one will find us here."

He sat on the ground, his plaid wrapped around him for warmth. It had stopped raining for the moment, but the wind blew cold from the mountains nearby, where snow still capped the peaks and choked the passes. He let his head fall forward onto his knees, exhausted by the flight.

I sat close by him, huddled within my cloak, and felt his breathing gradually slow as the panic subsided. We sat in silence for a long time, afraid to move from what seemed a precarious perch above the chaos below. Chaos I felt I had somehow helped create.

"Jamie," I said, at last. I reached out a hand to touch him, but then drew back and let it fall. "Jamie—I'm sorry."

He continued to look out, into the darkening void of the moor below. For a moment, I thought he hadn't heard me. He closed his eyes. Then he shook his head very slightly.

"No," he said softly. "There is no need."

"But there is." Grief nearly choked me, but I felt as though I must say it; must tell him that I knew what I had done to him.

"I should have gone back. Jamie—if I had gone, then, when you brought me here from Cranesmuir . . . maybe then—"

"Aye, maybe," he interrupted. He swung toward me abruptly, and I could see his eyes fixed on me. There was longing there, and a grief that matched mine, but no anger, no reproach.

He shook his head again.

"No," he said once more. "I ken what ye mean, *mo duinne*. But it isna so. Had ye gone then, matters might still have happened as they have. Maybe so, maybe no. Perhaps it would have come sooner. Perhaps differently. Perhaps— just perhaps—not at all. But there are more folk have had a hand in this than we two, and I willna have ye take the guilt of it upon yourself."

His hand touched my hair, smoothing it out of my eyes. A tear rolled down my cheek, and he caught it on his finger.

"Not that," I said. I flung a hand out toward the dark, taking in the armies, and Charles, and the starved man in the wood, and the slaughter to come. "Not that. What I did to you."

He smiled then, with great tenderness, and smoothed his palm across my cheek, warm on my spring-chilled skin.

"Aye? And what have I done to you, Sassenach? Taken ye from your own place, led ye into poverty and outlawry, taken ye through battlefields and risked your life. D'ye hold it against me?"

"You know I don't."

He smiled. "Aye, well; neither do I, my Sassenach." The smile faded from his face as he glanced up at the crest of the hill above us. The stones were invisible, but I could feel the menace of them, close at hand.

"I won't go, Jamie," I repeated stubbornly. "I'm staying with you."

"No." He shook his head. He spoke gently, but his voice was firm, with no possibility of denial. "I must go back, Claire."

"Jamie, you can't!" I clutched his arm urgently. "Jamie, they will have found Dougal by now! Willie Coulter will have told someone."

"Aye, he will." He put a hand over my arm and patted it. He had reached his decision on the ride to the hill; I could see it in his shadowed face, resignation and determination mingled. There was grief there, and sadness, too, but those had been put aside; he had no time for mourning now.

"We could try to get away to France," I said. "Jamie, we must!" But even as I spoke, I knew I could not turn him from the course he had decided on.

"No," he said again, softly. He turned and lifted a hand, gesturing toward the darkening valley below, the shaded hills beyond. "The country is roused, Sassenach. The ports are closed; O'Brien has been trying for the last three months to bring a ship to rescue the Prince, to take him to safety in France—Dougal told me . . . before." A tremor passed over his face, and a sudden spasm of grief knit his brows. He pushed it aside, though, and went on, explaining in a steady voice.

"It's only the English who are hunting Charles Stuart. It will be the English, and the clans as well, who hunt me. I am a traitor twice over, a rebel and a murderer. Claire . . ." He paused, rubbing a hand across the back of his neck, then said gently, "Claire, I am a dead man."

The tears were freezing on my cheeks, leaving icy trails that burned my skin.

"No," I said again, but to no effect.

"I'm no precisely inconspicuous, ye ken," he said, trying to make a joke of it as he ran a hand through the rusty locks of his hair. "Red Jamie wouldna get far, I think. But you . . ." He touched my mouth, tracing the line of my lips. "I can save you, Claire, and I will. That is the most important thing. But then I shall go back—for my men."

"The men from Lallybroch? But how?"

Jamie frowned, absently fingering the hilt of his sword as he thought.

"I think I can get them away. It will be confused on the moor, wi' men and horses moving to and fro, and orders shouted and contradicted; battles are verra messy affairs. And even if it's known by then what I—what I have done," he continued, with a momentary catch in his voice, "there are none who would stop me then, wi' the English in sight and the battle about to begin. Aye, I can do it," he said. His voice had steadied, and his fists clenched at his sides with determination.

"They will follow me without question—God help them, that's what's brought them here! Murtagh will have gathered them for me; I shall take them and lead them from the field. If anyone tries to stop me, I shall say that I claim the right to lead my own men in battle; not even Young Simon will deny me that."

He drew a deep breath, brows knit as he visualized the scene on the battlefield come morning.

"I shall bring them safely away. The field is broad enough, and there are enough men that no one will realize that we havena but moved to a new position. I shall bring them off the moor, and see them set on the road toward Lallybroch."

He fell silent, as though this were as far as he had thought in his plans.

"And then?" I asked, not wanting to know the answer, but unable to stop myself.

"And then I shall turn back to Culloden," he said, letting out his breath. He gave me an unsteady smile. "I'm no afraid to die, Sassenach." His mouth quirked wryly. "Well . . . not a lot, anyway. But some of the ways of accomplishing the fact . . ." A brief, involuntary shudder ran through him, but he tried to keep smiling.

"I doubt I should be thought worthy of the services of a true professional, but I expect in such a case, both Monsieur Forez and myself might find it . . . awkward. I mean, havin' my heart cut out by someone I've shared wine with . . ."

With a sound of incoherent distress, I flung my arms around him, holding him as tightly as I could.

"It's all right," he whispered into my hair. "It's all right, Sassenach. A musket ball. Maybe a blade. It will be over quickly."

I knew this was a lie; I had seen enough of battle wounds and the deaths of warriors. All that was true was that it was better than waiting for the hangman's noose. The terror that had ridden with me from Sandringham's estate rose now to high tide, choking, drowning me. My ears rang with my own pulsebeat, and my throat closed so tight that I felt I could not breathe.

Then all at once, the fear left me. I could not leave him, and I would not.

"Jamie," I said, into the folds of his plaid. "I'm going back with you."

He started back, staring down at me.

"The hell you are!" he said.

"I am." I felt very calm, with no trace of doubt. "I can make a kilt of my arisaid; there are enough young boys with the army that I can pass for one. You've said yourself it will all be confusion. No one will notice."

"No!" he said. "No, Claire!" His jaw was clenched, and he was glaring at me with a mixture of anger and horror.

"If you're not afraid, I'm not either," I said, firming my own jaw. "It will . . . be over quickly. You said so." My chin was beginning to quiver, despite my determination. "Jamie—I won't . . . I can't . . . I bloody won't live without you, and that's all!"

He opened his mouth, speechless, then closed it, shaking his head. The light over the mountains was failing, painting the clouds with a dull red glow. At last he reached for me, drew me close and held me.

"D'ye think I don't know?" he asked softly. "It's me that has the easy part now. For if ye feel for me as I do for you—then I am asking you to tear out your heart and live without it." His hand stroked my hair, the roughness of his knuckles catching in the blowing strands.

"But ye must do it, *mo duinne*. My brave lioness. Ye must."

"Why?" I demanded, pulling back to look up at him. "When you took me from the witch trial at Cranesmuir—you said then that you would have died with me, you would have gone to the stake with me, had it come to that!"

He grasped my hands, fixing me with a steady blue gaze.

"Aye, I would," he said. "But I wasna carrying your child."

The wind had frozen me; it was the cold that made me shake, I told myself. The cold that took my breath away.

"You can't tell," I said, at last. "It's much too soon to be sure."

He snorted briefly, and a tiny flicker of amusement lit his eyes.

"And me a farmer, too! Sassenach, ye havena been a day late in your courses, in all the time since ye first took me to your bed. Ye havena bled now in forty-six days."

"You bastard!" I said, outraged. "You counted! In the middle of a bloody war, you counted!"

"Didn't you?"

"No!" I hadn't; I had been much too afraid to acknowledge the possibility of the thing I had hoped and prayed for so long, come now so horribly too late.

"Besides," I went on, trying still to deny the possibility, "that doesn't mean anything. Starvation could cause that; it often does."

He lifted one brow, and cupped a broad hand gently beneath my breast.

"Aye, you're thin enough; but scrawny as ye are, your breasts are full—and the nipples of them gone the color of Champagne grapes. You forget," he said, "I've seen ye so before. I have no doubt—and neither have you."

I tried to fight down the waves of nausea—so easily attributable to fright and starvation—but I felt the small heaviness, suddenly burning in my womb. I bit my lip hard, but the sickness washed over me.

Jamie let go of my hands, and stood before me, hands at his sides, stark in silhouette against the fading sky.

"Claire," he said quietly. "Tomorrow I will die. This child . . . is all that will be left of me—ever. I ask ye, Claire—I beg you—see it safe."

I stood still, vision blurring, and in that moment, I heard my heart break. It was a small, clean sound, like the snapping of a flower's stem.

At last I bent my head to him, the wind grieving in my ears.

"Yes," I whispered. "Yes. I'll go."

It was nearly dark. He came behind me and held me, leaning back against him as he looked over my shoulder, out over the valley. The lights of watchfires had begun to spring up, small glowing dots in the far distance. We were silent for a long time, as the evening deepened. It was very quiet on the hill; I could hear nothing but Jamie's even breathing, each breath a precious sound.

"I will find you," he whispered in my ear. "I promise. If I must endure two hundred years of purgatory, two hundred years without you—then that is my punishment, which I have earned for my crimes. For I have lied, and killed, and stolen; betrayed and broken trust. But there is the one thing that shall lie in the balance. When I shall stand before God, I shall have one thing to say, to weigh against the rest."

His voice dropped, nearly to a whisper, and his arms tightened around me. "Lord, ye gave me a rare woman, and God! I loved her well."

He was slow, and careful; so was I. Each touch, each moment must be savored, remembered—treasured as a talisman against a future empty of him.

I touched each soft hollow, the hidden places of his body. Felt the grace and the strength of each curving bone, the marvel of his firm-knit muscles, drawn lean and flexible across the span of his shoulders, smooth and solid down the length of his back, hard as seasoned oakwood in the columns of his thighs.

Tasted the salty sweat in the hollow of his throat, smelled the warm muskiness of the hair between his legs, the sweetness of the soft, wide mouth, tasting faintly of dried apple and the bitter tang of juniper berries.

"You are so beautiful, my own," he whispered to me, touching the slipperiness between my legs, the tender skin of my inner thighs.

His head was no more than a dark blur against the white blur of my breasts. The holes in the roof admitted only the faintest light from the overcast sky; the soft grumble of spring thunder muttered constantly in the hills beyond our fragile walls. He was hard in my hand, so stiff with the wanting that my touch made him groan in a need close to pain.

When he could wait no longer, he took me, a knife to its scabbard, and we moved hard together, pressing, wanting, needing so urgently that moment of ultimate joining, and fearing to reach it, for the knowledge that beyond it lay eternal separation.

He brought me again and again to the peaks of sensation, holding back himself, stopping, gasping and shuddering on the brink. Until at last I touched his face, twined my fingers in his hair, pressed him tight and arched my back and hips beneath him, urging, forcing.

"Now," I said to him, softly. "Now. Come with me, come to me, now. Now!"

He yielded to me, and I to him, despair lending edge to passion, so the echo of our cries seemed to die away slowly, ringing in the darkness of the cold stone hut.

We lay pressed together, unmoving, his weight a heavy blessing, a shield and reassurance. A body so solid, so filled with heat and life; how could it be possible that he would cease to exist within hours?

"Listen," he said at last, softly. "Do you hear?"

At first I heard nothing but the rushing of the wind, and the trickle of rain, dripping through the holes of the roof. Then I heard it, the steady, slow thump of his heartbeat, pulsing against me, and mine against his, each matching each, in the rhythm of life. The blood coursed through him, and through our fragile link, through me, and back again.

We lay so, warm beneath the makeshift covering of plaid and cloak, on a bed of our clothing, tangled together. Then at last he slipped free, and turning me away from him, cupped his hand across my belly, his breath warm on the nape of my neck.

"Sleep now a bit, *mo duinne*," he whispered. "I would sleep once more this way—holding you, holding the babe."

I had thought I could not sleep, but the pull of exhaustion was too much, and I slipped beneath the surface with scarcely a ripple. Near dawn I woke, Jamie's arms still around me, and lay watching the imperceptible bloom of night into day, futilely willing back the friendly shelter of the dark.

I rolled to the side and lifted myself to watch him, to see the light touch the bold shape of his face, innocent in sleep, to see the dawning sun touch his hair with flame—for the last time.

A wave of anguish broke through me, so acute that I must have made some sound, for he opened his eyes. He smiled when he saw me, and his eyes searched my face. I knew that he was memorizing my features, as I was his.

"Jamie," I said. My voice was hoarse with sleep and swallowed tears. "Jamie. I want you to mark me."

"What?" he said, startled.

The tiny *sgian dhu* he carried in his stocking was lying within reach, its handle of carved staghorn dark against the piled clothing. I reached for it and handed it to him.

"Cut me," I said urgently. "Deep enough to leave a scar. I want to take away your touch with me, to have something of you that will stay with me always. I don't care if it hurts; nothing could hurt more than leaving you. At least when I touch it, wherever I am, I can feel your touch on me."

His hand was over mine where it rested on the knife's hilt. After a moment, he squeezed it and nodded. He hesitated for a moment, the razor-sharp blade in his hand, and I offered him my right hand. It was warm beneath our coverings, but his breath came in wisps, visible in the cold air of the room.

He turned my palm upward, examining it carefully, then raised it to his lips. A soft kiss in the well of the palm, then he seized the base of my thumb in a hard, sucking bite. Letting go, he swiftly cut into the numbed flesh. I felt no more than a mild burning sensation, but the blood welled at once. He brought the hand quickly to his mouth again, holding it there until the flow of blood slowed. He bound the wound, now stinging, carefully in a handkerchief, but not before I saw that the cut was in the shape of a small, slightly crooked letter "J."

I looked up to see that he was holding out the tiny knife to me. I took it, and somewhat hesitantly, took the hand he offered me.

He closed his eyes briefly, and set his lips, but a small grunt of pain escaped him as I pressed the tip of the knife into the fleshy pad at the base of his thumb. The Mount of Venus, a palm-reader had told me; indicator of passion and love.

It was only as I completed the small semicircular cut that I realized he had given me his left hand.

"I should have taken the other," I said. "Your sword hilt will press on it."

He smiled faintly.

"I could ask no more than to feel your touch on me in my last fight— wherever it comes."

Unwrapping the blood-spotted handkerchief, I pressed my wounded hand tightly against his, fingers gripped together. The blood was warm and slick, not yet sticky between our hands.

"Blood of my Blood . . ." I whispered.

". . . and Bone of my Bone," he answered softly. Neither of us could finish the vow, "so long as we both shall live," but the unspoken words hung aching between us. Finally he smiled crookedly.

"Longer than that," he said firmly, and pulled me to him once more.

"Frank," he said at last, with a sigh. "Well, I leave it to you what ye shall tell him about me. Likely he'll not want to hear. But if he does, if ye find ye can talk to him of me, as you have to me of him—then tell him . . . I'm grateful. Tell him I trust him, because I must. And tell him—" His hands tightened suddenly on my arms, and he spoke with a mixture of laughter and absolute sincerity. "Tell him I hate him to his guts and the marrow of his bones!"

We were dressed, and the dawn light had strengthened into day. There was no food, nothing with which to break our fast. Nothing left that must be done . . . and nothing left to say.

He would have to leave now, to make it to Drumossie Moor in time. This was our final parting, and we could find no way to say goodbye.

At last, he smiled crookedly, bent, and kissed me gently on the lips.

"They say . . ." he began, and stopped to clear his throat. "They say, in the old days, when a man would go forth to do a great deed—he would find a wisewoman, and ask her to bless him. He would stand looking forth, in the direction he would go, and she would come behind him, to say the words of the prayer over him. When she had finished, he would walk straight out, and not look back, for that was ill-luck to his quest."

He touched my face once, and turned away, facing the open door. The morning sun streamed in, lighting his hair in a thousand flames. He straightened his shoulders, broad beneath his plaid, and drew a deep breath.

"Bless me, then, wisewoman," he said softly, "and go."

I laid a hand on his shoulder, groping for words. Jenny had taught me a few of the ancient Celtic prayers of protection; I tried to summon the words in my mind.

"Jesus, Thou Son of Mary," I started, speaking hoarsely, "I call upon Thy name; and on the name of John the Apostle beloved, And on the names of all the saints in the red domain, To shield thee in the battle to come . . ."

I stopped, interrupted by a sound from the hillside below. The sound of voices, and of footsteps.

Jamie froze for a second, shoulder hard beneath my hand, then whirled, pushing me toward the rear of the cottage, where the wall had fallen away.

"That way!" he said. "They are English! Claire, go!"

I ran toward the opening in the wall, heart in my throat, as he turned back to the doorway, hand on his sword. I stopped, just for a moment, for the last sight of him. He turned his head, caught sight of me, and suddenly he was with me, pushing me hard against the wall in an agony of desperation. He gripped me fiercely to him. I could feel his erection pressing into my stomach and the hilt of his dagger dug into my side.

He spoke hoarsely into my hair. "Once more. I must! But quick!" He pushed me against the wall and I scrabbled up my skirts as he raised his kilts. This was not lovemaking; he took me quickly and powerfully and it was over in seconds. The voices were nearer; only a hundred yards away.

He kissed me once more, hard enough to leave the taste of blood in my mouth. "Name him Brian," he said, "for my father." With a push, he sent me toward the opening. As I ran for it, I glanced back to see him standing in the middle of the doorway, sword half-drawn, dirk ready in his right hand.

The English, unaware that the cottage was occupied, had not thought to send a scout round the back. The slope behind the cottage was deserted as I dashed across it and into the thicket of alders below the hillcrest.

I pushed my way through the brush and the branches, stumbling over rocks, blinded by tears. Behind me I could hear shouts and the clash of steel from the cottage. My thighs were slick and wet with Jamie's seed. The crest of the hill seemed never to grow nearer; surely I would spend the rest of my life fighting my way through the strangling trees!

There was a crashing in the brush behind me. Someone had seen me rush from the cottage. I dashed aside the tears and scrabbled upward, groping on all fours as the ground grew steeper. I was in the clear space now, the shelf of granite I remembered. The small dogwood growing out of the cliff was there, and the tumble of small boulders.

I stopped at the edge of the stone circle, looking down, trying desperately to see what was happening. How many soldiers had come to the cottage? Could Jamie break free of them and reach his hobbled horse below? Without it, he would never reach Culloden in time.

All at once, the brush below me parted with a flash of red. An English soldier. I turned, ran gasping across the turf of the circle, and hurled myself through the cleft in the rock.

PART SEVEN

Hindsight

47

Loose Ends

"he was right, of course. Bloody man, he was almost always right." Claire sounded half-cross as she spoke. A rueful smile crossed her face, then she looked at Brianna, who sat on the hearthrug, gripping her knees, her face completely blank. Only the faint stir of her hair, lifting and moving in the rising heat of the fire, showed any motion at all.

"It was a dangerous pregnancy—again—and a hazardous birth. Had I risked it there, it would almost certainly have killed us both." She spoke directly to her daughter, as though they were alone in the room. Roger, waking slowly from the spell of the past, felt like an intruder.

"The truth, then, all of it. I couldn't bear to leave him," Claire said softly. "Even for you . . . I hated you for a bit, before you were born, because it was for you that he'd made me go. I didn't mind dying—not with him. But to have to go on, to live without him—he was right, I had the worst of the bargain. But I kept it, because I loved him. And we lived, you and I, because he loved you."

Brianna didn't move; didn't take her eyes from her mother's face. Only her lips moved, stiffly, as though unaccustomed to talking.

"How long . . . did you hate me?"

Gold eyes met blue ones, innocent and ruthless as the eyes of a falcon.

"Until you were born. When I held you and nursed you and saw you look up at me with your father's eyes."

Brianna made a faint, strangled sound, but her mother went on, voice softening a little as she looked at the girl at her feet.

"And then I began to know you, something separate from myself or from Jamie. And I loved you for yourself, and not only for the man who fathered you."

There was a blur of motion on the hearthrug, and Brianna shot erect. Her hair bristled out like a lion's mane, and the blue eyes blazed like the heart of the flames behind her.

"Frank Randall was my father!" she said. "He was! I know it!" Fists clenched, she glared at her mother. Her voice trembled with rage.

"I don't know why you're doing this. Maybe you did hate me, maybe you still do!" Tears were beginning to make their way down her cheeks, unbidden, and she dashed them angrily away with the back of one hand.

"Daddy . . . Daddy loved me—he couldn't have, if I weren't his! Why are you trying to make me believe he wasn't my father? Were you jealous of me? Is that it? Did you mind so much that he loved me? He didn't love *you,* I know that!" The blue eyes narrowed, cat-like, blazing in a face gone dead-white.

Roger felt a strong desire to ease behind the door before she noticed his presence and turned that molten wrath on him. But beyond his own discomfort he was conscious of a sense of growing awe. The girl that stood on the hearth-rug, hissing and spitting in defense of her paternity, flamed with the wild strength that had brought the Highland warriors down on their enemies like shrieking banshees. Her long, straight nose lengthened still further by the shadows, eyes slitted like a snarling cat's, she was the image of her father—and her father was patently not the dark, quiet scholar whose photo adorned the jacket of the book on the table.

Claire opened her mouth once, but then closed it again, watching her daughter with absorbed fascination. That powerful tension of the body, the flexing arch of the broad, flat cheekbones; Roger thought that she had seen that many times before—but not in Brianna.

With a suddenness that made them both flinch, Brianna spun on her heel, grabbed the yellowed news-clippings from the desk, and thrust them into the fire. She snatched the poker and jabbed it viciously into the tindery mass, heedless of the shower of sparks that flew from the hearth and hissed about her booted feet.

Whirling from the rapidly blackening mass of glowing paper, she stamped one foot on the hearth.

"Bitch!" she shouted at her mother. "You hated me? Well, I hate *you!*" She drew back the arm with the poker, and Roger's muscles tensed instinctively, ready to lunge for her. But she turned, arm drawn back like a javelin thrower, and hurled the poker through the full-length window, where the panes of night-dark glass reflected the image of a burning woman for one last instant before the crash and shiver into empty black.

The silence in the study was shattering. Roger, who had leaped to his feet in pursuit of Brianna, was left standing in the middle of the room, awkwardly frozen. He looked down at his hands as if not quite sure what to do with them, then at Claire. She sat perfectly still in the sanctuary of the wing chair, like an animal frozen by the passing shadow of a raptor.

After several moments, Roger moved across to the desk and leaned against it.

"I don't know what to say," he said.

Claire's mouth twitched faintly. "Neither do I."

They sat in silence for several minutes. The old house creaked, settling around them, and a faint noise of banging pots came down the hallway from the kitchen, where Fiona was doing something about dinner. Roger's feeling of shock and constrained embarrassment gradually gave way to something else, he wasn't sure what. His hands felt icy, and he rubbed them on his legs, feeling the warm rasp of the corduroy on his palms.

"I . . ." He started to speak, then stopped and shook his head.

Claire drew a deep breath, and he realized that it was the first movement he had seen her make since Brianna had left. Her gaze was clear and direct.

"Do you believe me?" she asked.

Roger looked thoughtfully at her. "I'll be damned if I know," he said at last.

That provoked a slightly wavering smile. "That's what Jamie said," she said, "when I asked him at the first where he thought I'd come from."

"I can't say I blame him." Roger hesitated, then, making up his mind, got off the desk and came across the room to her. "May I?" He knelt and took her unresisting hand in his, turning it to the light. You can tell real ivory from the synthetic, he remembered suddenly, because the real kind feels warm to the touch. The palm of her hand was a soft pink, but the faint line of the "J" at the base of her thumb was white as bone.

"It doesn't prove anything," she said, watching his face. "It could have been an accident; I could have done it myself."

"But you didn't, did you?" He laid the hand back in her lap very gently, as though it were a fragile artifact.

"No. But I can't prove it. The pearls"—her hand went to the shimmer of the necklace at her throat—"they're authentic; that can be verified. But can I prove where I got them? No."

"And the portrait of Ellen MacKenzie—" he began.

"The same. A coincidence. Something to base my delusion upon. My lies." There was a faintly bitter note in her voice, though she spoke calmly enough. There was a patch of color in each cheek now, and she was losing that utter stillness. It was like watching a statue come to life, he thought.

Roger got to his feet. He paced slowly back and forth, rubbing a hand through his hair.

"But it's important to you, isn't it? It's very important."

"Yes." She rose herself and went to the desk, where the folder of his research sat. She laid a hand on the manila sheeting with reverence, as though it were a gravestone; he supposed to her it was.

"I had to know." There was a faint quaver in her voice, but he saw her chin firm instantly, suppressing it. "I had to know if he'd done it—if he'd saved his men—or if he'd sacrificed himself for nothing. And I had to tell Brianna. Even if she doesn't believe it—if she never believes it. Jamie was her father. I had to tell her."

"Yes, I see that. And you couldn't do it while Dr. Randall—your hus—I mean, Frank," he corrected himself, flushing, "was alive."

She smiled faintly. "It's all right; you can call Frank my husband. He was, after all, for a good many years. And Bree's right, in a way—he was her father, as well as Jamie." She glanced down at her hands, and spread the fingers of both, so the light gleamed from the two rings she wore, silver and gold. Roger was struck by a thought.

"Your ring," he said, coming to stand close by her again. "The silver one. Is there a maker's mark in it? Some of the eighteenth-century Scottish silversmiths used them. It might not be proof positive, but it's something."

Claire looked startled. Her left hand covered the right protectively, fingers rubbing the wide silver band with its pattern of Highland interlace and thistle blooms.

"I don't know," she said. A faint blush rose in her cheeks. "I haven't seen inside it. I've never taken it off." She twisted the ring slowly over the joint of the knuckle; her fingers were slender, but from long wearing, the ring had left a groove in her flesh.

She squinted at the inside of the ring, then rose and brought it to the table, where she stood next to Roger, tilting the silver circle to catch the light from the table lamp.

"There are words in it," she said wonderingly. "I never realized that he'd . . . Oh, dear God." Her voice broke, and the ring slipped from her fingers, rattling on the table with a tiny metal chime. Roger hurriedly scooped it up, but she had turned away, fists held tight against her middle. He knew she didn't want him to see her face; the control she had kept through the long hours of the day and the scene with Brianna had deserted her now.

He stood for a minute, feeling unbearably awkward and out of place. With a terrible feeling that he was violating a privacy that ran deeper than anything he had ever known, but not knowing what else to do, he lifted the tiny metal circle to the light and read the words inside.

"Da mi basia mille . . ." But it was Claire's voice that spoke the words, not his. Her voice was shaky, and he could tell that she was crying, but it was coming back under her control. She couldn't let go for long; the power of what she held leashed could so easily destroy her.

"It's Catullus. A bit of a love poem. Hugh. . . . Hugh Munro—he gave me the poem for a wedding present, wrapped around a bit of amber with a dragonfly inside it." Her hands, still curled into fists, had now dropped to her sides. "I couldn't say it all, still, but the one bit—I know that much." Her voice was growing steadier as she spoke, but she kept her back turned to Roger. The small silver circle glowed in his palm, still warm with the heat of the finger it had left.

". . . da mi basia mille . . ."

Still turned away, she went on, translating,

> *"Then let amorous kisses dwell*
> *On our lips, begin and tell*
> *A Thousand and a Hundred score*
> *A Hundred, and a Thousand more."*

When she had finished, she stood still a moment, then slowly turned to face him again. Her cheeks were flushed and wet, and her lashes clumped together, but she was superficially calm.

"A hundred, and a thousand more," she said, with a feeble attempt at a smile. "But no maker's mark. So that isn't proof, either."

"Yes, it is." Roger found there seemed to be something sticking in his own throat, and hastily cleared it. "It's absolute proof. To me."

Something lit in the depths of her eyes, and the smile grew real. Then the tears welled up and overflowed as she lost her grip once and for all.

"I'm sorry," she said at last. She was sitting on the sofa, elbows on her knees, face half-buried in one of the Reverend Mr. Wakefield's huge white handkerchiefs. Roger sat close beside her, almost touching. She seemed very small and vulnerable. He wanted to pat the ash-brown curls, but felt too shy to do it.

"I never thought . . . it never occurred to me," she said, blowing her nose again. "I didn't know how much it would mean, to have someone believe me."

"Even if it isn't Brianna?"

She grimaced slightly at his words, brushing back her hair with one hand as she straightened.

"It was a shock," she defended her daughter. "Naturally, she couldn't— she was so fond of her father—of Frank, I mean," she amended hastily. "I knew she might not be able to take it all in at first. But . . . surely when she's had time to think about it, ask questions . . ." Her voice faded, and the shoulders of her white linen suit slumped under the weight of the words.

As though to distract herself, she glanced at the table, where the stack of shiny-covered books still sat, undisturbed.

"It's odd, isn't it? To live twenty years with a Jacobite scholar, and to be so afraid of what I might learn that I could never bear to open one of his books?" She shook her head, still staring at the books. "I don't know what happened to many of them—I couldn't stand to find out. All the men I knew; I couldn't forget them. But I could bury them, keep their memory at bay. For a time."

And that time now was ended, and another begun. Roger picked up the book from the top of the stack, weighing it in his hands, as if it were a responsibility. Perhaps it would take her mind off Brianna, at least.

"Do you want me to tell you?" he asked quietly.

She hesitated for a long moment, but then nodded quickly, as though afraid she would regret the action if she paused to think about it longer.

He licked dry lips, and began to talk. He didn't need to refer to the book; these were facts known to any scholar of the period. Still, he held Frank Randall's book against his chest, solid as a shield.

"Francis Townsend," he began. "The man who held Carlisle for Charles. He was captured. Tried for treason, hanged and disemboweled."

He paused, but the white face was drained of blood already, no further change was possible. She sat across the table from him, motionless as a pillar of salt.

"MacDonald of Keppoch charged the field at Culloden on foot, with his brother Donald. Both of them were cut down by English cannon fire. Lord Kilmarnock fell on the field of battle, but Lord Ancrum, scouting the fallen, recognized him and saved his life from Cumberland's men. No great favor; he was beheaded the next August on Tower Hill, together with Balmerino." He hesitated. "Kilmarnock's young son was lost on the field; his body was never recovered."

"I always liked Balmerino," she murmured. "And the Old Fox? Lord Lovat?" Her voice was little more than a whisper. "The shadow of an ax . . ."

"Yes." Roger's fingers stroked the slick jacket of the book unconsciously, as though reading the words within by Braille. "He was tried for treason, and condemned to be beheaded. He made a good end. All the accounts say that he met his death with great dignity."

A scene flashed through Roger's mind; an anecdote from Hogarth. He recited from memory, as closely as he could. " 'Carried through the shouts and jeers of an English mob on his way to the Tower, the old chieftain of clan Fraser appeared nonchalant, indifferent to the missiles that sailed past his head, and almost good-humored. In reply to a shout from one elderly woman—"You're going to get your head chopped off, you old Scotch cur!"—he leaned from his carriage window and shouted jovially back, "I expect I shall, you ugly old English bitch!" ' "

She was smiling, but the sound she made was a cross between a laugh and a sob.

"I'll bet he did, the bloody old bastard."

"When he was led to the block," Roger went on cautiously, "he asked to inspect the blade, and instructed the executioner to do a good job. He told the man, 'Do it right, for I shall be very angry indeed if you don't.' "

Tears were running down beneath her closed lids, glittering like jewels in the firelight. He made a motion toward her, but she sensed it and shook her head, eyes still closed.

"I'm all right. Go on."

"There isn't much more. Some of them survived, you know. Lochiel escaped to France." He carefully refrained from mention of the chieftain's brother, Archibald Cameron. The doctor had been hanged, disemboweled, and beheaded at Tyburn, his heart torn out and given to the flames. She did not seem to notice the omission.

He finished the list rapidly, watching her. Her tears had stopped, but she sat with her head hung forward, the thick curly hair hiding all expression.

He paused for a moment when he had finished speaking, then got up and took her firmly by the arm.

"Come on," he said. "You need a little air. It's stopped raining; we'll go outside."

The air outside was fresh and cool, almost intoxicating after the stuffiness of the Reverend's study. The heavy rain had ceased about sunset, and now, in the early evening, only the pit-a-pat dripping of trees and shrubs echoed the earlier downpour.

I felt an almost overwhelming relief at being released from the house. I had feared this for so long, and now it was done. Even if Bree never . . . but no, she would. Even if it took a long time, surely she would recognize the truth. She must; it looked her in the face every morning in the mirror; it ran in the very blood of her veins. For now, I had told her everything, and I felt the lightness of a shriven soul, leaving the confessional, unburdened as yet by thought of the penance ahead.

Rather like giving birth, I thought. A short period of great difficulty and rending pain, and the certain knowledge of sleepless nights and nerve-racking days in future. But for now, for a blessed, peaceful moment, there was nothing but a quiet euphoria that filled the soul and left no room for misgivings. Even the fresh-felt grief for the men I had known was muted out here, softened by the stars that shone through rifts in the shredding cloud.

The night was damp with early spring, and the tires of cars passing on the main road nearby hissed on the wet pavement. Roger led me without speaking down the slope behind the house, up another past a small, mossy glade, and down again, where there was a path that led to the river. A black iron railroad bridge spanned the river here; there was an iron ladder from the path's edge, attached to one of the girders. Someone armed with a can of white spray-paint had inscribed FREE SCOTLAND on the span with random boldness.

In spite of the sadness of memory, I felt at peace, or nearly so. I'd done the hardest part. Bree knew now who she was. I hoped fervently that she would come to believe it in time—not only for her own sake, I knew, but also for mine. More than I could ever have admitted, even to myself, I wanted to have someone with whom to remember Jamie; someone I could talk to about him.

I felt an overwhelming tiredness, one that touched both mind and body. But I straightened my spine just once more, forcing my body past its limits, as I had done so many times before. Soon, I promised my aching joints, my tender mind, my freshly riven heart. Soon, I could rest. I could sit alone in the small, cozy parlor of the bed-and-breakfast, alone by the fire with my ghosts. I could mourn them in peace, letting the weariness slip away with my tears, and go at last to seek the temporary oblivion of sleep, in which I might meet them alive once more.

But not yet. There was one thing more to be done before I slept.

They walked in silence for some time, with no sound but the passing of distant traffic, and the closer lapping of the river at its banks. Roger felt reluctant to start any conversation, lest he risk reminding her of things she wished to forget. But the floodgates had been opened, and there was no way of holding back.

She began to ask him small questions, hesitant and halting. He answered them as best he could, and hesitant in return, asked a few questions of his own. The freedom of talking, suddenly, after so many years of pent-up secrecy, seemed to act on her like a drug, and Roger, listening in fascination, drew her out despite herself. By the time they reached the railroad bridge, she had recovered the vigor and strength of character he had first seen in her.

"He was a fool, and a drunkard, and a weak, silly man," she declared passionately. "They were all fools—Lochiel, Glengarry, and the rest. They drank too much together, and filled themselves with Charlie's foolish dreams. Talk is cheap, and Dougal was right—it's easy to be brave, sitting over a glass of ale in a warm room. Stupid with drink, they were, and then too proud of their bloody honor to back down. They whipped their men and threatened them, bribed them and lured them—took them all to bloody ruin . . . for the sake of honor and glory."

She snorted through her nose, and was silent for a moment. Then, surprisingly, she laughed.

"But do you know what's really funny? That poor, silly sot and his greedy, stupid helpers; and the foolish, honorable men who couldn't bring themselves to turn back . . . they had the one tiny virtue among them; they believed. And the odd thing is, that that's all that's endured of them—all the silliness, the incompetence, the cowardice and drunken vainglory; that's all gone. All that's left now of Charles Stuart and his men is the glory that they sought for and never found.

"Perhaps Raymond was right," she added in a softer tone; "it's only the essence of a thing that counts. When time strips everything else away, it's only the hardness of the bone that's left."

"I suppose you must feel some bitterness against the historians," Roger ventured. "All the writers who got it wrong—made him out a hero. I mean, you can't go anywhere in the Highlands without seeing the Bonnie Prince on toffee tins and souvenir tourist mugs."

Claire shook her head, gazing off in the distance. The evening mist was growing heavier, the bushes beginning to drip again from the tips of their leaves.

"Not the historians. No, not them. Their greatest crime is that they presume to know what happened, how things come about, when they have only what the past chose to leave behind—for the most part, they think what they were meant to think, and it's a rare one that sees what really happened, behind the smokescreen of artifacts and paper."

There was a faint rumble in the distance. The evening passenger train from London, Roger knew. You could hear the whistle from the manse on clear nights.

"No, the fault lies with the artists," Claire went on. "The writers, the singers, the tellers of tales. It's them that take the past and re-create it to their liking. Them that could take a fool and give you back a hero, take a sot and make him a king."

"Are they all liars, then?" Roger asked. Claire shrugged. In spite of the chilly air, she had taken off the jacket to her suit; the damp molded the cotton shirt to show the fineness of collarbone and shoulder blades.

"Liars?" she asked, "or sorcerers? Do they see the bones in the dust of the earth, see the essence of a thing that was, and clothe it in new flesh, so the plodding beast reemerges as a fabulous monster?"

"And are they wrong to do it, then?" Roger asked. The rail bridge trembled as the Flying Scotsman hit the switch below. The wavering white letters shook with vibration—FREE SCOTLAND.

Claire stared upward at the letters, her face lit by fugitive starlight.

"You still don't understand, do you?" she said. She was irritated, but the husky voice didn't rise above its normal level.

"You don't *know* why," she said. "You don't know, and I don't know, and we never *will* know. Can't you see? You don't know, because you can't say what the end is—there isn't any end. You can't say, 'This particular event' was 'destined' to happen, and therefore all these other things happened. What Charles did to the people of Scotland—was that the 'thing' that had to happen? Or was it 'meant' to happen as it did, and Charles's real purpose was to be what he is now—a figurehead, an icon? Without him, would Scotland have endured two hundred years of union with England, and still—*still*"—she waved a hand at the sprawling letters overhead—"have kept its own identity?"

"I don't know!" said Roger, having to shout as the swinging searchlight lit the trees and track, and the train roared over the bridge above them.

There was a solid minute of clash and roar, earthshaking noise that held them rooted to the spot. Then at last it was past, and the clatter died to a lonely crying wail as the red light of the end car swept out of sight beyond them.

"Well, that's the hell of it, isn't it?" she said, turning away. "You never *know,* but you have to act anyway, don't you?"

She spread her hands suddenly, flexing the strong fingers so her rings flashed in the light.

"You learn it when you become a doctor. Not in school—that isn't where you learn, in any case—but when you lay your hands on people and presume to heal them. There are so many there, beyond your reach. So many you can never touch, so many whose essence you can't find, so many who slip through your fingers. But you can't think about them. The only thing you can do—the *only* thing—is to try for the one who's in front of you. Act as though this one patient is the only person in the world—because to do otherwise is to lose that one, too. One at a time, that's all you can do. And you learn not to despair over all the ones you can't help, but only to do what you can."

She turned back to him, face haggard with fatigue, but eyes glowing with the rain-light, spangles of water caught in the tangles of her hair. Her hand rested on Roger's arm, compelling as the wind that fills a boat's sail and drives it on.

"Let's go back to the manse, Roger," she said. "I have something particular to tell you."

Claire was quiet on the walk back to the manse, avoiding Roger's tentative queries. She refused his proffered arm, walking alone, head down in thought. Not as though she were making up her mind, Roger thought; she had already done that. She was deciding what to say.

Roger himself was wondering. The quiet gave him respite from the turmoil of the day's revelations—enough to wonder precisely why Claire had chosen to include him in them. She could easily have told Brianna alone, had she wished to. Was it only that she had feared what Brianna's reaction to the story might be, and been reluctant to meet it alone? Or had she gambled that he would—as he had—believe her, and thus sought to enlist him as an ally in the cause of truth—her truth, and Brianna's?

His curiosity had reached near boiling point by the time they reached the manse. Still, there was work to do first; together, they unloaded one of the tallest bookshelves, and pushed it in front of the shattered window, shutting out the cold night air.

Flushed from the exertion, Claire sat down on the sofa while he went to pour a pair of whiskies from the small drinks-table in the corner. When Mrs. Graham had been alive, she had always brought drinks on a tray, properly napkined, doilied, and adorned with accompanying biscuits. Fiona, if allowed, would willingly have done the same, but Roger much preferred the simplicity of pouring his own drink in solitude.

Claire thanked him, sipped from the glass, then set it down and looked up at him, tired but composed.

"You'll likely be wondering why I wanted you to hear the whole story," she said, with that unnerving ability to see into his thoughts.

"There were two reasons. I'll tell you the second presently, but as for the first, I thought you had some right to hear it."

"Me? What right?"

The golden eyes were direct, unsettling as a leopard's guileless stare. "The same as Brianna. The right to know who you are." She moved across the room to the far wall. It was cork-lined from floor to ceiling, encrusted with layers of photographs, charts, notes, stray visiting cards, old parish schedules, spare keys, and other bits of rubbish pinned to the cork.

"I remember this wall." Claire smiled, touching a picture of Prize Day at the local grammar school. "Did your father ever take anything off it?"

Roger shook his head, bewildered. "No, I don't believe he did. He always said he could never find things put away in drawers; if it was anything important, he wanted it in plain sight."

"Then it's likely still here. He thought it was important."

Reaching up, she began to thumb lightly through the overlapping layers, gently separating the yellowed papers.

"This one, I think," she murmured, after some riffling back and forth. Reaching far up under the detritus of sermon notes and car-wash tickets, she detached a single sheet of paper and laid it on the desk.

"Why, it's my family tree," Roger said in surprise. "I haven't seen that old thing in years. And never paid any attention to it when I did see it, either," he added. "If you're going to tell me I'm adopted, I already know that."

Claire nodded, intent on the chart. "Oh, yes. That's why your father—Mr. Wakefield, I mean—drew up this chart. He wanted to be sure that you would know your real family, even though he gave you his own name."

Roger sighed, thinking of the Reverend, and the small silver-framed picture on his bureau, with the smiling likeness of an unknown young man, dark-haired in World War II RAF uniform.

"Yes, I know that, too. My family name was MacKenzie. Are you going to tell me I'm connected to some of the MacKenzies you . . . er, knew? I don't see any of those names on this chart."

Claire acted as though she hadn't heard him, tracing a finger down the spidery hand-drawn lines of the genealogy.

"Mr. Wakefield was a terrible stickler for accuracy," she murmured, as though to herself. "He wouldn't want any mistakes." Her finger came to a halt on the page.

"Here," she said. "This is where it happened. Below this point"—her finger swept down the page—"everything is right. These were your parents, and your grandparents, and your great-grandparents, and so on. But not above." The finger swept upward.

Roger bent over the chart, then looked up, moss-green eyes thoughtful.

"This one? William Buccleigh MacKenzie, born 1744, of William John MacKenzie and Sarah Innes. Died 1782."

Claire shook her head. "Died 1744, aged two months, of smallpox." She looked up, and the golden eyes met his with a force that sent a shiver down his spine. "Yours wasn't the first adoption in that family, you know," she said. Her finger tapped the entry. "He needed a wet nurse," she said. "His own mother was dead—so he was given to a family that had lost a baby. They called him by the name of the child they had lost—that was common—and I don't suppose anyone wanted to call attention to his ancestry by recording the new child in the parish register. He would have been baptized at birth, after all; it wasn't necessary to do it again. Colum told me where they placed him."

"Geillis Duncan's son," he said slowly. "The witch's child."

"That's right." She gazed at him appraisingly, head cocked to one side. "I knew it must be, when I saw you. The eyes, you know. They're hers."

Roger sat down, feeling suddenly quite cold, in spite of the bookshelf blocking the draft, and the newly kindled fire on the hearth.

"You're sure of this?" he said, but of course she was sure. Assuming that the whole story was not a fabrication, the elaborate construction of a diseased mind. He glanced up at her, sitting unruffled with her whisky, composed as though about to order cheese straws.

Diseased mind? Dr. Claire Beauchamp-Randall, chief of staff at a large, important hospital? Raving insanity, rampant delusions? Easier to believe himself insane. In fact, he was beginning to believe just that.

He took a deep breath and placed both hands flat on the chart, blotting out the entry for William Buccleigh MacKenzie.

"Well, it's interesting all right, and I suppose I'm glad you told me. But it doesn't really change anything, does it? Except that I suppose I can tear off the top half of this genealogy and throw it away. After all, we don't know where Geillis Duncan came from, nor the man who fathered her child; you seem sure it wasn't poor old Arthur."

Claire shook her head, a distant look in her eyes.

"Oh, no, it wasn't Arthur Duncan. It was Dougal MacKenzie who fathered Geilie's child. That was the real reason she was killed. Not witchcraft. But Colum MacKenzie couldn't let it be known that his brother had had an adulterous affair with the fiscal's wife. And she wanted to marry Dougal; I think perhaps she threatened the MacKenzies with the truth about Hamish."

"Hamish? Oh, Colum's son. Yes, I remember." Roger rubbed his forehead. His head was starting to spin.

"Not Colum's son," Claire corrected. "Dougal's. Colum couldn't sire children, but Dougal could—and did. Hamish was the heir to the chieftainship of clan MacKenzie; Colum would have killed anyone who threatened Hamish —and did."

She drew a deep breath. "And that," she said, "leads to the second reason why I told you the story."

Roger buried both hands in his hair, staring down at the table, where the lines of the genealogical chart seemed to writhe like mocking snakes, forked tongues flickering between the names.

"Geillis Duncan," he said hoarsely. "She had a vaccination scar."

"Yes. It was that, finally, that made me come back to Scotland. When I left with Frank, I swore I would never come back. I knew I could never forget, but I could bury what I knew; I could stay away, and never seek to know what happened after I left. It seemed the least I could do, for both of them, for Frank and Jamie. And for the baby coming." Her lips pressed tightly together for a moment.

"But Geilie saved my life, at the trial in Cranesmuir. Perhaps she was doomed herself in any case; I think she believed so. But she threw away any chance she might have had, in order to save me. And she left me a message. Dougal gave it to me, in a cave in the Highlands, when he brought me the news that Jamie was in prison. There were two pieces to the message. A sentence, 'I do not know if it is possible, but I think so,' and a sequence of four numbers—one, nine, six, and eight."

"Nineteen sixty-eight," Roger said, with the feeling that this was a dream. Surely he would be waking soon. "This year. What did she mean, she thought it was possible?"

"To go back. Through the stones. She hadn't tried, but she thought I could. And she was right, of course." Claire turned and picked up her whisky from the table. She stared at Roger across the rim of the glass, eyes the same color as the contents. "This is 1968; the year she went back herself. Except that I think she hasn't yet gone."

The glass slipped in Roger's hand, and he barely caught it in time.

"What . . . here? But she . . . why not . . . you can't tell . . ." He was sputtering, thoughts jarred into incoherency.

"I don't *know*," Claire pointed out. "But I think so. I'm fairly sure she was Scots, and the odds are good that she came through somewhere in the Highlands. Granted that there are any number of standing stones, we know that Craigh na Dun *is* a passage—for those that can use it. Besides," she added, with the air of one presenting the final argument, "Fiona's seen her."

"Fiona?" This, Roger felt, was simply too much. The crowning absurdity. Anything else he could manage to believe—time passages, clan treachery, historical revelations—but bringing Fiona into it was more than his reason could be expected to stand. He looked pleadingly at Claire. "Tell me you don't mean that," he begged. "Not Fiona."

Claire's mouth twitched at one corner. "I'm afraid so," she said, not without sympathy. "I asked her—about the Druid group that her grandmother belonged to, you know. She's been sworn to secrecy, of course, but I knew quite a bit about them already, and well . . ." She shrugged, mildly apologetic. "It wasn't too difficult to get her to talk. She told me that there'd been another woman asking questions—a tall, fair-haired woman, with very striking green eyes. Fiona said the woman reminded her of someone," she added delicately, carefully not looking at him, "but she couldn't think who."

Roger merely groaned, and bending at the waist, collapsed slowly forward until his forehead rested on the table. He closed his eyes, feeling the cool hardness of the wood under his head.

"Did Fiona know who she was?" he asked, eyes still closed.

"Her name is Gillian Edgars," Claire replied. He heard her rising, crossing the room, adding another tot of whisky to her glass. She came back and stood by the table. He could feel her gaze on the back of his neck.

"I'll leave it to you." Claire said quietly. "It's your right to say. Shall I look for her?"

Roger lifted his head off the table and blinked at her incredulously. "Shall you look for her?" he said. "If this—if it's all true—then we have to find her, don't we? If she's going back to be burned alive? Of course you have to find her!" he burst out. "How could you consider anything else?"

"And if I do find her?" she replied. She placed a slender hand on the grubby chart and raised her eyes to his. "What happens to you?" she asked softly.

He looked around helplessly, at the bright, cluttered study, with the wall of miscellanea, the chipped old teapot on the ancient oak table. Solid as . . . He gripped his thighs, clutching the rough corduroy as though for reassurance that he was as solid as the chair on which he sat.

"But . . . I'm *real*!" he burst out. "I can't just . . . evaporate!"

Claire raised her brows consideringly. "I don't know that you would. I have no idea what would happen. Perhaps you would never have existed? In which case, you oughtn't to be too agitated now. Perhaps the part of you that makes you unique, your soul or whatever you want to call it—perhaps that's fated to exist in any case, and you would still be you, though born of a slightly different lineage. After all, how much of your physical makeup can be due to ancestors six generations back? Half? Ten percent?" She shrugged, and pursed her lips, looking him over carefully.

"Your eyes come from Geilie, as I told you. But I see Dougal in you, too. No specific feature, though you have the MacKenzie cheekbones; Bree has them, too. No, it's something more subtle, something in the way you move; a grace, a suddenness—no . . ." She shook her head. "I can't describe it. But it's there. Is it something you *need,* to be who you are? Could you do without that bit from Dougal?"

She rose heavily, looking her age for the first time since he had met her.

"I've spent more than twenty years looking for answers, Roger, and I can tell you only one thing: There aren't any answers, only choices. I've made a number of them myself, and no one can tell me whether they were right or wrong. Master Raymond perhaps, though I don't suppose he would; he was a man who believed in mysteries.

"I can see the right of it only far enough to know that I must tell you—and leave the choice to you."

He picked up the glass and drained the rest of the whisky.

The Year of our Lord 1968. The year when Geillis Duncan stepped into the circle of standing stones. The year she went to meet her fate beneath the rowan trees in the hills near Leoch. An illegitimate child—and death by fire.

He rose and wandered up and down the rows of books that lined the study. Books filled with history, that mocking and mutable subject.

No answers, only choices.

Restless, he fingered the books on the top shelf. These were the histories of the Jacobite movement, the stories of the Rebellions, the '15 and the '45. Claire had known a number of the men and women described in these books. Had fought and suffered with them, to save a people strange to her. Had lost all she held dear in the effort. And in the end, had failed. But the choice had been hers, as now it was his.

Was there a chance that this was a dream, a delusion of some kind? He stole a glance at Claire. She lay back in her chair, eyes closed, motionless but for the beating of her pulse, barely visible in the hollow of her throat. No. He could, for a moment, convince himself that it was make-believe, but only while he looked away from her. However much he wanted to believe otherwise, he could not look at her and doubt a word of what she said.

He spread his hands flat on the table, then turned them over, seeing the maze of lines that crossed his palms. Was it only his own fate that lay here in his cupped hands, or did he hold an unknown woman's life as well?

No answers. He closed his hands gently, as though holding something small trapped inside his fists, and made his choice.

"Let's find her," he said.

There was no sound from the still figure in the wing chair, and no movement save the rise and fall of the rounded breast. Claire was asleep.

T he old-fashioned buzzer whirred somewhere in the depths of the flat. It wasn't the best part of town, nor was it the worst. Working-class houses, for the most part, some, like this one, divided into two or three flats. A hand-lettered notice under the buzzer read MCHENRY UPSTAIRS—RING TWICE. Roger carefully pressed the buzzer once more, then wiped his hand on his trousers. His palms were sweating, which annoyed him considerably.

There was a trough of yellow jonquils by the doorstep, half-dead for lack of water. The tips of the blade-shaped leaves were brown and curling, and the frilly yellow heads drooped disconsolately near his shoe.

Claire saw them, too. "Perhaps no one's home," she said, stooping to touch the dry soil in the trough. "These haven't been watered in over a week."

Roger felt a mild wave of relief at the thought; whether he believed Geillis Duncan was Gillian Edgars or not, he hadn't been looking forward to this visit. He was turning to go when the door suddenly opened behind him, with a screech of sticking wood that brought his heart into his mouth.

"Aye?" The man who answered the door squinted at them, eyes swollen in a flushed, heavy face shadowed with unshaven beard.

"Er . . . We're sorry to disturb your sleep, sir," said Roger, making an effort to calm himself. His stomach felt slightly hollow. "We're looking for a Miss Gillian Edgars. Is this her residence?"

The man rubbed a stubby, black-furred hand over his head, making the hair stick up in belligerent spikes.

"That's *Mrs.* Edgars to you, jimmy. And what's it you want wi' my wife?" The alcoholic fumes from the man's breath made Roger want to step backward, but he stood his ground.

"We only want to talk with her," he said, as conciliatingly as he could. "Is she at home, please?"

"Is she at home, please?" said the man who must be Mr. Edgars, squinching his mouth in a savage, high-pitched mockery of Roger's Oxford accent. "No, she's not home. Bugger off," he advised, and swung the door to with a crash that left the lace curtain shivering with the vibration.

"I can see why she *isn't* home," Claire observed, standing on tiptoe to peer through the window. "I wouldn't be, either, if that's what was waiting for me."

"Quite," said Roger shortly. "And that would appear to be that. Have you any other suggestions for finding this woman?"

Claire let go of the windowsill.

"He's settled in front of the telly," she reported. "Let's leave him, at least until after the pub's opened. Meanwhile, we can go try this Institute. Fiona said Gillian Edgars took courses there."

The Institute for the Study of Highland Folklore and Antiquities was housed on the top floor of a narrow house just outside the business district. The receptionist, a small, plump woman in a brown cardigan and print dress, seemed delighted to see them; she mustn't get much company up here, Roger reflected.

"Oh, Mrs. *Edgars*," she said, upon hearing their business. Roger thought that a sudden note of doubt had crept into Mrs. Andrews's voice, but she remained bright and cheerful. "Yes," she said, "she's a regular member of the Institute, all paid up for her classes. She's around here quite a bit, is Mrs. Edgars." A lot more than Mrs. Andrews really cared for, from the sound of it.

"She isn't here now, by chance, is she?" Claire asked.

Mrs. Andrews shook her head, making the dozens of gray-streaked pincurls dance on her head.

"Oh, no," she said. "It's a Monday. Only me and Dr. McEwan are here on the Monday. He's the Director, you know." She looked reproachfully at Roger, as though he ought really to have known that. Then, apparently reassured by their evident respectability, she relented slightly.

"If you want to ask about Mrs. Edgars, you should see Dr. McEwan. I'll just go and tell him you're here, shall I?"

As she began to ease out from behind her desk, Claire stopped her, leaning forward.

"Have you perhaps got a photograph of Mrs. Edgars?" she asked bluntly. At Mrs. Andrews's stare of surprise, Claire smiled charmingly, explaining, "We wouldn't want to waste the Director's time, if it's the wrong person, you see."

Mrs. Andrews mouth dropped open slightly, and she blinked in confusion, but she nodded after a moment, and began fussing round her desk, opening drawers and talking to herself.

"I know they're here somewhere. I saw them just yesterday, so they can't have gone far . . . oh, here!" She bobbed up with a folder of eight-by-ten black-and-white photographs in her hand, and sorted rapidly through them.

"There," she said. "That's her, with one of the digging expeditions, out near town, but you can't see her face, can you? Let me see if there's any more . . ."

She resumed her sorting, muttering to herself, as Roger peered interestedly over Claire's shoulder at the photograph Mrs. Andrews had laid on the desk. It showed a small group of people standing near a Land-Rover, with a number of burlap sacks and small tools on the ground beside them. It was an impromptu shot, and several of the people were turned away from the camera. Claire's finger reached out without hesitation, touching the image of a tall girl with long, straight, fair hair hanging halfway down her back. She tapped the photograph and nodded silently to Roger.

"You can't possibly be sure," he muttered to her under his breath.

"What's that, luv?" said Mrs. Andrews, looking up absently over her spectacles. "Oh, you weren't talking to me. That's all right, then, I've found one a little better. It's still not her whole face—she's turned sideways, like—but it's better nor the other." She plopped the new picture down on top of the other with a triumphant little splat.

This one showed an older man with half-spectacles and the same fair-haired girl, bent over a table holding what looked like a collection of rusted motor parts to Roger, but which were undoubtedly valuable artifacts. The girl's hair swung down beside her cheek, and her head was turned toward the older man, but the slant of a short, straight nose, a sweetly rounded chin, and the curve of a beautiful mouth showed clearly. The eye was cast down, hidden under long, thick lashes. Roger repressed the admiring whistle that rose unbidden to his lips. Ancestress or not, she was a real dolly, he thought irreverently.

He glanced at Claire. She nodded, without speaking. She was paler even than usual, and he could see the pulse beating rapidly in her throat, but she thanked Mrs. Andrews with her usual composure.

"Yes, that's the one. I think perhaps we *would* like to talk to the Director, if he's available."

Mrs. Andrews cast a quick glance at the white-paneled door behind her desk.

"Well, I'll go and ask for you, dearie. Could I tell him what it's for, though?"

Roger was opening his mouth, groping for some excuse, when Claire stepped smoothly into the breach.

"We're from Oxford, actually," she said. "Mrs. Edgars has applied for a study grant with the Department of Antiquities, and she'd given the Institute as a reference with the rest of her credentials. So, if you wouldn't mind . . . ?"

"Oh, I see," said Mrs. Andrews, looking impressed. "Oxford. Just think! I'll ask Dr. McEwan if he can see you just now."

As she disappeared behind the white-paneled door, pausing for no more than a perfunctory rap before entering, Roger leaned down to whisper in Claire's ear.

"There is no such thing as a Department of Antiquities at Oxford," he hissed, "and you know it."

"You know that," she replied demurely, "and I, as you so cleverly point out, do too. But there are any number of people in the world who don't, and we've just met one of them."

The white-paneled door was beginning to open.

"Let's hope they're thick on the ground hereabouts," Roger said, wiping his brow, "or that you're a quick liar."

Claire rose, smiling at the beckoning figure of Mrs. Andrews as she spoke out of the side of her mouth.

"I? I, who read souls for the King of France?" She brushed down her skirt and set it swinging. "This will be pie."

Roger bowed ironically, gesturing toward the door. "*Après vous,* Madame."

As she stepped ahead of him, he added, "*Après vous, le déluge,*" under his breath. Her shoulders stiffened, but she didn't turn around.

Rather to Roger's surprise, it *was* pie. He wasn't sure whether it was Claire's skill at misrepresentation, or Dr. McEwan's own preoccupation, but their bona fides went unquestioned. It didn't seem to occur to the man that it was highly unlikely for scouting parties from Oxford to penetrate to the wilds of Inverness to make inquiries about the background of a potential graduate student. But then, Roger thought, Dr. McEwan appeared to have something on his mind; perhaps he wasn't thinking as clearly as usual.

"Weeeel . . . yes, Mrs. Edgars unquestionably has a fine mind. Very fine," the Director said, as though convincing himself. He was a tall, spare man, with a long upper lip like a camel's, which wobbled as he searched hesitantly for each new word. "Have you . . . has she . . . that is . . ." He trailed off, lip twitching, then, "Have you ever actually *met* Mrs. Edgars?" he finally burst out.

"No," said Roger, eyeing Dr. McEwan with some austerity. "That's why we're asking about her."

"Is there anything . . ." Claire paused delicately, inviting, "that you think perhaps the committee should know, Dr. McEwan?" She leaned forward, opening her eyes very wide. "You know, inquiries like this are *completely* confidential. But it's so important that we be fully informed; there is a position of trust involved." Her voice dropped suggestively. "The Ministry, you know."

Roger would dearly have loved to strangle her, but Dr. McEwan was nodding sagely, lip wobbling like mad.

"Oh, yes, dear lady. Yes, of course. The Ministry. I completely understand. Yes, yes, Well, I . . . hm, perhaps—I shouldn't like to mislead you in any respect, you know. And it is a wonderful chance, no doubt . . ."

Now Roger wanted to throttle both of them. Claire must have noticed his hands twitching in his lap with irresistible desire, for she put a firm stop to the Director's maundering.

"We're basically interested in two things," she said briskly, opening the notebook she carried and poising it on her knee as if for reference. *Pick up bottle sherry for Mrs. T,* Roger read out of the corner of one eye. *Sliced ham for picnic.*

"We want to know, first, your opinion of Mrs. Edgars's scholarship, and secondly, your opinion of her overall personality. The first we have of course evaluated ourselves"—she made a small tick in the notebook, next to an entry that read *Change traveler's cheques*—"but you have a much more substantial and detailed grasp, of course." Dr. McEwan was nodding away by this time, thoroughly mesmerized.

"Yes, well . . ." He puffed a little, then, with a glance at the door to make sure it was shut, leaned confidentially across his desk. "The quality of her work—well, about that I think I can satisfy you completely. I'll show you a few things she's been working on. And the other . . ." Roger thought he was about to go in for another spot of lip-twitching and leaned forward menacingly.

Dr. McEwan leaned back abruptly, looking startled. "It's nothing very much, really," he said. "It's only . . . well, she's such an *intense* young lady. Perhaps her interest seems at times a trifle . . . obsessive?" His voice went up questioningly. His eyes darted from Roger to Claire, like a trapped rat's.

"Would the direction of this intense interest perhaps be focused on the standing stones? The stone circles?" Claire suggested gently.

"Oh, it showed up in her application materials, then?" The Director hauled a large, grubby handkerchief out of his pocket and mopped his face with it. "Yes, that's it. Of course, a lot of people get quite carried away with them," he offered. "The romance of it, the mystery. Look at those benighted souls out at Stonehenge on Midsummer's Day, in hoods and robes. Chanting . . . all that nonsense. Not that I would compare Gillian Edgars to . . ."

There was quite a lot more of it, but Roger quit listening. It seemed stifling in the narrow office, and his collar was too tight; he could hear his heart beating, a slow, incessant thrumping in both ears that was very irritating.

It simply couldn't be! he thought. *Positively impossible.* True, Claire Randall's story was convincing—quite awfully convincing. But then, look at the effect she was having on this poor old dodderer, who wouldn't know scholarship if it was served up on a plate with piccalilli relish. She could obviously talk a tinker out of his pans. Not that he, Roger, was as susceptible as Dr. McEwan surely, but . . .

Beset with doubt and dripping with sweat, Roger paid little attention as Dr. McEwan fetched a set of keys from his drawer and rose to lead them out through a second door into a long hallway studded with doors.

"Study carrels," the Director explained. He opened one of the doors, revealing a cubicle some four feet on a side, barely big enough to contain a narrow table, a chair, and a small bookshelf. On the table, neatly stacked, were a series of folders in different colors. To the side, Roger saw a large notebook with gray covers, and a neat hand-lettered label on the front—MISCELLANEOUS. For some reason, the sight of the handwriting sent a shiver through him.

This was getting more personal by the moment. First photographs, now the woman's writings. He was assailed by a moment's panic at the thought of actually meeting Geillis Duncan. Gillian Edgars, he meant. *Whoever* the woman was.

The Director was opening various folders, pointing and explaining to Claire, who was putting on a good show of having some idea what he was talking about. Roger peered over her shoulder, nodding and saying, "Um-hm, very interesting," at intervals, but the slanted lines and loops of the script were incomprehensible to him.

She wrote this, he kept thinking. *She's real. Flesh and blood and lips and long eyelashes.* And if she goes back through the stone, she'll burn—crackle and blacken, with her hair lit like a torch in the black dawn. And if she doesn't, then . . . I don't exist.

He shook his head violently.

"You disagree, Mr. Wakefield?" The Director of the Institute was peering at him in puzzlement.

He shook his head again, this time in embarrassment.

"No, no. I mean . . . it's only . . . do you think I could have a drink of water?"

"Of course, of course! Come with me, there's a fountain just round the corner, I'll show you." Dr. McEwan bustled him out of the carrel and down the hall, expressing voluble, disjointed concern for his state of health.

Once away from the claustrophobic confines of the carrel and the proximity of Gillian Edgars's books and folders, Roger began to feel slightly better. Still, the thought of going back into that tiny room, where all Claire's words about her past seemed to echo off the thin partitions . . . no. He made up his mind. Claire could finish with Dr. McEwan by herself. He passed the carrel quickly, not looking inside, and went through the door that led back to the receptionist's desk.

Mrs. Andrews stared at him as he came in, her spectacles gleaming with concern and curiosity.

"Dear me, Mr. Wakefield. Are ye not feeling just right, then?" Roger rubbed a hand over his face; he must look really ghastly. He smiled weakly at the plump little secretary.

"No, thanks very much. I just got a bit hot back there; thought I'd step down for a little fresh air."

"Oh, aye." The secretary nodded understandingly. "The radiators." She pronounced it "raddiators." "They get stuck on, ye know, and won't turn off.

I'd best see about it." She rose from her desk, where the picture of Gillian Edgars still rested. She glanced down at the picture, then up at Roger.

"Isn't that odd?" she said conversationally. "I was just looking at this and wondering what it was about Mrs. Edgars's face that struck me all of a sudden. And I couldn't think what it was. But she's quite a look of *you*, Mr. Wakefield—especially round the eyes. Isn't that a coincidence? Mr. Wakefield?" Mrs. Andrews stared in the direction of the stair, where the thump of Roger's footsteps echoed from the wooden risers.

"Taken a bit short, I expect," she said kindly. "Poor lad."

The sun was still above the horizon when Claire rejoined him on the street, but it was late in the day; people were going home to their tea, and there was a feeling of general relaxation in the air—a looking forward to leisured peace after the long day's work.

Roger himself had no such feeling. He moved to open the car door for Claire, conscious of such a mix of emotions that he couldn't decide what to say first. She got in, glancing up at him sympathetically.

"Rather a jar, isn't it?" was all she said.

The fiendish maze of new one-way streets made getting through the town center a task that demanded all his attention. They were well on their way before he could take his eyes off the road long enough to ask, "What next?"

Claire was leaning back in her seat, eyes closed, the tendrils of her hair coming loose from their clip. She didn't open her eyes at his question, but stretched slightly, easing herself in the seat.

"Why don't you ask Brianna out for supper somewhere?" she said. Supper? Somehow it seemed subtly wrong to stop for supper in the midst of a life-or-death detective endeavor, but on the other hand, Roger was suddenly aware that the hollowness in his stomach wasn't entirely due to the revelations of the last hour.

"Well, all right," he said slowly. "But then tomorrow—"

"Why wait 'til tomorrow?" Claire broke in. She was sitting up now, combing out her hair. It was thick and unruly, and loosed swirling on her shoulders, Roger thought it made her look suddenly very young. "You can go talk to Greg Edgars again after supper, can't you?"

"How do you know his name is Greg?" Roger asked curiously. "And if he wouldn't talk to me this afternoon, why should he tonight?"

Claire looked at Roger as though suddenly doubting his basic intelligence.

"I know his name because I saw it on a letter in his mailbox," she said. "As for why he'll talk to you tonight, he'll talk to you because you're going to take along a bottle of whisky when you come this time."

"And you think that will make him invite us in?"

She lifted one brow. "Did you see the collection of empty bottles in his waste bin? Of course he will. Like a shot." She sat back, fists thrust into the pockets of her coat, and stared out at the passing street.

"You might see if Brianna will go with you," she said casually.

"She said she isn't having anything to do with this," Roger objected.

Claire glanced at him impatiently. The sun was setting behind her, and it made her eyes glow amber, like a wolf's.

"In that case, I suggest you don't tell her what you're up to," she said, in a tone that made Roger remember that she was chief of staff at a large hospital.

His ears burned, but he stubbornly said, "You can't very well hide it, if you and I—"

"Not me," Claire interrupted. "You. I have something else to do."

This was too much, Roger thought. He pulled the car over without signaling and skidded to a stop at the side of the road. He glared at her.

"Something else to do, have you?" he demanded. "I like that! You're landing me with the job of trying to entice a drunken sot who will likely assault me on sight, *and* luring your daughter along to watch! What, do you think she'll be needed to drive me to hospital after Edgars has finished beating me over the head with a bottle?"

"No," Claire said, ignoring his tone. "I think you and Greg Edgars together may succeed where I couldn't, in convincing Bree that Gillian Edgars is the woman I knew as Geillis Duncan. She won't listen to me. She likely won't listen to you, either, if you try to tell her what we found at the Institute today. But she'll listen to Greg Edgars." Her tone was flat and grim, and Roger felt his annoyance ebbing slightly. He started the car once more, and pulled out into the stream of traffic.

"All right, I'll try," he said grudgingly, not looking at her. "And just where are you going to be, while I do this?"

There was a small, shuffling movement alongside as she groped in her pocket again. Then she drew out her hand and opened it. His eye caught the silvery gleam of a small object in the darkness of her palm. A key.

"I'm going to burgle the Institute," she said calmly. "I want that notebook."

After Claire excused herself to run her unspecified "errand"—making Roger shudder only slightly—he and Brianna had driven to the pub, but then decided to wait for their supper, since the evening was unexpectedly fine. They strolled down the narrow walk by the River Ness, and he had forgotten his misgivings about the evening in the pleasure of Brianna's company.

They talked carefully at first, avoiding anything controversial. Then the chat turned to Roger's work, and grew gradually more animated.

"And how do you know so much about it, anyway?" Roger demanded, breaking off in the middle of a sentence.

"My father taught me," she replied. At the word "father," she stiffened a bit, and drew back, as though expecting him to say something. "My *real* father," she added pointedly.

"Well, he certainly knew," Roger replied mildly, leaving the challenge strictly alone. Plenty of time for that later, my girl, he thought cynically. But it isn't going to be me that springs the trap.

Just down the street, Roger could see a light in the window of the Edgars's house. The quarry was denned, then. He felt an unexpected surge of adrenaline at the thought of the coming confrontation.

Adrenaline lost out to the surge of gastric juices that resulted when they stepped into the pub's savory atmosphere, redolent of shepherd's pie. Conversation was general and friendly, with an unspoken agreement to avoid any reference to the scene at the manse the day before. Roger had noticed the coolness between Claire and her daughter, before he had left her at the cab stand on their way to the pub. Seated side by side in the backseat, they had reminded him of two strange cats, ears laid flat and tails twitching, but both avoiding the eye-locking stare that would lead to claws and flying fur.

After dinner, Brianna fetched their coats while he paid the bill.

"What's that for?" she asked, noticing the bottle of whisky in his hand. "Planning a rave-up for later on?"

"Rave-up?" he said, grinning at her. "You *are* getting on, aren't you? And what else have you picked up in your linguistic studies?"

She cast her eyes down in exaggerated demureness.

"Oh, well. There's a dance in the States, called the Shag. I gather I shouldn't ask you to do it with me here, though."

"Not unless you mean it," he said. They both laughed, but he thought the flush on her cheeks had deepened, and he was conscious of a certain stirring at the suggestion that made him keep his coat hung over one arm instead of putting it on.

"Well, after enough of *that* stuff, anything's possible," she said, indicating the whisky bottle with a mildly malicious smile. "Terrible taste, though."

"It's acquired, lassie," Roger informed her, letting his accent broaden. "Only Scots are born wi' it. I'll buy ye a bottle of your own to practice with. This one's a gift, though—something I promised to leave off. Want to come along, or shall I do it later?" he asked. He didn't know whether he wanted her to come or not, but felt a surge of happiness when she nodded and shrugged into her own coat.

"Sure, why not?"

"Good." He reached out and delicately turned down the flap of her collar, so it lay flat on her shoulder. "It's just down the street—let's walk, shall we?"

The neighborhood looked a little better at night. Some of its shabbiness was hidden by the darkness, and the lights glowing from windows into the tiny front gardens gave the street an air of coziness that it lacked during the day.

"This won't take a minute," Roger told Brianna as he pressed the buzzer. He wasn't sure whether to hope he was right or not. His first fear passed as the door opened; someone was home, and still conscious.

Edgars had plainly spent the afternoon in the company of one of the bottles lined up along the edge of the swaybacked buffet visible behind him. Luckily, he appeared not to connect his evening visitors with the intrusion of the afternoon. He squinted at Roger's introduction, composed on the way to the house.

"Gilly's cousin? I didn' know she had a cousin."

"Well, she has," said Roger, boldly taking advantage of this admission. "I'm him." He would deal with Gillian herself when he saw her. If he saw her.

Edgars blinked once or twice, then rubbed an inflamed eye with one fist, as though to get a better look at them. His eyes focused with some difficulty on Brianna, hovering diffidently behind Roger.

"Who's that?" he demanded.

"Er . . . my girlfriend," Roger improvised. Brianna narrowed her eyes at him, but said nothing. Plainly she was beginning to smell a rat, but went ahead of him without protest as Greg Edgars swung the door wider to admit them.

The flat was small and stuffy, overfurnished with secondhand furniture. The air reeked of stale cigarettes and insufficiently taken-out garbage, and the remnants of take-away meals were scattered heedlessly over every horizontal surface in the room. Brianna gave Roger a sidelong look that said *Nice relatives you have,* and he shrugged slightly. *Not my fault.* The woman of the house was plainly not at home, and hadn't been for some time.

Or not in the physical sense, at least. Turning to take the chair Edgars offered him, Roger came face-to-face with a large studio photograph, framed in brass, standing in the center of the tiny mantelpiece. He bit his tongue to stifle a startled exclamation.

The woman seemed to be looking out of the photograph into his face, a slight smile barely creasing the corner of her mouth. Wings of platinum-fair hair fell thick and glossy past her shoulders, framing a perfect heart-shaped face. Eyes deep green as winter moss glowed under thick, dark lashes.

"Good likeness, i'n't?" Greg Edgars looked at the photo, his expression one of mingled hostility and longing.

"Er, yes. Just like her." Roger felt a little breathless, and turned to remove a crumpled fish-and-chips paper from his chair. Brianna was staring at the portrait with interest. She glanced from the photo to Roger and back, clearly drawing comparisons. Cousins, was it?

"I take it Gillian's not here?" Roger started to wave away the bottle Edgars had tilted inquiringly in his direction, then changed his mind and nodded.

Perhaps a shared drink would gain Edgars's confidence. If Gillian wasn't here, he needed to find out where she was.

Occupied in removing the excise seal with his teeth, Edgars shook his head, then delicately plucked the bit of wax and paper off his lower lip.

"Not hardly, mate. 'S not quite so much a slum as this when she's here." A sweeping gesture took in the overflowing ashtrays and tumbled paper drinks cups. "Close, maybe, but not quite this bad." He took down three wineglasses from the china cupboard, peering dubiously into each one, as though checking for dust.

He poured the whisky with the exaggerated care of the very drunk, taking the glasses one by one across the room to his guests. Brianna accepted hers with equal care, but declined a chair, instead leaning gracefully against the corner of the china cabinet.

Edgars plumped at last onto the rump-sprung sofa, ignoring the debris, and raised his glass.

"Cheers, mate," he said briefly, and took a long, slurping gulp. "Wotcher say yer name is?" he demanded, emerging abruptly from his immersion. "Oh, Roger, right. Gilly never mentioned ye . . . but then, she wouldn'," he added moodily. "Never knew nothin' about her family, and she wasn' sayin'. Think she was ashamed of 'em all . . . but you don't look such a nelly," he said, generously. "Yer lass is a looker, at least. Aye, that sounds right, eh? 'Yer lass is a looker, at least!' Hear 'at, eh?" He laughed uproariously, spraying whisky droplets.

"Yeah," said Roger. "Thanks." He took a small sip of his drink. Brianna, offended, turned her back on Edgars and affected to be examining the contents of the china closet through the bevel-cut glass doors.

There seemed no point in beating around the bush, Roger decided. Edgars wouldn't recognize subtlety if it bit him on the bum at this point, and there seemed a substantial danger that he might pass out soon, at the rate he was going.

"D'you know where Gillian is?" he asked bluntly. Every time he said her name, it felt strange on his tongue. This time, he couldn't help glancing up at the mantelpiece, where the photo smiled serenely on the debauch below.

Edgars shook his head, swinging it slowly back and forth over his glass like an ox over a corncrib. He was a short, heavyset man, about Roger's age, perhaps, but looking older because of the heavy growth of unshaved beard and disheveled black hair.

"Nah," he said. "Thought maybe you knew. It'll be the Nats or the Roses, likely, but I've no kep' up. I couldny say who, specially."

"Nats?" Roger's heart began to speed up. "You mean the Scottish Nationalists?"

Edgars's eyelids were beginning to droop, but they blinked open once more.

"Oh, aye. Bloody Nats. 'S where I met Gilly, aye?"

"When was this, Mr. Edgars?"

Roger looked up in surprise at the soft voice from above. It wasn't the photograph that had spoken, though, but Brianna, looking intently down at Greg Edgars. Roger couldn't tell whether she was merely making conversation, or if she suspected something. Her face showed nothing beyond polite interest.

"Dunno . . . maybe two, three years gone. Fun at first, hm? Toss the bloody English out, join the Common Market on our own . . . beer in the pub and a cuddle i' the back of the van comin' home from rallies. Mmm." Edgars shook his head again, dreamy-eyed at the vision. Then the smile faded from his face, and he frowned into his drink. "That's before she went potty."

"Potty?" Roger took another quick glance at the photo. Intense, yes. She looked that. But not barking mad, surely. Or could you tell, from a photo?

"Aye. Society o' the White Rose. Charlie's m' darlin'. Will ye no come back again, and all that rot. Lot of jimmies dressed up in kilts and full rig, wi' swords and all. All right if ye like it, o' course," he added, with a cockeyed attempt at objectivity. "But Gilly'd always take a thing too far. On and on about the Bonnie Prince, and wouldn' it be a thing if he'd won the '45? Blokes in the kitchen 'til all hours, drinking up the beer and arguing why he hadn't. In the Gaelic, too." He rolled his eyes. "Load o' rubbish." He drained his glass to emphasize this opinion.

Roger could feel Brianna's eyes boring into the side of his neck like gimlets. He pulled at his collar to loosen it, though he wasn't wearing a tie and his collar button was undone.

"I don't suppose your wife's also interested in standing stones, is she, Mr. Edgars?" Brianna wasn't bothering a lot with the polite interest anymore; her voice was sharp enough to cut cheese. The effect was largely wasted on Edgars.

"Stones?" He seemed fuddled, and stuck a forefinger into one ear, screwing it in industriously, as though in hopes of improving his hearing.

"The prehistoric stone circles. Like the Clava Cairns," Roger offered, naming one of the more famous local landmarks. In for a penny, in for a pound, he thought, with a mental sigh of resignation. Brianna was plainly never going to speak to him again, so he might as well find out what he could.

"Oh, those." Edgars uttered a short laugh. "Aye, and every other bit o' auld rubbish ye could name. That's the last bit, and the worst. Down at that In- stitewt day an' night, spendin' all my money on courses . . . courses! Make a cat laugh, ay? Fairy tales, they teach 'em there. Ye'll learn nothin' useful in that place, lass, I told her. Whyna learn to type? Get a job, if she's bored. 'S what I tell't her. So she left," he said morosely. "Not seen her in two weeks." He stared into his wineglass as though surprised to find it empty.

"Have another?" he offered, reaching for the bottle, but Brianna shook her head decidedly.

"Thanks, no. We have to be going. *Don't* we, Roger?"

Seeing the dangerous glint in her eye, Roger wasn't at all sure that he wouldn't be better off staying to split the rest of the bottle with Greg Edgars. Still, it was a long walk home, if he let Brianna take the car. He rose with a sigh, and shook Edgars's hand in farewell. It was warm and surprisingly firm in its grip, if a trifle moist.

Edgars followed them to the door, clutching the bottle by the neck. He peered after them through the screen, suddenly calling down the walk, "If ye see Gilly, tell her to come home, eh?"

Roger turned and waved at the blurry figure in the lighted rectangle of the door.

"I'll try," he called, the words sticking in his throat.

They made it to the walk and half down the street toward the pub before she rounded on him.

"What in bloody hell are you up to?" she said. She sounded angry, but not hysterical. "You told me you haven't any family in the Highlands, so what's all this about cousins? Who is that woman in the picture?"

He looked round the darkened street for inspiration, but there was no help for it. He took a deep breath and took her by the arm.

"Geillis Duncan," he said.

She stopped stock-still, and the shock of it jarred up his own arm. With great deliberation, she detached her elbow from his grip. The delicate tissue of the evening had torn down the middle.

"Don't . . . touch . . . me," she said through her teeth. "Is this something Mother thought up?"

Despite his resolve to be understanding, Roger felt himself growing angry in return.

"Look," he said, "can you not think of anyone but yourself in this? I know it's been a shock to you—God, how could it not be? And if you cannot bring yourself even to think about it . . . well, I'll not push you to it. But there's your mother to consider. And there's me, as well."

"You? What have you got to do with it?" It was too dark to see her face, but the surprise in her voice was evident.

He had not meant to complicate matters further by telling her of his involvement, but it was clearly too late for keeping secrets. And no doubt Claire had seen that, when she suggested his taking Brianna out this evening.

In a flash of revelation, he realized for the first time just what Claire had meant. She did have one means of proving her story to Brianna, beyond question. She had Gillian Edgars, who had—perhaps—not yet vanished to meet her fate as Geillis Duncan, tied to a flaming stake beneath the rowan trees of Leoch. The most stubborn cynic would be convinced, he supposed, by the sight of someone disappearing into the past before their eyes. No wonder Claire had wanted to find Gillian Edgars.

In a few words, he told Brianna his relationship with the would-be witch of Cranesmuir.

"And so it looks like being my life or hers," he ended, shrugging, hideously conscious of how ridiculously melodramatic it sounded. "Claire—your mother—she left it to me. But I thought I had to find her, at the least."

Brianna had stopped walking to listen to him. The dim light from a corner shop caught the gleam of her eyes as she stared at him.

"You believe it, then?" she asked. There was no incredulity or scorn in her voice; she was altogether serious.

He sighed and reached for her arm again. She didn't resist, but fell into step beside him.

"Yes," he said. "I had to. You didn't see your mother's face, when she saw the words written inside her ring. That was real—real enough to break my heart."

"You'd better tell me," she said, after a short silence. "What words?"

By the time he had finished the story, they had reached the car-park behind the pub.

"Well . . ." Brianna said hesitantly. "If . . ." She stopped again, looking into his eyes. She was standing near enough for him to feel the warmth of her breasts, close to his chest, but he didn't reach for her. The kirk of St. Kilda was a long way off, and neither of them wanted to remember the grave beneath the yew trees, where the names of her parents were written in stone.

"I don't know, Roger," she said, shaking her head. The neon sign over the pub's back door made purple glints in her hair. "I just can't . . . I can't think about it yet. But . . ." Words failed her, but she lifted a hand and touched his cheek, light as the brush of the evening wind. "I'll think of you," she whispered.

When you come right down to it, committing burglary with a key is not really a difficult proposition. The chance that either Mrs. Andrews or Dr. McEwan was going to come back and cop me in the act were vanishingly small. Even if they had, all I would have to do is say that I'd come back to look for a lost pocketbook, and found the door open. I was out of practice, but deception had at one point been second nature to me. Lying was like riding a bicycle, I thought; you don't forget how.

So it wasn't the act of getting hold of Gillian Edgars's notebook that made my heart race and my breath sound loud in my own ears. It was the book itself.

As Master Raymond had told me in Paris, the power and the danger of magic lie in the people who believe it. From the glimpse I had had of the contents earlier, the actual information written in this cardboard notebook was an extraordinary mishmash of fact, speculation, and flat-out fantasy that could be of importance only to the writer. But I felt an almost physical revulsion at touching it. Knowing who had written it, I knew it for what it likely was: a grimoire, a magician's book of secrets.

Still, if there existed any clue to Geillis Duncan's whereabouts and intentions, it would be here. Suppressing a shudder at the touch of the slick cover, I tucked it under my coat, holding it in place with my elbow for the trip down the stairs.

Safely out on the street, still I kept the book under my elbow, the cover growing clammy with perspiration as I walked. I felt as though I were transporting a bomb, something which must be handled with scrupulous carefulness, in order to prevent an explosion.

I walked for some time, finally turning into the front garden of a small Italian restaurant with a terrace near the river. The night was chilly, but a small electric fire made the terrace tables warm enough for use; I chose one and ordered a glass of Chianti. I sipped at it for some time, the notebook lying on the paper placemat in front of me, in the concealing shadow of a basket of garlic bread.

It was late April. Only a few days until May Day—the Feast of Beltane. That was when I had made my own impromptu voyage into the past. I supposed it was possible that there was something about the date—or just the general time of year? It had been mid-April when I returned—that made that eerie passage possible. Or maybe not; maybe the time of year had nothing to do with it. I ordered another glass of wine.

It could be that only certain people had the ability to penetrate a barrier that was solid to everyone else—something in the genetic makeup? Who knew? Jamie had not been able to enter it, though I could. And Geillis Duncan obviously had—or would. Or wouldn't, depending. I thought of young Roger Wakefield, and felt mildly queasy. I thought perhaps I had better have some food to go with the wine.

The visit to the Institute had convinced me that wherever Gillian/Geillis was, she had not yet made her own fateful passage. Anyone who had studied the legends of the Highlands would know that the Feast of Beltane was approaching; surely anyone planning such an expedition would undertake it then? But I had no idea where she might be, if she wasn't at home; in hiding? Performing some peculiar rite of preparation, picked up from Fiona's group of neo-Druids? The notebook might hold a clue, but God only knew.

God only also knew what my own motives were in this; I had thought I did, but was no longer sure. Had I involved Roger in the search for Geillis because it seemed the only way of convincing Brianna? And yet—even if we found her in time, my own purpose would be served only if Gillian succeeded in going back. And thus, in dying by fire.

When Geillis Duncan had been condemned as a witch, Jamie had said to me, "Dinna grieve for her, Sassenach; she's a wicked woman." And whether she had been wicked or mad, it had made little difference at the time. Should I not have left well enough alone, and left her to find her own fate? Still, I thought, she had once saved my life. In spite of what she was—would be—did I owe it to her to try to save her life? And thus perhaps doom Roger? What right did I have to meddle any further?

It isna a matter of right, Sassenach, I heard Jamie's voice saying, with a tinge of impatience. *It's a question of duty. Of honor.*

"Honor, is it?" I said aloud. "And what's that?" The waiter with my plate of tortellini Portofino looked startled.

"Eh?" he said.

"Never mind," I said, too distracted to care much what he thought of me. "Perhaps you'd better bring the rest of the bottle."

I finished my meal surrounded by ghosts. Finally, fortified by food and wine, I pushed my empty plate aside, and opened Gillian Edgars's gray notebook.

49

Blessed Are Those . . .

There's no place darker than a Highland road in the middle of a moonless night. I could see the flash of passing headlights now and then, silhouetting Roger's head and shoulders in a sudden flare of light. They were hunched forward, as though in defense against oncoming danger. Bree sat hunched as well, curled into the corner of the seat beside me. We were all three self-contained, insulated from each other, sealed in small, individual pockets of silence, inside the larger silence of the car and its rushing flight.

My fists curled in the pockets of my coat, idly scooping up coins and small bits of debris; shredded tissue, a pencil stub, a tiny rubber ball left on the floor of my office by a small patient. My thumb circled and identified the milled edge of an American quarter, the broad embossed face of an English penny, and the serrated edge of a key—the key to Gillian Edgars's carrel, which I had neglected to return to the Institute.

I had tried again to call Greg Edgars, just before we left the old manse. The phone had rung again and again without answer.

I stared at the dark glass of the window beside me, seeing neither my own faint reflection nor the massy shapes of stone walls and scattered trees that rushed by in the night. Instead, I saw the row of books, arranged on the carrel's single shelf in a line as neat as a row of apothecary's jars. And below, the notebook filled with fine cursive script, laying out in strict order conclusion and delusion, mingling myth and science, drawing from learned men and legends, all of it based on the power of dreams. To any casual observer, it could be either a muddle of half-thought-out nonsense or, at best, the outline for a clever-silly novel. Only to me did it have the look of a careful, deliberate plan.

In a parody of the scientific method, the first section of the book was titled "Observations." It contained disjointed references, tidy drawings, and carefully numbered tables. "The position of sun and moon on the Feast of Beltane" was one, with a list of more than two hundred paired figures laid out beneath. Similar tables existed for Hogmanay and Midsummer's Day, and another for Samhainn, the Feast of All Hallows. The ancient feasts of fire and sun, and Beltane's sun would rise tomorrow.

The central section of the notebook was titled "Speculations." That was accurate, at least, I reflected wryly. One page had borne this entry, in neat, slanting script: "The Druids burnt sacrificial victims in wicker cages shaped like men, but individuals were killed by strangling, and the throat slit to drain the body of blood. Was it fire or blood that was the necessary element?" The cold-blooded curiosity of the question brought Geillis Duncan's face before me clearly—not the wide-eyed, straight-haired student whose portrait adorned the Institute, but the secretive, half-smiling fiscal's wife, ten years older, versed in the uses of drugs and the body, who lured men to her purposes, and killed without passion to achieve her ends.

And the last few pages of the book, neatly labeled "Conclusions," which had led us to this dark journey, on the eve of the Feast of Beltane. I curled my fingers around the key, wishing with all my heart that Greg Edgars had answered his phone.

Roger slowed, turning onto the bumpy dirt lane that led past the base of the hill called Craigh na Dun.

"I don't see anything," he said. He hadn't spoken in so long that the statement came out gruffly, sounding belligerent.

"Well, of course not," Brianna said impatiently. "You can't see the stone circle from here."

Roger grunted in reply, and slowed the car still more. Obviously, Brianna's nerves were stretched, but so were his own. Only Claire seemed calm, unaffected by the growing air of tension in the car.

"She's here," Claire said suddenly. Roger slammed on the brakes so abruptly that both Claire and her daughter pitched forward, thumping into the back of the seat in front of them.

"Be careful, you idiot!" Brianna snapped furiously at Roger. She shoved a hand through her hair, pushing it off her face with a quick, nervous gesture. A swallow ran visibly down her throat as she bent to peer through the dark window.

"Where?" she said.

Claire nodded ahead to the right, keeping her hands shoved deep into her pockets.

"There's a car parked, just behind that thicket."

Roger licked his lips and reached for the door handle.

"It's Edgars's car. I'll go and look; you stay here."

Brianna flung her door open with a squeal of metal from the unoiled hinges. Her silent look of scorn made Roger flush red in the dim glow of the dome light overhead.

She was back almost before Roger had gotten out of the car himself.

"No one there," she reported. She glanced up at the top of the hill. "Do you think . . . ?"

Claire finished buttoning up her coat, and stepped into the darkness without answering her daughter's question.

"The path is this way," she said.

She led the way, perforce, and Roger, watching the pale form drift ghost-like up the hill ahead of him, was forcibly reminded of that earlier trip up a steep hill, to St. Kilda's kirkyard. So was Brianna; she hesitated and he heard her mutter something angrily under her breath, but then her hand reached for his elbow, and gave it a hard squeeze—whether as encouragement or as a plea for support, he couldn't tell. It encouraged *him*, in any case, and he patted the hand and tugged it through the curve of his arm. In spite of his general doubts, and the undeniable eeriness of the whole expedition, he felt a sense of excitement as they approached the crest of the hill.

It was a clear night, moonless and very dark, with no more than the tiny gleams of mica flecks in the starlight serving to distinguish the looming stones of the ancient circle from the night around them. The trio paused on the gently rounded top of the hill, huddling together like a misplaced flock of sheep. Roger's own breath sounded unnaturally loud to himself.

"This," said Brianna through her teeth, "is *silly*!"

"No, it isn't," said Roger. He felt suddenly breathless, as though a constricting band had squeezed the air from his chest. "There's a light over there."

It was barely there—no more than a flicker that promptly disappeared—but she saw it. He heard the sharp intake of her breath.

Now what? Roger wondered. Ought they to shout? Or would the noise of visitors frighten their quarry into precipitate action? And if so, what action might that be?

He saw Claire shake her head suddenly, as though trying to dismiss a buzzing insect. She took a step back, away from the nearest stone, and blundered into him.

He grabbed her by the arm, murmuring, "Steady, steady there," as one might to a horse. Her face was a dim blur in the starlight, but he could feel the quiver that ran through her, like electricity through a wire. He stood frozen, holding her arm, stiff with indecision.

It was the sudden stink of petrol that jerked him into motion. He was vaguely conscious of Brianna, head flung up as the smell met her nostrils, turning toward the north end of the circle, and then he had dropped Claire's arm, and was through the surrounding bushes and the stones themselves, striding toward the center of the ring, where a hunched black figure made an inkblot on the lighter darkness of the grass.

Claire's voice came from behind him, strong and urgent, shattering the silence.

"Gillian!" she called.

There was a soft, sudden whoosh, and the night lit up in brilliance. Dazzled, Roger fell back a pace, stumbling and dropping to his knees.

For a moment, there was nothing but the sharp pain of light on his retinas, and the blaze of brightness that hid everything behind it. He heard a cry beside him, and felt Brianna's hand on his shoulder. He blinked hard, eyes streaming, and sight began to return.

The slim figure stood between them and the fire, silhouetted like an hourglass. As his sight cleared, he realized that she was dressed in a long, full skirt and tight bodice—the clothes of another time. She had turned at the call, and he had a brief impression of wide eyes and fair, flying hair, lifted and tossed in the hot wind of the fire.

He found time, struggling to his feet, to wonder how she had dragged a log of that size up here. Then the smell of burned hair and crackled skin hit his face like a blow, and he remembered. Greg Edgars was not at home tonight. Not knowing whether blood or fire was the necessary element, she had chosen both.

He pushed past Brianna, focused only on the tall, slim girl before him, and the image of a face that mirrored his own. She saw him coming, turned and ran like the wind for the cleft stone at the end of the circle. She had a knapsack of rough canvas, slung over one shoulder; he heard her grunt as it swung heavily and struck her in the side.

She paused for an instant, hand outstretched to the rock, and looked back. He could have sworn that her eyes rested on him, met his own and held them, beyond the barrier of the fire's blaze. He opened his mouth in a wordless shout. She whirled then, light as a dancing spark, and vanished in the cleft of the rock.

The fire, the body, the night itself, disappeared abruptly in a shriek of blinding noise. Roger found himself facedown in the grass, clutching at the earth in frantic search of a familiar sensation to which to anchor his sanity. The search was vain; none of his senses seemed to function—even the touch of the ground was insubstantial, amorphous as though he lay on quicksand, not granite.

Blinded by whiteness, deafened by the scream of rending stone, he groped, flailing wildly, out of touch with his own extremities, conscious only of an immense pull and the need to resist it.

There was no sense of time passing; it felt as though he had been struggling in emptiness forever, when he at last became aware of something outside himself. Hands that gripped his arms with desperate strength, and the smothering softness of breasts thrust against his face.

Hearing began gradually to return, and with it the sound of a voice calling his name. Calling *him* names, in fact, panting between phrases.

"You idiot! You . . . jerk! Wake *up*, Roger, you . . . ass!" Her voice was muffled, but the sense of it reached him clearly. With a superhuman effort, he reached up and got hold of her wrists. He rolled, feeling ponderous as the start of an avalanche, and found himself blinking stupidly at the tear-streaked face of Brianna Randall, eyes dark as caves in the dying light of the fire.

The smell of petrol and roasting flesh was overwhelming. He turned aside and gagged, retching heavily into the damp grass. He was too occupied even to be grateful that his sense of smell had returned.

He wiped his mouth on his sleeve and groped unsteadily for Brianna's arm. She was huddled into herself, shaking.

"Oh, God," she said. "Oh, God. I didn't think I could stop you. You were crawling straight to it. Oh, God."

She didn't resist as he pulled her to him, but neither did she respond to him. She merely went on shaking, the tears running from wide, empty eyes, repeating "Oh, God," at intervals, like a broken record.

"Hush," he said, patting her. "It will be all right. Hush." The spinning sensation in his head was easing, though he still felt as though he had been split into several pieces and scattered violently among the points of the compass.

There was a faint, crackling *pop* from the darkening object on the ground, but beyond that and Brianna's mechanical ejaculations, the stillness of the night was returning. He put his hands to his ears, as though to still the echoes of the killing noise.

"You heard it, too?" he asked. Brianna went on crying, but nodded her head, jerky as a puppet.

"Did your—" he began, still laboriously assembling his thoughts piece-meal, then snapped upright as one came to him full-formed.

"Your mother!" he exclaimed, gripping Brianna hard by both arms. "Claire! Where is she?"

Brianna's mouth dropped open in shock, and she scrambled to her feet, wildly scanning the confines of the empty circle, where the man-high stones loomed stark, half-seen in the shadows of the dying fire.

"Mother!" she screamed. "Mother, *where are you?*"

"It's all right," Roger said, trying to sound authoritatively reassuring. "She'll be all right now."

In truth, he had no idea whether Claire Randall would ever be all right. She was alive, at least, and that was all he could vouch for.

They had found her, senseless in the grass near the edge of the circle, white as the rising moon above, with nothing but the slow, dark seep of blood from her abraded palms to testify that her heart still beat. Of the hellish journey down the path to the car, her dead weight slung across his shoulder, bumping awkwardly as stones rolled under his feet and twigs snatched at his clothing, he preferred to remember nothing.

The trip down the cursed hill had exhausted him; it was Brianna, the bones of her face stark with concentration, who had driven them back to the manse, hands clamped to the wheel like vises. Slumped in the seat beside her, Roger had seen in the rearview mirror the last faint glow of the hilltop behind them, where a small, luminous cloud floated like a puff of cannon smoke, mute evidence of battle past.

Brianna hovered now over the sofa where her mother lay, motionless as a tomb figure on a sarcophagus. With a shudder, Roger had avoided the hearth where the banked fire lay sleeping, and had instead pulled up the small electric fire with which the Reverend had warmed his feet on winter nights. Its bars glowed orange and hot, and it made a loud, friendly whirring noise that covered the silence in the study.

Roger sat on a low stool beside the sofa, feeling limp and starchless. With the last remnants of resolve, he reached toward the telephone table, his hand hovering a few inches above the instrument.

"Should we—" He had to stop to clear his throat. "Should we . . . call a doctor? The police?"

"No." Brianna's voice was intent, almost absentminded, as she bent over the still figure on the couch. "She's coming around."

The domed eyelids stirred, tightened briefly in the returning memory of pain, then relaxed and opened. Her eyes were clear and soft as honey. They drifted to and fro, skimmed over Brianna, standing tall and stiff at his side, and fixed on Roger's face.

Claire's lips were bloodless as the rest of her face; it took more than one try to get the words out, in a hoarse whisper.

"Did she . . . go back?"

Her fingers were twisted in the fabric of her skirt, and he saw the faint, dark smear of blood they left behind. His own hands clutched instinctively on his knees, palms tingling. She had held on, too, then, grappling among the grass and gravel for any small hold against the engulfment of the past. He closed his eyes against the memory of that pulling rupture, nodding.

"Yes," he said. "She went."

The clear eyes went at once to her daughter's face, brows above them arched as though in question. But it was Brianna who asked.

"It was true, then?" she asked hesitantly. "Everything was true?"

Roger felt the small shudder that ran through the girl's body, and without thinking about it, reached up to take her hand. He winced involuntarily as she squeezed it, and suddenly in memory heard one of the Reverend's texts: "Blessed are those who have not seen, and have believed." And those who *must* see, in order to believe? The effects of belief wrought by seeing trembled fearful at his side, terrified at what else must now be believed.

Even as the girl tightened, bracing herself to meet a truth she had already seen, the lines of Claire's tensed body on the sofa relaxed. The pale lips curved in the shadow of a smile, and a look of profound peace smoothed the strained white face, and settled glowing in the golden eyes.

"It's true," she said. A tinge of color came back into the pallid cheeks. "Would your mother lie to you?" And she closed her eyes once more.

Roger reached down to switch off the electric fire. The night was cold, but he could stay no longer in the study, his temporary sanctuary. He still felt groggy, but he couldn't delay longer. The decision had to be made.

It had been dawn before the police and the doctor had finished their work the night before, filling in their forms, taking statements and vital signs, doing their best to explain away the truth. "Blessed are they who have not seen," he thought again, devoutly, "but who have believed." Especially in this case.

Finally, they had left, with their forms and badges and cars with flashing lights, to oversee the removal of Greg Edgars's body from the ring of stone, to issue a warrant for the arrest of his wife, who, having lured her husband to his death, had fled the scene. To put it mildly, Roger thought dazedly.

Exhausted in mind and body, Roger had left the Randalls to the care of the doctor and Fiona, and had gone to bed, not bothering to undress or turn back the quilts, merely collapsing into a welcome oblivion. Roused near sunset by gnawing hunger, he had stumbled downstairs to find his guests, similarly silent, if less disheveled, helping Fiona with the preparation of supper.

It had been a quiet meal. The atmosphere was not strained; it was as though communication ran unseen among the people at the table. Brianna sat close to her mother, touching her now and then in the passing of food, as though to reassure herself of her presence. She had glanced occasionally at Roger, shy small looks from beneath her lashes, but didn't talk to him.

Claire said little, and ate almost nothing, but sat quite still, quiet and peaceful as a loch in the sun, her thoughts turned inward. After dinner, she had excused herself and gone to sit in the deep window seat at the end of the hall, pleading tiredness. Brianna had cast a quick glance at her mother, silhouetted in the last glow of the fading sun as she faced the window, and gone to help Fiona in the kitchen with the dishes. Roger had gone to the study, Fiona's good meal heavy in his stomach, to think.

Two hours later, he was still thinking, to remarkably little effect. Books were stacked untidily on the desk and table, left half-open on the seats of chairs and the back of the sofa, and gaping holes in the crowded bookshelves testified to the effort of his haphazard research.

It had taken some time, but he had found it—the short passage he remembered from his earlier search on Claire Randall's behalf. Those results had brought her comfort and peace; this wouldn't—if he told her. And if he were right? But he must be; it accounted for that misplaced grave, so far from Culloden.

He rubbed a hand over his face, and felt the rasp of beard. Not surprising that he had forgotten to shave, what with everything. When he closed his eyes, he could still smell smoke and blood; see the blaze of fire on dark rock, and the strands of fair hair, flying just beyond the reach of his fingers. He shuddered at the memory, and felt a sudden surge of resentment. Claire had destroyed his own peace of mind; did he owe her any less? And Brianna—if she knew the truth now, should she not know all of it?

Claire was still there at the end of the hall; feet curled under her on the window seat, staring out at the blank black stretch of the night-filled glass.

"Claire?" His voice felt scratchy from disuse, and he cleared his throat and tried again. "Claire? I . . . have something to tell you."

She turned and looked up at him, no more than the faintest curiosity visible on her features. She wore a look of calm, the look of one who has borne terror, despair, and mourning, and the desperate burden of survival—and has endured. Looking at her, he felt suddenly that he couldn't do it.

But she had told the truth; he must do likewise.

"I found something." He raised the book in a brief, futile gesture. "About . . . Jamie." Speaking that name aloud seemed to brace him, as though the big Scot himself had been conjured by his calling, to stand solid and unmoving in the hallway, between his wife and Roger. Roger took a deep breath in preparation.

"What is it?"

"The last thing he meant to do. I think . . . I think he failed."

Her face paled suddenly, and she glanced wide-eyed at the book.

"His men? But I thought you found—"

"I did," Roger interrupted. "No, I'm fairly sure he succeeded in that. He got the men of Lallybroch out; he saved them from Culloden, and set them on the road home."

"But then . . ."

"He meant to turn back—back to the battle—and I think he did that, too." He was increasingly reluctant, but it had to be said. Finding no words of his own, he flipped the book open, and read aloud:

"After the final battle at Culloden, eighteen Jacobite officers, all wounded, took refuge in the old house and for two days, their wounds untended, lay in pain; then they were taken out to be shot. One of them, a Fraser of the Master of Lovat's regiment, escaped the slaughter; the others were buried at the edge of the domestic park."

"One man, a Fraser of the Master of Lovat's regiment, escaped. . . ." Roger repeated softly. He looked up from the stark page to see her eyes, wide and unseeing as a deer's fixed in the headlights of an oncoming car.

"He meant to die on Culloden Field," Roger whispered. "But he didn't."

ACKNOWLEDGMENTS

The author's thanks and best wishes to:

the three Jackies (Jackie Cantor, Jackie LeDonne, and my mother), guardian angels of my books; the four Johns (John Myers, John E. Simpson, Jr., John Woram, and John Stith) for Constant Readership, Scottish miscellanea, and general enthusiasm; Janet McConnaughey, Margaret J. Campbell, Todd Heimarck, Deb and Dennis Parisek, Holly Heinel, and all the other LitForumites who do not begin with the letter J—especially Rober Riffle, for plantago, French epithets, ebony keyboards, and his ever-discerning eye; Paul Solyn, for belated nasturtiums, waltzes, copperplate handwriting, and botanical advice; Margaret Ball, for references, useful suggestions, and great conversation; Fay Zachary, for lunch; Dr. Gary Hoff, for medical advice and consultation (he had nothing to do with the descriptions of how to disembowel someone); the poet Barry Fogden, for translations from the English; Labhriunn MacIan, for Gaelic imprecations and the generous use of his most poetic name; Kathy Allen-Webber, for general assistance with the French (if anything is still in the wrong tense, it's my fault); Vonda N. McIntyre, for sharing tricks of the trade; Michael Lee West, for wonderful comments on the text, and the sort of phone conversations that make my family yell, "Get off the phone! We're starving!"; Michael Lee's mother, for reading the manuscript, looking up periodically to ask her critically acclaimed daughter, "Why don't you write something like this?"; and Elizabeth Buchan, for queries, suggestions, and advice—the effort involved was nearly as enormous as the help provided.

DIANA GABALDON is the #1 *New York Times* bestselling author of the wildly popular Outlander novels—*Outlander, Dragonfly in Amber, Voyager, Drums of Autumn, The Fiery Cross, A Breath of Snow and Ashes* (for which she won a Quill Award and the Corine International Book Prize), *An Echo in the Bone,* and *Written in My Own Heart's Blood*—as well as the related Lord John Grey books *Lord John and the Private Matter, Lord John and the Brotherhood of the Blade, Lord John and the Hand of Devils,* and *The Scottish Prisoner;* the nonfiction *The Outlandish Companion* and *The Outlandish Companion Volume Two;* and the Outlander graphic novel *The Exile.* She lives in Scottsdale, Arizona, with her husband.

dianagabaldon.com
Facebook.com/AuthorDianaGabaldon
@Writer_DG

To inquire about booking Diana Gabaldon for a speaking engagement, please contact the Penguin Random House Speakers Bureau at speakers@penguinrandomhouse.com.

And don't miss the next
installment of the acclaimed
OUTLANDER series . . .

DIANA GABALDON'S

VOYAGER

Read on for a preview. . . .

VOYAGER

on sale now

"Of course he's dead!" Claire's voice was sharp with agitation; it rang loudly in the half-empty study, echoing among the rifled bookshelves. She stood against the cork-lined wall like a prisoner awaiting a firing squad, staring from her daughter to Roger Wakefield and back again.

"I don't think so." Roger felt terribly tired. He rubbed a hand over his face, then picked up the folder from the desk; the one containing all the research he'd done since Claire and her daughter had first come to him, three weeks before, and asked his help.

He opened the folder and thumbed slowly through the contents. The Jacobites of Culloden. The Rising of the '45. The gallant Scots who had rallied to the banner of Bonnie Prince Charlie, and cut through Scotland like a blazing sword—only to come to ruin and defeat against the Duke of Cumberland on the gray moor at Culloden.

"Here," he said, plucking out several sheets clipped together. The archaic writing looked odd, rendered in the black crispness of a photocopy. "This is the muster roll of the Master of Lovat's regiment."

He thrust the thin sheaf of papers at Claire, but it was her daughter, Brianna, who took the sheets from him and began to turn the pages, a slight frown between her reddish brows.

"Read the top sheet," Roger said. "Where it says 'Officers.'"

"All right. 'Officers,'" she read aloud, "'Simon, Master of Lovat' . . ."

"The Young Fox," Roger interrupted. "Lovat's son. And five more names, right?"

Brianna cocked one brow at him, but went on reading.

"'William Chisholm Fraser, Lieutenant; George D'Amerd Fraser Shaw, Captain; Duncan Joseph Fraser, Lieutenant; Bayard Murray Fraser, Major,'" she paused, swallowing, before reading the last name, "'. . . James Alexander Malcolm MacKenzie Fraser. Captain.'" She lowered the papers, looking a little pale. "My father."

Claire moved quickly to her daughter's side, squeezing the girl's arm. She was pale, too.

"Yes," she said to Roger. "I know he went to Culloden. When he left me . . . there at the stone circle . . . he meant to go back to Culloden Field, to rescue his men who were with Charles Stuart. And we know he did"—she nodded at the folder on the desk, its manila surface blank and innocent in the lamplight—"you found their names. But . . . but . . . Jamie . . ." Speaking the name aloud seemed to rattle her, and she clamped her lips tight.

Now it was Brianna's turn to support her mother.

"He meant to go back, you said." Her eyes, dark blue and encouraging, were intent on her mother's face. "He meant to take his men away from the field, and then go back to the battle."

Claire nodded, recovering herself slightly.

"He knew he hadn't much chance of getting away; if the English caught him . . . he said he'd rather die in battle. That's what he meant to do." She turned to Roger, her gaze an unsettling amber. Her eyes always reminded him of hawk's eyes, as though she could see a good deal farther than most people. "I can't believe he didn't die there—so many men did, and *he* meant to!"

Almost half the Highland army had died at Culloden, cut down in a blast of cannonfire and searing musketry. But not Jamie Fraser.

"No," Roger said doggedly. "That bit I read you from Linklater's book—" He reached to pick it up, a white volume, entitled *The Prince in the Heather.*

"*Following the battle,*" he read, "*eighteen wounded Jacobite officers took refuge in the farmhouse near the moor. Here they lay in pain, their wounds untended, for two days. At the end of that time, they were taken out and shot. One man, a Fraser of the Master of Lovat's regiment, escaped the slaughter. The rest are buried at the edge of the domestic park.*"

"See?" he said, laying the book down and looking earnestly at the two women over its pages. "An officer, of the Master of Lovat's regiment." He grabbed up the sheets of the muster roll.

"And here they are! Just six of them. Now, we know the man in the farmhouse can't have been Young Simon; he's a well-known historical figure, and we know very well what happened to him. He retreated from the field—unwounded, mind you—with a group of his men, and fought his way north, eventually making it back to Beaufort Castle, near here." He waved vaguely at the full-length window, through which the nighttime lights of Inverness twinkled faintly.

"Nor was the man who escaped Leanach farmhouse any of the other four officers—William, George, Duncan, or Bayard," Roger said. "Why?" He snatched another paper out of the folder and brandished it, almost triumphantly. "Because they all *did* die at Culloden! All four of them were killed on the field—I found their names listed on a plaque in the church at Beauly."

Claire let out a long breath, then eased herself down into the old leather swivel chair behind the desk.

"Jesus H. Christ," she said. She closed her eyes and leaned forward, elbows on the desk, and her head against her hands, the thick, curly brown hair spilling forward to hide her face. Brianna laid a hand on Claire's back, face troubled as she bent over her mother. She was a tall girl, with large, fine bones, and her long red hair glowed in the warm light of the desk lamp.

"If he didn't die . . ." she began tentatively.

Claire's head snapped up. "But he *is* dead!" she said. Her face was strained, and small lines were visible around her eyes. "For God's sake, it's two hundred years; whether he died at Culloden or not, he's dead now!"

Brianna stepped back from her mother's vehemence, and lowered her head, so the red hair—her father's red hair—swung down beside her cheek.

"I guess so," she whispered. Roger could see she was fighting back tears. And no wonder, he thought. To find out in short order that first, the man you had loved and called "Father" all your life really *wasn't* your father, secondly, that your real father was a Highland Scot who had lived two hundred years ago, and thirdly, to realize that he had likely perished in some horrid fashion, unthinkably far from the wife and child he had sacrificed himself to save . . . enough to rattle one, Roger thought.

He crossed to Brianna and touched her arm. She gave him a brief, distracted glance, and tried to smile. He put his arms around her, even in his pity for her distress thinking how marvelous she felt, all warm and soft and springy at once.

Claire still sat at the desk, motionless. The yellow hawk's eyes had gone a softer color now, remote with memory. They rested sightlessly on the east wall of the study, still covered from floor to ceiling with the notes and memorabilia left by the Reverend Wakefield, Roger's late adoptive father.

Looking at the wall himself, Roger saw the annual meeting notice sent by the Society of the White Rose—those enthusiastic, eccentric souls who still championed the cause of Scottish independence, meeting in nostalgic tribute to Charles Stuart, and the Highland heroes who had followed him.

Roger cleared his throat slightly.

"Er . . . if Jamie Fraser didn't die at Culloden . . ." he said.

"Then he likely died soon afterward." Claire's eyes met Roger's, straight on, the cool look back in the yellow-brown depths. "You have no idea how it was," she said. "There was a famine in the Highlands—none of the men had eaten for days before the battle. He was wounded—we know that. Even if he escaped, there would have been . . . no one to care for him." Her voice caught slightly at that; she was a doctor now, had been a healer even then, twenty years before, when she had stepped through a circle of standing stones, and met destiny with James Alexander Malcolm MacKenzie Fraser.

Roger was conscious of them both; the tall, shaking girl he held in his arms, and the woman at the desk, so still, so poised. She had traveled through the stones, through time; been suspected as a spy, arrested as a witch, snatched by an unimaginable quirk of circumstance from the arms of her first husband, Frank Randall. And three years later, her second husband, James Fraser, had sent her back through the stones, pregnant, in a desperate effort to save her and the unborn child from the onrushing disaster that would soon engulf him.

Surely, he thought to himself, she's been through enough? But Roger was a historian. He had a scholar's insatiable, amoral curiosity, too powerful to be constrained by simple compassion. More than that, he was oddly conscious of the third figure in the family tragedy in which he found himself involved—Jamie Fraser.

"If he didn't die at Culloden," he began again, more firmly, "then perhaps I can find out what did happen to him. Do you want me to try?" He waited, breathless, feeling Brianna's warm breath through his shirt.

Jamie Fraser had had a life, and a death. Roger felt obscurely that it was his duty to find out all the truth; that Jamie Fraser's women deserved to know all they could of him. For Brianna, such knowledge was all she would ever have of the father she had never known. And for Claire—behind the question he had asked was the thought that had plainly not yet struck her, stunned with shock as she was: she had crossed the barrier of time twice before. She could, just possibly, do it again. And if Jamie Fraser had not died at Culloden . . .

He saw awareness flicker in the clouded amber of her eyes, as the thought came to her. She was normally pale; now her face blanched white as the ivory handle of the letter opener before her on the desk. Her fingers closed around it, clenching so the knuckles stood out in knobs of bone.

She didn't speak for a long time. Her gaze fixed on Brianna and lingered there for a moment, then returned to Roger's face.

"Yes," she said, in a whisper so soft he could barely hear her. "Yes. Find out for me. Please. Find out."

Also by DIANA GABALDON

THE COMPANION VOLUMES

THE OUTLANDER GRAPHIC NOVEL

THE LORD JOHN SERIES

Lord John and the Private Matter
Lord John and the Brotherhood of the Blade
Lord John and the Hand of Devils
The Scottish Prisoner

Continue the saga with original eNovellas,
engrossing tales to complement the Outlander series.

  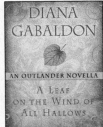 

A Plague of Zombies   The Custom of   A Leaf on the Wind   The Space Between
                       the Army   of All Hallows

DianaGabaldon.com
⬛ AuthorDianaGabaldon   🐦 @Writer_DG

Random House 🏛 Bantam • Dell • Delacorte • Del Rey

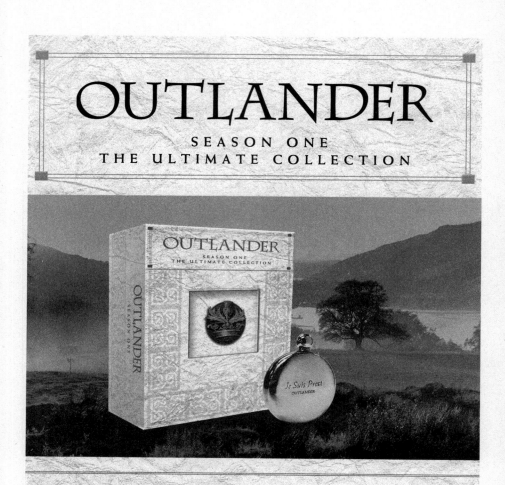

A STARZ ORIGINAL SERIES

OUTLANDER

STARZ